THE
STRIKERS

THE FIRST NOVEL IN
THE MORTHENSTAR TRILOGY

B. K. CAIN

Library of Congress Control Number: 2025913400

Hardcover: 979-8-9993353-0-2
Paperback: 979-8-9900069-9-7
Ebook: 979-8-9993353-1-9

Second paperback edition September 2025

Portland, Oregon

Cover and book design by Rosie Struve and Bailey Cain
Illustrations by Katrina Zarate
Map created with Inkarnate

www.morthenstartrilogy.com

FOR PIPER

TABLE OF CONTENTS

PROLOGUE I

CHAPTER ONE 9

CHAPTER TWO 32

CHAPTER THREE.. 4I

CHAPTER FOUR 58

CHAPTER FIVE 95

CHAPTER SIX... II7

CHAPTER SEVEN I32

CHAPTER EIGHT I5I

CHAPTER NINE I75

CHAPTER TEN 200

CHAPTER ELEVEN 220

CHAPTER TWELVE 236

CHAPTER THIRTEEN.. 250

CHAPTER FOURTEEN 256

CHAPTER FIFTEEN 265

CHAPTER SIXTEEN 275

CHAPTER SEVENTEEN 285

CHAPTER EIGHTEEN...294

CHAPTER NINETEEN...304

CHAPTER TWENTY...34I

CHAPTER TWENTY-ONE..351

CHAPTER TWENTY-TWO..360

CHAPTER TWENTY-THREE...378

CHAPTER TWENTY-FOUR...388

CHAPTER TWENTY-FIVE...415

CHAPTER TWENTY-SIX..445

CHAPTER TWENTY-SEVEN...468

CHAPTER TWENTY-EIGHT...480

CHAPTER TWENTY-NINE...490

CHAPTER THIRTY...500

ASHAN FOREST

THE MEADOWS

TWO FALLS

ALBASTER

THE WEST COUNTRY
IN
THE NEW AGE OF THE STRIKERS

RIDDLETON

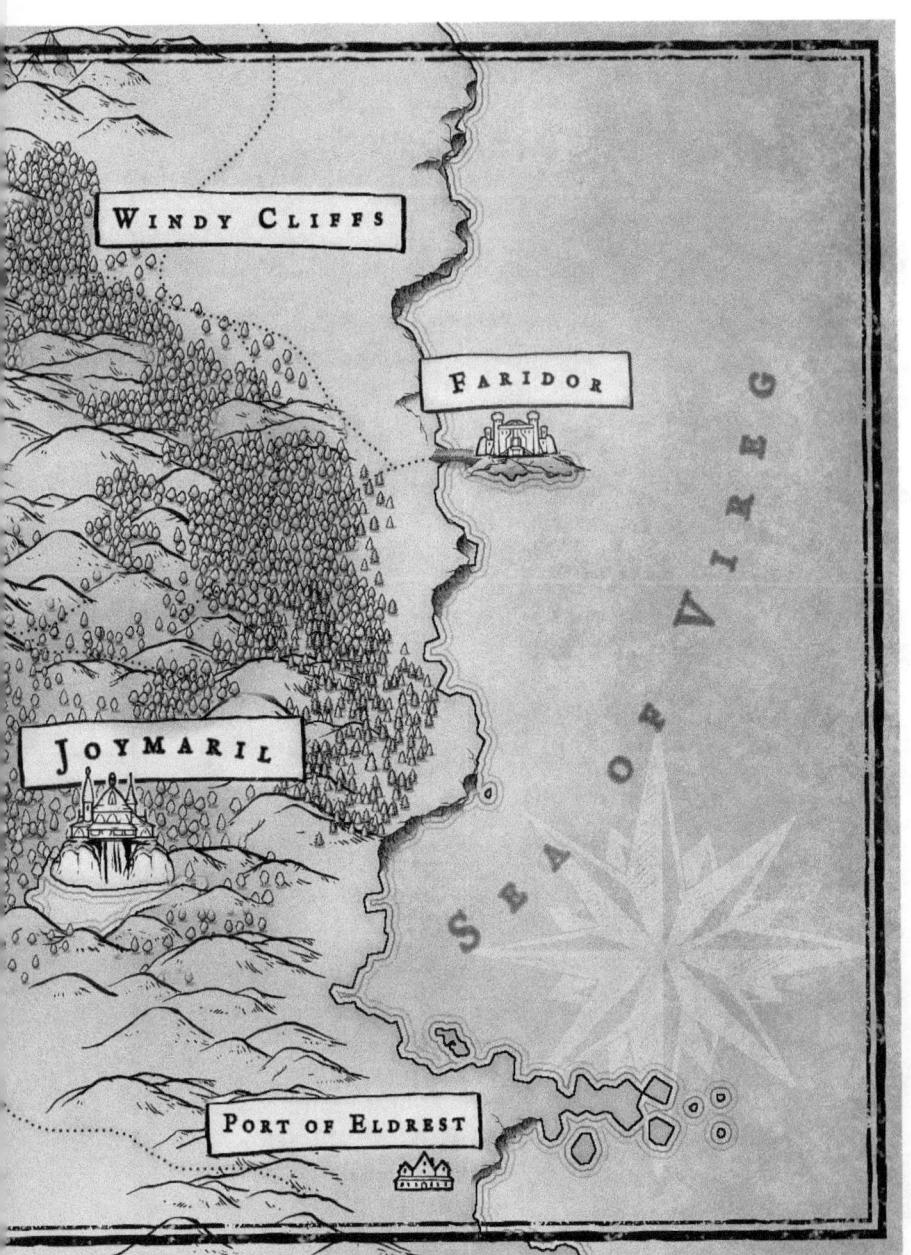

WINDY CLIFFS

FARIDOR

JOYMARIL

PORT OF ELDREST

SEA OF VIREG

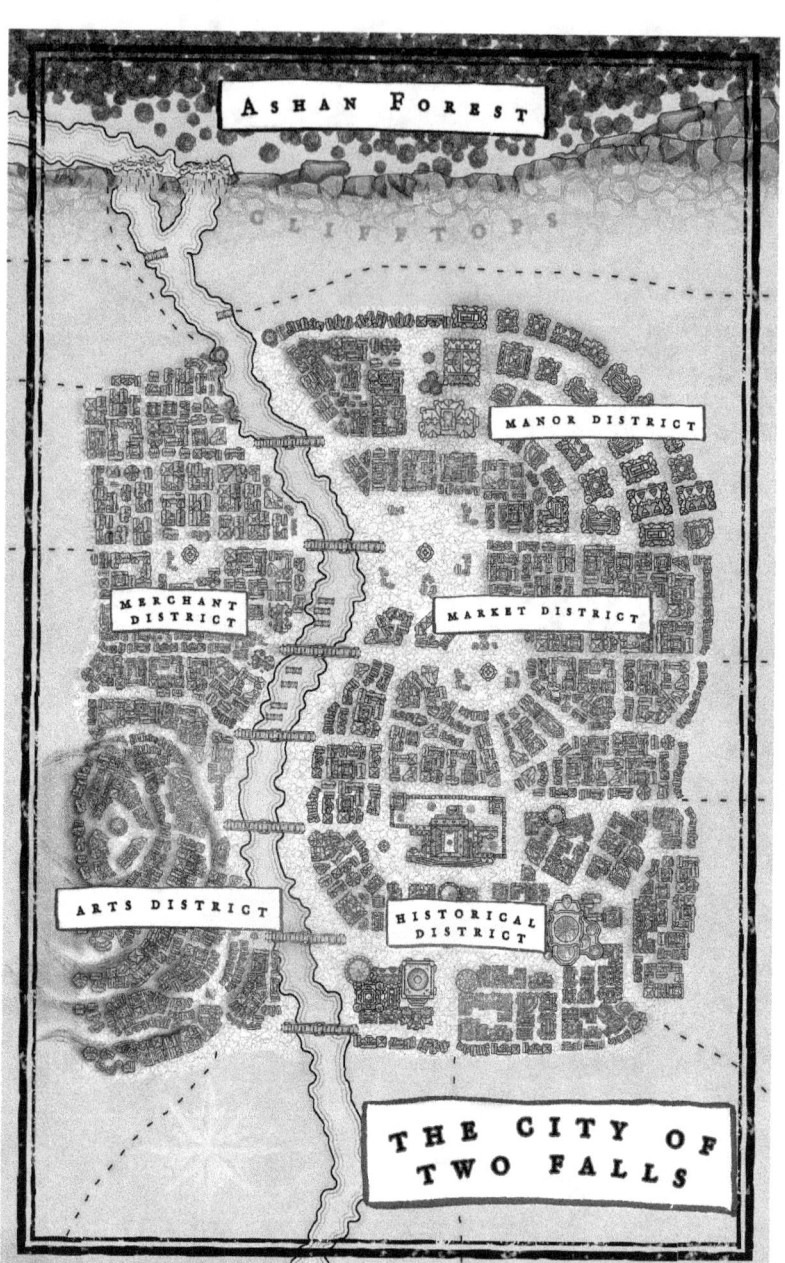

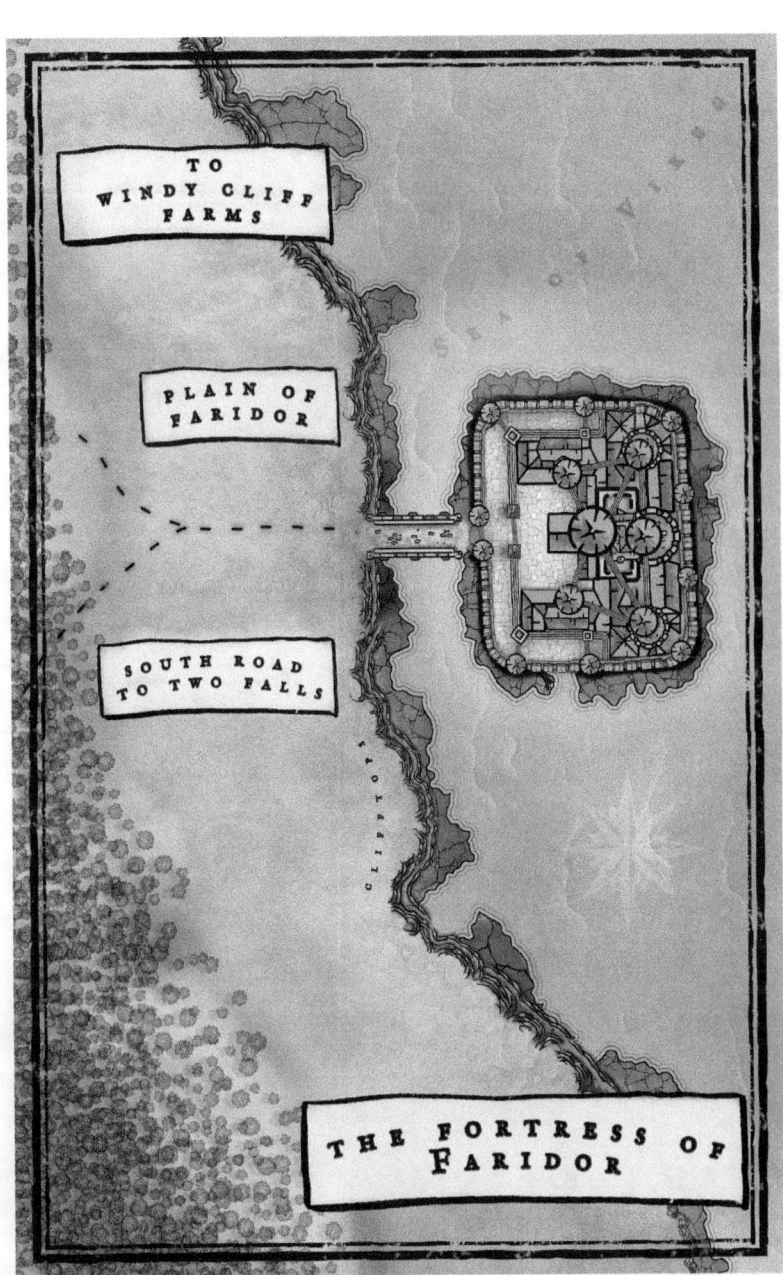

TO
WINDY CLIFF
FARMS

PLAIN OF
FARIDOR

SOUTH ROAD
TO TWO FALLS

THE FORTRESS OF
FARIDOR

PROLOGUE

TWO HUNDRED YEARS AGO

If the legends were to be believed, on the night before the final battle there was a lunar eclipse. The moon, hanging low and round like a great yellow ember, smoldered slowly and then was finally snuffed out, plunging the land below into inky shadow.

In the years that followed, no one could decide whether the eclipse was a naturally occurring phenomenon, a cosmic punishment for all that had passed, or a portent of things to come.

In the end, it didn't matter. The years came and went. The sea stretched out lazily beneath a gently turning wind. The sun swelled with heat and winced with cold. The memory of the moonless night slowly faded away.

Morning on the battlefield dawned gray, with a faint drizzle falling from the thick clouds in the skies, just as it had done every day for the past three months. The field itself held an eerie silence, as if everything that could have made sound had been wiped clean, like steam from a windowpane. All was quiet except the wind, which moaned softly over the plain, whistled through cracks in the battered armor of the dead soldiers, and ruffled the scarlet-red hair of Alder Morthenstar.

She was lying on her back in the churned-up mud, her sword lying a little way away from her, just out of reach. She couldn't move her legs, as she was under a pile of fallen foes. They kept her pinned down to the earth, their weight at once crushingly heavy and oddly comforting. She tried to open her eyes to see around herself, but found that she couldn't; something was sealing them shut. After a few moments of trying, one eye opened a tiny bit, letting in a thin sliver of morning. Alder squinted painfully but opened it successfully, blinding gray light pouring in, causing tears to spring forward. The other eye was more stubborn, closed tight with dried, caked blood. She blinked her good eye a few times as tiny drops of water fell against her face, and she tried to move again, but the weight was too much and the pain too intense. Suddenly, there was the sound of horses close behind her. An earthy thud; running footsteps.

"Holy...!" came a raspy voice from behind. Daemun. Alder relaxed, and her right-hand man came up, kneeling beside her, a look of barely masked horror on his face.

"Hullo, Daemun," Alder replied, and was momentarily startled to hear the weakness in her own voice. "How are you?" Her tone was light, as if she were greeting him in the middle of a street on market day. She almost laughed aloud at the idiocy of trying to feign casual nonchalance while lying bloodied and broken under a pile of dead soldiers in the middle of a battlefield.

But Daemun didn't laugh as he usually would have. He was purposefully avoiding her eyes. She felt a sliver of panic growing in her belly. "Alder, you're wounded," he said finally.

Morthenstar paused, raising an expectant eyebrow. "And...?"

Daemun glanced up to the sky and squinted a little before replying. "Well, frankly, my liege, you look like shit."

She relaxed ever so slightly and sighed. "I figured as much. Here, help me out," she asked. Daemun took her arm and pulled. Morthenstar felt a pain unlike any she had ever endured in her life. She nearly cried out, but stifled it and fell back, wincing, mouth open, unable to scream or even speak. Daemun's face changed immediately as he saw

Alder's reaction, whirling on the two soldiers standing awkwardly by their horses behind him.

"Didn't you hear me? I said she's wounded!" Daemun bellowed at his troops, already hoarse voice nearly giving way. He had been shouting battle commands to the soldiers for nearly a week straight, and by this point, the two retainers could recognize the extra charge in his tone. They nearly managed to knock themselves over in their haste to mount up and ride off. "Get a surgeon, quick!" Daemun added, then turned back to Alder and whispered, "Lie still. Don't move a muscle."

Morthenstar heard the horses turning and thundering off; the sound of their hooves escalated with her ear against the ground. The drumbeats did little to help the pounding in her head. Daemun was trying to shove some of Kagai's green riders off of her so that she could move. Good old Daemun. He was the best friend Alder had ever had. She was glad that he was there. Glad she could see him again, one last time.

One last time, she thought. *Is that what this is?*

Right as he lifted an arm off of Morthenstar's midsection, Daemun froze, bringing her attention swinging painfully back to the present.

"What?" Alder asked, alarmed at the expression on his face. Daemun looked sharply over to her and then looked back at what he was doing.

"We need to get some soldiers who can actually *ride,*" he complained. "We've had to make do with nothing but farm boys and milkmaids for the last six months." Morthenstar smiled. Griping about the troops was Daemun's favorite pastime. Her friend's voice lowered, and she heard him mutter, mostly to himself, "They won't get here in time." Daemun dropped the nearest soldier's arm and rocked back on his heels, looking up at the sky again, squinting his eyes though the sun was dim. Alder began to feel concerned. Daemun had never allowed an air of hopelessness to come upon him before. Even when they began this battle, outnumbered fifteen to one, Daemun had led the charge right beside her...their horses had been neck and neck, the sound of battle cries in the air. It had been as good a day as any for the end to come. Alder forced herself to concentrate on what was happening.

"Daemun, what is the matter? What do you see?" Alder asked hoarsely. Daemun didn't respond. Alder felt her patience growing thin, rage stirring beneath the pain. "That is an order, General! Tell me now!"

Daemun met her eyes, not liking the position she had put him in one bit. He took a deep breath and let it out slowly, then spoke matter-of-factly. "Alder, you are cut nearly in half. The only thing keeping you together is that rider. You are bleeding to death."

"Nonsense," Alder countered, grinning feebly. "I don't *feel* like I'm dying." *Ha*, she said to herself. *That was a good one. I've been feeling like I was dying for nearly three years.*

Daemun looked at her steadily and nodded. Alder's smile faded. Daemun always told her the truth. Alder lay back in the mud and stared up at the smoke-colored clouds above her. *The sun*, she thought. *I will miss the sun. How odd. Of all the things...No, Alder, keep yourself here. Keep looking at Daemun. Stare at his face.*

"We won the battle?" she asked. Daemun nodded. "And Kagai was killed?"

"Yes," Daemun replied, smiling as the spirit of victory rose within him. "Sedith did it. He and your warriors cornered him in his chambers after the army surrendered and yielded the fortress," Daemun paused and laughed, his tone rueful and bitter. "Kagai's mystics fled. They say they're crossing the sea to Vireg. And Kagai himself didn't even have the courage to come out on the battlefield and face you."

"Maybe he was the smart one," Alder mused thoughtfully.

Daemun paused briefly, consulting his mail-clad fingertips. "Sedith said he laughed," he said finally. "He laughed and laughed and vowed that it wasn't over. That he had been able to finish what he started. The...magic..." The fanciful word *magic* seemed to get stuck in Daemun's practical throat. "He said he'd done it."

"We knew this was a possibility. We knew what I saw. We did what we could, Daemun. It's out of our hands now," Alder told him firmly, and Daemun looked down. *He has fought harder than anyone in this war*, Alder mused. *He wants to undo what his family has done.* "I've asked the Serpens to do what they can. To counteract."

"I don't believe any of it," Daemun maintained. It was a familiar refrain, and Alder smiled to hear some of his old stubbornness coming back to the forefront.

"Not even my visions?"

"Nightmares," Daemun replied sharply, as he so often had over the past months. "Nightmares, nothing more."

A wave of sickness overcame her and she shook her head, clearing out the fog that had suddenly enveloped her eyes. *The charge...she* thought. *Oh, what a beautiful charge it was...soldiers and horses...I could hear every heart pounding beneath the armor.* She had always hated fighting. But that morning had been different. She blinked and looked again, and there was Daemun leaning over her, trying desperately to mask his worry. Alder smiled weakly at him.

"You know, for once, I think you're right," she told Daemun quietly. "Maybe this is it. Maybe this is goodbye."

"There could still be some chance," Daemun said desperately. "I'm not a surgeon..."

"You're right about that, too," Alder grinned. Then she stopped, suddenly solemn. "I never thought it would end this way."

"None of us did," Daemun murmured.

"You always said that after it was all over, you and I would live in two cottages side by side on a hill. A hill that would be covered in lilacs in the spring, like a carpet. Our houses would look over the meadow in the wintertime, everything frosted over with snow and the smoke falling out of the chimneys. And night after night, we would sit in our chairs beside our grandchildren and tell stories of the old times, and no one would have the nerve to tell us to shut up." Her voice cracked into a whisper. She could hear the way she was beginning to ramble, her mind becoming more and more unfocused, but she didn't mind it as much anymore. She looked up at the strong, noble face above her, with its thin layer of dirt streaked here and there by sweat and blood, the prematurely gray hair sticking out haphazardly this way and that. She met Daemun's dark eyes squarely, then spoke in a barely audible whisper. "For the first time in my life, I'll be going somewhere without you."

"I've followed you through worse," Daemun replied solidly, brow furrowing with emotion. His eyes darted away.

"You're staying behind this time, old man," Alder told him. "You and Sedith are going to be the war buffs who everyone wishes would just stop talking about the old days."

"No," Daemun told her, smiling sadly and taking Alder's head in his hands. "We're going to be the war buffs everyone wishes would just stop talking about *you*."

Alder smiled and held up an arm. Daemun grasped it and pulled it to his chestplate. A burning tear of sadness slid unheralded down Alder's cheek.

"The other Strikers," Alder asked him suddenly. "Are they all still alive?"

Daemun's face fell, and he shook his head. "Quenir fell near the wall, holding off twenty riders trying to let the Strikers into the fortress. Eva was hit by an arrow when she tried to save his body before it was crushed beneath the riders."

Alder digested this information, two hard hits against a heart that was already reeling. A sadness, thick and deep and blue, settled over her like a blanket. She shook her head, not sure whether the pain she felt was her wound or the news of her friends' passing. "It's all such a waste."

Daemun looked at her sharply. "Alder, the war is over. It's *over*. There will be peace now." But there was an uncertain look in his eyes that told her that he hadn't forgotten the words of their enemy. That somehow, some way, the wheel would turn, and the cycle would begin again.

"I know...but it doesn't feel any different." Alder felt her head getting light, and Daemun's face in front of her eyes was flashing in and out. She gripped Daemun's hand more tightly, and her general had to lean in close to hear what she had to say.

"Alder?" Daemun asked softly, looking worried. "What are you—"

"It wasn't for nothing, was it?" Alder whispered.

"No," Daemun assured him. "It wasn't for nothing. None of it was."

"Remember what I'm saying," Alder wheezed. "Remember..."

"Alder?" Daemun asked faintly.

"Take...take it when I'm gone. Hide it," Alder ordered. She could no longer see anything. Her hand tugged at a chain around her neck, trying to pull something up from beneath her armor. Daemun grasped her hand and nodded, telling her he knew what she wanted, that she didn't need to speak anymore. Daemun's face had vanished from above her. "Do you hear me? I can't see you."

"I'll take it. I'll hide it," Daemun assured her.

"You don't believe, but I do," Alder told him. "I believe what I've seen."

"I know. It's all right, Alder."

"And my visions?" Alder swallowed. "Tell me they're safe. I've written them down. What I've seen, the visions I've had. Keep them safe."

"They are safe. They are safe, Alder, I promise."

Alder stared out into space. "Do you think my family will be waiting?" she wondered, her voice far away and vague. "Will they have waited all this time?"

"They will," Daemun assured her. "Families always wait, no matter how long it takes. I know they will be there."

"I will wait for you, too," Alder whispered. "Someday. Someday, many, many years from now, when you're an old, old man, and it's your time." A peaceful smile rested on her cold, blue lips. "How nice it will be. To greet you once again as my brother."

"In everything but blood," Daemun agreed, smiling with her, squeezing her hand tight.

Alder closed her eyes and felt a rush of cold air sweeping through her body.

"In everything," she whispered.

Daemun saw Alder's life leave her. He held onto Morthenstar's hand until the other soldiers came and told him they had to remove her body. The general reached forward and undid the clasp of the broad silver medallion hung on a chain about Morthenstar's neck. He gripped it in his hand, his knuckles slowly turning white and blue, as the men carefully wrapped her abdomen with a black cloth, then drew a scarlet shroud over her body. As the shroud covered her face, Daemun had to look away. There was finality in that last glimpse. His friend was gone.

The soldiers lifted Morthenstar up onto their shoulders and bore her away from the battlefield, back to the encampment where the surviving Strikers were slowly trickling back to their tents, dazed and numb. Their faces were uniformly drawn and grim; as he slowly passed through their ranks in the wake of the pallbearers, the soldiers knew better than to offer him any aid or condolences. Their faces—such young faces— silently turned towards him. His expression didn't falter until he was out of sight of the soldiers and was in his tent alone, clutching the medallion close to his chest. His retainers knew not to enter.

Daemun had, by necessity, become a man at a very young age, and service on the battlefield had hardened him. He had not cried for many years. But that morning, as his tears fell to the ground, the rain stopped, and, for the first time in three months, the sun shone through the clouds onto the earth.

CHAPTER ONE

TWO HUNDRED YEARS LATER

A strong wind blew through the forest, bending the massive trunks from side to side as though the trees were nothing but stalks of grass. Amidst the treetops, the canopy looked more like waves on an ocean, rippling and pulsing, strong and alive.

Two Ashans sped along the upper branches with the ease and balance of forest cats—up one limb and down the other, launching their long, thin bodies into midair without the slightest moment of hesitation. Six-fingered hands burst out suddenly to catch a branch; a lean form catapulted itself recklessly into open space with an innate balance and grace that could only be learned after years of practice.

Abruptly, the whirlwind of motion paused and the two Ashans clung to their branches, bobbing and weaving like seabirds riding an ocean wave. "Is that all you can do, Tarr?" one Ashan called to the other. "You climb like a village Elder!"

"I was just testing you," her friend yelled back in their native tongue.

"And?"

Her companion seemed to wrestle internally for a moment, as if attempting to summon a truly cutting comeback from deep within. Then, somewhat lamely and with a sheepish smile, he shrugged. "You passed. Good job."

The first Ashan rolled her eyes at this pathetic attempt at competitive taunting. Her hair looked like bark: dark brown with streaks of gray. She had tanned skin and a plain but pleasant countenance. Her face had been almost perfectly round in her younger years, but now that she was fast approaching adulthood, the roundness had started to fade away, and a jaw and cheekbones had begun to emerge. "The border is that way," she called, pointing. "We will see who makes it first."

The young male Ashan coiled his skinny legs like springs and flew up into the air, soaring past two trees before landing with an elastic *swoosh* on the upper branches of another.

"Hey! I did not say go!" the female cried, but was up and on her way in a split second. She slid down a sloping branch and bounded off the end, catching the nearest outstretched limb in her callused, six-fingered hand, swinging herself up onto the next level. She ran along the branches as easily as if there were a marked path atop them, and not once did she glance down in fear at the hundred-foot drop to the forest floor.

"Come on, Juniper!" her friend yelled down.

She glared up at him. He was ahead of her, but just barely, skipping along the trees fifty feet above her head. She turned and scurried, hand over hand, up the trunk and leaped, with all her strength, out into the void. It did the trick. With a neat flip, she landed on a tree about ten feet in front of him.

Startled at her sudden appearance, his hand slipped and he fell through two branches before his feet thudded onto another, swinging farther below. There would be no catching her now. They had almost reached the border of their tribal land. Still, no harm in making it a close race.

With his feet dangling in the open air, he swung from branch to branch with his strong, wiry arms, flipping backwards and landing on a low bough only to be bounced elastically back up into the upper canopy. He landed squarely and ran along the limb before cartwheeling off the end, flipping and landing beside an extremely smug-looking

Juniper on the border tree.

"Not bad for a village Elder, eh?" he panted, slightly out of breath.

"Not bad, Tarr, not bad," Juniper acknowledged with a smile. "But you really need to work on your trash-talking."

Tarr gave a hopeless shrug, and Juniper hid a grin. Of all the young men in her tribe, Tarr was easily the most even-tempered, and what little competitive spirit he possessed manifested itself in tepid bouts of reluctant bantering. Juniper had informed him before they'd set out that day that if they were to race, he had to at least make some effort to pretend like he cared whether he won or lost.

They swung their legs contentedly back and forth as they caught their breath, listening to the rustle of the leaves in the strong wind and staring down at the mossy, earthy forest floor hundreds of feet below. Juniper glanced at Tarr out of the corner of her eye. His rectangular face was naturally thin and rather angular, but there was a look about his mouth and eyes that denoted a gentle nature and kind spirit. His irises were different colors: the right was a dark brown, and the left a bright forest green. They tilted down at the edges to give him a perpetual look of sweet melancholy, which tended to curry natural sympathy and extra treats for him from the more softhearted caretakers in the tribe. He had dark brown hair about the same color as Juniper's, but it was cut short and had gold flecks here and there that caught the sun when he passed beneath the dappled light that filtered its way through the forest boughs. The brown skin of his arm was even darker than hers, warmed and glowing in the spring sunshine; like all Ashans he had six fingers on each hand. He had a thoughtful way about him that belied his young years; once one looked past his preternaturally winsome expression, it was almost possible to see a keen mind ticking away behind his eyes as he regarded the world around him.

"Let us climb up," Tarr suggested. Juniper shrugged her agreement and so they set off, more slowly this time, enjoying the cold air in their hair, the feel of the smooth bark beneath their long hands. "Look!" Tarr said when they were nearly at the top. He pointed to a large amulet, roughly the size of his head. It was tied around the tree with a stiff piece of braided vine. Juniper drew up beside him.

"'The land of the Aspen, third tribe of the Ashans,'" she read, her fingers tracing it. A small charm dangled from the bottom of the amulet in the shape of an Aspen leaf. The same amulet hung from the doorway of the communal tribal house they shared with all of the other young Ashans their age.

"I have only been to the border a few times before," said Tarr thoughtfully. "And I do not think I have ever been up this high."

"Let us go all the way up," she suggested eagerly. Juniper was something of a daredevil. "Come on."

She scampered faster now, footholds and handholds flowing naturally beneath her. Tarr followed her up into the swinging point of the tree, swaying precariously with every gust of wind, the elastic wood bowing beneath their weight. Their heads peeked over the tops of the uppermost leaves, and they surveyed the extent of the forest around them.

"There!" Juniper said, pointing. "The mountains!"

Tarr had seen the mountains before, of course, but only on the rare occasions that he climbed to the very top of the forest. They were distantly cold and quite beautiful to look at, set against the pale blue of the sky. They looked so still compared to the rolling, rollicking canopy surrounding them.

"And there," Juniper turned and motioned in the other direction. "That is where the humans live. Where they have their cities." She used the Common language word for *city*; there was no equivalent word in Ashan.

Tarr looked curiously in the direction her hand indicated, then he cocked his head to one side. It seemed a long way away. He wondered if, at that very moment in the nearest town, there was a boy perched on his roof, staring towards the forest and the bowing tips of the trees to which Tarr was clinging. He shook his head, smiling mildly at his own folly. He was always thinking fanciful things like that. By this point, he had come to understand that many of his thoughts were rather strange. No one else in the tribe ever seemed to wonder about things the way he did.

It was another few seconds before he realized that Juniper was already descending down the tree and heading back towards the earth.

It was early afternoon as they followed the trail along the ground to where the other young Ashans were down by the river, doing the day's washing. The river spread through the trees, silvery and blue, shimmering brilliantly in the spots where it hit the light spilling from between the outstretched boughs of the trees. The water went rushing past, buoyed by melting snow that had come streaming down from the mountains towards the plains to the south, its sound intermingling with the noise of laughter and chatter from the other Ashans. A few of them glanced up as Tarr and Juniper swished beneath a low-hanging bough and picked their way down to the bank of the river. Both of them crouched down and grabbed a piece of cloth from a large woven basket that rested in the shallows. Tarr dipped his cloth in the water and dawdled a bit, dangling it against the flowing current before starting to halfheartedly scrub it against the smooth rock. He didn't mind chores as a whole, but for some reason washing always caused his mind to wander elsewhere.

"I am fairly certain I will be taken by the Martans," said a girl nearby, who had the advantage of having a rather bossy, self-important voice that was able to carry over the sound of the water. "They've all but told me they like my weaving. I'm sure it will be them."

Tarr let out an audible groan, which luckily was covered up by the river. The other young Ashans he lived with had talked of nothing but the Choosing for about two months, and he was fed up to the teeth with it. He considered mentioning an out-of-season bird he'd seen in the trees earlier that morning as a desperate attempt to change the subject, but then closed his mouth and sat back, resigned to traversing the same old path of wondering and postulating that his cohort had been endlessly treading.

"Well, *I* am hoping to be with the Huntars," said a boy, two months younger than Tarr, with glassy green eyes and a slight lisp. Tarr could tell that the boy's heart wasn't really in the scrubbing, either.

"Who do you think will choose you, Tarr?" Juniper nudged him teasingly. "Which family?"

Tarr rolled his eyes at her. She knew how tired he was of the conversation, how uncomfortable it made him. Juniper laughed to herself and turned back around to chatter amicably with the bossy-voiced girl. Juniper seemed to be able to talk to anyone, regardless of how irritating or self-important. It was not an ability with which Tarr was blessed.

The truth was that Tarr had been nervous about the Choosing ever since the winter had broken and spring had started to peek back up through the forest. It was the dawn of his twentieth year, which meant that it was time for him to be Chosen, along with all the others his age. Since they'd been born, as was the Ashan custom, the children had all been reared together—nursed by the caretakers, taught by teachers. They ate, slept, and played together in the same communal house in the middle of the village; took their lessons, did their chores, learned the skills needed to be good citizens of their tribe. There were records kept of biological parentage, of course, none of it was secret—Tarr, for example, knew that he had no blood-related siblings. But who an Ashan child was born to was beside the point. What mattered was the Choosing.

Tarr remembered the Choosing from the previous year. He'd paid closer attention to it now that it had begun to loom ahead in his own future. He remembered how glad he'd been that it was not his time to be Chosen, how he'd pitied the pack of nervous young Ashans, clustered together in the center of the village, staring down the elders of the village as they waited to be selected by one of the Ashan families in the village.

The Aspen tribe was composed of roughly fifty extended families; Tarr had come to understand through the course of his studies that their tribe was bigger than most due to its proximity to the border held by the humans to the south of them. Over the years, the placement of their tribal lands had led to quite a few Ashans (who had left their own home tribes for one reason or another) wandering back into the forest from various faraway lands to the south and being adopted into their tribe. Many, too, had been brought into the tribe as mates; custom dictated that when an Ashan wished to start a family, they would have to seek a mate outside the tribe's borders. These newcomers would have the trees of their families recorded and preserved in the village library, and the story of their lineage documented in their spinal tattoos.

Each year, the fifty Aspen families would come together and choose which of the young Ashans would leave the group of children and join them, to be knitted into the fabric of their family lines forever. Some families valued strength, some valued intelligence, others skill at crafts or labor. To hear the nervous chatter of his fellows, each of the other Ashans seemed to have a very clear idea of at least three families that would take them in on the night of the Choosing, but Tarr had to admit that he hadn't the faintest idea of who would choose *him*. As soon as he had matured and started to wrap his young mind around exactly what the Choosing entailed, he had been uncomfortably self-conscious around the adult members of the tribe. Did he smile too quickly? Could they tell he was nervous? Would they not find him skilled enough? Fast enough? He knew he was clever enough. But was something like cleverness as easy to pick out as skills like climbing or running? Should he have walked around loudly reciting facts he had learned in school? He had briefly considered the latter option, but then reasoned that if *he* were an Ashan Elder and one of the children had started walking around doing that, he would have dumped them in the nearest river.

The group of young Ashans were kept mostly to themselves as they grew up. The majority of their social interactions took place with each other, as well as the younger children and the various caretakers and teachers who helped them all to grow and flourish. Though they were all a part of the same tribe, there was a very definite divide between the adults and the young, and Tarr had never felt it quite as starkly as he did now.

"I wonder if the tattoos hurt," the boy with the lisp wondered aloud, snapping Tarr out of his meandering thoughts.

Every Ashan, once they had been adopted into their Chosen family, was given the beginnings of a tattoo that would start at the nape of their neck and, over time, stretch in a line all the way down the length of their spines, with flourishes and calligraphy and symbols branching off denoting partners, relatives, parents, children, even accomplishments like being made an Elder of the tribe. But those first marks, the ones at the nape of the neck, were the most important and would show the symbol of their home tribes and of their Chosen families. Tarr wasn't worried about the pain of getting the tattoo as much as he was worried about being Chosen at all.

"I do not want to go to the Choosing unless I can find my new comb," said another girl loudly, further down the river. "I want to wear my new comb to the ceremony, and I cannot find it anywhere."

"Sereph has it," Tarr said before he could stop himself. He winced reflexively, wishing he had kept his mouth shut.

The reaction was immediate. Almost all action ceased, and sixteen heads swiveled around to stare at him, eyes wide. The sound of the river seemed even louder in the silence that fell on them.

"*Tarr!*" Sereph, the girl with the bossy, loud voice whom Tarr had accused, whirled on him. Even though Tarr's insides were curdling with embarrassment, he felt a slight ping of pleasure to see that he had been right. Sereph darted a look over to Ren, the girl who had lost the comb. "I was going to give it back tonight before the Choosing," she said snottily, sending Tarr a furious glare.

"Fine," Ren said curtly, and returned to her washing. The chatter was less loud after that, with most of the other young Ashans muttering to each other, occasionally shooting Tarr a dirty look. Juniper gave him a bug-eyed expression that clearly said *why'd you have to go and open your mouth?* and Tarr helplessly shrugged.

It was hard to explain—Tarr just seemed to *know* things. He would know things like who had taken what, or where someone was, or why one of the Elders had gone away for three days under mysterious circumstances. Tarr hadn't understood why the others didn't know these sorts of things as well—all he did was watch and listen and put two and two together. He had noticed the way that Sereph had smiled secretly and ducked her head when Ren talked about the comb. It wasn't hard. Why hadn't the others *seen?*

He had always been able to do it, though the other young Ashans hadn't noticed or cared much when they were growing up. Things began to change, however, after they hit their teens and his former playmates began to forge their own identities and cliques, and to view each other with a sense of distance and suspicion rather than the uncaring amity of their youth. It was then they started to catch on, and began to think that it was odd that Tarr could see the things he could, and to think that Tarr himself was strange for knowing the things he did. And the most confounding thing of all was that any ire and irritation they felt when Tarr caught someone in a lie or found someone's piece of lost property, began to be directed at Tarr himself, rather than at any guilty party. So Tarr had tried to stop himself, tried to catch the words before they came out of his mouth, but it was difficult and he often tripped up. He wanted nothing more than to blend anonymously into the background, but often found himself at the receiving end of a chorus of bug-eyed stares, much as he just had.

He hoped that none of the adults in the village thought him odd. His teachers liked him well enough and knew him to be a conscientious student and an avid reader. He would spend many pleasant afternoons whiling away his time reading about the strange customs and lifestyles of the people who lived just beyond the border to the south, as foreign and fantastical-sounding as any of the legends that the Elders recited during the Fall and Spring gathering festivals.

All of a sudden, he couldn't take it anymore. He set down the sodden piece of cloth with a wet *flop* on the shining rock beside him, gave a tiny nod to Juniper (who was the only one who looked up at him as he rose), and swished back through the trees towards the village.

The village was set up in a circular shape only a short way from the river. Tarr automatically followed the familiar path through the trees around the north edge of the main part of the village. As he walked, his eye traveled along the pleasantly familiar pattern of the village buildings, all of them constructed as treehouses. Every treehouse was set at a height anywhere from six to ten feet off of the ground (depending on the size; the larger buildings tended to be closer to the ground.) They were formed onto and around the trees of the forest, so in any Ashan building there would be a number of trunks passing smoothly through the floor and up through the ceiling above. From the ground, it looked almost as though the trees had formed a strong set of fingers thrusting up from the earth, balancing the houses up on their tips. All the wood for the houses was carefully burnt black to preserve it from the weather. Sometimes, when Tarr approached the village at dusk, it seemed as though the Ashan houses were really a host of large black shadowy creatures crouching low in the trees, waiting to spring onto the floor below.

Tarr liked the way he could tell which buildings in the village were very, very old—the wood had a softer look to it, and the roofs of some of the houses were covered with crawling vines and moss that bloomed with white flowers in the springtime, almost like a verdant carpet of snow. He liked the soft paper screens that divided up the insides of the houses, the pleasant *shunk* sound they made when they slid closed. Any of the paper walls could be removed to create more space or added to create more rooms or more privacy. In the summers, the windows of the treehouses were fitted with gossamer-thin paper sheets to keep out insects and let in the breeze; the sunlight would filter through, turning the insides of the rooms a soft buttery gold. In the winter, it was dark almost all the time; the windows were replaced with reinforced layers to insulate from the cold, and fires were carefully lit in stone hearths on the floors of the houses.

He passed quickly by the main village circle where the adult Ashans lived and worked, and headed towards the young Ashans' lodgings, which were set in their own semicircle a short ways away from the main village square. The point of this arrangement, Tarr understood, was keeping the children's lives largely separate from those of the rest of the tribe—allowing them time and space to grow and flourish and learn. In the young Ashans' part of the village there were large communal sleeping and living areas occupied by newborns up to children about five years old, then five to ten, ten to fifteen, fifteen to twenty. There were seventeen Ashans living with Tarr in the "fifteen to twenty" building, though the house itself was empty at the moment; he had just left most of them down by the river doing their chores. Around the corner of one of the buildings was a playing and climbing area where a cluster of little ones were shimmying up ropes and swinging from softly bending low branches while three of their minders kept bemused watch. Occasionally, one of the children would fall with a fat *thump* in a heap to the earth, and then, after a few moments of wailing, would scamper merrily back off again.

Tarr halted in his step, his mind wandering as he watched the children at play. In another instant, he realized exactly where he wanted to go and turned back towards the village to the library at the far north end of the main square. The library was one of the few buildings in the central section of the village where the younger Ashans were actively encouraged to go and work on their studies, and was one of Tarr's favorite places to while away an afternoon. Especially since winter had recently broken and the days were slowly growing sunnier and more pleasant, the other young Ashans had found better and better excuses to spend their time out of doors. He was reasonably certain there wouldn't be anyone else there.

The library was a long, narrow building set low on its tree supports, with two cedars standing broadly like sentries at the front entrance. The double front doors had recently been exchanged from their heavy insulated winter editions to a warm-weather screen framed by the characteristically blackened preserved cedar wood favored by the Ashan builders in the village. As the doors closed behind him with a light *shunk* (Tarr smiled to himself), he saw the Keeper of the books straighten up from a row in the far corner of the library. Seeing that it was Tarr who had entered, she gave him a small wave and went back to her work. The paper screen beside her had been pushed back to fully let in the fresh, delicious breeze.

Tarr settled on a stool by one of his favorite sections and grabbed one of the rolled scrolls from the wall. The shelves were built in the shape of honeycombs, with the books rolled up in tight paper coils, each meticulously labeled at the end with a string and tag. When a gust of wind happened to blow through the library building, all of the tags would begin to flutter furiously at the end of their tethers like dozens of little white butterflies.

Tarr unfurled one of his best-loved scrolls (having to do with a legend about the Jelani, a near-mythical people who lived in a big white palace on the side of a mountain), but as his eyes passed carelessly over the familiar script, he felt his mind wandering once again. In a few seconds he was lost in another reverie, which was broken only by the appearance of the Keeper of the books, who popped around the end of one of the shelves.

"Well, Tarr, it is good to see you today," she said kindly. She was an older woman with gray hair pulled back into a braid, the bloom of her family tattoo creeping around the nape of her neck so that the whorls and loops of the Ashan calligraphy were almost visible at the front. Some of the Ashans in Tarr's age group had said that she could have become a village Elder if she'd wanted to but had opted instead to spend her life tending to the books in her library. The other young Ashans had seemed bewildered by this decision, but privately, Tarr thought it made a lot of sense.

"It is good to see you, Keeper," Tarr replied courteously. She had an Ashan name as well, but as was the habit for those who played a specific role in the tribe's infrastructure, she had taken the nickname of her profession.

She fixed him with a thoughtful expression and tilted her sharp, wizened head to one side. "Is something wrong, Tarr?"

"No," Tarr lied.

She frowned and pulled up a stool, sitting beside the shelf opposite Tarr and beginning to feign the pretense of checking some of the labels on the immaculately organized scrolls. "You are looking forward to the Choosing tonight, Tarr?"

"I suppose so," he shrugged one thin shoulder, aware of how glum his voice sounded in the stillness of the library.

Keeper hid a smile beneath a thoughtful nod. She was fond of Tarr. His uncommonly sweet expression, and the rather melancholy way his eyes tilted down at the edges, predisposed her to feel protective of him.

"I would not worry too much, Tarr," she said comfortingly. "Your teachers have made reports on all of you to the families in the village. Some of the family heads have even been invited to observe you during your lessons and activities. They know you and know your character."

"They have watched us in our lessons?" Tarr asked curiously. He hadn't been aware of anyone watching them, ever. The thought made him uncomfortable. He hoped he hadn't done anything embarrassing while they had been watching, like pick at his ear or doze off in class.

"Yes," she assured him with a smile. "But again. I would not worry about it."

"How can I not?" Tarr blurted out, the anxiety he'd been trying to tamp down within his chest suddenly burbling forth. "What if I am not Chosen? What if—"

He trailed off, but the unasked question hung in the air around them. He had never—not, at least, in the years he'd been actively paying attention to the Choosing—seen an instance in which one of the young Ashans was not chosen to become part of a family. But nevertheless, as the anxiety of the event mounted and the day itself loomed forward, the other Ashans in his class had started talking about those who hadn't been selected. According to his fellows, those who had remained unchosen were sent out of the village tribe for at least a year before returning. Many of them never returned at all. Tarr wasn't sure whether to believe the stories or not, as many of the other young Ashans had a flair for narrative embroidery, but if it was true, it was almost too horrible to be believed.

"Ah, I see," the Keeper said calmly, brushing her hands along the legs of her trousers in a businesslike manner. "Well, Tarr, I really do not think you need to be worried about that."

Tarr looked at her sharply, trying to discern whether there was some hidden meaning beneath her words. She regarded him kindly, her weathered eyes warm and comforting. And then, all at once, the realization came to him. *She was going to choose him!* Of course. It was a natural solution—she knew him better than any of the other adult Ashans in the village (other than their teachers, of course.) They got on well, so it only made sense that she and her family would be the ones to take him in. Perhaps he would apprentice with her and spend the rest of his life whiling away in the library, deep amongst the old tales and legends, smiling benevolently at the young Ashans who nervously made their way into the building to work on an assignment or project. He could see himself pointing them towards one of the honeycomb-shaped bookshelves, muttering, "Ah, yes, here's the one you want," beneath his breath, smiling beatifically as the student mumbled a nervous "thank you." It would be a good life, he thought. He would be content.

"Thank you," Tarr straightened suddenly, feeling immensely cheered. He tried not to crane his neck too obviously, but hoped that he could catch a glimpse of the family tattoo on the back of the Keeper's neck, to try and imagine it being transferred to his own. When he was adopted into her family, he would be given his own calligraphy character, which would be added to the tattooed lifelines of everyone in the family. "Thank you very much," he said in a rush, and stood. "I...I just remembered that I left some work down at the river. I should go down and finish."

"Right you should," the Keeper agreed with a patient smile. "I will see you tonight at the Choosing, Tarr."

"See you tonight," he echoed, and nearly stumbled over his own feet back out into the forest.

The Choosing began after sundown. Stone lamps were lit along the path leading the way from the young Ashans' living compound to the main square of the village. Tarr, Juniper, Ren (comb intact, twisted in her light brown hair) and the others trooped soundlessly together, trailing in the wake of two of their senior teachers.

The rest of the tribe was gathered around the perimeter of the center square and watched them soundlessly as they approached. A circle of stones had been laid in the direct middle of the village common, and it was into this circle that Tarr and the other young Ashans were nervously ushered. Even through his terror, Tarr could appreciate how pretty the square looked; it had been done up as they did for most of the major festivals, with strings of colored lanterns swinging low and heavy over their heads. Lights were flickering behind the paper windows of the houses, hunkered and dark in the trees just above their heads. The young Ashans stood silently beside each other. Tarr could hear nothing but the quiet night breeze rustling through the leaves of the trees and the pounding of blood in his ears.

He looked at the ring of faces surrounding them and saw many that he recognized. He wondered whether any of them had been the ones to sit in on his lessons with the other young Ashans. What had they thought of him? Had they even noticed him at all? He wasn't sure whether to smile or remain serious, whether to clasp his hands in front of him or to leave them loose at his sides. His limbs suddenly felt even more gangly and awkward than they usually did. He glanced over at Juniper, who was a little way to his right. Her face was illuminated by the lamplight, and he noticed the way her mouth, usually smiling and carefree, was set in an unusually thin line.

Off to one side, he could see a cluster of younger Ashans (the youngest group of babies and toddlers was already long in bed). Some of them were clearly bored and watching the lights above more closely than they were the Ashans who were about to be chosen. The older teens, Tarr could see, were watching with varying degrees of anxiety. He could almost see it dawning on them how relevant this ceremony was to become in just a few short years. If he hadn't been so terrified, he would have laughed ruefully at the expressions on their faces.

Suddenly, there was the sound of a drum off to one side, and the village Elders stepped forward. There were five of them, clad in deep gray-green cloaks that draped across the fronts of their chests and hung down their backs to the ground. Each of the Elders slowly exchanged the same greeting often performed between members of the same tribe: they clapped their hands over the napes of one another's necks to show deference and respect for their family tattoos, and briefly touched their foreheads together. One by one, after the greetings were exchanged, they turned around to survey the young Ashans gathered in the center of the tribal circle. Tarr swallowed, trying to pry meaning from their solemn expressions. *Did the Elder on the end look at me?* he wondered. *Does she know I'm going to be chosen?*

His eyes darted to the left, and there, in the back of the crowd, was the Keeper of the library. He could feel his shoulders loosen ever so slightly at the sight of her familiar expression. She was watching him softly, and Tarr could almost feel the assurance radiate out from her as she met his eyes and gave an encouraging smile. *It's all right*, he told himself, forcing a shaky breath down his throat. *It's all right. I'm going to be chosen. I will belong to her family.* He would have brothers and sisters, uncles and aunts, a great-grandmother. He squared his shoulders as the Elders began to speak.

"Welcome to all of you," the Elder Speaker said. He had long white hair braided back from his face, and though he must have been many decades old, he still had a strong stature and stood straight and tall as he addressed the crowd. He used an ancient Ashan greeting, appropriate for such an important ceremony. "Tonight, as you know, is the Choosing, when you will cease your lives as children and begin it again as true members of this tribe. There is great honor in this, and we know that you will serve your Chosen families nobly and with devotion."

Tarr shifted his weight to one foot, wishing this was all over already.

"We will call you forth one by one. The family who has chosen you will step forward and lay their family stone at your feet. Then you will be Chosen. Once the ceremony has concluded, you will gather your things from your former living quarters and then go to the house of your new family. Your tattoo ceremony will take place in three days, once your signs have been designed by our scribes."

All of a sudden, just as Tarr had wished for the ceremony to be over, it all seemed to be going much too fast. It looked almost as though they were about to begin calling names—

"Ren, step forward," called the Speaker.

Tarr heard an audible intake of breath behind him and felt a jostle against his arm as Ren pushed past him and stepped out of the circle. She stood with her hands clasped behind her back, and though her head was tilted proudly upward, Tarr could see the way her fingers were nervously fidgeting against each other behind her.

After a few excruciating seconds, the crowd of watching Ashans parted, and a tall man with jet-black hair stepped forward. In his hand he carried a flat, round stone with a symbol engraved into it. He smiled kindly at Ren and laid it at her feet.

"The family of Merh has chosen Ren," he announced.

Tarr, his eyes still on Ren's hands, saw them flex open and close, then flutter to rest at her sides.

"You may take the family sign," the Speaker told her.

Ren fumbled a little as she bent and picked up the stone from beside her feet. When she turned, Tarr could see all manner of emotions roiling on her face: happiness, relief, latent terror. He could feel his throat tightening as he braced for the next name. When it came, he jumped as if he'd been given a shock.

"Nera," the Speaker intoned. "Step forward."

The Choosing continued, and Tarr felt as though he were oddly floating somewhere outside of his body, listening numbly to the proceedings, being jerked back to reality every time a new name was called out, feeling both relief and mounting anxiety as the Ashans were called forward and chosen.

Finally, Tarr was one of only three left without a stone in his hand. He was actively shaking now, bracing for the next name to be called, dreading and hoping that it would be his.

"Tarr," the Speaker announced. "Step forward."

So shocked was Tarr to hear his name called that it was a full ten seconds before he responded; Juniper, who was also waiting to be

Chosen, dug a helpful thumb into his spine and basically thrust him forward out of the circle.

Tarr stood there as the seconds stretched interminably past. There was no movement in the crowd. Tarr took a rattling breath and tried to steady himself. *It took a few seconds for the others*, he reminded himself. *Just breathe. Stand up straight and breathe.* But still there was no one who stepped forward.

Tarr turned and looked towards where the Keeper was standing. He could see her face in the dim light of the lanterns, and as he watched, he could see the encouraging smile draining from her expression. She made no move to step forward. And then, as he watched, he saw her turn and look around at the rest of the crowd expectantly. *She's not going to step forward*, Tarr realized slowly. *She never had any intention of Choosing me. She was only trying to be nice.*

The weight of it hit Tarr so squarely on the shoulders that he nearly felt his knees buckle beneath him. He would have no family. He would have no home. He would be forced to leave the village and strike out on his own, knowing no one in the outside world, with no experience of anything beyond the trees.

Through the bleary haze of his vision, Tarr caught sight of movement and looked up hopefully. It was only the Speaker, though, who raised his hand above the crowd. "Tarr, you have not been Chosen," he announced solemnly, as a heavy stone settled in the pit of Tarr's stomach. "Tonight, you will leave the tribe for a period of one year before you may return. Step forward."

Tarr tried to walk, but his legs seemed to have melted beneath him. He stumbled, conscious of the aghast stares bearing down on him, the awful silence that permeated the air, stifling the breath that he was trying to force back into his lungs. He forced one foot in front of the other and managed to duck into and past the crowd just beside the Elders, into the blissful, blissful darkness where he didn't have to feel the heat of all those eyes on the back of his head. About twenty feet past the edge of the circle he fell to his hands and knees, the soft, cold earth beneath them oddly comforting. In the distance, what must have been a thousand miles away, he could hear Juniper's name being called. *Maybe she won't be Chosen either*, he thought, but then immediately felt guilty for even having the thought. Besides, Juniper was personable and charming, and she was bound to be picked by one family or another. As he'd suspected, as he half-crawled up to the embrace of the nearest tree root, he remained alone.

The Choosing ceremony continued for the next few minutes, but Tarr was conscious only of muffled voices far away. The fear of what almost immediately was to come began to burble up inside him as he faced the thought of the dark forest at night, now so forbidding and ominous when before he had gladly tromped through its foliage at all hours of the night and day. He had taken it all for granted, he realized: his warm bed in the treehouse, the food provided to them, the companionship of the other Ashans, the books he whiled away the day reading. It had all been snatched away from him in the breath of an instant.

He thought back again of the Keeper, and a new feeling, anger, began to well up like hot tears in the corners of his eyes. How could she have left him standing there like that? Had she no pity for him at all? Couldn't she have just stepped forward and saved him from the embarrassment, from the humiliation of being sent away? Had their long friendship meant absolutely nothing to her? Was there something so inherently *wrong* with him, with the person he'd become, that she couldn't bear to make him a part of her family?

There was the sound of footsteps, and the light of a lantern rounded the tree nearest him. Tarr found himself squinting up at the legs of three of the Elders, including the Speaker, who looked down on him with a mixture of pity and impatience.

"Well, young Tarr, you know the laws. You must leave now for a period of at least one year before you are welcome to return to the tribe."

"I have not done anything," Tarr maintained, figuring that he had nothing more to lose, so some mild protestation wouldn't hurt. "Why was I not Chosen? I have done nothing to merit being cast out of the tribe."

"This is not a punishment, Tarr," the Speaker said sternly.

"It feels an awful lot like one," Tarr muttered.

"You have been given a gift. A gift to venture into the outside world, to gather knowledge and experience and bring it back to us, to better the tribe and our people," the Speaker told him.

Can't someone else do it? Tarr wondered.

"In any case," the Speaker said sharply, as if he'd heard the thought in Tarr's head, "you were not Chosen, and now you must leave. This is the law."

Tarr could see that he wasn't going to make a lot of headway with this line of argument. He hunkered back against the comfort of the tree, unable to think of what more he could possibly say. Another Ashan came up behind the cluster of Elders, carrying a large bundle in her arms. She handed it to the Speaker, who unfurled the bundle, revealing it to be a traveling cloak and a full knapsack.

"We have gathered your things," the Speaker told him, extending Tarr's belongings with one arm.

Tarr's mouth fell open, and he was numbly aware of raising one hand to take the cloak and knapsack from him. "Now?" he whispered. "I have to go now? May I at least go back and say goodbye to—"

"No," the Speaker shook his head. "There is a time for all things. It is the time for this now."

"But," Tarr's limbs were wobbly again as he struggled to his feet, leaning against the tree behind him for support. "Where do I go?"

"Two Falls is to the south," said the Speaker. "There are other Ashan tribes to the east and the west."

Tarr slowly, disbelievingly, pulled the cloak over his head and settled the drape over his chest. A small carved wooden Aspen leaf was pinned to the shoulder. He looked up and around at the faces regarding him, looking for an ounce, even a shred of sympathy. This was not the first time they had done this, and the time in which they might have empathized with Tarr's plight had long passed.

"We have made provisions for you for some days—food and some money, which is used as currency in Two Falls, should you choose to go in that direction."

"Money?" Tarr echoed. He had read about it, of course, but never used it before. His head was spinning.

"There are clothes as well. And a knife."

Silently, he took the knapsack and slung it over his shoulder. The Speaker, clearly relieved that Tarr had given up his feeble protestations, indicated the path behind Tarr and made a motion that he should follow.

As Tarr turned, he fought back the urge to suddenly drop to the ground and refuse to move a step further, perhaps grabbing onto a nearby trunk and knotting his fingers together like a child throwing a tantrum. Instead, realizing that dignity was perhaps the only thing truly left to him, he balled his hands into fists and forced himself forward, keenly aware of the lights of the village fading behind him, the forest growing darker and darker.

They traveled silently down the path leading out of the tribal lands, towards the main road that led south through the forest towards the human village of Two Falls. "We will leave you here," the Speaker said finally, coming to a halt. Tarr slowly turned and faced him, resigned that there was little else to do or say. "Good luck on your journey, Tarr. We hope to benefit from the insight and wisdom that you will glean from your time away. When the year is ended, we will welcome you back into the tribe. You will be able to choose your own vocation. Start your own Family."

Tarr nodded mutely, and with that, the small group of Elders turned and left him. Tarr stood and watched until their silhouettes melded into the inky black of the forest night. He was completely, utterly alone.

Only he wasn't. There was a small rustle in a tree a short ways to his left, and his attention instantly snapped into place. It would be a fitting cap to the evening, he thought to himself ruefully, if he was eaten by a mountain lion three minutes after leaving the village. He hadn't even had time to unpack the dagger that the Speaker had told him was in his knapsack.

He hunkered lower to the earth, bracing himself to be eaten. "Tarr!" hissed a voice from somewhere up in the trees. "It is me."

Tarr straightened, a wash of relief and gratitude crashing over him. "Juniper?" he whispered back.

"I wanted to come and say goodbye to you," she told him, dropping down from the tree above and landing like a feather on the loamy ground below. She clasped her hand over the nape of his neck, and he did the same. Briefly, their foreheads touched. "I did not think...I do not know what I can say..."

Tarr could sense her genuine distress, and somehow it made the pain of his worry less acute. "It is all right," he assured her, releasing her and taking a step back. "You were Chosen, then?" he asked, trying to make his voice sound casual.

"Yes," she said, looking uncomfortable. "It is a good family. It—"

"I am glad for you," he said, trying to keep the bitterness from his tone.

"Maybe we could find some way...some loophole," she suggested desperately. "Some way to keep you here."

Tarr smiled wanly. "I know. We could come up with some sort of situation where I wind up owing you a life debt, and then you could order me to stay. And not even the Elders could say anything."

Even though Tarr had been joking, the situation was desperate enough that the two of them paused and considered it. An Ashan life debt was the highest law, even higher than the laws of Choosing. But with every passing second, the momentary levity drained from the air. There was no way out, and both of them knew it.

"Where will you go?" she asked.

"I only learned I would be leaving about fifteen minutes ago, Juniper," Tarr said wearily. "I do not know yet."

"You speak the Common language, correct?"

"Hello, how are you, I'm fine," Tarr said immediately, switching languages smoothly from Ashan to the Common tongue. They had all learned it when they were young; the tribe's proximity to the human lands made it practical to do so. For some of the young Ashans, like Tarr, it had come easy and stuck. For others, it had been more difficult.

Juniper wrinkled her nose. "I hate the sound of it," she grimaced. At that moment, Tarr did, too.

Silence fell around them, and suddenly Tarr felt uncomfortable. It was clearly time for them to part, and he wasn't sure how best to do it. Should he hug her? Was she expecting something more? They had been friends since childhood and there had never been any awkwardness between them before. Already, he could feel the distance growing.

"One year is not such a long time," Juniper pointed out.

"No," Tarr agreed, though from where he stood, a year stretched out to almost an interminable length.

"Keep yourself well, Tarr," Juniper clasped him on the shoulder with one hand, using the formal Ashan farewell.

"Keep yourself well, Juniper," he replied.

And with that, he turned away and walked into the deep of the black forest.

Tarr awoke the next morning in the crook of a tree off the main path that wound its way south through the forest. He had wept for an hour or more before falling into an exhausted slumber; jerking himself awake into the cold periodically through the night, feeling each time the crushing disappointment that it had not all simply been a dream.

For the first time since the almost nightmarish events of the previous night, he allowed himself to take a moment and actively consider his options. To the south lay Two Falls, which sat squarely on the border between the human lands and the Ashan forest. To the west lay other Ashan tribes, who might or might not offer Tarr refuge. Most of the other tribes, Tarr had been led to believe, were less liberal in their beliefs and practices than Tarr's. The Aspen tribe had, out of practicality due to its contiguity to the humans, been more open to non-Ashan customs and traditions. This was why Tarr had been taught the Common language at an early age; many other tribes farther away from Two Falls had refused to teach the language at all, and actively discouraged Ashans from learning it. The northernmost Ashan tribe, the Birch, lived in the snowy forests and mountains at the far reaches of the Ashan lands and were so private and insular that their reclusiveness was the stuff of legend, even among the other Ashan tribes.

The prospect of venturing onto other Ashan lands was just as daunting to Tarr as the idea of traveling further south to Two Falls. He couldn't be sure of a warm welcome, or even of being admitted into the other villages at all, and the thought of aimlessly wandering through the forest with limited knowledge of foreign food and water sources wasn't something that Tarr particularly relished. So south it must be. Though he had read about the customs of humans and knew their language, he had never really considered the prospect of being among them, especially on his own. He hoped that the village would be large enough that he would blend in and go unnoticed.

Investigating the contents of his knapsack, he found the knife, which he strapped to his boot, a loaf of unleavened bread (which he tore into gratefully; having a plan apparently made one hungry), some dried, smoked river greens in a small paper parcel, and the few items of clothing he owned. There were a few strange gold coins jingling at the bottom of the knapsack, which he investigated curiously and then returned. Chewing thoughtfully and assessing his situation as he gazed out through the lightening blue haze of morning through the treetops, he slowly began to feel a bit better.

CHAPTER TWO

The next day at midmorning, Tarr began to purposefully wind his way southward towards the human city of Two Falls, faced with nothing but the quiet of the forest and open hours spread before him. Fully confronted with his new, strangely solitary reality, he felt his mind turning back to the events of the night before, and almost without realizing it began churning them over and over, imagining alternate scenarios and trying to project how it might have all gone differently if he'd said or done something else. Perhaps he should have stood up more to the Elder council when they had commanded him to leave. Perhaps he should have found a solid-looking tree, wrapped his arms around it, and refused to budge. Perhaps he should have appealed to the Ashan families directly. Perhaps he should have turned towards the Keeper and looked her straight in the eye and asked her why she hadn't chosen him. If only he had had the courage to do one of those things instead of foolishly standing there and then stumbling out of the circle like a frightened child.

The more he thought about it, and the more he tried to imagine how he could have changed the outcome of the Choosing, the more unhappy he felt. So, after a time, he turned his mind around to focus on what lay before him rather than what lay behind. However, in pointing his mind towards Two Falls, he found himself wishing that his teachers and the other adult Ashans had left him feeling more prepared for what he was about to face; wished that they had told him more about human customs and how to pass through the city without raising any comments or inviting any unwelcome attention. How did humans forage for food? He understood that they all lived closely together. Perhaps they shared foraging lands? Was there someone he could ask once he got there?

These thoughts, combined with a tendency to revert back to the events of the night before, twisted together around his chest until he was feeling quite gloomy indeed. Even though the woods were lovely, and the spring sunshine was dancing through the leaves and dappling the path that lay before him, he felt as though there was a dark, cold cloud following just behind his head as he made his way down the hill.

He couldn't quite put his finger on the emotion he felt. There was the anger he'd felt the night before, yes, and hurt. But there was also a sense of *betrayal*, which he couldn't remember ever feeling before. He had trusted them—trusted his teachers, trusted the Keeper, trusted the Elders—to protect him, to take care of him, to look after his well-being until he was ready to do so himself. And they hadn't done it. There he was, minimally outfitted, facing an unknown future in an unknown civilization, with only the basic tools required to keep him alive. And he felt angry.

This realization made him pause for a minute, and he settled himself at the base of a large, spreading tree, trying to gather his thoughts. He would not let this happen again, he decided. If he managed to overcome the difficulties of his situation, if he somehow managed to survive and make it through a year away and then return back to the Aspen village, he would never trust any of them ever again. He would not trust anyone in Two Falls to keep him alive, either. He was the only one he would rely on from this moment forward.

He glanced around himself, trying to see if there was something ceremonial he could break or cut in order to make this newfound pact with himself more official, but he saw nothing but a rock and a cluster of drying berries on a withered vine. For a moment, he considered mashing up some of the berries into a brown paste and making some kind of mark on the nearby tree trunk to commemorate the occasion, but decided after a moment or two that it was a stupid idea. Instead, he glumly shook the vine and a few of the dried berries plopped off and fell to the earth. It wasn't nearly as satisfying as he'd hoped. He sighed and stood, brushing the leaves and moist earth from the backs of his trousers and slinging the knapsack once more over his back.

A few hours later, he stopped and reassessed his direction. Two Falls lay somewhere due south of the Aspen tribe, which was where he'd been heading, but he was fairly certain that there was supposed to be an actual road close by that led to the southern border of the Ashan forest. He frowned and glanced at the sun; he was certainly heading in the right direction. Perhaps he just had to press on a bit farther. The thought of having a clear road to follow after so many hours of shuffling through the leaves and dodging under low-hanging branches was certainly appealing.

He hadn't taken ten steps before something prickled on the back of his neck and he instinctively turned, shading his face against the noon sun. Silhouetted in the top of a tree about fifty feet away was a figure watching him.

Another Ashan! he thought with interest. He was well past the border of his home tribe, the Aspen, so this had to be an Ashan from a different tribe, perhaps the Redwood, or maybe the Yew, though he didn't think he was far enough west to be near their border. He raised his hand and called out a greeting, but the figure remained immobile. There was something slightly threatening in the way the figure just sat there and watched him. It made Tarr uneasy, and so after another moment he took a few hesitant steps back and began walking again, trying not to be too obvious about the glances he continued to steal over his shoulder to check if the Ashan was still there watching him.

Tarr was silently followed for nearly the next half hour along his way, and continued to check every minute or two to be sure his shadow was still there. Tarr had surmised by this point that the mysterious Ashan in the trees was a scout from a neighboring tribe, which meant he must just be skirting the border of their lands. He rather wished that the scout would just give up stalking and come down to walk with him to have a proper chat and escort him to the edge of the border in a more straightforward fashion. It had struck him anew how lonely his new situation truly was. He had grown up surrounded by a pack of friends and peers; their absence, which he had never really considered before, was now an enormous chasm. The prattling in the mornings, hushed giggles and whispers in the night before they'd gone to sleep in their shared lodging, the tattling, the murmuring...it had been as constant and natural as his own breathing. And now there was only a great vacuum of silence. He would give anything to hear their voices again. Even the high-pitched annoying ones would have sounded positively melodic to his ears.

He reached the southern road by midafternoon. Glancing over his shoulder one last time, he saw that the mysterious Ashan, whoever they had been, had vanished back into the forest. For a moment, he felt a pang of jealousy that the scout had a home of his own to return to, but he forced himself to look ahead and take his first steps out onto the path.

As he had anticipated, it was easier going on the open road than it had been through the forest, and he made good time for the rest of the afternoon. On three occasions, he actually saw other travelers coming up the road in the opposite direction. The first was an Ashan woman carrying a baby and leading a small child, all of whom avoided meeting his eyes as they passed. Next, he saw a hooded man leading a small wagon pulled by a dispirited-looking horse (Tarr kept well clear of the horse, as he'd heard of them but never seen one before), and lastly, there was a pair of young Ashans roughly his age, who looked at him curiously and began whispering to each other almost as soon as Tarr had gone by. Tarr wondered vaguely if perhaps the two young Ashan men hadn't been Chosen either, and were returning to their tribes after their year away. *Maybe I should just follow them and try my luck*, he thought, but by then it was too late, and the Ashans had disappeared around a bend in the wood.

By nightfall, he began scouting around for a good place to make camp and sleep, though nothing in the woods by the road particularly beckoned to him. He wasn't sure whether it was safer to leave the road and head out alone into the woods where he wouldn't be bothered by any passersby (though, he reasoned, he didn't have much that would make stealing an appealing prospect.)

As he walked along, the gloom of night falling heavily through the boughs, he saw the glimmer of a light flickering orange and red through the trees. Curious, he ventured closer. As he drew near, he could see that it was a campfire set a little ways off the road. An Ashan man was sitting by the fire, feeding it with bits of twig and old leaves. He had dug out a rudimentary pit in the earth and lined it with stones to keep the flame from spreading, and held out his hands to warm them by the light. Beside his right foot was an enormous white fur pelt, folded and curled in a ball. As Tarr passed, the man looked over at him and, to Tarr's great astonishment, the white fur pelt began to move. A moment later, a canine head twisted round, regarding him with cool, detached interest.

Tarr completely forgot himself and stopped still. "Is that a wolf?" he asked, openmouthed.

The strange Ashan looked down at the animal beside his feet and shrugged. "Yes, I suppose so." He studied Tarr for a few moments, clearly sensing his hesitation. "He's tame enough. He won't attack you."

Tarr laughed nervously and took a step back. The stranger looked him up and down. "You can come up here if you like. I have food if you want some."

Tarr's stomach, as if in response, gave an unmistakable grumble. The meager provisions that had been provided to him by the Elders had run out around lunchtime earlier that day and it was already too late to forage for anything else.

"I have no goods to trade," he said cautiously, remembering that now that he was out of his tribe, he would be expected to trade or pay for whatever he needed. He thought briefly of the few coins jingling at the bottom of his knapsack, but didn't fully understand their value and didn't want to offer the Ashan man the wrong thing.

The stranger shrugged as if this was little surprise to him. "Come on. You can stay here, if you like. The wolf will take care of anything that might want to harm us."

Tarr cautiously picked his way off the side of the road and clambered up to the outcrop where the stranger and the wolf were sitting. He scooted around the edge of the fire, keeping a respectful distance between himself and the wolf, who mercifully hadn't barked or growled at him, but was still watching him coolly, as if sizing him up. Tarr had seen wolves in the forest before, but never this close. The animal was much, much bigger than he'd imagined.

The stranger reached into his knapsack and drew out some bread and a hunk of yellow cheese, which Tarr set about devouring gratefully. The stranger watched him eat with a bemused sort of detachment, then after some consideration, he withdrew another small roll and tossed it to him.

"Where are you heading?" the stranger asked.

"Two Falls," Tarr said through a mouthful of bread. It was all rather undignified and impolite, so he forced himself to swallow before continuing. "My name is Tarr," he volunteered, though the stranger had made no attempts to inquire after it.

"Been to Two Falls before?" the stranger inquired, but the tone of his voice implied he already knew the answer.

Tarr shook his head. The taut pull of his hunger momentarily slackened, he took the opportunity to study the stranger over the last few bites. The Ashan sitting opposite was a well-preserved, athletic individual of perhaps fifty years of age. He had dark hair and eyes, and an air that he had seen many things in his time, to the extent that it would take a great deal to shock him. He wore a dark gray cloak over his head and shoulders, different in style from the traditional Ashan traveling cloak. Tarr got the sense that he had lived among the humans for a long while. *Perhaps I should ask him for advice*, he thought, but was too embarrassed to do so.

"Where did you find the wolf?" Tarr asked finally, his gaze traveling down to the enormous white animal, who was still looking back at Tarr with his placid, searching stare. The wolf's eyes were blue, Tarr noticed.

Tarr had been expecting some sort of long, meandering tale about lifelong friendship between the stranger and his pet, something that would temporarily relieve Tarr of the burden of drumming up conversation, but instead, the Ashan merely shrugged a shoulder and glanced down at the wolf beside him. "He just sort of showed up one day. I've been traveling along the southern border, and he just appeared out of the woods. Been following me ever since. He seems tame enough. Must have belonged to someone and just wandered off one day. I feed him a little, but he generally hunts on his own." The Ashan shrugged again.

Tarr got the sense that if the wolf were any more high-maintenance than he had just described, the stranger would have severed all relations a long time ago.

"How nice," Tarr said politely. He cleared his throat, glancing around at the dark trees stretching upwards into the vault of the sky. "Is it long to Two Falls?" he asked.

"Another day or so," the stranger replied. "There's a gate at the bottom of the cliff, and then a path that goes upward, and then you go a bit farther, and there's the city. You can't miss it."

"I see," Tarr replied, though he didn't see at all. He wondered whether the stranger would be amenable to their traveling to Two Falls together, but was too timid to suggest it. Instead, he tried to sort the stranger's instructions into some sort of order that would be helpful to him when trying to find his way to Two Falls, but was especially perturbed by the assurance that he "couldn't miss it." In Tarr's limited experience, when these sorts of guarantees were given, the opposite was likely true.

The stranger stretched his arms above his head and began settling back. Realizing that he was preparing for sleep, Tarr immediately felt awkward and made a movement to pack up his things. He even began stammering out his gratitude for the meal. Without looking up, the stranger settled back against his bag, pulled his hood down over his head, and nonchalantly said, "Stay if you like. It will be safe enough with the wolf there. No one is likely to come close."

Tarr considered for a moment, imagining the night spent cold and damp teetering in the crook of a tree versus there by the fire with the watchful gaze of the wolf (who at least seemed to tolerate him.) "Thank you," he said finally, and settled down on the ground. It had been a long day of walking, and sleep crept over him quickly. He drowsily toyed with the carved wooden Aspen pin that had been affixed to his cloak. He had only a few moments to spare a thought for what the next day might bring.

Show me the right way to go, he thought dimly, turning the leaf over and over in his hand. *Show me where to go so someday I can be home.*

The last thing he remembered seeing before closing his eyes was the wolf's cool blue stare, studying him thoughtfully from behind the dying flames.

The embers of the fire were still smoking when Tarr awoke to the blue light of morning. The day was cool and overcast, and a strange gray haze hung low in the sky, like a blanket had been drawn over the tops of the trees, enveloping everything within. Rubbing his eyes and glancing around, Tarr could even make out the wisps of a ghostly mist creeping between the trunks of the trees, dissipating up into the air.

He pushed himself up blearily, relieved to find that his knapsack (which he'd used as a pillow) was still intact. Remembering the stranger from the night before, Tarr twisted around to wish him a good morning, but was stunned to find the stranger had gone. His brow furrowing a bit, Tarr wiped the last bit of sleep from his eyes and leapt to his feet, searching the surrounding forest for any sign of the stranger. *Perhaps he's gone to forage some wood to start the fire again, or maybe he had to relieve himself*, Tarr reasoned. He waited there for a few minutes, but the stranger did not return. He listened carefully. Other than the hush of the forest, he could hear nothing.

Suddenly, a twig cracked directly behind him and he whipped around, a smile already affixing to his face as he prepared to greet the stranger and ask him how he'd slept. To his utter astonishment, though, he found himself face to face with the enormous white wolf. Standing, he was even larger than Tarr had thought; the animal's head came up nearly to his own elbow. His mouth fell open as the wolf looked up at him with the same level, blue-eyed gaze from the night before.

"Hello," Tarr said after a moment. "Where did your master go, then?"

The wolf remained immobile.

Tarr looked around at the empty woods one last time. They were quite alone. There weren't a whole lot of options left to him, so he decided to default to his usual route of courtesy. "I'm traveling to Two Falls," he informed the wolf. "You're welcome to come along if you like."

The wolf merely looked back at him.

"I'd like to give you a name," Tarr told the wolf, well aware that after a day of walking by himself he was already starting to sound like he was losing his grip. "How about Wolver? There was a character in an old Ashan story I used to love with a character named Wolver."

The wolf wasn't much of a conversationalist one way or the other, but Tarr was nevertheless glad to finally have someone to talk to. He covered the smoldering embers with dirt and set off down the small hill back onto the main road. When he turned around to look over his shoulder, he half expected to find that the wolf had vanished once more into the trees, but was astonished to find the animal trotting along in his wake. He was no judge of the creature's facial expressions, but it seemed to be quite content to walk along with him. Feeling as if the day couldn't get much stranger, Tarr gave a shrug and continued along the southern road, the white wolf following twenty paces behind.

CHAPTER THREE

That same day, Lady Cira, one of the Jelani Princesses of Joymaril, returned to her palace after six months in the Meadows, ready to exact her revenge on those who had wronged her.

She was heralded from the palace's gleaming white towers with the sound of trumpets, and basked unabashedly in the silvery sound and the golden light filtering down on her upturned face. Who really cared about the circumstances under which she had been sent away? None of that mattered. She was wiser, much wiser than she had been when she had left. She would make things difficult for her enemies. She would have her revenge.

Upon dismounting from her horse, carelessly tossing the reins to the nearest attending servant, she walked forward up a winding marble staircase, her long traveling robe brushing behind her feet as she walked. She didn't trip on it. She made it her practice to never err, never take a false step. As she walked through the once-familiar hallways, glowing with soft white refracted sunlight, she reflected that they all seemed strangely small now, as if she had grown beyond them.

Gliding through to the soaring royal entrance chamber, she saw with a smug twinge that her mother and father, the King and Queen of Joymaril, had come down themselves to greet her with their habitual formality: sterile brushes on the cheek with their lips, a pleasant exchange of words and nothing more. Her father, the King, had the perpetual look of someone whose mind was elsewhere; Cira knew from experience that this was not just an expression. It was unlikely that he had even noticed her absence at all in the six months she'd been gone.

"Welcome back," he said vaguely, placing a paternalistic hand on her head.

"Thank you, Father," she said sweetly.

"You are most welcome, daughter," said her mother in a low voice, her face almost a mirror image of her daughter's. The Queen was the ruling power in the Jelani court, and lucky it was, too; she was sharp and calculating in every way that her husband was vacant and disinterested. Cira regarded her anew, as if seeing her familiar visage for the very first time. Her mother's shrewdness would be a difficult obstacle to overcome. Cira would have to figure out the best way to worm her way back into her mother's confidence, to get to the point where she could whisper words in her ear and have the Queen repeat them aloud, never realizing they weren't her own. It would be difficult, but not impossible.

Cira turned while the crowd behind her applauded politely at their tepid exchange of familial affection. Cira kept a winning smile fixed upon her face, a smile she had learned and practiced and could keep up without the slightest effort, while inwardly her mind seethed and schemed.

The three of them set off together in a procession towards the receiving rooms. It seemed as if the entire staff of palace servants had all been enlisted to throw flowers in front of her feet as she and her parents made their way together through the pearly white palace towards the royal lounge, where she would be greeted by the officials and the nobles. Only after the stiff formalities were over could she retreat to her spacious apartments (which, she assumed, had been decked out in their full splendor on the occasion of her return) and put her feet up after a hard week's ride. Cira wouldn't rush things, however. She didn't want to look *too* tired, too eager to take off her boots, to change out of her spotless riding habit. She had to keep up appearances at all costs, and an extra hour or so of standing around and conversing wittily with sycophantic courtiers was something at which she had always excelled.

The courtiers of the palace crowded the hallways as she and her train made their way forward, gawking at her, whispering to one another behind their hands. Cira flipped her sheet of white-blond hair over her shoulder, straightening her shoulders ever so slightly as she felt the eyes staring at her as she passed. She turned up her nose disdainfully at their admiration. She knew how the light caught her hair. If she wanted to, she could work her charm upon any and all of the people in attendance. She could have the entire court eating from the palm of her hand.

All of a sudden, she became aware that a certain pair of eyes had fastened upon the back of her swaying traveling cloak. She gave a half-shiver at the familiar eerie sensation, but she kept her jaw firm and defiant as she turned to greet her elder sister, Athela.

Athela was skulking in the shadows, her black curly hair fading seamlessly into the darkness she habitually inhabited. There was little, if any, familial resemblance between the two siblings, or indeed any resemblance between Athela and the other fair-colored denizens of the city. Her wild black hair, the deep brown of her skin, the expression currently knit between her brows—everything about her was darker than those around her. Temperamentally, Cira was all too aware that the same determination and strength she valued in herself had also been imbued deeply in her sister. They had never, however, seen eye to eye on anything and had been set firmly at loggerheads almost since the day Cira was born.

The King and Queen, who had been walking on either side of Cira, stopped and turned towards their other daughter, waiting for Athela to come out and greet her and pay her the respects that etiquette demanded. However, it seemed that Athela had no impetus to comply. She remained motionless against the wall, arms folded impudently, one knee bent, foot resting against the wall, the other leg bracing her at an angle. She stared, unblinkingly, with her light gray eyes. The very informality of her stance was a challenge.

"Athela, won't you come over to me and at least say hello?" Cira said in her sweetest, most engaging voice. There were dozens of people watching them. She had to keep up her appearance, though the animosity between the siblings was common knowledge throughout the palace and the surrounding city. "I've been away for half a year; surely that warrants a greeting."

Athela snorted audibly. "Hello, then," she conceded.

"Hello," Cira retorted sharply, letting her temper get in the way for a moment. *Easy does it,* she reprimanded herself. *Be polite. You have an audience.* She relaxed her posture a little bit, smiling and spreading her hands out wide, welcoming. The smile felt awkward on her face. Athela let out a bark of a laugh.

"Oh, wipe the grin, Cira, it makes you look sick. Not to say that that isn't an improvement."

Cira let the mask drop and angrily stepped forward. She wasn't afraid of Athela, though her elder sister was two inches taller. There wasn't anything Athela could do to her. Cira was her parents' favorite child, whereas Athela had spent the majority of her life in social and familial exile.

There were the sounds of running footsteps echoing through the expansive dome of the hallway, and the attention of the watching courtiers swept from the two sisters to a pair of newcomers. "My lady Cira," came a sudden familiar baritone voice from behind her, low and with the richness of honey, halting her every thought. There was a soft but distinctly audible intake of breath from the people watching, and she knew who it had to be. She turned and saw her cousin Lord Argolaith fast approaching, his chestnut eyes warily taking in the unfolding scene.

Laith, as he was known casually to his friends (and the flocks of girls who imagined they were on intimate terms with him), had been a beautiful child and, upon his return from ten years of formative campaigns in the Meadows, had matured into a young man whom many believed to be the most handsome Jelani ever born. Tall, athletic, and inherently graceful, he had light sandy hair brushing the tops of his dark eyebrows and a face reminiscent of the sculptures of old kings, with a slightly curved aristocratic nose, a wide jaw, and a long, slender neck. Cira noted with amusement how many of the gawking members of the court had abandoned all interest in watching the argument in favor of staring unabashedly at Laith. Cira, too, found it hard to look away or do anything but smile rather stupidly.

Still, she knew better than to think that Laith was happy to see her. He was dressed simply in a loose black shirt and riding trousers; his black boots were scuffed and unpolished. He must have rushed back to the palace from an afternoon ride to divert the inevitable confrontation between Cira and her sister, with whom Laith shared an inexplicable and rather unfortunate friendship. It was a testament to his popularity that his association with Athela had done nothing to tarnish his reputation in the eyes of the court. Laith gave a respectful nod to the King and Queen, who were watching them with narrowed eyes. He stopped in front of Cira, a full foot taller than her.

"Cousin Cira. It is good to see you again." Laith leaned in to kiss her cheek, and Cira felt Athela shift uncomfortably behind her. While Athela would never confess to having affection for anyone, everyone knew that Laith was her favorite relative, and seeing him even put on the façade was enough to make her spitting mad. Seeing an opportunity for a delicious bit of provocation, she moved in closer than she had to, making sure her hand lingered against his muscular arm so that Athela was sure to see. Laith brushed Cira's rosy cheek with his lips and took a few steps back. She breathed in his scent deeply, full of sun and the smell of woods.

"You look well," he said guardedly. "I hope you enjoyed your time away. The Meadows are lovely this time of year."

Laith's quick eyes darted back to Athela in the shadows and returned to Cira. Around his shoulder, she saw Marc, Laith's bodyguard and best friend, remaining a few strides away from the prince. Marc's ice-blue eyes were trained on the scene before him, looking for any danger to Laith, his hand resting carefully on his sword. He wouldn't dare draw it. Not in front of the King and Queen.

Well, well, Cira thought to herself. *Quite the homecoming reception I'm having.* The courtiers might as well have brought large tubs of roasted nuts so they could snack while they watched the matinée that was unfolding.

Cira matched Laith's smooth tones with her own. She could fill the air easily with empty courtier's platitudes about the weather and the pleasantness of travel. "I did enjoy my time away. I was so eager to return home, but I was just greeting Athela here, and it seems she's not terribly happy to see me." Cira put on a mock face of injury.

"I wouldn't take it personally, Milady," Laith assured her evenly.

"*I* would," Athela muttered.

"Is lunch being served soon?" asked the King vaguely from behind them.

"Soon, darling," the Queen replied distractedly. "Athela, you have greeted your sister; now you may go." The Queen could clearly see the storm of a full-out brawl brewing between her daughters and was eager to head it off. The courtiers leaned in eagerly, their eyes like hungry birds, waiting for a crumb to drop at their feet.

Athela's face took on a sour expression, and she bobbed a sarcastic curtsy. As she made a pretense of turning to go, she looked over her shoulder. "You'll be sorry to hear that I changed all the locks on my apartment doors, Cira," she growled in a low tone, below the earshot of her parents farther away. "It will make it that much harder for your spies to go through my things looking for signs of treason."

"I don't think they'll have to look *that* hard," Cira hissed back, her eyes flashing.

"What a shame it is that *you* were the one who was sent away, though," Athela retorted, her voice rising. The courtiers around them were now staring at the escalating scene with expressions of unabashed delight.

We should have charged admission, Laith thought to himself with an inward sigh.

"I can assure you," Cira said heatedly, her voice rising to the level of Athela's, quite forgetting her own resolution to come across as calm and collected, "that the next time it shall be *you* who is sent away, and it won't be for a mere six months."

"At this point, I'd welcome it if it meant not having to see you ever again," Athela snarled. Laith laid a hand on her arm, but she shook it away.

"I would suggest," Cira's voice took on a dangerous, silky quality, "that you keep a civil tongue in your head when you're talking to me, Athela. If you want to continue walking around with a head on your shoulders at all."

Athela blinked, and Cira was pleased to see that she looked taken aback by this. "Was that a threat?" she asked. "You're threatening me in front of the entire court?"

Dozens of wide, greedy, saucer-like eyes staring at them from all edges of the room confirmed that, yes, the entire court had heard the threat and that they were absolutely delighted by this new development.

"Call it friendly advice," Cira retorted. "You'd do better to remember who wields influence here. To show the appropriate respect. And to remember your place."

"*My place,*" Athela echoed, looking at Cira as though she were some form of insect that had crawled out from underneath one of the nearby drapes. "I'm your elder sister."

"Not that it matters," Cira shot back smugly. "You lost your place in line."

"Stop this *at once,*" the Queen ordered, and such was the edge in her voice that even Cira felt herself falling silent. Cira glanced over at her parents. The Queen looked livid, her face taut and her eyes glittering dangerously. The King was regarding them quizzically. He had likely only tuned in once she and Athela had begun raising their voices and probably had no idea what the fuss was about. "Athela," the Queen snapped, "bow before your sister and kiss her hand. Do as you're told."

Athela swallowed, and Cira enjoyed the sight of her sister physically wrestling with the revulsion this order provoked in her. She knelt before Cira, who daintily extended her slip of a white hand for Athela to take. With the barest minimum of physical contact, Athela touched Cira's fingertips with her own and hovered her lips above Cira's pearly pink nails. Cira could feel her heated breath against them. For a fleeting moment, she wondered whether Athela would take the opportunity to take a solid bite at her index finger.

"If you think it's bad now," Cira murmured, her lips barely moving, voice so quiet that not even the Queen could hear her, "just wait until I am Queen. You'll never have a peaceful night's sleep again."

"I haven't had a peaceful night's sleep since the day you were born," Athela growled back, slowly rising to her feet. "And I wonder how long you'd really last without Mummy over there to fight your battles and wipe your nose for you."

At that, Cira's composure fell like a discarded cloak at her feet, and she started towards Athela, her small hands bared, nails ready to connect with whatever exposed flesh they could reach. But something moved out of the corner of her eye, and, in another confused second, the room was spinning and she felt herself falling, before a strong pair of arms caught her.

"My lady, you must be careful," Laith's soothing deep tones. "You are overly tired after your long day of travel. Let me help you up."

Cira's green eyes flashed angrily, realizing that Laith had managed to make it look as though she'd tripped and he'd caught her as she fell. A moment later, though, she recovered herself and allowed a grateful smile to play around her lips, enjoying the breathy sighs she'd heard from the ladies around the room as Laith's strong arms bore her up back to stand on her feet. His dark brown eyes looked at her coldly.

"My thanks, cousin," she purred, letting her hand linger on Laith's arm. "I *am* tired. It has been a long day. Perhaps," she said, batting her eyelashes at him, "you'd be so good as to escort me back to my room? I would hate for another dizzy spell to catch up with me again."

"Did Cira fall?" asked the King. "What, is she sick?" He looked around hopefully. "Maybe she's hungry. Perhaps we should serve lunch."

"No," snapped the Queen irritably. "Athela, your behavior has been outrageous. Guards, take her to her room and hold her there until we summon her later. Cira, walk with me and leave your cousin be." With that, the Queen stalked away, her entourage in tow. Cira paused only a moment, turning to Laith and smiling sweetly. She lifted a hand and placed it intimately against his hard stomach, then swept off after her mother. Laith's jaw clenched, but he held himself still. He glanced off to his side, where his bodyguard, Marc, shivered and made a retching motion.

The crowd around them dispersed, buzzing happily at the scene they'd just witnessed. Two guards walked forward to stand on either side of Athela and lead her to her room, where she would await the summons of the Queen. Rane, Athela's own bodyguard, paused by the doorway and made brief eye contact with Marc before ducking along behind Athela as she was escorted out. Laith let loose a long string of pent-up breath. Silence fell blissfully into the once-packed reception chamber. Laith and Marc stood alone.

"That went well. Lovely to have Cira back home," Marc remarked matter-of-factly in his usual slow, almost drawling rate of speech. He shook his head.

Laith couldn't muster up much more than a chuckle. He rubbed his hands tiredly through his hair, letting some stick up at the top. He laced his fingers behind his neck, breathing evenly through the length of his long, lean torso. "Leave it to Cira to instigate a brawl after being home for approximately three and a half minutes. Athela's going to be spitting mad."

"Can't say I blame her," Marc remarked as they began to amble along slowly, following the guards to Athela's room. "The peace and quiet with Cira gone was far too good to last."

"The courtiers got bored with nothing to gossip about," Laith concurred. "That should keep them going for a while."

Marc shook his head, sending his pale, silky hair cascading around his face, brushing down almost to the tops of his broad shoulders. During his training as a soldier and bodyguard with Laith in the Meadows, Marc had excelled as one of the best boxers the regiment had ever seen, and his build certainly lent him an advantage. He was shorter and stockier than his willowy relatives and would likely list towards stoutness in his later years. Now in his early twenties, Marc was built as squarely as a bull, with his bulk entirely made of muscle. Marc had ice-blue eyes with white frost around the outer edges, a curved nose like a bird's beak, and a long white scar that split his face in two from his left temple down to the edge of his right jaw. The combination of the scar and muscular build gave him an intimidating air to strangers; they masked, however, an inherent gentleness and good humor.

He looked up at Laith, who was thoughtful and silent beside him. "So, did you trip her when she lunged at Athela? Is that why she fell?"

"Yeah," Laith shrugged, grinning smugly.

"She won't hold it against you too long," Marc predicted. "It gave her the opportunity to dramatically swoon into your arms in front of the entire court. She can coast on that for another two weeks."

Inside her rooms, as Laith had suspected, Athela was fuming.

"Don't tell me; I don't need to hear it," she said sharply, pacing restlessly beside her half-open window. "It was stupid of me to lose my temper with her, I know it full well."

"I wasn't going to say anything," Laith said soothingly, walking forward. "But there's going to be hell to pay when your parents think of something nasty enough to do to you."

"My parents never think of anything themselves, she whispers in their ears and they do exactly what she tells them to do," Athela shook her head. "I wonder if I could learn to imitate her voice, maybe I could go tell them to jump off of the top of the falls."

"Worth a shot," Marc shrugged.

As she was almost perennially out of favor with the King and Queen, Athela's apartments were the smallest and comparatively shabbiest of any of the royal family's. But because almost no one paid attention to what she did or worried whether her appointments were in keeping with the standards set by the court, she had been free to arrange them and furnish them as she liked, at least as far as she could afford through her relatively tight allowance. Her bedroom faced the west, and she had positioned her bed so that she could watch the moon rising through the balcony window. She had stripped the bed of any of the customary frills and hangings that were usually in fashion so that it stood, stark and sturdy, against the far wall facing the window. The bed was handsome and exquisitely carved with the images of running horses coursing through a forest of entwining ivy; she had a thickly embroidered cobalt blue coverlet for warmth in the winter and light linen sheets in the summer. There was a worn-out rug from her early childhood that she refused to have replaced even though there were patches of floor visible through some of the threads and a few leather cushions tossed haphazardly on the floor where her cousin and Marc could usually be found lounging on the long afternoons. Her other possessions—leather riding boots, a saddle, sundry clothes—were all stashed in a closet off the main room. Even though it would have made more sense for her to keep her equipment down by the stables, she liked to have her things close, to better keep an eye on them.

Laith gave her a small shrug, as if to say *it's all right, and* then the three of them headed out onto the balcony, where Athela gazed balefully out at the comparatively cheery waterfall cascading in the distance.

"Why did she have to come back?" Athela said grumpily.

"Good things never seem to last," Laith admitted.

"At least my parents ignored me while she was gone," Athela folded her arms on the balcony railing and leaned her curly black head against them. "Now that she's back, she'll just go stirring things up and making up more excuses as to why my parents should banish me for good."

"It's her first day back," Laith said soothingly. "Maybe she's just in high spirits and wanted to assert her position. Maybe things will settle down after today."

The three lapsed into a gloomy silence, well aware that such an optimistic viewpoint was unlikely to actually come to pass. Cira's temporary departure for the Meadows had come at the conclusion of a rather considerable dust-up between the sisters. Athela had discovered that Cira had set spies on her to try and find evidence of treachery against their mother, the Queen, with the apparent end goal of having Athela permanently banished or even executed. The whole affair had culminated in Athela's senior bodyguard catching one of the spies in Athela's rooms late at night and, mistaking the intruder for an assassin, killing them. The trail had led straight and rather obviously back to Cira, but to avoid making the scandal any bigger than it already was, the Queen had quietly removed Athela's bodyguard, replaced her with another, and sent Cira away from the palace, ostensibly for combat training with the Queen's legions in the Meadows.

This type of training wasn't unusual for members of the royal family, so no one outside the inner court thought much of it (though some gossip and speculation were inevitable.) The Meadows were the richest holdings in the entire country, grown even richer under the careful governance of the Queen. The Queen had a palace there as well, which was familiarly referred to as her "hunting lodge," though she neither hunted in nor around it, and the sprawling estate was by no stretch of the imagination a "lodge." Nevertheless, the Meadows were set quite far away from the coast and the major trade routes, so the Queen typically kept her residence in Joymaril near the coast and had her cavalry keep order in the Meadows. It was customary for children in the royal family to serve with the Meadows army for a period of five to ten years during their upbringing, unless they were direct heirs to the throne (as Cira and Athela were), for in that case the risk was considered too great for them. However, as in Cira's case, if the Queen needed a quiet place to temporarily ferret away one of her misbehaving daughters, the Meadows provided a very convenient option.

"I guess we'll have to go back to testing all my foods for poison," Athela grumbled.

"Probably," Laith smiled faintly.

"And don't think you're going to connive me into pulling a shift as your taste-tester by making me feel guilty about my sworn duty to protect your family," Marc told her narrowly. "That only works twice."

"Four times, Marc," Laith corrected.

"Is it four? Are we up to four already?" Marc asked, giving a beleaguered sigh.

They spent the rest of the day pottering around Athela's rooms as usual, playing cards and chatting about the classes Laith was teaching at the Academy. At sunset, a servant was sent to Athela's quarters, bearing a rather unwelcome summons. "My Lady Athela, Lord Argolaith, sir, and Lord Marcus," the servant inclined her head respectfully to each of them in turn. "The King and Queen wish Lady Athela's presence in the throne room. Lord Argolaith and Lord Marcus may come if they wish, but must promise to stay silent." The servant bowed again and departed.

"'We have to stay silent?'" Marc echoed. "What are we, three years old?"

Athela rolled her eyes so hard that Laith thought she might strain an ocular nerve, but the three nevertheless rose and followed the servant out of the room and through the winding, labyrinthine corridors to the gigantic domed throne room where the Queen was seated imperiously at the head in her throne of state. Behind her stood Cira, smirking coldly like a sliver of moonbeam. Athela walked forward and stood straight before them, her refusal to bow an insult that echoed through the silent room.

"Athela," the Queen said coldly, eyeing her from her high seat, green cat's eyes so much like Cira's, her pale blond hair streaming down her shoulders like a river. "I was in the mind of ordering you to serve time in the dungeons for your insult to your sister today, so grievous I find your behavior towards her. However, she has pleaded with me to change my mind about my punishment for you, a kindness which I feel you most certainly do not deserve." Behind her mother's shoulder, Cira's self-satisfied smirk deepened. Athela had the strong urge to walk up and smack her soundly across the face to get rid of it.

Her mother cleared her throat and continued. "Instead, I wish you to ride to Two Falls and pick up some supplies for your sister."

Athela was stung, and felt her sister's hand behind her punishment. Unlike her mother, who didn't know Athela well enough to understand, Cira understood that time in the dungeons would have little or no effect on her psyche. She was used to isolation and would probably regard the change of scenery as a point of interest. Instead, Athela loathed the pedestrian idea of running errands for her sister, the way in which such a task served to enforce her inferiority and inequality. She had her pride, and could feel the heat rising like steam in her chest.

"Well?" the Queen snapped. "What do you have to say for yourself? Don't you wish to thank your sister?"

"No," Athela said, mustering as much self-control as she could.

"Dismissed," the Queen ordered curtly. "And mind you learn this lesson."

Laith, Marc, and Athela bowed and withdrew from the chamber. Cira smiled after them as smugly as she could without bursting into open cackling. The Queen, however, was watching her out of the corner of her eye.

"Dear," the Queen said, addressing her husband. "Leave us, would you?"

The King, who was an avid collector of potted plants, had been thinking about an orchid he had acquired recently that was looking rather poorly in one corner of his greenhouse. He was temporarily startled by the direct address from his wife, and with a pleasant nod to Cira retired without much complaint.

"Cira," the Queen said when he had left, "stand before me."

Cira did so. She tilted her green eyes up to read her mother's expression, but the Queen's face was completely blank.

"I have brought you back home because I had hoped that this animosity between you and your sister had died down. Rivalry is to be expected. But this bickering is common," the Queen said finally. "I had hoped that we would have no more embarrassing public scenes between the two of you. I have had enough of the servants and courtiers gossiping about my squabbling daughters. It has to stop."

"Yes, mother," Cira grumbled through gritted teeth.

"It is much easier for me to punish your sister than it is to punish you. She has never been a favorite at court, and, except for her relationship with your cousin Laith, she doesn't have a friend among our people."

"I know," Cira replied.

"What I am trying to say to you is that you need to bide your time, Cira," the Queen told her. "There will be time enough for vendettas and plotting later on in life. You have power here, and you have the favor of many at court. Don't taint your image by picking fights with someone beneath you."

"Thank you, mother."

"Good," the Queen sat back and rested her hands on the sides of her chair. She looked satisfied. "Now, I have not had a chance to speak to you about your training in the Meadows. Were your instructors adequate?"

"Yes."

"You feel you have improved in your studies?"

"Yes." *More than you know*, Cira thought to herself smugly.

"Good." She paused. "We have started to discuss the possibility of a marriage."

Cira's head snapped up, her mouth opening and closing a few times. "Marriage?" she stammered. "To whom?"

"A prince," the Queen said casually. "Or a higher rank. It's of little importance, as you're the heir to the throne anyway. Would you like that?"

No would have been the most obvious answer to her mother's question, but Cira could tell that such a response would not be welcome. "I hadn't considered it," Cira said tactfully. "It is simply a surprise."

"It is useful to have someone to rule beside," her mother intoned, then her expression shifted and she cast a weary look towards the side door where her husband the King had departed to be with his plants. In an undertone, she muttered, "For the most part."

Cira felt an angry spark within her chest. *I want to rule alone,* she thought. *I want to rule by myself and only for myself.* Instead, she gave another sweet smile. "I am sorry for my immaturity, mother," she intoned, lifting her head once again, her voice apologetic. "You must remember that I am only a girl."

"Not for much longer," the Queen said fondly. "Try and be more controlled, Cira. Don't let your feelings get the better of you. Like I said, there is still much for you to learn and still room for you to grow. You are not queen yet."

"No," Cira agreed, smiling slowly. "Not yet."

As they stalked back through the halls and headed up to Laith's apartments, Athela opened her mouth, ostensibly to let fly a particularly round oath, but found her vocabulary lacking in a curse profound enough for her emotion.

"It will be fine," Laith said quickly, reflecting that if Cira kept things up, he would probably have to tattoo the phrase on his forehead. "She's just trying to get a rise out of you. We could always send someone to run the errands ourselves. Or better yet, we'll come with you to Two Falls too, and make a proper outing of it. We can leave tomorrow morning, get day drunk, and come back nice and sauced just in time for another blow-up with Cira around dinnertime."

"Works for *my* schedule," Marc grinned.

Beside him, Athela said nothing, just whipped her black curls over her shoulder with a vindictive twist of her hand. Marc sent Laith a taut grimace.

Laith sighed. "Oh, cheer up, Athela, it's better than being forced to sit in your room for hours on end with nothing to do."

"Excuse me," a light female voice called out from behind them. "Did I hear something about you getting *drunk*, Laith?"

"Of course not, darling," Laith responded automatically.

They turned. At the foot of a flight of stairs behind them stood Laith's wife, Ilaina. She was tall and athletic, dressed in trousers and a high-necked dueling shirt, removing a pair of fencing gloves from her large, tapered hands; a curl of red-golden hair had shaken loose from the bun at the nape of her neck and had drifted over her shoulder. She was vibrantly lovely in a way that had an intoxicating effect on those around her, and the tension in the hallway seemed to dissipate somewhat as she ironically cocked an eyebrow and regarded them all.

"Cira still as charming as ever?" she asked drily. "I heard she was back." Ilaina had been teaching at the Academy for most of the day and had thus managed to avoid being summoned for Cira's welcome at the palace.

"Charming as a swamp adder," Athela growled.

"Cira has bestowed upon Athela the great honor of going and picking her up some supplies from Two Falls tomorrow," Laith said sarcastically.

"Ah, naturally, it's nothing that could be conveniently purchased here in the city, like privy paper or socks," Ilaina agreed sagely. "Only something that sucks up an entire day will do."

"That's about the gist of it," Laith confirmed.

"She really prefers *Two Falls* privy paper," Marc interjected. "Her tastes have become more refined since she went to the Meadows."

"Her tastes and her bottom both, it seems. Well, it's my day off tomorrow, and here you all are, planning to desert me," she said with mock severity as Laith drew close. She was standing two steps from the bottom of the stairs and, from her perch, was almost as tall as he. She clasped her arms around his neck. He looped an arm around her waist and one under her knees and picked her up. She laughed as he turned to the others.

"I have her now, people, run for it while you can! Drink a pint in my honor and remember me," he called. Athela rolled her eyes. Laith turned back and arched an eyebrow coyly at Ilaina. "I think I'll just have to surrender and let her deal with me as she will."

"Well, don't surrender here, for heaven's sake, at least make it up the stairs," Athela said grumpily. Laith paid her no mind; public displays of affection made her intensely uncomfortable, and he was used to it.

"You heard her," Ilaina smiled at Laith.

"*Do* you want to come on some boring, idiotic, pointless trip to the village tomorrow?" Athela asked her abruptly. Laith swiveled Ilaina around in his arms so that she could talk to Athela face to face.

"You make it sound almost *irresistibly* tempting, Athela. But I'm actually tutoring tomorrow," Ilaina said regretfully. "One of my nieces is having trouble with her history studies, and I said I'd come by and help her so my sister can do the shopping." Ilaina's family wasn't high-born and still lived in the main section of the city, outside the palace walls.

"Next time," Athela said dismissively. "Heaven knows this likely isn't the last time Cira will send me on some wild goose chase."

"See you tomorrow, then, we're going to bed," Laith announced. He hadn't taken his eyes from Ilaina for some time and the intimate look in his eyes made Athela feel as though she were intruding.

"Good," she assented, pulling back from the group. "Don't keep him up too late, Ilaina."

"I'll do my best," Ilaina replied with a slow smile at her husband.

"See you, Laith!" Marc called jubilantly as he fell into step behind Athela. He paused, a thought occurring to him. "Hey!" he yelled. "Are you sure you won't need any bodyguarding up there?"

"Shove it, Marc," Laith called back pleasantly, beginning to climb the stairs.

Marc chortled to himself and headed off to his chamber.

CHAPTER FOUR

By the end of Tarr's and Wolver's day of traveling, the trees had begun to thin and the ground was getting ever and ever steeper. Dusk was fast approaching, but even in the dim light he could see the border gate that stood at the base of the cliff. Beyond the gate was a steep, winding road that zigged and zagged its way up to the top. Over the lip of the cliff face gushed a river, cleaved in half by a jutting elbow of rock so that it cascaded down in two enormous waterfalls to a roiling pool below. From where Tarr stood at the trees' edge, he could see that there were two guards manning the gate and that there was a short queue of people waiting to be let through. He swallowed, hoping that he would say and do the right things, that he would be admitted into the city. He took a cautious step forward.

By this time, he and Wolver had become amiable companions, especially after Tarr had verified that Wolver's chosen food was not Ashans. Tarr often found himself talking to Wolver beneath his breath, though he knew the wolf could make no reply.

"It is this way, I think, Wolver," he muttered in Ashan. "No need to be concerned. There is no reason for us not to be allowed into the city." Even as he said it, though, he could feel the doubt creep in. Something had kept him from being Chosen by one of the Ashan families. Perhaps the same thing would keep him from being allowed entry into Two Falls.

A short field lay before the edge of the trees, edged on the far side by a dirt road that led the way up to the entry gate. Along the side of the road, large red and orange lanterns hung on tall poles, looking almost like glowing bubbles that spilled their light onto the packed earth. With a pang, he realized that they reminded him of the lanterns that had been strung across the village square during the Choosing. As they approached the gate, Wolver got quite a few strange looks from the passersby, and most people kept their distance. Nervously, Tarr patted the top of Wolver's silver head and tried to look as though he had any idea what he was doing.

The guards at the gate were short and wheezy, as if glancing at people now and again and beckoning with one hand was about as much exercise as they could take. Once they caught sight of Tarr and Wolver, they stopped them abruptly.

"What is that thing?" the other man asked, voice high and strained as if it took all he had to push the air out of his lungs to speak.

"Are you bringing a wolf into Two Falls?" asked the other suspiciously.

"Hello," stammered Tarr, his tongue tripping nervously over the first few words in Common. "I—er..." He wasn't sure how to respond. The man's tone sounded as though it were not permissible to bring a wolf into Two Falls, but there wasn't much else to describe what Tarr was doing. He briefly considered saying "no" and seeing what results that yielded.

The other man, sporting a large brown beard, arched an eyebrow at Tarr. "Is he a weapon of some sort?"

"Well, he's got teeth," Tarr observed. "And claws."

The men shook their heads. "Sorry, can't let him in."

"Why not?" Tarr asked, annoyed.

"Danger to the public," the first man huffed. "He could eat someone."

Tarr glanced around, hoping that the use of logic would have some effect on the gatekeepers. "Look at all of the horses that have passed through here. They have teeth. And hooves. If they stepped on you, it would hurt, now wouldn't it? Why aren't horses a threat?"

Beard eyed the wheezer. "He's got a point."

The wheezing man attempted to take a deep breath, but failed abjectly. "Maybe we should make a report?" He sounded desperate to pass along any actual responsibility.

"About the horses?" Beard wrinkled his nose.

"We must have let twenty by so far today."

"I'll just go," Tarr said quietly, and he and Wolver stole by, leaving the two checkpoint guards still debating behind him. His heart was hammering a bit, but as they pulled away from the checkpoint and no one came rushing after them to throw them back out into the forest, he let himself relax ever so slightly.

The path zigged and zagged back and forth up the face of the cliff. It would have been much faster if Tarr had simply hopped off of it and scaled the rock outright, but everyone else seemed to be walking, and he didn't want to attract attention. The ascent strained the muscles of his legs and shortened his breath, so that he was panting ever so slightly as the forest floor fell away beneath him and the path lifted him up and deposited him onto the flat clifftop above. Having reached the summit, he turned around and gave the shadowy expanse of the forest one last look and said a silent goodbye to it. Then, steeling himself against everything that was to come, he faced forward down the road towards Two Falls.

At the lip of the cliff, the land had abruptly flattened out into a broad grassy field, rimmed here and there by trees and split by the broad river that flowed down towards the twin falls spilling into the forest below. The rocky path Tarr had traversed up the face of the cliff was now paved with large, flat flagstones, signaling a subtle sort of change, a shift towards urbanization. Tarr peered closer through the gathering gloom as a few travelers went by, staring curiously at him and his wolf as they passed.

Across the field, Tarr could dimly see the silhouettes of huge black buildings with lights flickering in the windows. They looked imperious there on the ground, so different from the treehouses perched among the branches in his village. They were larger than any treehouse he had seen, and he felt pulled in two directions at once: his curiosity rising more and more while his fear of the unknown still clawed at him.

Almost unconsciously, he stepped forward down the paved path, his eagerness to get his first glimpse of this strange new world beating out the anxiety he felt. As the first dwellings drew closer, the path grew more crowded and in short order he was jostling past other travelers on the road, muttering "Excuse me's" when appropriate. He stopped and gaped up at the first structure he came to; it rose a full three stories high above him, stretching up into the blue night sky. Someone pushed past his arm, nearly sending him off balance, forcing his attention momentarily back down to earth. He allowed himself to be swept along the current into the city.

The moment he stepped inside the city's border, Tarr could feel the hum of life that emanated from Two Falls, and he wished that he could somehow take in everything at once. Though it was well after dark, there was no sign that anyone in the town had gone to sleep or, indeed, was going to anytime soon. The streets jostled with people; he seemed to have found himself on a main thoroughfare that wound beside the gentle wash of the river. Somehow, the people of the city seemed to have carved out a stone bed for the river to lay in; it swished merrily along, and unconcerned passersby traversed its bank over numerous stone bridges that spanned it, barely looking around themselves as they went. Gaily colored lanterns were hung on the sides of the streets; there were shops and houses and people, people everywhere. It was so overwhelming that after a minute or two, Tarr left the street and sat down on the low stone railing above the river embankment, giving himself a moment to catch his breath and take it all in.

He remembered what he had read about the city, what seemed like two lifetimes ago in the library back in the village. He could almost recite it by heart: Two Falls was well known as the crossroads of the country, and anyone going anywhere would have to pass through it sooner or later. There were people of all kinds—some who even looked Ashan, men and women, children, young and old, every size, shape, and color. They all seemed to know what they were doing and where they were going. Everyone except him.

Unconsciously, one hand reached out to stroke Wolver's fur. The wolf had dutifully come to sit beside him, and the touch calmed Tarr's beating heart. After five minutes, during which he allowed himself to grow used to the loud clamor and sudden movements everywhere, he rose to his feet and set out once more down the main street.

All of a sudden, there was a gigantic crash behind him and Tarr whipped around, ready to defend himself, but it turned out to be only two men being ejected from a small house in which there seemed to be a great many people gathered. *Perhaps it's their equivalent of a tribal council building,* Tarr reasoned. A nearby door opened up, nearly hitting him, and he got a whiff of a strangely sweet odor that he could not identify. The colors around him were overwhelming; some people wore brightly colored dresses, and others sported baggy shirts and high, polished boots, so different from the regular earth tones that all the Ashans wore in his tribe. He tugged down the drape of his traveling cloak, feeling suddenly self-conscious.

There was another noise, and Tarr managed to stop himself from starting and running for the nearest tree. In the middle of the street, a man had taken out a small round tool and had begun playing it and singing. Tarr froze in his tracks, suddenly hypnotized. The sounds weren't anything familiar, but he knew in theory what he was hearing for the first time: *music.* The Ashans didn't have much in the way of their own music; there were some ritualistic chants for ceremonies and so forth, but this was the first time that Tarr had ever heard someone sing a song. A woman walking by the singing man stopped and smiled, then began dancing, her purple dress fluttering around her legs as she spun, and Tarr briefly glimpsed gold bands around her ankles with little bells on them. He leaned up against the wall behind him and listened with rapt attention as the people around them milled and passed through.

Once the man had finished the song, he put away his instrument, and the woman smiled and pressed her lips to the man's. Tarr turned his head to one side, confused. If that was a sign of affection like it was in the Ashan tribes, then he must be very far away from home indeed; in his culture, the kiss was only something that Ashans who had been joined in a lifelong ritual could do, and then it was only in the privacy of their own trees. He wondered faintly what he would do if someone tried to kiss *him* and made a resolution to resist as politely as possible.

Tarr continued along his way down the road and eventually surmised that there must be a holiday or a celebration of some sort going on; even the most decadent human city couldn't possibly be this extravagant every night. Banners were draped across the faces of the buildings and across the tops of alleyways, a rich red fabric whose color and texture entranced him so much that he spent about five minutes in front of one of the banners, fingering the material. Ribbons hung down from long poles that vendors were selling from the sides of the streets, alongside ornaments with the same picture of a weeping woman on it. Tarr debated briefly about whether or not he should ask someone what the party was for, but eventually decided that he should not. He wasn't sure whether those sorts of questions could be interpreted as an invitation to kiss him or to start dancing.

As he continued, with Wolver trailing behind him and waiting patiently every time he was distracted by a new sight or sound, the streets became wider and he reached an open square paved with cobblestones. After a moment of consideration, Tarr nearly laughed aloud. It was almost exactly like the main square in his village! He imagined that this must be where markets and councils were held, but for the time being there were just clusters of people passing through, laughing and talking and singing together. Tarr watched them, Wolver at his side, deeply conscious of his own isolation from the comings and goings of the townspeople.

Amid all the hubbub, he saw that there was something like a stone spring in the center of the square, burbling forth water. He went up to investigate it and found that it was ornately shaped like some sort of fish fighting with a man; spurts of water burst forth as if spat out by an unseen mouth. Tarr stood there for a long time but couldn't figure out how the device worked, so he settled for just sitting on the edge of the spring and enjoying the familiar sound of the water. He wondered whether it would be acceptable to drink from the stone spring, as by this point he was quite thirsty, but he didn't see anyone else doing so; fearful of breaking some sort of social taboo, he held back.

After watching from his perch for some time, Tarr realized that although it was late into the night and early morning, the townspeople were showing no signs of stopping and found that the long day of walking had rendered him exhausted and quite hungry. He stood and wandered until he saw another house (how did they build their houses so tall?), where he could see people eating and drinking at tables in the room on the ground floor. Quietly, he opened the door and was hit with a blast of clamor and clinking from inside and immediately found himself faced with a harried-looking woman whose expression reminded him of some of the watchers of the very young Ashans after the children had had too many sweets at the spring festival.

"Your dog waits outside," she said tersely, pointing at Wolver.

Tarr nodded and gestured to Wolver to wait. The wolf, for his part, looked rather put out at being referred to as a dog, and Tarr wondered briefly whether he would be there when he came back out. He closed the door behind him, unslung his knapsack from over his shoulder, and withdrew a few coins. "Please," he asked her politely, "I would like some food. Is this enough?"

She looked from the coins to his face with renewed interest; took in the trusting expression, his melancholy tilted eyes. "You an exile?" she asked.

Tarr couldn't help but bristle. Only Ashans who had committed the worst possible crimes were exiled; their names and memories were struck from the tribes, and they were no longer allowed to set foot back in their homeland. It was forbidden for a tribal Ashan to even *speak* to an exile, or even to accept a piece of food handed by one. To be an exiled Ashan was to be counted among the worst individuals in the world. "No," he replied stiffly.

She looked at him again shrewdly, grappling with some inner debate. Finally, something relented, and she pointed to the coins. "This is a lot of money. You will want to be careful. This smaller coin here is ten marks; half of that will be enough for food and drink. The other is fifty, and you will want to hang on to that and not go showing it around too freely. There are some who might want to take it from you."

Immediately, Tarr handed her the smaller coin and stowed the other away, far down in the bottom of his knapsack. "Thank you," he said gratefully. "May I have a little water, too, please?"

She stared at him a moment and laughed. "Someone certainly taught you good manners, lad. Give them my compliments."

Tarr wasn't sure what to make of that, or whether he had said something wrong and she was making fun of him, so he was relieved when she turned from him and went off across the room and vanished into a passageway at the back. Regardless, he was grateful that food and water was on its way and that he had successfully overcome at least one of the major hurdles in surviving through the night.

He found an empty table apart from most of the other diners, and when the food was brought out to him, he eyed it gratefully. "Excuse me," he asked the woman, remembering suddenly an anecdote he'd once heard about the eating habits of humans in Two Falls. "Is there meat in this food?"

The woman gave him the same inscrutable look, almost as if he had said something funny. "No, young man. Usually, it would, but I know most of you tribal Ashans are vegetarians. I asked them to leave it off the plate."

"Thank you," he said, relieved. He wasn't sure what would have been worse: having to eat the meat or having to send the plate of food back to the kitchens and go away hungry. His tribe was almost exclusively vegetarian, with the exception of fish on special occasions; it was interesting to know that those habits extended to other Ashan tribes as well.

The woman had clearly decided that Tarr needed some looking after, and kept coming back to check in on him. After the third or so visit, when Tarr had efficiently cleared every last morsel off his plate, she sat down opposite him, a small bag in her hand.

"I put some food for your dog in this pouch," she said, passing it to him.

"You're very kind," Tarr said gratefully, accepting it.

"Did you really live in a bark hut in the forest?" she asked abruptly, her tone overwhelmingly curious, as if she'd been holding the question in for some time.

There was something Tarr didn't like about the phrase "bark hut;" it almost made the Ashans sound impoverished and uncivilized. But the woman had been kind to him, and he decided to give her the benefit of the doubt. "No," he said, wishing there was a way to tell her how beautiful Ashan homes were, how the light turned gold when filtered through the buttery yellow paper screens, the beautiful black wood, and the gentle padding of feet from one room to another. "We have houses, too. Different than this, more open. But they are good houses."

He thought that he might not have done enough to fully convince her, for she looked a bit skeptical. But thankfully, she changed the subject. "Did you get enough?"

"Yes, thank you."

"Do you have somewhere to sleep?"

He didn't, and hadn't really considered it, but her question about the bark huts had made him uncomfortable, and he wanted to leave as soon as possible. "Oh, yes," he lied. "Yes, I do."

He could tell that, once again, she didn't quite believe him, but she didn't press him any further. He bid her goodnight and headed back out into the street, where he was pleased to find Wolver waiting dutifully by the door for him. Passersby were staring and skirting away from him as far as they could.

Perhaps it was finally being satiated, perhaps because it had been a long and taxing day, but Tarr felt all at once overwhelmed with sleep. He hadn't any idea where to go, though, and wondered whether there was a place to pay for a bed, just as he had paid for dinner. It was comforting to know that he had enough money to eat at least for a few days, and perhaps by tomorrow he could figure out where to find more permanent lodgings and how to begin to earn a wage to pay for it all.

He began to wander around. He spotted a tree beside one building and made for it hopefully, then remembered that to the people of this city sleeping in trees was generally uncommon. Tarr wanted to blend in as best he could. He took one street, then another, then another, and they began to grow smaller and more narrow, almost as if they were closing in on him. Finally, when he was down a road that was pitch dark, with no lights on in any of the windows nearby, he spotted a small gate, and beyond it was a pile of dried grass sheltered by a shabby wooden roof. A shovel and a few other tools lay nearby. *It'll have to do,* Tarr thought to himself, hoping that he would awaken before anyone caught him there.

Tarr felt exposed and uneasy about having to sleep this close to the earth, but he tucked himself into the pile of hay, reckoning that it would still be more comfortable than sleeping on the stone road. Wolver curled up in a white mound of fur beside him with his tail tucked comfortably beneath his chin; Tarr opened the bag the woman had given him in the tavern and found a meaty soup bone within. He gingerly extended it to Wolver between thumb and forefinger. The wolf accepted gratefully, beginning to tear and chew methodically from one end to the other. The night was cold, but with the insulation from the hay and warmth from the wolf, Tarr wasn't terribly bothered. It seemed as though every two seconds there was another loud noise coming distantly from the main street that jolted him just in time to keep him from actually falling asleep, but soon his anxiety at being found lessened, and the stillness of night stole over the city, and Tarr fell into a deep, exhausted sleep.

Tarr awoke late, nearly at midday judging by the placement of the sun, and bolted upright, wary that at any moment someone might come by and catch him sleeping in the hay. His head felt fuzzy, as though someone had dropped a pound of bricks on it in addition to bunging him full of a sleeping draught. His vision was bleary at first, but soon it cleared, and he glanced around. Wolver was nowhere in sight, and Tarr sighed, feeling more lonely than ever. Maybe the wolf had left him for good. *You have only yourself to rely on*, he reminded himself sternly and clambered unsteadily to his feet and walked out onto the main street.

The road was not nearly as busy as it had been the previous night, but there were still a large number of people, more than Tarr had ever seen together in one place at one time, aside from the village councils back in the forest. Despite his aches and latent exhaustion, it was a fine day, golden and springlike, but with the fleeting bite of the past winter still in the air. Tarr took a deep breath, feeling his head clearing already, and then decided to take a proper look around this strange town in the light of day. He turned left and started walking towards what seemed to be the busiest hub of activity, wending his way back through all the narrow streets until they gradually grew wider and wider and spilled him out back into the central thoroughfare. Tarr, who had given up any hope of ever finding his way around a place as big as this, was surprised and a bit pleased with himself for accidentally stumbling onto the main street and even more pleased that he had found somewhere he halfway recognized.

He seemed to have come out in the middle of a noon market; for a moment, he thought that he had again found the square with the burbling spring and the statue of the fish creature, but this was different. Instead of the fish, there was a statue of a six-pointed star, two long ends at the top and bottom, and a cluster of four points around the middle. From all sides, he was greeted by street vendors who waved bright fabrics of cotton, wool and even silks in his face, barking out their prices. There were stalls selling sweet fruits and meats, and a number of farmers with fresh vegetables. Tarr was surprised to see no sign of the rowdy people who had been carousing the previous night. Perhaps they were still in bed.

He heard a four-legged tap-tapping behind him and turned to see Wolver trotting up behind him. "Hello," he said, greeting the wolf with a friendly pat, overwhelmingly relieved at the sight of him despite his renewed commitment to self-sufficiency. "Where did you get off to? Breakfast?" Tarr was still fairly full from his meal the previous night. Wolver's tongue lolled out of his mouth, and his bushy tail swished once or twice in reply.

Tarr set out, feeling infinitely lighter and much more confident than the day before. He had made it successfully through the night; his stomach was full, his eyes bright with keen interest. They began to wander aimlessly up one street and down the other, and as Tarr grew more and more accustomed to the sights and smells of the city in the daytime, he began to take note of the differences he saw. There were definite *neighborhoods*, areas of the city where the buildings looked the same or were built in the same style. It was interesting, Tarr thought, to see how the houses had sprung up; the city was extremely old, founded centuries ago, and in some ways he thought he could read the story of the city by examining the buildings. Here and there were the remains of a pillar or a stone archway, which must once have been impressive in its grandeur but had been allowed over the years to crumble into ruin. Some of the buildings had foundations made of stone that slowly evolved into wooden structures on the upper floors, as if someone had simply pasted a new house on the base of an old one.

They reached a section of town that Tarr deduced was very, very old. Almost all the buildings were made of stone, rather than brick or wood, and the scope of them was much grander than the ones in the other part of town. They were so tall that Tarr's neck went all the way back when he looked up at them. He couldn't imagine how such structures had been built; it would have taken a long, long time and a great many people all working together towards the same purpose.

It was this part of the city that he enjoyed the most. There was a sense of history here that pervaded the atmosphere and a majesty that made an onlooker want to whisper. There were buildings with pillars as big as tree trunks and broad, sweeping steps that led up to their entrances. Though Tarr was overwhelmed with curiosity, he couldn't quite get up the courage to go up and peek inside. Rounding a corner, he saw an open square crowned by a big fortified building with a golden-domed ceiling that gleamed like the sun. There were many riders on horses out in the front, passing to and fro, some stationed at the ends of the staircase. All were wearing matching yellow cloaks that had some sort of flower on the back, which Tarr took as a symbol of some sort of tribe. *Perhaps this is where the rulers of the city live*, he thought, impressed. He was too nervous to get much closer, lest he make some sort of error and get thrown in prison, which he had read about as a punishment common in human civilizations.

Tarr and Wolver wandered around the city for almost four hours, gradually making a large circle that took them back to the central market square with the star statue. Tarr was glad to have managed to find his way back again and was just starting to think about perhaps going back to the house where he'd eaten the previous night when there was a commotion ahead of them, and Tarr saw people begin to scurry back and forth across one of the streets on the opposite side of the square. He peered forward with interest, trying to see from where the noise was emanating. Pedestrians were frantically running to clear the road, and a number of dogs were barking in harmony with the general yelling coming from the far side of a corner. Thinking that there may be some sort of pageant or demonstration going on, he and Wolver walked forward to stand in the center of the market square, directly beside the star-shaped statue. Tarr rose up on his tiptoes, craning his neck to see what all the fuss was about.

The fuss, it turned out, was due to the sudden appearance of four riders moving at a fast clip through one of the more congested market streets. People were shouting at them in protest and shaking their fists in the riders' direction; even Tarr, who hadn't the faintest notion about the laws governing riding speeds through the center of town, knew that it wasn't the best idea to be careening around on horseback in a densely populated area.

The four riders spilled out into the central market and drew to a halt. The horse that mainly seemed to be causing the hubbub was a light dapple gray with a black mane and tail. The horse looked extremely excited and appeared to be doing everything it could to unseat its rider and go charging off through the city. The rider was sticking with the horse with remarkable poise, even as the horse snorted and knocked into the rider beside it.

"For goodness' sake, Athela, calm him down," Tarr heard one of the other riders say. It was a deep voice, soothing and pleasant to listen to. The mysterious group were all dressed in nondescript brown cloaks, hoods pulled over their heads, and unusual purple scarves of some sort of gossamer-looking fabric covering their noses and mouths.

"It's not my fault that dog spooked him," snapped the rider on the gray horse as her mount gave a terrific plunge into the air, small hooves slipping haphazardly on the cobblestones. She hauled on one rein, and the horse was forced to spin around in a tiny circle. "Calm down, you nut," she ordered, a directive presumably aimed at the horse.

The gray horse, after doing about five tiny circles at the end of his tight rein, eventually shuddered to a quivering, highly charged halt. Its rider sat for a few protracted moments to see if everything was all right, then swung her leg over the back of the horse and landed springily on the street. By now, the commotion around the riders had died down, and all that remained of the disturbance were a few sour looks shot in their direction from the locals.

This was one of the most interesting things Tarr had happened upon that morning, and he was in no hurry to move away. There was something strange about the group of four riders. Their cloaks were drab and nondescript, but the purple cloth that covered their noses and mouths was a brilliant color and had clearly been made using expensive dye. The horses, too (even to Tarr's untrained eye), were large and glossy and looked well cared for; there was the hyperactive gray, an enormous black charger standing like a mountain, and two bays off to the back. The polish on their bridles and saddles glinted in the midmorning sun. Everything about the group indicated a kind of wealth and gleaming prosperity different from the townspeople around him.

In the midst of his observations, Tarr suddenly noticed that the male rider beside the huge black horse had stopped still and was staring straight at him. Tarr turned and glanced over his own shoulder to see if there was anything behind him of particular interest, but there was none. Rather nervously, he turned back around. The rider nudged the woman on the gray horse, who swiveled around and looked at Tarr, too.

Maybe they don't like Ashans, he thought uncomfortably, and took a hesitant step back. He glanced down at Wolver, who didn't seem at all alarmed. The wolf's ears were pricked towards the group of riders, an interested look on his face. Wolver's comparative congeniality was of little comfort to Tarr, who quickly decided it would be best if he beat a hasty retreat. He turned on his heel to go.

"Wait! Stop!" came the commanding, deep voice of the first male rider.

Reluctantly, Tarr halted and swiveled back around as the first three riders left their horses and began striding up to him, a sense of urgency in their step. The fourth, a smaller figure Tarr assumed to be a woman, hung back with the horses. She, too, was watching him with keen interest over the top of her scarf. A few of the local pedestrians shot Tarr and the riders curious looks as they passed, giving them all a wide berth.

"I'm sorry," Tarr said automatically as the first rider approached, though, to his knowledge, he hadn't done anything wrong.

"Are you an Ashan?" the rider asked urgently. At this point, Tarr could still only see his eyes. He was tall for a man, almost as tall as Tarr was himself, and had large dark eyes that at that very moment were scanning Tarr's face like he was trying to read it.

Tarr wasn't sure what the best response would be, so he decided to be honest. "Yes," he replied. "I've only just arrived in Two Falls yesterday."

The rider blinked at him in what Tarr assumed to be astonishment (since he could only see half his face.) One hand raised and pushed the hood back, revealing a head of short, sandy blond hair that brushed over his forehead. The other hand reached up and pulled down the purple scarf covering his face. "And...is that your wolf?"

Tarr was so taken aback by the rider's face that for a full ten seconds, he completely forgot to reply. The rider was easily the most beautiful person Tarr had ever seen, with dark eyes and a well-sculpted head set atop a long, graceful neck. Tarr goggled at him, eyes wide, then recovered himself enough to answer. "No—er—yes," he stammered. "He's not really *mine*. We're sort of just traveling together." He laid a six-fingered hand atop Wolver's white head.

Beside the beautiful young man, the second rider, the woman who had been riding the excitable gray horse, drew up and pulled down her scarf, though she left her hood in place. A black ribbon of curly hair licked over her forehead, and she brushed it impatiently back with one hand. Her gaze wasn't as open and welcoming as the handsome young man's; in fact, she seemed to regard Tarr with a sort of innate hostility and suspicion. Tarr had to consciously stop himself from taking another step back away from her. Her face was strong and full of character, with a remarkable pair of light gray eyes that were rimmed with lashes so thick and dark it looked as though she had outlined them with kohl.

"Do you think...?" the young man muttered under his breath.

"Maybe," the woman replied.

"It's too much of a coincidence," he shook his head. "We have to ask him to come with us."

"What?" Tarr said nervously. "Come with you where?"

The young man's face relaxed into a pleasant smile. "I'm so sorry for not introducing myself. My name is Laith."

"*Prince* Argolaith," the woman beside him interjected, her steely glare still boring into Tarr. "Of the Jelani."

A Jelani prince? Tarr thought, blinking in surprise. He had read about the Jelani royalty in some of the books in the Ashan library but never for a moment thought that he would meet one in person. The young man certainly looked the part.

"My companions and I are from the city of Joymaril. We would like...we would like to ask you to accompany us back to the palace. As a guest," he added hurriedly, clearly seeing the look of apprehension on Tarr's features.

"Why?" Tarr asked. Two Falls couldn't have been so short on Ashans that these Jelani needed *him* to come with them. There were plenty of others. He shifted uncomfortably, placing his weight on the other foot, wishing that Wolver was doing a better job at appearing impressive and threatening. The wolf had been regarding the newcomers with a placid, genial sort of interest since they'd first approached.

"There's actually quite a good reason why," Laith said somewhat evasively and glanced around them as if on guard for anyone listening. "But we can tell you on the way. Where do you live?"

Tarr fidgeted for a moment. He didn't think that the Jelani prince would be very impressed if he replied, "Someone's shed." Finally, he straightened up. "I've only recently come to Two Falls from the Ashan forest, as I said. I'm currently looking for lodging." *There*, he thought. *That sounded respectable enough.*

The prince's face cleared. "Wonderful, then you can come with us. You can see the palace, and we have plenty of room for you to stay." He gave Tarr a rather calculating look, sizing him up. "And plenty of food."

This, in particular, was appealing. The need for food was looming larger and larger in Tarr's mind. *But I've only just come to Two Falls*, he thought to himself. *What good would it do to just go gallivanting off to a palace?*

Listen to yourself, another voice said. *You are being given an invitation to a Jelani palace. Two Falls has been standing on this spot for centuries. It will still be here once you get back. And you may not get such a chance ever again.*

"All right," Tarr said slowly. "All right. We'll come with you." He looked down at Wolver. "As long as the wolf can come."

"Absolutely," Laith agreed, and Tarr was shocked to see relief wash over the prince's face. *Why on earth does he want me to ride with them back to the palace?* he wondered again, and tried to remember whether he'd ever read anything about Jelani conducting ritual sacrifices requiring Ashan blood. *If that's the case*, he thought grimly, *Wolver had better shape up to be a better guard dog than he has been in the last ten minutes or so.*

His gaze slid over to the woman, hoping to see some softening in her expression now that he had accepted the prince's offer to accompany them to the palace. But her stare was still hard and searching and devoid of any friendliness or welcome. Instead, one hand tersely jerked the purple scarf up over her nose, and she spun on her shining leather heel, marching purposefully back to where the horses stood.

The third rider, who hadn't yet revealed himself, turned towards Laith. "Cira will be needing her supplies," he reminded him.

Laith brushed the words aside, pulling the hood back over his sandy head of hair. "We're coming back with more than we expected," he said in a low voice. He had meant the last bit to be only for his companion's ears, but Tarr overheard him anyway and, with every footfall, felt himself growing more and more bewildered. *No one in the forest is going to believe me if I tell them that this is how my first day in the human city turned out*, he reflected and almost smiled to himself at the thought of it.

They drew up to the horses, and Tarr faltered. "I've...I've never ridden before," he stammered, dodging nimbly out of the way as the high-strung gray horse leered at him and aimed a bite at his elbow.

"You can ride with Marc," the prince gestured towards the third rider, who raised a hand and gave a cheery wave. Over the top of his face covering, Tarr could see a twinkling pair of ice-blue eyes, white like frost around the edges. It was a much more pleasant greeting than he'd been given by the woman, and made him feel a little better.

"Climb up behind, there you go," Marc said, indicating that Tarr should put his foot in the stirrup and swing up behind him on the saddle. It was all rather clumsy and awkward, and Tarr, who hadn't been this close to a horse in all his life, clung close to Marc, peering over the side of the animal at the unfamiliar sight of the ground below. Marc, fortunately enough, was very broad-shouldered and stockily built, and Tarr had the impression that he would not topple over very easily. "We'll go slowly," Marc assured him, seeming to sense his unease. "You'll get used to it."

Tarr gave a nod and twisted around to see if Wolver was still following, which the wolf was. They set out at a walk, and Tarr's heart gave a lurch as the horse moved beneath him, the stride unnatural and strange beneath his seat. "Well done!" Marc complimented him. "That's the hard part."

Even through his bewilderment, Tarr couldn't help but appreciate

Marc's kind encouragement. "Thank you," he stammered.

"I'm Laith's bodyguard," Marc informed him as they passed out of the market center and headed down one of the nearby streets. It was odd seeing the same sights from the back of the horse, and more than a few townspeople stopped to gawk at them as they passed. Tarr felt like shrugging at them as he went, as if to say, *I don't know what I'm doing here either.*

"Who is she?" Tarr asked, taking a risk by loosening his hold and pointing towards the woman on the gray horse.

"Athela, his cousin. She's a princess, the daughter of the King and Queen. That's her bodyguard, Rane, behind us," Marc replied.

Tarr twisted around. The fourth rider, who had not revealed herself or spoken yet, trailed silently at the rear of the party. All Tarr could see was a pair of blue-gray eyes staring back at him, cool and even like a clear lake. Tarr turned back around, watching as Athela, the princess on the gray horse, managed to stop her mount from rearing up and colliding with a fruit vendor on the side of the street.

"Her horse is mental," Marc grumbled.

"I noticed," Tarr agreed, feeling fervently glad that as far as horses went, the one he was currently sitting on seemed relatively disinterested in such exhibitionist theatrics.

He must have been gripping Marc's shoulder rather hard, for Marc suddenly said, "Don't worry. We're not dangerous. I'll tell you more once we're out of the city. We mean you no harm."

"All right," Tarr agreed, and, feeling more reassured, sat silently and watched the city roll past. After a few minutes, he almost began to enjoy the sight of the saucer-like pairs of eyes turned his way as their odd little procession wound its way east and out of Two Falls.

Once they had passed the city's eastern border, Tarr peered over Marc's bulky shoulder and saw a small group of riders clustered in a meadow below. The riders were all outfitted in purple cloaks and seemed to belong to the same group, as they all wore shiny protective armor on their arms and legs, and had thick leather tunics embroidered with the image of an egret. "Who are they?" Tarr asked Marc curiously.

"Jelani guards, they just came with us from the palace," Marc told him casually, as if it was an everyday occurrence that a host of armed guards should accompany them on their errands. Laith rode up to the guards on his big black charger and exchanged a few short words; some of the riders' heads turned in Tarr's direction, and Tarr felt himself growing nervous. Finally, two or three of the riders with purple cloaks broke away and headed past them back towards the city of Two Falls, regarding Tarr curiously as they passed.

"Athela was sent down here to run errands for Athela's sister Cira as a sort of punishment," Marc told Tarr. "Laith and I came because we thought it would be a fun sort of distraction. Laith's sending those guards to get what we needed, now that we've got you."

None of this made any sense to Tarr, but he worried he would sound stupid if he asked Marc to elaborate any further.

The riders fell into line. Laith rode in front on his enormous charger, his graceful back swaying slightly in time with his horse's stride. Athela came up behind him, her gray horse tossing his head and squealing impatiently every few feet. Then came her bodyguard, then Tarr and Marc with Wolver beside them, and the other guards coming up behind. Tarr felt like he had undergone a kind of mental whiplash, so quickly had he gone from the reality of carving out survival in Two Falls to being unexpectedly whisked off to the city of the Jelani.

They were making their way across a broad sort of meadow towards a distant, gently sloping hill framed at the top by trees. The day had grown quite lovely indeed, with the spring sun shining beatifically on all that lay below it, and the fresh grass reflecting the shining rays upwards like dazzling, shifting green water. Tarr took in a deep gulp of the fresh air, still scented with the edge of rain and moist earth, and let himself relax. Perhaps this wouldn't be so bad after all.

By this point Marc, Tarr's riding companion, had pulled back his hood and lowered his scarf and was looking appreciatively out over the rolling countryside. He had long, silky yellow hair the color of straw, which Tarr had to occasionally brush away when a breeze blew it up into his face. When he turned his face slightly to the side, Tarr was shocked to see that the young man's face was split by an ugly scar, straight, thin, and deep, as if drawn there by the edge of a blade. The line split his face diagonally from the left temple to his right jaw. His scarf and hood had done a good thing of hiding it, but now that it was out in the open, Tarr couldn't help but stare. Marc had a curved nose like the beak of a bird, and there was a neat slice of it missing right where the white scar passed over its bridge. Tarr swallowed and pretended to be looking elsewhere as Marc twisted in the saddle to face him straight on.

"Now then," he said. Despite the terrible scar, his manner continued to be extremely friendly and engaging in a laid-back sort of way. Tarr wondered what on earth he had gotten up to that had resulted in a wound of that sort. "I suppose you want to know why we picked you up."

Tarr nodded mutely, and Laith, having heard what Marc had said, pulled back his black charger to fall into step alongside them. Tarr still couldn't help but stare at the sight of him, his almost unearthly beauty framed against the bucolic splendor of the meadow beyond. Athela, the woman with curly black hair, rode before them, her ramrod-straight back unflinching and unforgiving. She made no effort to turn around or engage with him.

"Have you heard of Alder Morthenstar?" Laith asked.

Of course, Tarr had. The legend of the great warrior had spread to all the corners of their country; there was not a single child of any race who had not heard the legend before being put to bed at night. A star was carved into the doorframe of nearly every house in Two Falls for the protection that Morthenstar gave to her followers from the afterlife. The Ashans in Tarr's tribe gathered once a year to retell her story within the clan. It was one of Tarr's favorites.

Almost two hundred years before, there was a Jelani whose mind had turned to the ways of evil, and his entire soul seemed to plummet into darkness. His name was Lord Kagai, and he was banished from the halls of Joymaril when he tried to convince the Jelani to wage a campaign to overtake the peoples of the entire country and subject them to his rule. He built a fortress on the island of Faridor off the coast and made plans to realize his vision. He amassed an army of followers and, with them, set about burning and killing entire villages, bringing fear in their coming and destruction in their wake. Kagai became particularly obsessed with the extermination of the Ashan people, whose resistance had prevented him from seizing valuable timber from the forest. His vendetta against the Ashans aside, Kagai also had no qualms about killing men or other Jelani to get at the Ashans.

It was in one of the outlying villages that a girl escaped after witnessing the death of her father and sisters. She was only fifteen years old, but was determined to find a way to stop Kagai and began to travel the outlying country to raise support for a resistance. Though she was young, she commanded such a presence that even men who were four times her age decided that they would follow if she would lead. The girl, Terran Morthenstar, eventually went to the palace of Joymaril to ask for help. There, she met Daemun, a Jelani who was to become her general and most trusted friend and who was, ironically, Kagai's nephew. The Jelani adopted Morthenstar as one of their own.

The girl's fame grew. The Jelani gave her the name *Alder,* and soon after, they joined forces with the Ashans. An Ashan artisan tattooed the image of a star upon her forearm, a symbol that Morthenstar claimed as her sigil. After she and Daemun successfully led a surprise attack on one of Kagai's strongholds, she and her closest followers collectively became known as the Strikers. With her Strikers and army of Jelani, humans, and Ashans, Alder began to beat back the riders of Kagai. Their war lasted over five years until it culminated one day on the plain in front of Faridor, Kagai's island. Kagai was killed and the battle won, but there were other casualties: several Strikers were lost, and Morthenstar died from her battle injuries, leaving behind her best friend Daemun, and a centuries-long legend.

"Yes, of course, I've heard of her," Tarr replied. "What about her?"

"Well, it's a little-known fact that Kagai predicted that he himself would have an heir who would come back years later and finish what he began. Morthenstar also said that if that came to pass, new Strikers would emerge who would oppose Kagai's heir."

"Oh," Tarr said, for lack of a better response. It all sounded fine, like the coda to a fairy tale. "I see." Then, more tentatively: "What does that have to do with me?"

"It's said that Morthenstar had visions. She told all of these visions to Daemun, her general, who wrote down what she said. She said that three people would lead a new army against Kagai's heir, and at first, everyone believed what she had predicted. Then, when no threat arose from Faridor, year after year, the people had their doubts. Kagai was dead, they said; he wasn't married, the prophecy that Morthenstar made was merely rambling."

"Just a complete fabrication, no truth to it at all," Marc chimed in.

"My parents, for example," Athela interjected suddenly, turning in her saddle, "think it's all a load of nonsense."

"Anyway," Laith interjected, "Morthenstar said that one of these Strikers would be a Jelani woman with black hair and gray eyes."

Tarr looked sharply over to Athela. She stared back at him.

"Odd..." Tarr said slowly. "Is it strange for Jelani to have black hair?" he asked, looking around at the other fair-haired riders surrounding him.

"Not unheard of," Laith conceded.

"But rare," Marc added. "You'll get a brunette here and there, but Athela is unusual. Very unusual."

Tarr glanced over at her. She was back to staring stonily ahead, as if she was completely ignoring the rest of them. Tarr wondered again why she was so unfriendly to him. *Does she also think I lived in a bark hut?* he thought. He wondered if there was a way he could organically work in some facts about Ashan ingenuity and craftsmanship into the conversation.

"There are humans with dark hair," Tarr pointed out. "Aren't..." he lowered his voice a bit, unsure of whether his question would be offensive to his hosts, "aren't Jelani and humans basically the same?"

Marc laughed as if at a private joke. "You'd better not say something like that in front of the Queen," he cautioned Tarr. "But yes, Jelani and humans are essentially the same. The Jelani are like...like their own tribe and came together from a different part of the world, long ago. And so Jelani tend to think they're..."

"Superior," Laith volunteered. "Which is mostly nonsense."

Tarr nodded, still not completely following but appreciative of Marc's suggestion not to mention the subject in front of the Jelani Queen.

"Wait," he said and blanched. "I'm going to meet the *Queen*?"

"Probably," Marc shrugged, as if meeting the Jelani Queen was as commonplace as brushing his teeth. Tarr looked to the side, torn agonizingly between tantalizing curiosity and the urge to scoot off the back of the horse and go running straight back to Two Falls.

"Anyway," Laith interjected, "Morthenstar predicted that another of the Strikers would be an Ashan standing at the heart of Two Falls with a white wolf," Laith finished and paused for effect. He swung around and met Tarr's gaze straight on. "So you see, that's why you perked our interest."

Tarr's mind went blank for a moment.

It was actually so funny that he burst out laughing, unable to stop himself, even though he could see the way his reaction caught Laith by surprise. "There's been a big mistake," he chortled finally. "This isn't my wolf, for one thing. He belongs to another Ashan I met in the forest. That Ashan is the one that you want. I'm no warrior; I've never fought anything in my life."

Laith looked a bit put out by his reaction, but shrugged a shoulder and turned back around, swaying gently in the saddle. Athela continued to stare straight ahead, as if she'd heard nothing. Tarr immediately felt abashed, but the whole thing was almost too ridiculous for words.

"Marc," he said in a lower voice. "You should let me off right now, this is a complete mistake. I'm not the one you're looking for. I should go back. This is a waste of time for all of you."

"Don't worry about it," Marc assured him in the same low voice. "You live in the forest, right?"

"Yes," Tarr said hesitantly, wondering if Marc was also going to make some sort of crass comment about Ashan living arrangements.

"This is your first time out?"

"Yes."

Remembering suddenly the money in his knapsack, he wasn't sure whether the protocol at the palace would be the same as it was in Two Falls. He wrestled with whether to ask Marc about whether he would need to pay for his food and lodging, as it was probably impolite to do so. But Marc had been so kind and easygoing so far (unlike Athela, Tarr thought unhappily) that he decided to risk it. "Marc, I have some money...but don't know if it will be enough to pay for my food."

Marc laughed, and Tarr immediately felt slightly ashamed to have asked. "There is no need to pay for anything," he assured him, and through his embarrassment, Tarr felt a wash of relief. "You are our guest, and at the palace, guests do not need to pay for their board. You will have as much food as you like, and a room to yourself."

"Thank you," said Tarr politely. He looked behind him to where Wolver was trotting happily through a spray of cornflowers, his tail held high in the air. Tarr, too, felt his heart lifting ever so slightly, and sat back to silently take in the rolling landscape as it passed them by.

It was a fine afternoon and the field seemed to stretch out, lazy and green for as far as the eye could see, with distant hills rising blue and sloping off in the distance. Flowers had begun to spring up amid the grass, blues and yellows and whites, delicate and soft and liable to crumple against the breeze. The horses' hooves crushed them underfoot and sent a delicious aroma wafting up into the air around him.

They crossed the large swath of open meadow and followed the meandering path upwards towards the first thicket of trees, smaller and more delicate than those Tarr was familiar with in the forest. Once they struck through the trees, all Tarr could see in front of him was the trail they were following and a thick curtain of boughs that hid their destination from view. The path wound them steadily up a thickly wooded slope, the ground between the trees a carpet of grass, velvety green moss, and hardy woodflowers that beckoned up to the sun.

Eventually, the ground tapered out again, and the party began to trail its way along the well-worn path to their unseen destination. Tarr still could not make anything out through the top of the trees surrounding them, though they were nowhere near as tall as the trees among which he had lived in the forest. Finally, the trees began to thin, and Tarr could see the blue glistening of a large body of water ahead of them. He began to wonder where exactly they were. At last, they passed through the last dense thicket of wood, and Tarr saw that the glimmering water was actually a huge lake, so stunning in its vastness and serene beauty that it took him a few moments before he looked up and saw, for the first time, the glistening palace of the Jelani. When he did, he caught his breath and seized Marc's shoulder reflexively in his hand.

The palace was pure white, settled like a beautiful pearly shell into the rock cliff. There were interconnecting domes and archways carved out of stone that, in some places, caught the late afternoon sun and turned the white building a blinding reddish-pink. Just looking at it, Tarr had absolutely no idea how big the palace and the surrounding city really were, for as he looked closer, he could see balconies and windows jutting out from the cliff itself, which told him that Joymaril lay not only *atop* the cliff but *inside* it as well.

Through the center of the main building ran a wide current of water that continued to the edge of the cliff and then cascaded all the way down to the lake in a brilliant waterfall; Tarr could see smaller falls shimmering in the light down the sides of other buildings as well. The entire place took Tarr's breath away, and he had to blink a few times to make sure that he wasn't imagining the entire thing. In fact, he stood there staring at it for so long that it was quite some time before he realized that the rest of the party had continued on and that the horse was moving beneath him.

They approached the edge of the lake, and Tarr began to wonder what the plan was—whether they would swim atop the horses to the palace on the other side. To Tarr's utter amazement, the train of riders began to walk straight through the middle of the lake, the horses' hooves only about a foot underwater. Tarr knew that the lake could not actually be that shallow, so as he and Marc approached on their horse, he made it a point to peer over the side and look beneath the water. What appeared to be a submerged sort of bridge had been formed across the lake; a mound of high earth and paved stone that made a safe path for the horses to walk across. This was, he realized, a very clever defense mechanism. Had he not known that the bridge was there, he would have abandoned all hope of getting across the lake to the palace.

Wolver trotted through the shallow water, sloshing merrily, tail held jauntily behind him. As they walked closer and closer to the palace, Tarr craned his neck upwards to peer at the top of the cliff where the palace was situated, and thought that he could see a few figures watching them from the archways, though it might have been just a trick of the light. Soon, however, the train went through an opening at the cliff's base, and as they passed into the shadow, Tarr looked eagerly ahead, wondering how they were going to get up the mountain and into the palace, for he could hardly wait to get off the horse, stretch his legs, and go exploring.

Tarr's eyes adjusted as they entered the dimly lit interior. As the long train traveled up a steeply spiraling dirt pathway in the belly of the cliff, Tarr saw other passages leading off to separate areas, as well as rooms built right next to the path, though Tarr only saw one or two Jelani inside, and the light was so dark that he could not get a really good look at any of them. As the group traveled higher and higher, the light became paler. Wolver was panting, the air snuffling in and out of his nose with each step. After about a ten-minute climb, the passage opened up into blinding light, and Tarr shielded his eyes as the full force of the sun hit his face. He looked around himself as soon as he could, eager to take it all in.

A few guards, wearing the token purple Jelani cloaks, had stepped forward and taken the reins of the royal family's horses. Some of them stared at Tarr and Wolver, but Tarr was getting used to this by now and hardly noticed them, so eager was he to look around the palace.

The room in which they found themselves was one of the most mind-boggling spaces Tarr had ever seen (how could his companions seem so casual about it? They barely glanced around themselves as they dismounted.) Arched panels of glass surrounded them, the light from the setting sun spilling in and casting lilac shadows on the marble floor. In the center of the circular room bubbled a spring like the one with the fish back in Two Falls, from which formed a tiny stream that ran along a canal that had been carved into the stone beneath their feet. It went rushing off to the wall to pour out into the lake below.

"What is that?" Tarr asked eagerly, pointing at it.

Marc blinked a few times. "That's a fountain." He gave Tarr a sideways look, as if surprised Tarr didn't know what a fountain was.

"How does it work?" Tarr asked.

Marc's mouth opened, and his pale brow furrowed. He exchanged a glance with Laith, and then both of them gave little shrugs. "I actually have no idea," Marc grinned a bit sheepishly.

Tarr didn't mind. He peered down the course of the burbling water to where it spilled over into the open air. It was indeed a long way down. The tops of the rock surrounding them had turned a creamy yellow in the sinking sun, and Tarr wouldn't have minded very much at all if he had had to remain in that room for a long time until he was needed again to save the world, or whatever nonsense Laith and the others expected him to do.

"What is *that?*" one of the guards blurted out, motioning towards Wolver.

"A wolf," Laith told him impatiently, and Tarr was rather relieved not to be the only one asking stupid questions. "Where are my aunt and uncle?"

"With your cousin over in the throne room, m'Lord," the guard replied, his eyes still on Wolver.

"Thank you. Stop staring, please; this Ashan is our guest," Laith instructed in a calm tone that was clearly at home with issuing orders, then turned to Tarr, who was still gaping out at the view.

"Sir," came a voice beside him that snapped him out of his reverie. It took him a moment to realize that the voice belonged to a purple guard, and that they were addressing *him*. "Would you like me to take your...animal...and give him housing?"

Tarr opened his mouth, unsure of how to reply, and looked quickly over to Laith.

"I will give Tarr the guest apartments below mine," Laith requested. "Please take the wolf there and give it food and water and a bed to lie on. Tarr will come for him later."

"Thank you, if you don't mind," Tarr concurred politely, not put out by the bizarre look the guard shot him. He was still too thrilled to be embarrassed. He looked down at Wolver. "Don't worry," he told the wolf. "I'm sure it'll be a nicer place than where the horses sleep." Wolver grunted but followed the guard obediently out of the room, claws clicking on the marble floor, tail waving lazily behind him.

"Come with us," Laith told Tarr, walking off in one direction. Tarr was momentarily distracted by the engraved details on a nearby doorframe but caught himself and jogged a few feet to fall into step behind Athela and her bodyguard, Rane. He looked over at Rane, who seemed to feel his gaze and looked back for an instant. Her eyes were blue, he noticed, rather like the cornflowers they had ridden past on their way to the palace. It was a nice face; he couldn't tell much about her as she wore a hood that masked her hair, with a gold circlet over her head to keep it in place. The hood had a strange way of making her seem anonymous, which Tarr sensed was intentional. He gave her a small smile and was pleased to have it returned. *At least she seems more friendly than Athela*, he thought.

As they crossed the marble halls, Tarr noticed that some of the people walking through cast him odd glances as he passed, and became instantly aware of how out of place he looked. He awkwardly tugged at the drape of his traveling cloak and tried to straighten up and tighten the knapsack to his shoulder. Each of the halls was gleamingly, pristinely white, and Tarr began to lose track of where they were, immensely glad that he had the others to follow.

Finally, they came to a halt in front of two massive mahogany doors, manned by a guard who instantly swung the door open upon seeing Athela and Laith. "Follow me," the prince ordered and swept away in a ripple of cloak. Tarr complied amiably.

The throne room was more vast than anything Tarr had imagined. It was almost like standing in the midst of the forest and looking up towards the tips of the trees. The ceiling was domed like the curve of the sky itself, held in place by arching branches of stone that crossed and crisscrossed one another in ever more intricate patterns. Framing the room were columns of pure white, with vines of golden ivy shimmering their way up to the roof. The floor was so shiny that Tarr could nearly see his reflection in it. The furniture was sparse, especially given the grandeur of the setting, just a few tables and chairs pressed up against the walls. Tarr got the sense that, as in an Ashan home, furnishings in this room could be moved in or out to suit the requirements of the event.

At the moment, the room was scattered here and there with clusters of brightly-dressed people, who, once they caught sight of Tarr, quickly leaned together and began whispering. Tarr immediately began to feel uncomfortable and wondered what they were saying about him. He wished he could duck down behind Marc to hide, but as Marc was almost a foot shorter than him, this didn't seem like a feasible option. As his group of companions moved farther into the room, Tarr could see that at the other end there was a raised platform with two import-ant-looking rounded chairs upon it. It was here, Tarr surmised, that the King and Queen must sit when there were meetings at hand.

Laith went over to a cluster of five people near the chairs' platform, all of whom were chatting in an intimately small group. From the resplendence of their clothing and the deference with which Laith greeted them, Tarr realized that they must be other members of the royal Jelani family. He wished he knew the etiquette so as not to give the impression that Ashans were coarse and uncultured, and watched carefully to see what the appropriate behavior was. Laith sank to one knee and dipped his head. A gesture of respect, apparently. Tarr wondered if he could manage it without falling over.

"You're back, I see, Prince," noted one of the women. She was maybe fifty years old, with a cold sort of beauty, rather like the edge of a knife. She wore a shimmering gold dress that Tarr had to resist reaching out and touching; it looked almost like water. She carried herself with such a haughty air that Tarr immediately felt smaller just standing before her.

"Who is that?" asked one of the men in a dark purple cloak. He had slightly curling light-brown hair that was graying at the temples and at the ends of his beard. The corners of his eyes were wrinkled, and he had an indifferent air about him.

"King, this is Tarr, an Ashan from the forest," Laith answered, rising to his feet and motioning in Tarr's direction.

A Jelani king! Tarr's eyes widened, and immediately he reassessed the man. The King looked at him with interest, then his gaze slackened and his eyes drifted off into one corner of the room. Tarr followed where he was looking, but didn't see anything. If this was odd behavior, none of his companions gave any indication that it was so.

"Why did you bring *him* here?" a young woman in a dark green dress asked coldly. She was obviously related to the Queen, perhaps her daughter. She had a sheet of white-blond hair and eyes like green ice. She was regarding Tarr with cruel derision, as if he were already the butt of an unspoken joke.

"My Queen," Laith said, ignoring her and turning to the Jelani Queen in the gold dress, "When I met him, he was standing in the center square of Two Falls, right on the heart stone. Beside a wolf."

Silence greeted this. Tarr shifted uncomfortably, well aware that everyone else in the room seemed to think that the situation was just as ridiculous and far-fetched as Tarr found it. He felt embarrassed for

Laith and even more embarrassed to once again be the focus of everyone's stares. *It's not my wolf,* Tarr wanted to say. *He belongs to someone else. Even if this whole thing has a shred of truth to it, you've got the wrong Ashan.*

"The prophecy?" one of the other people nearby asked dubiously.

"There is no truth to the prophecy," the Queen snapped sharply.

"The prophecy predicted a Jelani matching Athela's description and an Ashan with a white wolf," Laith insisted. "It can't be mere coincidence. And if this half of the prophecy is true," he gestured to Tarr and Athela, "then it might also stand to reason that Kagai's heir is out there, too. Somewhere. Potentially gathering his strength."

The Queen glared down at them. "Argolaith, this is foolish, and this...thing...should be returned to his village where he belongs before he sullies these halls with his dirt."

Beneath Tarr's astonishment, anger stirred. *Thing? Dirt?* He was conscious that there was literal mud on his boots, yes, but no more than were on Laith or Athela's. He stirred and straightened up, feeling the same surge of discomfort and indignation as he had felt when the woman serving him his meal had asked him about Ashans living in bark huts.

One of the Jelani who had spoken before, the young woman dressed in the lush green gown, began laughing icily. Tarr sensed distaste in Laith's shoulders as he turned around to face her.

"Yes, my *lady*?" Laith asked. Tarr noted the sarcastic tone in his voice. "Is something funny?"

"Look at his clothes!" she chortled, nodding towards Tarr. "So dirty."

Tarr's jaw clenched, and his hands tightened. Laith laid a calming hand on his arm as the woman in green stepped forward. She had wide-set eyes, gleaming like a cat's.

"You're still so convinced that the prophecy is true, aren't you, Laith?" the young woman asked, a cold smile framing her delicate pink lips.

Laith shifted uncomfortably. Tarr wished he could just tell the prince to stop trying. He stared at the girl with the green cat's eyes, filled with a sense of loathing that he had never truly felt before. She stared right back at him, unyielding, a cruel smirk on her lips.

She took a step towards Laith and laid a hand on his arm as if to comfort him. "We didn't take you for such a gullible fool. It will be all right."

The prince's back was as stiff as a board. Tarr could sense the furious energy emitting from him. He pulled his arm away from her as politely as was humanly possible, gave an extremely short bow to the King and Queen, turned on his heel, and stalked off. Tarr, not knowing precisely what to do, followed him and saw the Lady Athela do the same. However bad Lady Athela might be, she was nothing compared to the girl with the green eyes.

"Hell!" Laith growled explosively, stopping abruptly outside of the door. Tarr skidded to a halt, Athela mirroring him. "It's like talking to the backside of Marc's horse!"

"Hey!" Marc exclaimed, insulted.

"My parents are idiots, Laith, you know that," Athela told him soothingly.

"They won't listen, will they?" Laith vented. "And the way they spoke to Tarr!" he swiveled on his heel and faced the Ashan. "I apologize. It was completely indecent for them to have behaved that way towards you."

"You and I are intelligent enough to know that we can't know everything, and that there might indeed be some truth to the prophecy," Athela told him calmly. "Now, come on. Usually, it's my job to complain and yours to tell me to shut up."

Laith still looked grumpy but seemed slightly more pacified at her words. Tarr, sensing that perhaps the cousins wanted time to talk without his prying ears, allowed himself to be drawn away by a magnificent tapestry hanging on one of the walls, depicting what Tarr assumed to be a Jelani king. It was very different than the type of decoration favored by the Ashans, which tended to be more simple, graphic, and austere. But Tarr loved the way that the threads melded together to create tones of flesh, earth, and flowers. He couldn't imagine how long it must have taken to create.

A few minutes later, he turned back around and noticed that everyone but Marc had left. The bodyguard was watching Tarr with a rather bemused look on his face. "Where did everyone go?" Tarr asked him.

"Laith has gone to see his wife, and Athela has gone off to talk to her horse about something," Marc shrugged. "I'll take you to your rooms if you like."

"Thank you," Tarr said nervously. "Do I need to...stay in my rooms?"

Marc shrugged again. "Not as far as I know. You can have the run of the place." He considered Tarr for a moment, clearly taking a dim view of Tarr's ability to fend for himself. "You might get lost, though," he added.

"Oh," said Tarr unenthusiastically.

"Just ask one of the servants to show you back up to your room. Dinner's in a few hours, and you're invited, of course," Marc announced with a smile.

"The young woman with the blond hair..." Tarr asked hesitantly, remembering the cruel laughter and the green feline eyes.

"Athela's sister? Cira? Just our bright little ray of power-grubbing, backstabbing sunshine," Marc quipped cheerfully.

"She probably wouldn't want me there," Tarr grumbled.

"Probably not," Marc agreed. "All the more reason for you to go."

Tarr considered for a moment. Marc had begun leading him through the hallways, and so wrapped up was he in his thoughts that Tarr barely spared a moment to gape at each towering new room they passed carelessly by.

"Marc," Tarr said quite seriously, trying a new tack, "Laith has made a great mistake. I don't like to agree with what his family said, but they're right. The wolf isn't even mine; he belongs to an Ashan I met in the forest, and he just sort of followed me here." Tarr didn't know why, but it felt very important to him to make the others understand this particular point.

Marc smiled. "Laith believes in things very deeply, Tarr. He's got his convictions, and they're hard to shake out of him. This happens to be one of them."

Tarr tugged unhappily at his draped travel cloak. "But he's wrong."

"He's been wrong before," Marc said with a dismissive gesture. "And he admits it when he is. He'll be wrong again, I reckon. As I said on the road, you have free room and board and a chance to explore. Don't worry about it."

"All right," Tarr agreed, wishing he could feel as cavalier about the whole thing as Marc seemed to be. Suddenly, he stopped. "Wait, you said that there was a dinner tonight?"

"That's right."

"Is it..." Tarr groped for the right word. "Formal?"

"Yes, of course," Marc replied, as if it was ridiculous that Tarr had to ask in the first place. "Once you're in a palace, pretty much everything is formal. Brushing your teeth is formal."

If this was a joke, it was hard for Tarr to follow, though Marc seemed amused by his own words. "Well, I'm afraid I don't really have anything proper to wear," Tarr told him anxiously, already imagining the judgmental stares of the courtiers as he shambled nervously into one of their great halls. "These are my only clothes."

"We'll dig you up a jacket or something," Marc said kindly, stepping back and sizing him up. "Our clothes will probably be a bit short on you, but I'm sure you'll be able to manage. You can say it's some sort of fashion statement. They'll let it pass; you're foreign-looking enough. Maybe you'll start a new trend."

"Maybe," Tarr agreed dubiously, feeling overwhelmed.

"Now, follow me; I'll show you to your room."

And feeling like he was treading water at the end of a very deep pool, Tarr followed.

An hour later, Cira slunk along the marbled corridors from her sprawling apartments to Laith's on the other side of the palace. She was already dressed in her finery for dinner and felt her heart beat faster as her slippered feet padded along the floor. She tossed her hair, knowing full well how lovely she looked.

Laith's door was a gigantic, ornate piece of work, and Cira paused momentarily to adjust the bangles on her wrist before throwing the doors open and entering Laith's entrance chamber. A dozing manservant leaped to his feet at her entrance and gave her a steep bow, looking rather abashed.

"I wish to see Lord Argolaith," she ordered.

"He is...occupied," the manservant informed her awkwardly.

Cira's stomach raced. "Do you want to go and get him, or shall I?" she demanded, glaring at the manservant with her piercing green eyes. His resolve faltered, and he fell back a few steps before turning and hurrying off to do her bidding.

Cira was in no mood to wait, so she decided to give Laith only a minute or so to prepare himself. She swept out of the entrance chamber and into his inner sanctum. The room was undeniably masculine, decked out in mahogany wood, though there were a few feminine flourishes here and there: a spare, elegant arrangement of flowers beneath a gilt mirror, a pair of beautiful lambskin riding gloves on a side table. She came around a corner and found Laith, half-dressed in a loose pair of drawstring pants, standing with his manservant, who was handing him a shirt. The bed beside him was recently unmade, and Cira heard a door close in the distance. She smirked to herself.

At the sight of Cira, Laith waved his valet away and took the shirt. He eyed her warily as she approached him, not taken in for a moment by the coy smile playing across her mouth.

"Don't bother with the shirt, Laith," she purred. "You show up like that down at dinner, you're likely to start a riot."

"Thank you for all your help earlier with your parents, Cira. Now, did you actually have something important to say to me, or did you just come barging in on a whim?" Laith threaded his lean body through the shirt and walked off to dig his boots out from beneath a nearby chair. Cira was close enough now so that she could see the mist of sweat on his forehead, catch the vestiges of heavy breathing.

"And what might I have been interrupting?" she asked innocently.

Laith gave her a sarcastic look. "I was looking over last month's exchequer reports."

She laughed and turned away. "No need to be like that, Laith. Come and sit by me." She arranged herself on a small couch just beside his balcony. A cool breeze flowed in through the open windows, fluttering through her white-blond hair. Laith approached her cautiously and sat beside her.

"I've been away so long," she began slowly, her voice smooth.

"I know," Laith agreed, not sounding terribly sorry about it.

"I thought of you often," she said, leaning towards him.

"Cira," Laith said slowly. "I'm not exactly sure what you're hoping to accomplish by all of this."

"I'm in a position of power now, Laith," she smiled and leaned back. "The next queen. It would behoove you to be friendly towards me. I'm in a position to make your life either very comfortable or very unpleasant."

He stared at her blankly for a few seconds, then his face cracked into a genuine smile of astonishment. "Are you *threatening* me?" he asked disbelievingly. "First Athela, and now me? What on earth happened to you while you were away, Cira? Before, it was pulling off the wings of dragonflies and throwing cats over the waterfall or making Athela's life a living hell. Now you're threatening *me*?"

"It was *one* cat," Cira snapped. She took a step back and then considered the best way to irk him. She decided on some flirting, which always seemed like a good provocation. "How long have you been married, Laith?" she asked. "And no children, how sad."

She could see by a twinge in his jaw that she had hit a nerve. Satisfied, she reclined back, staring up at the ceiling. "Though," she conceded with a vicious grin, "it doesn't seem to be for lack of trying."

"You are not going to succeed in provoking me, Cira," Laith said evenly, and when she looked at him she could see that his face was completely calm. "My relationship with my wife is absolutely no business of yours."

"I just hate to see you wasting your time, Laith," she shrugged a white shoulder and laid her hand on his. He didn't flinch. "It all must get terribly boring after a while."

"Stop it," he pulled his hand away and stood, walking out towards the balcony. She watched him for a moment and followed. He was silent for a few minutes, staring out at the tops of the trees, the light dipping below the horizon, the shushing waterfall falling beside his apartment window. He turned to her, and his face was grave.

"Cira, I don't know if you're too wrapped up in your petty games and little torments to actually register any of what I'm about to say to you, but I want you to know that I am perfectly serious." He faced her. "I don't know what it is inside you that goads you into treating people the way you do. Perhaps it's due to my aunt and uncle and the way they raised you, I don't know. But you are smart. You are ambitious. You can read people, you can predict what they're going to do, and you can help them or hinder them. Every one of those qualities I've just described is the hallmark of a potentially great leader. You're not a nice person, but you don't *have* to be a nice person to be a great leader—my aunt certainly isn't, and she's one of the greatest Queens we've ever had. But you can't let this..." he groped for a word, "*obsession* with humiliating others, with proving you're superior, be all that you focus those talents on. Ambition is useful—helpful, even—but not in the sadistic way you seem to want to wield it."

"Are you finished?" Cira snapped, feeling slightly off-balance.

"I have some advice," Laith continued, unperturbed.

"I can't wait to hear it," she retorted sarcastically.

"Find a teacher you trust and listen to them. Let them help you harness your potential. Don't always be concerned with being the smartest, the best, the most adored in the room. Learn the humility of knowing that others may have more wisdom than you. Find what you can do to help, not just to rise higher. Otherwise, sooner or later, you'll rise as high as you can go, and there will be nothing below you to hold you up."

"Boring," Cira spat. "I never knew you were so *boring*."

Laith shrugged. "Perhaps. But if you listen to what I'm saying, you won't have to *prove* you're great. People will *know* it."

Cira fumed silently and took a step back to go, her eyes flashing.

"You have a choice, still, Cira. A choice that I sense is coming to a head. Maybe the prophecy is playing some part in that. Do you remember Lord Seth?" Laith asked. Of course, Cira did: Lord Seth had been one of the most ruthless, merciless, psychopathic killers ever spat out by the city of Joymaril. "He's rotting away now in prison because he had these same impulses you do and couldn't control them. But you can. You have a mask you can pull over that pretty face of yours. At this point, unless something changes in you, I honestly don't know who scares me more, you or him."

Laith took her arm and pulled her close; normally, Cira would be thrilled by the proximity, but she felt herself flinch reflexively. "It's not too late, though. I believe that."

With that, he released her. Cira stepped away from him, her head held high and her back straight and immobile. She walked to the door of his chamber and turned around to face him. Her white dress pooled at her feet, and her blond hair hung like a sheet down her back. Her green eyes glistened bright and hard like emeralds as she stared at him. Laith could feel a change in the air, something dark and cold; he let go an involuntary shiver.

"See you at dinner," she murmured and was gone.

Laith stood still for at least five minutes before his wife came back in from the bath. Her hair was wet and smelled sweetly of jasmine oil, and she wore a scarlet silk dressing gown cinched around her waist. "That was a close one," she grimaced. "Hasn't she ever heard of knocking?"

Seeing the look on her husband's face, she approached him, standing on her tiptoes to kiss him softly on the cheek. Laith stirred as if from a dream, and looked down on her face. He pressed his lips to her forehead and ran his fingers lovingly through her damp, curly hair. Ilaina smiled softly.

"Let's not go to dinner," Laith said abruptly.

"Five minutes with your cousin spoiled your appetite?" she demanded mockingly. When he only managed a small half-smile at her joke, she touched his cheek, her brow furrowing in concern. "What's wrong?"

"I'm afraid," Laith said hollowly.

CHAPTER FIVE

His first morning in the palace, Tarr awoke at the crack of dawn and had a few protracted moments of confusion before he sorted out exactly where he was and what he was doing there, and why there was a majestic waterfall cascading just past his balcony window. The day before had been such a whirlwind that it had taken on the hazily surreal qualities of a dream, but as the minutes ticked by and he recounted the events in his head, the reality of his situation dawned fully. *I'm really here*, he thought to himself. *I'm sleeping in a bed in a Jelani palace.* It was almost too absurd.

He had managed, through some rather clever subterfuge, to beg his way out of attending the formal dinner to which he'd been invited the night before, pleading a fairly plausible case of exhaustion. He'd antici-pated that this would mean he'd have to skip another meal, which wasn't a terribly appealing prospect but was still better than having to feign his way through Jelani table manners while being glared at by various members of the royal family. Marc, he supposed, had seen through his ruse but had complied with his request after only minimal amounts of persuasion. Tarr had been astonished, after he'd ensconced himself in his new lodgings, to find that food had actually been brought up for him and was waiting on a small table by his bedside. He ate gratefully, picking his way around the meat at the center of the plate. Afterward, he paced around the room as night fell swiftly around him, and soon began trying to figure out how his bedside lamps worked. They were quite different from any lights he had used in the Ashan village. Eventually, he was eating the final bits of his dinner while sitting on the floor of his bedroom in the pitch black of night, too shy to go out and ask one of the guards or to try and find Marc to help him. It was all slightly ridiculous. He tried to avoid Wolver's judgmental stare, the reflections of the wolf's glassy blue eyes glinting in the dark as if to say *the lamps aren't that hard to figure out. I could do it.*

"You don't even have thumbs," Tarr had said aloud. Shortly after this pronouncement, he rolled into bed, sleep covering him like a blanket.

He soon found the disadvantage of having awakened so early in the morning. He was still too apprehensive and unsure of the proper etiquette to venture out of his room alone, so he contented himself for the first few hours of wakefulness by exploring every inch of the apartment in which he found himself, and which he'd had little opportunity to examine the night before.

Looking out of the balcony off his room, he gazed around at the city stretching along the length of the top of the cliff. He was pleased to make out one or two moving specks of people winding their way through the slumbering city streets. He wondered how many people lived in the palace and in the city beyond it.

Tarr, having grown up in the forest among Ashan craftsmanship, inspected the wood furnishings—the canopied bed, the tables, chairs, stools—with a keen eye and sharp interest. It was all beautifully made and fitted, though the ornate carvings that decorated the bedposts and the backs of the chairs were more fussy than the spare and simple Ashan aesthetic. The posts of his bed, upon examination, were carved to look like cascading water, splashing down into waves of mahogany wood that surrounded the frame, so that it almost appeared as though the sleeper were adrift on a boat. The bed was hung with tapestries, minutely embroidered with silk thread made to look like silvery raindrops falling from blue clouds. Wolver, who had been set up with a lovely velvet cushion on the floor beside Tarr's bed, was momentarily disarranged as Tarr investigated the meticulous edging on the seams. *They must have dedicated teams of craftspeople*, he mused, *whose sole job it is to create these elaborate fabrics and furnishings. They must not need to forage for food at all.* Ashan homes were beautiful in their minimalism and served quite a practical function: the adults were often ranging through the forest gathering supplies and food and certainly didn't have months on end to sit around embroidering fabrics, even in the winter months.

There was a small washroom outfitted with a pump and a basin of steaming hot water (though how it had got there was beyond Tarr's realm of guessing). The balcony off the side of his room offered a lovely, sweeping view of the edges of the Jelani city built into and on top of the rock, as well as the side of the cliff down to the lake below. As the sun rose in the east, Tarr contented himself with watching the ways the colors changed on the sides of the white buildings, soaking up and reflecting the glorious pinks, golds, and lilacs of the sky above, and was gratified to see more and more denizens of the city coming out of their homes and moving through the streets like distant pinpricks.

After a few hours of this, Tarr felt himself growing restless and impatient. He wanted very much to see the other Jelani again and to continue to explore the palace. He was also feeling quite hungry and had absolutely no idea how his dinner had come to his room the night before or how to go about getting breakfast. Laith had assured him that he did not need to pay, which was a relief as he had no idea whether Jelani even recognized the marks typically accepted in Two Falls as currency. At one point, he grew so impatient that he even opened the door of his apartment and peeked out at the hall beyond, but it seemed so large and imposing that he shut the door at once and went back to sit beside the balcony window.

Have they forgotten I'm here? he wondered.

After a time, he was relieved to hear a soft knock at the door, and jumped to his feet as Marc's friendly countenance peeked around. "Ah, good! You're here," he said jovially, and strode in.

"Yes," Tarr smiled nervously. *Where else would I be?*

"Well, I thought I'd take you down to get some food. We're all a bit busy today, so you can explore the palace as you like on your own."

Tarr was surprised and a bit disappointed by this, but tried to hide it. "All right. You...you'll be busy as well?" He didn't relish the thought of trying to find his way around the enormous palace all by himself.

"Laith and I are both teaching today and most of the days this week, so you'll be by yourself for a bit, I'm afraid," Marc clapped him on the shoulder, seemingly unconcerned at the prospect of leaving Tarr adrift in the enormous palace.

"What about Athela?" Tarr asked tentatively, hoping he had her name right.

"Oh...er...she..." Marc looked momentarily uncomfortable, and at once Tarr knew the underlying reason. *Athela doesn't want to spend time with me.* He again wondered why, or what he had done to offend her. Perhaps she didn't like Ashans either, just like her mother and sister.

As if he'd read Tarr's thoughts, Marc shook his head. "Athela's a tough one to crack. She doesn't warm up to anyone easily. It's not just you. She'll come around." He glanced down at Wolver, who had rather huffily resumed his spot on his velvet cushion after Tarr had moved him off to examine it. "I'll have some food sent up for your wolf."

"Thank you," Tarr said gratefully.

The two of them headed out into the soaring hallway beyond the room, and Tarr couldn't help but crane his neck up at the ceilings as they walked. "Now, don't worry about getting lost. Your room is on the west side of the palace, next to the royal apartments. Laith's room is up there," he made an unhelpfully vague gesture towards the upper left ceiling, "and Athela's is on the other side. All the guards and servants and everyone know who you are, of course."

"They do?" Tarr asked nervously, tripping slightly as they began descending a broad, sweeping marble staircase. He focused on a statue of something that looked like an enormous twisting feather at the bottom of the stair and committed it to memory. *Look for this statue at the bottom of the staircase leading up to my room*, he told himself.

"Everyone knows who you are," Marc chuckled. "It's not like we have a lot of Ashans wandering around the palace all the time. Not too many people will come up and try to talk to you, but the servants and guards can help point you in the right direction if you get lost."

Asking strange guards for directions didn't sound like the most appealing idea, and Tarr wasn't even sure that he could identify one of the servants if he tried, but he kept his worries to himself.

"Here we are," Marc announced finally and ushered Tarr in through a door. This room wasn't nearly as large as the one in which he'd met the King and Queen; it was actually only about twice as big as his bedroom. There were panels of gold and silver on the walls, with inlaid sections of mother of pearl in the shapes of flowers and vines that gave the room a soft, otherworldly sort of glow in the morning light streaming through the long, narrow windows. The room was almost empty, except for Marc and Tarr and one or two guards in purple livery standing by doors on the opposite sides of the room. Each of the guards had a white egret embroidered on the front of their sashes. *Those must be the palace guards*, Tarr thought to himself.

In the center of the room was a table laden with a bounty the likes of which Tarr had never before seen, except for perhaps on the spring and autumn feast days back in the forest. Platters of fruit were mounded up a foot high, wheels of buttery yellow cheese stood next to rolls and crusty loaves of bread; there were meats and what looked like smoked fish arranged in colorful geometric patterns, garnished with sprigs of herbs.

"This is the informal royal dining room," Marc told him, completely oblivious to the almost mind-melting opulence spread before him. "There's usually some sort of spread in here, so if you're hungry, this is the place to go. The Queen has her own dining chamber, so don't worry; it's unlikely that you'll run into her or Cira when you come in here."

For that, at least, Tarr was grateful. Marc handed him a plate, and Tarr went around the table, taking some fruit and bread and cheese, and some exquisitely sliced vegetables that had been arranged beside a vat of sauce.

"No meat?" Marc asked curiously.

Tarr shook his head. "I'm a vegetarian, most Ashans are. Sometimes we have fish, but no meat."

"Huh," Marc said, as if he couldn't quite wrap his head around the concept.

Tarr arranged himself on a gilt chair next to one of the walls and ate quickly, conscious that Marc (and probably the guards, though he couldn't see their faces behind their curving helmets) were watching him do so. When he had finished, he felt much better and thanked Marc as he stood.

"Just leave the plate," Marc said casually. "There are servants in and out of here all the time. They'll clean it up for you."

Feeling embarrassed, Tarr did as he was told and left the plate on his chair. He had always been taught to clean up after himself and was used to washing his own eating utensils. It felt impolite to leave it for someone else to do, but he trusted Marc's word.

"Right, I'm off then," Marc told him briskly as they left the dining room.

Tarr, who had turned to try and fix the location of the dining room in his mind's eye, snapped back around. "What?" he asked. "So soon?" He was deeply conscious of the twinge of anxiety in his own voice.

"You'll be fine," Marc said, with the casual dismissiveness of someone at home in his surroundings. "There's lots for you to see, I imagine. You can go anywhere you like. If it's the Queen's chamber or somewhere you *can't* go, the guards will point you in the other direction. Otherwise, you have the run of the place. There's a library if you get bored."

Tarr's ears perked up. "A library?" he asked. "Where—"

"Sorry, I've got to run," Marc told him, turning on his heel and heading in the opposite direction. "We'll find you around dinnertime. The library is that way," he added, with another unhelpful gesture to the left.

And with that, the sound of his footsteps receded down the hall and Tarr found himself quite alone. For a moment he considered just going back up to his rooms, but realized he didn't know the way there, either. *There's nothing for it,* he told himself firmly. *If Marc said you're allowed to explore, then you're allowed to explore. Laith and the others will help get you out of trouble if someone complains.* The voice in his head sounded decidedly more confident than he felt in real life, but he nevertheless set out and began to walk up and down the halls of the palace.

Almost instantly, he was completely and irrevocably lost. After the first anxious hour or so, though, he ordered himself to relax and began to just enjoy the feeling of wandering, of not knowing where he was or where he was going. The halls were all beautifully white and pristinely clean, with paintings and statues set into small alcoves, perfectly placed so that the sun hit them and filled the space around them with a serene white glow. Everything in the palace showed the evidence of someone's care, artistry, and thoughtful, intentional design. Also dotted here and there along the otherwise deserted hallways were guards in purple livery. As he passed by the first few, Tarr felt a pang of nerves, wondering if one of them would stop him and demand to know what he was doing there in the palace, but after they had let him pass with no comment, he let himself breathe easier.

Now and again, he would find himself in a more common area where members of the court gathered (*who* were *these people?* he wondered. *Were they all relatives of the King and Queen?* If so, it was the largest family group he had ever seen in his life.) Deeply conscious of the stares directed towards him, he eventually began to skirt the public forums and content himself with keeping to the back passageways.

At seemingly random intervals, a hallway would spill out into a resplendent, perfectly manicured garden, with the trees pruned just so and the buds of flowers beginning to spread along their branches. Around noon, he took a rest on a bench in one such garden. It was beautiful, he acknowledged, but there was something almost *too* meticulous about its care. Everything that grew had been carefully selected, specifically placed, fretted and fussed over to maintain the absolute maximum expression of aesthetic beauty. There was nothing wild, nothing random, about any of it. Tarr thought of the forest, and the way it felt to turn a corner and come face to face with a downed tree trunk, spread with a velvet carpet of green moss and just beginning to bud little white flowers. That was the kind of beauty he preferred, he decided, as a brilliantly plumed bird twittered away from atop a cascading rosebush. He liked the kind of beauty that didn't care whether or not there was anyone there to look at it. It just *was.*

He continued his aimless wanderings for much of the day, conscious that he was likely just going in circles but increasingly content to do so. Around evening, when the sun began to set over the trees, Marc appeared as if by magic and retrieved him to bring him up to Laith's room for dinner. Laith's rooms were much more impressive than the guest quarters in which he was housed, and Tarr wished he had the freedom to roam about and examine the prince's things. He stayed quiet for most of the meal, which was shared with Athela (who pointedly did not speak to him the entire time), Marc, and Laith. Laith had a wife, Tarr was told, but she was away visiting family for a few days in the city. Tarr didn't imagine that he was much of a scintillating dinner guest, as he barely spoke at all, and when he was asked questions about his day at the palace, he answered with uninteresting phrases such as "Oh, yes," and, "Yes, thank you."

The next day and the day after fell into much the same pattern. Tarr had the general feeling of being a sort of neglected pet; something that had been brought home in a moment of high excitement, then forgotten about as soon as some of the novelty had worn off. But after three days or so, he found that he didn't mind very much. The palace, which seemed so huge and forbidding and impossible to navigate, had begun to fall into a generally recognizable layout; he could find his way to the breakfast room, the gardens, and to the audience chamber, which many of the courtiers seemed to inhabit.

After those first self-conscious days, he grew more bold about walking through the general audience chambers, too, watching and listening to the courtiers as they milled around and talked, ignoring the looks of suspicion that were shot his way. None of the Jelani bothered to speak to him, so he found after a time that he could disregard their obvious disdain with little to no effort. They, too, grew bored with him after a few days, and soon he was able to pass through the crowds of people with minimum comment.

Figuring out how exactly the world of the palace operated was almost akin to learning a new language through immersion. By quietly watching and listening, Tarr began to see how it all worked: the courtiers who inhabited the palace were from "noble" families (he was still only dimly aware of what this meant, but he assumed that it had something to do with wealth), who by virtue of their status asked the Queen for a place at court. From there, the Queen chose her favorites to perform certain roles in the palace, and there was always a sort of seething intrigue, just below the surface, between the courtiers attempting to vie for the most coveted positions. One courtier was in charge of city maintenance and worked with a delegation of individuals from the city itself. One was in charge of overseeing supplies and the food needed to feed the court; still another was in charge of watching over the Queen's treasury and making sure that they had enough coin to pay for all the servants who bustled in and out of seemingly every room, hooded and silent. One day, Tarr overheard something that sounded a great deal like one of the courtiers had been appointed to assist the King in his daily bathing, but he decided he must have heard wrong.

Whether or not any of the courtiers who held these positions were actually *good* at their jobs, or whether they had been appointed by virtue of their quick wits or good looks, was anyone's guess. Tarr had to admire the Queen, though; after observing her (from a safe and remote distance) a number of times during her public audiences, he saw that she ruled with absolute confidence, and not a single detail seemed to slip past her. The King, however, was almost the opposite. He always seemed to be about three counties away, deep in some faraway reverie that often seemed to involve lunch. After two days, Tarr had observed that the meals always followed the same schedule, but the King seemed not to have yet come to this realization after fifty-odd years of living in the palace. Out of all the characters in this colorful court, Tarr decided, the King was his favorite.

Tarr had not forgotten Marc's mention of a library, and after a full two days of steeling his courage, he politely asked one of the purple-cloaked guards to show him the way. She had seemed surprised at first to be addressed so directly by him, but initial awkwardness aside, she turned out to be quite nice (much nicer than an armed, helmeted palace guard would appear to be) and led him around to a separate circular building to the southeast of the palace. She even stayed behind to help Tarr devise a path to return to the main palace building when he was done at the library. Tarr had a feeling that acting as a tour guide was much more interesting than her usual duties of remaining motionless by various doors and entryways.

After bidding the helpful guard farewell, he turned and faced the library. It was located across a footbridge stretching the narrow width of a rectangular pool of water, which reflected up the beautiful domed building above it. The library was very grand indeed, and Tarr felt a thrill of excitement as he laid his hand on a cool, carved ivory handle and stepped inside.

The library was largely empty, except for two younger Jelani (students, he imagined) off in one corner at a desk, a pile of books next to them. His eyes traveled upward, taking in the grand scope of the building, seemingly endless rows of books all around the circular room, with staircases and multiple floors. The ceiling was stone, carved into the shape of an enormous blossoming peony. Tarr was gaping up at it when there was the sound of someone's throat clearing beside him. He looked down and saw that at a grand marble desk beside the front door was an elderly gentleman with wispy white hair and the crinkled eyes of someone who had spent their life peering down at books.

"Can I help you?" he asked, with the slightest edge of suspicion.

This must be the Jelani Keeper, he realized, and the sudden familiarity brought with it a wash of relief. "I am a guest of Lord Argolaith," he said carefully, wanting to make sure the Keeper could understand his southern accent. "I am interested in exploring the library."

"An Ashan!" The Keeper exclaimed and stood up creakily. He regarded Tarr with distinct interest, not the sort of dismissive disdain with which he'd been met by the Queen and Princess Cira. "It's nice to meet you. I am the librarian here."

"Librarian?" Tarr repeated slowly. *That must be their word for the Keeper.*

"Yes," the man answered, still looking Tarr up and down as though he were some interesting rare species of animal that had come wandering blindly into the library. "If you are looking for anything in particular, I can help you find it. I know all these books. They are like my family."

"You have a big family," Tarr said, still awestruck. He turned and surveyed the nearest shelf lining the side of the circular wall. The books looked funny to him, straight and rigid, with sheaves of paper inside a hard cover. They were not at all like the scrolls back home, and the shelves were the same sort of straight up-and-down, not honeycombed like the ones in the Ashan library. He observed as much to the Librarian.

"Ah, yes," the little man said, a secretive smile playing on his face. "This way, the text is more protected by the cover, and the pages are less likely to be torn. And see here?" He took a volume off a nearby shelf and indicated the book's edge, where all the binding joined together.

This is called the *spine*."

"The spine?" Tarr asked. He wasn't sure he knew the word.

"The...er...backbone," the Librarian said.

This word Tarr knew, and he regarded the book with new appreciation. *Spine*, he thought to himself. *Backbone*. Almost as if the book was a living thing. He liked the term very much.

"If you have time during your visit," the Librarian said, falling into step beside him and leading him towards a nearby rack of books, "I have a few texts in Ashan that I would love to have translated. Would you...?" The question was open-ended, and his look was shrewd.

Tarr hid a grin. "I'd be glad to help."

"Wonderful." The man's face relaxed. "Now, over here..."

Out of all the Jelani he'd met thus far, Tarr felt most at home with the old librarian and his rows and rows of strange, hard-bound books. It was nice to think that some things translated directly across cultural lines, and he supposed that a love of books was one of those things. He spent the rest of that afternoon in the library, perusing the shelves and asking the Librarian questions about their organization, how they were printed and bound, who had written them, and when. The Librarian answered all his many questions patiently and, in turn, sent him off back to the palace with a sheaf of texts in Ashan for him to translate. (Tarr was deeply amused, later on that night, to discover that the texts were mostly concerned with seedling cultivation and were likely not to be of much use or interest to the Jelani people.)

Having made these few inroads, the next set of days fell into a pleasant pattern of exploring, visits to the breakfast room (which, regardless of when he visited, always seemed to be outfitted with an obscene amount of fresh food, almost entirely untouched), and long hours spent at the library under the helpful observation of the Librarian. The four Jelani who had brought him to the palace in the first place met with him for dinner every day, though Tarr still had trouble feeling as though he were contributing anything substantial to their conversation. Their talk oftentimes fell to the subjects of people or places about which he knew nothing. *Soon they'll ask me to leave, and I'll return to Two Falls*, he assured himself. He had enjoyed his time at the Jelani library so much that he thought perhaps upon his return to

Two Falls, he would try to get a job apprenticing in the library there or perhaps at the house of a book publisher, of which he had learned Two Falls had at least three.

It was in the middle of this pleasant, leisurely routine that Tarr made two unexpected acquaintances. The first he made one morning as he was leaving the morning breakfast room, stashing an orange in one pocket. He looked up as he closed the door behind him and was surprised to see a young man standing opposite him in the hall, leaning against a wall. He had pale hair and small delicate features and bore a remarkable resemblance to Princess Cira, so Tarr deduced that he must be some member of the royal family and was, therefore, almost immediately on his guard. He was a few years younger than Laith and the rest, though, likely in his mid-to-late teens. Trying to remember the proper protocol, Tarr gave a half-bow, the gravity of which was undermined somewhat by the orange tumbling out of his pocket and plopping heavily onto the marble floor.

"Sorry," Tarr apologized, hurriedly stashing the orange back in his pocket.

"You're the Ashan Laith brought back from Two Falls?" the boy asked. He was looking at Tarr quite closely, but Tarr was pleased to see that this boy, too, looked more interested than scornful.

"My name is Tarr," he introduced himself.

"I'm Cade," the boy replied. "Laith's younger brother."

This caught Tarr by surprise. The family resemblance was there, certainly, but Cade didn't at all have the physical presence or charisma of his elder brother. He was slight and delicate where Laith was tall, capable, and athletic. "It's nice to meet you," Tarr said politely, hoping that Cade didn't notice how taken aback he'd been.

"I've never met an Ashan before," Cade observed thoughtfully.

Tarr wasn't sure what to say to this. "Well," he said after a moment, "here I am. And we've met."

"Your people really live in treehouses?" he asked.

By this point, Tarr had learned the word "treehouses" from his chats with the Librarian. He considered the young man's tone, probing it for hints of the derision with which he'd been met before. It was curiosity only, he decided, and replied, "Yes. Though likely not what you're picturing in your mind. They're set in the trees, but are quite beautiful and carefully made." He felt a swell of pride. "Simpler and smaller than all this, but still quite exquisite."

"Interesting," Cade said thoughtfully.

Tarr looked to the left and right, unsure of what to do. He had intended to go out and eat the orange in the gardens overlooking the lake where there was a lovely view of the city, but he wasn't sure whether Cade expected him to stay there and continue to talk with him. Cade seemed to sense his uncertainty and indicated the hallway with his hand.

"Here, I'll walk with you," he said. "What do you think of the palace so far?"

Tarr considered his answer carefully, still not sure how honest he could be with the young man. There was something very clever, very calculating about him that told Tarr to be on the alert. And even as he felt his suspicions burbling beneath, there was some ringing of pleasure, too. It was a new sensation for him to meet someone who also liked to observe, to listen. It was almost like some sort of unspoken game had broken out between them: who could say the least while learning the most?

Cade watched him, waiting for Tarr to make the next move.

"It's much bigger than any place I've ever been," Tarr said finally. "Very beautifully...decorated."

"Mm," Cade mused, his hands in his pockets. Shafts of light illuminated his white-blond hair into a kind of glowing halo every time they passed a window. "And you've met my cousin Cira and Athela. And my aunt and uncle, the King and Queen."

This statement seemed to be an invitation for Tarr to pass judgment on Cade's family members, but Tarr wasn't foolish enough to impart what he really thought. "They've been very hospitable," he said carefully. "I'm grateful they've allowed me to stay. I've enjoyed the library here, and exploring the palace."

To this, Cade gave a derisive snort. "You'd make a good courtier," he observed.

Tarr was taken aback. "What do you mean?"

"The best courtiers know how to talk without saying anything at all. It's a skill many of them have to learn. For *some*," he said with pointed emphasis, "it comes naturally."

Tarr wasn't sure whether or not to feel complimented by this. He had a dim view of the courtiers in general and got the sense that Cade did as well, so he merely nodded and continued to walk.

"You don't have to say nice things about my relatives on *my* account," Cade said abruptly. "Athela's all right, but the rest of them are fairly terrible. I intercept Cira's letters and read them, just for fun."

Tarr stared at him, surprised that he should be so forthcoming. "They don't seem to like Ashans very much," he volunteered slowly.

Cade glanced at him with interest. "Oh?"

"They're quite wrong about us, in fact," Tarr drew himself up, happy to finally get the chance to speak up on behalf of his own people. "Our homes and practices are no less civilized than those here." *A great deal* more *civilized, in some cases*, he said to himself privately, thinking of the courtier in charge of the King's bathtub. "They're just different. That's all."

Cade seemed to mull this over and nodded. "They haven't met many Ashans, either, I daresay. Maybe they'll change their minds now that they've met you."

I doubt it, Tarr thought drily. He didn't think that he'd made much of an impression, skulking about in hallways and asking for directions. Moreover, he didn't get the sense that Cira or the Queen were likely to change their opinion in anyone else's favor unless it directly benefited them. He was quite sure that the King had no idea he existed.

Once they reached the garden, Cade left him on the flimsy pretense of having to examine a shipment of musical instruments that had just come into the palace. Walking past a beautifully curved reflecting pool, Tarr decided that their meeting had been no accident; Cade had specifically sought him out in order to get a sense of him. Tarr found himself thinking about the young prince for much of the rest of the day. He hadn't *liked* him, per se, but he had enjoyed the glimpse he'd gotten of the keen mind ticking along behind those eyes. And at least he had come up to Tarr to talk, which was more than he could say for about ninety-five percent of the Jelani population. If Tarr was, indeed, the first Ashan he'd ever met, at least Cade had come away from their conversation with a good impression of his people.

The second unexpected meeting that occurred was on Tarr's eighth day at the palace. It was midmorning, and Tarr had gotten a late start after staying up far too late translating the Ashan sapling guides the Librarian had given him. There was a light knock on the door, and Tarr looked up in surprise, not expecting Marc or any of the others to come to his room that day.

He blinked in surprise as a young woman entered, beaming at him as though they were already fast friends. He found himself reflexively smiling in response, though he had no idea who on earth she was.

"Hullo!" she said pleasantly. "Tarr, isn't it?"

"Yes," Tarr replied, feeling bewildered. Wolver was looking interestedly at the young woman from his cushion, as if he'd never seen the like of her either.

"I'm Ilaina, Laith's wife," she smiled even more broadly.

As he had done with Cade, Tarr felt himself take a mental step back and reassess her. He had been surprised to learn that Laith was married, for he seemed rather young for it—Ashans weren't paired together until much later in life, around the time they were thirty years old. He had conjured a vague mental picture of Laith's wife as being very soft and quiet and refined and perhaps given to light, delicate bouts of coughing when the morning dew was especially heavy, but the person standing before him was quite different than he had imagined. She was tall and athletic, with a blazing head of reddish-gold curls that were casually thrown up at the back of her head, though some of the curls had escaped to tumble haphazardly down her back. There was something about her that gave Tarr the impression that he could immediately sit down with her and tell her his life story. All of it, all his trials and troubles and woes, the hurt and betrayal he had felt at not being Chosen; she would sit and listen, offering consolation where needed and advice where requested. He liked her at once.

"It's very nice to meet you," he said cordially.

Ilaina crossed to Wolver and held out a hand for the wolf to inspect. After a moment, Wolver thumped his tail, and she patted him on his white head. Turning back up to face Tarr, she squinted an eye at him. "I wanted to see if you'd come with me this morning to the stables. Marc said you were unused to riding, and I wanted to offer some lessons if you like."

Normally, Tarr would have been abashed at the thought of clumsily bumping around on the back of a horse in front of a beautiful, intelligent young woman, but such was her manner that he was sure she wouldn't think less of him for his awkwardness. Besides, it might be useful to be able to better ride a horse. "Yes, please," he said gratefully.

"Wonderful," she beamed.

"I don't have any fancy riding clothes or anything," he pointed out, assuming, from what he had gleaned of Jelani culture, that there was a "correct" outfit in which to go riding.

"Just trousers and boots with a heel; you'll be great," she said, indicating her own simple, practical attire. "I'm a fan of black; it shows less mud when you're tromping back home at the end of a ride." She grimaced. "In case you hadn't noticed, the people in this palace aren't huge fans of dirt."

Tarr hadn't yet been to the stables and was glad to have Ilaina with him to lead the way once they had progressed out past the now-familiar sections of Joymaril. She was easygoing and chatty and asked him many questions about what he'd done and where he'd gone in his days alone in the palace. Far from the reserve he'd felt when Cade had asked him the same things a few days before, he found himself relaying his adventures in the breakfast room and the friendship he'd forged at the library. "I'm sorry you've been left to your own devices," she said after he'd described his routine. "You came here during a rather odd week, with my being out on a visit and the boys having to teach. And Athela being, well...Athela."

"I don't mind at all," Tarr told her, the memory of those first lonely days in the palace dissipating.

The stables were a sprawling set of buildings to the west of the palace and city, abutting a broad swath of hilly, forested land through which pastures, warm-up arenas, and riding trails were scattered. The stable compound was almost as big as his entire village back home; when he pointed this out to Ilaina, she shook her head and laughed.

"It's a bit much, isn't it? All of this," she waved her hand around at the rolling hills, the shining equine heads popping curiously out of stall doors, the palace set like a glimmering pearl on the edge of the cliff behind them. There was something in the way she said it that made her sound as though she were something of an outsider, someone like him who had grown up elsewhere and could take all the splendor in with a critical eye.

"You weren't born here," Tarr observed.

Ilaina looked at him, surprised. "No, I wasn't. I'm from the city, originally. I met Laith at the Academy where he was teaching." A faraway swell of affection and remembrance arose in her eyes, and Tarr was amused to see a retroactive flush arise in her cheeks. She coughed, regaining some of her composure. "As you might imagine, he was utterly repulsive and unpleasant and hard to get along with—much less look at—but somehow I fought through it, and here we are."

"How nice for you both," Tarr laughed. "Is it usual? For a prince to marry someone from the city?"

"Oh, no," she frowned. "I think he was supposed to marry a distant cousin or something. But he got special permission from the Queen and got out of it. He owes me for that."

"I hope you don't let him forget it."

"Never."

After a short time, she was introducing him to his horse, a quiet, placid little mare with a slight potbelly and a fondness for apple peels. She showed him how to saddle the horse and how to lead her out (all the while, Tarr was aware of a swarm of royal grooms hovering anxiously around them, seemingly appalled that Ilaina was attempting to do all the tacking up herself.)

They found themselves in a small paddock set away from the stables, where a dirt exercise ring had been carved through the grass. The ground was even and the day was pleasant, and after a short time, Tarr forgot some of his self-consciousness and actually began enjoying the sensation of riding. Ilaina was a good teacher and managed to make him laugh, even when he made mistakes. His natural Ashan balance, he soon found, worked well in his favor, and after only a short time, he was able to sit his horse at a jog and even for a round or two at a slow canter. The mare seemed reluctant to do much in the way of exercise, which suited Tarr just fine.

"Marvelous," Ilaina concluded as the two of them walked back out of the stable, Tarr's mount happily bathed and shuffled back into her stall. Tarr's rear end and legs were in so much pain from the ride that they had nearly buckled into a jagged heap beneath him when he'd dismounted, and was doing his best to hide it. He was conscious, however, that he was walking as though he had something stuck up his rear end; if Ilaina noticed, she was kind enough not to point it out.

"You'll be an expert in no time, as good as Athela, I reckon." He could tell by her smile that this last bit was something of an exaggeration.

"Ilaina," he said slowly, feeling comfortable enough to ask her outright what had been nagging at him for days. "Does Athela not... like me?"

"Not like you?" she blinked in surprise. "Not at all. Though you shouldn't feel bad for thinking so. She takes a while to warm up to people. She'll come around, I promise. You are one of the most inoffensive people I've ever met."

"She doesn't ever talk to me, though," Tarr persisted. "Not at dinner, not..." He trailed off, frustrated. This was roughly the third time that someone had assured him that "Athela would come around," but so far, there'd been no indication that any such transformation would ever take place.

Ilaina smiled, a little secretive smile that only she seemed to understand. "Don't you worry," she assured him. "I have a good feeling about it."

The riding lessons progressed for another four days before Tarr began to see what Ilaina meant. In the middle of one of their sessions, still out in the same exercise paddock, he was shocked one day to look up and see Athela watching him ride from a perch atop a distant rail near one of the stable buildings. The surprise of it all nearly set him reeling out of the saddle, but luckily, the mare had grown accustomed to his lapses and slowed to a walk before he could come toppling off. He resolved himself to focus more on the lesson at hand but couldn't help but look up every now and again to see whether Athela was still there. She watched him for the entire lesson, but vanished by the time they made their way back to the stable.

The next day she was there, too, and the day after that, only this time she had inched forward to another fence that sat closer to the paddock, still far enough away as to not be an official part of the proceedings. At the end of the lesson, when Tarr pointed his horse into the center of the ring and drew up next to Ilaina, he could have sworn that she glanced over in Athela's direction and gave him a cheeky wink.

This proceeded for another few days, and each day Athela would come a little bit closer, like a wild animal slowly being coaxed out of its den. After a week or so, she was sitting on the railing of their arena, her black curls blowing in the spring breeze, surveying him closely, but still saying nothing. Neither Tarr nor Ilaina had acknowledged her presence there; it was almost as if they didn't wish to startle her or frighten her off.

He was decidedly more aware of his mistakes and faults underneath her watchful gray gaze, but resolved to do the best he could under the circumstances. Rounding a corner and coming up to where Athela was perched on the fence, he signaled his mare to canter, but instead of breaking into the faster stride, she gave a few bobbing steps of a trot and tossed her head in refusal. A bit abashed at his failure, he ducked his head as he walked next to Athela's post, gathering up his reins to try again.

"Pull her nose in a bit," Athela said suddenly, and Tarr's head flicked up. She was studying him thoughtfully, her gray eyes observant, her tone helpful rather than condescending. Tarr slowed the mare to a full halt so that he could better listen as she continued. "She's a lazy thing, and she'll try to pull one over on you if it means getting out of having to do some work. Gather her head in like this," she demonstrated, sitting up taller and motioning with her hands, "and then ask her. And *mean* it. They can tell when you don't mean it."

Tarr nodded gratefully and did as she suggested. It wasn't as smooth as it could have been, but the trick worked: the mare could clearly see no way out of having to go faster and lurched forward in a resignedly slow canter. When Tarr rounded the circle again, Athela gave him a nod of approval. Tarr felt his heart soar as high as if she'd leaped off the fence to embrace him and hand him an award for achievements in horsemanship. When he glanced at Ilaina, there was a private smirk of satisfaction on her face that Tarr suspected had little to do with his riding. It was clear that this had been her aim all along, and that the fastest way through Athela's armor was to plop Tarr on a horse and send him off in her direction.

Athela was there every day after that, only now she came with them to saddle up and stood in the center of the ring beside Ilaina as she taught. Horses were Athela's favorite subject, and one on which she felt completely comfortable discoursing. Once she had talked to him about horses, it seemed, she was comfortable talking about other things as well. He had been worried at first that she would deride his feeble efforts, but just like Ilaina, she was patient and constructive. She was more reluctant with her praise, but when she did compliment a transition or his seat, he felt absolutely elated.

The two women, he eventually realized, were best friends. They had such different temperaments that it took him a while to fully grasp the depth of their friendship, but the more he got to know them both, the more it seemed to make sense. They were as different in personality as in looks, but there was a genuine, palpable affection between them that was quite touching to witness. He would walk behind them, watching their retreating backs as they ambled back to the barn after a lesson, their two curly heads—one ebony black, one red-gold—turned towards one another conspiratorially as they chatted easily back and forth, their strides naturally mirroring each other as they walked.

Finally, a day came that seemed to conclusively confirm the fact that Athela had finally warmed to him and accepted him into her small circle of companions. He was walking with Wolver out by the stables on a day when he had no lesson; Ilaina was teaching at the Academy and had postponed their ride for the following day. He had grown to love the quiet fields behind the palace, where the hint of wildness was still allowed to encroach just a little across the manicured lawns. Following a short walking path between the paddocks, he rounded the top of a hill and found himself looking down on a spread of open pasture, divided here and there by perfect lines of white fences, alongside which Wolver was gamboling merrily. At the base of the hill just below him he saw Athela, instantly recognizable by her mane of tumbling black curls. She was leaning forward against a fence, looking out at the horses in the paddock beyond.

Tarr came up behind her hesitantly, unsure of whether or not she would welcome his company. She only glanced at him as he drew up next to her, but made no move to leave or avoid him as she once might have done. Tarr leaned his skinny arms on the top railing of the gate and rested his head on his arms, looking out at the paddock. The silence, he noted, was comfortable and companionable, not at all strained or difficult. Indeed, Athela seemed quite content to have him there.

Closest to them, only a foot or so from the gate, was a small gray donkey with enormous ears that flipped back and forth every now and again to ward off a fly. It wore the patient, rather resigned expression of its species, not wanting for anything, its long lashes unhurriedly blinking. Further afield, Tarr saw a cluster of horses at the far edge of the paddock. He wasn't an expert, but they looked young to him: leggy and unsure, each with a bright, wide-eyed look that suggested that the world to them was still fresh and new. There were four of them, but none looked particularly relaxed or were eating any of the lush green grass spread at their feet. All were clustered together in a tense little group, their heads thrown up, their ears alert. Every once in a while, one of them would utter a piercing whinny that split the air around them with its shrill desperation.

"Weanlings," Athela said by way of explanation. "Still calling for their mothers."

As if to punctuate, another one of the horses let out its high-pitched call, which was picked up by two of the others. Then there was a long pause as they waited. There was no reply. Frustrated, two of the horses pushed back from the fence and trotted around in an anxious circle before settling once more into line, staring out at the trees.

"Where are the mothers?" Tarr asked curiously. He'd felt an odd pang looking at the distressed young horses, and didn't quite know why.

"When we wean them, we take the mothers down the hill to another stable, out of earshot. It's better if they can't see or hear one another. Helps them adjust faster," Athela told him. She reached down with one hand over the top of the gate and smoothed the donkey's forelock gently between her fingers. "We put the donkeys with them to keep them company. They'll fight off any predators that might come close."

"Really?" Tarr was surprised. The donkey seemed, if anything, catatonic—not the most effective bodyguard he would have imagined.

"You'd be surprised," Athela said.

The donkey, spurred into action by some unseen force, took a few shuffling steps closer to them and nudged at the gate with his nose. The metal bar clanked tiredly one time and eased into place. The donkey, having made its halfhearted bid for freedom, sank back into a stoic sort of immobility.

"Donkeys always want out," Athela observed sagely.

Tarr looked over at her. She raised her eyebrows, frowning thoughtfully as if acknowledging a universal truth. The donkey flipped an ear. Athela smiled fondly and scratched its forehead.

It was at that moment Tarr decided that he liked Athela. And he began to suspect that she liked him as well.

CHAPTER SIX

A few days after Tarr and Athela communed with the donkey in its paddock, Tarr received the rather unwelcome news that there was to be another formal banquet in honor of some religious holiday or another (Marc was rather vague on the details) and that Tarr and the others would be required to attend. Tarr had grown quite comfortable with the relaxed dinners taken in Laith or Athela's apartments, and though by now he had spent more time in the palace and grown accustomed to its sights and people, the prospect of attending a royal dinner was no less intimidating than it had been when he first arrived.

He'd had a rather anxious notion that it would be Marc who would outfit him for the event as he was deeply self-conscious about his clothing, especially when compared to the finery of the Jelani. The best Marc had offered him was a few indeterminate comments about procuring him a jacket, which Tarr didn't think would be at all suitable, given Marc's shoulder-to-torso ratio. On the night of the dinner, however, he was overwhelmingly relieved to hear a knock at his door and for Ilaina and her maid Nadia to come sweeping briskly and capably into the room, bearing with them armfuls of Laith's old clothes.

"Thank goodness," Tarr remarked as the women spread out the

clothes over his bedspread. "I thought I was going to have to wear something of Marc's."

Both of them laughed, even Nadia. Marc was a fraction of Tarr's height and twice as broad-shouldered. The effect would have been quite comical. "That would have been something to behold," Ilaina agreed, holding up a forest-green jacket and squinting thoughtfully as she examined it. "But Laith is about your height and was skinnier a few years ago than he is now. We'll find something that works." She tilted her head and consulted Nadia in a low tone. "This one might bring out his eyes," she frowned. "Here. Try it."

In due course, Tarr was outfitted for the banquet, and at Ilaina's invitation he gathered up his things and followed her to her private rooms to wait while she got ready. On the way she informed him that she had appointed herself to be Tarr's date for the evening.

"What about Laith?" Tarr asked curiously.

"He'll fend for himself," she waved her hand, unconcerned. "They love him at these sorts of gatherings, you'll see. I usually wind up spending half the time with his little brother Cade throwing food at the backs of people's heads."

Tarr couldn't find words to express to her how grateful he felt for her companionship that evening. Out of all the Jelani, he was most at ease with Ilaina. He felt pleased when his jokes made her laugh, or when she asked him questions about his former life in the forest. He watched her graceful arms appreciatively as she twisted her red-gold curls up and out of the way on the back of her head, chatting merrily with Nadia as she went.

Ilaina's dressing room, located in her own private suite adjoining Laith's, was one of the most beautiful places he'd been in the palace. The panels of her walls were similar to those in the breakfast room (Tarr imagined they must have been crafted by the same artisan), only hers were gilt in silver, with inlaid patterns of mother of pearl depicting water lilies and rippling waves that spanned the entire length of the room. The space had a gentle, almost otherworldly shimmer, reflecting the soft light of the rising moon over the distant trees. Long, gossamer curtains of pale turquoise hung down over her balcony windows, which were thrown open to invite in the delicious spring evening. Tarr lounged with a goblet of sweet wine on a small velvet settee just around the corner from where Ilaina and Nadia were rooting through her closet, and felt himself actually quite looking forward to the night's events and the prospect of a date with his friend.

My friend, he realized suddenly. *I've made a friend.*

"You won't need that," Ilaina said suddenly, gesturing to the Ashan traveling cloak he had brought with him up to the room. "Give it here, I'll stash it for you back in my closet. You can wear Laith's old cloak to walk into dinner."

They went down to the party together a short while later. Ilaina had dressed to match him in a dress of pale, shifting green that set off the red undertones in her hair, which was twisted and braided at the back of her head and held up by a delicate, draping net of tiny seed pearls. Tucked in her hair was a little pin shaped like a cornflower, glinting with brilliant blue sapphires and tiny diamonds that fell off the petals like dew; Tarr leaned in and admired it up close, complimenting its beauty.

"It was a gift from Laith," Ilaina told him, trying to sound casual but failing. She blushed.

Tarr actually felt almost confident as they strode together through the hallways, her hand looped around his elbow. It was as if her presence was a suit of protective armor he was wearing. He could see the guards' eyes following them as they went, and felt rather proud to have such a lovely young woman with him. At one point, they passed by the guard who had helped him find the library days before, and Tarr gave her a slight wave; she gave him an infinitesimal wink in return.

This place isn't so bad, he thought to himself, and breathed a contented sigh. *I wonder what they do after parties here. Maybe we can go to the library.*

As they approached the great hall, the palace seemed to gradually grow more and more crowded; lights were blazing high as night approached, and members of the Joymarillian court began pouring out of their apartments dressed in all of their finery, ready for the evening's festivities. Many of them stared at Tarr and Ilaina, but before Tarr could even begin to feel uncomfortable, Ilaina would sweep them up to one Jelani or another and say something along the lines of, "Don't *you* look wonderful tonight? Have you met my friend, Tarr? He's visiting from the Ashan forest and has graciously offered to escort me for the evening." At this, the Jelani would be forced to smile and greet Tarr with courtesy; if they harbored any of the same prejudices as the Queen or Princess Cira, they had to swallow them down.

Tarr had to catch his breath as they entered the dining hall. Dozens of chandeliers had been brought in and hung at various heights throughout the room, dotted with seemingly endless candles and shimmering petals of glass, so that the effect was almost as if someone had taken a thick handful of tiny glowing stars and scattered them across the ceiling. The room was crowded with Jelani in glistening colors of every shade; Tarr felt himself saying a silent prayer of gratitude for Ilaina's efforts in outfitting him, for his attire blended in seamlessly with the others. As if she'd heard him, Ilaina gave his arm a squeeze.

Beyond the sea of milling Jelani, Tarr could see dozens of long tables set in rows beneath the throne platform, with coverings of pale cream fabric embroidered with enormous egrets, the symbol of the royal family. The tables glittered with golden goblets and cups of chiseled glass, and spilled over the edge with flowers and leafy vines that cascaded to the floor. Tarr's ears perked as he heard distant music emanating from one corner, and craned his neck over the crowd to try and catch a glimpse. There was a group of musicians, outfitted in the royal purple, rather listlessly plucking at their instruments, clearly aware that no one was really listening to them. After they finished a song, Tarr applauded rather loudly, and one of the musicians (as well as several nearby guests) looked over at him in surprise. Ilaina laughed at Tarr's enthusiasm, but before he could feel embarrassed she gave the musicians her own encouraging, very unladylike hoot. It was much louder than his applause had been (inspiring a few scandalized whispers from nearby dinner guests.) Eventually, the musicians returned to their instruments, this time with slightly more gusto.

Ilaina's hand still draped easily in the crook of his elbow, the two of them steered slowly through the chatting members of the crowd and headed gradually towards the head of the room, distantly skirting the platform atop which the King and Queen sat. The Queen had a courtier whispering in one ear, whom Tarr recognized as the individual in charge of managing the Queen's money. Noting the rather harried look on the man's face, he tried to imagine what the banquet had cost and couldn't help but grin. While the courtier spoke, the Queen regarded the entire gathering with the haughty superiority of a bad-tempered cat; the King, who after weeks of observation had remained Tarr's favorite of all the royal family, seemed to be singing something under his breath, tapping his knee aimlessly with one finger and, Tarr imagined, wishing he was elsewhere.

Tarr would have been quite content to spend the rest of the night strolling around the great hall with Ilaina's hand tucked against his arm, but before long there was a stir and Laith walked in, flanked by Marc, Athela, and Rane, Athela's bodyguard. Tarr spotted a knot of young women gaping openmouthed at Laith, who seemed completely oblivious to all the attention. He glanced over at Ilaina, who seemed to understand his unspoken question.

"He's used to it by now," Ilaina said with a fond chuckle, her eyes not leaving her husband. "As am I."

"Is it usual for bodyguards to come to these events?" Tarr asked curiously.

"No, not usually. But Athela and Laith are important enough in the royal family that even their bodyguards are also royal or royal-adjacent. Marc and Rane are both distant cousins, a few steps removed here or there." She crinkled her nose. "What's the Ashan word for 'cousin'?"

Tarr smiled. Ilaina had asked him to teach her a few Ashan phrases, and though her accent was abysmal, she had caught on to the vocabulary quite quickly. He opened his mouth to reply, but before he could, the others came up to greet them. Ilaina disentangled her hand from Tarr's arm and gave her husband a soft kiss, then brushed her cheek lightly against Marc's and Athela's. Tarr had never seen this kind of welcome before and was momentarily worried that he would be expected to do the same, but the others made no movements towards him. Athela looked lovely in shining silver, and even greeted him with a small, reserved smile and a minuscule nod, which was a vast improvement over where their friendship had stood only a week before. Laith cut a rather dashing figure in a high-necked black jacket embroidered with gold thread, and Marc stood behind him, cobalt blue. Tarr looked around with interest at Rane, Athela's bodyguard, who he'd only glimpsed here and there on the occasions he had dined in Athela's apartments. If anything, she seemed even shyer and more reserved than he was. She always wore a rather traditional hood that covered every part of her head except for the round oval of her face, so he had no notion as to the color of her hair, but her face was quite pretty in his estimation: delicate-featured, with calm gray-blue eyes like a placid lake. He'd never heard her speak before. He gave her a nod, which she barely returned, the edges of her eyes creasing ever so slightly.

"Well, here we are again," Laith observed, looking out around the heads of the Jelani surrounding them. "Same old nonsense. I—"

At that moment, an older man in burgundy-colored robes touched Laith's arm in greeting, and at once the prince was pulled off into a conversation with a very boring-looking group of older Jelani, who seemed to hang on Laith's every word and punctuate every sentence with a rather sycophantic chorus of laughter.

"See?" Ilaina muttered to Tarr. "I told you."

"Now what do we do?" Tarr asked. He was surprised to note how many of the faces in the chamber he now recognized from his days wandering around the court. Over in one corner, off by himself, he could see Laith's younger brother Cade, who met Tarr's eyes and raised his goblet in an ironic salute.

"What do we do?" Athela echoed grimly. "We wait for it to be over."

"Now, now, Athela, they haven't even served dinner yet," Marc said placatingly.

Suddenly, an unpleasantly loud sort of honking sound came from the musicians' platform, loud enough that all the Jelani ceased talking and turned to look. The crowd parted, and Cira, Athela's sister, entered from one of the antechambers to the side of the great hall, sweeping past the royal purple drapery and gliding up to the dais where she greeted her mother and father. She was in a glimmering long dress of sky blue fabric, pale hair falling in a swath down her back, with bits twisted away from her porcelain face by clusters of tiny pearls.

"We welcome you, daughter," the Queen intoned, and Cira sank into a deep, respectful curtsy, a smug smile on her face, clearly reveling in the attention from the court. It was all so solemn and theatrical that Tarr almost let a helpless giggle escape his lips.

The pomp of the moment was suddenly shattered by the loud sound of a scuffle behind them all. Surprised, Tarr swung around and could see that at the opposite end of the hall, towards the entrance through which they'd walked, there was a small knot of struggling figures: guards in purple and someone between them. *Is someone trying to start a fight?* Tarr wondered. The Jelani nearest the scuffle skittered back, clearing the area like a fighting ring. Out of the corner of his eye, Tarr saw Marc and Rane instinctively move closer to Laith and Athela.

"What is the meaning of this?" the Queen's voice boomed out, dripping with displeasure. Cira's face was absolutely livid, clearly furious at having her grand entrance spoiled by someone else's theatrics.

The nexus of the scuffle seemed to be one small individual, who was squirming in the grasp of four or five of the royal guards. From what he was able to glimpse, the figure appeared to be small and delicate, almost like that of a child. *Has a Jelani child escaped to try and break into the party?* Tarr wondered. If they had been back in the Ashan village, it would have been most unsuitable for a child to appear at an adult's gathering like this, and from the reactions of those around him, it seemed to be similarly taboo here. He looked around at the faces of his companions but could see by their expressions that they had no idea what was going on, either.

The crowd parted as the guards dragged the struggling figure up to stand in front of the dais. They came to a halt, and the figure ceased its wriggling. The guards stepped to the side. In shock, Tarr could see that the figure *was* a child—a boy of ten years of age or so. He had a comically large, ornate sword strapped to his back, so big that Tarr was surprised he could carry it. All at once, Tarr saw Laith's hand shoot out and urgently grip Athela by the forearm.

"We found this boy prowling around the first floor," one of the guards announced. "He broke into the palace. He's from Two Falls."

"Is that so?" the Queen asked silkily, eyeing the boy with disdain as though he were a particularly unpleasant kind of insect. "And what, pray tell, were you doing here in our palace?"

"Nothing," the boy's voice was light and breathy and almost hard for Tarr to hear, though they were not too far away.

"Nothing?" the Queen repeated. "I find that hard to believe."

Tarr began to have a very bad feeling that the Queen's limited mercy did not extend to include trespassing children, and wondered (with a rather sick sort of dread) what she was going to do to him.

"The sword," Laith muttered. "The *sword*, Marc."

Marc blinked in surprise, and his ice-blue eyes narrowed as he peered closer at the relatively enormous weapon buckled to the boy's back. "That's a Whitsun sword," he muttered.

"Not just any Whitsun," Laith hissed.

Marc's eyes grew wide. "Morthenstar's?" His voice was hoarse.

Ilaina and Tarr gaped at him. "That little boy is carrying *Morthenstar's sword*?" Ilaina demanded, her voice low.

Laith nodded, his face pale.

Tarr looked towards the weapon. He knew very little about swords, but it certainly seemed to be finely made. He could see a spray of rubies inlaid at the hilt; they tumbled down the length of the white scabbard like falling rose petals. It didn't seem at all the type of weapon that a young boy from Two Falls would be carrying. He began to get the feeling that whoever the boy was, he hadn't come by the sword honestly.

"You dare," the Queen rose to her full height, her dress glimmering down off of her lap and pooling at her feet, "to break into the palace of Joymaril, *armed*, and then lie to *me*? What is your purpose in coming here? Speak!"

The boy muttered something. Tarr couldn't see his face, just his back, but his head was bowed and Tarr could tell that he was trying to avoid making eye contact with the Queen. He had a head of shining copper-colored hair and a slight, weedy frame, as if he hadn't grown up with much nourishment or care.

The guard to the side of the boy seized the sword and twisted it around so that the Queen could get a good look at it. "He is carrying *this*," the guard informed her with some satisfaction. The boy was now facing towards their group, and for an instant, his eyes locked with Tarr's. Tarr could see a frightened face and a smattering of freckles across his nose. A moment later, he was turned roughly back around to face the ire of the Queen.

"What are you doing with a Whitsun blade?" the Queen demanded, her voice a sharp hiss.

"What?" the boy asked feebly.

"That sword," the Queen demanded, pointing. Tarr was startled to see her finger shaking ever so slightly.

She recognizes it, Tarr realized suddenly. He still wasn't sure what the significance of the sword was in the grand scheme of things, but it was clear that the sword scared her.

"It's mine," the boy said, his voice a little stronger. He stood up taller. "I found it."

"*Found* it?" the Queen repeated sarcastically. "You do not just *find* a Whitsun blade."

"Whitsun swords are among the rarest and most coveted weapons in existence," Ilaina muttered to Tarr under her breath. "There's no way he would have just *found* it. And there's no way he could afford to buy it. Whitsun swords are priceless." She glanced sidelong at Laith. "And if that *is* Morthenstar's sword," she added, lowering her voice even more, "that makes it the rarest, most valuable of them all. The sword has been lost for centuries."

"I *did* find it," the boy protested stubbornly, raising his voice even louder. "Hidden in an old shoe shop in Two Falls." There was a smattering of laughter around the hall.

"A shoe shop," the Queen repeated, her voice deathly quiet. The entire hall fell so silent that if one of the glasses had toppled to the floor and shattered, the noise would have been like lightning splitting the air. Every pair of eyes in the hall was trained on the Queen and the boy, even the King's, who looked as though this banquet was shaping up to be far more engaging than most of his royal duties tended to be. The Queen leaned forward like a falcon readying for a dive. "You came here to steal."

"I just wanted to look around!" the boy insisted. "Can I go now?"

"I believe the intention was worse than theft, Mother," Cira said smoothly, drawing forward a step and looking down at the boy with a mirror image of the Queen's disdain. "I fear he has been sent here to spy." Momentarily, her green cat's eyes flicked up towards Tarr and his group, and he felt himself grow uneasy. *What is she up to?*

"I'm not a spy!" the boy exclaimed. His voice was more indignant than fearful, as if he were almost offended by the accusation.

"Ever since my return from the Meadows, I've been watched," Cira said. "I have been followed. My letters have been open and read." There was a flash of genuine fury on her face at this, and Tarr couldn't help but glance across the room to where Laith's brother, Cade, was standing. He remembered Cade saying that he'd been intercepting and reading Cira's letters for his own amusement. Not meeting his eyes, Cade took a long, deliberate sip of his wine and continued watching the unfolding events with a sort of innocent, benign interest.

"I believe, Mother, that this boy had been hired to infiltrate the palace during our celebration tonight, and to ransack my rooms under the guise of thievery," Cira announced dramatically, with a sharp movement of her hand. "But with the true motive of espionage."

A small gasp followed this announcement. The boy was silent, and Tarr got the impression from looking at the back of his copper head that he was goggling at the ludicrousness of the charge. Tarr was surprised that no one in the hall had burst out laughing. It all seemed fairly far-fetched, but the courtiers were keeping their faces studiously blank. Tarr began to feel truly uneasy.

"Marc, Rane," Laith said suddenly. "Get Athela and Tarr out of here."

Tarr blinked, confused, and felt Marc's hand move to his arm. He met Ilaina's eyes and was shocked to see that her face, too, was draining of color. "What do you—" Tarr began.

"And on whose behalf do you believe he is acting as a spy?" the Queen asked. Tarr stopped still and turned to face Athela, whose face was steely and resolute, staring stonily up at the throne platform towards her parents.

Tarr could feel the trap tightening even before Cira replied. "I'm afraid it is on behalf of my sister, Athela," Cira said, a note of mock remorse in her tone as she met her sister's eyes, triumph blazing out of her every pore.

"I see," said the Queen slowly. *Surely, she can't really believe any of this,* Tarr thought to himself. With a feeling of dread, he began to see that it didn't matter. *She doesn't care,* he realized. *She doesn't care that that is Morthenstar's sword. She doesn't care that Athela clearly had nothing to do with this boy appearing at the palace. She's going to do exactly what Cira wants her to do.*

"Moreover, I believe that this is not the first time such a thing has been attempted," Cira continued, and Tarr could feel the cold edge of fear begin to claw at him. "They have already brought in a spy from the outside."

Me, he thought wildly. *They mean me.*

"The Ashan," Cira continued, and raised a delicately tapered finger to point directly at Tarr. "A spy."

"No," Tarr said reflexively, before he could stop himself. He saw the sweep of heads in the crowd turn in his direction like a wave.

"Speak up, Ashan," the Queen ordered him, her sharp gaze turning to bear down on him. "For whom are you spying? Are you spying for Athela? For the Ashans?"

"Neither," Tarr replied.

"Athela employed you to spy on us. On her sister."

"She didn't," Tarr answered, his voice a bit stronger. *No way will you get me to incriminate Athela,* he thought firmly.

"Then you are a spy for the Ashans."

"I assure you, the Ashans are not *remotely* interested in anything you all are doing here," Tarr shot back, feeling himself grow heated. Before, he would not have dared speak to the Queen that way, but the bubbling resentment of her initial treatment of him—as well as the days he'd spent observing the court and its ridiculous obsessions with status and appearance—had lessened some of the intimidation he had once felt. He was now more angry than anything.

The Queen glared at him, as if the greatest insult he could have uttered was to say that someone somewhere in the world didn't care what the Jelani people thought or did. "Guards," she ordered. "I want you to arrest this boy, Lady Athela, and the Ashan. I want them held in the dungeons for questioning and," here she gave a nasty little pause, as if to savor the moment, "for sentencing."

In an instant, all the heroism Tarr had felt in his exchange with the Queen evaporated, and a wave of bewilderment overtook him. He swayed in his place as guards in purple cloaks began descending on them from all sides.

Laith swung around and met his and Athela's eyes. "We'll figure out something," he assured them in a low voice. "I promise. We'll get you out." He looked over to Rane. "Rane, we've got to get our hands on that sword. Do what you have to do, but I need you to recover it."

Rane mutely glanced at Athela, who gave her a curt nod. "Go. Do as he says. I'll be alright." She turned to Tarr as Rane seemed to evaporate silently into the shifting, muttering crowd. "We'll stick together, okay?"

Tarr nodded. "Okay." He was glad, suddenly, to have Athela there with him. *She knows what to expect, and she may know a way to get us out*, he reassured himself.

The guards had reached them, and Laith and Ilaina stepped reluctantly to the side. "My Queen, I must protest," Laith spoke up, as if he couldn't contain the indignation he felt at the entire situation.

"Must you?" Cira sneered.

"There is absolutely no evidence to support Cira's claims," Laith pointed out, as Ilaina laid a placating hand on his arm. The guards took rough hold of Tarr's bony elbows and pushed them behind his back. Tarr could feel his heart beating up in his throat and looked over to where the young intruder, now relieved of his ornate sword, was being shoved over to them, his thin face pinched and anxious. Even through his fear, he met Tarr's eyes and managed a smile.

"The evidence of Athela's treachery will be left for us to determine, Lord Argolaith, not you," the Queen rebuked him. "And I might remind you that unless you wish to join your cousin in the dungeons, that you should learn to hold your tongue and remember your place as a servant of this crown."

Laith looked stunned, and Tarr could tell that the prince was unused to being rebuked in such a forceful way. The crowd was shocked as well, and whispers burbled up even louder at the Queen's words. Laith looked helplessly over to Tarr and Athela, his large brown eyes filled with concern. Beside him, Ilaina's jaw was set in a resolute line. *She's already thinking of ways to save us*, Tarr realized, and the thought brought him a small amount of comfort.

"Take them away," the Queen ordered, and a moment later Tarr felt himself being shoved forward by his flanking guard. The stares from the crowd of onlookers were almost oppressive in their intensity; he had to fight the urge to duck his head and study his shoes as his feet shuffled forward. However, a short ways ahead of him, he glimpsed Athela's ramrod-straight back, her proudly lifted head. *If she can manage it at a time like this, so can I,* he thought, and lifted his chin, forcing himself to stare boldly out over the heads of the Jelani spectators as he was ushered past. To his surprise, almost as soon as he changed his posture, people began to step back out of his way, almost as if they were intimidated. He kept up the same attitude as they left the room and were led through the adjoining hallway, where a few members of the crowd had slipped out to watch them be escorted down to the dungeons. Once free of the crowd, Tarr desperately wanted to turn towards Athela to ask her where the dungeons were, what they were like, and how long they were to be kept there, but something in her fierce, focused stare told him that his questions would have to wait.

So he bit his tongue and allowed himself to be led down, down and down, staircase after staircase, until the soft white gleam of the palace had faded behind him and was replaced instead by jagged walls of living reddish rock, the only lights emanating from intermittent torches mounted along the walls. Jagged, ominous shadows filled the stairs and danced on the faces of the guards.

After what seemed like an eternity, they reached the bottom of the last stair and were pushed roughly out into a narrow, dark passageway. From what Tarr could gather, they were now squarely in the belly of the cliff, with seemingly no way to escape—no windows, no light. The air was stale and oppressive, as if it were pressing out against the stone, pushing against his face, trying to escape. Tarr could barely breathe. *This must be where they keep their prisoners,* he realized. He had read of such things before, though there was no Ashan equivalent. Small infractions in his village were punished by the Elder council; the perpetrators were ordered to carry out acts of service to atone for what they'd done. Greater crimes resulted in the individual being exiled outright from the tribe, unable to ever return or claim kinship with any Ashan. But this practice of holding the offender in a tiny room apart from the rest of society, unable to see the daylight, unable to breathe, struck Tarr as particularly barbaric.

A purple-cloaked guard emblazoned with the royal egret was waiting for them down the hallway, standing by the open door of what appeared to be a small room. Athela was shoved in first, followed by Tarr, and then the boy, who tripped over Tarr's heels in the dark and sent them both sprawling clumsily onto the wall opposite. Then the door slid shut with a resounding finality, and all was silent.

There was a small grate at the top of the door, just big enough that a small shaft of light shone through. Tarr could at least make out the dim shadows of Athela's face as his eyes adjusted to the darkness of the cell.

"On the whole," Athela said after a protracted silence, "I'd say that was one of our better parties."

Tarr couldn't help but laugh. He groped around in the darkness until he felt the wall and pushed himself back up into a standing position. He walked to the door and peered out at the hall beyond, but it appeared to be deserted. He was glad that they had left a torch burning. It was almost overwhelmingly claustrophobic to be there in the cramped cell in the center of the cliff; he couldn't imagine what it would be like in the pitch darkness.

Remembering the boy, he turned around. "Are you all right?" he asked.

"I think so," came the boy's voice, soft and breathy, light as air. "You people aren't very nice, I must say."

"Don't judge us all just from this evening," Athela said ironically. "Usually, we're quite hospitable."

"I'll take your word for it," the boy said dubiously.

"What's your name?" Tarr asked.

"Si," the boy replied. "It's spelled S-I, but pronounced like the word 'sigh.' People make that mistake a lot. When I was little I stayed with a lady, and every time I broke something she'd roll her eyes and give what she called a 'Si sigh.' Get it?"

"All right, then, Si," Athela settled back against the far wall. "What *were* you doing here?"

"I'd heard about the palace from a fellow in Two Falls, and I wanted to have a look for myself," Si said with all the logical-sounding irrationality of someone very young.

"And you made your way all the way up here?" Athela asked dubiously. "By yourself?"

"Yes," Si replied with no small amount of pride.

"And the sword?" Athela pressed.

"I told you, I found it," the boy said defensively. "And I didn't want to leave it in my lodgings. People steal things, you know."

Tarr heard Athela let out a long, exasperated sigh. "Well, you'd better cross your fingers that my cousin comes up with a clever way to get us out of here, or you may be in for an extremely short visit."

Tarr's stomach fell at her words, and he glanced towards the door. For a few seconds, he willed it to open and for Ilaina and Laith to suddenly appear, swords drawn, ready to rescue them. But no one came.

He had to hand it to Cira, he thought. She'd effectively managed to turn a bit of unexpected breaking and entering to her absolute advantage, had set Athela up for attempted espionage, and gotten rid of their pesky Ashan visitor all in one fell swoop. She'd been clever.

Or had she been? Tarr wondered. It was, at the end of the day, all complete nonsense, and the only reason she'd gotten away with it was because it was also convenient from the Queen's perspective to have them locked up. Cleverness was one thing. Opportunism was quite another.

"They can't kill you, though," he said abruptly, facing Athela in the darkness. "Even if it were true, and you did hire Si to go poking around Cira's rooms, that's not something they could *kill* you for, is it?" Tarr had been guilty enough of the same thing from time to time back in their Ashan common rooms when he was young, and it was almost unthinkable that someone should be executed for such a thing. "Besides, you're a princess, too."

"Sort of. I wouldn't put it past them," Athela said levelly. "My mother can do what she likes. My old bodyguard caught Cira's servants red-handed going through *my* rooms, and what did Cira get? A six-month vacation to the Meadows." She heaved a resigned sigh. "If Cira wants to leverage this into getting me out of the way, once and for all, she'll do it. Maybe they won't kill *me*," she added. "Maybe just exile. But you both are in for it for sure."

This was not as comforting a response as Tarr had hoped.

CHAPTER SEVEN

Tarr hadn't quite known what to expect of his night in the dungeon. He wasn't sure whether it was the Queen's intention to let them sit there for days, suffering in the darkness, the oppressively heavy air weighing in on them, or whether she intended to be done with them quickly and have them executed in short order. He wasn't sure which prospect was worse. These unsettling thoughts, plus the stifling atmosphere and the cramped, uncomfortable conditions, led to a strange night of half-dozing, jerking awake after being seized by strange intangible terrors. Athela and the boy spoke very little throughout the night and seemed to be in a similar mental space as Tarr. His eyes having adjusted to the gloom, Tarr could steal glances over at Athela once in a while. She leaned back in the crook of a corner of the cell, her eyes staring sightlessly into space. From what he could see, she didn't sleep a wink throughout the night.

Once, the boy was allowed out to use the privy down the hall, and for a brief moment Tarr hoped that he might be devising a means of escape, but upon his return, he had shaken his head grimly and informed Athela and Tarr that there was little to no hope for escape by that route. The dungeons were an airless maze; it would be nearly impossible to find their way out, and they were too well guarded.

Though they had no real way of telling the passage of time, there came a certain point where Tarr was sure it must be morning. He had been wrong to think that the room was solid rock. Now that it was daylight, he could see that there were thin horizontal slits at the top of their room, too thin for him even to slide his hand through, that admitted tiny cracks of light into the cell. While the cracks provided little in the way of illumination, they did something to bolster his spirits. *What an awful place to keep people*, Tarr thought to himself again. He had been trapped in the cell for a matter of hours, and already he felt suffocated and so claustrophobic that he was having to continually fight down a welling spring of terror that threatened to burble up and tear his chest apart. He couldn't imagine what it would be like for prisoners who had to spend weeks, months, even years trapped in those tiny rooms. The physical punishment was one thing. The mental punishment was something else entirely. If someone was locked in one of those rooms for any considerable length of time, there was no way that they could come out with all of their sanity still intact.

On the opposite end of the cell, Athela tiredly raised up her hands and twisted her hair on top of her head. She was still rather incongruously dressed in her silver gown from the banquet the night before; Tarr had helped her loosen the laces on the bodice so that she could breathe more comfortably while slouched against the wall. There were dark circles under her gray eyes and she shot Tarr a wan smile when she noticed him looking at her.

Abruptly, her expression changed, and she slowly sat up, her gaze fastening on the small opening in the door. Tarr straightened up, looking in the same direction, trying to see what she saw. And then he heard it: voices talking down the hallway. Not the low, monosyllabic mutter of the guards as they exchanged shifts, but a strange voice, higher-pitched and with an insistent tone.

Tarr rose to his feet and walked towards the door, where Athela was now on her tiptoes, peering out into the hallway. He looked over her head, but could see no one yet.

"What is it?' the boy Si asked curiously, leaning up and rubbing his eyes.

"Shh," Athela cautioned him, her dark brow knit in concentration, straining her ears to hear what was being said.

The voices down the hall began to take distinctive shape, and with a jolt, Tarr realized that he recognized the voice of the newcomer. "What I'm saying is that if the Ashan *is* to be executed later today, we might as well try and use his knowledge to our benefit while we still have him here."

It was the Librarian. Tarr's heart leaped at the sound of a familiar voice, but was almost immediately hit with a wave of bewilderment. *What on earth is he doing here in the dungeons?* Tarr wondered. And then, with a lurch: *Am I really sentenced to be executed later today?*

Tarr could now make out the voice of the guard approaching down the hallway, irritation dripping from every syllable. "I tell you, you cannot see the prisoner without *express* permission from the Queen."

"I passed Lady Cira on my way through the dungeons; why don't you ask *her*?" the Librarian replied primly. "These translations are important, and it may be our last chance to have them completed, seeing as how we're unlikely to have any native Ashan speakers visiting our palace in the near future. You may speak to the Queen yourself if you have any objections. I demand to see the prisoner."

Tarr wasn't sure what was going on. It sounded as though the Librarian had some remaining texts of importance that he wanted Tarr to translate, but this made little sense. Almost everything Tarr had translated so far had been nearly useless. Athela faced him, her eyes questioning, and Tarr gave a helpless shrug. *I don't know what he's on about.*

The door creaked and groaned, and Tarr and Athela took an immediate step back, trying to appear as if they hadn't been listening too closely to what was being said. One of the purple-cloaked guards peered around the edge of the heavy door, his expression exasperated.

"You," he ordered, pointing at Tarr. "Out."

Tarr swallowed and stepped forward, meeting Athela's perturbed gaze for a split second before the door was closed and fastened behind him, the keys on the jailor's chain clanking heavily as he turned. "You have five minutes," the guard informed them curtly, then strode off down the hallway and settled himself on a stool against the wall. Tarr could see that he was keeping one eye on them as he waited. The guard out of the way, Tarr tried to keep his face neutral as he faced the Librarian.

"Ashan," the Librarian continued, addressing Tarr with a harsh tone in his voice. "I need you to look at this book and translate the passage I have outlined as best you can."

Tarr was slightly bewildered at being addressed in such a fashion, when before the Librarian had treated him with nothing but courtesy. He decided, however, to play along, and gave a meek nod before looking down at the book the librarian held out. There was a bookmark indicating a particular page, but before Tarr could begin to read, the guard watching them straightened up, his gaze narrowing suspiciously.

"What is that?" he demanded.

"Just a book," the Librarian held it up, turning smoothly on his heel. "Would you like to inspect it?"

The guard made no response, but came up and snatched the book out of the Librarian's hand. He examined the marked page the Librarian had proffered Tarr, but could clearly make neither heads nor tails of the foreign language. He grunted and then began to flip roughly through the other pages, and even felt along the bound cover of the book. It took Tarr a moment to catch on, but he quickly realized that the guard was checking the book for any tools or devices smuggled within its pages, something that could help Tarr and Athela escape. *Is that really what he's trying to do?* Tarr wondered. He glanced at the Librarian's face, trying to get a sense of whether he, too, should be nervous, but the little man's face was completely blank. If he was concerned about the guard finding contraband within, he was doing a good job of hiding it.

After a few seconds of general inspection, the guard grunted and held the book back to the Librarian, who seemed to breathe a small sigh of relief, barely perceptible but to Tarr's attuned eyes. *There is something in the book*, Tarr realized. *But the guard didn't find it. How am I going to find it?*

"Thank you," the Librarian said politely, and handed Tarr the book again, indicating the same marked page as before. Eagerly, Tarr looked down, scanning the Ashan script. His heart dropped. It was the same nonsense as before, something about pruning and transplanting. He glanced up at the Librarian helplessly, but the little man merely raised his eyebrows and blinked down at the pages. Tarr looked again closely.

In the margin of the page was written one small word in Ashan:

backbone.

Backbone? Tarr thought, his brow furrowing.

Spine.

He remembered the Librarian teaching him about the spines of the bound books in the Joymarillian library. He took a deep breath, glancing over to the guard, who was still eyeing them closely from the comfort of his stool.

"I can read this aloud, if you care to take notes," Tarr said carefully.

"That would be excellent," the Librarian agreed, momentarily forgetting to treat Tarr with suitable disdain.

"'Begin by cutting the young tree at the base of...'" Tarr began to read, but even as he did, he moved his left hand to hold the book along its spine. There was a tiny opening at the base of the book where the binding gaped open, and as he continued to dictate, one of his long, nimble fingers poked inside. There was what felt like a long metal implement tucked up into the crease of the book's spine, and (his peripheral vision trained all the while on the watchful guard) smoothly withdrew it and tucked it up into the sleeve of his jacket. His heart was pounding wildly the entire time; it was a lucky thing that the guard stood no closer to him, for he was sure that he would be able to hear the sound of it.

"...bark grafting may be done most successfully in early spring," Tarr concluded, swallowing and closing the book.

"Thank you," the Librarian said, then caught himself. "And now, I hope you will stand in the shadow of the Queen's justice for your crimes," he added, though even Tarr could tell that his heart wasn't really in it. Other than his ability to keep a straight face, the Librarian wasn't much of an actor.

"*That's* the critical document you found?" the guard demanded.

Tarr swallowed, his throat dry, certain that they were going to be found out. His mind traveled down to the thin metal rod in his sleeve, trying to think of some way to hide it again should the guard come to inspect him more closely. He didn't know what the thing was, or how it could possibly be of use in getting them out of the prison, but he trusted that Athela might have some idea.

"Her Majesty the Queen takes the maintenance of her gardens very seriously," the Librarian lied. "These instructions will be of great use to us."

The guard looked unconvinced, but Tarr could see that they had an advantage in that he clearly didn't know much about gardening—or trees, for that matter. "Get out," the guard ordered. "I will inform the Queen that you were here. If you did not come at her bidding, you will be brought here yourself to answer for your actions."

"Please do," the Librarian said easily, sounding decidedly unconcerned. "I can't wait to see Her Majesty's reaction when one of her prison guards comes up and demands that she justify her own orders. It should end well for you."

Even the guard looked somewhat put out at this prospect; Tarr had to give the Librarian credit for his quick thinking. Without so much as a backward glance, the little man set off back down the dungeon hallway, and Tarr was summarily thrown back into the cell alongside Athela and Si, with perhaps more force than was truly necessary.

Once the door had screeched into place and the key was turned sharply in the lock, Tarr waited until the metallic clanking of the guard had receded all the way down the hall before turning back eagerly to his two companions.

"Sapling care?" Athela asked in a dubious voice. She had clearly been listening at the grate in the door.

Tarr silently shook his head. He didn't want to say anything, as he couldn't be totally sure that there wasn't someone listening at the door. He pulled open the cuff of his jacket, and the metal rod slid smoothly out. He held it up triumphantly.

For a moment he felt dismayed, for rather than immediately seizing it, Athela's forehead knit in confusion and he could tell that she had no idea what the thing was or how they could use it to get out. But then, to his great surprise, the boy Si snatched the thing from Tarr's hand, his expression brightening.

As Tarr and Athela watched in astonishment, the boy took the metal rod and, his freckled nose crinkling in concentration, began to bend the end into a pliable shape. He quietly tiptoed to the door, inserted it in the lock, and moved it around here and there, making adjustments to the curve of the rod, before he looked back at them, his gray eyes wide and a smile of excitement blooming wide across his face. He gave a hurried nod. *He can pick the lock,* Tarr realized, his heart lifting. *He can get us out.*

"Good," Athela whispered. "Wait to pick the lock. The guard might hear the sound."

Lock aside, there *was* still the difficulty that the hallway was still under heavy guard and that it would be almost impossible for them to find a way out of the dungeons (much less sneak through the palace) without being seen. All three of them were immediately and almost comically identifiable: an Ashan over six feet tall, a human boy with blazing red hair, and the only raven-haired Jelani woman in the city. It was not remotely likely that they would be able to creep out of the palace or blend into the crowd.

The prospect of a way out, though, had galvanized their spirits, and Tarr and Athela now waited at the door, eager for any chance to make their escape.

Athela's face was only a few inches from Tarr's, and she whispered to him so low that it sounded just like a faint breath. "If we steal some of the guards' cloaks, we may be able to sneak out."

"Do you know where they keep them?" Tarr replied just as quietly.

"No," Athela shook her head, frustrated. "I don't know the layout of the dungeons. But we will find a way. If we can find a sword, I can at least get us past one guard, maybe two."

Tarr felt somewhat guilty that he had nothing to offer in the way of fighting prowess, but nodded. They remained there as the minutes ticked by, slowly rolling along into an hour, their bodies tensed and ears pressed close to the opening on the door.

Then, suddenly, they had their opportunity. There was the sound of distant footsteps far away down the hall, and Athela straightened up taller.

"Lady Cira is requesting a prisoner," said a voice.

"A prisoner?" asked the now-familiar voice of the guard.

"Highest level security."

"Can't I just give you the key?" the guard inquired tiredly. The morning had clearly already been more trouble than he was used to.

"Not for this security clearance; we need the highest-ranking officer on duty," the other replied. "That's you."

"All right," their guard said reluctantly. "You stay here, then."

"I can't, I'm afraid," the other informed him. At once, Tarr and Athela's gazes snapped together. *This is it,* Tarr thought with a rush. "There's been an order for a phalanx of guards to report up to Lord Argolaith's rooms. We're short-staffed as it is, and they're calling up other dungeon patrols."

"Fine," their guard snapped. "This better not take long. What on earth does Lady Cira want with a high-security prisoner?"

Still grumbling, the two voices faded off into the distance. Athela and Tarr whirled around to Si, who was waiting wide-eyed, his makeshift lockpicking tool held up and at the ready.

"Now, Si, hurry!" Athela urged, and the boy leaped forward. For a few agonizing seconds, Tarr thought that nothing was going to happen and that their opportune moment would be wasted, but suddenly there was a resounding *click,* and the door lurched forward an inch, a thin shaft of dim light from the hallway breaking in.

Tarr and Athela heaved on the door and it creaked open enough to let them out, and all three of them piled into the hallway, the stiflingly stuffy air of their cell rushing out behind them. Athela closed the cell door as best she could, then whirled around, her gray eyes searching the sparse, rocky hallway for anything that might be of use.

"Break the stool," she ordered, pointing to the seat where the guard had ensconced himself during Tarr's meeting with the Librarian. Tarr did as he was told, cracking the wood against the rock wall. He drew back up holding three short wooden sticks—not much, but better than nothing. He handed one of the sticks to Si. He felt rather foolish holding one himself, as he was fairly sure that if someone came charging up at him, the best he could do would be to hurl the stick and run in the opposite direction.

Athela immediately took charge, Si scrambling close behind and Tarr bringing up the rear. The guard had unfortunately not left them any extra capes or swords lying around with which they could fashion a convenient disguise, so Athela gave up and motioned them towards the stairs. Tarr's heart was beating so hard that he felt as though his legs might buckle and give way, but forced himself to follow as Athela bravely turned the corner and began making her way out of their wing of the dungeon.

"Keep low," she told them, crouching down and proceeding silently up the stairs, almost on all fours, her ears trained for any sound of approaching footsteps. Tarr, much taller than either of his companions, hunkered down as best he could, his head swimming with adrenaline and the fear of being caught. He admired Athela's bravery more than he could say.

Towards the top of the stairs, Athela paused, still low enough so that only the top of her black, curly head would be visible to someone on the floor above. She peeked up and surveyed the hallway.

"No one's there," she told them.

"Do you know the way out?" Tarr asked anxiously.

"No," Athela replied. "But we have a better chance of running if we're out of that dead-end hallway down there." She gestured down the stairs to the prison wing in which they'd been kept.

The thought of having no concrete direction filled Tarr with a fresh wave of nerves, but he forced the feeling down and felt himself give a resolute nod. Athela was right. At least on the floors above they would have places to run, and on the off-chance they encountered a lone guard, the three of them would be able to overcome them—perhaps taking their weapon and cloak.

Athela rose and ran forward, and Tarr and Si charged after her. As Athela had ascertained, the halls were surprisingly empty, perhaps because of the order of guards to Laith's rooms. *Were they going to arrest him, too?* Tarr wondered. *Or was this also some sort of ruse?*

The air on this floor was far less stifling than it had been down in their cell, which gave Tarr some hope that they might be headed in the correct direction. They kept against the wall, though this tactic would offer them little cover if they were seen.

The dungeon hallways were all blank and anonymous, the walls a long expanse of craggy reddish stone; so much the better, Tarr imagined, for keeping prisoners from escaping. They went down one and around another, unsure of their direction, except that when one passage ended and joined a larger hallway, Athela would point them in that direction, the thinking being that the larger the path, the closer they would be to a clear way out.

Heading up a large, vaulting corridor, they barely managed to hide around the corner of a wall as a small troop of purple guards went past and turned down the hall in the opposite direction. Athela peeked around the corner and was readying for a fresh sprint when Si's face blanched, and his hand shot out to catch the hem of her dress.

Following his gaze, Tarr turned as well, feeling the blood draining from his head. Coming up behind them in the hall was a group of three purple-cloaked guards, their steps insistent and brisk, their focus intent. There was no question about it—they had been seen. Tarr tightened his grip on the piece of broken wood and raised it slightly, and in his peripheral vision saw Athela shift around and face the oncomers.

Athela pushed past him to the front of their group, brandishing her makeshift weapon and readying herself to fight. Tarr's heart was beating a sharp tattoo against the edges of his chest. "There's three of them and three of us," Athela growled beneath her breath, holding a protective arm up in front of Si. "We can take them." This was a more optimistic view of the odds than Tarr was inclined to give.

"Athela!" one of the guards hissed, just as she was about to lunge forward with her weapon. The voice caught her so by surprise that she nearly tripped over the edge of her dress and tumbled to the floor.

"Laith?" she asked, dumbfounded.

Tarr had never been so glad to see anyone in his entire life, and sweet relief blossomed in his chest. As the three guards drew closer, he could see that it was, indeed, Laith, Marc, and Rane, all disguised as Jelani troops. He realized he'd been holding his breath and let it out in a long, thin stream.

"What on earth are you doing?" Laith demanded, looking bewildered.

"Escaping," Athela answered. "What are *you* doing?"

"Rescuing you," he replied. Beneath the sweeping visor of his helmet, Tarr could see his face cracking into a relieved smile. "Ilaina has horses saddled and supplies waiting down at the bottom of the cliff."

"And Wolver?" Tarr asked anxiously. He'd spent a number of unpleasant hours in the cell the night before imagining what would happen to the wolf.

"She's got him, too," Laith assured him. "We've had quite a

morning setting up a bunch of different diversions to make sure all the guards were called off in different directions."

"Not as thrilling as *our* morning, I'll wager," Athela said sarcastically, "But we can compare notes later. Someone please tell me that they brought along some riding trousers so I can change out of this ridiculous dress."

"First, let's get out of here," Laith told them firmly. "Turn around, and I'll bind your hands so it looks as though we're escorting you."

Athela, Si, and Tarr complied. As Marc was wrapping a rope around his wrists (more for show, it seemed, than actual restraint), Tarr twisted around. "Do any of *you* know the way out of here?" he asked. Glad as he was to see the others, it wouldn't do them much good if they all spent another half hour wandering aimlessly through the twisting dungeon tunnels.

"Rane does," Laith answered, with a jerk of his head towards Athela's bodyguard. Tarr glanced at her and she favored him with a small smile, her lake-blue eyes calm as ever. They might as well have been heading off to the weekday market, for all the nerves she seemed to project.

The "prisoners" safely secured, the group set off together at a brisk, deliberate pace. Occasionally, Rane would mutter "left" or "right" beneath her breath, and together they would smoothly sweep in one direction or another, for all intents and purposes looking as though they knew exactly where they were going. Tarr was relieved that their plan had developed somewhat from "haphazardly wander around and hope for the best" to at least some level of actual subterfuge, and though he hadn't yet had the opportunity to see them in action, he was reassured by the tales he'd heard of the others' fighting prowess.

He tensed up slightly as a group of other Jelani guards rounded a corner and came towards them, but they merely nodded at Laith and shot Tarr a curious look as they swept past. "Almost there," Rane muttered. "We have to turn right, and then there's a long flight of steps and then a short passageway. That should take us down to the bottom of the cliff where Ilaina is waiting with the horses."

Tarr was impressed with Rane's ability to find her way through the seeming maze of the dungeons. He wondered whether learning the layout was all a part of becoming a bodyguard, or whether she was preternaturally gifted with remembering those sorts of details. He was inclined to believe the latter, as Marc had given no indication that he had any idea where they were supposed to be going, and he was a royal bodyguard as well.

Marc gave him a short nudge with his burly arm, and Tarr snapped to attention. A fresh group of guards was coming up to intercept them on the left as they made a turn towards the stairwell. Tarr stiffened and tried to find an appropriate expression to sell the deception. *Should I look angry?* he wondered. *Penitent? Afraid?* Afraid wouldn't be too much of a stretch for him at the moment. Much like the Librarian, he had a feeling that his own acting skills wouldn't be able to stretch past a certain point.

"Where are you taking those prisoners?" called the lead guard, and Tarr's heart dropped. Marc's grip tightened on his forearm, and out of the corner of his eye, Tarr saw the bodyguard's other hand slowly go to the hilt of his sword. The group that approached them was much larger than any he'd seen patrolling the dungeons thus far. There looked to be about twelve of them, all armed, bearing down on them like a swarm of hawks.

Their group rounded and faced the oncomers so that Tarr, Athela, and Si were pushed safely to the back, away from danger. "Escorting them to the Queen," Laith replied gruffly, masking his voice.

The officer who'd stopped them studied them suspiciously. Beneath his curving helmet, Tarr could see a pair of eyes sizing them up and down. Tarr began to feel quite nervous indeed; though they were disguised, it wouldn't take a lot of brains to recognize Laith and Marc. "Why are you taking them in this direction?" the officer inquired, his hand creeping towards the weapon hanging from his belt.

"We were told of a disturbance in the dungeons," Laith answered in the same low, rough voice.

"We heard of no such alert," the guard countered. Tarr could feel the tension ratcheting up around them. *They're not going to let us pass,* he thought. *They're going to take all of us. And who will be left to save us then?*

"It was...ah...a very recent development," Laith lied, faltering ever so slightly.

"What is your name, soldier?" the officer demanded. "Give me your report and your commanding officer's name."

It was over, and everyone seemed to know it. Tarr looked over his shoulder, down at the long flight of stairs behind them. Though he had had no experience in combat whatsoever, he could understand perfectly well what a precarious situation they were in, how badly placed they were for a fight. They were cornered. There was no room to make a stand. And his group was outnumbered two to one.

"Lord Argolaith," the head officer intoned, and there was a distinct sneer in his tone. "I am placing you under arrest. You and all your co-conspirators."

Tarr caught his breath. Every muscle in his body pulled taut, ready for whatever was about to come next. Laith's shoulders seemed to relax now that the charade had been dropped. He straightened up, pulled back the purple hood, and drew off the curving helmet, revealing his sandy head of hair. He dropped the helmet to the stone floor, where it fell with such a loud clatter that all of those present jumped slightly. He scanned the faces of the officers opposite him and shook his head.

"No, I don't believe that we *are* under arrest," he said calmly.

"I assure you, you are," the officer snapped, though Tarr thought he could detect a note of hesitancy in his voice. *Why hasn't he ordered the other soldiers forward to arrest us?* he wondered. He looked at the face of the female guard standing just beside the officer, and to his shock, he could see fear on her face as she looked at Laith. Her hand was clenched around the hilt of her sword.

"I order you to comply," the guard snapped. "You all are traitors to the crown."

"I'm not!" Si piped up. "I don't think I really fall under your jurisdiction."

"Shut up," the guard barked.

"I do not have to comply with your orders at all. As a Joymarillian war prince, I outrank you," Laith smiled easily. With one hand, he made a flapping motion behind his back, urging the others to start edging down the long staircase. Tarr took one step down, and then another, never leaving the scene unfolding above. *What was Laith playing at? Why didn't he run?*

The officer and his guards still seemed unsure about advancing towards them, and Laith seemed to sense their trepidation. "Athela, Rane," Laith said under his breath, "take the others down. Marc, stay with me." Then, with one graceful sweep, he withdrew the sword hanging at his side. This time, Tarr was certain that he saw multiple guards take nervous steps back.

"They aren't going to fight all of those guards *alone*?" Tarr hissed to Athela under his breath, still edging towards the stairs, Si between them. The boy was clinging fearfully to a shining drape of Athela's dress; she hadn't seemed to notice.

"They'll be fine," Athela assured him nonchalantly, taking the opportunity to stoop down and tie the lace on her boot.

How? Tarr felt like yelling. *How will they be fine?*

And then, in the space of a split second, the long, protracted moment of tension seemed to crack and was overrun by a flurry of motion. Rane whirled, her sword out and ready, and began charging down the stairs, motioning to Athela and Si to follow in her wake. The officers and his guards gave a united shout that shook and echoed through the cold stone walls of the hallway, and darted forward toward Marc and Laith, who faced them, swords out and drawn. Tarr dove down the first few steps, then chanced a look over his shoulder, certain that in those few seconds Laith and Marc had been summarily cut down beneath the blades of the advancing patrol.

But the sight that met him instead made him stop dead in his tracks. He had never seen anything like it.

Laith moved first, stepping up from the stair to the landing, facing the onslaught head-on. He gave his sword an absentminded twirl with the barest flick of his wrist, almost as if the weapon were an extension of his own arm, then lightly bounded back so that his foot struck the first step and bounced up and forward, springlike and easy. As the first Jelani guard approached him, purple cloak billowing back, armor glinting in the dull light, Laith's easy stride came to life, and he fell on them. He darted to one side and dipped down, his sword raised in an attack position. Blades sang over and around him as he darted forward into the melee of soldiers, their swords missing him by bare centimeters. Like a striking snake, with three graceful moves of his arm three soldiers went down, though even in the frenzy of the moment Tarr could see that he hadn't killed them, merely stunned them with the hilt of his blade. He whirled, and Tarr caught a brief glimpse of his face: absolutely calm and completely in control, as if he were listening to music. Even Tarr, who had no knowledge of fighting, could see that Laith had the poise and art of a dancer as he cleaved his way through the hoard, soldiers falling left and right as if he were a blade through a field of wheat. It was something both beautiful and terrible to behold.

And, just like that, it was over. Laith stood in the hallway at the end of the column of fallen opponents. A few of them groaned and stirred, but none stood up. He paused only for a moment, then relaxed and stood, his sword loose at his side.

"Shall we go, then?" he suggested. He was barely breathing hard.

Marc, who had only had to parry a blow or two during the course of the entire skirmish, re-sheathed his sword and brushed his silky yellow hair back from his eyes. "You could have left me a *couple*," he complained, his tone accusatory.

"I have a feeling there'll soon be more on the way," Laith murmured grimly, replacing his weapon and jogging through the field of felled guards to the top of the stairs. "You may still get your chance."

All this while, Tarr realized he'd been standing and watching open-mouthed about ten steps from the top of the stairs. Marc jogged down to him and gave him a quizzical look, glancing over his shoulder as if to try and ascertain what Tarr was looking at that had shocked him so. After a moment, his expression cleared.

"Oh! That. Yes, Laith is pretty much the deadliest Jelani swordsman..." he considered, calculating. "...Ever."

"I see," Tarr said weakly. He watched Laith go by down the stairs, a newfound awe taking over him. He was quite glad he'd had no idea of Laith's prowess when they'd first met. As intimidated as he was already, he didn't think he'd have been able to muster up the courage to even speak to him had he known what he was capable of.

Shaking his head to clear the shock of what he'd just witnessed (and conscious that a few of the stunned and incapacitated guards were starting to stir and groggily attempt to clamber to their feet), Tarr sprinted as quickly as he could after the others down the long flight of stairs, following them to a dark passageway below. He didn't recognize it as the way they'd come up when he first arrived at Joymaril, but figured that a palace of that size must have multiple entrances leading to the city above.

They tumbled breathlessly out onto the dim landing below and charged forward through an almost completely black passageway before they suddenly rounded a corner and burst forth into a blaze of morning sunlight. Shielding his eyes and squinting back tears, Tarr got his bearings and glanced around. They were still just beneath the cover of the cliff in what appeared to be a small alcove beside the edge of the lake. There were a number of horses to one side, tethered and waiting. Tarr's heart lurched as a purple-cloaked figure emerged from behind the horses, but a moment later its hood was pulled back, and Ilaina grinned out at them. Wolver emerged at her side, sweeping his tail back and forth as he came up to greet Tarr.

"Glad you made it. I thought that if you were much longer, I'd have to come back in there and rescue the rescue party," she said, with a twinkle in Tarr's direction.

"You very nearly did," Athela said darkly. The four Jelani spread out, businesslike, checking saddlebags and dispersing weapons to those who didn't have them. Athela dove into her saddlebag, withdrawing a pair of riding trousers, a sense of relief washing over her face. She pulled them on beneath her dress, then took a dagger from her bag and slit the front and back of her dress down the middle so that she would be better able to ride.

"Never again," Athela muttered, shaking her head. "No more dresses."

"I put your riding boots by the wall," Ilaina informed her.

Marc strode back from investigating his own saddlebag and held out a knife to Tarr, who took one look at it and raised his hands.

"I don't know how to use it," Tarr told him.

"Take it anyway, just wave the pointy end at anyone who gets too close," Marc insisted, pressing the knife into his palm.

Tarr obeyed and tucked the knife into his belt. Beside him, Ilaina withdrew the weapon Laith had identified as Morthenstar's sword, which Si had brought with him to the palace. The craftsmanship on it was even more dazzling up close; a shower of rubies at the hilt glinted and winked like drops of blood.

"I'll take that, thanks," Si smiled and reached over. Ilaina hesitated, raising an eyebrow in Laith's direction.

"Did you really steal that?" Laith inquired.

"Yes," Si replied after a moment's pause. "Sort of. I found it. In a shoe store."

"A shoe store in Two Falls," Athela repeated tiredly.

"That's right!" the boy agreed cheerfully. "You remembered!"

"Know how to use it?" Marc inquired hopefully.

"Nope."

"Figures," Marc muttered. "Well, same as goes for Tarr. Pointy end faces out."

"We'll hang onto it for now," Laith told him firmly, buckling the sword to the back of his own saddle. Si looked momentarily crestfallen, but was soon cheered when Ilaina handed him a long, thin dagger.

"This one's lighter," she told him.

"And pokier!" he exclaimed, brandishing it enthusiastically until Ilaina, alarmed, coaxed him to replace it back in its scabbard. He looked over to Laith and buckled the dagger to his belt, adjusting it so that it hung at exactly the same angle as the prince's sword.

"Hurry," Rane urged them suddenly in her soft voice. Tarr wheeled around and saw that she was standing watch beside the passage from which they'd emerged. "They'll be coming down after us shortly. They may try and warn the lower guard, block off the lake bridge."

"I wasn't able to get horses for everyone; I didn't want to attract too much attention," Ilaina told them apologetically. "Tarr, Si, you'll have to double up with someone."

"Ride behind Rane, Si," Marc said kindly, and gave the boy a boost up into the saddle. He turned around and motioned to Tarr, who followed him and, with slightly more grace and agility than he had the first time he and Marc had ridden together, managed to settle himself on Marc's horse.

Moments later, they were all mounted up and ready. Wolver had turned towards the passageway, growling low and steady, hackles beginning to raise along his white back. They didn't have much time.

"Hurry!" Athela ordered, wheeling her horse around. The horse was the same one Tarr had seen her ride before, a gray with a black mane and tail and black stockings on its legs. Its neck was bunched up into a thick arc, and it made little bounding steps, half-rearing with each stride as Athela held him back.

Laith wheeled his black charger around, directing him with a heel to the flank. He thundered forward past Athela, who then gave a shrill hiss into her horse's ear and let the reins loose. Her horse darted back his ears for a split second, jerked his head up into the air, and bounded forward like a deer, pulling past Laith with three springing strides.

The single column of horses ran at top speed out of the alcove, then spun to the side and sprinted down the bank of the lake beneath the soaring cliff, the sunshine hitting them full blast as they emerged from the cover of the rock. Tarr, deliriously grateful that Ilaina and Athela had taken the time to teach him to ride, clung desperately to Marc's back, trying hard not to be jostled off. It was one thing to maintain one's balance *in* a saddle, Tarr soon realized, and quite another thing to try and hold on *behind* a saddle. Even so, he couldn't help but look behind them and saw with a thrill that they had barely made it out in time: a fresh set of guards had emerged, barely twenty feet behind them, shouting and waving and calling for reinforcements. Tarr looked back around just as Athela banked a hard left at the center of the lake and began to charge across the hidden submerged bridge that led to the safety of the woods and open land beyond.

Ilaina pulled off to the side as they passed, holding back her snorting buckskin horse, her eyes trained on the cliff face behind them. Tarr tightened his grip as Marc turned their horse and aimed him straight down the underwater bridge. They hurtled across, spray and wind burning the riders' eyes and whipping the horses into higher speed. Tarr chanced a look down at the ground and nearly became dizzy from the sight of the plunging hooves, the explosions of water rising up all around them. Wolver, he was relieved to see, was keeping good pace with them, dodging the spray where he could, his white fur soaking through and his blue eyes squinted against the torrent.

Nearly halfway across the bridge, his fingers still clenched tightly in the fabric of Marc's tunic, Tarr swung back around to see whether they were being pursued. Ilaina had pulled out after them and was bringing up the rear of their group, and from the looks of it was clearly planning to buy the others some time by blocking the guards' way across the bridge. Tarr felt like shouting to her, but knew his voice would be lost in the furor of the water and the horses' pounding hooves. As he watched, a column of purple-cloaked riders poured out of the bottom of the cliff and began to set out in pursuit across the submerged lake bridge. At their head were two riders, not dressed in purple cloaks, whom Tarr didn't recognize through the spray and the jostling stride of the horse. What he could see, however, was Ilaina's face: intent with focus and concentration, completely devoid of fear. She sat back and slowed her horse to an abrupt halt, a cascade of lake water swirling around her horse's hooves like a whirlpool. She spun her horse around on its hind legs and, in one smooth arc, withdrew her curved sword from its sheath, brandishing it at her side so that it caught the light. Turning her head, she caught Tarr's eye.

"Go," she urged, her voice barely audible over the tumult. "I'll catch up. I'll follow!"

And with that, she spun around, facing the oncomers. The bridge was narrow enough that they couldn't all rush her at once. *It might work*, Tarr thought. *She could slow them enough that not all of them can get across. Then she can flee. Get through the forest by a different route. She must know a way. She's a fast enough rider. She can outrun them.*

Tarr could still not quite make out who the two riders at the head of the column were, as they had hoods drawn over their heads. He and Marc were rapidly approaching the opposite bank of the lake, so he wouldn't have an opportunity to find out. He watched as Ilaina lifted her curved sword in challenge, kicking her heels against her horse's side and springing forward to meet the oncomers. Tarr didn't have a chance to see what happened next. A moment later, his horse pounded off of the bridge, across the muddy bank of the lake, and flew into the trees like a gust of vanishing wind.

CHAPTER EIGHT

The run that followed their escape was probably the most exhilarating experience of Tarr's entire life. He highly doubted that any guards could have gotten past Ilaina, but regardless of how long she was able to hold them off, there needed to be as much distance between them and the palace as possible. The trees sped past at lightning speed; it was all Tarr could do to duck and dodge out of the way as branches and twigs came singing through the air, whizzing past his head with only a hair's breadth to spare. Tarr had his long, skinny arms wrapped around Marc's bulky waist, grateful again that the bodyguard's low center of gravity seemed to make it impossible for him to topple over.

Athela remained the pace-setter, and actually seemed to have to choke her horse back from going full speed so as not to outrun the others. She sped beside them through the trees just off the main path, jumping logs and maneuvering around trunks at a velocity that Tarr found nauseating. Finally, after about twenty minutes of solid running, the horses' sweaty flanks began to heave, and Athela and Laith eased their mounts out of the gallop and into a canter, then down into a leisurely lope and finally into a walk. The horses huffed and snorted, with froth ringing their bits and around the outside of their saddles and breastcollars, and their riders gasped breaths with similar exhaustion showing around their faces.

"Off the path," Athela panted, indicating with a jerk of her head, and their column turned off the main road and went down a nearby hill, where they paused beneath the cover of an outcrop.

"Do you think it's the Third?" Marc asked through ragged breaths. "Did the Queen send the Third after us?"

"No," Athela shook her head. "No, those were just house cavalry. I saw the insignia on their cloaks."

Tarr looked from one of them to the other. Marc saw his confusion and clarified. "The Third is Joymaril's most dangerous cavalry troop. Our special forces," he said. "We're lucky they're not the ones chasing us."

Lucky? Tarr thought faintly.

"Where's Ilaina?" Laith asked immediately, his dark eyes anxiously searching in every direction for a sign of his wife.

"I saw her," Tarr replied, trying to catch his breath. Even though it had been the horse doing the running, he was every bit as winded as if he'd sprinted up a flight of stairs. "She pulled off behind us and held back to try and slow the guards down."

Laith's face contracted, and he swore lustily under his breath. "Why did she *do* that?" he hissed through tightly clenched teeth, searching again around the woods. "I'm going after her," he told the others and began turning his horse back up to the road.

"Laith, *no,*" Athela snapped, wheeling her nimble gray to cut him off. "We need to stay together as long as we can." She surveyed the rest of them and dropped her voice into a lower, more soothing register. "It's all right; she can take care of herself. She can hold off a few of them, buy us some time. *But,*" she said with emphasis, "they're going to be after us sooner or later. We have to figure out what we're going to do. Where we're going to go. And quickly."

Wolver lay panting on the ground beside Marc's horse. Other than general fatigue, he seemed largely unconcerned with their plight. Tarr had a somewhat dim view of Wolver's abilities as a guardian, but he figured that the wolf would at least indicate if the sounds of the Jelani troop were in earshot. Momentarily reassured, Tarr found himself also scanning the woods for sight of Ilaina. *She can't be that far behind,* he thought again. *Unless she had to take a different path.*

"We should probably find a town or something where we can stay the night," Athela continued, then turned to face Si, whose thin, freckled face was streaked with perspiration, his copper hair plastered to his forehead. Tarr felt a pang of sympathy for the boy. *Quite a day you've had.* "You," Athela addressed him sharply. "Do you know of any villages that would be safe for us to stay in?"

Si tilted his head to one side. "Well, there's Two Falls, of course."

"Not Two Falls," Laith shook his head immediately. "That's the first place they'll look."

Si considered. "Well, I lived in Riddleton, that's the only other town I really know. It's slightly more than a half-day's ride south of here. It's...ah...a colorful place," he concluded rather vaguely. "If you're looking for adventure."

In Tarr's opinion they had quite enough adventure on their hands already, but Athela seemed to seriously consider the suggestion. She met Laith's eyes, and for a few moments they seemed to silently communicate.

Finally, Laith nodded. "We need a place to hide. And what's more, we're going to need a guide, someone familiar with the human villages around these parts, someone with connections, especially if we're going to be laying low for a while."

"Laith and Marc and I have been to Two Falls a few times, but never for very long. We've never been outside of the town, so we don't know anything about the outlying country. And Tarr's only just arrived from the forest, so he's no help," Athela added.

Thanks, Tarr thought wryly.

"I'm sure that you'd be able to find a guide if we went to Riddleton," Si suggested. "There's lots of people who know how to do all sorts of things. There's nothing there that you can't buy. And I mean *nothing*," he continued eagerly, his voice getting breathier as he built up some momentum. "I once saw a man who was selling bottles filled with jellied—"

"That sounds great," Laith agreed, mercifully cutting Si off. "We'll go to Riddleton to find someone who knows the lay of the land," he looked around to where Tarr was still clinging to Marc on the back of his horse. "And another horse or two."

"Come on," Athela urged, turning her horse around and pointing its nose south. The gray, seemingly possessed of boundless energy, snorted eagerly and attempted to take off again through the trees. The others were more reluctant to pick up the pace. Laith, especially, seemed to dawdle a bit, looking back over his shoulder every few moments, clearly expecting his wife to materialize behind them.

"Don't worry, Laith," Marc assured him, pulling his horse up alongside Laith's black charger. "She'll be alright. She'll catch up with us, find our trail where we pulled off. She'll follow us to Riddleton and meet us there. I know she will."

"I'm sure you're right," Laith agreed, though his eyes continued to anxiously scan the woods around them even as he urged his black horse forward.

Tarr, too, felt uneasy. He had a momentary flashback to the sight of Ilaina on her horse, facing down the phalanx of Jelani guards, the two strange hooded riders at their head. And he thought of what Marc had said: if Ilaina was able to follow their trail off the main road and through the forest towards Riddleton, so would the Jelani guards attempting to track them down. Which meant that even with some semblance of a head start, it would only be a matter of time before the Jelani caught up with them, regardless of where they went.

His fingers unconsciously gripped more tightly to Marc's tunic as the bodyguard moved his horse up into a canter. He squinted his eyes at the dappled sunshine and dodged neatly beneath a low-swinging bough, trying not to look back over his shoulder as they began to weave their way south through the trees.

They arrived in Riddleton well after dark, tired, sweaty, and exhausted after a long, hard day of riding. The trek had taken considerably longer than anticipated, as Athela had insisted on keeping off the main roads and riding through the trees where possible to try and confuse their tracks and put off any Jelani guards who may be coming in pursuit. Tarr had a bad feeling that it was only a matter of time before the Jelani regrouped and came after them in a more focused attack. The Queen wasn't likely to lose face by letting not one but three prisoners escape from the palace right under her nose without making a concerted effort to drag them back and force them to face her wrath.

What Tarr wanted most in the world at that moment was a hot bath, a fresh change of clothes, a soft bed, and some sort of abrasive scouring pad that could effectively scrub away the thick coating of sweat and grime that he had accrued after a night spent in the prison and a long day on horseback. Laith's handsome dinner jacket, which he was still rather incongruously wearing, was coated with mud kicked up by Marc's horse's hooves, and one of the underarms of the sleeves had torn a bit. He was too tired to care what anyone in Riddleton would make of them, but they certainly must have looked like a strange group.

All afternoon, Tarr had turned whenever he could to look over his shoulder, both for signs of their Jelani pursuers and also for any glimpse of Ilaina. Each time, he was met by an expanse of wood, dimming gradually as the afternoon waned, and couldn't decide whether to feel relief that they had so far eluded capture or worry at Ilaina's continuing absence. *Ilaina must have taken a different path, led them off on some sort of chase,* Tarr thought again. *She'll be with us again before long. She's clever. She'll know that we likely didn't go to Two Falls. Riddleton must be the next logical choice.* He tried to force himself to feel comforted by this.

Riddleton itself first appeared as a mere spattering of lights in the distance, where it remained for some time until they drew close enough that the edges of buildings and the slopes of roofs began manifesting out of the pitch-black of night. Tired as he was, bobbing listlessly on the back of Marc's horse, he peered forward with interest as they crossed the city border and headed into the main street. He wondered whether there would be any real discernible difference between Riddleton and Two Falls, or whether one human city was much the same as another.

It only took about five minutes before Tarr concluded that Riddleton had a character all its own, and it was not a character with which Tarr wanted to interact for any great length of time. The differences weren't as apparent at first; many of the buildings were stylistically similar to those in Two Falls, with tiled roofs and criss-crossing beams of wood supporting the exterior walls. But there were no merrily swinging colored lanterns strung across the tops of the streets. The entire place seemed intentionally shrouded in darkness, with great pools of inky black shadow spilling around every corner, giving the buildings and each passerby a shifty, jagged appearance. The plaster on some of the houses had chipped and crumbled, with no thought or consideration given to their repair, and in some cases huge gouges in the buildings' sides revealed the skeleton of the brick or wood beneath. The signs outside the buildings, to a one, seemed to creak and groan in protest as the night breeze blew them back and forth on their hinges as if they hadn't been oiled for decades. Every few streets, there was a house that seemed to have burned or crumbled into nothing but rubble and had been left there like carrion thrown to the vultures.

The people, too, were of a different ilk. There were a great many of them out and about on the street, even though the hour was considerably late. There was no music, no laughter, no sounds of carousing emanating from the open windows of the taverns; instead, they either walked down the streets with their shoulders hunched and their coats drawn tight against their faces, or they conversed in low tones against the sides of buildings. As Tarr's strange group of riders passed by, some of the locals stopped to watch them. The looks the locals gave were rather predatory, as if they were trying to size them up as a potential meal. It all made Tarr considerably uneasy, though it was again a comfort to be riding with Laith and Marc. Tarr hadn't forgotten the rather stunning display of swordsmanship Laith had demonstrated earlier that day and was fervently glad to be on the prince's side.

Si and Rane were riding alongside Athela now, and the boy was giving her instructions about which road to take and where to go. At his direction, they went up a long, narrow road that spilled them out into a square, much different—cramped, dark, and uninviting—than the ones Tarr remembered in Two Falls, which had seemed to be hubs of activity and excitement. As they pulled to a halt at the corner of the square, a few denizens of Riddleton scuttled to and fro. In their uniformly black cloaks, they almost resembled little spiders scurrying for cover.

"Charming," Athela observed, casting an unimpressed eye over their new surroundings.

"It's better in the daytime," Si protested defensively.

Athela looked unconvinced.

"Si, do you know of somewhere we can stay the night? And where we can board the horses?" Laith asked. His voice was tired. Tarr had noticed that he, too, had been periodically swinging back around in his saddle to look for any sign of Ilaina.

"Maybe," Si said dubiously.

"Do you have a house here?" Athela asked curiously. "A family?"

Si shook his head, seemingly unperturbed by the question. "Nope, nothing. I've been on my own for as long as I can remember. I went to Two Falls for a short bit before I decided to come up and try and see the palace, but otherwise, I've been here."

The others stared at him. "Then where do you...live?" Marc asked, as if he couldn't quite fit the pieces of Si's existence together in his mind.

Si scratched his freckled nose and shrugged. "Attics, mostly. The odd shed. I was with another group of boys for a little while, and they had a pretty great setup in the loft of an old stableyard towards the south side of town."

Silence greeted this. Si seemed completely unruffled by his rootless, unprotected existence, and it was a shock to Tarr how sweet and rather innocent he still seemed to be, especially after what must have been a very difficult childhood. Tarr had only spent a single night in a shed, and that was enough for him.

"What about an inn? Somewhere that won't ask questions?" Athela pressed him.

Si thought for a moment and then pointed them down another street. In short order, they found themselves stopped before a rather derelict old building, but there were at least some lights in the windows, and there seemed to be enough rooms in the inn to accommodate all of them. They dismounted wearily, and Laith went in to make inquiries while Rane and Marc led the horses around the back of the building to stable them. Tarr felt his hips and knees creak a bit as he straightened them after many hours in the saddle, and gave Wolver a short pat on the head. The formerly white wolf was now a dingy brown color after their day of travel, and had a rather put-upon expression on his face as if he couldn't quite believe that following Tarr had led him to such a lowly state.

"Sorry, friend," Tarr apologized. "I'll try and find you some food."

All at once, his own stomach gave a resounding gurgle, as if to remind him that he was in need of sustenance as well. He hadn't eaten since early the day before; there hadn't been time for much at the Jelani party.

"What do you think the odds are that they have a bath here?" Athela asked, with a dubious look up at the creaky building.

Laith reappeared a moment later, and Tarr wondered immediately what they would do about money. It must cost a lot of money to afford lodging for such a big group. But Laith seemed unconcerned and went back to his saddlebag, withdrawing a few coins from inside. *Ilaina must have thought to pack him some coin to bring along*, and at the thought of her he immediately rotated on his back heel to stare around at the black streets beyond, just in case she chose that moment to suddenly appear.

"We'll be able to stay here for tonight, but I don't trust it much. I doubt that any Jelani will be here; they'll likely wait till morning if they decide to search for us in Riddleton at all. Hopefully, we lost them back in the forest," Laith shrugged. "A group such as ours in a place such as this is bound to call attention. People here will be only too eager to tell Jelani guards where to find us."

"But you think we're safe for tonight?" Tarr asked.

"Tonight, yes," Laith assented. "If we like, we can take turns on watch."

No one seemed to particularly relish this idea.

Tarr found himself sharing a room with Si that night, which wasn't bad at all since it turned out that the boy was more than happy to do most of the talking, and all Tarr had to do was sit and listen and occasionally grunt to show that he was still conscious. Upon examination, it turned out there was no bath after all, but there was an area out back of the inn by the water trough with a pump and a basin, so Tarr wound up stripping to his trousers and having a makeshift bath with buckets of cold water in the chilly spring night, all the while resolving that he would never take hot water for granted ever again.

He was glad to be able to finally change out of his grimy riding clothes into the fresh ones Ilaina had packed. He slid into the lumpy bed; the mattress had a strange dip in the center so that he constantly felt as if he were rolling inward and being pulled down, but it hardly mattered. So relieved was he to be there, to be alive, to be clothed and housed and bathed (if not fed), that sleep soon overtook him, even as Si's breathy chatter carried on through the still darkness.

The first thing that struck Tarr when he awoke the next morning was a rumbling sense of almost ravenous hunger, followed by momentary disorientation as he again tried to suss out where he was and with whom. He saw with a jolt that Si was gone from their room, but after a moment or two of listening, he thought he could hear the boy through the wall, prattling merrily away to someone who sounded like Marc.

He dressed and went out into the hall, still sore and creaky from the long day before. He ducked his head into the next room and exchanged a loose wave with Marc, seated on the floor next to Si, who was apparently regaling Marc with the story of his life. Tarr debated going down to the entrance of the inn, but he didn't much relish the prospect of running into the innkeeper, a man with a scraggly, unkempt beard and a soiled apron pulled tightly and rather defiantly over his round belly.

"Food in Athela's room," Marc called out after him. Gratefully, Tarr went down the hall one room more and found Laith, Athela, and Rane seated on the floor enjoying a makeshift picnic of bread and cheese and a few pieces of weedy-looking fruit that Laith had somehow managed to procure.

"There's some sort of market happening in the main square," Laith informed them through a mouthful of bread. "That's where I got this lot. I think I saw a few places with horses for sale, so that might be the place to start. And we can ask around to see if anyone can think of a suitable guide."

This seemed like an adequate enough plan, and so after they had had enough to eat and were dressed and cloaked as best they could be (leaving their larger weapons at the inn so as not to attract attention to themselves), they went out to explore Riddleton in the daytime. Wolver remained in Tarr's room, seemingly grateful for a day off after their trek the day before. At the water pump by the stables, Tarr had done his best to get some of the mud off of Wolver's legs and belly, but even after his efforts the wolf was still a rather sallow shade of off-white, and Tarr wasn't entirely sure what more he could do to restore him to his former glory.

Once on the street outside, Tarr eagerly turned his attention to the new town in which they found themselves. Tarr's expectations for Riddleton had been significantly lowered after their first introduction to it on the previous day, and though it was much easier to see where they were going, the sunlight did little to make the town seem more cheery than it had the night before. The derelict buildings—while less haunted-looking by day—were still to be found everywhere they went, and the general seediness and unpleasantness of the town and its people pervaded the air around them. Tarr couldn't be sure whether people simply didn't care whether their homes were well-kept, or whether a cheery, upkept building would become the immediate target of thieves (of which, he suspected, Riddleton had its fair share.)

Having traversed the same route only a few hours before, Laith led them with ease to the main market, which was indeed in the center of some sort of square. This, at least, was more lively and bustling than the reserved, suspicious air of the rest of the town, and Tarr felt himself slightly cheered. Si, who had apparently grown up in the middle of Riddleton, seemed oblivious to its unwelcoming atmosphere and was walking beside Marc, merrily pointing out notable landmarks ("That's the place where my friend Alan found a hair in his soup," "That attic up there has a floorboard with a big nail poking out and I tore my sock on it.") Si had clearly taken a shine to Marc and had glommed onto him with all the intensity of a limpet. Marc, Tarr was surprised to see, seemed perfectly content to listen to Si's nattering on, and seemed to regard him with the benevolent affection and bemusement of an older brother or uncle.

Here and there, Tarr would turn around, both scanning for signs of Ilaina and trying to catch a glimpse of Rane, who, as always, walked towards the back of their group and kept to herself. He could see that she, too, seemed to be on the alert, though he imagined that she was looking out more for signs of the Jelani troops than for Ilaina. At the thought of the troops, his heart fell. *Laith said they would likely regroup and try to come after us in the morning*, he thought to himself. They had to be on guard. The Jelani were unlikely to let them escape again, and he didn't want to think of how quickly and efficiently the Queen would have them dispatched once they'd been brought back to her.

Tarr was soon glad that they'd taken precautions to cover their faces and cloak their heads; even disguised as they were, they attracted a few stares from locals who clearly recognized them as outsiders. The market square was fairly crowded, though strangely quiet given the number of people crammed into the space together. Irritated-looking vendors stood beside their fruit stands, occasionally snapping at people who tried to reach out and poke items of produce, and bored-looking young women gazed off into the distance at the backs of their jewelry stands, perking up now and then when they caught sight of Laith (who seemed to be able to attract interest even with his face half-covered.)

Laith steered them purposefully to the far end of the market square, where a long gray tent had been erected, under which stood a line of horses tethered to a stretch of rope that ran along the length of the enclosure. The horses seemed to alternately be sleeping and munching on strands of hay that had been tossed down at their feet; two of the horses at the end were having some sort of disagreement and were trading sour faces back at one another with swings of their upturned heads.

"Athela, come with me," Laith murmured, and his cousin broke away from the others to go and talk horsy things with the tent's manager, an extremely tall, broad young man with shoulder-length black hair and a rather impassive expression.

Tarr, who over the course of his riding lessons with Ilaina had gradually begun warming to the animals, approached the line of horses with his hand outstretched in welcome, looking for any of the telltale warning signs that one of them was going to take a bite of him. These horses, unlike seemingly everything else in the entire city, were brushed and shining and clearly well-cared for: their whiskers had been clipped down, and their manes had been neatly combed. Tarr turned, about to remark on this to the others, when a young woman of about twenty came around the end of the tent carrying a woven horse blanket in her arms. She saw them and stopped, smiling brightly at the sight of them.

"Hullo!" she said. "I'm Silva."

From this cheery greeting alone, Tarr got the sense that she wasn't a Riddleton local. She was small, shorter than Athela or Rane, and had long, straight, silvery-gray-blond hair that flowed loosely down her back. She had one of the most outright feminine faces Tarr had ever seen:

a heart-shaped face with a pointed chin, soft pillowy lips, and bright green eyes framed in light lashes.

"How are you?" Marc replied. "We're hoping to purchase two horses."

The girl rose slightly on her tiptoes to look over to the opposite end of the tent. "Ah, yes, it seems my brother is helping you," she observed. Athela, Laith, and the burly tent manager were all grouped around a nearby horse and apparently deep in conversation. Athela was crouched down and poking expertly at the horse's foreleg.

Silva glanced down at Si. "Is one of the horses for you?" she asked kindly, setting down the blanket she'd been carrying. Si nodded mutely, clearly somewhat taken by her. She walked down the row of equine heads and paused at one. The horse's coat was a lovely creamy golden color, and he appeared to be deep in the midst of a nap, blond eyelashes fluttering gently.

"This is Kip," Silva told him. "He's quite sweet, you'd like him."

Si looked up and rubbed the palomino's golden forehead. Kip's sleepy eyes blinked open and he nuzzled Si's neck, blowing hot breath into his ear. Si smiled and pinched the horse's nose between his thumb and forefinger; Kip wiggled it happily, displaying his upper row of strong teeth. Si kissed the horse firmly on the nose.

"I like this one," Si announced.

"That was fast," Marc observed with a fond, paternal sort of smile. Tarr was beginning to see distinct strains of a mother hen running through Marc's makeup. Marc looked over to Silva and gave her a bit of a wink. "We'll see what the experts over there decide on."

Out of the corner of his vision, Tarr could see that Rane had positioned herself a short way away from them, up against the cracking wall of a nearby building. Her eyes were trained on the milling crowd in the market square, poised and alert for any sign of danger. Tarr felt comforted knowing that she was there, and allowed himself to relax a bit more. He turned back around to Silva.

"Your name?" she asked, extending her hand.

"Tarr," he returned, taking it. "You're not from here," he observed. Silva looked up, surprised. "How did you know?" she asked.

Tarr grappled around with a more polite way to say "your apparent will to live" but thought better of it. "I don't know," he said vaguely. "Are you from Two Falls, then?"

She shook her head. "My brothers and I have a farm on the northern cliffs. Do you know it? It's just off the road up to the mountains past Faridor Island. We're the third farm past the road to Faridor. A horse on the sign."

Tarr was taken aback by how casually Silva mentioned Faridor, which had been the island fortress of Lord Kagai hundreds of years before. However, he reasoned that for her, the island was merely an everyday landmark, nothing more. Though he had no idea what part of the country she was talking about, he decided to play along. "Oh yes," he said easily. "The cliffs. Absolutely."

"It's mostly farms around there, vegetables and the like, you know, but all of us come down to do the market rounds once or twice a month. Riddleton and Two Falls are always the best places to sell, and then there's some sort of military outpost on the edge of the Meadows, but I haven't been out there much yet," she told him.

It struck Tarr once again how little of the world he had actually seen in his life. So many of the places Silva mentioned—the cliffs, the mountains, the Meadows—all were completely foreign to him; he had no frame of reference to even begin to imagine them. "I haven't been out there either," he said, which in itself was true, but the way he said it carried the implication that he was far more worldly than he truly was.

"I've been to the Meadows," said Marc, coming up beside Tarr and facing Silva. Behind him, Si was demonstrating his ability to make the palomino's upper lip wiggle to Laith and Athela, seemingly as an argument in favor of the horse's purchase. Laith looked bemused while Athela had her arms crossed over her chest and one black eyebrow raised, seemingly unconvinced. Marc brushed a few strands of long, silky yellow hair over his ear.

"Oh, have you?" Silva said, raising again on her toes to see who Marc was referring to. Then, as Tarr watched, she caught her first real sight of Laith, and the effect was almost comical. Her eyes widened, and she stopped blinking for a full ten seconds, then a rosy blush flushed into her cheeks and up her throat. She slowly lowered back down and ducked her head as if trying to re-orient herself, but even so, Tarr noticed that she started to steal little glances in Laith's direction every few seconds after that.

"Tell me," Marc said conversationally. "You may not know this, but we're looking for a guide. Someone to show us around, tell us where to go and where not to go. To keep us out of trouble. We're not as familiar with Riddleton or Two Falls as we'd like. Do you know of anyone?"

She frowned, thinking (even as her green eyes continuously darted to the left towards Laith), "I don't know for sure. There's someone who might be right for what you need. I hear him talked about in the pubs a lot after the markets. He's sort of...someone you hire if you need a job done. For instance, if you need something smuggled out of town, or you need to hide someone, or even," she dropped her voice. "If you need someone *killed*. I've heard them say he can do it."

Marc chortled evasively. "Well, we certainly don't need anyone killed. But the other bits sound like they might be a good fit. Do you know his name?"

She frowned again. "I think his name is Archer or something. Funny name, isn't it?"

"Well, Laith's horse is named *Arfolasth*, so..." Marc replied with an eye roll. He stopped and considered. "Archer, eh? How would someone get a hold of this Archer?"

She shook her head. "I wouldn't know that. I think it's fairly hard to find him, considering the line of work he's usually in. Here in Riddleton, people tend to turn a blind eye to that sort of thing, but even so, it won't be as easy as walking into his office and plunking down some money. But my brother may have a better idea of how to contact him," she mused. "We had one of our horses stolen from the market a few months back, and my brother Cass was able to recover it, though he never told us how he managed it. One day, the horse was gone; the next, it was back in our paddock at home. Like magic."

All of this sounded rather exciting to Tarr's ears. He didn't hold with killing anyone, and whoever this Archer person was, they would clearly have to treat him with some amount of caution, but otherwise, he sounded almost ideal for their purposes. He was curious what such a person would look like, how they would behave, how they would talk. Before he'd met Laith and Athela, he'd had no idea what princes and princesses were like, and yet here they were, and it was now almost commonplace to be around them.

The business of buying the horses was soon concluded, and Si was overjoyed when Athela informed him that Kip was one of the purchases. "You've got to brush him at least once a day," Athela chided Si sternly, but as the boy eagerly turned away to pet the palomino on the forehead, he thought he detected a soft twinkle in the corner of her eye. As the horses were being readied and money exchanged, Tarr could see that Silva was whispering something in her brother's ear. Shortly thereafter, the brother approached them, his beetle-black brow knotted a bit.

"My sister Silva tells me that you're looking for someone to act as a guide," he said. Behind his arm, Silva was positively radiant and was gazing unabashedly at Laith. If the prince noticed her staring, he had the good manners not to draw any attention to it.

"That's right," Marc agreed. "Someone by the name of Archer?"

Si's jaw dropped. "*The* Archer? I thought he was made up."

Silva's brother considered and folded his arms. "He's hard to find, and he doesn't come cheap. But Archer's the best. I heard that he operated mainly in Two Falls before it got too dangerous for him to live there. I don't know if acting as a guide would be attractive to him, but..." he trailed off as he took in the sight of their group: the four well-clad, clearly wealthy Jelani, an Ashan, and a young boy. Tarr could almost see the wheels rolling around in his head. "If the assignment is interesting enough, he may take it. You'll never know."

"How do we find him?" Laith asked. Tarr could tell that he, too, was keenly interested in the sound of this Archer fellow.

"Odds are, he'll be the one to find you. But you can let him know you're interested. There's a tavern called the Blackburn that way," he jutted one finger to the left of the market square, "where all the vendors usually stop and have a pint after closing. You take a three-mark piece, give it to the bartender, and order a bottle of the honey wine." He smiled faintly. "They don't actually make honey wine, you see."

"And then?" Laith pressed him, intrigued.

Silva's brother shrugged his big, square shoulders. "And then you wait. Either he finds you and agrees to help you, or he doesn't."

"We leave no names, nothing about what we wish to employ him for?" Laith asked.

"No," he replied. "None of that. He'll find out. I'd be surprised if he doesn't know you're here already. And what you're looking for."

This was all so mysterious and intriguing that Tarr would have been tempted to go to the pub and try the trick with the coin and the honey wine even if they *hadn't* been looking for a guide. On some level, he knew that it was all likely some form of theatrics and a clever way to drum up business, but he nevertheless couldn't wait to see if the little ritual Silva's brother had described would summon this mysterious person to actually appear in front of them, perhaps with a dramatic flourish of a cloak and a wave of his arm.

Laith thanked Silva's brother for his help and turned to the young woman, proffering his hand. Tarr thought for a moment that she might faint, but she managed to keep her footing and even whispered a tiny, "My pleasure."

Their business concluded, they set away from the tent with their two new mounts: Kip, the amiable palomino, and a dark bay whose lead Athela handed to Tarr. "Name him what you like," she told him with a smile. "He's yours."

Tarr reached out, then hesitated awkwardly. "I can't pay you for him," Tarr told her quietly, feeling embarrassed.

"A gift," Athela insisted, pushing the lead into his hands.

"Thank you," Tarr said appreciatively, looking at the horse in surprise. Other than the small knapsack of belongings that he'd brought with him from the forest, he had never owned anything himself, much less anything as grand as a horse. He patted the horse's neck and was rewarded with a gentle whicker as the horse turned and tried to nibble the side of his belt. He felt a pang of guilt as he realized that, eventually, he would have to return the horse or at least pass it along to a new master. He would have no use for it once he returned to his life in the Ashan forest.

Since Laith seemed keen to track down Archer, they headed towards the tavern Silva's brother had indicated. To make it less attention-grabbing, they broke off into groups of two and kept apart from one another, walking on opposite sides of the winding streets. Tarr was aware at all times of people watching them: eyes that followed them behind half-shuttered windows, figures slung against doorways, heads slowly revolving as they went by.

They stopped outside the Blackburn tavern, which stood at the west side of its own small square. In keeping with the town's general aesthetic, the building seemed about two years away from crumpling completely into sawdust; the sign outside the door had a broken hinge and swayed drunkenly back and forth whenever there was a breeze. It certainly didn't look very promising.

"Right," Laith said, his tone businesslike. "I'll go in, and we'll see if all of this leads anywhere. If we don't hear from this Archer fellow by tonight, I vote that we strike out for Two Falls by tomorrow morning on our own and try our luck there. I don't much like the look of this town, and the sooner we're out of here, the better."

Beside Marc, Si squinted and looked around at their surroundings as if he couldn't quite understand what was so distasteful. "There's a spring fair," Si said defensively. "That's loads of fun."

"Oh, yes?" Marc inquired politely, though his expression was dubious.

"Yes, they bring people out of the jail for the day and you get to throw soft tomatoes at them!" Si informed him enthusiastically.

"Sounds lovely," Marc said with a sidelong glance at the others.

Laith shook his head. "I'm going in," he announced briskly, handing his reins over to Athela.

"Why doesn't Tarr go with you?" Athela asked casually. Tarr was taken aback. *How could Athela have known I wanted to go?*

Laith blinked around at the Ashan as if he had half-forgotten he was standing there. "Yes, wonderful," he agreed and motioned Tarr forward. "Let's go." He paused. "Marc, if we're not back out in ten minutes, come in after us."

At this Tarr gulped, but nevertheless found his excitement mounting as they came up to the door of the tavern and ducked inside. The air in the tavern bore the acrid smell of stale yeast, which Tarr recognized from the place where he'd eaten on his first night in Two Falls. He had to catch his breath for a few moments before he became accustomed to it. The Blackburn was a single large room with a fireplace at one end and a scattered assortment of rickety old tables and chairs in the center. Tarr imagined that much of the tavern's business would come after the market closed for the day; at that particular time, the room was almost completely empty, just a few cloaked individuals huddled conspiratorially over tankards in the far corner.

Just beyond the entrance of the tavern was a long bar, perhaps the only handsome piece of construction in the entire place. It was a long, solid piece of wood that had been well cared for in its day, polished and cured to protect against stains. Behind the bar was a sour-looking woman brandishing a filthy graying dishrag, who appeared to be in the midst of "cleaning" a row of mugs. Casting an eye over the rag and the crusted drinking vessels, Tarr made a solemn vow not to actually touch any nearby surfaces.

"Whaddyou want?" the woman asked as the door groaned shut behind them.

"Good afternoon," Laith said courteously, pulling back his hood and shaking his hair loose. Tarr thought that he saw the woman's expression soften slightly as he stepped closer. Laith's hand went down to his pocket, and he withdrew a small brass coin and slid it across the bar. The woman stared narrowly down at the coin, and one of her eyebrows arched as she looked up to the prince's face. "We would like to order a bottle of honey wine," Laith told her, keeping his voice low.

Tarr waited with bated breath to see what the woman would do. Half of him expected it all to be a hoax and for the woman to stare at them and laugh, or perhaps even throw them out. For all he knew, she might also shrug and turn around and actually produce a bottle of honey wine. But she did none of these things. With a quick flick of her wrist, she flipped the cleaning rag up and over her shoulder, then with a sweep of her hand she nimbly caught the coin and stowed it away out of sight.

"Honey wine it is," she replied. "I'll have to check on that for you. I'm not sure we have any in stock. If we do, my delivery man will find you."

"Shall I leave my address?" Laith asked.

The woman shook her head, a thin smile on her lips. "He'll find you."

"Right," Laith said slowly. He pushed back from the bar, met Tarr's eyes, and gave a little shrug as if to say, *I suppose that's it, then.*

Tarr was glad to be out of the tavern, and though he liked the coded exchange between Laith and the bartender, the interaction hadn't been nearly as thrilling as he'd hoped, and he felt rather deflated. He'd imagined that perhaps Archer would come bursting out of the door as soon as they'd paid. All there seemed to do now was wait. It was disappointing.

The others' expectant expressions met them as they made their way back outside, but again, all Laith could do was shrug and tell them that he had done as Silva's brother had suggested and that it had seemed to work well enough.

"Now what?" Athela asked impatiently. She also seemed to be slightly put out that there hadn't been a more satisfying ending to Laith's efforts in the tavern.

"Perhaps we'll go back to the inn. I want to be sure that no one's been asking around for us. If they have, we should get our things out and move lodgings," Laith suggested.

So their group began to head back towards the inn where they'd stayed the night. And though nothing had happened yet to indicate that Archer had received their summons, Tarr couldn't help but imagine that they were somehow being watched, perhaps even followed. Everywhere he glanced, he thought he could see someone just disappearing around a corner or the edge of a cloak vanishing into the cover of a doorway. After about five minutes of snapping his head this way and that, trying to catch a glimpse of their imaginary pursuer, he told himself that he was being stupid and that he was letting his imagination run away with him.

They came up to the inn from the back side, where the horses were stabled. They hung back for a few seconds, watching closely for any signs of a disturbance.

"I don't see anything," Marc said in a low voice. "Do you think it's safe to go up?"

"Rane, check it out. If you don't mind," Laith suggested.

Silently, Rane stepped forward, brushing Tarr's arm as she passed. He felt a thrill race up his spine and watched as she silently slipped along the edge of the building and vanished behind a tower of empty crates that had been stacked up in the middle of the alleyway. He didn't see her again after that. He couldn't understand how a person could move so softly, so confidently, or could seemingly vanish into thin air as she had. It was completely beyond him.

Tarr and the others led their horses around to the back of the stable behind the inn, where Laith's black charger was taking a midday nap. The other animals seemed quite comfortable (except, of course, Athela's excitable gray, who perked up the moment he saw her and began pawing dramatically at the stable floor.) The other horses sniffed curiously at the newcomers, but seemed to accept them with little ado. Si gave Kip a tickle on his nose and then swung around to face the others. "Well," he said brightly. "Shall we go up to the rooms?"

All at once, three things happened in quick succession. Tarr glanced over to Athela, whose eyes were trained on something metallic glinting against the door of a stall. Tarr peered into the gloom and saw that it was a sword, but not any that he recognized. Peering closer, he thought he saw the symbol of an egret engraved on the hilt, and his stomach dropped. Then there was the sound of light footsteps behind them, and Rane bolted around the corner of the inn, running as fast as she could, a look of warning in her eyes.

Then, much louder, there was the sound of metallic clanking, and a Jelani officer, fully outfitted in armor and a purple cloak, came walking around the far side of the stable. He was in the midst of flicking his hands free of water, having clearly just washed them at the pump. At the sight of them, he stopped dead, and there was an almost comical moment of protracted silence as the two sides sized one another up.

Rane slid to a halt just as Laith made a lunge towards the officer, but it was already too late. The officer reached down and grabbed his sword from where he'd leaned it on the stall door, and raised his voice in a full cry. "They're here!" he called. "They're here!"

Tarr and the others locked eyes, momentarily frozen. "Run!" Athela shouted, and, galvanized into a sudden flurry of action, they sprang forward and took off back down the path from which they'd come.

Tarr's heart beat in time with his flurried footsteps as they crashed through the stack of empty crates and dove down the alleyway beside it. They had only a few seconds' head start, and Tarr could hear a loud rumbling, almost like a metallic roll of thunder, as the Jelani came after them, the footsteps soon comingling with the sound of troops on horseback. Tarr's mind went blank with fear. *We can't outrun riders on horseback*, he thought to himself desperately. *They're going to take us. They're going to catch us and take us back to Joymaril, and there won't be anyone left there who can save us.* The thought gave him an extra burst of speed.

Tarr and his friends were at a distinct disadvantage in that (other than the path back to the marketplace) they had no idea where they were going and no options for where they could possibly hide. Tarr expected Si to take the lead, as he was most familiar with the city, but his solution seemed to be to flat-out run and hope for the best. Rounding a sharp turn, Athela caught him by the wrist and pulled him back just as he was about to go sailing by, and in turn, the others stopped, panting, taking shelter behind the corner of the wall.

"They were waiting for us," Rane told them through gulps of air. "Waiting for us in our rooms."

Wolver, Tarr thought with a pang. *What would they do to Wolver?*

"What do we do?" Si asked, his gray eyes frightened.

"Scatter? Split up?" Marc suggested, straining his neck to look over the top of Si's head.

"How would we find each other again?" Athela asked. "I say we stick together as long as we can."

"We could meet back at the tavern tonight?" Laith suggested.

A loud cloud of clomping feet rose just a few streets away. They were almost out of time. Tarr could feel every muscle in his body tense as he waited for the others to decide what to do.

"Si, you've lived here all your life, surely you must know of some place we can go," Athela urged.

Tarr could see the boy's mind racing. "There's a sewer grate where I liked to hide," he suggested tentatively.

"A *sewer grate?*" Athela demanded exasperatedly. "How are we all supposed to fit in a *sewer grate?*"

"You asked him where he liked to go, don't bite his head off," Marc countered. "He's just a boy; his old hiding places probably aren't going to be what we need."

"And if we try and sneak into a building, anyone who sees us is going to give us up almost immediately," Laith muttered.

Suddenly, there was a shout almost immediately to their right, barely a foot or two around the edge of the corner. Every one of them gave a start, and then, almost without thinking, Laith barreled forward just as a Jelani guard rounded the corner. Laith shoved the astonished guard off his feet, and the two of them grappled on the ground for a moment; as soon as they drew apart, Marc leaped forward and dealt the guard a swift blow that sent him reeling senselessly back to collapse in a heap on the ground.

The call went up around them, and Tarr knew that they'd been sighted by the other Jelani. They scurried like fleeing animals down the alleyway, turning one way and then another, not knowing exactly where they would come out. Once in a while, Si would point them to the left or the right, but with nowhere to go and no place to hide, Tarr was acutely aware that all they could do was continue to run in circles until the Jelani caught up to them. All Laith, Marc, and Athela had brought with them were their daggers, which wouldn't be much use against the Jelanis' broadswords. Tarr had a terrible sinking feeling that their time was running out.

News of their chase had evidently swept through Riddleton, as before long Tarr became aware that the streets had become oddly deserted, as if all the denizens of the city had taken shelter inside their homes. He even began to notice people peeking out from behind the shutters of their windows, as though the chase and imminent arrest was some sort of eagerly anticipated afternoon entertainment. Tarr got the feeling that this wasn't the first time the citizens of Riddleton had watched a high-speed pursuit unfolding through their streets.

Crossing through one intersection, Tarr chanced a glance to the left. Far down the end of an alley, he could see the still-bustling market square. He slid to a stop and grabbed Laith by the arm, pointing in that direction with an unspoken question. Breathing heavily, Laith nodded silently and beckoned the others to follow.

They plunged into the market, which, while giving them the temporary advantage of the cover of a great many people, also hindered their ability to run. They now had to dodge around and between great thickets of shoppers, who Tarr could have sworn began to close in around them as if to keep them in, indignant voices rising like a cloud of smoke as they shoved and pushed their way through. He ducked under the canopy of a small tent selling jars of pickled vegetables, and thought he heard a little old woman swear at him and pelt a dried bit of fish at his head as he went charging heedlessly through the middle of her display.

Pausing ever so slightly to cast a look over his shoulder, he saw that this ploy had worked at least somewhat in their favor. The Jelani mounted on horseback were unable to follow them through the milling crowd, and those on foot weren't having much more luck than Tarr and his friends were. The crowd seemed to have little or no respect for the uniformed armed guards, and were making no efforts to part a way for them through the market. Their reticence had bought Tarr and his friends a few precious seconds at least.

At the east end of the market the scattered runners met up again, not before upsetting a display of withered-looking oranges on a nearby cart. To Tarr's great surprise, the vendor—slumped over to the side with his head leaning against one fist—seemed completely nonplussed by the disturbance and even seemed to give a small resigned sigh and a shrug, as if to say, *well, this might as well happen.* He made no effort to right the display or collect his spilled fruit, and even seemed to halfheartedly wave them along on their way.

Tarr couldn't wait to get out of Riddleton.

They charged down the street, ducking beneath a low-swinging tavern sign that nearly whacked Si in the face as it recoiled. Following Athela's lead, they dashed to the right down a residential alleyway where all of the windows in the buildings were shut tight and boarded up. Tarr's throat and lungs were burning from the effort of running, and his head was swimming with the dizzying dose of adrenaline that had sent him hurtling through the city. *We've got to find some way out*, he thought to himself. *We can't keep this up all day.*

At the end of the alley, they stopped and turned to the left, where there had looked to be another small passageway leading away from the alley, but Tarr's stomach dropped as he realized that they were faced with a dead end. They looked up and around at the buildings. Tarr, with his Ashan climbing abilities, could have perhaps scaled the wall himself, but he wasn't about to leave the others behind. Sickeningly conscious of their precious seconds ticking away, he spun on his heel, looking for any way out. The only apparent exit was the alleyway from which they'd come, but that would lead them directly into the waiting arms of their pursuers. They were trapped.

Off in the distance, there was the sound of a distant crash.

Athela's gray eyes were wide and grim as she whirled around to face the others. Her hand was already going for the dagger at her hip, and a note of resolution crept over her features. They were going to have to make a stand, Tarr realized, and his heart dropped. They would be captured or killed for sure. He was no fighter. He would surely be one of the first to go. He tightened his fists into balls, determined that if this was where it would end, he would do his best. *I should have stayed in Two Falls*, he thought. *Found a job at the library and hunkered down until the year was over.*

"Hullo," came a sudden, unfamiliar voice from somewhere above them. "I hear you've been looking for me."

CHAPTER NINE

As one, Tarr and the others swung around, searching for the origin of the voice. Flat against the drowsy midmorning sun high above them was a black silhouette, head ringed like a halo against the light. The figure seemed to pause for a moment to enjoy the stir he'd caused, then he moved down the roof with swift, assured nimbleness, scaling the side of the building as easily as if there had been a ladder set against it for him to climb. A bow and embroidered leather quiver filled with black and white fletched arrows hung from his back. As the figure descended, Tarr caught a glimpse of six fingers on his left hand, and realized with a jolt of shock that he was Ashan.

But as the stranger sprang neatly to the ground and turned to face them, Tarr realized that he was unlike any Ashan he had ever seen, so much so that he found himself taking a reflexive step back. The Ashan's skin was white—not just pale brown, but *white*—with a bluish tint, almost like freshly fallen snow. He had a pair of glittering golden eyes and spiky white hair tipped in black, rather like a bird's feathers. The face that regarded them was all long, chiseled angles: a sharp jaw, pronounced cheekbones, a straight, diving nose. Between his bone structure and his strange coloring, the overall effect was that of a bizarrely humanoid bird of prey. Looking around at his friends' expressions, Tarr could see that he wasn't the only one taken by surprise.

Nevertheless, Tarr's heart leapt at the sight of one of his country-men, and he tried to surreptitiously catch a glimpse at the nape of his neck to see what family he belonged to. He was clearly a few years older than Tarr—and maybe even Laith and Athela—so perhaps he had been Chosen into a family already. But the Ashan wore a coat with a tall black collar, hiding any of his family tattoos from view. For a moment, Tarr's friends and the strange-looking Ashan surveyed one another, sizing each other up. Tarr, a step or two behind Laith's shoulder, was rather startled when the piercing golden eyes seemed to come and rest on him for a few seconds, as if the strange Ashan was taking his measure.

"Well, then," the Ashan said finally. "I'm Archer. It seems you lot are in a rather tight spot." His accent was strange to Tarr's ears; he had never heard anything like it before. There was a singsong lilt to it that he couldn't quite place.

"You might say that," Laith concurred, with a nervous glance towards the far end of the alleyway. "We have some people after us."

"You don't say," Archer said. "You cut a neat swath through half the weekend market."

"You've been following us?" Athela blurted.

The Ashan swiveled his gaze around to her and seemed to take her in. After a moment, he smiled. "With interest. I should thank you all for bringing some entertainment value to an otherwise dull morning."

Anxiously, Laith and Marc both sent nervous looks back down the alleyway, as if expecting the guards to come bursting around the corner at any minute. The Ashan followed their gazes and gave a casual shrug. "I tipped over a big stack of crates across the road up there. Should buy us a minute or two. At least enough time to negotiate my fee." He gave a toothy, rather wolfish grin. There was something inherently sardonic in his demeanor, an innate sense of wry humor that faced the world with an ironically cocked eyebrow. Tarr wasn't sure whether he liked him or not. He became acutely aware of a nagging feeling of unease. *Why would an Ashan be in the trade of smuggling or killing?* he wondered. *Those activities are strictly forbidden. He wouldn't be permitted to do such things, unless...*inwardly, Tarr's line of thought trailed off, as if the thought was too awful to truly consider.

Was this Ashan an exile?

"Your fee," Athela cut in, her tone brisk and businesslike. "What is it?"

Archer considered. "I don't come cheap. But..." Here, he stopped and seemed to survey the Jelanis' comparative finery. "I have a feeling it won't be a problem for all of you."

"What about this," Laith suggested. "You get us out of here in one piece, we'll take it as a demonstration of your abilities, and we pay you whatever you ask. If you don't, you'll be missing out on a fairly lucrative opportunity."

Archer stretched his long arms and didn't seem much moved one way or the other. Tarr suddenly remembered what Silva's brother had said about Archer not taking on a mission unless it interested him. Tarr could see that promises of money weren't going to be enough.

"Did you recognize the guards who were chasing us?" Tarr asked quietly.

Archer took another long, slow, appraising look at him. Off in the distance, closer to them now, there was shouting and another crash. They were running out of time.

"Not directly," Archer replied slowly, yellow eyes searching Tarr's face. "I imagine they're Jelani, though, right?"

"That's right," Tarr confirmed. "This is a Jelani prince," he said, indicating Laith with one hand, "and *this* is the daughter of the Queen herself," he motioned to Athela. "We escaped from the palace and are being hunted by the Queen's soldiers because we believe that Morthenstar's heir may be amongst us." He silently prayed that Archer's suspension of disbelief would extend to include all the nonsense about heirs and Morthenstar. The Ashan didn't look like a fool. But instantly, he could tell that his ploy had worked. Archer looked intrigued.

"Who's the heir, then?" Archer asked keenly.

Laith opened his mouth to reply, but Tarr cut him off. "That's all we can say for now," he replied firmly. He could sense Laith staring at him.

Almost as if they were two duelists circling around one another in a ring, Archer took a step back, a slow smile creeping across his face as if acknowledging that Tarr had the upper hand. "Well, isn't that a cunning little mystery," he mused appreciatively. "Tell me, is *anything* you just said remotely true?"

Tarr opened his mouth to hotly protest the notion that he was in any way capable of lying, but Archer waved a dismissive hand. The yelling was even closer now, and Tarr heard a shrill horse's whinny pierce the air like a blade. The Jelani guards would round the corner of the alleyway at any moment, and they would all just be standing there haggling.

"Right, then," Archer said with a grin and the air of a tour guide. "If you'll be so kind as to follow me, let's see about getting you safely hidden away."

There was a collective sigh of relief around the circle, then Si's breathy small voice piped up. "Where can we go?" he asked, squinting up towards the sheer wall of the building from which Archer had descended. "We can't all climb up onto the roof."

"No," Archer agreed. "But you can run, can't you?"

"Yes," Si said dubiously.

"Then you'd better start," Archer suggested. "This way."

It was lucky that they had had those few moments to rest and catch their breaths, for Archer took off with all the speed of one of his own arrows towards the street's dead end. It wasn't a moment too soon. Behind them, a thick knot of purple-cloaked guards, both on foot and on horseback, came charging around the corner, their collective cries of victory rising in the air as they spotted their prey.

Tarr had no idea how Archer planned to get them out of their predicament, but a moment later, his way out became apparent. On the ground by one of the rearmost buildings was a locked double door that apparently led down to some sort of cellar. Archer paused a moment, then raised the heel of his boot and, with one swift movement, kicked the rusty lock off the doors so that they flapped open.

"Where does this go?" Si peered down interestedly into the gloom below.

"Basement, I think," Archer said, flinging open the doors and motioning them inside.

"You don't *know*?" Athela demanded, as if aghast that he didn't have more of a concrete plan in mind.

"Look, *I* didn't manage to trap myself in a dead-end alleyway," Archer pointed out impatiently. "If you'd like, you are free to wait and discuss the pros and cons of my strategy with your friends back there." He gestured towards the rapidly approaching guards. Athela shot him a rather sour look, but did as she was bidden and lowered herself down into the gloom of the cellar, the others quickly following.

The floor of the cellar was about six feet below the ground, at the base of a flight of very narrow, very rickety stairs; the air was damp and musty and very, very cold. Behind them, Archer banged the cellar door shut, blocking out all light and there were a few confused seconds of groping around in the darkness before Archer lit a match and by the tiny pinpoint of light began to lead them speedily forward through the belly of the cellar.

"The horses won't be able to follow us, obviously, they'll have to go around," he informed them. "It'll be better if we get them to split up. I have a few places around town I use for hiding smuggled goods, so I'm going to divide everyone up. You'll stay where I tell you till it's safe again."

Tarr wasn't sure he liked this plan. He didn't trust Archer, certainly not now that he'd considered the possibility that he could be an exile. Perhaps he would stow them all safely away in the safehouses only to immediately turn them over to the Jelani and collect some sort of handsome reward. Their options, however, were limited—Tarr had already heard the cellar door behind them being thrown open by the pursuing Jelani—so he bit his tongue and resolved to be on his guard.

The passageway ended in another set of stairs, these carved out of stone. Archer, his match long since extinguished, sprinted up and threw himself bodily through the door at the top, the others piling out behind them.

The scene that met them was so comical that Tarr could almost have burst out laughing. They had emerged into some sort of tavern or pub, in which every person in the entire establishment was crowded around the windows, looking out towards the street and clearly hoping to catch sight of the high-speed chase that had reportedly been taking place outside. At the sound of the cellar door bursting open, they all spun around and froze in a shocked stupor, their eyes as wide as dinner plates.

Archer, too, had frozen in place, though he recovered himself a bit faster than the tavern's patrons. "Hullo," he said, trying to sound casual. "Can someone tell me which pub is this?"

A few seconds of startled silence followed his question. "The Boar's Hide," mumbled a nearby woman, her face immobile with shock.

"Ah!" Archer exclaimed, his expression clearing. "Yes, that makes sense. Thank you."

He beckoned, and the others followed him out the front door of the tavern, past the startled patrons, and into the street. Tarr imagined what the taverngoers' faces would be only a few seconds later when a troop of Jelani footsoldiers poured out of the cellar, too, and had to stop himself from collapsing into laughter then and there.

Archer quickly aimed them down the street—much larger than the alleyways through which they'd been sprinting—and turned them towards an odd apartment building with tiny square balconies and multiple levels arranged almost like enormous stepping stones up to the rooftops. "This place is very handy—here, follow me; you should be able to climb it," he told them, hoisting himself up onto a platform that had evidently once been intended as a raised curbside garden but was now a graying, browned cluster of dead weeds. The building was arrayed in a way that made it easy to clamber up from the street to a balcony, up to a roof, and so on over the face of the building. Climbing it outright would have been as easy as skipping for Tarr, but he hung back and ensured that Si and Marc were able to scramble up.

In short order, they had reached the top level of the building and were now balanced along the rooftop, which mercifully didn't have much of an angle to it and was therefore easy to cross. Below them in the street, Tarr saw the slew of Jelani horses slide to a frustrated halt beneath the building, and even saw a few of the furious faces of the guards pointing up towards him, calling for the footsoldiers to catch up and go after them. Tarr turned away and followed the others along the length of the building, aware that the riders would plan on circling around beneath them and catching them whenever they decided to descend. Perhaps it was his innate Ashan instincts, but he felt much safer now that they were high above the ground.

"This way," Archer coaxed them, and led them across a narrow beam slung between the roofs of two of the residential buildings. Si scampered to the other side like a mouse, and Tarr followed after, comfortable as a cat on the narrow footwalk.

Archer motioned them to a square stone structure jutting out of the roof on which they stood. It was about hip-height, with a grated metal top. Tarr realized that it was a chimney to allow smoke to escape from the fireplace in the dwelling below. They had similar structures in some of the larger Ashan buildings back home.

"This isn't really a chimney," Archer informed them, swinging the grated top open. Tarr peered down and could see that there were metal handholds bolted into the stone leading all the way down into the darkness. "It connects to a small safe room that I use to hide contraband. Big enough for three people, I'd say."

"How about three and a half?" Laith asked, eyeing Si.

"Possibly. It'll be tight."

"Right. Tarr, Marc, Si, come with me," Laith ordered and swung his legs over into the opening of the chimney shaft. Hand over hand, he lowered himself down into the darkness below. Marc and Si obediently followed, and Tarr (sending one last suspicious glance towards Archer) followed suit.

Once they were situated, Archer swung the grate closed and bolted it into place. He leaned over the side of the building, searching for any signs of the Jelani below. A glimmer or two of purple flashed in the street, and he rocked back on his heels, swearing beneath his breath, his mind quickly turning.

Rane quietly cleared her throat. "With your permission, milady," she murmured, "I would like to go back to the inn and see what I can do about collecting our things. I imagine that anyone guarding them might be otherwise occupied at the moment."

Athela momentarily paused and looked from Rane to Archer, clearly torn between the logic of Rane's words and the prospect of being alone with the strange Ashan. "All right," she agreed. "See what you can do."

Rane smoothly turned away. Light and assured on her feet, she tiptoed silently along the ridge of the roof and, after a few seconds, disappeared like a wisp of smoke into the void beyond. Archer and Athela listened for a few seconds with bated breath, waiting for any yell or alarm from the street below indicating that she'd been seen or captured, but there was none.

"Impressive," Archer said appreciatively.

"So, what, are we going to stay up here on the roof all day?" Athela asked curtly. "Or do you have a plan for us, too?"

"So little faith," Archer sighed. "I think I've done a pretty good job thus far."

"You kicked a cellar door in and shoved my cousin down a chimney," Athela pointed out.

"But knowing *which* chimney to shove your cousin down," Archer observed, swiveling around on his heel and beginning to negotiate his descent to the street below. "*That's* the real trick."

Athela rolled her eyes, but followed nonetheless. Wisps of her curly black hair had blown free of the twist on the back of her head and blew around her face and in her eyes. She wasn't as fast or as nimble as Archer, but she was able to follow him down the side of the building, holding onto a drainage pipe for leverage and gruffly accepting his help when she had to leap the last few feet onto a roof below.

Brushing herself off, she looked up at Archer and was surprised to find that he was watching her with an appreciative look on his face.

"You know, you have very striking eyes," he observed.

Automatically, she lowered them and made a great show of wiping more dust from her trouser leg. Finally, sensing that he hadn't yet looked away (and furiously aware of the blush that had spread up her neck), she looked boldly back up at him. His face and coloring were so strange and alien, yet there was a charm and an undeniable appeal to be found in the planes of his angular face.

"What happens if you cut your hair?" she asked curiously.

"It's all white for a while, and then the tips turn black," he responded.

"Is that an Ashan thing?"

"No. Just me." There was a flirtatious edge to his smile, and Athela felt her heart do a little turn.

An instant later, however, she snapped herself out of it and leaned over the side of the building, looking for any way to break the sudden, unexpected tension. As if in reply, a shout went up. They'd been spotted. Cursing herself for being so careless (and for the way her head had been spinning a moment before), she whirled around.

Archer grabbed her hand as if it were the most natural thing in the world, and pulled her along the rooftop, then crouched down and vaulted to a balcony below. In another bound, he landed lightly on the street. Athela did her best to keep up, which she managed to do (albeit somewhat less gracefully). Once she had both feet on the ground, Archer took her hand again and led her down the winding street.

They turned a corner, and suddenly a horse and rider burst out in front of them, a drawn sword swinging through the air, missing Archer's face by inches as it went past. The horse, spooked at the sudden appearance of the runners, gave a frightened whinny and scrambled back, its shoes slipping on the slick stone.

"I've got them!" the rider exclaimed, whirling the horse and readying herself for another swipe in Athela's direction. "Over here!"

In the frenzy, Archer pulled Athela to the side and they slipped past the rider, running as fast as they could to the next street's intersection. Dodging beneath a low-hanging string of laundry, Archer increased his speed, sending a dark look over his shoulder towards the rider who had nearly caught them, who at that moment was disentangling herself from the laundry line.

"They're persistent, I'll give you that," Archer panted.

They passed by another street, and with a clutch of panic, Athela could see that the guards on foot were only a few feet away from turning after them. She felt herself unconsciously grip Archer's hand a little harder.

"Wait! This way!" Archer exclaimed and pulled her to the right.

"You have a plan?" Athela demanded.

"Don't sound so surprised."

"I'm so sorry. Do you have a plan *other than* running around in ever-narrowing circles?"

"Yes, and I have a feeling you're really going to love it," Archer muttered sarcastically, and with another turn they found themselves in yet another anonymous-looking back street. Suddenly, he pulled them to a halt. Athela looked around, searching for wherever it was he intended for them to hide, but there didn't seem to be anywhere. All that the street had to show for it was a little storage trunk pushed up against the side of a building, far too small to house the both of them, and too short to accommodate Archer's long limbs.

"It's still here!" Archer exclaimed happily, taking a long stride to stand over the storage trunk. "Wonders never cease."

"Wait a second," Athela's brow furrowed. "What on earth are you talking about? There is no way we're both going to fit in there."

With a dramatic flourish, Archer flipped open the top of the storage trunk, propping it open on a metal hinge. Inside, there were a few coils of rope and what looked like a hammer. Athela frowned at the contents and looked back up to Archer, her expression still quizzical. There didn't seem to be much in the trunk that would aid in their escape.

"What, we're going to string them up and pound them? *That's* your plan?" she pressed.

Archer rolled his eyes exasperatedly. He leaned in and pushed the back side of the trunk, which was pressed up against the wall of the building. To Athela's shock, she saw that the trunk had a false back and that the rear panel actually flipped up into a small crawl space beneath the building behind it.

"*You* hide in there?" Athela asked dubiously, looking from the seemingly tiny space to the tall Ashan beside her.

"Not habitually, no," Archer conceded, unbuckling his quiver and bow and tossing them into the hideaway. "But needs must. Today, it'll have to do. After you." He made a welcoming sweep of his hand towards the little hideout.

Athela still hesitated. Archer rolled his golden eyes and, with some effort, clambered into the storage trunk, folded up his long limbs, and then slithered himself through the false back into the crawl space beneath the building. He rolled onto his side and peered up at her expectantly from the gloom within. Athela could see that it would, indeed, be very snug in there, but she wasn't sure what else they could do. Footsteps were rising behind her. In a few seconds, it would be over.

She hopped one foot and then another into the trunk, then crouched down and threaded herself into the little hole leading to the opening beneath the house. Quickly, she discovered that the only way they would both fit is if she, too, lay on her side so that her body fit against Archer's. She twisted herself around, her head resting on her bent elbow. The instant she settled herself into place, Archer extended one long arm over the top of her head and dislodged the top of the trunk from the metal hinge holding it open so that it closed with a *thunk*. Then, with another quick sweep of his arm, he lowered the trunk's false back, effectively hiding them from view.

They lay there together in the pitch-black darkness, listening for the sounds of their pursuers. *Had the guards seen the top of the trunk close?* Athela wondered. The floor beneath them was a slab of cold, hard stone, and though she was warm from all the running they'd been doing, she nevertheless felt a shiver go through her. She was also deeply conscious of Archer behind her, and could feel the soft warmth of his breath on the back of her neck. She usually hated being touched; she'd only ever occasionally exchanged a hug with Laith or Ilaina, and even then only at weddings, funerals, and once when Laith had helped her get out of teaching beginner's horsemanship to a group of five-year-olds. And yet here she found herself, crammed intimately against a strange young Ashan man she'd met not half an hour before.

She felt Archer's body tense up against her as the unmistakable sound of footsteps came clanking up the street outside their hiding spot. She tucked her head against her hand to stifle the sound of any breath. *Just keep walking,* she willed the footsteps. *Just keep walking and pass us by.* But the footsteps slowed, and soon, other pairs followed and halted. She thought she heard the sound of hooves and the babble of voices, indistinct until they got close enough for her to pick out the words. Judging from the noise, there must have been upwards of ten guards standing only about three feet away from where she and Archer were hidden.

"Where the hell did they go?" one of the guards yelled. "We were blocking the other end of the street, and you came down here. Where could they have gone?"

"Maybe they went up to the roofs again," a female voice volunteered.

The first voice swore lustily, and Athela could hear vague murmurs from the other guards. She could feel Archer's heart drumming furiously against her back. *He's afraid, too,* she thought, and the realization made her even more anxious.

"Wait a minute," a deeper male voice growled.

There was a loud creak seemingly just above their heads, and Athela realized that one of the guards had opened the top of the trunk. Archer's hand flew out over Athela's side and pressed against the false back shielding them from the guards' view. A moment later, their little hideout exploded in thunder as the guard dealt the trunk a few swift kicks with his foot. Athela let out a cry of shock, and her hand shot out beside Archer's to press against the secret door, her whole body shaking with fear and with the deafening noise of the blows, amplified by a hundred as though they were sitting in the belly of a drum.

"Don't be stupid," growled the first voice, and the dreadful explosive pounding stopped.

Behind her, Archer gave a small chuckle and punctuated the moment with a small, distinctly uncomfortable shift of his weight. Athela silently repeated to herself, *close the trunk and walk away. Close the trunk and walk away.*

As if in response to her chanting, there was a creaking groan and a thump as the top of the trunk closed again. Athela let out a thin sliver of breath, realizing that her entire body had gone absolutely rigid with fear.

"Looks like they scattered," the female guard observed. "We'll have a tough go of it finding them now. With enough of a head start, they may be able to escape the city altogether."

"We'll keep searching," the first guard ordered. There was another thump against the trunk, and Archer and Athela both jumped. The Ashan's arm was still over her, long six-fingered hand pressing protectively against the trunk's false back. Athela guessed that one of the guards had delivered the trunk another frustrated, spiteful blow.

"The Queen won't take it well if we come back empty-handed," another guard observed gloomily.

"They can't have gone far, and there's nowhere for them to hide in this town," the first countered. "No one will shelter them here who won't give them up again for a price. We'll find them. Now, move out. We'll meet up with the second group and patrol the area. They're eventually going to have to show their faces again." And then, with as much relief as if she'd plunged herself into a cool river, Athela listened as the footsteps passed by and gradually faded into the distance. Soon, all was completely silent.

The danger now gone, Athela's senses began to slowly recover, and she took in her surroundings. It was pitch black where they lay, but Archer's skin was so pale that he seemed to glow ever so slightly, so that she could almost see the outline of his white hand as it slowly, tentatively withdrew from holding the false back of the trunk. His hand hovered awkwardly in the air over the side of her body, as if he didn't know where to rest it. The sight of his uncomfortably poised arm filled her with relief, as she was acutely aware of the compromising situation in which she had found herself.

"Excuse me," he whispered. "May I rest my arm—"

The ceiling of their crawl space wasn't high enough for him to rest his arm on his own side. "You may," Athela conceded. "On my waist. No hands."

"No hands," he agreed, and she felt his forearm settle comfortably against the dip of her waist. To her surprise, the weight of it felt rather comforting, and she felt the strangest urge to nestle back against him. She could still feel his heart beating against her back, but the speed of it had slowed. His face was pressed against her hair just beside the curve of her neck. She wasn't sure whether it was their near escape or the frenzy of all the running, but all at once her stomach felt quite fluttery. The silence between them seemed to build and build.

"So. You're a princess, then?" he asked, and the tension lessened somewhat.

"Believe it or not," she said wryly.

"Do all princesses have such pointy elbows?"

She was glad he couldn't see her stifle a grin. "I keep mine sharpened. To ward off predators."

"You may be surprised," he said, shifting his weight, trying to find a more comfortable position, "but this is the first time I have found myself shoved underneath a building with a princess."

"I'm shocked," Athela rejoined. His hips were snugly hugged

against her. She continued, pleased with how steady her voice sounded, "For all I know, you led me here on purpose."

She felt his hard belly flutter behind her as he chuckled softly. "You should count yourself lucky. I usually only bring people here after the third date."

The silence between them resumed. Her mind racing, she forced herself to swallow and cleared her throat. "Do you think it's safe for us to go out?" she asked.

"Oh, no," he said easily. "I think we'll need to hunker down here for a while longer. Give them some time to patrol around and give up trying to find us."

The thought of it was dizzying. "How *much* longer?" she asked crossly.

"What's your name?" he asked suddenly.

"I *asked* you..."

"Half an hour," he said.

"Half an *hour?*" she repeated. "In *here?*"

He made no response, as the answer to her question seemed somewhat obvious, even to her. She sighed and thought for a moment. He had to be even less comfortable than she was, being much taller and longer-limbed. And he was probably right. They had been fortunate to find their hiding space, and they risked giving it all up if they ventured out too early.

"Athela," she said finally.

"Athela," he repeated, turning over the sounds of it in his mouth. His tone sounded satisfied. "Does it mean anything?"

"It means 'one who deeply values her personal space,'" she shot back, then paused, feeling strangely gratified as he chuckled again. "Does Archer mean anything?"

"Yes, it means 'one who shoots things with a bow and arrow,'" he retorted.

She rolled her eyes. "Where are you from?"

"Here and there," he said vaguely.

She heaved an exasperated sigh. "If we're going to be stuck in here for half an hour, you might as well start telling me your life story so we have something to talk about."

"Who is the Ashan?" he asked suddenly. "The one who's traveling with you? With the melancholy eyes?"

"That's Tarr," Athela said. "We found him in Two Falls." She hesitated, considering bringing the prophecy up, then decided against it. Prophecies of any kind sounded pretty far-fetched from the cramped darkness of their hiding spot. "He's quiet. Smart, I think, but he's only just come from the forest. He doesn't know much about the outside world."

"What tribe is he?" Archer asked curiously.

"I don't know," Athela admitted, suddenly realizing that she'd been living in close proximity to Tarr and hadn't bothered to find out such an elementary piece of information. She wasn't even aware that Ashans *had* tribes.

"He doesn't really look like much, does he?" Archer mused. "But he watches things..." he trailed off, and she felt him shake his head. "Interesting. Interesting fellow." He moved his arm slightly against her waist.

Athela cleared her throat, desperate to avoid another tension-filled silence. "Where *are* you from?" she asked curiously. She'd never seen anyone like him before. None of the Ashans or half-Ashans who she'd seen in her excursions to Two Falls or the surrounding areas had borne any resemblance to him.

"The north," he replied shortly, and swiftly changed the subject. "Well, Athela, this seems like as good a time and place as any for a job interview," he observed briskly. "Tell me why you all were looking for me."

She noted the way in which he'd again dodged the topic of his origins, but let it pass. "We need a guide," she said, inwardly noting the absurdity of conducting an interrogation with him talking at the back of her head. "Someone who knows Two Falls. Who can show us around. Connect us with the right people."

She felt him shrug behind her. "You can hire people like that for a fraction of what I cost."

"Our mission is slightly more...sensitive than just a bit of sightseeing," she said delicately.

"Finding the heir of Alder Morthenstar?" he said, his voice rife with skepticism. "Like your friend the Ashan seemed to suggest?"

"Maybe," she said evasively.

"Do you know who she is yet?" Archer pressed. A strand of Athela's curly hair had fallen over her forehead. With one hand he reached up and brushed it back from her eyes. As he did, his hand touched her cheek; his skin was smooth and incredibly cool, almost like marble.

"Not yet," Athela conceded, forcing herself to keep her mind on their mission. "But we have reason to think she's out there."

"Intriguing," he murmured. "And you already have troops from Joymaril after you. And maybe Kagai will be, too, if he happens to come back."

Archer's casual tone made it sound like the whole idea was a big joke. Athela gritted her teeth and refused to rise to the bait. "Probably," she agreed shortly. Then she twisted around as far as she could in the confined space, so that she was looking up at the milky blue line of his face above her. "It would be helpful to have someone with a knack for finding hiding places."

"It *is* a gift I have, isn't it?" he agreed with a grin. "I'm so glad you noticed."

Their eyes locked for a moment in the gloom, and then Athela caught herself and hurriedly twisted back around to face forward, acutely aware that he'd be able to feel her heart beating faster. For a frantic second, she thought that he would point it out and perhaps tease her for it.

Instead, he merely fell silent and seemed to think for a few moments more. Finally, he stirred. "Well, Athela, I have to say that meeting you all has so far made for an interesting morning. Can't wait to see what you all get up to by dinnertime."

"You'll help us!" she exclaimed, forgetting herself and turning back to look at him.

"I'll help you," he agreed. "And what's more, this has been such an enjoyably unconventional start to my day, I'll throw in a discount on my usual rate."

"My cousin Laith will be delighted to hear it."

Athela turned to face forward again, wondering why she should possibly feel so elated at the prospect that Archer had decided to join them, and why she was starting to feel the slightest edge of regret that she'd ordered him to keep his hands away. *You are being an idiot*, she told herself firmly. *Clearly, there is something in the trapped air beneath this house that is impairing your judgment.* Sternly, she resolved to put her personal guard right back up just as soon as they had extricated themselves from their ridiculous predicament.

When finally Archer murmured that it was safe for them to venture out, Athela had to admit that they had been right to wait. The streets around them were completely deserted and blissfully devoid of the clanking of armor or the pounding of horses' hooves. They slipped from their hideaway without issue, relieved to be able to stretch their limbs and take deep gulps of cool spring air. For all the forced intimacy of the past half hour, Athela found herself suddenly feeling strangely embarrassed, and had trouble making eye contact with Archer or even answering his questions with anything more than a clipped monosyllable. If he noticed a change in her behavior, he said nothing. With his help, they once more took to the roofs and began to make their way back to where their companions were stowed safely away in the false chimney across town. The Jelani guards were nowhere to be seen.

Laith, Tarr, Marc, and Si were duly extricated and spirited swiftly across town to Archer's safehouse. Their voyage this time was much smoother and easier without a troop of Jelani soldiers chasing after them. Archer was rather vague about the details of who exactly owned the safehouse or how he'd first come across it (evidently, it wasn't his primary place of residence), so Tarr didn't know quite what to expect, having never seen a safehouse before. Upon arrival, he was overjoyed to find that it was outfitted with a delightful hidden entrance located behind a trash chute, and found himself wondering why all human homes didn't bother to have secret entrances when they made the act of coming and going so much more enjoyable.

Also key to the security of the place was a dour-looking woman keeping watch over the street from the balcony above. The woman made no gesture of welcome as they approached, merely took a deep inhale of smoke from a long, curving pipe fixed firmly within her withered grasp. This woman, Archer informed them in a low voice, was eternally indebted to him as he'd been instrumental in helping her husband "disappear" the year before.

The safehouse itself wound up being much more comfortable than any of the other hiding places they'd endured so far that day. It was clearly a place where Archer stayed only when he was on the move or needed a quick place to hide, for it was spartanly outfitted with only the barest necessities of survival. It was one large room plus a narrow hallway lined with shelves leading to a lavatory tucked at the far back of the house. There was a single bed, a couple of chairs, a table, but almost no other furniture. There were, however, a number of stiff cots stacked under the bed that Archer drew out and placed around the floor for them to sit on. He lit a few oil lamps and went to the fireplace in one corner to start a fire and boil some water. He offered them all tea, and once he'd seen to it that they were comfortably situated, he quickly departed to try and track down Rane, who had earlier left them to go and try to recover their things from the inn where they'd been staying.

Tarr couldn't help but feel worried about Rane. He hadn't any doubt of her abilities, but the thought of her having to manage hiding six horses, all their knapsacks and saddlebags, weapons, and Tarr's white wolf—all without being spotted by the Jelani guards—seemed like a tall order.

The others were exhausted from the day's events, so they talked very little, and Si actually fell asleep on his cot a short while after Archer left. Athela especially was acting even more reserved than usual and seemed to be deeply absorbed in her own thoughts. Tarr wondered what had happened when she'd gone off to hide with Archer after they'd had to separate. He hoped Archer hadn't tried anything with her, but he knew Athela well enough to get the sense that if he had, Archer would currently be missing some of his limbs.

After about an hour, there was a small noise at the door and Tarr and the others immediately tensed up. A moment later, Archer's tall frame filled the door and he entered, followed by Rane and, to Tarr's relief, Wolver.

Tarr leapt up immediately and walked over to the wolf, patting him gratefully on the head and scratching him behind one ear. Wolver gave a single, rather irritated sweep of his tail but accepted Tarr's welcome, as if to say *you've no idea of the day I've had.*

"Sorry, old fellow," Tarr muttered. "Things took a turn after we left."

Archer had two knapsacks slung over his shoulder. He set them heavily down by the door, then disappeared and reappeared a few more times until all their weapons and belongings were arrayed on the floor. As the edge of a bag fell back and revealed Morthenstar's glittering ruby sword, Tarr saw the Ashan's golden eyes flick up and down its length, and his gray eyebrows rise ever so slightly. Rane came in like a quiet shadow and made for the corner of the room, where a stone pitcher and wash basin sat next to a water pump. She poured the water and splashed a few handfuls over her face and neck, then rubbed her face with the edge of her sleeve. Whatever she had done and wherever she had been that day, it had taken a great deal of work.

Archer latched the door and locked it carefully behind him, then turned away and began to distribute the saddlebags and knapsacks to their owners. As Tarr reached out for his, Archer gave him a curious, searching look with his piercing yellow eyes before wordlessly handing him the bag and turning back around.

Tarr resumed his seat and glanced around at their group. Athela seemed to be fixated on one of the buckles on her saddlebag, and was pointedly not making eye contact with anyone else. Over on his cot, Si momentarily sat up and rubbed his eyes, then almost immediately lay back down and went to sleep. Tarr felt a sudden, unexpected wave of grateful affection for them. They'd all been lucky to survive.

"So?" Laith prompted expectantly, his dark eyes following Archer across the room.

"All is taken care of," Archer sat down with a heavy creak on the side of the bed, removing his coat and beginning to unlace one of his boots. His neck curved against the lamplight, and Tarr peered towards him with interest. There was no family tattoo on the back of his neck, not even the tattoo of his own tribe. *Odd,* he thought. Perhaps, like him, he had not been Chosen by one of the Ashan families in his tribe. Maybe he had been sent out and simply stayed away. This was common enough; many of the Ashans living in Two Falls and the surrounding area had done the same. But Archer was only a few years older than he was, and from the bits of information he had been able to glean, it sounded as though he had been living in the human cities for much longer than only a handful of years. Perhaps whichever tribe he was from did their Choosing at an earlier age. Tarr was dying to pepper Archer with these questions, but had to satisfy himself by stealing glances at him every now and again.

"Everything is taken care of?" Laith repeated. "Meaning...?"

"Meaning Rane over there did much of the work," Archer nodded in Rane's direction. As the others turned around to look at her, she gave an ironic salute with the stone pitcher. "Apparently, your wolf," he nodded towards Tarr, "did a good job of watching over that big old sword in your room; the guards didn't want to go near him. And then they all lit out after you, leaving your belongings unprotected."

"I moved them to a secure location," Rane murmured.

"A dustbin," Archer clarified.

"You put Morthenstar's Whitsun sword in a *dustbin*?" Laith asked, aghast. Rane and Archer raised their eyebrows expectantly, as if to say, *what else should we have done?* Laith swallowed a bit, and Tarr could see him forcibly trying to push aside the indignities that the sword had suffered. "Well, it's safe, at least," he sighed. "Go on."

"How did you hide the horses?" Marc asked keenly, as if Rane and Archer were a pair of magicians about to unveil the secret behind their latest sleight of hand.

"The girl, Silva, who we met at the market today," Rane said with a shrug. "I went to see her and explained the situation, and she and her brother took a different route on their way out from the market when they brought their horses back to stable them for the night. And they just happened to collect our horses along the way."

"They're staying out towards the north end of the city, where there's a large stable with stalls to rent," Archer added. "We can collect your horses from there anytime."

"That's a rather neat job," Laith said appreciatively. "Well done, both of you."

"My guess is that once the Jelani guards who were after you return to the inn and find your things gone and the stable empty, they'll assume that you took off and left town. Only once they get to the north road to Two Falls, there won't be any of your tracks for them to find. That

particular trail will have gone cold. And I..." here, Archer coughed delicately, "may have suggested to a few of my favorite malleable tavern-go-
ers that your group rode southwest. It's reasonable to assume that that
information will reach the people looking for you."

For the first time since they'd escaped from Joymaril, Tarr let out
a truly liberated sigh of relief.

"Archer, there hasn't been word of another Jelani rider arriving in
town, has there?" Laith asked suddenly. "A young woman? She wouldn't
have been part of the troop coming after us. She would have been on
her own."

Archer frowned thoughtfully, but shook his head after a moment.
"Not as far as I know," he said slowly. "I would have heard by now. The
whole town lit up at the news that you lot had come in. There would
have been talk about someone else." His look was quizzical, as if he
expected Laith to explain further, but the prince merely looked down
at his hands, his face crestfallen.

"She must have gone to Two Falls," Marc consoled him. "Maybe
she's waiting there for us."

"Maybe," Laith agreed, sounding unconvinced.

"So, you're coming with us, then?" Marc asked Archer with interest.

"You all made a very persuasive argument today," Archer agreed,
and Tarr thought that he saw the Ashan send a glance towards Athela,
who was studiously facing the other way.

"Good," Marc said, sounding relieved.

"How much?" Laith asked, his tone suddenly businesslike.

Archer waved a long hand. "Negotiable. We can talk about it on
the way there."

"He promised a discount," Athela said suddenly. Tarr thought he
detected a fraction of warmth in her expression before it flickered away.

"That I did," Archer grinned. "A pointy elbow discount."

This was obviously some sort of inside joke, and neither Tarr nor
Laith asked what he meant, though Tarr detected a blush rising in Athela's cheek as she turned.

"When do we leave?" Marc asked as he rolled up his coat and carefully wedged it under Si's sleeping head as a sort of pillow.

"I'll check with my informants later tonight to confirm that the

Joymaril guard is indeed heading southwest looking for you. And then we should leave under cover of darkness tomorrow morning." Archer stretched his long arms behind him, and Tarr couldn't help but feel a twinge of relief that they would soon be leaving Riddleton.

"That's awfully soon; don't you have to wrap up your affairs here? Say goodbye to friends? Let out your apartment?" Marc inquired.

Archer made a noncommittal movement with his shoulders. "That's one good thing about Riddleton," he grinned. "People come and go all the time, and no one thinks much of it." His yellow eyes traveled down to Si's makeshift pillow and over to Wolver, curled up by the fire, then to Laith, who barely stifled a yawn. "Here," he volunteered. "I have a few sheets and pillows and things in the cupboards back there. I'll bring some out, and you all can get some rest before we leave tomorrow."

"I'll help," Tarr volunteered suddenly, springing to his feet.

He followed Archer across the living room and down the narrow hallway towards the lavatory. Archer paused in front of one of the hallway cabinets and pulled the doors open. There were stacks of linens neatly folded inside, and he began to withdraw them and pile them onto Tarr's waiting arms.

"Been a while since I've had need of these," he observed, counting the sheets beneath his breath. "I think I had pillows back here somewhere..."

"I'm Tarr, by the way," Tarr said.

"Nice to meet you," Archer said pleasantly. "Do you think we'll need coverlets? I think I only have two." He glanced over towards Athela, clearly trying to determine whether or not she was the type of person to need a coverlet.

Tarr was somewhat disappointed. He had hoped that Archer would start speaking in Ashan to him once he'd introduced himself. He was determined to try again and switched to his native language. "What tribe are you..."

"I don't speak it," Archer said curtly, not looking at him. "I've forgotten."

"Oh," Tarr said, momentarily abashed. He couldn't imagine forgetting how to speak Ashan. Archer must have left his tribe a very, very long time ago. *But why?*

"I think Kai left me a quilt back here," Archer muttered to himself, leaning forward into the linen cabinet so that he was half obscured from view.

"What tribe are you?" Tarr asked, this time in Common. He had no idea why Archer was being so evasive.

Slowly, Archer withdrew and turned to briefly meet Tarr's eyes. He seemed to think for a long time. "Birch," he said finally.

Tarr was shocked, but did his best to hide it. If Archer was indeed a member of the Birch tribe, that did something to explain his strange looks. The Birch were the northernmost Ashan tribe and lived in the foothills of the mountains. They were the most insular, the most exclusive, and also the strictest tribe. Other than the vaguest of details, not much was known about them, even to other Ashans. Tarr had certainly never heard of one of their members making their way so far south. Even when the Birch left to find mates, it was said that they ranged further north to the uncharted lands beyond the mountains.

"How did you end up—" Tarr began, but quickly stopped when Archer heaved a sigh, swung towards him, and faced him straight on with another piercing stare from his yellow eyes. That look told Tarr everything he needed to know.

How do you think I ended up here? his expression said.

Tarr felt his throat go dry and stood there, immobile, as Archer turned away and laid the last sheet atop the pile he'd accumulated. "That should do it," he concluded, and without another word, he walked past Tarr and back into the main room. Mutely, feeling as though his legs had gone numb, Tarr followed, almost unable to stop staring at the back of Archer's head.

He was exiled from his tribe, he repeated to himself. *He's an exile. A real exile.*

Being exiled from one's tribe was the very worst punishment reserved for only the worst sort of Ashan criminal. Exiles, Tarr had been taught since birth, were not to be trusted; they were held up as characters to frighten children into good behavior. Exiles were the kind who would lie, steal, cheat, or kill. The kind who always placed their needs ahead of those of others or the needs of the tribe. Tarr was now uncomfortably aware of the presence of evil standing there in the room only five feet away from him, and watched him walking around handing out bedsheets to his other companions as if he were the most innocent creature in the world. Only Tarr seemed to be aware of the mask he was wearing, the ravenous beast behind the virtuous face.

He had to do something. He had to warn the others against trusting Archer, against having anything more to do with him than they already had. *But would they understand?* he wondered. His friends knew so little about Ashans and their culture that the magnitude of who and what Archer was might not resonate with them as soundly as it should. Were they already tainted, just from the brief amount of contact they'd had with him?

With a rush of fear, Tarr wondered suddenly whether having consorted with an exile as much as he had already would be grounds for the Aspen tribe not to let him back in once the year was up and he could return home. It was forbidden to speak with or to associate in any way with an exile in the forest, but did the same hold true outside the tribal borders? He simply couldn't be sure. There seemed no way of avoiding him now, not without completely abandoning the others, quitting the safehouse, and wandering out into the night to find alternate lodging in Riddleton alone. That idea didn't hold much appeal.

Laith and the others were set on having Archer as their guide, and he was doubtful as to whether or not he could convince them of Archer's capacity for evildoing, at least not without concrete evidence to show them. He would simply have to be careful, that's all, and would have to convey his tacit displeasure to Archer by not speaking to him and having as little to do with him as possible. He would hold his head high and maintain the standards and laws set by the tribe so that when he returned, he could speak of his actions with pride.

Thus resolved, he made his way back to the cot, where Archer had already dropped an extra sheet for him. Gingerly, using his thumb and forefinger as though the sheet were already soiled, he shook it out flat and laid it over the cot, thinking with a sudden rush of homesickness of the sleeping mats where he and the other young Ashans had slept throughout his childhood. *Make them proud*, he told himself firmly. With great dignity, he bunched up his knapsack beneath his head for a pillow and settled himself down to sleep.

But he soon found that, now that he knew who Archer really was, his mind was much too active to allow himself to drift off easily. He decided to keep an eye on the other Ashan for as long as he could stay awake, just in case the Archer made some attempt to kill the others in their sleep and perhaps make off with Morthenstar's sword to sell it for money. It was exactly the sort of thing, Tarr thought grimly, that an exile would do.

So he kept the sliver of one eye open, and followed Archer with his gaze as he crossed the room, blew out one of the lanterns, and crouched beside Athela, who also was turned away from him and also seemed to be pretending to sleep.

"You're welcome to the bed," Archer whispered to her in a low voice. "I can take the cot."

"I'm quite all right, thank you," Athela told him, her tone icy. *At least Athela seems to have the right idea about him,* Tarr thought with satisfaction. Perhaps he'd be able to convince her, if not the others.

Archer gave a nonplussed shrug and stood back up. He padded silently in his long bare feet back over to the remaining lantern, which was perched on a rickety table across the room. He leaned over and fiddled with the knob for a moment or two. Suddenly, Tarr felt Archer's yellow gaze turn on him, and for an instant he imagined that the corner of the Ashan's mouth twisted up in a smile, as if he could sense that Tarr was watching him. Then, a moment later, Archer gave a little puff of breath and the light was extinguished in a twisting curl of blue smoke.

CHAPTER TEN

Archer insisted that they leave Riddleton under cover of darkness (the better to avoid being seen by unfriendly eyes), so a few hours before dawn, they slipped out of the safehouse and made their way to the north side of the city, where their horses had been hidden in the stable alongside those belonging to Silva and her brother. All was quiet, and no one appeared to be watching the stables very closely, so Athela and the other Jelani had them saddled and ready in record time. Archer hung close by the entrance of the stable, keeping a lookout for any suspicious-looking passersby. The city, fortunately, appeared to be fast asleep.

A short while later, they were all assembled outside. The horizon had just begun to grow pink, silhouetting the sharp, jagged edges of the houses spreading off to the east. It took Laith and Marc two minutes to hold Athela's horse still enough for her to leap onto the saddle. Once they let go of their grips on the bit, the gray bunched its neck against Athela's firm hold on its mouth, pawing the stones beneath its sharp black hoof and giving little bounding leaps. Athela sat quietly, and Tarr marveled at another display of her excellent balance and patience with the excitable horse. Wolver, sitting beside Tarr, watched the horse's antics with an aloof sort of dignity, as if to say *I would never resort to such base theatrics.*

"Keep him quiet!" Laith cautioned Athela with a nervous glance around at the surrounding houses. Tarr looked up, swallowing anxiously. No lights had been lit behind the shuttered windows; with any luck the neighbors were still fast asleep.

Athela gritted her teeth and hauled on Aria's head until there was nowhere else for him to go. The horse snorted angrily and vented his frustration by slamming his hindquarters skittishly into Laith's and Marc's horses, who dealt with it with the equine equivalent of an eye roll, clearly used to this sort of behavior.

Archer eyed Athela's horse warily and cleared his throat loudly. "I have an announcement," he said. "I don't really do horses. I'll walk."

"You can't ride?" Laith asked.

"I *can* ride," Archer replied. "I choose not to."

"Come on," Athela snapped as Aria made another circle, tossing his head angrily. "It'll take less time if you're on horseback."

"It won't if your flighty nutter kills me first," Archer said darkly, shooting Aria a look of deep suspicion. The horse pinned his ears back and leered unpleasantly at him.

"Ride behind me," Laith suggested. "I'll steer. You sit."

Tarr could see that Archer didn't like this, but he sized Arfolasth up, decided the black horse looked placid enough, clenched his teeth, and walked forward. "The minute we're not running," he said, "I am on the ground walking like I was designed to do."

They set off at a good pace, the horses' hooves raising what seemed like an enormous racket to Tarr's ears as they trotted down the winding stone streets of Riddleton. At first, Tarr was concerned that the noise would wake the entire town and bring them straight to their windows to see what the fuss was about, but there was barely any movement in the city at all. Here and there, a shopkeeper was wandering out of the front of his or her building, sleepy-eyed and bleary, but otherwise the streets were blissfully deserted. Archer gave them instructions regarding the fastest way out of the city, and it was a significant relief when they left the paved roads and emerged onto a dirt path leading them north towards Two Falls. As the buildings of Riddleton fell behind them and slowly disappeared around a bend in the path, Tarr took a deep breath, overwhelmingly glad to leave Riddleton behind him. The city had given him an uneasy feeling, like someone had been watching him out of the corner of their eye the moment he had set foot within its borders. It had neither the grandeur of Joymaril nor the sense of history of Two Falls, and had always seemed as though it were about one strong wind away from crumbling into utter decay. *Good riddance*, he thought, and looked ahead up the path that lay before him.

Once they had cleared Riddleton and joined the main road towards Two Falls, they settled into a brisk walk to save the horses' energy and Archer, true to his word, slid immediately off of Arfolasth to walk beside them on foot. He had a long stride, being well over six feet tall, and was able to easily keep pace. The seven of them grouped close together to hear the ongoing conversations better.

"Why exactly are we going to Two Falls again?" Si inquired.

"Our priority right now is to try and find the heir of Morthenstar," Athela informed them. "She's out there somewhere. We have to find her and help her. That's the most important thing. And the biggest clue we have to go on is that Morthenstar hid the prophecy leading to her heir somewhere in the Two Falls library."

"The *library?*" Si asked dubiously. "Why did she hide it in the *library?*"

Because the library is the best place of all, Tarr thought fondly.

"Two Falls existed before Morthenstar was born, but the modern layout of the city and many of the major buildings there were designed by Morthenstar herself," Laith pointed out. "Including the library, which is one of the oldest surviving buildings that she commissioned. And all of that makes it more likely that if there are more clues leading to the heir's identity, they will likely be hidden somewhere in Two Falls as well."

"Not to mention that from a tactical standpoint, Two Falls is right in the center of everything—close to Faridor, relatively close to the palace of Joymaril, right on the border of the Forest...we want to be placed so that if something happens, we'll be the first to hear about it," Athela added.

"True," Marc agreed. "More eyes and ears, though, make it likely that someone will pass along who we are and what we're doing to people who might want to know that information."

"Then we have to be careful," Laith said simply. "We take

precautions with who we decide to trust. Who we tell."

This struck Tarr as a problem. How on earth would any of them know who could be relied upon and who couldn't? The Jelani had lived their whole lives in the palace and were probably only slightly more familiar with Two Falls and its people than *he* was. Si had been born and raised in Riddleton and had seen little of the outside world. The only person who might have any real connections to the city was Archer, and Tarr wouldn't trust him any farther than he could throw him. Perhaps even less.

Almost as if he'd heard Tarr's train of thought, Archer piped up. "I still have quite a few friends and acquaintances from the time I lived in Two Falls. It should be easy enough to reach out to them."

No, Tarr thought forcefully, and nearly opened his mouth to say so aloud. After a moment, though, he hesitated and sat back on his horse. *Maybe I'll try to warn Athela.* He remembered the coldness with which she had addressed Archer the night before, and hoped that her predisposition not to like or trust strangers would work in his favor.

"Good," said Laith. "It's very important, all of you, that when we get there you make efforts to create connections with different people throughout the city. People who hear things and will be likely to pass on any rumors or gossip to us. If all this is true, and if the prophecy is real—"

It's not, Tarr thought to himself reflexively.

"—then while we're looking for Morthenstar's heir, we have to be just as wary that Kagai's heir might be somewhere as well."

Tarr was amused to see Si's face go slightly pale. The boy glanced over his shoulder, seemingly concerned that Kagai's heir might be lurking behind one of the nearby thickets of wild primroses.

It still seemed quite unlikely to Tarr that anyone's heirs were likely to come popping willy-nilly out of the woodwork, but he was nevertheless happy to be returning to Two Falls. His first sojourn there had been cut short by the unexpected arrival of the Jelani and being whisked off to the palace of Joymaril with them. There was still much of the city that he wanted to see and explore, and it pleased him to think that he might have a chance to do so—especially that there may be some work to do in the library. Perhaps once they reached the city and settled in, they could discontinue Archer's services as well. Tarr would feel much better once the other Ashan had left them and returned to the dregs of Riddleton where he belonged.

As the hours slid by, Tarr enjoyed the sight of the sun slowly creeping up over the eastern hills and morning settling upon the countryside, fresh and dewy. In their frenzy to flee Joymaril, he hadn't given himself much time to enjoy the beauty of the spring that had come to bloom across the land, but now he could take it in at his leisure. The road had brought them into the basin of a broad, shallow valley and ran along the high bank of a beautiful blue rushing river (the same river, Tarr realized eventually, that must run through Two Falls and cascade down to the forest.) Along the banks of the river, dotted here and there beside the path and up the gently sloping hills around them were coarse thickets of wild roses, blooming yellow and white and blushing pink. Beyond that, in the spread of the valley's shallow basin, were carpets of wildflowers: bluebells and sunny little yellow buds, waves of shimmering grass rippling to and fro in the breeze. Clusters of aspen leaves flickered in the wind like clouds of fluttering green butterflies. Tarr could see Athela and Laith taking in the sights around them with deep appreciation. He was glad they seemed to like it, too.

He remembered suddenly one afternoon in the gardens at Joymaril when he'd gone up to a brilliantly spreading rose blooming boldly out from a carved white trellis. It had clearly been showered with love by its keepers, and had been pruned and primped and carefully cultivated to look its best, yellow petals blushing into rose just at the tips. Tarr had gone up to it and taken a deep inhale, expecting the lovely peppery fragrance to come wafting up in a cloud over him, but to his surprise, the rose had had no scent at all. It was no match for the beauty of a wild primrose, he thought.

And then, almost unconsciously, his mind slid to Rane.

Startled by the abruptness of the change in his train of thought, he caught himself and stole a glance at her. She swayed quietly in her saddle, regarding the landscape with her level gaze. Smiling at his own folly, he shook his head and gazed back out over the sweep of the land, watching contentedly as Wolver gave a buoyant leap over a large plume of grass.

By late afternoon, Tarr could make out a thin line of buildings appearing at the bottom of a sloping hill. With a sweep in his chest, he realized that they were drawing close to the city of Two Falls. Their path began to diverge slightly from the riverbank they'd been following and pointed them out into an enormous open field, across which Two Falls slowly began to pull into view and take form.

All at once, there was a flurry of motion out of the corner of Tarr's eye, and he realized that Marc was pulling up his horse on the side of the road, a look of concern on his face.

"What's up, Marc?" Laith asked.

"Give me a second," Marc said, and dismounted. He bent down and began inspecting the path beside them. He turned and ran off to the right, eyes still on the ground. Tarr tried to look around and find what it was he had seen, but nothing came to him. He watched in bewilderment as Marc ran off about twenty yards away, then knelt and faced the sloping hill that led up to the faraway line of woods beyond.

"Fascinating little ritual," Archer observed, his folded arms resting atop Si's horse's neck. "Does he perform this often?"

"Something's up," Laith murmured, looking after his bodyguard.

Marc finally came running back down to them and stopped beside Laith's horse. "Riders," he said. "A gigantic troop of them. Passed by a few days ago and tried to do their best to cover up their tracks."

"That's not so unusual," Archer countered. "There's a lot of traffic into Two Falls. It could have just been a band of peddlers or something."

"This is different," Marc shook his head. "The horses were all shod, and they didn't actually go into Two Falls. They came along this road just until they were in sight of the city, then they veered off into those trees." He motioned to the grove at the top of the hill.

"More riders from Joymaril?" Athela asked tentatively.

"Maybe. If there are as many as Marc says there are, it wouldn't end well if it came to a confrontation," Laith pointed out.

"They may have a harder time getting their hands on you in Two Falls," Archer pointed out. "The city government is less friendly to anyone who wants to ride into town and make arrests. They wouldn't look kindly on troops of Jelani riders cruising around. They have their own officers, their own law enforcement. It's not like in Riddleton, where everyone can pretty much do what they like."

"That's comforting," Athela muttered.

After a few more moments of searching, Marc mounted back up on his horse. Tarr remained motionless, his brow furrowed as he looked at the ground. "Marc," he said suddenly, "how old would you say these tracks were?"

Marc pulled up and faced him. Beside him, Archer ventured off the path and examined the tracks himself.

"Three, four days, maybe?" Marc suggested.

"I'd make it three," Archer corroborated, peering down at the ground.

"It can't have been the Jelani troop that came after us, then," Tarr said slowly. "We were only in Riddleton yesterday and the night before that."

Tarr noticed out of the corner of his eye that Rane was now staring at him curiously, an interested expression knitting a slight crease between her eyes.

"Maybe they sent out two patrols. One to Riddleton, one to Two Falls," Athela suggested.

Tarr hesitated to reply, realizing that the others all probably knew much more about tracks than he did. But the timing simply didn't add up, and he couldn't help himself. He pointed. "If it was three days, then they would have left *before* we even tried to escape from Joymaril."

"I could be wrong," Marc shrugged.

"Even so," Tarr persisted, "Once they found our trail towards Riddleton, they would know where we went. And if a troop of Jelani *was* riding towards Two Falls, why wouldn't they just take the path into the city? Why did they leave it to go hide up in the woods?"

"Maybe they were heading back to Joymaril," Athela replied, and Tarr could hear that she was beginning to get exasperated with him. He decided to let it drop, and gave a shrug before picking his reins back up, taking longer than he needed to so he wouldn't have to meet the others' eyes.

"He's right, though. If someone was riding from Riddleton to Joymaril, they wouldn't go this way. It'd be completely illogical." Archer said slowly, and Tarr's eyes shot up. Archer had his arms folded across his chest now and was regarding Tarr with an expression almost identical to Rane's, thoughtful and assessing. "I don't think these tracks were made by the Joymarillian riders who came after you lot back in Riddleton."

"I suppose we can't know *who* it was, so we'll just be careful," Laith asserted firmly. He, too, was ready to move along.

"It could be nothing," Athela pointed out. "Some group of travelers or a patrol from the city. Merchants. Nothing related to us."

There was finality in her tone, and Tarr could see that the conversation was over. Their group moved forward and continued along the road towards Two Falls. But even as they did—and even as he pretended not to be aware of it—Tarr was deeply conscious that Archer was still watching him, golden eyes boring into the back of his head.

After another hour's ride, they pulled up to the southern limits of Two Falls, which consisted of a small, mostly ornamental gate where two guards stopped them and asked them their business. It was strange to think that it had only been a month before that Tarr had emerged from the forest at the northern border, worrying about whether the guards would admit him into the city. It seemed like three lifetimes ago.

Laith spoke directly to the guards himself, and his manner was so steady and reassuring that it was barely a few seconds more before they were waved through. Tarr noticed that Archer was purposefully keeping himself somewhat obscured from the guards' view; he had his hood up over his head, and he had let his gaze wander off in a distant direction so that he could face away from them. Tarr wondered again, with a sickened lurch in his stomach, what sort of crimes Archer was guilty of committing to have been exiled from his tribe, and what sort of crimes he might still wind up committing against them.

Cleared to enter, the group moved forward. The guards looked curiously at Wolver, but otherwise let them pass without further comment.

"Where's a good place for us to stay, Archer?" Athela asked.

Archer turned back around, sweeping the black hood off of his hair with one hand. His white and black tipped spikes were mussed and sticking out here and there, giving him the appearance of a bird that had ruffled its feathers. He squinted, thinking, then his expression cleared. "It's been a while since I've been back here, but I know of a nice old lady who'd be happy to put us up," he said finally. "She runs a boardinghouse, mostly for students at the Two Falls Academy, but with any luck, she has some rooms open as the spring term is likely out. It's this way, follow me."

Archer began to lead them north through the streets, some of which Tarr realized he recognized from his brief wanderings in the city the morning before he'd met up with Laith and the others. But whereas Tarr could only identify a shop window here or there and knew major landmarks like the main square and the fountain with the carved fish, Archer skimmed through the back alleyways with the greatest of ease, like he was following some sort of internal map. Whatever his past life had been, it had obviously given him a close familiarity with Two Falls' layout, and Tarr begrudgingly had to admit that they were lucky to have him as their guide.

After making their way through the western neighborhoods of the city, they stopped in front of a homey-looking house with no name sign over the door, just the traditional six-pointed star carved into the frame.

"Place for the horses is out back," he told them, dismounting. "I'll go in and see if Ma is inside." Everyone followed his example and began to dismount. Marc was keeping a wary eye and ear on the street behind them. Looking back, Tarr briefly locked eyes with Rane, managing a nervous smile at her before her head disappeared behind the side of her horse.

"This is a boarding house," Archer said behind Tarr. "It's a bit like the inn where you stayed in Riddleton, only the people tend to live here for a longer period of time."

Tarr said nothing, merely watching Archer in stony silence for a few seconds before the Ashan gave him a sideways smile and turned away. Tarr was shocked at being addressed so directly, and felt that he had done the right thing by making it clear to Archer he would have nothing to do with him. Still, he had to admit that he was grateful for the information about the boarding house. It was one less thing for him to feel stupid about. Humans and Jelani, he reflected, seemed to have an infinite variety of places to stay and sleep: taverns and inns and boarding houses and palaces and apartments—even safehouses and hideaways.

The inside of the boardinghouse was cheery and cluttered, meticulously decorated with poufy little chairs and candles and bunches of flowers gathered in vases at the windows and at the tables, some of which were drooping slightly and had dripped leaves onto the carpet. Tarr immediately got the sense of the personality that had decorated the house: someone fond of pretty things, a bit fussy, with a tendency to collect and hoard both belongings and old memories. It was a far cry from the stark but beautiful austerity of Ashan homes, and an even farther cry from the opulent grandeur of the Jelani palace, but Tarr at once felt at home. The chairs looked like they were almost begging to be sat in, a hearty fire roared away on one side of the room, and bookcases were lined up against the wall, crammed full of papers and old, worn books. A tinkly bell tolled away as the door closed, and a cheery voice called "Com-ing!" from another room.

"This is very nice," Laith commented appreciatively, looking around the room. There was a smell wafting in tantalizingly from the general direction of where the voice had been, a smell that was warm and full that Tarr recognized from home.

"Fresh bread baking," Archer said, almost as if he had read Tarr's mind. Tarr shot a glance over at him again, and realized that Archer had been watching him out of one eye. Tarr ignored him and took a step back and away, under the pretense of examining a small cup resting atop one of the tables. He wished Archer would leave him alone.

"You can put the bag down," Archer instructed Marc, who was standing at the door with one of the saddlebags. No sooner had he done so but a small, rotund little woman with wispy gray hair tucked away in a bun came bustling in and positively clapped her hands with delight at the sight of the tall white Ashan in her room, waddling forward to be received into the gigantic bear hug that Archer presented her.

"Archer! You'll knock my hair loose!" she chortled, backing away.

"Good to see you, Ma," Archer beamed at her.

"She's your *mother*?" Si wrinkled his nose incredulously.

"Strange forces are at work here," Marc raised his eyebrows suspiciously.

The tiny woman laughed. "Oh, no, not really, everyone calls me that. Do you think that if he was my child he'd ever get to be that skinny?" She looked disapprovingly at Archer's tall, slim frame, shaking her head. She beamed again, looking around at all of the others clustered around her living room. "Have you brought some friends to see me? And a wolf, how nice!" She seemed equally delighted by the prospect of both the visitors and the large carnivorous animal sitting solemnly beside the stairwell.

"Yes, Ma, these are my friends. Think you could put all of us up for a little while?" Archer asked earnestly. "And don't try to give us the rooms for free, that never works."

The woman had stopped with her mouth open, ready to offer just that, it seemed. She gave Archer a glare, then sniffed. "Of course, dear, we're all open at the moment. Is anyone hungry?"

"Ma—" Archer began and shot the others a warning look.

"Look at *you*!" Ma shrieked, bustling forward and pulling Tarr's arm with surprising force, yanking him out of the group of others and inspecting him closely, measuring the size of his wrists with her thumb and forefinger and pulling his shirt tight over his stomach to see how small his waist was. She looked up at his face, took one glance at his sweetly tilted, melancholy-looking eyes, and seemed to make up her mind that he was in dire need of mothering.

"You're so thin!" she exclaimed. "Haven't they been feeding you, you poor dear?" Tarr, feeling decidedly uncomfortable, was unsure of what to say or how to protest without seeming rude to the kind little woman. She wasn't at all what he'd expected Archer's acquaintances to be. He'd anticipated a horde of unpleasant, unkempt, leering individuals not unlike the denizens of Riddleton. This woman was the polar opposite.

"He's fine, Ma, I promise," Archer said patiently.

The tinkly bell tolled again as Rane walked in and shut the door, eyes widening slightly as she took in the scene of Tarr being accosted by the tiny, plump little woman. Ma smiled kindly at Rane, who took up her usual position two strides behind Athela's left shoulder. Laith walked forward, leaning down slightly to be more in Ma's field of vision.

"We would be very honored if we could stay in your home for a while, it's a lovely place," he said politely. "We promise we won't take up too much space, and we won't cause you too much trouble."

"Aren't you polite? Such a handsome boy!" Ma's cheeks turned bright pink and she relinquished her hold on Tarr, who stepped back, blinking fast. She turned on Laith and pinched his cheek. "What's your name, young man?"

"Laith," he replied, blinking. Tarr guessed that Laith had never had his cheek pinched before in his life.

"Well, Laith, you can tell your parents from me that they did a good job raising you to be so well-behaved. Food is on the table in the kitchen, and heaven knows I'm not going to eat it all," she waved a hand around in a broad sweep, smiling indulgently.

An hour later they were all reeling, gripping their stomachs, filled to bursting with breads, cheeses, fruits—enough food to feed a group three times their number. Ma had been momentarily put out when she discovered that Tarr didn't eat any meat other than fish, but immediately redoubled her efforts by bringing out seemingly every non-meat food item housed in her kitchen. Archer, Tarr noted, ate meat without any qualms and actually seemed not to notice his food at all, as he was wrapped up in conversation with Laith and Athela.

Tarr himself had never been fretted over like this before. Ma stood hovering above his plate to cram in a new item of food every time that he managed to clear off a section so that he could see a glimmer of the dish below. It took some getting used to, but after a brief struggle of one-upmanship in which Tarr and Ma had both attempted to outdo the other with sheer politeness (Ma insisting he eat more, and Tarr kindly refusing), Tarr had relented. He wondered briefly whether all human homes operated this way, whether all children were tended to with such care and concern. It wasn't at all what he'd been used to back in the forest.

The rest of the day was spent settling into their new home. The house, which seemed fairly modest from the ground floor, had many more floors stretching above it, and though Ma had recently had a few student boarders, they had all left for the spring holidays and she was able to offer them the top three floors all to themselves. "The rooms will be small, but there will be almost a room for each one of you," she told them, ushering them up a twisting, rickety staircase without a banister. "The girls can share if they like, or Archer, you and your Ashan friend can bunk together."

Tarr sent her a wild look, but was comforted when Archer instantly demurred and changed the subject.

Once they'd reached the top step, Archer looked up and out of the window on the landing. "We'll stay here for a while and then go out once it's dark," he told her. "We'll be back before dawn."

"Be careful, dear," she said and bustled back down the stairs.

The others had already split up to go find their rooms, and Archer and Tarr were left standing awkwardly on the landing.

"Why don't you take that one?" Archer asked, indicating the room to Tarr's right. "I'll see if there's still one open below."

Tarr nodded silently. He wondered why Archer didn't seem put out by his clear refusal to speak to him. Maybe he wasn't conveying his disapproval strongly enough. Resolving to be even more firm in his convictions, he opened the door to his room and went inside, Wolver close on his heel.

The room within was small and simple. A bed, a chair, a small table—everything spotlessly clean and neatly kept. Tarr laid his knapsack on the floor and sat down on the mattress, which creaked and groaned as it gave way. Over his shoulder, the evening moon began to peek out over the tops of the roofs of the city, intermingling with the light from the setting sun.

The evening was settling into an inky blue as they walked, and a night mist crept along the alleyways and around the corners of the houses like a silvery snake wending its way through the city. Tarr stood on the stoop beside Ma's house and watched transfixed as the townspeople went about lighting the yellow lanterns strung along across the tops of the streets, casting their pretty pools of light down to the ground. The glowing orbs swayed back and forth in the wind, and Tarr stood beneath them for a good minute or so before he realized that the entire group had left him—save Archer, who was watching him with a curious look on his face.

"Reminds you of the forest, doesn't it?" Archer asked quietly.

"Beautiful," Tarr smiled before he could catch himself. Then he snapped back to reality, and almost angrily tried to think of something to say to Archer to put him in his place, but Archer merely watched him for a moment or so with that odd, almost wistful half-smile on his face before turning away.

"Don't fall behind," he said over his shoulder. "This place is hard to navigate after dark."

Tarr gave an Ashan curse under his breath and jogged to catch up with the others.

Their path led to a different side of town, which Tarr hadn't visited in his previous exploration of Two Falls, an area just west of the older section of town. In this area, Archer insisted, the real heart of Two Falls' nightlife lay, and would be the best place to lay the groundwork and make connections that could alert them to any important developments related to their search. "There's an even seedier district if the need arises," he informed them as they all passed beneath a stone archway that led into this new part of the city. "But you'll find there are more musicians here and fewer bounty hunters out for blood. Both have their uses."

"Musicians?" Athela asked drily. "We'll definitely need musicians."

"Anyway, we absolutely have to stop by this one place first, as long as she hasn't moved or changed locations—"

"Where's Laith?" Marc asked suddenly.

The group stopped. The tall, handsome prince was nowhere in sight.

Marc grew visibly agitated. "Where could he have got to, that great idiot?" he snapped, glancing over his shoulder as though Laith was lurking there, waiting to spring out and make a fool of him. "He's basically got beams of sunlight radiating out of his ears; he's hard to miss, how could he have slipped out on us like that?"

"Better question is, why would he *want* to slip out on us like that?" Athela twisted around, squinting. "Well, if I know my cousin as well as I think I do, if he doesn't want to be found, then he won't be. He probably just wanted to look around town for himself."

"He could have *told* us," Marc grumbled, hands twisting anxiously on the hilt of his sword. Si, standing by Marc's side, began to look frightened and glanced over his shoulder before hunkering even closer to Marc.

"He'll be fine, I bet we'll see him again tomorrow morning," Athela assured them all firmly and began walking forward resolutely, indicating for them to follow along behind her. Archer frowned, but then shrugged it off and jogged a few steps to catch up with her, pointing out the route that they were going to take.

This district, whatever it was, had a unique feel to it that was different than the other areas of town Tarr had seen. It boggled his mind how one single city could have so many distinct neighborhoods. The one word Tarr could think of to describe it was *cluttered*. Pubs and inns were no longer just on the ground floor of buildings—there were taverns on the second and third floors, parties spilling out onto balconies, discordant music fighting for supremacy across opposite ends of the street. Some of the buildings looked quite old, as they had in other areas of town. Whereas in other sections of the city it seemed like new buildings had just been pasted atop the foundations of the old, here it seemed as though there had been a concerted effort to preserve the feeling of the ancient stone edifices. It was somewhat incongruous in Tarr's eyes to see a raging party echoing down from a stately stone balustrade that had likely stood there for the past three hundred years or so, but there was something charming and rather romantic about it, too. Tarr read the names of the establishments as they passed, his legs aching from the steady hike up the winding streets on the hill. He liked the fact that each of the buildings seemed to have a name. *Orion*, he read. *Rose and Thorn*. There was a sense of mystery and of glamour about this district, something both alluring and slightly dangerous, though the danger felt different than the seedy sort of lingering threat of Riddleton. This kind was exciting and thrilling.

In and out of pools of light they walked. Here, the streets were lit not by red and yellow lanterns hanging over the tops of the streets but by torches encased in iron cages and mounted on the tops of very tall poles placed at intervals along the roads. Tarr wondered if it was someone's job to go along and light them every night and to snuff them again in the morning.

"Many artists and musicians live around these parts," Archer breathed deeply in the cool night air. "Poets...songwriters. It's a wonderful place for the arts, and many of these old buildings have been here since the town was first built. They don't allow horses up here either, except in sanctioned stables."

"No horses?" Athela asked, sounding affronted. "Why no horses?"

"Something to do with keeping the integrity of the buildings and roads; horses are too rough on the streets. Ah...it should be around here..." he murmured, mostly to himself. He led them inside a building, under an archway that formed itself into a dark, narrow corridor. At the end of the passage, Tarr and the others found themselves in an octagonal courtyard with doors leading to different establishments on every side. Archer, not missing a beat, led them straight into one with a dark purple cloth over the entrance, the star of Morthenstar carved into the doorframe.

Inside, the club was packed but relatively quiet, with most of the patrons talking amongst themselves in hushed, respectful tones. There was a long, unending stream of solemn, quiet music emanating from a woman in one corner, who was holding some sort of flute and had a long braid over one shoulder. A few people at tables appeared to be painting; Tarr tried to peer over as inconspicuously as possible, but even with the advantage of his height couldn't see what it was they were working on. He got the sense that this place was the domain of artists and thinkers rather than those who wished to drink excessively and throw wild parties.

The club was divided into two levels. One was on the ground floor, and then there were a series of steps that led up to a higher platform with more tables and chairs. Tarr, by this point, had started to wonder what they were doing there or who they possibly could need to meet in such a place, and reluctantly followed the others up the stairs to the higher platform. They wound back through another doorway into what seemed like a very exclusive, private room tucked at the very far back of the building. There was a guard sitting by the door, ostensibly to keep unwanted visitors out, but to Tarr's surprise, they were admitted with a curt nod. Archer, it seemed, could go anywhere he liked. As they passed, Tarr was conscious that the man's watchful gaze had fastened upon the rest of them as they passed by him into the darkly lit room.

"Archer," came a female voice to the side. "I heard rumors you'd come back. It's been a long time."

Out of the shadows emerged a woman, whom Tarr immediately recognized to be Ashan (or was she? She had to have been part-Ashan at least.) She wasn't quite as tall as most Ashan women, but upon his close inspection he saw that she had the telltale sixth finger on one hand. She was a few years older than most of them, about the same age as Archer. She was a remarkable-looking young woman with thick black hair like the wing of a raven and lovely brown skin. She was wearing a dark purple dress that clung to her form, almost the same color as her eyes. In fact, purple seemed to be a theme with her, for as she turned her head to greet Archer, Tarr could see a purple birthmark blooming like a flower on the right side of her neck. After greeting Archer with a cordial kiss on his white cheek, she scanned the others with interest. Tarr shifted, slightly scandalized by their public intimacy.

They parted, and Archer swept his arm around the group. "Everyone, this is Rowan," he introduced her to each one in turn. Rowan's eyes peered out under black bangs, and then they stopped and rested squarely on Tarr.

"Pleasure to meet all of you," she murmured. "I'll remember your names, don't worry. I'm quite good at it." She was very pretty, Tarr noticed with a lurch in his stomach. Some of her raven hair slipped to one side off her shoulder and caught the light. "An Ashan, eh?" she said, looking him up and down with some surprise. "Straight from the forest, too, I'll wager. You have that look about you. Archer, where did you find him?"

"I'm from the Aspen tribe," Tarr said sharply, then, with a pointed jab in Archer's direction, added, "*Not* an exile."

"I see," she said silkily, not batting an eye.

"You'd already heard I was back, eh?" Archer asked with a rueful shake of his head. "Still got ears at every door, do you?"

She spread her hands innocently. "When it's news about *you*, Archer, I can assure you that I'm the first person anyone thinks to tell. And after you've been so long away, you must have a good reason for coming back."

Archer demurred, making an evasive gesture with his head. "How is Kai? Joris? The others?"

Rowan shrugged. Tarr didn't recognize the names of any of the people Archer had mentioned and felt his attention beginning to drift slightly. "Kai is in Vireg; I haven't heard from her for six months. Joris comes here when he can; you know how his parents are, always trying to shuttle him here or there to keep him out of trouble. I did see Persefea a few days ago. Apparently, she's fallen on hard times..."

They continued chatting as the others shifted listlessly and started staring around the room, trying to occupy themselves while Archer and Rowan caught up. A thought suddenly occurred to Tarr, and he took the opportunity to pull Marc and Athela to the side, out of earshot from Archer and Rowan. Si was across the room examining a sculpture on the mantelpiece; Rane was standing by the window, her eyes trained down on the street below.

"I wanted to warn you," Tarr said in a low voice, chancing a look over his shoulder to ensure that Archer was still occupied. "I don't think we should be too quick to trust Archer."

"Why not?" Marc shrugged casually. "He seems all right."

Tarr felt like shaking him. He rooted around for the words that could effectively convey who Archer truly was. "He's a criminal. An exile. To be exiled from your tribe, you must commit an unforgivable crime, one so bad that you lose all ties to your people and your family. You can barely be considered an Ashan anymore."

Marc still looked unconvinced, but Athela seemed to be listening to him closely. Tarr looked over his shoulder again and could see that Rowan's violet eyes were trained on him. Tarr turned urgently back to the others. "We need to be careful, that's all. We don't know what he did to be exiled, and we don't know what he's done since. And we don't know where his true loyalties lie."

"You think he'd betray us somehow?" Marc asked incredulously.

"If the opportunity arose," Tarr confirmed grimly.

"He saved us back in Riddleton," Marc persisted.

"Because it benefitted him to do so," Tarr rejoined. "We're paying him."

Athela jerked her head towards Rowan. "Kagai hates Ashans. It's unlikely she or Archer would ally themselves with Kagai."

"You can't know *what* an exile will do," Tarr said darkly. "Or how low they will stoop."

"All right," Athela cut in before Marc could reply. "At this point, Archer's the best chance we have to get around the city and start a network. He's set us up with lodging. We'll just have to keep an eye on him, that's all."

Tarr nodded. "Tell Laith what I said, too. When he comes back."

"Wherever he is," Marc muttered darkly.

Shortly thereafter, Rowan and Archer motioned the others back over to join them, with apologies for taking so long and reminiscing about old times without including the rest of them.

"I met Archer when he first came to Two Falls," Rowan said with a private smile in Archer's direction. "When he was just a young slip of a thing."

"Yes, those were certainly the days," Archer said. Tarr got the sense that he wished to move past the subject.

"There's very little that goes on in Two Falls without my knowing," Rowan informed the rest of them with smooth self-assurance. "If I hear of any unusual activity in the city, I'll invite you to come back and visit." Her gaze lingered a bit longer on Tarr as she said so, and he felt his cheeks flush red.

A short while later, they left Rowan's club and piled out into the comparatively cool spring night. Athela, who'd keenly eyed the way in which Archer and Rowan had bid each other farewell, kept stealing covert glances over at Archer as they walked, bracing herself to say something. Finally, she arched an eyebrow and, in a loaded tone, said, "Well. Your *friend* certainly seems obliging."

"Ex-girlfriend, actually," Archer said lightly, skipping over a jutting cobblestone. "A long while ago. We were together for a few years, and then I...ah...took up with her sister, Kai."

"Her *sister?*" Athela exclaimed, looking scandalized. Tarr met her eyes and raised his eyebrows, as if to say *see? I told you what Ashan exiles are like.*

"Kai is her *older* sister," Archer countered defensively. "It wasn't my proudest moment, to be sure. But everyone's allowed to be a bit of an idiot when they're younger."

"Hear, hear," Si agreed enthusiastically.

They visited a number of taverns that first night, stopping by another three up in the artistic district of Two Falls, then journeying back down the hill and across town for a brief foray into the seedy district Archer had mentioned. It was an excursion that Tarr felt nervous about, but Archer seemed to regard it as an exciting sort of field trip. They'd only gone a block or two into the new neighborhood before Marc had pointed out in a low voice that they were being followed. This revelation was shortly before someone tried to sell Athela something resembling a dried bunch of newts that they had hanging from a string inside their cloak. After this encounter, Athela indicated that she'd had enough immersion in Two Falls nightlife for one night, and so Archer steered them back out of the district and towards the safer central neighborhoods.

As they walked easily through the streets, the lanterns swinging lazily overhead like lines of drunken fireflies, Tarr only took in half of the conversations swirling around him. His mind was too busy spinning, toying with all the puzzles spread before him. Where had Laith gone? Who was Rowan, really, and would she actually help them? And above all, what was Archer's angle in all of this?

They piled into Ma's house in the wee hours of the morning. Tarr couldn't remember ever being more glad to see a bed in his life, and patted Wolver gratefully on the head as he settled in. He noticed, though, that Marc didn't go up to bed with the rest of them. He made some pretense of saying goodnight, but Tarr suspected that he was going to wait and make sure that Laith returned safely from his mysterious outing. And though Tarr tried to stay awake and listen as long as he could, he never heard Marc come back up the stairs.

CHAPTER ELEVEN

To Tarr's extreme relief, the next morning found Laith sitting in his usual seat beside the others, one long leg slung across the other, smiling placidly at them across a steaming platter of freshly baked rolls. Marc was seated next to Laith, the bodyguard watching him with an annoyed look on his face, his own plate of food ignored, and his arms folded across his chest. Laith looked up amiably at Tarr as he entered and took a seat.

"Morning," the prince muttered. Tarr could see no physical signs of what Laith might have been doing the previous night; there were no scars or cuts on his smooth face, and except for some darkness around his eyes from obvious lack of sleep, he looked none the worse for wear. Tarr reached over for one of the rolls, and Marc rather aggressively slid a tin of homemade elderberry jam over to him from across the table.

"Thanks," Tarr took up a knife and began applying liberal amounts of homemade jam to his bread. This was followed by a few moments of eyeing Laith suspiciously across the table while wondering how he had gone so long without experiencing the combination of bread and jam before.

The prince was innocently chewing, dark eyes turned up to look at the ceiling. Seeing that Laith wasn't going to start up a conversation,

Tarr murmured, "So, can you tell us where—"

"No, he *can't*, apparently," Marc snapped, his ice-blue eyes narrowed as he stared at Laith. "I asked him last night when he got in but he hasn't said a word, just that he wasn't hurt and he wasn't in any danger, so don't worry about it."

"*What?*" Laith inquired defensively, looking over at Marc with disbelief and taking a bite out of his roll. "We're not in the palace anymore. Cira doesn't know where we are. I can take care of myself."

"That's not the point," Marc hissed.

"Then what is?" Laith asked fairly, slinging his free arm up to lay it on the table. Marc made no answer. He just shook his head disdainfully, flaxen hair slipping about his ears, and re-folded his burly arms more tightly. He wasn't used to being excluded from Laith's confidence.

Athela sat back, looking around the table as the others groggily shoved food in their mouths. "Right. Here's what I think we should do today. Rane and I are going to head over to the library and start looking for clues to find out who the heir of Morthenstar is."

Library! Tarr perked up and opened his mouth to ask if he could come, too. But Athela hadn't noticed his interest and continued. "But what we really need is to go to the main meeting place, you know, the seat of the kingdom—"

"Town hall," Archer interjected.

"That's right," Athela agreed. "Town hall. We need to find some way to let the Two Falls government know that there may be a threat. Our work will be a lot easier if we can get them on our side."

"Here's hoping they're more receptive than your parents," Marc grumbled into his mug of tea.

"You think it's safe to tell the government that you're the Strikers?" Archer asked, a dubious note in his voice.

The others looked around at the table at each other. "Why?" Athela asked narrowly, trying to suss out whether Archer was pulling one over on them. "They're the ones in charge, aren't they?"

We have no idea what we're doing, Tarr realized with a sinking feeling. *We are a bunch of children wandering around with no idea what we're doing.*

"Why?" Athela asked again. "Do you think we shouldn't go to

the town hall?"

Archer made a noncommittal noise in the back of his throat. "Do what you like," he said finally, with a dismissive gesture of his long hand. "In my experience, governments are not to be trusted."

Tarr stifled a snort. *I'll bet they're not, when you've spent your life on the wrong side of the law.*

"I'll go," Laith volunteered. "Marc, Tarr, why don't you both come along as well? " Tarr, who had been about to volunteer again to accompany the expedition to the library, closed his mouth, feeling disappointed. He forced a small smile and nodded. "Great," Laith smiled. "Archer, Si? You coming with?"

Archer let out a choking little cough. "Laith, I would absolutely love nothing better than to go straight with you down to Town Hall, but there are, ah, one or two small extenuating items I may have on my record that certain officials...may or may not have forgotten...when I may or may not have...ah..."

"Let me guess," said Athela. "Loitering?"

Before Archer could reply, Laith cut him off. "Right, then, just Marc and Tarr. Si, you hang around with Archer. See what you can find out."

To Tarr's immense surprise, he realized that he had actually already seen the town hall building in his brief previous visit to Two Falls. It was in the oldest section of town, near the enormous library that Morthenstar had built. It was set at the head of its own broad square, a large golden dome atop the building shining like a beacon against the sky. The three friends stared at it for a few moments, duly impressed.

"Seems reputable enough," Marc squinted. "Better than that place we went last night, with the stalking and the dried newts."

"Hopefully," Laith agreed and started forward, squaring his shoulders. "If you all don't mind, I'll take the lead. I've read about the cities here and how they're run."

"Do they have a king and queen?" Tarr inquired curiously.

"No, not at all. The council is made up of elected officials from the different districts of the city. They all stay here and discuss the problems in the city and what to do about them."

"Sort of like an Ashan village," Tarr murmured.

"Seems like it would lead to a lot of bickering," Marc observed.

Tarr shrugged. Living apart from the rest of the village with the other young Ashans, he had only a dim idea of how problems had been resolved among the adult members of the tribe. He'd always assumed that the governance of their village was smooth and unanimous, though now, looking at it from an outside perspective, he realized that it couldn't possibly have been so.

The stately doors of the building were thrown open to admit the fresh spring air, so they passed easily inside. The interior of the town hall was like nothing Tarr had ever seen before. Had he not grown so used to the grandeur and opulence of Joymaril, he might have been completely overwhelmed, but his recent palatial living conditions had prepared him. The ceiling rose up into the curve of the huge golden dome, crowning an enormous open gathering place below. Groups of robed individuals spoke in hushed clusters around the chamber; everyone seemed very important and had the appearance of being bearers of extremely crucial business. While he might have been impressed a month or so ago, Tarr was immediately reminded of the Jelani courtiers who had made careers out of looking very self-important while actually doing almost nothing. He wondered if it was the same thing here.

There were different colored robes on different people; some of them wore sashes with insignia almost reminiscent of the Jelani guards at the palace. Tarr had no idea what color robe denoted what. Every sound in the massive room was magnified by a hundred so that the mere scuffling of a shoe echoed up to the top of the great dome. The effect of nearly a hundred people scuttling to and fro across the room was nearly deafening. Tarr suddenly had a great urge to give a shout to hear it reverberate off of the columned walls, but understood that that wouldn't get them off to a very auspicious start.

To one side of the enormous entry hall there was a broad wooden desk the length of three dining tables, where seven or so scribes were busy scrabbling words down on stacks and stacks of creamy white parchment. One of the scribes eyed Laith tiredly as their group approached, scratched the last few sentences with a great flourish of his pen, and raised his eyebrows.

"Yes, what's your business?" he asked in a bored voice.

"We wish to speak before the council," Laith said. Tarr was impressed at Laith's seeming self-assurance. He sounded like he addressed the Two Falls council all the time.

"Right, that'll be a five-mark filing fee, and you'll receive your appointment date by post within two weeks," the scribe said automatically. "Thank you for visiting town hall."

Laith blinked his large eyes. "I beg your pardon?"

The scribe looked over his glasses at the prince as if he were an imbecile. "That—will—be..."

"I heard you the first time," Laith cut him off with the slightest twinge of irritation, unused to being spoken to in so flippant a manner. "We don't have two weeks to wait."

The scribe shrugged helplessly and gestured around them at the scurrying flood of people. "You think you're the only people in this city with urgent problems?" he asked with the world-weariness of someone twice his age. "Look, we have a sewer blockage in Eastgate and all the shops are flooded with a foot of water; someone's reported that they think they saw a crocodile, and crocodiles don't even *live* in this part of the world. The council is very busy. Please step back so I can help the next person in line."

Abashed, Laith stepped down from the stair and walked bewilderedly back over to Marc and Tarr. "This is moronic," he shrugged. "I guess we can't do anything but go back home."

"I wish we'd brought Athela," Marc said morosely. "She'd scare him into letting us in."

"Excuse me," came a small female voice behind them. They swiveled around. It was a tiny middle-aged woman wearing an official-looking robe of silver and blue. She didn't wear a sash, though whether this meant she was *more* important or *less* important in the grand scheme of things, Tarr didn't know. She smiled kindly at them. "I heard you talking to the scribe right now. I just wanted to let you know that some members of the Lesser Council have a small open session where they open the floor to public petitions. It begins in ten minutes."

"Why didn't he just tell me *that*?" Laith asked irritatedly.

The woman laughed and pushed her glasses back up her nose.

"Well, you see, if he told everyone, then there'd be a stampede of people to get into the session. This way, it's much more controlled."

Laith and Marc looked at one another in utter bewilderment as if mutually searching for some semblance of logic in this approach. Tarr had to bite his lip to keep from grinning.

Laith sighed and gave the woman a knee-buckling smile. "I truly appreciate your help," he said in his smooth voice.

The woman, to Tarr's amusement, let loose an extremely girlish giggle that belied her seeming maturity. "The line is right over there," she pointed. "Good luck." Tarr watched in astonishment as she actually gave Laith a cheeky wink before walking away.

"Wow," Tarr muttered aloud.

Laith gave a helpless shrug, as if to say *I don't know why this works, but it always does.*

They stood in line for at least half an hour before they were admitted into the council chamber to state their case. The room, Tarr could feel, was extremely old (he remembered that the woman had referred to this as the "Lesser" council, and the state of the room certainly reflected this.) It was a circular dome, though only a fraction of the size of the entry hall, with long windows from the top of the room almost halfway down, draped with heavy velvet curtains that, on closer inspection, seemed to be rather torn and tattered at the bottoms. Tarr could see a few places where small piles of dirt from the floor had just been swept and half-hidden behind the drapes. The ceiling was probably a grand sight back in its heyday, painted with images of heroes atop chargers, swords drawn, but had been allowed to fade and peel over time without proper care given to its preservation. Tarr tried surreptitiously to stare up at the paintings, but this resulted in his nearly tripping over Marc's heel as they walked in.

A group of black-robed council members, twenty or thirty of them, sat behind a tall mahogany desk in a semicircle facing them from the opposite side of the room. Tarr gulped, suddenly very nervous.

If Laith was anxious, he hid it beautifully. He strode up into the center of the room, flanked by Marc, and paused for a moment before beginning to speak. His deep voice soared through the vastness of the dome, sounding right at home as it filled the room. "Honored council members," he began, "My name is Prince Argolaith of the Jelani." At this, a few of the council members began to whisper and buzz amongst themselves.

We should have lied, Tarr realized suddenly. *We shouldn't have said who we are.* But it was too late. He studied the faces of the council members, who were eyeing them with a mixture of curiosity and suspicion.

Laith waited patiently for the murmurs to settle before he continued. "I bring a warning that Kagai's heir may have been chosen. That he may be planning to move against Two Falls."

This time, a large smattering of outright laughter broke out. Laith didn't flinch, but Tarr could see from the ramrod set of the prince's back that he was displeased. The head council member, who wore a silvery-looking sash and white stripes down the front of his robe, pounded the front of his desk, and the chuckles subsided.

"Oh yes? What proof do you have?" he demanded.

Laith swallowed, and Tarr began to feel nervous. "Over the years, I have studied the prophecies of Morthenstar," he said. "And in the last month, individuals matching the descriptions of Morthenstar's Strikers have begun to come together. If the Strikers are assembling, then we believe Kagai's heir is as well."

Tarr reflexively winced as he did every time Laith brought up the prophecy. He wished he could find some way of talking the prince out of mentioning it at all. Laith seemed so blissfully unaware, so *certain* in his convictions.

"And?" returned the councilor. "Are there any other fairy tales you'd like to wish into existence while this council is in session?"

"This is absurd!" another member shouted. "Show him out!"

"I have a right to speak," Laith maintained evenly.

"Are you a citizen of Two Falls?" an elderly woman demanded.

"No," Laith conceded, his assurance faltering slightly.

"Then you have *no* right. Get out!" she yelled.

Laith's jaw clenched. "Honored council," he said slowly, a slight sarcastic emphasis on the word *honored*, "I have not come here to stir up trouble or cause a riot. Some signs have simply become apparent, and I have come here in friendship and support to share this information."

"Please, everyone," came a new voice. Tarr looked around. It came from an older man, the only one who was watching them with a thoughtful look on his face rather than a sneer. "We should at least listen to what this young man has to say."

"Why?" demanded the angry woman. "What right does he have?"

"If you remember, Mara," the man maintained quietly, "Two hundred years ago, this council did a good job of ignoring warning signs, and it resulted in the city being overrun by Kagai's soldiers."

"It won't happen again," said another man.

"It's just an old legend," chimed in another councilor.

The old man shrugged and looked intently at Laith. "You say the Strikers have begun to assemble?"

"Yes," Laith replied. "An Ashan with a white wolf, a Jelani with gray eyes and black hair. I have even seen the sword of Morthenstar resurface."

"Who is the heir of Morthenstar, then?" a man called tauntingly. "Why doesn't she come here herself?"

"I don't know who the heir is yet," Laith said, not rising to the bait. "But if this council acts now and takes steps to protect its people, we may be able to combat whatever may rise against you."

"You're just a boy," the woman snapped. "What do you know?"

Tarr could clearly see how they must appear in the eyes of the council. Three youths of only about twenty, inexperienced, and outsiders to boot. *If I were in their place, I'm not sure I would believe us, either,* he thought. *But I wouldn't laugh. I wouldn't hurl insults.*

"Look at this young man," the sympathetic council member said. "You all have been unspeakably rude to him and his friends, and he has dealt with it with patience and diplomacy. I should say that he's much better behaved than half the members of this council."

"You're only sore because we vetoed your civic reform bill last week," Mara sneered.

"I assure you, I am still 'sore' about that, but that has absolutely nothing to do with *this,*" the older man said patiently. "This may be very important."

"It's a waste of time," another council member called. "Children reading too many books and believing their bedtime stories. Show them out. We still have to vote on the immigration tax."

"Argue about it, more like," the old man sighed. "Vote as you will. I would like to excuse myself from the proceedings for the rest of the day. My aide will take over for me."

"You may be excused," the chief council member called, and struck the desk with his hand once again. Tarr wondered whether being able to loudly pound the desk was the major determining factor in being elected to the chief council position.

Laith's shoulders slumped as if the sound had been a physical blow. He turned his back and stalked out, Tarr and Marc close behind. The gigantic doors of the council chambers closed firmly behind them. Tarr put a hand on Laith's arm and the prince swallowed a few times, then shook his head and rolled his eyes.

"Not unlike giving a toast at one of my family gatherings," he muttered. "Maybe even a slightly warmer reception."

"Young man," came a quiet voice behind them. They turned to see the council member who had advocated for them during the hearing. He was standing with his arms folded thoughtfully beneath his robes. "What was your name again?"

"Argolaith," Laith replied, turning. "Or Laith, for short."

"Laith," said the older council member, shaking his hand. "And your friends?"

Laith introduced Tarr and Marc, and the council member shook their hands slowly, studying them over his glasses. "Pleased to meet all of you. My name is Pieter, and I am a council member here in Two Falls. I would like to speak with you. Could you please come to my office?"

Pieter's office was small but elegant, filled to the brim with books, in a style closer to the Jelani than Ashan, with hard covers and bindings on the spines. Tarr ran his finger along them as they entered the room, pleased with the sensation and his memories of the Jelani library, and found himself wondering whether he'd ever go back there again. Pieter motioned them into chairs and asked Laith to recount his story, which the prince did, beginning with Athela and continuing on about their meeting with Tarr (at which point Tarr had awkwardly toyed with the laces on his boot and avoided eye contact with the rest of them) and seeing the sword that Si carried when he made his unexpected arrival at the palace.

"You say the boy stole it?" Pieter interjected.

"Yes," Laith replied, then reconsidered. "Well, he says he found it in a shoe store here in Two Falls, but we can basically interpret that to mean that he stole it. So, it would be difficult to find out exactly where it came from. I nevertheless regard it as significant."

Tarr looked swiftly at Pieter, trying to assess whether Pieter also thought that Laith's belief in the prophecy was a lot of nonsense. But the old man's expression was calculably noncommittal. *I supposed he has to be able to keep his thoughts to himself,* Tarr mused, *if he is a member of the governing council.*

"Indeed," Pieter steepled his fingers beneath his nose. He had a kindly, rather jowly face and thick bushy eyebrows. "I am not a superstitious man, you understand," he began slowly, "but I have always believed in learning from the past. And, like you said, I believe it is better to err on the side of caution. However," he sighed and began to polish his glasses. "As you may have ascertained, our council is filled to the brim with its own squabbles and infighting, too much to even hope to achieve something productive. Even if Kagai himself was marching across the bridge at this moment, they would be arguing about who should stay behind and watch the council building and who should go out and fight. And still others would argue about whether the bridges had been engineered to properly hold the weight of an entire army. But," he glanced through his glasses and replaced them on his nose, "this doesn't mean that we don't hear things and see things. We just choose to ignore them. So, if you would like, I will keep my eyes and ears open here. At the first sign of trouble, I will send word to you. Where can I reach you?"

Laith opened his mouth to begin answering with Ma's address, but Tarr felt a twinge in the back of his mind.

"Rowan's," he muttered abruptly. "Send word to Rowan's club." Laith looked at him curiously, but did as he suggested.

Pieter repeated the address until it was safely in his memory. "Better than writing it down," he smiled, then leaned back in his chair. Tarr glanced at him with interest. He looked them all over, his expression carrying a touch of sadness. "You're very young," he murmured. "All of you."

"We're used to responsibility," Laith replied squarely.

I'm not, Tarr reflected.

Pieter stood from his chair, and the others did likewise. "Contact me at any time. My aides are trustworthy; you can leave a word with them. I will do what I can for all of you." He reached out his hand, and Laith shook it. "I do hope you're wrong," he said with a rueful smile.

"So do I," Laith agreed.

You're both in luck, Tarr thought.

A short while later they made it back to Ma's house and met up with Archer and Si in the comfy, squashed-seat living room, where Archer was in the midst of tightening his bowstring. The pair of them had apparently had a grand time prowling around the artistic district on the hill. Laith gave a short recap of the morning's events, which were met with no small amount of derision from Archer, who seemed to have a rather dim opinion of government and authority in general.

Marc watched as Archer tightened the tension on his bow, his golden eyes intent with concentration, nimble white fingers twisting and adjusting with expert precision.

"You really know how to use that thing?" he asked curiously.

Archer grinned his wolfish grin. "How d'you think I got my name?"

Marc shrugged. "Well, I didn't know whether or not your skill with a bow was inherent at birth or whether your parents were just very fortunate in their choice of name."

Tarr looked closely at Archer's face. "Archer isn't an Ashan name," he said finally. Archer glanced towards him with a brief flick of his golden eyes, but said nothing. Tarr shook his head. "It's not even an Ashan word."

"Ashan word?" Si asked blankly. "You mean, you all have a language and everything?"

"Of course," Tarr said with a bemused smile. Somehow, Si's ignorance about Ashan culture wasn't as offensive to him as a grown adult's. "I'll teach it to you, if you like."

"Do you speak it, too, Archer?" Si asked with keen interest.

"No, I've forgotten how," Archer said shortly, laying down his bow. "Let's get a bite to eat, shall we?"

He stood up rather abruptly and headed back to the kitchen. Although his words had been welcoming, something in the finality of his manner did not invite the others to accompany him.

Silence settled around them, companionable and easy. Si was fiddling with the corner of one of the pillows on the couch and stealing sidelong glances at Marc. Tarr could tell that he was steeling himself up to ask Marc something. "Marc," Si asked finally, his breathy voice tentative, "where did you get your scar?"

"Cut myself shaving," Marc joked immediately, and the others chuckled automatically. Tarr could see, though, from the lack of mirth in Marc's eyes that this was a rote answer he must have come up with years ago to deflect the question. Tarr had been curious about the scar as well but hadn't drummed up the courage to ask; he was almost grateful for Si's innocent lack of tact. Hoping he wasn't being too obvious about it, he stole another glance at Marc's face. The scar was deep, diagonal, and white, stretching from Marc's left temple to his right jaw, bisecting his face in a clean line.

"It was *supposedly* an accident," Laith said, though his voice was dark.

"Someone did it on purpose?" Si asked, aghast.

"In all likelihood, yes," Laith replied, his eyes grave. "There was a boy who'd served with us in the Meadows—"

"What's that?" Si asked curiously.

"Every child from a noble family where we come from serves for a certain amount of time in the Meadows in our army," Laith explained patiently. "So starting when I was four or so, I began my training and was there for about ten years. Marc was there, too. And there was another boy with us while we were serving...there was always something a bit... *off* about him. Something not quite right."

"How do you mean?" Si asked.

"Things would happen around him...people would get hurt, and it would look for all intents and purposes like accidents, but we could never be sure."

"And he cut Marc?" Si asked curiously. Tarr was again glad to have

Si there to ask all of the obvious questions.

"Not then," Marc shook his head. "It was after we'd come back."

"We were doing some training at the Academy back in Joymaril. Nothing special, nothing different, just combat exercises. Marc was with me." Laith glanced over at his bodyguard. Marc folded his arms, his usual ebullient demeanor suddenly dimmed. Archer reappeared from the kitchen and took a seat opposite Tarr as Laith continued.

"I was paired with Marc and had my back turned. And this other boy, the one we'd been with in the Meadows, was coming up closer and closer behind me, just practicing, swinging his sword. He said later that he didn't realize how close he'd gotten—"

"But it was impossible," Marc interjected. "I only saw him out of the corner of my eye. And I could see that he was going to hit Laith. Across the back of his neck. Would have badly wounded him, if not killed him,"

"Marc didn't have a sword at that moment; he'd lent it to one of the other trainees for the drill. He barely even had time to react; it all happened so fast," Laith said quietly. "He stepped in front of it. The blade hit him in the face."

The room fell into silence as Si, Archer, and Tarr slowly stared around at Marc, who shifted in his chair. "Hey," he said brightly, spreading his hands and trying to diffuse the tension somewhat, "at least I didn't lose my eye. Not sure I could pull off an eyepatch."

This seemed to Tarr to be another practiced way to diffuse the conversation, and it worked. Si even let out a laugh, though his eyes were still large and impressed. Tarr could scarcely fathom the courage it had taken Marc to save Laith in such a way. It was as if the scar on his face had taken on a different, more profound meaning. *I wouldn't be able to do that*, he thought to himself.

"What happened to the boy who tried to cut Laith?" Si asked, his breathy voice in a hushed whisper.

"Seth?" Laith shook his head. "He tried to play it off as an accident, but there was no way, and everyone knew it. He was far too talented with a sword. Easily as good as I am. If he cut someone, it was because he meant to. But his family had influence at court and begged him out of any real disciplinary measures, managed to pass it off as a momentary lapse. He was forbidden to attend Academy classes for a year, but it didn't seem to matter. Later on, we all found out just how sick he really was, and he was imprisoned for life. He's still in prison, actually."

Tarr gave an involuntary shudder at the image of Seth there in the dungeons beneath the cliff at Joymaril, knowing full well the feeling of claustrophobia and the pervasive darkness in those cramped cells. He thought about the night he, Athela, and Si had spent in captivity. *I could have been standing directly next to him*, he realized.

Suddenly, there was a loud bang at the front door as it was thrown open. Tarr jumped and twisted around, relieved to see that it was only Athela and Rane, newly returned from the library.

"What an exhausting day," Athela griped as she stomped loudly into the room, glancing over to Archer before collapsing dramatically into one of the armchairs and flinging one arm over her forehead. Rane softly entered and shut the door behind her, like the quiet stillness following a thunderstorm. Tarr sent Rane a shy smile, which was softly returned.

"I don't expect *you* lot to understand," Athela declared with an accusatory look towards the rest of them. "You've been mincing around the town all day."

"I resent the term *mincing*," Archer countered. "For your information, it was thoroughly masculine stomping."

"Fine, while you've been masculinely stomping about, *I've* been trapped in a library all day, and I haven't found a single thing that can help us. I walked in there, this really huge solemn place with this librarian who looked about as old as the building itself. I ask if she has any lore about Morthenstar and she takes me to a room with a big old statue of Morthenstar reading outside it, just to set the mood. An entire room! An entire room full, and then she tells me when the library closes, and shuts us in there with a couple of candles to read by. And we're not talking about a small room either, but one with shelves and ladders, and they're not organized in any civilized way that I know of, and so basically, I'm having to read through them one by one."

Tarr could empathize perhaps with Athela's frustration after hours of fruitless searching, but the day she had just described sounded fairly close to his ideal. "Athela…" he said tentatively, about to volunteer to go with her on the next search.

"Surely if there are that many books about her, you'd be able to find what we're looking for with no problem at all," Laith told her soothingly.

"There's an entire book devoted to Morthenstar's eating habits, Laith," Athela said in a deathly grave voice. "Her *eating habits*. And nothing yet about the prophecy or the heir."

"Did she like cabbage soup?" Si asked suddenly. "*I* like cabbage soup."

"Well, you should be able to skip all those books that have nothing to do with what we're looking for, Athela," Laith pointed out sensibly. "Just look for some with big important titles like *Where Morthenstar Hid Her Prophecy*."

"Or maybe *Ten Ways to Discover Whether You are Morthenstar's Heir*," Archer suggested with a grin.

"I looked in those," Athela retorted sarcastically. "All we have to go on is that the clue to find the heir is hidden in a book in the Two Falls library. It gave no mention of anywhere else."

"Morthenstar built that library herself," Laith agreed. "It makes sense that any clues would be there."

"Athela," Archer asked suddenly, a thought occurring to him. "Was Morthenstar married?"

Athela stared at him. "Why do you ask?"

Archer shrugged. "Well, if we're looking for her heir, then maybe it would be easier to trace her lineage than go on a probably fruitless treasure hunt through the Two Falls library."

"Well," she frowned, considering. "That's a possibility, but I don't think it would make things any easier. Alder wasn't ever married, but there are also rumors that she may have had cousins somewhere."

"Vague cousins," Archer observed wryly. "Sounds promising."

"Many Jelani claim to have some distant relation to Morthenstar," Laith added. "Though whether it's anything more than empty boasting is anyone's guess."

"That means that you could all be related to Morthenstar, doesn't it?" Tarr asked curiously. The thought hadn't occurred to him before.

"Exactly," Athela pointed her finger at him to indicate that he got the point she was trying to make. "And, technically, so are Marc and Rane. Rane is my second cousin or something along those lines."

"Twice removed," Rane murmured. Her sudden speech caused the others' heads to flick around and look at her in surprise. It was a nice voice, soft and slightly husky.

"Marc is...oh, I don't know, we're far more distantly related than they are," Laith squinted, thinking hard. "But he's technically house of Cade, like me."

"Cade like your brother?" Tarr asked, feeling out of his depth.

"My brother is named after our family house," Laith explained.

Athela shrugged. "So, the heir could come from Morthenstar's Jelani family, in which case one of the four of us would seem a likely candidate, or it could be one of the race of humans. Really, there's no way to definitively trace Morthenstar's bloodline."

"Especially because who's to say that one of her descendants didn't marry an Ashan? Perhaps a distant relative of yours, Tarr," Laith pointed out.

"I hope not," Tarr murmured.

"If, indeed, the heir *is* a relative. There's always a chance it could just be *anyone*," Laith pointed out. "Anyone worthy."

Archer threw up his hands. "Ah, well. Rules out *that* idea."

Though they were no closer to finding out the identity of the heir than they had been an hour before, Tarr nevertheless felt a nagging discomfort. He hadn't ever considered the possibility that *he* might be the heir if, indeed, there was such a person.

Which, of course, there isn't, he reminded himself, though for some reason he felt far from assured.

CHAPTER TWELVE

The days eventually fell into a comfortable pattern, one after the other: Athela went to the library with Rane to try to discover more information about Morthenstar's prophecy, and the others went out through the town, where Archer had a seemingly endless list of former contacts and acquaintances with eyes and ears in every walk of life of the city. Tarr enjoyed getting to see different parts of Two Falls, which gradually became less foreign and more familiar as the weeks went on. But day in and day out, the response was always the same: no one had heard anything strange, no one had seen anything strange; there had been no word from Pieter, the city council member, left for them at Rowan's establishment.

Tarr, who hadn't believed in the truth of the prophecy in the first place, had begun to grow more and more certain that there was nothing to it and that they were running rapidly towards a dead end. Still, he couldn't complain. It had been an interesting adventure thus far, and he liked his companions. Even Archer, who he had continued to avoid as studiously as possible, was amiable enough and hadn't murdered or betrayed any of them yet (though it had only been a few weeks, and Tarr wouldn't put it past him.) There was no sign of the Jelani troops who had pursued them through Riddleton; Tarr supposed that they'd given up. They were safe for the time being.

He had no idea what the others thought of *him*. They probably found him pleasant enough, if somewhat shy, timid, and ignorant of anything that could possibly be of help to them in their quest to find Morthenstar's heir. The thought that he was more or less useless in their quest didn't concern him much, as he didn't believe in their mission to begin with. The entire situation was temporary, after all. His needs for shelter and food had been met, and he would at least have a story or two to bring back to the tribe when he returned at the end of the year. Already a few months had passed since he'd left, and in no time he would be heading home.

The real puzzle in Tarr's mind was that, just as he had done their first night in Two Falls, without fail every week or so Laith would manage to slip away from the others and go about some sort of mysterious private nocturnal business of his own. Tarr marveled at how adept he was at doing it—one minute he would be there having a lively argument with Si or Archer, and the next minute he was nowhere to be seen and his horse was missing from the stable. Marc had given up hope of catching him after the first few slips, and had even suggested that Tarr send Wolver after him. Tarr himself thought that he had a vague inclination of where Laith was going all the time but kept it to himself. Laith's business was his own.

Tarr still hadn't quite managed to get up the courage to ask Athela whether he could accompany her and Rane to the library to help with their research. Oftentimes, he would practice what he wanted to say with Wolver, who spent most days sleeping up in Tarr's room and most nights out prowling around the city. Out of all of his new companions, Athela was still the most intimidating to him, but he also found himself feeling rather foolish around Rane whenever she was near (though it was a very different kind of foolishness than he felt around Athela.) Rane was so quiet and self-possessed, and her movements were so spare and graceful that he always felt like a large, awkward bird by comparison. He never seemed to know what to say to her, though he desperately wanted to find some excuse to strike up a conversation.

One morning, he resolved to finally get over his nerves and ask Athela whether he could go with them on their next research excursion.

Gathering his courage, he mounted the stairs up to Rane and Athela's room. Once out front, he squared his shoulders, knocked briefly, and opened the door quickly lest he lose any momentum.

Inside was a young woman in a chair by the window, wrapped in a blanket with her back to him, head tilted down, a mane of beautiful reddish-brown hair hanging down in waves nearly to her elbow. Tarr was momentarily struck dumb, and it took him a full few seconds to realize that it was Rane. It was the first time that he had seen her without her hood and circlet. Rane started at the sudden noise, then scrambled to her feet, as startled as if Tarr had happened upon her while she was stark naked. Her hands went self-consciously to brush her hair back, as if she wished to hide it from him.

"I'm sorry!" Tarr apologized quickly and made as though he would close the door and leave, but thankfully, her voice stopped him.

"Just a moment; I wasn't expecting anyone," Rane cast off the blanket, revealing a simple red sleeping shift that revealed no skin and very little of her figure. Throwing a dark black robe over her shoulders and pulling the tie close around her waist, she went to the top of her dresser and pulled off a familiar piece of fabric. She expertly twisted her hair round and pulled her hood over her head, affixing the silver circlet in place around her head to keep the hood still. She turned around to face him, the expressionless, anonymous bodyguard once again.

"Please—you don't have to do that on my account," Tarr said, hopeful that she would dispense with the hood.

"It's all right," Rane said. Her voice was incredibly soft, almost like Si's, but she had an odd accent reminiscent of Laith and Athela, perhaps even slightly more pronounced than theirs. Her eyebrows rose expectantly. Tarr suddenly remembered that he should probably have a reason ready for why he had decided to go barging into her room. He at once felt awkward about asking whether he could tag along with them to the library.

"Er—Athela told me that there was a book she had that I could borrow, I just came up to see if it was here," he lied, frantically hoping that Athela had remembered to bring along some literature with her back from the library.

"Of course," Rane replied, standing and moving across the room to the wall against which Athela's saddlebags were propped. She flipped open the top of one and removed a thin book. Tarr took it anxiously, scanning the title, which turned out to be *To War: The Collected Memoirs of Celebrated Jelani Queens.*

Thanking the heavens that it wasn't a florid romance novel, Tarr waved the book and smiled. "Thanks; I'm trying to brush up on my history."

Rane said nothing, merely nodding politely, keeping her eyes fastened around the level of his ankle. Without another word, Tarr backed out of the room, shutting the door behind him and closing his eyes.

Well, that went well, he thought sarcastically. *What on earth could I have been thinking?* He walked forward a step, prepared to go downstairs to the den once more and discover whether or not Athela's book was actually any good, when a feeling of rebellion stirred somewhere deep in his chest. With sudden resolve, he turned around and prepared to heroically burst through the door once again and demand a conversation. An instant before he threw open the door, he remembered his sense of propriety and checked himself, almost bonking his head on the door with his momentum while managing to knock softly with his knuckles against the hard oak paneling.

"Come in," came Rane's soft voice. Tarr took a deep breath, opened the door, and re-entered. Rane looked at him square in the eyes this time, with a faintly bemused look on her face.

"It's me again," he announced, in case she hadn't noticed. She nodded, still smiling, but it began to look rather strained, as though she were inwardly struggling against something. Tarr realized that he actually had nothing to talk to her about. Every possible interesting subject of conversation had completely fled from his mind. "I was wondering," he said slowly, "if you would like some tea."

Rane regarded him solemnly, though Tarr thought he could see the faintest twitch at the corner of her mouth. "Some tea would be lovely."

"Excellent," Tarr exclaimed, relieved.

He walked out the door, paused a moment, and walked straight back in.

"Hello," he declared. "I was wondering how you take your tea?"

"Lemon and some honey?" Rane suggested. This time, he could definitely tell that she was fighting back laughter.

"Excellent choice," Tarr complimented her. "I've always enjoyed honey in my tea, too."

"Do you drink a lot? Of tea, I mean?" Rane inquired, and there was an almost desperate note to her voice, which was shaking ever so slightly.

We're having a conversation, Tarr realized with a surge of excitement. This new positive development momentarily threw him for a loop, and it was a full ten seconds before he could gather his wits to reply. "Well, no," he admitted. "We really didn't drink a lot of it back where I came from. It's more herbal water. You know," he concluded weakly. "Herbs...steeped. In hot water."

Rane nodded, her smile still oddly strained. And then, after a few more protracted moments of anguished silence, she actually began to giggle uncontrollably, to the point where she had to hide her mouth behind her hand for a couple of seconds before she could regain her composure. Tarr wasn't sure what to make of it. He didn't *think* he'd said anything funny, but apparently something had tickled her. He was relieved, though, that her laughter wasn't cruel or mocking; she really seemed unable to govern it. Through his bewilderment, he noted how lovely the sound was, how beautiful her smile.

He wasn't sure what the most graceful way to extricate himself would be, especially not with Rane barely in control of her laughing fit. Summoning up what nobility he could, Tarr gave her a nod of finality and ducked back out of the room again, tripping eagerly and a little dazedly down the stairs and into the kitchen, dimly aware of a fresh peal of helpless laughter loosed almost as soon as the door had closed behind him.

It was only while he was straining out the tea leaves from the water that he realized how idiotic he must have seemed. However, he couldn't just hide in the kitchen and leave Rane upstairs without her beverage—that would be possibly the most idiotic move of all—so he steeled himself against any further outbursts and firmly told himself not to say more than three words when he saw her. He mounted the stairs again with a resolute sense of his own dignity.

"Here you go," he said sternly, handing her the steaming mug.

Rane nodded with a small smile, but her gray-blue eyes were twinkling as she watched him.

"It's all right, you know," she whispered conspiratorially.

Tarr relaxed and heaved a sigh. "I'm really sorry," he apologized, perching lightly on the end of her bed, ensuring that he was far enough away from her that he didn't seem forward. "Usually, I don't talk very much."

"I know," Rane murmured. Tarr could tell she was teasing him, but it was playful. He rather enjoyed it.

"Were you born in the palace?" Tarr asked, relieved to have remembered one of the questions he'd wanted to ask her.

She shook her head. "In the city." She took a long, deliberate sip of her tea and met his eyes squarely. Tarr felt a pleasant little jolt. He bounced up and down a bit on the bed and, as all words, phrases, and questions had temporarily fled his brain, looked over and smiled.

"I'd best be off, then. Read my new book."

Rane nodded. Her eyes became upside-down *u*'s when she smiled. "Thank you for the tea," she murmured. "And the chat."

"My pleasure," Tarr replied. Even though the encounter had been heady and slightly bewildering, he left her feeling light as air.

"Wait, everyone, stop here; I'm going to check the news," Laith told them. They drew up close to the news board, on which was tacked the daily sheets announcing major announcements of the day. After their fruitless trip to the Two Falls city council, and with no word from Pieter, Laith had taken a proactive interest in keeping up with what was going on around the city. At first, Tarr himself had been fascinated by it all. Before the aide at town hall had mentioned it, he had never heard of anything like a sewer blockage or flooding. His initial interest had given way once Tarr had realized how many rather blasé items made it to the news board. Recently, there had been an epidemic of broken wagon wheels going around, the newest development of which seemed to be that the transportation guild had accused the paving guild of sabotage. It wasn't much use to them in their search.

Laith leaned closer to the board, dark brow furrowing with interest. "This one's new, must have been posted this morning...we know him, don't we?" Laith inquired of Archer, tapping a tapered fingertip against one fluttering sheet. Archer leaned in beside Tarr as he took a closer look; Tarr shifted only slightly to move away from him.

"Yeah, I saw him the day before yesterday at Rowan's," Archer murmured, surprised.

"What is it?" Si inquired, reaching up and leaning over Archer's elbow. The paper had a notice on it, which read:

> The innkeeper of the Dog's Head would like to inquire as to the whereabouts of one Fadith, who was until yesterday a long-standing resident of the inn. Fadith was reported missing by the innkeeper, who insists that his things are still in his room but has not checked in in two days and has missed paying his rent. Fadith is described as being half-Ashan, six feet four inches, with dark black hair and hazel eyes. He has a tattoo on the nape of his neck. Anyone who knows the whereabouts of Fadith is asked to report their knowledge to the Town Hall, so as to get to the bottom of this.
>
> Thank you.

"That's odd," Archer frowned. "I've known Fadith for a while; he's not the type to skip out on his rent like that or just leave town without saying. Bit of a moron, it's true, but not irresponsible."

"Those notices are tacked all over this thing. I guess someone wants to find him pretty badly," Laith observed.

"Probably the innkeeper. Fadith was always bragging about how nice his digs were," Archer glanced across the street. Marc walked up beside Laith and bent down, looking low on the board.

"Wait, here's something else!" Marc exclaimed, ripping off another sheet of paper and standing back up, tucking his shining hair behind his ear. "Gaven. We know her, too, don't we? At the Blue Lounge? Last week, wasn't it?"

"Yes, that's right," Archer looked over his shoulder. "She's missing too..."

"Both Ashans," Laith observed. Archer looked up swiftly, meeting his eyes.

"Or half-Ashans," Archer pointed out.

"Could be coincidence," Marc suggested tentatively. Laith shrugged in agreement, though his eyes were unmistakably grave.

"I want Athela to have a look at these," Laith said slowly. "We'll bring her back here tonight. Maybe there will be even more notices up by then."

They turned to go, but as they did, something struck Tarr. He squinted at the board and saw that there were multiple copies of the missing person flyer. He reached out and pulled two of them off, tucking them carefully in his back pocket. He didn't know why, but he had a funny feeling that he should keep them.

As he rounded the board to catch up with the others, he could see that Archer's face was uncharacteristically sober. "We should check with Rowan, too, to see if she's heard anything," Archer suggested, pulling his black coat tighter over his shoulders.

As planned, once Athela and Rane had returned from another day of fruitless searching at the library ("They might as well rename that awful room the Athela's Patience Memorial Wing," Athela growled on her arrival back at the house), they set almost immediately back out to show her the news board. Tarr had been about to procure the leaflets he'd secretly taken, but Athela seemed so relieved at the prospect of an outing to somewhere other than the library that he had remained silent. For his part, he hadn't decided yet what to make of the disappearances. As with so many things relating to their search for Morthenstar's heir, they could either be an easy coincidence or a portent of doom, depending on how one looked at it.

As he trailed behind his group of companions, watching them flow easily through streets and around corners together, Tarr suddenly felt grateful that they all were there, that he was part of their little group. How nice it felt to have others to walk beside, to have a mystery (however inconsequential it might wind up being) to solve together. He even felt a sudden wash of affection for Archer, who was cracking jokes. (Though, he reflected with a small internal grin, however hard he might try, Archer couldn't make Rane laugh as hard as he had just by bringing her a cup of tea.)

Eventually, they turned into the market square that housed the news board, and Archer strode confidently up to it. After a second's glance, his eyes grew concerned and his brows knit close together as he walked around the pole, closely examining every sheet of paper tacked to it, even running his hand up and down the lengths of the sheets a few times. "They're not here," he said finally.

"They're not?" Marc asked blankly.

"What's not there?" Athela demanded.

"There were notices for missing Ashans today, but it looks like someone's taken them all down," Archer stepped back, hands on his slim hips, as if he wasn't quite sure what to make of it all.

Heart thumping faster, Tarr stepped forward and withdrew the papers from his back pocket. "Here," he held them out. "I took these earlier. Just in case."

The others all faced him with identical wide-eyed stares, as if Tarr had suddenly sprung forth and done a cartwheel. "Good thinking, Tarr," Archer said slowly as he took the papers. Tarr shrugged uncomfortably, still feeling Archer's eyes watching him after he turned. He pretended to examine the board.

"They were tacked all over this thing today," Si insisted. "D'you think perhaps the Ashans were found? And that's why the notices are gone?"

"Probably," Tarr said.

Athela frowned. "Archer, have you checked in with your lady friend yet?" Athela very rarely called Rowan by name, instead referring to her through epithets imbued with references to her and Archer's past relationship.

Archer shook his head, not rising to the jab. "Not recently. But Fadith used to go there pretty often. We can head up there now, see if she's heard anything."

They made the long trek across the town and up the hill to Rowan's club. She was holding court, resplendent in her usual purple, and batted her eyelashes beguilingly in Tarr's direction before Archer pulled her off to one side to ask some questions. Eventually, after about ten minutes of hushed conversation, Archer bid her farewell and ushered the others back into the street with the disappointing but not entirely unpredictable news that Rowan hadn't seen or heard anything unusual. Fadith occasionally went away on business, she said, and besides, people came and went so quickly in Two Falls that if one of her regular customers didn't show up, she didn't think twice about it.

"She'll be on the lookout now, though," Archer shrugged. "Best we can do. Tell you what, I'm going to stay around here tonight and see if I can see anything. You all head back to the house."

"Be careful," Marc warned.

Archer grinned and flipped his black hood up over his head, then spun on his heel and was gone. Tarr watched him go. Something was gnawing at him, and he couldn't quite place it. *He can take care of himself*, Tarr thought. *Besides, what does it matter what happens to him? He's an exile.* But even as he thought the words, they rang hollowly in his head. The fact of Archer's banishment didn't loom quite as large as it once had.

The rest walked along beside each other in an amicable silence save for the sound of Si's whistling. Here and there were people Tarr recognized, but few of them bothered to say hello; everyone had a strange pinched look on their face, as if they were preoccupied with something. One man, whom Tarr recognized to be one of Archer's friends, walked straight past them.

"Hello, Bearn," Laith said politely, but the man just stalked into his house and slammed the door.

This reaction caught them so suddenly that they all stopped and stared at one another. "That was odd," Athela said slowly. "Laith, did you do..."

"Do you smell that?" Marc said abruptly. They all stood still and inhaled the cool night air. There was the smell of beer and wine, of something baking in a nearby house. And something else...something out of place.

"Horses," Athela whispered. "And didn't Archer say something..."

"Horses aren't allowed in this district," Tarr remembered immediately. "To preserve the older streets and buildings."

Marc had his ice-blue eyes narrowed at Bearn's door. "I'm going to have a quick look," he muttered. "Stay here." He jogged around the side of the building and returned a few moments later. "There's a covered area behind the house, all right, but it's behind a big gate. I couldn't see through."

"I can fit through the gate and open it from the inside," Si said pleadingly, his eyes entreating Marc. "Let me go!"

Marc debated for a moment or two. "Fine," he agreed, and Si gave a triumphant pump of his small fist. "Keep very quiet and stay out of sight."

"I know what to do!" Si said eagerly and scampered off.

They crept around the corner and slunk down the narrow alleyway toward the back of Bearn's house. The houses on that street stood back to back, and there was a small enclosure between his dwelling and the house on the other side of the street, blocked by an enormous black gate. Without any difficulty, Si slipped right under the gate. After a moment, there was a slight creak and the door opened.

Tarr and the others peeked inside. There, munching contentedly on a few flakes of hay, were three horses.

"So what?" Athela muttered. "So he's keeping horses at his house illegally. Why?"

"Why is he keeping *three*?" Laith asked. "They're expensive. I doubt he could afford it."

Si had moved even closer. One of the horses snorted, smelling a stranger, but Si gave it a quick pat on the chest and the horse went back to his hay. "There's a bag back here!" he called excitedly. "With lots of shiny stuff in it!"

"Bring it here!" Athela whispered.

"I can't, it's too heavy."

Marc skirted the horses and went around to where Si stood. There was a small clinking sound, and Tarr distinctly heard voices growing closer in the house.

"Hurry up!" he hissed.

"Oh...Athela, you're not going to believe this," Marc breathed.

The door to the back of the house swung open, and a man walked down the back stairs to the horses. Athela and Tarr flew around the corner and hunkered down in the shadows. Tarr managed to peek around. The man was dressed in a green cloak and inspected his horse's cannon bone. He straightened and—even though Tarr was praying against it—saw Marc and Si.

"What the—"

Marc barreled forward and put all of his considerable heft into a strong right hook that sent the man flying back against the wall. The horses started and whinnied nervously, hooves clattering; Si scampered nimbly around the horses' legs with something clutched in his hand and ran past Tarr and Athela.

"Go!" Si yelled gleefully.

The guard effectively stunned, Marc slid beneath the hitching post and bolted down the alleyway behind his friends. They ran until they could be sure that there was no one behind them, then stopped to rest.

"What...is...it?" Athela panted. Si handed her what he had in his hand. It was a horse's breastcollar, and on the front was a silver seal engraved with a green *K* with a constellation behind it. Athela seemed to have stopped breathing for a good few seconds before Tarr nudged her. She audibly inhaled.

"That's Kagai's symbol," she whispered hoarsely. "Which means that those were Kagai's guards."

That's impossible, Tarr thought. *Impossible.* And yet there it was, glinting back up at him from the palm of Athela's hand. *Kagai is real?*

"What were they doing in Bearn's house?" Si wondered.

"Perhaps Bearn supports Kagai," Marc suggested.

"I don't think so," Tarr said slowly, remembering the look on Bearn's face as he'd passed them. The others turned to him. "You saw how he looked. I'll bet you anything that he was forced." Something slid into Tarr's memory, something far back when they had first rode up to the city. He remembered the gate with the guards, Archer hiding his face. And just before that... "Remember those strange tracks you saw the first day we came here, Marc? The day we arrived in the city?"

"Yes," Marc said, watching him wide-eyed.

"I'll bet you anything they started coming almost the same time we got here. Two Falls won't have any warning when Kagai attacks. We've been waiting for something from the outside—an invasion. But it won't be. It will come from within."

Tarr stopped speaking and the others continued to stare at him for a few moments as if they'd never quite seen anything like him. It reminded him of how the young Ashans in his tribe used to look at him when he'd say something unexpected. He couldn't quite believe that Kagai's name had come out of his mouth, either, not when he'd spent so long believing it all to be just an old legend. But as farfetched as it was, it made sense to him.

Laith looked up, a stubborn set to his jaw. "Marc, Rane, I think you should search the district and see how many troops you find. We'll go with this information to the city council tomorrow. They wanted proof. I think we may now have it."

Rane and Marc nodded, but before she vanished, Tarr was almost sure that Rane gave him a quick smile of admiration. His heart did a few flip-flops.

Archer was aloft, high above the world below, tucked against the base of a statue on one of Two Falls' edifices. He was invisible to anyone who passed. His sharp golden eyes surveyed the familiar spread of the city around him. He took in everything: the movement of the people below, patterns in groups as they walked.

And then he spotted what he'd been looking for.

A few shadowy figures were standing across the street, eyeing the tavern opposite. There was something in their manner—stiff, unsmiling, barely speaking to one another—that told him to be watchful. They could have just been run-of-the-mill thieves, but they'd already let much more tempting targets pass undisturbed.

Archer remained still, and when an Ashan finally came out of the front door of the club and proceeded down the deserted street, the shadows moved. He followed, slinking along the rooftops like a cat, yellow eyes glinting as he passed through thin shafts of lamplight. If the Ashan on the street was aware that he was being followed, he seemed oblivious to it. The shadows moved closer.

All at once, in a coordinated surge, the figures made their move and lurched toward the Ashan down in the street. Archer reared up and fitted an arrow to his bow with the speed of lighting and sent it hissing down into the alley. It hit its mark and one of the figures fell. Archer leaped off of the roof, taking out his knife, expecting the thugs to run away. But there were about six of them, more than Archer had initially thought, and they were in no mood to run. Three turned to face him while three more grabbed the felled Ashan, who had startled and turned when Archer shot the arrow. Not willing to let them get away, Archer launched himself towards them, knife out, but to his great surprise they were all fully armed, and three swords came singing out of scabbards.

This may not have been the greatest idea, Archer thought to himself mid-leap. He was never as comfortable fighting with a knife or sword as he was with a bow, but he was capable enough to knock one of the fighters' swords to the ground. Another one of them leaped atop him, and a moment later Archer felt a sharp pain on his arm as a blade sliced through it. With a yell, Archer tossed his attacker from his back and kicked her to the ground, only to look up and see the other abductors making away with their quarry.

Furiously, Archer darted forward, only to have a third blade come singing toward his head. He ducked just in time, his black coat whirling around him, and used his unwounded arm to land an elbow into the swordsman's neck, felling him temporarily. In the blink of an eye, another black and white fletched arrow was sighted and released after the retreating abductors. One of them fell, but the other two managed to hold on to their captive and pull him struggling around a corner.

Cursing, Archer barreled after them, but when he turned the same corner, they had already vanished into the night. He did a peripheral jog around the area, but it was as if they had never been there at all. He stopped and glared angrily about him with his bright golden eyes, out of breath, scarlet blood dripping down his white hand.

Reluctantly, he turned to go home and tend to his wounds.

CHAPTER THIRTEEN

"Did you get a look at them?" asked Marc the next morning as he inspected Archer's wounded arm. "You know, for someone who gets into as much trouble as you do, you're lacking in basic first aid."

"Poisons, yes," Archer grimaced as he pulled the bandage tight. "Bandages, no. Usually don't have to bother with them if I do my job right. Anyway, I didn't get a good look at them, no. There were six of them."

"Wearing cloaks?" Laith asked.

"Yes, though everyone does at that time of night," Archer winced again.

"What color?" Tarr inquired.

"Green, I think," Archer said.

"Green cloaks," Marc said significantly.

"What?" Archer demanded. "We don't like green?"

Marc and Laith filled him in on the horses they'd found in the arts district and the breastcollar Si had managed to steal.

"Cheeky fellow, this Kagai," Archer breathed, impressed. "Can't say he lacks originality. All right. What do we do?"

"I'm going straight to Pieter," Laith announced. "The town hall wanted evidence, and now they're going to get it. Si, fetch me that breastcollar, would you?"

Si, overjoyed at being able to run an errand for Laith, scampered from his seat and hurtled up the stairs.

When they arrived at the town hall they found that Pieter's council was in session, so they unobtrusively made their way up to his office, which was unlocked. Marc skulked around the door to keep an eye out for trouble. Laith had told them that they had to be especially careful nowadays, as they never knew quite when they might be followed or by whom. It was the type of precaution they should have taken from the beginning, Tarr thought privately, though it did little good to say so now. *And for that matter, Pieter should keep his office locked,* he thought, thumbing through a few papers on the desk.

Tarr found himself in something of a quandary. The breastcollar they'd found with Kagai's insignia was undeniable proof that all was not well, but the more he thought about it in the clear light of day, the more it could all be explained away, and he felt rather foolish for losing his head the night before and buying into all of it and planting wild ideas in Laith's head about some sort of covert coup. Perhaps they'd stumbled upon a rogue band of Kagaian supporters, nothing more. Marc and Rane hadn't turned up anything new when they'd gone to search the rest of the arts district for soldiers and horses. Perhaps the Ashan disappearances were all coincidence. Perhaps the breastcollar hadn't meant Kagai at all; perhaps it just belonged to someone with the initial *K.* And what did it matter if someone wore a green cloak or not?

Either way, he wouldn't be much use. The narrow escapes they'd made from the palace of Joymaril and Riddleton had been thanks to the ingenuity of the others.

Pieter came up to his office after about forty-five minutes, and if he was surprised to see two Jelani and an Ashan lurking in his chamber, he hid it well. He made his way unhurriedly to his seat and smiled at them. There was something comforting about him, something that reminded Tarr of the council elders back home, the sense that he had the knowledge and authority to take care of their problems.

Laith recounted the previous night's happenings as thoroughly as he could and showed Pieter the breastplate that Si had stolen from the bags.

"So the council has to listen now, don't they?" Marc asked hopefully. "Now that there is physical evidence? There's the breastplate, and a whole lot of Ashans have mysteriously gone missing."

Pieter sighed and leaned back in his chair. "They may see it, but that doesn't mean for an instant that they will acknowledge it. They will say that the breastplate is a forgery. You could have had one made to prove your story."

Tarr grimaced inwardly; he hadn't even considered that.

Pieter smiled mildly. "They'll say I'm growing old and need to abandon my seat on the council for believing in such nonsense. They'll say that a few missing Ashans here or there don't point to anything, much less a greater conspiracy."

"But," Laith said, his soldier's mind of action momentarily overcoming his diplomacy, "the council has got to *do* something! For no other reason than the missing Ashans. They ought to be found."

Pieter made a helpless gesture with his hands. "People go missing every day."

Laith stared at him. There was a long silence. "The seven of us can't fight this battle alone," he said finally.

"No. No, you shouldn't have to do that," Pieter said softly. He thought to himself. After a moment, an expression of resolve settled on his face. "And you won't have to. I will speak to the council. This will be enough to reason with some. Some may be all we need. I can try to motivate a few of the home guards, some of the police force, and the city militia. Have them start searching homes for any horses or troops—best not to mention Kagai, that will get people too worked up. But I will tell them that Ashans are going missing. It will take time."

"It's better than nothing at all," Laith agreed.

"You know, you're not the only ones who have noticed things going awry," Pieter mused. "There was a young man in here yesterday with his father. They run a blacksmith shop towards the north gate, and the Ashan who worked with them had vanished without a trace. They have been asking around and found out about the others who were missing, just as you did. They came here and had much the same reaction that you got when you tried to speak before the council. Curt dismissal, much to my annoyance."

"What's the young man's name?" Laith asked. "They sound like they would be good people to get in touch with."

"The father's...oh, what was it?" Pieter pinched the bridge of his nose between his thumb and forefinger. "Orro, I think it was. The son's name was Ari. Big, serious fellows, both of them. Not a smile to split between them. They didn't leave me any contact information, but keep your ears open. If they come back, I'll point you their way."

"When will you speak to the council?" Laith asked.

"We've adjourned for the day, so I will speak tomorrow. I hope that it will be enough," Pieter smiled. "Thank you for coming to me."

Laith nodded and stood. "Please be careful of yourself as well. If there is any hint of danger, be sure that you have a place to go."

"I have already made arrangements," Pieter smiled. "Not everyone in this city is unable to look to their futures."

They stood outside in an unseasonably cold drizzle. Spring was on its way out, and summer was just around the corner, but it could have been late fall for how dreary the day was. Laith strode out into the plaza, where the dull light fell on him, making him look almost like one of the statues posed nearby at the foot of the town hall steps. After a moment's pause, he stirred.

"I want to have a look around," he said, clearly fed up with sitting and talking. "Perhaps we'll try to find that blacksmith Pieter mentioned."

They flipped their hoods up over their heads. Laith took them on a crisscrossing route through the streets and eventually came to the north side of the city near the gate through which Tarr had first come to Two Falls from the forest. To his right, Tarr recognized one of the bridges and the merry street that had been decked out in lights for the festival when he'd first arrived. The thought of it made him smile fleetingly. It already seemed so very long ago.

But things were not all the same. Where the bridges had been open and free for anyone to use, some were now being guarded by individuals wearing the yellow livery of the town council. Three of them were stationed by the far end of the main road, right at the entrance to the city, and were speaking to everyone trying to leave, while waving in whoever cared to enter.

"That's odd," Marc murmured.

"Let's have a closer look," Laith suggested. "Tarr, keep your hands in your pockets."

Tarr did as he was told, realizing only after a moment that Laith was telling him to hide his six fingers, the evidence that he was Ashan. Tarr swallowed and looked sharply about him for anyone watching them strangely and wondered if there was a way to make himself appear shorter and bulkier than he actually was.

An Ashan couple approached the officers guarding the exit. "Halt," one of them ordered, and they stopped, looking nervous. They were both middle-aged and clung to one another as if for physical support. "Why are you leaving the city?" the guard demanded.

"To see my relatives near the Meadows," one of the Ashan men said hesitantly.

"Names?" the officer demanded.

"Cedar," he replied. "My husband's cousins. They have recently had a baby and have invited us to stay with them."

"Where is your travel permit?" the guard asked with a fair amount of relish.

"Travel permit?" the second man asked blankly. "What travel permit?"

"The Ashan travel permit," she responded.

"We didn't know we needed a travel permit," the first said fearfully. "We've never needed a travel permit in Two Falls. We always just came and went as we pleased."

"The law has changed," the guard replied. "It was announced last week."

"We didn't hear of it!" the first Ashan exclaimed, challenge in his voice. The guard looked back up at him coolly.

"It was announced last week. I'm afraid I will have to detain you for attempting to leave without a permit." She motioned to two other guards, who stepped forward and laid their hands on the second Ashan's arms. He let out a cry.

"This is a free city! We have committed no crime!" he yelled angrily as the guards set upon him. "We are not criminals! You have no right to take us away!"

The guard waved her hand, bored, and the two Ashans were led off, still shouting and protesting. Laith turned to Tarr, who felt sick. The prince looked as though he were about to speak when suddenly his face blanched. Tarr whipped around and found himself face-to-face with another guard.

"Going somewhere?" the guard asked suspiciously.

"Merely getting the details of applying for a travel permit," Laith said swiftly, laying his hand on Tarr's arm. "Let's go back to town hall."

"Loitering is not permitted," the guard sneered. "Leave, or I'll have you arrested."

They walked as swiftly as they could from the checkpoint. Tarr was at a loss for words. So, it seemed, were Marc and Laith. Suddenly feeling as though they were being hunted by some threatening, unseen force, Tarr jammed his hands down into his pockets as far as they would go, stooping slightly and hoping he would pass unnoticed.

CHAPTER FOURTEEN

That night, after a good bit of coaxing, Archer convinced Ma to leave Two Falls and pay an extended visit to her cousins outside of Riddleton. It wasn't easy. Archer had to be rather vague about his reasoning and evasive about what exactly it was that he and his friends had been up to. But Ma clearly trusted him, and after he'd assured her that her house would be safe and that the others would have enough to eat, she assented.

Tarr had been listening to their exchange from the living room couch—the door to the kitchen had been open, and it would have been nearly impossible not to overhear. As Ma and Archer stood, there was the scraping of chairs against the floor, followed by the quiet sound of a shared embrace.

"I'm proud of you, Archer," Tarr heard her say, so quietly that he had to strain to hear her. "I remember the first time I saw you. Just a little boy, unable to speak. So lost. And now look at you. So handsome. And with such nice friends."

"Thanks, Ma."

Ma came through the door and gave Tarr a weepy smile as she passed, dabbing at her eyes with her apron. She vanished towards the back of the house.

Tarr continued to stare at his book, but his mind was churning. It sounded as though Archer had been young—*very* young—when he'd been exiled. *What on earth could a child have done to be thrown out of his tribe like that?* Tarr wondered. And then, much to his own surprise, he thought, *it couldn't have been right for them to do so. The tribe must have been wrong about him.*

He blinked, shocked at his own audacity. It was almost impossible to conceive that an Ashan elder council had erred, and even more impossible to consider an Ashan law or ruling to be unjust.

Then he remembered: *My tribe sent me away. Maybe they were wrong, too. Perhaps I should give Archer a chance.*

Almost like a clenched fist releasing, he felt something in his chest relax.

Only a moment later, Archer emerged from the kitchen bearing an expression of weariness on his long, angular face. He spotted Tarr on the couch and, accustomed to Tarr's studied avoidance, continued on towards the staircase.

"Evening," Tarr said hesitantly. "Archer."

Archer stopped still and slowly swiveled around to face him. His eyes searched Tarr's quizzically, surprised by this sudden acknowledgment. Tarr gave him a tentative smile, a small olive branch from one Ashan to another.

"Tarr," Archer said slowly, and Tarr was pleased to see that the corners of his mouth were creasing into a smile. He reached into his pocket and withdrew a tiny note. "One of Rowan's associates just passed this to me on the street."

Tarr rose from the couch and walked over to Archer, taking the note from him and uncrumpling it in his hand.

Meet me as soon as you can at the club.

Bring the others. Rowan.

"Want to come with me?" Archer asked. Tarr was shocked to hear the note of vulnerability in his voice. He sounded slightly nervous even to ask.

"Sure," Tarr replied, and couldn't help but feel a little pleased at the way Archer beamed back at him. "It says 'bring the others,' though, shouldn't we fetch them?"

Archer waved a hand. "They're all asleep, anyway, no need to wake them. We'll fill them in later."

Tarr had the strangest suspicion that, for some reason, Archer wanted to go with him alone. If it had been a month ago, he would have guessed that Archer was trying to betray him and lead him into some sort of trap. But now the thought barely registered as a possibility. Nodding, he rose and fetched his cloak from his room.

They didn't talk much on the walk up to Rowan's club, but to Tarr's surprise, it wasn't strange or awkward; he didn't feel the usual need to try and think of something to fill up the silences, and Archer seemed perfectly content to let them pass as well. Archer was different one-on-one than he was with the group of others. Rather than finding clever jokes or quips as he usually did with Laith or Athela; instead, he would occasionally point out a landmark or historical building that he thought Tarr would find interesting. His knowledge of the city was immense, which made sense after what Tarr had overheard in the kitchen. If he truly had come to Two Falls first as a young boy, he would have lived there for at least a decade or more. Tarr was fascinated by all of the things Archer pointed out, like an inn where a Jelani Queen had once stayed and gotten food poisoning from a bad oyster (which apparently had almost led to an outright human-Jelani war) or a bakery that had smuggled secret messages for Morthenstar in their cakes. After ten minutes or so, Tarr began to wish that they had more time just to wander about the city together; how silly his one-sided vendetta now seemed.

Eventually, they made it safely up to Rowan's club. They ducked through the now-familiar passageway into the courtyard and under the purple cloth covering the entrance. Inside, the two Ashans found it mostly empty, with only a few patrons here and there. One was snoring away into his tankard, and the other two were conspiring across a bowl of what looked like a thick, steaming stew. Tarr supposed that Rowan was up in her private rooms as usual and wove behind Archer through the tables, up the stairs, and back into the area where she usually entertained. Rowan was sitting upon a soft couch and rose immediately when she saw him, a slight smile playing around her curved lips. She looked from one of them to the other. A flicker of surprise flitted across her features. Tarr noted it and began to feel uneasy.

"Archer, you have brought your friend, how nice," she said in Ashan.

"I don't speak it, Rowan," Archer said tersely.

She gave a strange sardonic chuckle while Archer looked stonily ahead. Something about the exchange struck Tarr as odd. *Is Archer lying?* he wondered. It had always seemed strange to him that Archer insisted he didn't speak Ashan, when Tarr couldn't imagine actually forgetting the language himself. But Rowan didn't press the issue any further.

She came up and took Archer's hand, and Tarr could see him relax a bit. She was undeniably lovely; her dress was again the same color as the purple birthmark on her neck. She wore a thin line of smoky black makeup around each eye and the faintest hint of rouge on each high cheekbone. Her irises were a dark violet.

"Rowan, why did you call us here?" Tarr asked suddenly.

Archer looked curiously over at the sharp tone in Tarr's voice. As Tarr had begun to suspect, Rowan immediately looked quizzical. "Call you here?" she asked, a puzzled smile playing on her mouth.

"Archer—" Tarr began, but there was a noise behind them.

The door burst open, and a man Tarr recognized from previous visits to Rowan's club flew in. "Khan!" Archer said jovially, clearly expecting a greeting in return, but the man, who had sharp, plunging dark eyebrows and a curling head of black hair, simply nodded swiftly at Archer and took Rowan urgently by the arm.

Hissing between her teeth, Rowan bade Archer and Tarr wait as Khan pulled her roughly out into the hallway, closing the door behind them. As soon as she was out of sight, Tarr leapt to his feet, feeling as though he wouldn't be able to contain himself just sitting there. He drew up beside the window and looked out. Archer came up right behind him.

Standing below the tavern in the courtyard was a rider cloaked in green. Beside it were two other horses, similarly arrayed but with no riders in sight. Tarr's breath caught, and his unease was replaced by a swelling fear. He whipped around and caught Archer's expression, which had similarly shifted.

"Is that—" Archer's eyes narrowed.

"I think so," Tarr whispered.

"Come on," Archer grabbed his arm. "I'll get us out."

Overwhelmingly relieved that Archer was there beside him, the two bolted out of the private area to the balcony overlooking the main room. Below them, Rowan's club was completely empty; even the few patrons who had been there before had vanished.

"Back," Archer ordered through his teeth, pulling on Tarr's arm. "Through the window."

Suddenly, there was the clanking of boots and spurs on the floor below, and the sound galvanized Tarr into sudden action. The two Ashans flew back into the private room. Archer bolted to the window and slammed the pane up and open. Like a cat, he leaped up and crouched on the sill, calculating the best way to get down. He glanced at Tarr to make sure he was ready to follow, then twisted around and headed up onto the rooftops.

The sound of the window had alerted the rider in the courtyard, and as Tarr thrust his head out into the cool night air he heard an indecipherable shout from the street. He slithered his body out of the window and found a handhold on the stone gutter of the building. After that, the terror of the moment seemed to dissipate entirely. *Just like climbing trees back in the forest,* he thought, and then swung out into space.

There was the sound of a whistle and Tarr realized that an arrow had gone sailing past his head. Stifling an audible cry of fear, he hoisted himself up onto the roof, and keeping low, he scrambled up the tiles to where Archer was crouched, silhouetted against the dim light of the night sky.

"Did you see Rowan?" Archer hissed. "Did she get out?"

"No," Tarr shook his head breathlessly. "They'll be after us, though; they saw us."

"They can't get us up here," Archer shook his head. As Tarr's eyes adjusted to the darkness, he could see that Archer was scanning the street below, looking for any sign of Rowan or Khan. "I have to go down. I have to try and help them."

"Khan may have gotten her out," Tarr reassured him. He certainly didn't want to wait there on the rooftops alone, and didn't like the idea of Archer heading back down into the club either. It was much safer there, high above the street.

All at once, there was a clamor down below, and a troop of three riders rounded the corner of the street, pointing upwards to where Tarr and Archer were silhouetted against the night sky. Archer cursed beneath his breath and seized Tarr by the arm, forcing him down just as another arrow whizzed past. "I should've brought my bow," he muttered, mostly to himself. "Come on, this way."

He pointed Tarr towards the long edge of the rooftop, and the two Ashans scrambled forward, balancing easily just at the razor edge of the roof, twenty feet above the street below. The riders were still tracking them from the ground, and twice Archer stopped and pushed Tarr down just as arrows were loosed past their ears.

At the corner, Archer stopped. "Jump first, that building there."

Tarr swallowed, nervously eyeing the riders below, but a moment later gathered his strength and launched himself through the night air, landing with only a short skid on the angled roof of a nearby apartment building. He wondered briefly what the inhabitants of Two Falls must be making of the sounds of two fully-grown Ashans skittering up and over their rooftops in the middle of the night. The riders, alerted to Tarr's jump, were now waiting for Archer to do the same so that they could get a good shot at him. *He sent me across first so that I would be safer*, he realized, with no small amount of shock.

He cast about for something that might help and, with his long, nimble fingers, managed to pry up one of the clay roof tiles, which had been hanging loose and at an odd angle a foot or two from his handhold. He kept his eye on Archer, and just as he saw Archer prepare to crouch and spring for the jump, he threw the tile bodily at the nearest guard he could reach. It shattered into dozens of pieces, spooking the horses and creating quite a sizable commotion, in the midst of which Archer was able to safely leap through the air and land on the roof right by Tarr.

"Thanks," Archer panted, recovering his breath.

"Anytime," Tarr returned.

"We can lose them now, no problem," Archer glanced over his shoulder down to where the riders in the street below were still trying to regain order. Their horses clearly hadn't anticipated the possibility of large projectiles being hurled at them from the night sky, and weren't terribly keen on cooperating any further.

With one hand Archer motioned Tarr forward, and the two Ashans began picking their way across the rooftops of Two Falls.

"With all the danger building up for Ashans lately, you two clearly need to start laying low," Athela said gravely the next morning, after Tarr and Archer had filled the others in on the events of the night before.

The house was already feeling dimmer with Ma's departure at the crack of dawn on a wagon bound southward. Tarr had been so exhausted from the night's activities that he hadn't remembered to wake up to tell her goodbye, for which he felt more than a little guilty after the generous hospitality she had shown them. Archer had managed to see her off himself and, therefore, had had maybe an hour of sleep at the most. This explained why he was looking blearily down at a slice of buttered toast, and had been doing so for the past five minutes.

"Did you get word on what happened to Rowan?" Laith asked.

"I went by Khan's apartment after I saw Ma to the city border," Archer shook his head. "It's not good. Rowan's gone. Khan barely got away."

"Where did they take her?" Si asked, his eyes wide.

"If it's who we think it is, probably Faridor. That's Kagai's fortress," Laith said gravely.

This statement was greeted with a dark stretch of silence. According to legend, it was all but impossible to break free from the dungeons of Faridor. They were located in the belly of the fortress, below the waterline of the ocean. No prisoner had ever been known to escape before.

"Maybe...she'll get away *on the way* to Faridor?" Tarr asked tentatively, trying to infuse a small bit of optimism into the proceedings.

"Maybe," Archer echoed, but there was a dubious note in his voice. He rubbed his forehead tiredly with one hand, and Tarr felt a sudden pang of sympathy. Archer had known Rowan for many years. For all the anxiety Tarr felt about the prospect of her being taken by Kagai's forces, Archer must have felt it tenfold.

It felt as though the jaws of an invisible trap were closing around them, and they had no way to slip free. *We should try to save who we can while we can,* he thought suddenly. He leaned forward.

"If all of this is true, and Kagai—or whoever—really is on the rise, we've got to try and protect Pieter," he said. He was surprised by the force in his own voice. "Someone will remember the day we came to speak to the governing council, and someone will remember that Pieter agreed to meet with us. They may have seen us going in and out of his offices. He's in danger. He should find somewhere to hide. Somewhere safe."

"You're right," Laith agreed thoughtfully. "We should get word to him."

"Si and I can do it today," Marc suggested. "Si can deliver a note to him. No one will suspect a boy of having anything to do with the Strikers."

Beside him, Si straightened up a little taller at the table, looking self-important and puffing his chest out a bit.

"I can pretend to have an accent," Si suggested.

"Good instinct," Archer agreed. "An accent always helps."

"In the meantime," Athela cut in, "it won't do much good having you and Archer going traipsing around Two Falls out in the open anymore, not with all of Kagai's riders snatching Ashans out whenever they can. You'll have to lay low as well."

The prospect of pottering aimlessly around Ma's deserted inn (comfortable though it was) seemed somewhat gloomy to Tarr, who exchanged a brief glance with Archer. The other Ashan seemed similarly unenthused.

Suddenly, Tarr realized he was no longer nervous about asking Athela to follow her to the library. He swiveled towards her, wondering what on earth had taken him so long. "Could I come with you and Rane and help with your research? I could wear a cloak when we travel to and from, and I'd be safe enough with you both there."

Athela blinked as if she honestly hadn't considered it before. For a few moments, Tarr could see Athela inwardly wrestling with her naturally cautious instincts and with her deep-set desire to have another set of eyes and hands helping to sift through all the material at the library. "Fine," she said, after a few moments' grappling. "You can come with us. Archer, though, you stick out like a sore thumb and everyone in town knows what you look like. You'll have to stay here for now, at least during the daytime."

"Fine by me," Archer said with a yawn. "Nocturnal life it is."

Tarr focused his attention once more on the slice of toast before him, trying not to betray his inner joy at the prospect of losing himself beneath a pile of books. And if it meant an opportunity to sneak a few sidelong glances at Rane—or perhaps even talk to her again—so much the better.

CHAPTER FIFTEEN

The library itself was one of the great old buildings in the ancient part of town, its sweeping flight of stairs leading up to an intimidatingly majestic front entrance. Tarr remembered that Morthenstar had actually designed the library herself, and the weight of that history loomed above him as he mounted the steps, carefully hooded and cloaked against any prying eyes.

Inside, the air was cool and musty, the ceiling soaring up above them and magnifying the sounds below like a drum. Tarr had never seen anything quite like the inside of the building before, not even at Joymaril palace. The sheer number of books contained within was almost overwhelming; there were rooms and rooms filled from top to bottom, enormous shelves that rose above him like the walls of a cliff. In one room, there was an entire wall—an entire wall!—that looked exactly like the Ashan library back home, with honeycomb structures and scrolls tucked inside, only these shelves ran from the floor all the way up to the vaulted roof. Just as at home, each scroll was marked with a fluttering white tag explaining what sort of information it contained. Tarr felt a sudden, unexpected pang of homesickness just seeing them, and pretended to be distracted by something else as they passed so he didn't have to look.

While pretending not to see the Ashan wall of scrolls, he noticed a funny little room tucked to one side of the main hallway. It had a heavy oak door and a carved woman with outstretched arms over the top of the door, as if she was welcoming any passersby into the room.

"What's that?" Tarr asked, pointing and feeling very much like a young child on a trek with an elder, seeing new trees for the first time.

"That's the portrait room, I think," Athela replied dismissively, her mind clearly on the task at hand. Behind her, Rane was staring up at the face of the woman with the open hands above the door. When Tarr continued gawking, Athela paused. "The library houses a rather large collection of portraits and landscapes that were painted all the way back from when Morthenstar was still alive. There are sculptures, too. Everything's very, very old."

"Are there any pictures of Morthenstar in there?" Tarr asked.

"I don't know, I haven't gone in," Athela admitted, then flapped a hand at him. "Come on, this is going to take all day if we just stand here."

Tarr followed Athela and Rane around the circular alleyway between the rows and rows of books until they reached a stone staircase with a curved railing. Athela purposefully trotted her way up it, followed by Rane, who glided silently along, the pads of her fingers lightly skimming over the gritty stone as she passed. Tarr took it more slowly, staring at the pillars and stained glass that seemed to stretch up and up above him, high as any tree in the forest. They reached the landing above, and Athela led them around the side of the wall. Every few feet was another door leading into what Tarr supposed were rooms full of books devoted solely to one subject. Athela paused in front of one of these. As she had described, there was a large statue of Morthenstar reading outside.

Tarr stopped beside the statue, inspecting it curiously. It was life-size and incredibly detailed, so much so that it looked as though she had just come to sit down for a brief rest and had a thin layer of stone painted over her features, holding her in place. She was depicted sitting on a high chair with her feet crossed down in front of her. Her face was mostly obscured, hair cascading down before her eyes, and she held a stone book up with one hand in her lap, head resting on a fist made by the other.

"Bit eerie, isn't it?" Athela asked, voice breaking the silence like a whip.

"Very," Tarr agreed, and followed her into the room.

Morthenstar's bookroom was a two-story affair with a small table and chairs at the center for reading purposes and a ladder propped up against the shelves, all of which bore placards explaining the contents of the section.

"We've been all through those up there, and down along that side, and over on that wall, and still we've found nothing. If it's not in here then we have to start searching the rest of the library." She closed her eyes as if to banish the thought itself. "I don't even want to think about it."

They settled quickly down to business, Athela and Rane already used to the routine. Rane went about in her quiet way and pulled down three books at once, and they all leafed through, looking for any mention of Morthenstar's heir. A number of times, Tarr found copies of the prophecy, all of which claimed to be the exact words spoken to Daemun by Morthenstar, but Tarr noted with amusement that each account was slightly different.

> Three Strikers were predicted by Morthenstar to her general, Daemun. One was spoken of to carry her sword, another to have gray eyes, and a third to have a wolf. There has been much speculation as to whether or not these are to be the only Strikers in existence if and when the prophecy is fulfilled, but suffice it to say that had there been more Strikers, Morthenstar would probably have predicted them.

Tarr tossed the book aside, taking up another and flipping through, eyes scanning along the yellowed pages. Here, another retelling:

> Morthenstar's prediction of a number of Strikers to follow in her footsteps was clearly mirrored by the band that was with her at the time, a group of nine or ten Ashans, Jelani and humans, Morthenstar being chief among them. There is no real detail on record about which of the Strikers should follow in Morthenstar's footsteps upon the second

coming, but there is definite evidence to suggest that a Jelani with gray eyes and an Ashan with a wolf will certainly be amongst them.

Tarr sighed, throwing the book aside to land on top of the other. He wondered, not for the first time, just who that mysterious traveler had been in the forest, the one who was clearly meant to be the subject of the prophecy (if there was indeed any truth to be found in the prophecy at all.) He squinted up at a clock hanging down from the wall. They had already spent two hours in the library, and it was getting late. He needed to stretch his legs.

"I need to take a walk," he informed Athela, who grunted in response. Rane merely flicked her eyes up to Tarr once and then returned them down to the book she was reading.

Tarr stepped out into the main hold of the library, knowing exactly where he wanted to take his break. He headed down the stairs, across the circular center, nodding at the watchman, who returned his gesture with a yawn, past another gigantic statue of Morthenstar that crowned the exact center of the library, and wandered in through the portrait room door where the woman with open arms welcomed him, her face blank and tranquil.

The room was one story, slightly larger than Tarr had initially judged by the size of the door, and was poorly illuminated by only a single light, though Tarr could see unlit torches mounted up in holds against the wall. Though he had been expecting a room full of paintings based on Athela's description, he was surprised to see that the room only housed one portrait. He walked eagerly up to it. The inscription beneath the frame read "*Portrait of Alder Morthenstar,*" and Tarr was rather touched to see that there were some flowers (a few fresh, some brown and wilting) and candles left on the stone floor beneath the portrait, perhaps as an offering. He wondered if the flowers held the same meaning as they did in Ashan culture, where the pyres of Ashans who had passed away were covered entirely with boughs, berries, and wildflowers before they were set aflame, a symbol of the life that had passed and the life that was to come.

Tarr's eyes traveled up from the offerings and locked eyes with the most famous woman in the history of his country.

He hadn't had much experience with artwork, only the paintings and sculptures he had seen at the Jelani palace, but out of all of those he'd seen, he liked this one the best. Alder Morthenstar was posed in what looked like a study, a stack of books on a table beside her hand and one opened in her lap. He peered forward curiously, but the writing in the book was illegible. She was dressed not in armor but in trousers and a simple shirt, a red cloak tossed casually over her shoulder, almost the same shade as her scarlet hair, which was held halfway up by a comb that glinted warmly out of the shadows of the room in which she sat. Through the illustrated window Tarr could make out a few buildings, one of which he recognized as a tower near the entrance of Two Falls, a waterfall, and a thick forest spreading out into the distance. It all seemed to suggest her connection to the founding of Two Falls and to the forest of the Ashans. Tarr smiled, pleased with what he'd uncovered. *Perhaps paintings hold clues to things, too,* he realized. *The painters must have chosen what is presented, after all. It all must mean something.*

With this newfound realization, he eagerly leaned forward, scanning the canvas for other such hints. The only bit of the painting that seemed to denote her life as a warrior was her sword, which was still in its scabbard and held loosely in her hand, down by her side. Tarr looked closer and felt a rush of goosebumps run up his arms and a chill go up the back of his neck as he realized that the sword in the painting was the exact same—the *exact same*—as the sword Si had brought with him to Joymaril. He recognized immediately the pattern of red scrollwork on the hilt, the cascade of rubies falling like rose petals down the length of the scabbard. Tarr swallowed, his throat suddenly dry.

No, he told himself firmly. *Just because it's the same sword doesn't mean that the rest of that nonsense about Ashans with wolves and Jelani with gray eyes and black hair is true.*

Thus reassured, he leaned in and examined Morthenstar's face. He had no frame of reference as to whether or not the artist's depiction was accurate, but he had the sense that whoever had painted it had captured her spirit. It was odd how much personality could be conveyed through paint and a few careful brushstrokes. The expression that looked back at him was noble and serious, to be sure, but there was a hint of a cheeky edge to the corner of her mouth, a glint in her eye that told him she would have been ready with a joke or a laugh, regardless of how dire her circumstances. He liked her.

A moment later, he gave a start and realized that he'd been dawdling in the portrait room for more than fifteen minutes. He turned to hurry back to Athela and Rane, but paused and straightened one of the flowers on the floor beneath the portrait, which had fallen out of its vase onto the stones below. With a last smile at Morthenstar, he hot-footed it back up past the statue of Morthenstar reading (a popular pose, apparently) to their room, where little to no progress had been made.

"You haven't found anything, then?" Tarr inquired in an attempt to be polite, settling back into a chair and feeling relieved that Athela wasn't angry with him for taking such a long break. Rane was rummaging around in the stacks again on the other side of the room.

"No, we haven't," Athela groaned, clawing her fingers a few times through her curly black mane of hair. "We're on the last two books and Rane's looking around for anything we might have missed, but we *haven't got a single clue*." She sighed heavily, leaning forward and resting her hands on her bent knees. "I guess all that we have left to do is to start looking in books outside the room." She looked morosely around at the library's solemn grandeur.

Suddenly, with a small *click*, Tarr's mind slid two puzzle pieces into place.

The books outside the room.

He thought of the portrait he had just seen, of the open book in Morthenstar's lap, and suddenly he knew. His breath caught, and a thrill of excitement nearly bowled him over.

"Athela!" he bellowed and grabbed her by the wrist, all vestiges of his usual decorum gone. Above them, Rane had appeared at the sound of his yell. She leaned over the railing, watching with astonishment as Tarr dashed towards her.

"There's nothing in here..." she called down. "What happened?"

"I have no idea!" Athela yelled helplessly, letting herself be dragged along by Tarr's wiry grip. He threw open the door of the room and flung Athela bodily out into the hall, then stood beside the statue of Morthenstar reading and turned back to Athela with a triumphant grin on his face.

"There you go, Athela."

She approached, face screwed up in puzzlement. "What on earth do you mean?" she asked.

"The book," Tarr replied.

"Stop being an ass and tell me what you're talking about!" she yelled. "What book? You don't have a book!"

"*That* book!" Tarr responded, still grinning, and pointed to the statue of Morthenstar behind him. Athela's jaw dropped.

"I don't *believe* it," she walked forward and peered over the Morthenstar statue's shoulder. "I can't see...there's something written, Tarr, you were right! Hand me that light!"

Rane deftly moved to one side and yanked a torch out of its grating and passed it over to Athela, who grabbed it and held it in front of her. Tarr met her eyes and she actually smiled at him, looking almost faint. His head felt like there was an explosion of joyful sparks going off inside.

On the stone pages of the book that Morthenstar was reading was an inscription engraved in tiny, meticulous lettering. Tarr couldn't read what it said, as it appeared to be in a very old sort of language, but something inside him *told* him that he'd found what they were looking for. Athela leaned back and turned to look up at Tarr, who was still grinning, so proud of himself that he looked nearly idiotic. "Tarr..." she groped for words, obviously struggling to find praise expansive enough to convey the depth of her feeling. Finally, she clapped a hand on his shoulder. "Well done," she told him. "Rane, get me some paper; we're going to copy this down."

Two hours later Athela sat back in her chair in the boardinghouse, holding up the old piece of parchment proudly in front of her face, scanning it up and down with a triumphant smile lighting up her usually stern features. Tarr rubbed his eyes, feeling them burn in the lamplight, and gave an enormous, satisfied yawn. Even Rane, whom Tarr had never known to show any sign of fatigue, was looking slightly worn out.

"This answers everything," Athela announced. Tarr looked up hopefully.

"It does?"

"Well, to a point," she conceded and lowered it. "Here's hoping the others come back soon so I can brag about how clever we've been."

As if on cue, the front door banged open, and their friends piled into the living room. One by one, the poufy little chairs swallowed them up as they flung their arms and legs out in ungainly, exhausted sprawls.

"So?" Athela asked them. "Success?"

"Some," Laith conceded. "And you?" He sounded as though he didn't expect much.

"As a matter of fact, yes," Athela said primly.

The others sat straight up and listened with rapt attention as Athela described how they had found the inscription in the book. When it came to the part where Tarr had realized the book in which the prophecy was written, the others all swiveled around to stare at him, undeniably impressed. Tarr felt his ears flushing scarlet, and he ducked his head modestly to avoid their gazes. Out of the corner of his eye, he could see Archer studying him appraisingly.

"So, what did the translation say?" Si asked eagerly. "Is it the prophecy? Does it say who Morthenstar's heir is?"

"Well, it's pretty rough; it's written in a very old dialect," Athela reasoned, and Tarr could tell that she was building up to some less-than-stellar news. She took a deep breath. "Basically, it tells us that this is only one half of the puzzle. We've got to find the other."

The collective groan in the room was so great that Athela looked momentarily deflated. She glanced over to Tarr, who gave her an encouraging smile.

"Great," Laith grunted, slumping backwards. "So where is this next piece hidden?"

Athela gave a nervous chuckle and masked it with a small cough. "Don't worry, it gives instructions about where the other half is located," she assured them, "And then there are a bunch of funny lines below that I'm assuming are clues about how to access the other half. 'A poppy in a field,'" she read, trying to sound jovial. "That sounds nice, doesn't it?"

"Athela," Laith said slowly, his brow furrowed suspiciously. "Where is the next piece hidden?"

She coughed again, and Tarr got the sense that she was hedging. "Well, see, that's the not so terribly good news. This gives detailed instructions as to where the next part can be found, but unfortunately, the next part is concealed in the fortress of Faridor."

Laith sat straight back up, Marc's head whipped around, and Si nearly fell out of his chair. "Faridor?" he asked, flabbergasted. "As in, Kagai's fortress Faridor?

"Well, that's just wonderful, Athela; why don't we wrap ourselves up with a big red ribbon and just present ourselves to Kagai's heir while we're at it?" Marc asked.

"Look, *I* didn't make the stupid prophecy, so there's no need to yell at *me*," Athela snipped, smoothing out her pant leg and looking dignified. "I'm sure there's a perfectly safe way that we can get into the fortress and have a look around. It's not really like we have a choice, we've *got* to find out who the heir is supposed to be."

An atmosphere of gloom settled down around the cozy living room, extinguishing all the buoyant good spirits that had occupied it only moments before.

"Anyway," Athela continued, trying to recover a bit of their lost enthusiasm, "how did your prowling go?"

"Well, we snuck into town hall during their lunch hour, which was a great deal of fun, I can tell you," Laith began. Beside him, Si let out a few conspiratorial giggles. "We went into Pieter's office, but it looks as though he's already gone into hiding; no one had seen him, and his office was closed. So," Laith coughed delicately, "Naturally, Si picked the lock, and we went in and searched around."

"Naturally," Athela assented laconically.

"We didn't find anything at first," Marc chimed in, "but then Laith found his appointment book."

"He had a luncheon scheduled yesterday," Laith said.

"And at first we didn't think anything of it," Marc went on, "But then Laith turned to today's page, and it just had a name written down. *Nicolas.* And we didn't know who that was, but we thought it was strange there'd be a name left out so obviously, and scheduled on a day after he went into hiding."

"We figured it was a clue," Si said importantly.

"So we got Archer and very subtly asked around, and found out that he has a nephew-in-law named Nicolas who lives in the very posh section of town. He's a count or something, I don't know."

Archer ran his fingers through his hair. "The address was familiar. I think he used to be neighbors with a friend of mine."

"Anyway," Laith continued, "that took the greater part of the day, having to find out without anyone really realizing we were trying to find out."

"I'll bet," Athela agreed. "So?"

"So we staked out his house for hours, and finally we saw someone matching his description leaving the house," Laith continued. "And Si went up to him pretending to be a street urchin or whatever, then after a while told him that he was working for the Strikers. And Nicolas said that yes, he was hiding his uncle, and if we needed to get in touch with him, he could arrange it."

"So, did you arrange it?" Athela asked impatiently.

"We didn't have time," Laith shook his head. "Nicolas was meeting some people, and they came right up at that moment. Bad luck. But, still, at least we know now where he is and how to get in touch with him."

"Good work," Athela said approvingly. "Let's hope that he was able to motivate those idiots at town hall to actually *do* something."

But, unbeknownst to Athela, it was already too late.

CHAPTER SIXTEEN

Tarr was pulled roughly out of sleep the next morning into what seemed like a nightmare.

"Get up," a strange voice snarled, and Tarr started awake to the terrifying image of a rider dressed in Kagaian green standing over him, a huge black shadow blotted against the light of his window.

Heart racing, Tarr whirled around. Wolver was nowhere to be seen. The rider pulled Tarr upright by the neck of his clothing and pressed a sword to the small of his back, throwing him out towards the door, not uttering a word to him. Tarr made no outcry, too disoriented to do so, but raised his hands helplessly and walked out, the rider close behind him. Tarr could feel the sharp steel tip poking through his thin shirt into his back. He wasn't even cogent enough to put up a struggle, and his groggy mind struggled to comprehend what was going on. *They've got us, they've found us, it's too late. Not yet. A few more days, not yet.* He twisted around and tried to see out in the hallway. *Maybe the others made it out in time. Where's Wolver?*

To his despair, only a few moments later there was a skirmish behind him and Tarr twisted around, watching Archer being led down the stairs behind him. His golden eyes widened as he saw Tarr and he let out a low growl, leaping forward as if he was going to attack the rider behind Tarr, but the one pulling him hit him hard across the face with the flat of the blade he was carrying and roughly pulled Archer up to stand on his two feet again.

"It's all right," Tarr tried to say, but the rider jerked him and pushed him down the stairs.

As they were pulled out into the morning sunlight, Tarr saw that he and Archer weren't the only two people who seemed to be under arrest. The street was packed with displaced villagers, who were being herded out in large packs into the open roads by the riders at swordpoint. Confusion was everywhere; no one seemed to have the faintest idea what was going on, and there was a barely controlled hum of hysteria burbling up from the voices in the street. For some reason, the sight of the townspeople acted as a small comfort. *Perhaps they don't know who we are,* Tarr thought. *Maybe everyone is getting sent out here.* Laith, Athela, and the others were nowhere to be seen.

A moment later, his suspicion that the riders were unaware of their identities was confirmed: as soon as they were outside, they were released into the crowd and shoved unceremoniously to the ground. Archer was tossed next to Tarr, and the two picked themselves up slowly, brushing dirt off of their clothes. Archer's shirt was unbuttoned, and his cheek was bleeding from where the edge of the blade had cut him.

"You all right?" he asked Tarr, who nodded dumbly. Archer rubbed one hand against his face, his dark red blood standing out starkly against his bluish skin. His eyes flashed, and he offered Tarr a tapered hand to help him up, which the other Ashan accepted gratefully. Archer straightened, staring out over the crowd. Beneath the edge of his shirt, Tarr noticed a green tattoo in the shape of a birch leaf resting directly over Archer's heart.

"The others aren't anywhere over there," Archer told him. "When that rider came in on me I thought someone had got the drop on us for sure, but it looks like everyone's out."

"Archer! Tarr!" sounded a familiar voice from behind them. Marc and Si came jogging out from behind a nearby building, Marc's silky hair glinting in the sunlight. "We were going to try and creep away, but Si saw you."

"Athela, Laith, and Rane are coming; we were going over to meet up with them," Si added. "What on earth is going on?"

"Haven't the faintest," Archer replied. They were soon joined by the rest of the Strikers, still dressed in their sleeping clothes. Rane was missing her usual hood and circlet, and her hair shone red-gold in the burnished light of the morning. She stared about herself, silent and watchful. Even within the peril of the moment, she looked lovely.

"We heard them coming in," Marc said. "We were all up and made it out the back way, but there wasn't enough time to come and warn you."

"I couldn't find Wolver," Tarr said, agitated.

"He was in the kitchens with us; I let him out to hide in the barn," Marc assured him. "He's all right."

Around them, people were buzzing and milling, frightened. Families clutched together in little clumps. Heads twisted this way and that, looking for means of escape.

"So, what do we do?" Athela asked, rubbing her bare arms with her hands to try to warm them. "We could try and make a run for it."

"Won't do any good," Laith shook his head grimly. "They've got us penned in. Just like Tarr predicted they would. They placed riders all around the city, and then this morning they simply took the place. Simple. Elegant, almost." With dark eyes, he surveyed the frightened crowds, growing larger and larger by the second as more villagers were pulled out of their homes and cast into the main square. *Are they going to try and kill us?* Tarr wondered wildly. He looked around for any means of escape, but could see none.

"Where are the town guards?" Marc wondered. "Why aren't they coming to fight?"

"Maybe there's no reason to," Laith muttered darkly. "Maybe it's too late."

"They're not going to have a mass execution, are they?" Si asked anxiously, echoing, as he often did, Tarr's own unspoken worries. His boyish face was pinched and strained.

"No, not while I'm here, don't worry," Marc said comfortingly. Si drew closer to him, his frightened young eyes staring out at the chaos surrounding them.

Tarr turned and looked behind them and began to see some flurry of movement farther down the street. The riders began closing in around them, and slowly, like a shifting wave, they herded the towns-people through the streets towards a small platform set up at the town's center. Like sticks adrift in the current, Tarr and the others could do nothing but be carried along with them. The crowd was pressed in close together, squishing shoulder to shoulder so that the riders could fit as many people as possible into the square. Tarr felt someone being pushed up against him and turned, seeing Rane trying to resist the weight of hands on her back, shoving her forward. She was smaller than many of the people around her and was having a difficult time staying on her feet, so Tarr twisted as best he could and pulled her under his arm so that she could stand in front of him. He looked over to be sure that the others were still with them and saw Laith and Marc doing the same thing he was for Athela and Si, Marc's bull-like shoulders bent backward against the influx of bodies around them. Archer had somehow acquired a child: a small girl with brown curls who was crying against his neck, fingers in her mouth, obviously having been separated from her parents in the pandemonium. The tall Ashan was rocking her back and forth, murmuring comfortingly, one arm wrapped protectively around her small body and the other shoving people away from him when they became dangerously close.

Finally, when it seemed that an outright brawl was bound to begin, a man climbed the platform at the square's center. He held up a hand for silence, and the people around Tarr obeyed. The man took out a rolled-up sheet of paper, held it in front of his face, and began speaking. The area suddenly fell deathly silent, apart from the sounds of bated breathing and the crying of a few small children.

"People of Two Falls," the speaker intoned loudly. "This procla-mation has come by order of Kagai, sovereign ruler of this country."

His words fell like a stone, and Tarr could feel the blood draining from his head. *It can't really be true.* His eyes met Archer's, golden and grave.

The herald continued. "A bloodless coup has been staged this morning, and Kagai has become supreme ruler of this country. The separate towns, cities, tribes, and lands that have before been apart have hereafter been united under the rule of Kagai. As there is a new govern-ment, there are also regulations that have been set in place, and any deviation from these regulations can result in fines, seizure of homes, or death for the perpetrators."

At this announcement, the crowd began buzzing angrily, but the speaker went on as if he hadn't heard them. "After the dissolution of this conference, all Ashan or part-Ashans are to report to Kagaian riders for processing. All citizens of this town are to remain in Two Falls unless the appropriate paperwork is completed and special permission for travel is granted by the town's Kagaian riders. Ashans are never to receive permission to travel outside of the city. This country's borders have been newly established and will be run by Kagaian riders; town mayorships, councils, and governments are hereby dissolved and new government officials will be put in place by Kagai. Riders will now act as the executive peacekeepers. The outlying lands and forests will now be marshaled by the riders. Anyone found outside their hometown or recorded residential area without the proper travel permits will be arrested immediately. And, twice a year, all residents of towns must pay homage to Kagai. Those failing to pay the tax and those who deviate from these instructions set down by the hand of Kagai will immediately have their lands seized and will be arrested to face execution. A wall will be built in the coming weeks to fortify the city against intruders and against those trying to escape. In the meantime, the city is surrounded by our riders. Anyone trying to escape will immediately be killed."

"This can't be real," Tarr heard Athela faintly mutter through gritted teeth, and he couldn't help but agree with her. And, it seemed, many of the townspeople were of the same mindset.

"Who is this Kagai?" one man yelled furiously. "Who is he to dictate to us who we are and where we can go? We're free!"

Shouts of assent greeted the outburst. Tarr, a sick feeling of dread enveloping his stomach, backed away as far as he could, for he saw where the man couldn't that the riders were slowly beginning to steal their way through the crowd, bearing down on him like hawks. The man began to yell something else when he was clubbed forcefully by one of the green-cloaked guards; his words swallowed in his throat as he dropped like a stone. The guard drew his sword.

Resistance dissolved into an agitated frenzy. People began screaming and tried their best to get as far away as they could. A wave of people surged against Tarr, nearly knocking him off balance and dragging Rane underneath them.

"Stop!" yelled the herald, holding out his hand. As if by magic, the crowd paused and the heads flickered back to look at the podium. "There will be no pandemonium here," he ordered. "We will have order."

"The council!" came a voice from the crowd. "Where is the council?"

"Where is Morthenstar?" came another. A glance passed between Tarr and the others.

The man smiled, but it was the least comforting expression Tarr had ever seen in his life. "As a matter of fact, I'm glad you asked about the well-being of the council. Bring them out."

There was not a single sound in the square as the crowd parted slightly to accommodate a long row of bound individuals being led into the square. Tarr's eyes widened disbelievingly. He recognized some of them. The council members who had mocked them when Laith tried to appeal for their help were now standing in line before the entire city. Rather than feeling any sort of smug validation, Tarr felt sick.

"Who are they?" Athela whispered.

"The city council," Marc grimaced.

Her expression was taut. "We've got to do something. We've got to do something."

"Athela, you stand right here," Laith ordered, clearly sensing that Athela was about to barrel forward and plunge herself into some sort of desperate unarmed combat. "We can't help them. The only advantage we have right now is that the riders don't know who we are. We make one move to help the council, and we'll be killed faster than you can think, not to mention start a stampede. They've got us completely surrounded."

Athela could see that Laith was right, but didn't like it one bit. The line of city council members was marched up the stairs to the top of the platform, their feet thudding hollowly on the dry wood. They formed a line, and Tarr scanned their faces quickly. Pieter was not amongst them. He saw the woman who had been so rude to Laith during their meeting with the council. Her face was ashen, and her eyes were racing left and right as though searching for someone to swoop in and rescue her.

The lead guard walked up to the first city council member. "Do you accept Kagai as your sovereign ruler, and do you swear fealty for the rest of your life?"

"I do not," said the first city council member.

Almost before anyone could think, an arrow whizzed through the air and into the council member's chest. They reeled and fell. The crowd cried out, and there was a surge against Tarr's back as the people ducked in unison, pressing against each other. Tarr grabbed Rane's arm and helped steady her as the crowd slowly straightened back up as one.

The other members of the council looked at the body of their fallen comrade in disbelief. Tarr felt a lurch in his stomach and felt as though he was going to be sick; his head began buzzing unpleasantly, and he felt his knees buckle slightly beneath him as he retched. Archer's hand was on his shoulder as he stood back up, embarrassed. He had never in his life seen someone killed before. *I don't belong here,* he thought wildly. *I have to get back to the forest. I don't care whether it's been a year or not. I have to get back.*

"I'm sorry," he muttered aloud, trying to still the racing horror in his mind. Archer made no response but squeezed his shoulder. It was comforting, and Tarr was grateful.

Calmly, the guard walked to the second member. "Do you accept Kagai as your sovereign ruler, and do you swear fealty for the rest of your life?"

"I...I...do," the woman whispered, her face still turned to the fallen man on the platform.

"Louder," the guard ordered.

"I do!" she shrieked.

"Good," he said and continued down the line.

"And just like that, Two Falls is lost," Laith muttered, his jaw clenched. "Out of hope and filled with fear."

The speaker moved to the next councillor and asked for her fealty.

"I do not," she said, her mouth in a thin line and her eyes full of resolve. Another arrow sang through the air and she fell. The crowd gasped in dismay and looked away.

By the end of the grim spectacle, four council members lay dead, and the rest stood quaking in their shoes. Tarr's head felt curiously numb, and he felt himself swaying on his feet like he was clinging to a thin branch in the wind.

The guard turned about and faced the crowd. "I hope you understand the importance of what you have witnessed today," he announced. "And I hope that you will cooperate with us fully or face the consequences. You may go."

"Laith!" Athela screamed as the crowd turned and began to stampede in all directions like a nest of insects hit with a rock. The prince and his bodyguard flanked Athela and Si as best they could, while Tarr, who weighed comparatively little, did his utmost to shield Rane. Archer was bent protectively around the small girl he'd picked up during the fracas. She had abandoned her crying and was now clinging desperately around his neck, brown eyes wide and small, face as white as Archer's. All around Tarr, people were tripping, falling, being trampled. Thinking only of getting himself and Rane to safety, he grabbed her by the arm and managed to half-pull, half-carry her through the running crowd to shelter behind one of the buildings.

Archer managed to slip out of the throng and joined them, arms around the girl as the three of them ducked down a nearby side street. Hearing something, he whipped around and gave a yell. Behind them, a rider was approaching on foot, sword out and voice raised in an audible challenge. He had clearly recognized them as Ashans, and was planning to take them away to be processed.

Tarr was unarmed and braced himself for the worst, but Rane darted forward beneath his arm like flashing quicksilver. In a moment, a dagger was drawn from her robe and she cut down the rider with a deft stab. The green-cloaked rider fell to the ground, and after a moment of stunned silence, Tarr leaped forward to help. He and Rane kicked and pulled the rider so that he was concealed in a low stairwell leading down to a basement apartment beneath the foundation of the nearest house.

"That was a close one," Archer panted, looking over his shoulder at the street. The crowd was beginning to thin, though a number of riders were advancing, swords out. "We've got to find the others and make sure they're safe."

"Who's the child?" Tarr asked. The girl was still clinging for dear life to Archer's neck, her small fingers clutching strands of his black and white hair.

"No idea, she was wandering around when they started shoving people together. I thought she was going to get trampled for sure, and I didn't see her parents around, so I picked her up, and it's a good thing I did."

Tarr looked around behind him to check and see that Rane was all right. She was gazing keenly out at the main street, where it appeared that no one was running anymore. Just as quickly as the pandemonium had begun, it seemed to have stopped as everyone scattered into the safety of their homes.

They slid out of the side alleyway, keeping close together, Rane resting her hand on her hip where her dagger was once more concealed. A short ways down the street, Tarr saw Laith skirting a wall and whistled to get his attention. The prince pointed, and soon all the Strikers were grouped together in the shallow cover of an awning, tucked safely back from the main street. For a few moments, they silently scanned one another up and down for any sign of injury. It was plain on everyone's faces that they were relieved that no one had been hurt in the melee.

Archer unpeeled the small arms from around his neck and set the little girl in the crook of his elbow so that she was facing the others. "You're fine now. See? Isn't that man funny-looking?" Marc stuck his tongue out and bugged out his eyes, and the girl let the smallest flicker of a smile cross her face. "See, there, Marc's funny face will make it all better. What's your name?" The girl responded by staring at Marc and sticking her thumb in her mouth.

A shriek sounded in the street beside them, and a woman darted up to them, her eyes wide and frantic. The little girl held out her arms and was scooped into her mother's embrace. The woman shot the others an accusing, frightened look as if they had purposefully taken the girl and rushed away before Archer could explain.

"You're welcome," he grumbled under his breath.

"Did you see that woman's face?" Si asked in wonderment, as if he couldn't believe how suddenly the normal order of things had been inverted. "Everyone's so afraid now."

"It'll be all right, Si," Marc said comfortingly, patting him on the shoulder. "We're together again, and we're all alive. It will be all right."

Si nodded and tried to smile.

"Kagai's certainly not wasting any time, is he?" Laith asked.

"Which means we shouldn't, either," Marc pointed out.

"Archer," Athela said suddenly, turning towards the Ashan, who straightened. "It looks like this is the change of the tide. But this isn't your fight anymore. If you want to leave, you can."

Tarr stared at Archer, his breath bated. *Exiles have no loyalty,* he thought, bracing for Archer to look them in the eye and abandon them all without a moment's hesitation.

"I told you," he said, with the ghost of a grin. "My rates are negotiable."

Tarr was puzzled. To his knowledge, Archer hadn't actually been paid yet for acting as their guide around Two Falls. Laith, however, seemed to be in on the joke. "What's your going rate for joining the Strikers in a possibly futile battle against an evil overlord?" he asked.

"Reasonable, I assure you," Archer smiled. "I'm not going anywhere." He turned to Tarr and there was a challenge in his eyes, almost as if he had been able to hear what Tarr had been thinking.

"So," Marc inquired after a moment's pause. "What's the plan?"

"We have to get to Faridor and get that prophecy," Athela said firmly. "Now more than ever."

"Oh, wait, I forgot that the next part of our plan involved breaking into our enemy's impenetrable fortress," Archer quipped. "Is it too late for me to opt out again?"

"Yes," Athela replied.

"We have to meet with Pieter right away," Laith said. "Maybe he'll have some ideas."

CHAPTER SEVENTEEN

Pieter's hideout, where he had been ferreted away by his nephew Nicolas, was far from the dank little cave that Tarr had initially imagined. It was tucked into the basement of Nicolas's family mansion, located in an affluent neighborhood in the northeast of the city. By this point, Tarr felt that he was getting a better sense of the different kinds of human homes and what they said about the owners, and what this home seemed to say was *riches* and *comfort*. It suddenly occurred to Tarr that, as in the Jelani palace, the conspicuous display of so many precious objects—paintings, vases, tapestries—was intended to convey the power and wealth of the owners more than it was to create an environment of beauty. Feeling somewhat disillusioned, Tarr was nevertheless delighted to discover that the mansion featured a number of paintings that swung around on their frames to reveal secret passageways, as well as a fireplace that turned in place to open onto a long stairway that led down into Pieter's new residence. The hideout itself bore a striking resemblance to Ma's cozy home, with armchairs and tables, a small wood-burning stove, and a good many bookshelves adorned with well-preserved leather-bound volumes.

The Strikers sat across from Pieter as he enjoyed a cup of steaming subterranean tea. His nephew Nicolas, dark and intense, stood off in one corner, watching them with his arms folded.

"Now then," Pieter said as soon as he had finished his cup, "my nephew has told me about what went on today in the city. I must apologize profusely for not coming to you all sooner."

"Were you able to talk to the council?" Laith asked. "Before Kagai took over?"

"I spoke with them, yes, but as we predicted, most were still skeptical. I could see that raising a force great enough to investigate and counter the type of power you described was going to be next to impossible. My guess is that Kagai had already started to infiltrate the branches of our government and turn loyalties wherever possible. I then noticed a few individuals skulking around my place of residence, and I knew that it was time for me to disappear. My nephew was kind enough to find me this comfortable safehouse."

"Well, as far as hideouts go, I've been in places a lot more smelly and drippy than this," Archer said, gazing around with approval.

"I can attest to that," Athela concurred.

"I was lucky," Pieter smiled, then his face grew grave. "Very lucky."

"We've managed to decode the first part of the prophecy," Athela announced proudly. "My translation is a bit rough, but as far as I can tell, it points us to Faridor. I've made a copy for you as well."

Pieter's nephew stirred in his corner and looked with interest at the paper in Athela's hand. Tarr watched him closely for a moment or two.

"May I have it?" Pieter leaned forward, raising his eyebrows over his glasses and quickly scanning the lines of Athela's neat script. Pieter passed the sheet to Nicolas, who perused it carefully.

"Anyway, what's happening now," Athela leaned towards him, "is that we need to find a way to somehow get into the fortress of Faridor—"

"And not get killed within the first three minutes," Marc muttered.

"—and find the rest of Morthenstar's prophecy. It's imperative that we discover who Morthenstar's heir is. He or she may be given powers that will enable us to win against Kagai."

Pieter thought carefully for a few moments, then a smile spread across his face. "As it just so happens," he said slowly, "I think I may have just the thing. Nicolas," he called, and his nephew stepped forward, taking the offered seat beside his uncle. "Ah. There, you see? Nicolas, being of some social standing in this city, has received a very interesting invitation today. Why don't you show it to them?"

Nicolas silently withdrew an envelope from his jacket and handed it to Athela, who unfolded it. She read it aloud. "Queen Kagai requests the honor of your presence at a coronation banquet to be held on the fifth day of the month at the fortress of Faridor." She looked up. "*Queen* Kagai, eh?"

"Kagai is married?" Si asked.

"Maybe Kagai is a woman," Pieter shrugged. "There's no mention of any other person."

"Well, that eliminates half of the population," Archer said sarcastically.

"A banquet?" Marc scoffed. "Sounds charming. Let's go around terrorizing the citizens of the city and shooting down its council members and then throw a large party to celebrate."

"She's probably trying to impress the ones she couldn't intimidate with sheer force," Tarr mused, thinking of the opulence on display in the mansion just above their heads. The others stared around at him with what were becoming rather habitual expressions of surprise.

"So," Archer said slowly, "Are you suggesting that we go to the banquet in Nicolas's place and infiltrate the fortress that way?"

"I am indeed," Pieter said with a serene smile.

"It's in two days," Laith pointed out. "We have no time to plan."

Beside him, Archer muttered something along the lines of, "That's never stopped us before."

"Laith, that party may be the perfect opportunity for us to find the rest of the prophecy that's concealed at Faridor," Athela exclaimed excitedly, and Tarr could tell that she was rapidly warming to the whole idea. "Imagine it: a huge party, delegations from all over the country and the surrounding lands. She wouldn't notice if seven people went on a little excursion around the fortress and just happened to take themselves on a self-guided tour of the old Faridor library?"

"Not all of you have to go and find the prophecy," Pieter pointed out reasonably. "Only a few need go. It might be safer."

"Yeah," Archer agreed. "Some can go prophecy hunting, while the others can stay and keep a lookout while sampling a varied selection of appetizers...to blend in, of course," he added quickly.

"So, we're in agreement?" Athela asked around the circle eagerly.

"Why not?" Archer grinned in his wolfish way. "If we die, at least we'll have gotten free food."

"That's the spirit," Pieter agreed, a twinkle in his eye.

"The one problem I can see..." Laith murmured.

"*One* problem?" Marc asked sarcastically.

"Is that we have absolutely no idea what the layout of the fortress is. How are we going to find our way around? It's all well and good if we get in at all, but once we're in, we've got to know how to find what we need."

"Not to mention we'll have two Ashans in tow," Archer pointed out. "Bound to raise some eyebrows."

"Also, won't they be suspicious if all seven of us show up with only one invitation?" Tarr asked, hoping the question wasn't too stupid.

"These sorts of social events, it comes as expected," Nicolas put in, speaking for the first time. "I once went to a party with nine servants. No one batted an eye."

"Here's hoping you're right," Laith muttered.

"That still doesn't help solve the small problem of how to find our way around," Marc pointed out. "We need to get our hands on a plan of Faridor. A blueprint, or a layout, or something else we can use."

Beside him, Rane stirred for the first time since they'd sat. "If you don't mind," she said in her quiet, almost scratchy voice, "you can leave that to me."

The next night, Rane slipped out of the front door of Ma's house and walked noiselessly down the street. The bustling nightlife that had once been so characteristic of the city had completely vanished since Kagai's takeover, and a frightened silence permeated the balmy summer night air. Here and there, a cluster of green-cloaked Kagaian guards walked across the street. At each instance of this Rane froze in the shadows, and the guards strode by, oblivious to her presence. She waited, patient, still as a stone, until she saw a glimmer of metal around a corner down the street. In the small sliver of moonlight, she saw the edge of a solitary green cloak. A lone guard. Perfect.

She slunk through the shadows behind the house and calculated the angle of her attack. From behind the guard it was no good. They would have a chance to escape to her left. Better if she turned. Rane picked up a stone from beside her foot and threw it across the road beside the guard, who whipped around and found the hook of Rane's elbow already wrapping around her throat. She twisted and slumped to the ground, but Rane caught her before she fell. It was all done without so much as a whisper.

The cloak and regalia were slightly big for her, but she could manage. She had luckily picked a target not much taller than she. She searched along the inner lining of the cloak, and looked inside the front of the thick leather vest that had been worn by the officer. *C. Bishop* was embroidered on the hem. Satisfied, she rearranged the vest and swung the cloak about her shoulders. She buckled the sword around her waist and strode purposefully through the streets, not bothering to keep to the shadows. When another guard saw her, he ducked his head in a salute, which she returned without breaking her stride.

The soldiers' barracks had been erected temporarily in a large, newly vacated manor townhouse beside the Two Falls town hall (which was being converted into the new Kagaian headquarters). Rane had heard rumors that the owners of the manor had managed to flee the city on the day of the takeover. It was easier for those with money to escape than those without.

Guards off-duty were talking outside the manor, and gave her nods as she walked calmly up to the front door and went inside. The manor was handsome and had a masculine edge to it; the interior was in the old style, with rich accents of gleaming red wood set against walls of white stone. A large announcement board by the entrance showed the night's schedules and commanding officers; Rane scanned it with interest as she slowly unbuckled her sword from her belt, repeating a few names to herself. Satisfied, she headed inside to the main foyer of the converted manor, where a desk had been set up on the main floor close to a window. A woman was waiting behind it, holding a pen.

"Report," she ordered curtly, not looking up.

"Officer Bishop, patrol in the west district, coming off duty. One curfew breaker, who was duly reported and arrested. We've taken him into custody. Other than that, all quiet," Rane said easily. The woman before her looked up.

"Where's Jenkon?" she asked suspiciously.

"Commanding officer met us in the street, told him to go and help patrol the northern district. I was to finish Jenkon's shift," she replied. Though her tone was relaxed and her body held casually, she was carefully scanning the room with her blue-gray eyes.

"Which commanding officer was that?" the woman narrowed her eyes.

"Tobias," Rane replied without hesitation, reciting from memory the shift list by the front door. "Said he'd do another round before heading back in."

"Very well," the woman replied, and wrote her name and the time of her arrival in a small ledger before him. "Be sure and drop your uniform off before you head to the bunks."

Rane saluted and walked out of the room. She smiled to herself.

She'd seen the way the room was set up, how against the wall, just behind the woman at the desk, was a table bearing a document-sized box with an intimidating-looking lock on the front. She headed through the door and up the stairs towards the bunks, which were two long, narrow rooms at the very top of the stairwell. They were directly above the entrance hall where the desk and safe box were located. Rane headed to the left, unbuckling the clasp on her cloak and folding it a few times over her arm.

The barracks were mostly full as the day's patrols were winding down for the night. Some were sleeping and a few reading by candle-light; the bunk beds had been crammed in closely together, more in the interest of efficient accommodation than comfort. There was a narrow window near the entrance of the room. Rane walked quietly over to it without attracting so much as a glance from the other inhabitants as she did. She looked down at the road below. She had watched them all the night before and hoped they would keep to the same schedule. It would be only a few minutes now.

To her relief, they did. After about ten minutes, she saw the woman who had been manning the desk below come out the front door of the barracks and order the chatting soldiers to report back to their rooms for curfew. Rane waited patiently until she heard every last one of them tromp, grumbling, up the stairs into their rooms, closing the doors firmly behind.

Once that was done, Rane stood smoothly upright and opened wide the window of the barracks. A gust of balmy wind billowed in, blowing out the candle of one reader.

"Close the damn window!" one woman yelled to her from her bed. "What are you trying to do?"

"Oh, I'm sorry," Rane said sarcastically. "I was just trying to air out the stench from the room. This place stinks. Maybe it's *you.*"

About twenty female faces turned to stare disbelievingly at her. The woman in the bed rose up. She was quite intimidating, with dark black hair and large eyebrows. She was a good deal bigger and older than Rane. "What did you say to me?" she said in a deathly low voice.

"I mean, if I want a spot of fresh air, not even a cow like you can stop me," Rane sneered. This was all it took.

The woman burst forward and launched herself onto Rane, who spun neatly out of the way. She planted a punch in the woman's stomach, only to be grabbed by another girl. By now, the room was pure chaos. In the midst of the fray, Rane darted nimbly to one side, subtly blowing out the largest lamp as she went and plunging the room even further into darkness. Shrieks went up in the room as the women scrambled to lay hold of Rane. But Rane was not to be found.

She shimmied out of the open window completely unnoticed and slowly lowered herself down an exposed wooden beam on the exterior of the barracks until she was even with a window that looked into the entrance hall below. As if on cue, the woman bolted out of her chair and up the stairs to see what the ruckus was all about. Rane didn't waste a second. She darted back through the front door of the manor house, leaving it open just a crack in case she needed a quiet getaway. She sprinted soundlessly around the vacant desk to the safe box in the back. She inspected the lock closely and moved it around a little. It was remarkably light, and she tried turning the dial for a moment or two. Her sensitive fingers were trained for any sort of click or hint of a spring releasing, but there was none. She sat back on her heels, calmly thinking. The rumpus continued upstairs; evidently, some of the men had joined in as well.

She cocked her head to one side, studying the safe. From what she could see from the construction of the box, the lock appeared to not actually bolt two halves of the box together; it just sat on top. If the lock wasn't real...just a ruse to put someone off the scent...she felt around the sides of the safe and the bottom, and there she found what she was looking for. A tiny button that she pressed in, and the top of the box came unlatched. She pulled it open. There was more yelling and then a general sense of the pandemonium subsiding upstairs. She was running out of time.

There were a good many papers in the safe, but she flipped quickly through them and found what she was looking for. A plan of Two Falls with an intricate layout of postings and of guard schedules, the districts divided up neatly into different areas. And, more importantly, a detailed floorplan of the fortress of Faridor from the ground up to the tip of the tower. It spanned many pages, which she hadn't anticipated. Oh, well. Too late to do anything about it.

She reached under her shirt where she had tucked a sheaf of papers into the back of her pants, her estimation of what the documents would look like. They were crude, to be sure, but a casual observer wouldn't notice the difference. They certainly wouldn't be able to find the substitution before the next day. She exchanged the papers, tucking the real plans safely beneath her shirt, and closed the top on the safe box.

She stood back, hearing the stomping of feet on the landing above and down the stairs. She didn't have enough time to bolt for the door. Thinking quickly, she jerked open the nearby window. Then, in one fluid motion, she tucked herself up into a ball and rolled beneath the desk.

"Nonsense, utter nonsense," the woman muttered to herself as she walked back in, but stopped as soon as she felt the draft from the window. "What the hell is this?" she demanded, stalking across the office to the window. Her back was to Rane.

"Nonsense is what it is," she continued. "Windows falling open at all hours of the night. Troops starting bloodbaths in their nighties." She reached up to pull the window closed, but it stuck. She began to grunt and force it down.

Rane took her chance. Keeping low to the floor, she silently slid out from beneath the desk, scuttled across the floor, and pushed through the slightly opened door and out into the night, closing it almost completely behind her. She crouched low by the entrance, listening for any sound of alarm. All was quiet. Crossing the small courtyard at an even jog, she dissolved into the deep blue shadows, grinning to herself to think of what the woman would say when she found the front door open, too.

At breakfast the next day, Athela was having a rather morose staring contest with an apple, and the others looked similarly deep in thought. For the second time that week, troops had searched the house for Ashans, and Tarr and Archer had had to spend a couple of early morning hours hiding on the roof (where they'd spotted a few figures doing the same thing atop other buildings.)

The banquet was that night and they had no plan.

"I guess we'll have to wing it," Laith sighed. "Not exactly my chosen mode of operation, but nevertheless..."

Rane came softly into the room, a sheaf of papers in her hand. She laid them down in front of Athela, who started out of her reverie.

"These might help," Rane said in her soft voice.

The six others looked at her, dumbfounded. For a fleeting second, Tarr thought she looked at him and gave him a tiny wink. Athela began to sift through the papers, her expression growing ever more joyous by the second. "Rane!" she exclaimed, quite beside herself, "this is fantastic! Where did you find them?"

"The Kagaian barracks," Rane replied. "A lucky hunch. They have troops moving back and forth between Faridor and Two Falls; I guessed they'd have a floorplan to map out patrol routes and assignments."

"How on earth did you lay your hands on them?" Laith pressed her.

"I asked politely," she replied with a straight face, then walked quietly out of the room, the others staring open-mouthed after her.

CHAPTER EIGHTEEN

"She's been in there for three hours at *least*," Si complained noisily, throwing a piece of ripped-up paper at his feet and sighing. "Does her dress have some sort of rope and pulley system involved?"

"Everyone knows what to do tonight, right?" Laith asked for what must have been the fourteenth time. His soldier's brain, trained since childhood, was obviously keeping up some form of detailed interior monologue. He remained silent and unresponsive unless an idea occurred to him, at which point he would break out in questions or instructions completely unrelated to the subject the others were discussing. "And what our plan is in case she finds out? Where we're supposed to go? Where to meet outside the fortress if we're separated?"

"For the thousandth time, *yes*," Marc rolled his icy eyes, flicking a tiny wadded-up piece of paper towards Si and hitting him squarely on one copper eyebrow. Laith nodded distractedly at them as though they had responded acceptably and then tuned them out again, staring up with a furrowed brow at the ceiling, lips moving slightly as he muttered under his breath.

"He'd better blink soon; I'm about three seconds away from having him committed," Archer said sardonically, his long, spindly fingers steepled beneath his nose.

"The stairs!" Laith exclaimed suddenly, then shook his head and retreated back into his trance-like state. Tarr smiled and shifted uncomfortably, tugging on his jacket. They were all dressed up in varying levels of finery for the night's events. Tarr was outfitted as Laith's "valet," which he was told was some sort of person in charge of making sure that Laith had a handkerchief if he needed to sneeze. The advantage of this, Laith had informed him, was that no one would think much of it if Tarr walked around with his hands clasped behind his back, thereby giving him a way to hide his telltale Ashan sixth finger.

Hearing something behind him, Tarr twisted around and watched as Athela made her way down the stairs in a shining silver dress, stomping aggressively and arching a self-conscious eyebrow as if daring the others to make a joke at her expense.

"Wow," Si's breathy voice came appreciatively, gray eyes wide, breaking the astonished silence.

"I know I said no more dresses," she said curtly. "So tonight had just better go smoothly." Archer frowned thoughtfully and poked a long finger at the net draped over her hair as if it were some strange breed of insect until Athela caught him at it and slapped him away.

"Pretty," Archer said appreciatively. Athela opened her mouth to try and retort with some sort of witty rejoinder, but after a few seconds closed it.

"Thank you," she said with dignity, and for a moment their eyes locked together. Si grinned at Marc from behind her back and batted his eyelashes exaggeratedly. Marc attempted to stifle a snort that he managed to turn into something resembling a cough.

Tarr turned his eyes away from Athela to the staircase where a different figure was hanging back reluctantly, not wanting to come out of the shadows. Tarr looked to each side and saw that he was the only one still paying attention and raised his eyebrows. With a visibly deep breath Rane walked down the stairs, her auburn hair flowing down her back, outfitted in an emerald green dress that covered her shoulders and neck.

"Right," Athela said briskly. "Is everyone armed?"

"Yes," Si replied eagerly. They'd allowed him to take what was essentially the equivalent of a butter knife from Ma's kitchen, but he still seemed thrilled at the prospect of wielding some sort of weapon.

Tarr shifted ever so slightly, aware of the dagger he had strapped to his boot. Archer had shown him how to pull it out, but he hoped fervently that the opportunity to use it would not arise as he didn't think it would do him much good. He wasn't sure whether or not he would be able to bring himself to harm anyone.

He had only a dim conception of what a fortress even was. When he tried to imagine Faridor, he pictured a building along the lines of Joymaril palace. It seemed like it would be difficult to find one small room in such a large place, and he hoped that the floorplans Rane had recovered, along with the instructions he and Athela had found in the library, would be sufficient enough to point them in the right direction. He was nervous, certainly, at the prospect of skating so close beneath the heir's nose, but the others seemed relatively assured that Kagai would be so busy that they could go by unnoticed. He was glad, too, that he would be paired with Athela for most of the night's activities. She was practical and capable, and he got the feeling that she would keep her head in the midst of a crisis.

Tarr, as he had already a few times in the last five minutes, brushed aside the window curtain and looked out into the street beyond to see if he could catch a glimpse of the carriage that would be conveying them to the fortress. If he was honest with himself, the prospect of riding in a carriage was almost as exciting as stepping inside Faridor; he had seen carriages from afar (they were usually only used by the wealthy families of Two Falls) but had never seen one up close, much less ridden in one. Nicolas had arranged for his family's carriage to meet them at their residence and take them to Faridor.

Finally, he saw it draw up to the front of their boardinghouse and stop outside. It seemed much larger up close than he expected. He whipped around excitedly. "It's here!" he exclaimed, and was only momentarily abashed by the bemused looks his friends were giving him.

He dashed to the door (giving Wolver a fond farewell pat before he went outside) and looked up at his new conveyance. The carriage was glossy black, with a fancy sort of gold crest at the back; the inside, from what he could see just by peering in the window, looked quite comfortable, with cream-colored upholstered seats and curtains pulled back from the windows. It was drawn by a team of horses, a gray and a dark bay. A small woman was perched on the top of the coach and skipped down nimbly to open the door for them as they emerged to clamber into the carriage.

Tarr pulled himself inside first, surprised by the way the carriage rocked and sprang a bit with his weight as he entered. He settled himself by one of the windows and peered forward eagerly as the others piled in around him. With a snap the door was shut, and the carriage lurched forward.

Tarr found the experience of riding in the carriage to be incredibly thrilling for the first five minutes or so, but with the six of them inside (Archer, posing as a hooded, scarved groom, was riding on the back of the carriage as a lookout for danger) it was more than a little cramped. Still, he looked with interest out of the window as the now-familiar streets of Two Falls rolled by; it was almost novel seeing the marketplaces and statues from inside the carriage.

"When we reach the gate, try to look like you do this all the time," Laith was watching him, amused. Tarr nodded, more abashed now that some of the novelty had worn off, and leaned back in his seat, trying to act nonchalant as the carriage rattled and rolled uncomfortably over the cobbles.

They were stopped at the city border, and Tarr could hear snatches of conversation outside as the guards conversed with the driver. A face appeared at the window, seemingly to inspect the contents within. Tarr tried to attempt a nervous smile of reassurance and was sure to keep his six-fingered hands well out of sight. The guards at the gate continued to circle around the carriage until they caught sight of Laith, who looked imperiously down his nose at them from behind the glass. His physical beauty seemed to startle them for a moment (Tarr even saw one of the guards' mouths fall open slightly as they stared at him), then in another instant, the letter of transport was being folded and handed back up to the driver, and they were off.

"I will never understand why everyone assumes that good-looking people are always on the up and up," Athela shook her head disparagingly. Laith shrugged helplessly.

The carriage rolled along its path. Slowly, the city of Two Falls fell away behind them, and they went through a wide meadow into a stretch of forest. The monotony of the woods tamped down Tarr's enthusiasm somewhat, so he settled back in his seat, enjoying the others' nervous chatter around him and stealing the odd glance at Rane beside him whenever he was able. She had a small smile playing on her lips, as if she knew what he was up to, though she herself was looking through the opposite window and never seemed to catch him outright.

The journey was a couple of hours on a bumpy dirt path, and after a while of being jostled back and forth and up and down, Tarr began to feel rather impatient to reach their destination. The trees passing by the window had an oddly lulling effect; he felt his mind drifting off here and there, thinking about the Aspen village and his friend Juniper, then worrying about their mission to retrieve the prophecy and whether he would be found out and revealed as an Ashan.

All of a sudden, the line of trees ended and they emerged out onto an open plain. He could see where the land ended a little ways away, but beyond that was something else. He furrowed his brow and watched the way it seemed to move. It was water. It had to be water. But it was more water than he had ever seen, stretching on and on, all the way to where the sky met the horizon. It was impossible.

"Stop," Tarr whispered. "Stop the carriage."

"Tarr, what—" Athela looked alarmed.

"Stop!" Tarr yelled, his hand on the handle of the carriage door. Laith raised up one hand and thumped twice on the roof of the carriage, giving the signal to stop, but Tarr was already halfway out.

A bracingly strong salty wind hit him square in the face as he descended from the carriage and ran out towards the cliff. The road ran up along the edge of the coast, where the land fell away in a dramatic near-vertical drop down to the shore; beyond that was the sea. It was more vast, more overwhelming than anything Tarr had ever seen before, bigger than the Jelani lake, more enormous than the entirety of the Ashan forest. It was absolutely staggering. He couldn't take his eyes away from it.

"Beautiful, isn't it?" came a voice from behind him. Tarr whipped around and saw Archer approaching. To his surprise, his expression wasn't mocking or amused, as the others' generally were when Tarr became excited about something that to them was commonplace. Archer instead looked...wistful. Almost sad. Tarr turned back around, shaking his head in disbelief.

"I never knew...I never knew how big it was," he breathed.

"There's land on the other side of it, too," Archer told him. Tarr stared at him.

"There's another side?" Dimly, he remembered what he'd read about lands beyond the sea, but that concept had always seemed so abstract, so distant. Seeing the wide blue expanse in person put things in stark perspective. "But I can't see anything." He peered as hard as he could towards the horizon. "Where is it if I can't see it?"

Archer shook his head. "You have to start traveling. You can't see the land until you've been at sea for a while."

A thousand questions crowded into Tarr's mind. "But how do the people who go there know the way? How can they find their way across?" he asked, the words tumbling out of his mouth in an ungainly heap. "There aren't any roads, no path to follow."

"There are ways," Archer assured him. "I don't know much about it myself, but I'm led to understand that those who travel on the sea can read it, just as you or I could read a tree or a trail through the woods."

"Are you done?" Athela barked from the carriage behind them, her silver dress slithering out over her feet. She was hanging halfway out the door, shouting against the wind.

"Coming!" Archer called back.

The spell was broken somewhat, but Tarr could still barely tear his eyes away from the sight before him, the strangely reassuring shushing of the waves striking the shore far below them at the foot of the cliff. He gave Archer a curt nod of thanks and turned away, looking over his shoulder every few feet, trying to fix the image in his mind. Clambering back into the carriage and avoiding Athela's reproachful gaze, he stared once more out of the window at the water beyond, until the light had dimmed and all the shades of blue and gray had faded together into the blur of dusk.

"We're nearly there!" Marc shouted excitedly about an hour later, gesturing at the curtain. Tarr snapped to attention. He had been dozing, his head lolled back against the cushioned headrest of the carriage seat. All at once, a flurry of butterflies alighted in his stomach, and he peered out once more into the cobalt-blue gloom beyond the carriage's interior.

About five hundred yards away was the silhouette of a gigantic castle perched high on the top of a rock set out to sea. With surprise, he realized that he'd been quite wrong when he tried to imagine it in his mind's eye. It wasn't nearly as large or extensive as the Jelani palace of Joymaril, but it was twice as intimidating: black and ominous, with sharply pointed turrets thrusting up to pierce the bellies of the low-hanging clouds above.

The fortress of Faridor was built into and onto the rock of the island on which it sat, and was connected to the mainland by a long stone bridge that was supported from the bottom by massive columns set into the water. Twinkling lights flickered along the bridge, lighting the way towards the main gate of the castle. Tarr continued watching out of the window as they drew closer and closer to the beginning of the bridge, and saw in one frantic second that there were guards checking each of the carriages before they crossed.

What am I doing here? he asked himself wildly.

"Tarr," Laith said softly. "Drop the curtain."

Embarrassed, Tarr hurriedly obeyed and flattened his back against the seat, breathing rather hard, wishing he could find a way to stop his legs from shaking. All at once, he felt a warm hand slide over onto his and give his first two fingers a minuscule squeeze. Upon realizing that the hand belonged to Rane, Tarr's butterflies vanished, and nerves of an entirely different sort took their place. To his surprise, he felt his knees stop quivering, and his breathing slowed back to a normal rate. He tried to catch her eye, but she continued staring ahead, nothing but the soft weight of her hand on his leaving any hint that she had moved at all. Their carriage rolled to a halt, and the gold handle on the side opposite from Tarr opened. A man in a green robe and hood stuck his head into the carriage.

"Invitation," the guard demanded. Tarr was fervently glad that it was dark there in the carriage; the guard was less likely to identify him as Ashan. Laith quickly procured the requested paper. Athela kept her eyes lowered and her hood covering her hair, and Tarr took her lead, ducking his face down modestly.

The guard inspected the invitation closely. "Which one of you is Nicolas?" he asked finally.

"I am," said Laith.

The guard took a look at him, digested the noble bearing of the face staring back out at him. "And these are?" the guard demanded, motioning to the others in the cramped interior. Tarr felt his heart hammering. He gripped Rane's hand tightly.

"My guests and servants," Laith said, with a voice so aristocratic that Tarr could almost feel the haughty disdain dripping down from it. "I was under the impression that this was a *high-class* event and that we could bring everything we require. If this is not the case, I have a number of other engagements on which I could bestow my presence."

The guard eyed them sharply for another moment or two, but that seemed to have done the trick. Tarr breathed a shallow sigh of relief as the guard stepped back out and closed the carriage door. "Continue on, then; the guards at the other end will direct your driver." The carriage door closed again with a bang, and every person inside let out a long, lingering breath. The wheels creaked shrilly, and they lurched forward.

"Sheer nonsense," Athela shook her head. "You do have a way."

"Thank you," Laith said with a prim inclination of his golden head. "Eight years listening to idiot courtiers blathering all day came in handy after all."

They rolled across the long bridge, a sharp clattering sound filling their ears and rattling their teeth as the wheels moved over the flagstones. After what seemed like all too short a time, the carriage again drew to a halt and before Athela could manage to offer any last-minute words of advice, the door was opened again from the outside and was held ajar for them to get out. Tarr felt Rane's hand move away from his, and his spirit dropped back down a couple of notches.

Athela stepped out onto the stones first, daintily, head thrown back, the very image of royalty. Rane followed, more in her shadow, but her demure, ladylike manner effectively conveyed the same kind of refined upbringing as Athela. The others followed; Tarr was the last out, the cramps in his legs from having sat in the carriage for so long blissfully unfolding as he paced back and forth a few times by the carriage's back wheel. The black walls of the fortress loomed high and forbidding around them. Tarr had an ominous sensation that they almost seemed to be moving in to enclose them. A gust from over the sea blew up; the strong smell of salt hit his nose, stinging it, filling his lungs. He wanted to wander over to the side of the bridge and gaze down again at the rippling ocean, and was about to do just that when Archer nudged him in the side of the arm and Tarr at once leapt to attention. A guard was speaking to Athela, and Tarr craned his neck to hear. He kept his eyes downcast, hands cupped behind his back as Laith had instructed. Archer, in the livery of a groom, had his hood up to cover his singular hair and to hide most of his Ashan features.

"Continue in through those gates," the guard was ordering, motioning into the inner keep where Tarr could vaguely see an octagonal courtyard lit by torches hung on the walls, another huge doorway at the far end. "When it is your turn, you will pay your respects to Queen Kagai and move on into the reception hall where you will wait until all the guests have arrived and dinner is ready to begin."

"And our carriage?" Athela asked imperiously.

"It will await you here in the courtyard."

Athela nodded sharply and extended her hand to Laith, who tucked it in the crook of his elbow. "Follow," Athela curtly ordered over her shoulder to Tarr and the others, and together they passed through the outer wall into the open-air courtyard. The ground was cobblestoned, and groups of people were clustered here and there, talking amongst themselves and obviously waiting for the opportunity to continue through the far gate. Tarr squinted slightly and could see a smallish figure shaking hands with those who passed through the entryway, surrounded by three towering guards. People were bowing, heads bobbing up and down. Tarr couldn't make out a face, merely a figure. It was certainly a woman. The Strikers moved over towards the wall, away from the other groups of talking guests.

"Pay attention, all of you," Athela ordered, and the others turned towards her. "We all know the plan? Everyone clear on when and where we split up? And where we meet?"

"We meet at the carriage across the bridge," Marc and Si chorused in unison.

Tarr looked over his shoulder at the shadowy figure at the entrance of the castle. People were still streaming in. Tarr gulped, feeling a rising bit of fear in his throat. Something wasn't right. Something more than the fact that they were about to go walking into their enemy's stronghold with nothing but winning smiles as disguises.

"Before we go in," Tarr suggested timidly, "maybe we should get a little closer, get a good look at whoever it is, size her up."

The others glanced around, looking for a consensus. "Good idea," Athela agreed.

They slowly moved towards the brightly lit entryway, the area around them gradually becoming more crowded as they neared Kagai.

"I still can't see anything," Marc muttered. "We need to be closer."

They drew closer still, and finally Tarr could get a good view of Kagai. His eyes gobbled up the face, eager to know his enemy. A long sheet of white-blond hair, small features, wide-set green cat's eyes. Recognition hit him hard across the face, and his breath caught in his throat. To be sure he wasn't mistaken, he looked around at the others and, to his dismay, saw that he wasn't dreaming. Athela's face was as white as a sheet, and Tarr could see the blood physically draining from Laith's normally tan face.

"Get back!" Athela hissed.

"Why, what's wrong?" Archer asked, confused. Laith silently grabbed the Ashan's arm, and they slid back into the shadows, safely out of sight.

"It can't be," Athela gasped, her voice deathly hoarse.

"What the hell's going on?" Archer asked irritably.

"My sister...that's my sister," Athela choked.

CHAPTER NINETEEN

"Your *sister?*" Archer's face lost any vestige of his usual innate mirth. His mouth opened once or twice, but eventually could find nothing to say.

"How did she...How could she...?" Athela asked blankly. "There's no way that it could be her. It couldn't be, there must be some mistake." Tarr could see her struggling to recover from the shock, the wheels in her head turning. For some reason, Laith didn't seem to be as surprised as Athela was.

Marc's ice-blue eyes were wide. "What are we going to do now? Are we just going to go back? I mean, there's no way we could possibly get past her now; she's sure to recognize us."

"Not all of us," Athela said distractedly, biting her lip as she worked out what to do next. Her eyes slowly traveled upwards and came to rest. "She didn't meet Archer."

Tarr looked over back towards the entryway. About one in five of the people were actually talking to Cira as they entered; the others merely passed by her with a polite nod. "There is a way we can get in," Tarr said hesitantly. "We can't just leave now that we're here. We have the cover of being with a lot of people; there won't be many other opportunities like this coming up anytime soon. What we need to do is let Archer go up and start talking to her. While he's got her distracted, we pass by, hoods up. A lot of those people over there aren't even greeting her; they're just going inside while she talks to the others. There's a chance."

"Archer's Ashan," Laith pointed out.

"And well-known in Two Falls," Marc pointed out.

"Not in these kinds of circles," Archer grinned.

Athela shook her head. "If you're charming enough, she'll let it pass, and no one will dare say anything to you if it looks like you're in her favor, Ashan or not." She looked to Laith for confirmation, and after a moment, the prince nodded. Athela faced Archer once more. "Archer, you up for it? Just do what you usually do in these types of situations."

He sent her a cheeky wink. "Usually, I find excuses to cram in next to them in small trunks underneath buildings."

"What?" Marc asked, bewildered.

"It's all right," Archer continued easily, surveying their surroundings. "I don't think that particular opportunity is going to present itself here."

It must have been some sort of inside joke, for to Tarr's surprise, Athela gave Archer a glare (without much actual animosity behind it), then blushed and found an excuse to adjust the hem of her dress around her shoe.

"I'd meant to ask you about your fee for flirting with the heir to the most supremely evil leader in history," Laith asked drily. "But it must've slipped my mind."

"Negotiable," Archer replied. "As always."

Tarr had to admire him in that moment. There hadn't been a single instant of hesitation. There was some jostling in the shadows as Marc, Archer, and Laith exchanged a few items of clothing so that Archer could at least give the impression of being a high-born guest rather than a groom ("I love a good cravat," Archer had mused.) Then, once they had all settled, the Ashan cast them a wink and turned, striding confidently with his long, swinging gait over to the main entrance, standing behind two other people who were waiting to shake Cira's hand. The others stole along the shadows and then found a spot near the gateway where they could safely loiter without being spotted. Tarr's heart was beating hard against his ribs, a sick feeling in his stomach.

One slip from Archer—if Cira happened to sneeze and look up in their direction—they were all as good as dead.

"We'll have to wait until he turns the full charm on," Athela murmured to the others, drawing her silvery hood over her hair, Laith and Marc mimicking her motions. Si remained quiet, peeking out from behind Marc's elbow. Tarr guessed that Si was almost certainly as nervous as he was. As they watched, Archer moved up, shaking Cira's hand. She didn't look at him at first, but Tarr saw Archer say something to her, though he couldn't hear exactly what. She cast another look up at him, his tall, slender frame, broad shoulders, casually messy hair, golden eyes, and Tarr saw something in her expression click. A slow smile spread across her features. Archer continued talking, pausing for her response, then followed it up with something that made them both laugh. Cira folded her arms and leaned back against the wall. The people who had been waiting behind Archer saw that they wouldn't have much of a chance to shake her hand anytime soon and began to move behind them. Archer casually sidestepped to lean against the wall beside Cira, forcing her to turn around sideways to look at him. The crowd began streaming in past them; Cira didn't seem to notice.

"Now," Athela hissed, and slipped forward into the crowd, melding in perfectly with her medium height and build. Tarr and Laith found themselves in more of a predicament, ducking down and keeping to the far wall to try to conceal their heights. Rane and Si were a little ways behind them, keeping their faces lowered to the ground. It only took a few seconds to pass through the entryway, and Tarr kept expecting Cira to shriek, to notice them, for some alarm to go up, but none came. When they had gone safely through, Tarr chanced a look back over his shoulder and saw that Cira was still speaking animatedly to Archer, who met Tarr's eyes for a sliver of a second and registered that the others were safe. Athela caught Tarr's arm, pulling him to one side.

"Change of plan. We're dividing up now," she informed him. "You and Si are going to come with me, and we're going to try to find the library and sort out this clue. Laith, Marc, and Rane are going to stay here and blend in and keep an eye on Archer if they can. I'm just hoping that no one else from my family is at this pleasant little gathering, or else the rest of this mission is going to be very short-lived."

Tarr nodded, heart still pounding from their near escape. They were standing in an adjoining hallway that led into the gigantic dining hall. Tarr couldn't help but stare. He had expected the interior of the fortress to be all gray, dull rock, similar to its outer walls, but it was like a geode that had been cracked in half. The hall itself drew up into an enormous arched ceiling, a splendid chandelier hanging like a glittering, shimmering globe above their heads. The floor was black, polished stone, so shiny that Tarr could see his reflection in it. Tables with refreshments were set up on one side of the hall while a long dining table was set up on the other side, at that moment unoccupied. Musicians played in one corner of the room, and there were a few couples dancing. Mostly, the guests seemed to be milling about and talking amongst themselves, marveling at the grandeur of the surroundings. There was a viewing area on the second floor; Tarr could see guests looking out over the railing at the people on the floor below, laughing and pointing.

Tarr ducked his head down. Beside him, Athela and Laith were pulling off their hoods and giving them to a nearby servant who was waiting patiently with outstretched hands to receive them. Tarr mimicked their actions, but felt an inward stab of nervousness; the cloaks had been their only disguises. Athela caught Laith's eyes, and he nodded as she slipped away to the side of the wall, Tarr and Si keeping close to her. Laith, followed at length by Rane and Marc, slid easily back into the crowd, and the three of them slowly faded into the anonymity of the gathering. The prince approached a knot of chatting young women, who, at one glance, immediately enfolded him into their circle, giggling madly.

Athela, who had extensively studied the Faridor plans that Rane had stolen, seemed to have at least some idea of where they were supposed to be going. Hallways led off from all corners of the dining hall, and Athela took the one nearest them. It was completely deserted and eerily dark, lit like the rest of the castle with torches in twisted metal grates affixed to the sides of the walls. There were tapestries hung here and there depicting in grotesque shapes and forms the images of dogs, warriors, and horses in battle and on the hunt. Tarr could tell how old the fortress was; everything was dank and rather damp and eerily still.

After they had left the large group behind in the hall, the atmosphere had grown steadily colder and the air more stale, as if the castle had been boarded up for centuries (which, from what the others had told him, it probably had.) The tapestries on the walls were all faded, the breath of their color having long since given out. Through the hallways there were narrow rugs laid out along the floor, everything a sickly shade of green.

All at once, Athela let out a gasp and Tarr jumped visibly, looking around for what could have been the matter. Athela changed course and made a beeline for something mounted on the nearest wall. As Tarr drew up behind her, he saw that it was a sword, inlaid with gold and sapphires in the same curved style as Athela's.

"Look at the craftsmanship on that thing!" Athela whistled.

"Athela!" Si hissed, his normally soft voice suddenly harsh and tense. "Focus!"

"Right, sorry," Athela apologized, then stopped. "Hang on, I need to check the plans. This place was purposefully constructed like a maze, so that it would be harder for Kagai's enemies to escape."

Charming, Tarr thought.

She reached down into the top of her boot and drew out a thin sheet of paper, upon which Tarr recognized her own handwriting.

"Read it out loud," Tarr suggested.

"According to Rane's map, we're to go to the south from the center of the palace, which is easy. The dining hall is smack in the middle, and we went down the south passage. According to the code in the clue, it should be somewhere around here." She looked up from the paper and squinted around, light from a nearby torch dancing off of her silver dress and the delicate filigree netting in her hair. "'Honor the foe,' our clue says. I don't know what that's supposed to mean."

"Me neither," Si wondered. "I suppose we should go back and walk up to your sister and shake her hand or maybe offer a toast—"

"That would probably be the most efficient way to end the war," Athela said wryly. "We'd be dead in two minutes."

Tarr, however, wasn't quite ready to give up. He started walking forward down the hallway. It came to a perpendicular intersection with another, larger passageway. Tarr wandered down to the left a little bit, but found nothing of interest. *Honor the foe. Honor the foe.* He made up a chant beneath his breath, spinning on his heel and walking back down the passageway to the right. Athela and Si were watching him as though he had lost his mind. All of a sudden, Tarr halted and whirled around, pointing to something on the wall. A small portrait was hung to the right of a pair of crossed swords, a miniature image, so tiny Tarr wouldn't have noticed it had he just been walking casually down the hallway. He strode forward quickly and inspected the picture. A handsome man stared back at him, sharp-featured with plunging eyebrows shades darker than his hair and light red-hued eyes.

"Athela, would you know Kagai if you saw his portrait?" he asked eagerly. Athela approached quickly, her boots tapping lightly on the stones, a slow smile spreading across her face, gray eyes glinting eagerly. She stooped to inspect the portrait and then leaned back, nodding.

"I have to hand it to you, Tarr," Athela said, impressed. "You're a handy fellow to have around on these treasure hunts."

"That's all well and good, but what about the *honoring the foe* part?" Si inquired, casting his eye over the picture.

"That's what I'm trying to figure out," Tarr replied, leaning forward.

Back in the dining hall, the final guests had arrived. Cira was the last person in, and Laith was both relieved and anxious to see that she was still chatting animatedly with Archer, who searched the room until he managed to locate Laith and catch his eye with an infinitesimal nod. Rane was a step or two behind Laith, graciously and quietly declining offers to dance with hopeful-looking young men and women. Marc was talking exuberantly in a group close to Laith's, turned so that his back was almost touching the prince's. Cira and Archer parted, and she went to one side of the room. Laith and Archer unobtrusively wound their way through the crowd and met in the back of the room at the farthest point away from her that they could manage.

"We shouldn't stay together too long," Laith cautioned in a low voice. "If she comes looking around and sees Marc, Rane, or me, we'll be done for."

"That occurred to me," Archer agreed. "Have the others gone off, then?"

"We got past without a hitch, thanks to you," Laith smiled. "She seemed to like you."

"I'm her official date for the rest of the night," Archer rolled his eyes ruefully. "Athela was right. The fact I'm Ashan hasn't even come up."

"It's beyond hypocritical," Laith shook his head. "Rounding up Ashans in Two Falls and twirling with you on the dance floor here. It's all just an excuse to stir up conflict. A distraction."

"Well, it's saving us tonight, at least," Archer pointed out.

"Milord," Rane said softly, her gray-blue eyes focused on something ahead. Cira had ascended to the top of a platform where she faced her guests. She wore a shimmering green dress almost the same hue as Rane's, and her long hair flowed loose and pale against her skin.

"I'll keep my eye on you; I can see you over all these people. Signal me if you need me, and I'll try to break away from her," Archer muttered hurriedly as all the people around them hushed themselves into a stark silence. He moved away from Laith through the crowd, his head standing out from the others like the beam of a lighthouse on a dark night. Laith was immediately thankful that they had separated when they did as he saw Cira's eyes latch onto Archer's moving form, staying on him until he came to a halt. She then took a deep breath and faced those around her.

"My distinguished guests," she began. Laith was shocked to hear the all-too-familiar voice, the same one that had gone complaining to her parents about Athela pulling her hair when they were teenagers, now addressing an assembly of dignitaries from around the country. There was something different as well—an air of absolute confidence that Laith had never heard before. Cira paused, allowing a measured smile, flashing her small white teeth before she continued. "It is my distinct pleasure to welcome you to the castle of Faridor. I hope you will enjoy yourselves tonight. If I may give you a brief outline of the events that we have scheduled, we will begin with dinner and then continue with dancing and refreshments, then those who wish to may participate in a discussion with me about my intentions and visions for this country. However, first things first. If you will please make your way in an orderly fashion towards the dining tables, there will be enough seating for everybody." Cira lowered her hands and inclined her head, then tossed her hair over her shoulder and turned, descending down the side of the platform, where Laith saw her wait for Archer to come up to her.

"She's certainly playing the part," Marc muttered beneath his breath. Laith had to agree. It was as if Cira had been practicing for this moment her entire life.

The guests began to slowly drift in the direction of the tables, Marc, Rane, and Laith keeping far to the back, getting seats the farthest down possible. They found themselves between a fairly bulky pair of individuals, which was just fine as they were then very effectively hidden from Cira's view. Cira, however, didn't even seem to want to chance a look down the table, so involved was she in talking with Archer, who was seated at her right hand. Marc nudged Laith softly on his arm and motioned slightly with his head, ice-blue eyes wide. Laith twisted and saw a number of guards go down each passageway.

"Do you think they've found them?" he inquired in a low voice.

"No," Laith swallowed. "Cira would have been alerted, but no one except Archer has gone up to her yet. They're probably just under orders to round up any stragglers to come down for dinner, that's all. They haven't found them." He said this to assure both Marc and himself.

He reached for the silver goblet of clear spring water that was in front of him, taking a heavy swig, swirling it around in his mouth until his teeth were cold, then swallowing. Across the table a woman in a large hat was making eyes at him. He sent her a curt nod distractedly, and then turned around in his seat to look for the guards again. They were nowhere in sight.

"There's got to be something we're missing," Athela frowned as she studied the portrait, Tarr still pacing back and forth behind her. "Honor your foe. Should we bring some fruit and lay it down in front of him? I don't understand. Do we have to say something? Surely, that can't be it. *Why*," she said exasperatedly, "does this all have to be a big puzzle? Why couldn't she have just plastered the name of her heir across the front of the Two Falls library?"

"Athela!" Si hissed. "Someone's coming down the passage!"

Athela leaped back as if a bolt of lightning had run through her, grabbing Tarr's arm. Athela pulled them over to a nearby painting depicting a warrior queen with her foot placed on the throat of her vanquished and bleeding enemy. Tarr, too, could hear the footsteps now and was fervently thankful for Si's quick hearing.

Si cocked his head impishly, eyes fixed on the grisly painting. "She sort of looks like you, Athela," he observed. Athela glanced at the painting and wrinkled her brow, as if she couldn't quite decide whether to feel complimented or insulted.

The footsteps in the passage grew louder, and around the corner came three guards in green cloaks. Tarr was all too aware of the gigantic swords strapped to each of their backs and thought anxiously of the piddly little dagger in his boot.

"Dinner has been served in the main hall," one told Tarr, who they had, for some reason, picked out as the leader. "My Lady would be pleased if you would join us."

"Please give her our compliments, and we shall adjourn as soon as we are done sampling this fine piece of artwork," Tarr gestured grandly towards the writhing depiction of the dying man beside them. If the guard found any humor in this, he hid it well and continued past them, flanked by his two cronies. Athela kept her face tilted down, the picture of demure refinement. As soon as they were out of sight, she whirled around to the two standing beside her. "Great!" she gasped. "We need to have figured this thing out by the time they come back for a second pass. If they find us here again, they're bound to become suspicious." She turned towards the Ashan, a plaintive look on her face. "Come on, Tarr, you're good at this sort of thing. Think..."

Tarr walked forward, a new resolution in his mind. It had to be behind the painting. Suddenly, he remembered the manor owned by Nicolas, Pieter's nephew. How some of the paintings had hidden passageways behind them, and how, with a special mechanism, the fireplace turned to reveal a staircase leading to the safehouse below. It had to be something similar. The hidden library had to be behind the wall. He just had to find the key.

Honor your foe. As to that, he confessed that he found himself at a loss. Ashans had no foes that he knew of. He thought back to the first time he had met Laith and Athela, the first time he had seen the

King and Queen of the Jelani...he remembered something that Laith had done...

Tarr stepped forward so that he was standing right in front of the portrait. The floor below him was cut into square stones, with one of the swirling green rugs thrown over it. Tarr felt with his toes until he was standing two stones from the portrait, then sank down on one knee in a bow, his head lowered. His right knee pressed the stone closest to the wall, directly below the picture. With a loud grinding sound, the stone suddenly sank down deep into the floor, and Tarr nearly lost his balance.

"Oh!" Athela yelped, quickly clapping a hand over her mouth. The section of wall they were in front of slid back a few feet and went to the side as if pulled back by an unseen hand, revealing a dark room past them.

"You did it!" Si exclaimed, astonished.

"Hurry!" Tarr said, grabbing Athela and Si's arms and yanking them into the room.

No sooner had they stepped over the threshold of the room than the huge stone door slid back into place behind them, sealing them in like corpses in a tomb. Tarr couldn't see a thing in the pitch black, his other senses immediately heightening to compensate. There wasn't a carpet beneath his boots, and the air smelled even staler and musty than the rest of the castle had. Tarr imagined that he could actually hear the beating hearts of his friends. Fingers, which Tarr supposed belonged to Athela, were digging into the flesh of his arm.

"Do you think this is a trap?" Athela whispered, fear sharpening the edges of her voice. "Could Cira have known about this, and now we're trapped here for her to find?"

"I don't think so," Tarr said, surprised at how calm he sounded. "We followed what Morthenstar wrote. This is where we're supposed to be. There must be a next part to the clue. Can you remember what it was? Think of the next line, and maybe it'll tell us what to do."

"*Step towards the light.*"

"There is no light," Si's voice quivered in the old stale air.

"Exactly," Athela snapped. "How are we supposed to get to the light if there is none? It's pitch black! I can't even see my hands in front of my face!"

"The light came from the door when we went in. That was the only source of light we had," Tarr mused out loud. "Step backwards toward the door with me, both of you." He felt the two bodies on either side of him take steps backward in sync with his own strides. No sooner had his foot touched the ground, but small flickerings of light quivered and burst into full fruition, almost blinding him. He raised his hands protectively in front of his face.

When he finally chanced a peek through his fingers, he saw that they were in a vast room that was half-library, half-mausoleum. It was lit by torches, with walls covered in shelves and shelves of books, the open floor of the room filled with enormous statues of humans and animals, twisting and writhing with lifelike realism. Si took a few cautious steps forward, touching the foot of the nearest statue. The torchlight made his copper hair burn even redder in the low light.

"The door," Athela said abruptly, looking behind them. "The stone door closed, but it's still all sunken in. Anyone who walks through that hallway will be able to see that a random stone doorway just appeared in the wall. I don't think we'd be able to make the entrance fully disappear again unless we were standing back outside and could kneel on the flagstone to close it."

"Hopefully, no one will notice that it appeared there," Tarr suggested. "And even more hopefully, they won't know how to actually open the door to the chamber."

"All they have to do is step down in front of it," Athela persisted.

"Which they won't," Tarr countered.

"Hopefully," Si added.

"Right," Athela agreed with a long intake of breath. "In that case, we have to work very quickly."

Tarr stepped closer to inspect the statue nearest him: three girls facing each other in a circle, their hands lightly clasped and crowns of flowers around their heads. Their faces were strangely at peace, mere hints of smiles around their lips. The effect, Tarr concluded, was altogether rather eerie.

"Statues," Athela said, profoundly unimpressed. "*More* statues."

Tarr remembered the figure of Morthenstar outside of the library in Two Falls where they had found the first clue. He withdrew his hand. "What was the next line?" he asked.

Athela squinted at the parchment. "A poppy in a field." She wrinkled her nose. "Field? What on earth is she talking about?"

"Well, we've got to look," Tarr shrugged. "Spread out."

He walked up and down the rows of statues, but nothing leaped out at him. There were images of warriors, of hunters, of beautiful expressive figures draped in lifelike stone fabric.

"*Field?*" Athela demanded irritatedly. "Where are we supposed to find a field in here?"

"Athela!" Tarr exclaimed, frustrated. "Keep it down!"

"Tarr!" Si called from across the hall. "Come look at this!"

Tarr jogged over and stood beside Si, who pointed at the base of one of the statues. It was the one Tarr had seen first, the one of the three young girls dancing in the round.

"Well, isn't this cheery," Athela murmured, coming up behind them. "Matches the fortress perfectly."

"Look," Si said, pointing to the base of the statue. At the foot of one of the girls was a single carved flower.

"How on earth did you find *that?*" Athela exclaimed indignantly.

"I saw it," Si shrugged.

Athela gave Tarr an exasperated look, then motioned him forward. Tarr reached out slowly and felt around the edges of the carved flower. He pushed it gently, but nothing happened. He leaned forward and saw a tiny seam threading around the base of the flower bulb. He hesitated for a moment, then turned the bulb of the flower around. There was a slight click.

"You did it!" Athela breathed.

Behind them came a loud grating sound of rock on rock, and, to their astonishment, a single brick seemed to have shifted to the right on the blank stone façade behind them, leaving an empty hole gaping in its place.

"Don't tell me," Athela said, the smile dying from her face. "We have to move all the stones. *All* the stones to see what's behind."

"No time to lose," Tarr said. His heart was still racing from having figured out the first clue. "Si, what's next?"

"And then my husband told me that he had used the entire amount to buy a fleet of ships to trade with, and I told him, I said, 'Have you lost your mind? You expect to make your fortune trading tea leaves?' Well, he was right and I was wrong, and I suppose I have him to thank for all the things I have today, but heaven knows that he hasn't let me forget that day for the entire rest of time we've spent together."

The countess had a nasal laugh and an elaborate hat with a stuffed bird on it that still bore in its character its last agonizing moments of living. Laith had known before she had opened her mouth that he preferred it shut.

He nodded politely for the umpteenth time and turned away to face Rane, whom he noticed was tensely shoving her vegetables around her plate. The countess across the table had made it her personal mission to hold Laith's attention for the entire duration of the dinner, completely ignoring her husband, who was sitting on her left and chatting up a rather buxom blonde in a cleverly cut dress.

He chanced a glance behind him and saw that the house guards were returning through the passages and back into the dining hall. Laith breathed a slow sigh of relief through his teeth as he saw that they had come back in alone, meaning that Athela, Tarr, and Si hadn't been found. He nudged Rane softly with his foot to see whether she had noticed them, too, and she gave a tiny nod in response.

A loud peal of laughter came from the far end of the table, and Laith poked his head forward ever so slightly. Archer and Cira were smiling broadly, both acting as if there were no other people around. Laith couldn't help but be impressed with Archer's flirtation skills.

Across the table, the countess was inhaling sharply as she took deep swigs of wine from her goblet, alternating her beady gaze from Laith to her husband and back again. Remembering that she had failed to say anything to him for at least forty seconds, she opened her mouth to speak. Laith sighed and started thinking about anything to keep his mind occupied. He wondered how his wife was doing, whether she had cut her hair, as she'd hinted she was going to do before he left. He missed hearing her laugh.

Soon, he thought to himself. *Just a little longer.*

He shook his head a few times and took a sip of water. He was determined not to be tempted by the overflowing goblets of wine that had been set in front of them. Most of the food on his plate was untouched, as was the same for Rane's and Marc's, neither of them having much of an appetite. Marc was deep into conversation with one of the broad men sitting on his right, and though Laith only caught snippets of their conversation, he deduced that it had something to do with goat herding. While Marc seemed to be genuinely exploring the topic with fervent enthusiasm, Laith himself was grateful that he didn't have to take any part in it. *Good old Marc*, he thought to himself.

"...And then the entire room exploded, and I figured that it was a good time for me to just take the wench and run for it," the heavyset man guffawed and took a long drink. Marc shook his head disbelievingly, silky blond hair swishing from side to side with his movement. Laith considered the possibility that maybe they weren't, in fact, discussing goats.

"Milord," Rane's softly accented voice came. Laith immediately turned around, cursing himself for being lax in his surveillance of the guards' actions. They were slightly to the side of him, so he found he could easily push back his chair a few inches and act like he was reclining and still be able to see them. One guard was intently whispering to the other, and they seemed to be looking over all the faces of the guests. As their curious eyes reached him, Laith hurriedly leaned forward, tapping Marc on the arm to look as though he was in a productive conversation.

"So, what were you two talking about?" Laith asked in what he hoped was a casual tone.

"Goat herding," Marc replied, ice blue eyes watching Laith over the rim of his goblet as he took another swig. "Something wrong, then?"

"Maybe."

At that precise moment, the three guards put their heads together and conferred for about a minute and a half, their green cloaks reflecting dully on the polished black floor. At long last, one straightened up and approached Cira from behind, lightly tapping her on the shoulder. Laith, uncaring of who was watching, stared at them. Cira at first looked irritated that the guard had disturbed her conversation with Archer, but after they had whispered in her ear for a few seconds, she looked up sharply and spat out an order. Archer, who was right beside both of them, chanced a hurried glance at Laith and gave him a nod that could only mean one thing: something had happened. The plan was in jeopardy.

"What's going on, Laith? I can't see properly," Marc whispered urgently.

"They must have seen Athela, Tarr, and Si in the corridor, and they just noticed that they aren't at dinner. Cira's probably going to order her guards to go and search the hallways again for them. She suspects something."

Marc nodded sharply and straightened back up, turning to the man beside him and striking up a conversation once more. Laith drummed on the tabletop with the pads of his fingers, and was suddenly aware that the countess was still talking to him, oblivious that he had been engaging with other people during her soliloquy. He worked his jaw forwards and back, agitatedly dipping his finger in his water goblet and spinning his finger around the rim. His cousins were all able to produce a high-pitched whine when they did the trick, but Laith himself had never been able to. The guards passed behind them. Laith felt the swish of their motion on the nape of his neck as if a cold wind had suddenly blown across his back. There was still a chance that Athela, Si, and Tarr would make it out safely, just as long as Laith and the others did nothing to attract attention. Laith shifted in his seat uncomfortably. Sitting and doing nothing was never something that he had been terribly good at.

The minutes were ticking by faster than Tarr cared to acknowledge, while their progress through the series of clues left by Morthenstar—each one revealing a tiny segment of the prophecy concealed on the wall—was painfully slow. He tried not to think of it as they worked from statue to statue, but was conscious of a nervous buzzing rising higher and higher in the back of his mind as they went.

"This has got to be it," Tarr decided firmly, furrowing his brow and looking around the room. "This has to be the next statue."

"Thank goodness," Si grunted. He was teetering on the edge of a plinth displaying a woman in a long, flowing robe, the folds of fabric caught in motion so perfectly by the sculptor that she could have been ready to walk off her pedestal. Si clung onto the smooth stone arms beside him as he peered over the still shoulder. Morthenstar, Tarr thought to himself, must have had a sense of humor.

"Nothing wrong with being thorough," Athela sniffed, bringing the parchment closer to her nose and inspecting the writing closely. "This does, however, seem to be a bit of overkill."

"Found it!" Si crowed, pressing in a piece of stone on the statue's belt, watching with satisfaction as the button caught. Another stone slid back on the wall. About three-quarters of the inscription carved on the wall behind was now revealed—not enough to fully decipher. Si stood up, smoothing his copper hair back behind his ears and looking proud of himself. "This is getting to be easy. Give me the next one."

Tarr walked around the pedestal of another statue, running his hands over the carving, feeling the texture grate against the skin on his fingers as they probed the imperfections in the stone. Noticing something, he stopped. There were six fingers on the statue's hand. It was an Ashan. Tarr smiled to himself.

"Your next clue, Si," Athela stood up straighter, holding the parchment a little farther away from her face. "is an archer who has struck his target."

"That'll be...simple..." Si's face fell as he looked around at the statues and realized that there were three archers. One was a man, standing to one side as though he was running, a bow and a quiver buckled across his back. Another was a woman, her bow raised and an arrow drawn far back, her eyes wide as she sighted down the shaft. The last was a man who was kneeling and in the middle of nocking an arrow to his bow.

"I don't understand," Athela groaned, "*why* it needs to be this complicated."

"Nothing wrong with being thorough," Tarr echoed mildly, and she glared at him.

"It's got to be one of those three," Si nodded, folding his thin arms and biting his lip as he thought. "Bow of an archer...should I just press each of their bows and see whether or not I find one of the triggers?"

"Remember, Si, we don't know whether or not this has to be done in order, but knowing how meticulous Morthenstar has been with her other clues, I'd have to assume that they would be," Tarr cautioned. "We can't take the chance that they'd be out of order. We could jeopardize this whole situation if we do something careless like that. We just need to think about this carefully."

"We don't have much time," Athela warned. "Something's bound to have happened by now. They're going to notice we've gone."

"Do you think Athela's sister knows about this place?" Si asked.

"I don't know," Tarr frowned.

"Why would Morthenstar even *hide* part of the prophecy in here to begin with?" Athela wondered aloud. "You'd think she'd want to keep it as far away from Kagai as possible."

"In some ways, it might be safer just to keep a clue right under Kagai's nose," Tarr pointed out, shrugging.

"Nuts," Athela shook her head disparagingly, as if Tarr and Morthenstar had somehow conspired to make the clues as obscure as possible. "Both of you are nuts. Either way, we need to hurry. We can argue about the logic of Morthenstar's hiding places once we're safely back in Two Falls."

"Right," Tarr agreed. "The clue said that they had just struck their target?"

"That's right," Athela confirmed, looking back at the parchment. "It's odd, though..."

"...None of them seem to have struck a target," Tarr finished. "Yeah, I noticed that, too. Those two are about to shoot, and he doesn't look like he's aimed or anything."

"We don't know that," Si pointed out. "He could have just shot one and is looking off into the distance."

"Why is the bow strapped to his back, then?" Tarr asked. "No, Morthenstar wants us to look below the surface. There has to be something else here. Something else that we're missing..." At that moment, he turned and found himself face-to-face with the shield of one of the warrior statues. It was the form of a woman, though her face was concealed behind a battle helmet. Her sword was up in a defensive position in one hand, her shield raised to the side of her crouching body as she looked over the top of it. On her shield was a decorative floral border, and in the center was the image of an archer kneeling down, bow raised. An arrow was lodged in the trunk of a tree at the other end of the shield; the tree's branches spread up and joined in the pattern around the sides.

Tarr turned around to the others, pointing. "There. I found it."

"Not fair," Si pouted, jogging forward to inspect the shield. He had clearly come to regard their treasure hunt as a game rather than the life-or-death mission it actually was.

"You'll get the next one," Tarr smiled as Si kneeled beside the statue, stroking the engraved bow of the archer on the shield. A section of the bow slid back into the shield under the pressure of his fingers, locking itself into place. Athela came to stand beside them, shaking her head in amazement and patting Tarr affectionately on the back.

"There we go," Si straightened up, looking back at them eagerly. "What's next?"

"We've only got five more to go," Athela informed them, skimming down her list of clues. "We can make it."

The party's program had once more moved to dancing. Laith, Marc, and Rane were all rotating around the fringes of the crowd so that they could take turns keeping an eye on Cira and Archer. Archer, due to his considerable height, was easy to spot over the heads of the crowd.

The countess who had taken a liking to Laith had unfortunately not been dissuaded by the fact that dinner had ended and that she and Laith were no longer obliged to be in close quarters; indeed, she tailed him like a hound on a rabbit. Marc, sensing his prince's rising level of stress, attempted gallantly to distract the countess's attentions to himself so as to allow Laith some unfettered thought, but the woman proved to be as tenacious as a crab. Rane was on full alert, standing so close to Laith that he could feel her breath on his shoulder blade, one step behind him, staring around at the other guests in case Kagai's guards ambushed them. The other guests, by this point, were all getting slightly tipsy and were far too interested in their own conversations to pay them any mind.

Laith's dark eyes slid over to the hall's entrance, where a group of guards were slinking in, keeping out of the way of the partygoers. They were probably under strict orders to keep their actions subtle so as not to create a disturbance and ruin the facade of absolute control that Cira was trying to maintain throughout the occasion. Laith felt a small inner twinge of satisfaction knowing that their operation was causing her some chagrin.

He stared unblinkingly over the rim of his glass and watched as the guards moved towards Archer and Cira. Marc approached him, nudging him slightly in the elbow with one hand. Laith glanced over his shoulder and saw that the countess was at the drinks table. He looked forward and adopted a genial smile, as if he and Marc were having a pleasant conversation about someone at the party.

"You saw them, too?" Laith murmured.

"Yes, and so did Rane. Doesn't look as though they found Athela and Tarr, did they? There would have been more of a commotion."

"Not now, at least, though I doubt Cira's going to drop it. She's not very likely to let there be even the slightest chance that her party will be ruined. She'll investigate this as far as it will go."

"But even if she did find them, you don't think she'd make a public show of arresting us? I mean, causing a disturbance and letting the guests know that we managed to get in? Maybe she'd just want to take care of us *after* the party. We might have a bit of time to find a way to sneak out."

"She'll look at it as an even bigger victory if she captured us red-handed trying to infiltrate. The Strikers getting caught would only cement her takeover of the country. No, I have no doubts that if we're found, it'll be the end of it. The end of *us*. And she'd do it publicly."

Marc swallowed.

"They were seen, though, weren't they? Athela and Si and Tarr? That's how the guards know they weren't at dinner? Cira might recognize Athela from her description."

Laith managed a small smile. "I doubt she did, or else they'd be combing the place for the rest of us."

"She knows we have to be out here somewhere. I'm surprised she hasn't gone stomping through every house in every city looking for us already."

"Me too. My guess is that she expected us to go into hiding, not to come barging straight into Faridor." Laith smiled faintly. "It is not, after all, a very tactically sound move."

Marc made a conciliatory motion with his hand and turned around to intercept the countess, who was coming sloshily up to them bearing drinks in each hand.

Across the room, the guards had sidled up to Cira and Archer, clearly obeying her order not to raise any alarm among the guests. Rane noted their position, then looked silently over to Laith and Marc. Though Marc appeared to be chatting amiably with the countess and his prince, his eyes were just as open as hers for trouble.

She took a small step back away from Laith's broad shoulder and slipped off through the throng of people, keeping her head ducked, her eyes just low enough so as not to invite conversation but not guilty enough to inspire suspicion in anyone who might look at her. She was smaller and more lightly built than many of the other guests, and she didn't find it hard to conceal herself behind some of them. She halted within what she calculated was about two yards from Archer and Cira, tuning her ear to the sound of their hushed voices, ignoring the chatter of the people around her.

"We haven't found anything, Your Highness," came an overly apologetic voice. Rane could almost hear the cringe in the guard's tone. "We've searched both the upper and lower stories. We have guards posted around the hallways in case they try to move their positions. No one is there."

"Oh?" Cira's all-too-familiar voice snapped. "Are they ghosts? Is this place now haunted? Are these special ghosts who only come out during parties?"

"Perhaps your guards have been partaking of that punch, which, might I add, is aptly named," Archer's familiar sardonic tone chimed in. "My head's reeling already, and I've only had one and a half glasses."

"Liar, you've had three," Cira's voice was silky, flirting.

"See? Can't even count correctly."

"There may be one or two places where you haven't looked yet, but I doubt I can trust you to look there by yourselves," Cira sighed dramatically.

"What's going on?" Archer asked innocently. "I heard your guards mention something about guests being missing."

"Yes, they were seen earlier in the hallways but never turned up at dinner."

"Perhaps they nipped off to a broom cupboard."

"There were three of them."

There was a beat of silence, and Rane could almost see the slow, wolfish smile creeping across Archer's face. "Surely, my Lady, I don't have to enlighten you as to *those* implications."

There was another small moment of silence.

"No, I don't suppose you do," Cira cooed. "I will have to go and look after this, though, can't have people nipping off to the broom cupboards, as you so eloquently put it. Causes quite a stir with the custodial staff."

Buy them time, Rane thought under her breath. *They need more time. Tarr and Athela are going as fast as they can, but they need more time.*

"Dance with me first?" Archer inquired, as if he had heard Rane.

"Why, I thought you said you couldn't dance," Cira exclaimed.

"Get enough of that punch in me and I'm game for anything," Archer said heartily. A moment later, the people who were screening Rane from Cira and Archer's views were moved aside as he and Cira moved through them. Rane sped as fast as she dared go backwards through the crowd as they quickly spread out to allow Cira and Archer room to dance. Smatterings of applause were here and there, though Rane could see many of the guests looking suspiciously in the direction of Archer's hands, where his telltale sixth finger was on full display. Cira may not have actually cared about the Ashans, but there were obviously guests at the party who did.

Archer spun Cira around, her green dress fanning out around her legs as she twisted, her blond sheet of hair swinging as Archer pulled her back against his chest, smiling as though he knew something that she didn't. Rane moved even farther backwards through the crowd so that she was on the very outside of the circle and walked around it until she found Laith and Marc towards the rear of the group.

"Much more of this, and he'll be our *in-law*," Marc shook his head.

Rane ducked her head next to Laith. "They haven't found Princess Athela or the others yet. Lady Cira is going to go out after her dance with Archer and look for them herself."

Laith nodded. The crowd around them gasped at some antic Archer and Cira were performing. Marc was clapping appreciatively along with the other guests. "We'll all try and keep an eye on them," Laith said in a low voice. "Archer will probably be able to go along with her, and if worse comes to worse, he can try and intervene even if it does mean blowing his cover."

The dance ended with Archer pirouetting Cira around into a low dip, then raising her up. Cira was flushed from dancing and smiled, nodding gracefully to the guests who came up to bow sycophantically and congratulate them for their skill. After about a minute of small talk and tiny whispers in Archer's ear, she held up her hands for silence. Laith noted with dismay how easily she controlled the guests, how they obeyed her within a matter of seconds. It was just as it had been back in Joymaril, only on a much grander, more dangerous scale. She looked around, flashing a bright, winning smile.

"I would like to thank you all for your kind applause, and I would also like to thank my friend here, Urk, for the dance."

Laith and Marc both snorted loudly and bent over double, hands clasped over their mouths. Even Rane felt a small twitch around the edges of her mouth, though she had an easier time concealing it than did Laith or Marc.

"*Urk?*" Marc gasped in a strained whisper. A few of the guests chuckled and more than a few gave disapproving or condescending glances over towards Laith and Marc. Laith coughed a few times to try and hide his laughter.

Indeed, Archer stood up rather proudly when Cira announced his name, and Laith was sure that he had seen their reaction from above the heads of the other guests. The Ashan casually clasped his hands behind his back and looked innocently up at the ceiling as if nothing had happened. Cira continued, not having noticed a thing.

"There is a small matter which I must now attend to, nothing more than some housekeeping, but I hope you will forgive my temporary absence. In the meantime, I would like to ask you all to please adjourn to the next room, where I will be conducting a small question-and-answer session. You all will be free to ask me whatever you choose. I assure you that I will answer everything to the best of my knowledge and ability. If you will excuse me now, I will try and get this done as fast as I can."

Cira let down her hands, and the crowd moved forward, milling about and gradually moving towards the door that Cira had pointed out to them during her speech. The countess gave a few hopeful tugs on Laith's arm, but he ignored her. Marc patted her on the back and assured her that they would be in momentarily. Looking happier, the countess promised that she would save them seats and followed the other guests out into the adjoining room.

"What do we do, Laith?" Marc hissed. "Do we follow Cira, or do we join the other guests?"

"If she didn't know who we were, I'd say follow her," Laith replied through gritted teeth after a moment's reflection. "But if we slip up even a little bit, everything goes up in smoke."

The banquet hall was almost empty, and Laith and the other two began walking hurriedly toward the other room, keeping close behind the final stragglers. Cira was following the guards out of the hall on the other side, flanked by Archer, who seemed to have cajoled his way into coming along.

"Good man," Laith murmured. "Now, keep an eye on her for us."

"This is it," Athela crowed, taking eager strides forward. "Last one."

"Well, read it already!" Si said eagerly.

Athela fumbled with the parchment for a few moments. "'The answer you will find is in her place and in her hands.'"

"I think I know what it is already," Tarr announced, walking back up to them. "There are only a few statues that we haven't used in the clues, and I think Morthenstar is one of them."

"Good thinking," Athela agreed, folding up the parchment.

"She's over here," Tarr told them, striding off so quickly that Athela and Si had to jog to keep up with him. Tarr stopped proudly in front of the statue of Morthenstar, who had one hand raised and was pointing off into the distance as if she was motioning her troops onward. Her stone cloak swirled around her legs, and her sword was held low by one side. Her hair flowed around her face as if an invisible wind was moving it. Athela nodded with satisfaction.

"This has to be it," she agreed.

"That's what I thought. Now, what the rest of the clue probably means is that someone has to get up on the pedestal with the statue and stand in her position with their hands in hers. Athela and I are probably slightly too tall to do it."

"I'll give it a go, though I'm not much shorter than you are, Athela," Si volunteered cheerily, clambering up onto the pedestal. He shifted his thin shoulders back and forth a few times, hunkering back, fitting his body against Morthenstar's, and placed one of his hands around the statue's. He raised the other in the air, pointing ahead. He was almost exactly as tall as the statue was, and he turned his face to one side.

"Nice pose," Athela said sarcastically. "Very heroic."

Tarr stared at it for a few moments, knowing that this had to be what they were looking for. "Si, did you find the button on Morthenstar's statue?"

Si glanced around for a few moments, ducking under the statue's elbow, then finally stood up, triumphant. "Yes, here it is, on the hilt of her sword."

"Press it."

Si obeyed. Immediately, there was the grating of rock on rock and the last stone pulled away, revealing the inscription in its entirety. Athela let out a low cry of delight and sprang forward, copying down the remainder of the prophecy on a parchment she'd brought. Tarr and Si stood back and watched her scribbling away furiously, arms folded, both content.

Suddenly, Si stopped stock still, hands out to the side on Tarr's arm.

"What?" Tarr asked in a whisper, alarmed at the look of fear on Si's face.

"Someone's outside," Si replied hoarsely.

"Athela!" Tarr called, leaping forward and laying his hand on her arm. She shook him off angrily.

"It's almost finished! Let me just—" she waved him off, irritatedly looking back up at the stone and squinting her eyes.

"Athela, if someone's coming, that can only mean Cira's here and they've seen the door; we don't have time, we have to leave now!" Tarr insisted, tugging on her arm. He himself could hear them now, voices outside the door. His heart began pounding, fear creeping up his throat. Si was standing to one side, frozen, his eyes wide open, staring at the door. "Athela, please!" Tarr begged again. When she didn't respond, scribbling down the last word of the prophecy, he took her by both arms and hauled her bodily to her feet. Her yell of rage was caught somewhere in the back of her throat as there was a booming sound of stone grating against stone; the door opened, and the lights blew out on them, plunging them into the dark. A loud grinding sound from the opposite side of the room told Tarr that the wall had once again rearranged itself to cover the coded prophecy that they had worked so hard to reveal.

Tarr, still holding Athela by both arms, took a step back so his spine was bumping along the stone wall behind them. Si was beside him. Athela pressed against Tarr's chest. He heard the parchment rustle ever so slightly in her hand.

A vertical sliver of yellow light showed at the other side of the room, gradually growing wider and wider until Tarr could see the silhouettes of at least seven people. The light behind the people at the door allowed him little ability to identify their faces, though one of the people stood a head taller than anyone else, and the long neck and spiked hair told Tarr that it was Archer. *Thank goodness,* Tarr thought fervently. *Maybe he has some idea how to get us out of here.* The people at the door took a hesitant step inside until all of them were standing just in front of the doorframe when the stone again slid back into place, casting them all into utter darkness.

"Your Highness!" a strange man's voice called out.

"I'm right here," came an irritated reply. "Didn't any of you think to bring any lights?"

"No, Your Highness," another voice replied timidly. "We didn't know we would need them."

"How will we get out?" asked a third voice, more panicky than the others. "Are we trapped in here?"

"Stop whining," Cira snapped. "Right now, I want you to search this room as best you can. This is absolutely the last place they could be hiding; the other guards have confirmed they haven't gotten past this corridor. They're in here, somewhere." Tarr, his eyes straining against the darkness, saw dim forms of people beginning to stumble forward, arms outstretched. Athela flattened herself against Tarr, pressing so hard that he could even feel her heart beating through her back.

"Where are you?" Cira called, though her tone was different, more seductive, obviously meant for a different person.

"Right here," came the familiar lilt, so close to them that Tarr nearly jumped. He turned towards the voice and could see Archer's translucent skin glowing slightly in the darkness. He was stretching out a hand towards them, groping, obviously trying to find where his friends were. He had rolled up his long sleeves so that the pale skin of his arm was just barely visible in the black vacuum of the cavern. *He must have done that so that we would know where he was. But how on earth did he guess that we were over here?* Tarr wondered. Archer took another step close to Si, who was trembling like a leaf. Tarr reached out and grabbed Archer's arm. The other Ashan started, then twisted his grip, sliding down Tarr's forearm, feeling along the other Ashan's hand for his sixth finger. Upon finding it, he released Tarr's hand and took a step back. "There's nothing against this wall that I can feel; I've gone all up and down it." Archer's voice paused. "What on earth *is* this place?"

"Some sort of statue room. Kagai built loads of hidden passageways and trick entrances all throughout the fortress," Cira replied impatiently, as if such behavior were commonplace. "I've found most of them by now. The rest of you look along the other walls."

"There are things in the way!" the first guard whined.

"They're the statues, you idiot; we have more important things to worry about than whether or not you stub your toe," Cira snapped.

Tarr saw Archer quickly pass his hands over Athela and Si, who both flinched at the touch. The heat from Si was vibrating beside Tarr's neck, and he realized that he was shaking. Tarr felt Archer's hand on his shoulder again, this time gently pressing him to one side, guiding him. Tarr responded, sliding along the wall slowly, still holding onto Athela and grabbing Si's forearm to tug him along. They moved silently along the stones to the far corner closest to the door. Archer placed both hands on Tarr's shoulders, pushing him down into a crouch on the floor.

"Urk?" Cira's voice was dangerously close. Archer whirled around, hands outstretched, feeling through the darkness for her.

"Where are you?" he asked.

"Right in front of you."

Archer grabbed her arms and took her to one side. "I haven't found anything, and I don't think the others have either. They would have let out a call."

"That's not why I came over," Cira purred. Tarr felt Athela tense up against his chest. He gave her arm a small squeeze, though it did little to relax her. Everything was silent for a few horrible seconds (except for the slightest sound of slurping), and Tarr didn't have to use much imagination to see what was going on a few feet in front of them. Finally, after what seemed like an eternity, Tarr could faintly hear Archer murmuring to Cira, and her giggling.

"Milady!" a voice called from the other side. "I think I've found something!"

"I'll go," Cira said and slid off through the darkness. Archer let her walk a few feet away from them then rushed silently back over to the corner where Tarr, Athela and Si were crouched. He knelt down beside them, leaning forward so that his mouth was only about an inch from Tarr's ear, whispering.

"Tarr, do you know how the door opens?"

Tarr closed his eyes, forming a mental picture. Having it securely in mind, he turned his face slightly so that he was next to Archer's cheekbone, whispering just as quietly as the other Ashan had. "There are seven tiles in front of the door. The one in the middle, the fourth one, turns the lights on. The one directly in front of that should open and close the door."

"Right, here's what we'll do," Archer leaned forward, resting a hand on Si's shoulder and pulling him over so that he could hear. "I'm going to draw them off to the other side of the cavern. Tarr, you open the door. They won't make it out in time to catch you."

Tarr and Athela nodded their understanding. Si leaned up close to Archer's other ear. "What about you?" he whispered.

"If I go with you, as soon as they see I'm gone, they'll know that something's not right and they'll start combing the place." Angry yells came from the other side of the mausoleum, evidently from the guard's mistake.

Archer turned to them. "Be sure you close the door again once you're out."

Tarr patted Archer softly on the shoulder to let him know that they understood. Tarr could almost feel the glint of Archer's smile. "By the way, Athela, your sister kisses like a horse." With that, Archer leaned back on his heels and vanished into deeper darkness.

Tarr slid his hands along the wall, feeling for the crevice where the wall ended and the door began, Athela and Si edging along beside him. Finally, his deft Ashan fingers found it and he slid them down the groove to where it met the floor. He traced the cut around the flat stone on the floor. He moved left horizontally, counting the other edges as his fingers found them. One, two, three...His hand stopped on the stone.

Suddenly, behind them, a dark shadow loomed forward, and an arm shot out, grasping Si's shoulder. It wasn't Archer.

"Milady! I've got them!" one of her guards shouted out, his voice echoing around the room. Tarr, mind completely blank, could think of nothing else to do but flatten himself back against the wall, keeping his hand pressed to the stone. Athela sprang forward, catlike, and landed with a dull thud squarely onto the guard's chest, knocking him back onto the ground. She struck him with a stablike motion on the neck with her hand. He shuddered and fell quiet. Voices and footsteps were coming towards them, the dread sound of feet echoing in the wide room. Closer...closer...

"The parchment!" Athela hissed in Tarr's ear. "I dropped the parchment!" He felt her strain beside him, groping in the absolute darkness.

"Where?" Tarr whispered. "On the floor?" He bent down and waved his fingers over the cold stone.

"I don't know!" Athela replied. "Turn on the lights and I'll find it!"

But if they turned on the lights, they were done for. They'd have no time to go searching around for the parchment, which could have gone flying in any direction during Athela's scuffle with the guard.

"Over here!" Archer called from the other side of the hall. "They're making a run for it. I felt one on the wall, but they got away!"

The footsteps closest to them halted and began running off in the opposite direction. Thinking quickly, Tarr tried to disguise his voice and called back, "Coming! Our archer dropped something by the front door!"

It was their only chance. He had to hope that Archer would know the message was for him and understand what it meant. It was a long shot. He stepped onto the stone in front of the door. With a loud groan, the door grated open and Tarr plunged forward out of the room, pulling Si and Athela with him.

"They're getting out! They're going out the door!" a guard howled from behind them. Tarr squinted his eyes and chanced a glance over his shoulder. He saw the dim forms of the two others beside him. He quickly stepped on the center stone; with a groan, the rock door slid firmly into place. Tarr didn't even bother to wait but ran down the hallway from which they had come, the world around him sliding more and more into clarity, the dim light stinging his eyes. Athela and Si were running beside him, both unscathed. They turned a corner and collapsed, panting. No sooner had they stopped than Athela rounded on him.

"We left the parchment inside," she snapped. "All that *for nothing.*"

Tarr shook his head. "We had to get out. Archer will find it."

"*If* he knew that was you shouting and *if* he understood what you meant," Athela rejoined icily.

Tarr didn't bother to argue. Athela had worked so hard to get the prophecy. He understood her disappointment.

Si was doubled over, hands on his knees, red hair hanging towards the ground. Athela looked over at him, concerned. "Si, you okay?"

He gave a small cough and nodded.

"You're fine," Athela assured him with a reasonable approximation of a comforting tone.

"They've probably locked down the rest of the fortress by now," Tarr pointed out. "They'll be searching everywhere for us. Any other ideas?"

"Window?" Athela suggested.

The nearest window they found was around the next corner and across a short walkway that brought them over the keep to the outer wall of the fortress. Old and ill-kept, the shutter took some convincing to open. Scaling down the wall was another challenge; they were on the ground floor but the terrain below them was made up entirely of enormous jagged rocks. The wind blew fast and sharp past their ears, seeming to pick up speed as it raced up from the sea across the wall.

Tarr went first. The descent was laughably easy for him, but Athela and Si needed steady coaching to clamber down the few jutting stones to reach the rocks below.

Once they'd made it down, they picked their way around the side of the fortress, slipping here and there on the salt-slicked terrain. In due course, they came around a last curve and spotted the front gate and the bridge across to the mainland.

"Here's a pretty problem," Athela observed. "We seem to be out here, and the carriage is in the courtyard."

"Can you climb up and over the wall, Tarr?" Si asked. "To get inside?"

Tarr looked up. The sheer stone wall loomed above them, high and intimidating. It would be tricky, though not impossible. "Maybe," he said dubiously. Getting down from a first-story window was one thing. Scaling the entire wall in the dark was another.

"I could try and distract—" Athela began.

"Wait," Tarr cut in. "Si, go up to the guard. Tell him you're Cira's page and that our carriage has been summoned back to Two Falls immediately. The Queen has requested the presence of another guest. They're to be brought here without any delay."

Athela glanced at Tarr, then back to Si. "Can you do it?"

Si squared his thin shoulders and gave a resolute nod. " I can do it."

They watched as he scampered off, hugging the wall as closely as possible so that he could approach the guards at the gate without them seeing him.

"A bit of a risk, isn't it?" Athela asked tensely.

"A young boy is less suspicious than you or I," Tarr shook his head. "And with any luck, the search for us is going on inside. They won't have alerted the outside guards yet."

They watched in silence as Si crept up to the guards at the door. Clearly, his experience as a pickpocket served him well; neither of them noticed him or turned as Si came up behind them. For all they knew, he had come straight from inside the fortress. He tugged on one guard's cloak, and when he turned, Si gesticulated earnestly back at the courtyard, speaking quickly and animatedly.

For a few protracted seconds, Tarr held his breath as he and Athela watched the pantomime unfold. Finally, however, the guard gave a curt nod and waved an arm, taking a few steps back towards the inner keep of the fortress where the carriages were stationed. Athela nudged Tarr in the ribs with her elbow.

They kept low and used the rocky ground as cover as they inched towards the bridge and the front gate of the fortress. Finally, they stopped, flat on a cold slab. They were hidden in the black shadow of the wall above, as near as they dared go without attracting any notice.

"Remind me never to wear a dress again," Athela growled. She'd had to knot the silvery fabric at her knees to keep from tripping over it.

"If we make it out of here, I will personally burn every dress in your closet," Tarr vowed.

A minute or so later, there was a loud clatter of hooves and wheels and their carriage pulled forward out of the front gate. The same small lady driver was perched atop it, and a few steps before the head of the bridge she hauled on the reins to stop the team. Tarr watched as the bridge guards walked around the far side of the carriage to exchange words with the driver before departing. Tarr could hear traces of Si's breathy young voice on the wind. He'd clearly led the guards away from them on purpose.

"Now!" Athela hissed and scrambled to her feet.

Tarr rather clumsily lurched up behind her, and the two of them dashed to the door of the carriage nearest them, opening it as quietly as they could and scrambling inside, trying to rock the vehicle as little as possible. The carriage curtains were still lowered, and the interior was dark and cool. Tarr and Athela huddled together on the floor, trying not to make a sound.

"Take the boy with you," the guard said, presumably to the driver. "See that the guest is given the message and is brought back to the Queen."

The carriage gave a minuscule bounce as Si alighted on its back and an instant later there was a broad lurch as they began rolling forward, the blissful racket of the wheels on the bridge filling the air.

Like steam escaping, Tarr slowly let his breath out through his teeth.

The stone door of the hidden statue room opened and Cira and her guards spilled out, blinking owlishly in the lamplight. Archer looked swiftly about him for any sign of the others, and tried to hide his relief when he saw that they were gone. "Search every room," Cira growled, and stalked down the hallway. "I want them found."

Shortly before they reached the empty dining room, Archer stopped abruptly in his tracks. "Wait!" he exclaimed. "I left my cravat back in that room."

Cira turned slowly and gave him a searching, narrow look. Archer saw the slightest edge of suspicion flickering in the corner of her eye. "Your cravat?" It was more a statement than a question.

"Yes," Archer insisted. "It must have come off when we were... you know..."

She considered. "Guards, take him back," she said slowly, then added, "Stay with him."

Archer sighed. "It's so hard to find a good cravat these days, and that one brings out my eyes. Come on then," he said jauntily to the other guards, and turned on his heel. Cira remained motionless, watching his retreating back.

She paused and brushed back a strand of her hair, ever so slightly adjusting the sleeve of her green dress higher up her shoulder. Then she appeared, perfectly poised and unruffled, in the lounge just off the main dining hall. Her guests—who had all been chatting merrily—fell silent as she and her entourage entered the room. The room itself was, like the rest of the castle, ornately decorated with sparkling chandeliers hanging down from the ceiling and lighting the interior. The roof was gilded with swirling gold patterns that ran down onto columns lining the walls. There were a number of velvet-cushioned couches and chairs (all of which looked newly made) upon which a few guests were perched; still more were standing around in small clusters. A slightly raised dais stood at one end of the room, a draping blue tapestry hung behind it.

Laith and Marc were tucked away in the farthest corner, sitting in a group of standing guests so that they were effectively shielded from sight. As the crowd parted to allow Cira space to glide to her gilded chair in the front of the room, Laith slowly rose, looking over the shoulders of those around him. There was no sign of Athela or Tarr—or, worryingly,

Archer—and Laith couldn't ascertain from Cira's expression whether his friends had been caught or had escaped. As Cira sat, the rest of the guests followed her example in one smooth ripple of motion. His path of vision cleared, Laith hunkered down once more.

"What do you think happened?" Marc inquired in a hushed voice.

"I don't know," Laith replied.

"I am sorry for the slight delay, there was a minor inconvenience that needed to be attended to," Cira began. "It is all taken care of now, I assure you." Her face gave nothing away. Laith couldn't be sure whether or not she was bluffing.

"I have been looking forward to this moment for some time," Cira continued, the epitome of effortless poise and eloquence, her hands folded neatly across her lap. "You may now feel free to ask me any questions you wish, and I will be glad to answer them."

One of the guests across the room from Laith and the others stood and gave a small bow. "Your Majesty, I have come to inquire about the tax which you say must be visited upon every city." The man gave another bow and sat down.

Cira laughed airily. "Oh, that. That is a fee to pay for the protection I will provide our country from neighboring kingdoms. It is highly necessary, and I assure you that all funds will go towards the benefit of my subjects."

Another guest rose and gave a bow. "Milady, what are you planning to do about the Ashans?"

Cira smiled, reminding Laith somewhat of a wolf baring its fangs. "That is probably the most important thing we will discuss tonight. As you well know, the Ashans have all but invaded our land, taking valuable resources away from the honest human citizens of this country and amassing great wealth at their expense. They have their own lands, and now they have set their sights on ours. My aim is to rectify this great problem. I will enact laws to control the Ashan population in Two Falls and elsewhere, and thereby create a balance that will be much more beneficial to my people."

"What about that fellow you were dancing with?" one man asked boldly.

"He is an Ashan who has agreed to work for me," she said smoothly.

"It is best, I think, to understand one's enemy from the inside out."

Laith looked around at the other faces to gauge their reactions. Some were watching her with blatant skepticism, others seemed more interested, or were even nodding.

"I have already begun to take steps to manage the Ashans by containing and limiting their ability to travel in and out of the capital city of Two Falls," Cira continued. "Once they have been registered, further action will be taken. No more will the people of this country have to compete for wealth that should rightfully be theirs."

A slow round of applause began around the room. Marc and Laith exchanged looks, their eyes grave. Cira nodded her demure appreciation. At that moment, the door opened again, and Archer entered, flanked by three of Cira's guards. He gave a faint nod to Cira, then Laith could see him begin to scan the room.

"What about the Strikers?" asked another voice from the audience.

"The Strikers..." Cira said slowly, "are a legend. Nothing more."

Archer locked eyes with Laith, finally having seen him. He shook his head and gave a small wink, which could only be noticed if someone had been watching him closely.

Which was exactly what Cira was doing.

She stared at Archer and then followed his gaze straight over to Laith. His heart skipped a beat in his chest as he saw recognition flash across her face. Her eyes widened in absolute shock, then narrowed to mere slits. She opened her mouth to call for her guards—

"Oh, no," Laith muttered.

All at once, Archer grabbed the guard nearest him and slammed him into the wall. There was a flurry of yelling and stomping feet and crashing as the guests leaped to their feet, and pandemonium effectively broke out as each guest tried to find the nearest exit.

"Marc, Rane, we've got to get out now!" Laith bellowed. He grabbed Marc by the shoulder, hauling him into the stampeding wave of guests.

Just outside the room, as guests began to scatter through the dining hall, Laith nearly collided squarely with Archer.

"This is one of the best parties I've ever been to," Archer panted.

"Rane, you had a chance to look at those plans of the fortress,"

Laith said urgently. "Please tell me you can find us a way out."

"This way," she said and motioned towards the opposite side of the dining hall, against the flow of the other guests who were running towards the front door.

"Rane, stay in front," Laith ordered as they jogged across the chamber. The yelling and shouting were echoing from all corners now; the chaos was absolute. It was startling to see slightly intoxicated high-born men and women in evening dress screaming like banshees and colliding bodily into one another.

They sprinted across the open dining hall, conscious of the pounding of footsteps behind them; it was too much to hope that they weren't being pursued. Rane pushed open a small service door, almost camouflaged in the wall, intended for use by the kitchen servants. They crashed haphazardly down a small staircase and came to a landing and a long passageway. This was a darker area of the fortress, not so well furnished as the public-facing rooms above. The rooms and corridors were like a maze; Laith hadn't the faintest idea how Rane could find her way through them; they all blended together into one. She led them down a corridor to their left and burst through a double door.

About five women and men looked sharply up at them, startled. One was frantically whisking a large bowl of what looked tantalizingly like clotted cream; the other was in the midst of slicing a small mountain of strawberries. The kitchen was a long, low room with a broad countertop and a huge fire roaring in the hearth. Its walls were hung with dozens of pots and pans, the stove was laden with cooking utensils, and all available surfaces were filled with vegetables and fruit. Long tables, clearly intended for staff to use at mealtimes, were lined up across the room.

"This way," Rane motioned. Behind them, the unmistakable sounds of dozens of footsteps were coming down the corridor.

They piled through a small door across the kitchen, leaving the bewildered cooks still staring after them mid-chop. Archer hung back for a moment.

"My compliments," he said, leaning his head back into the kitchen. "The appetizers were fantastic. I'm sorry to have missed dessert." He shut the door politely behind him.

A short while later, Tarr, Athela, and Si were waiting in the dark interior of their carriage, concealed in the shadows a safe way down the road from Faridor. The lamps on the sides of the carriage had been blown out; they were all but invisible. They were taking turns peeking beneath the curtains when Tarr saw a group of four figures approaching, two of them stripping off green Kagaian cloaks and casting them into the brush.

"It's them!" Tarr called, and pushed back from the door as Laith swung it open. The prince, Archer, and the others piled into the carriage, and a moment later, Laith pounded on the roof of the carriage, signaling the driver to start. With a lurch, they set off.

Tarr had never been so glad to see anyone in his entire life. All four of his friends were thoroughly out of breath, but from what he could make out of their faces, they were otherwise none the worse for wear.

"How on earth did you get out?" he asked curiously.

Laith, Marc, and Archer's words tumbled over one another rather breathlessly as Rane stared serenely out the carriage window.

"We found a service door down by the kitchens—"

"—and then there was a covered wagon with some empty crates on it right outside the door—"

"—so Archer, Rane, and Laith hopped in the back, and I threw the blanket over them and drove it round—"

"We got stopped, but Marc bopped them on the head before they could say anything—"

"—took the guards' cloaks, Rane and I put them on, and when we got round to the front gate, we said we'd been delivering wine to Faridor and were supposed to go back to Two Falls right away, but no one cared. Everyone was running around like mad—they thought we were all still trapped somewhere inside the fortress—so in the hubbub, we just slipped out across the bridge." Marc chortled richly. "No one noticed. Almost all the bridge guards had been called inside to look for us."

Athela slowly turned to Archer with an almost desperate look of entreaty. Milking the moment for all it was worth, Archer slowly withdrew a paper from his jacket pocket and handed it over to her.

"You dropped something?" he grinned.

Athela let out a low cry and snatched the paper from his hand. She looked back up at him, her gray eyes shining. For a prolonged second, it looked as though she were about to plant a kiss right on Archer's lips. But she recovered herself—perhaps remembering where his lips had been an hour earlier—and looked down at the treasure in her hands, smoothing it out on her lap.

"Ew," Si wrinkled his nose, smirking.

"Look," Laith said suddenly, pointing out the carriage window towards the fortress.

The others leaned in and watched the distant melee unfolding on the island. Tarr could almost hear the dim sound of yelling, and saw the pinpricks of light rushing to and fro atop the fortress walls as the Kagaian guards scrambled to try and find them. One by one they broke out into laughter.

"If that doesn't get the whole city talking by tomorrow morning," Archer raised his eyebrows with an elated sigh, "I don't know what will."

CHAPTER TWENTY

Tarr and Rane strode along together in the cool morning air, basking in the sunlight and the freshness of the day. Two Falls was not yet awake, and they kept to the back streets, away from the patrol of the Kagaian guards. For the first few minutes of their walk, Tarr had worried about what to say, but when he glanced over and saw the peaceful smile of happiness on Rane's face, he realized that, just as he had felt with Archer, he didn't have to fill their silence with empty conversation. She was so lovely, he thought suddenly, and wondered why everyone else seemed not to see it.

"Tell me about where you're from," she said suddenly, in her husky voice. Tarr began his response about five times before he managed to get the words out properly. And to his surprise, instead of just blurting out "a tree," he began to talk. Slowly, at first, then more freely. He told her about their treehouses, their soft glow, the quiet way the breeze blew through them in the summertime, the golden light at sunset. He spoke of climbing through the trees during a snowstorm, everything blinding white and cold, and how they would heat enormous stone baths of water with hot rocks so that he and the others could bathe while the snow fell around them and steam rose off their bodies like mist off a lake. He told her how the trees would bend like stalks of grain in the wind and how he clung to them, as minuscule as an insect on the back of a giant's hand. And when he stopped, he felt a yearning in his chest that had lain dormant for weeks and weeks. He turned suddenly and looked to the north where the forest lay.

"You miss it," Rane said quietly. Tarr nodded mutely, and she studied him with her soft gray-blue eyes.

"And what about you?" he asked. "And the others? It must be different, not living in a palace."

"Certain things were easier there, to be sure," she agreed. "But there...there was always something lurking behind a corner. We could never be sure from day to day when Athela would be safe or when the Queen would turn on her. It was...unsettling."

"You said you were born in the city, right?" Tarr asked curiously. "Not the palace?"

Rane nodded. "That's right. I began my training when I was quite young, though. So I sort of half-grew up at the palace."

"What about your parents?"

"They knew that being a royal bodyguard would be a good life for me," she shrugged. "So I started training there part-time when I was five years old. By fifteen, I lived at the Academy full-time."

"Are they still there in the city?"

Rane shook her head. "My father is originally from the Meadows. He's deaf, and much of his family is, too. So, once I was living at the Academy, they went back to the Meadows so that he would have more of a community. He and my mother were older when they had me. I think it was good for them."

"Oh," Tarr was surprised. "So can you speak..."

"Sign language?" Rane prompted with a faint smile. "Yes. Both my mother and I can. And there was a deaf teaching aide at the Academy. He and I would talk together quite a lot. I haven't been able to speak it as much since I started guarding Athela, though."

They left the relative security of the back streets to walk through the main square, and checked to make sure that their hoods were up and mostly obscured their faces. They had to be careful after the Strikers' excursion to Faridor a few days before. Cira was furious that they'd escaped and was on the lookout for them. He remembered the feeling of Rane's hand taking his as they'd sat in the carriage on the way to Faridor; tentatively, he reached out, and was thrilled to feel her fingers entwine with his.

Soon the city awoke, and they lost themselves in the midmorning crowds. Tarr stooped slightly every time they went past a guard so that they wouldn't fall under suspicion. The open markets were still doing business, but to Tarr's ears, the vendors hawking their wares were slightly muted and the general mood of gaiety had dissolved, an odd shared anxiety in its place. Tarr kept Rane's hand close in his, and they wandered without any real destination for quite some time, around the bottom districts and back up to the river, strolling along its banks until they were at the north gate, closest to the forest. Before they had realized it, they were only about twenty feet away from the guards on duty.

"Tarr," Rane said warningly, shaking his hand and stirring him out of his complacent state of satisfaction. "We should turn back. They're likely to start searching anyone who comes close."

They took a step to turn around, but Tarr abruptly found himself face-to-face with a sneering Kagaian guard. "What's this, then?" she demanded. "Looking for a way out, are you?"

"Out for a walk," Tarr said. It was the first thing that came to mind. Rane tensed up beside him.

"Let me see," the guard snatched out a hand and caught Tarr's forearm, wrenching his hand away from Rane's. She grinned as she counted the sixth finger on Tarr's hand. "An Ashan. Where are your papers and your permit to be out and about in town this time of day?"

"He has none," Rane said calmly. "And he needs none. He's free, as are all Ashans."

"Don't know where you've been, but that's not the way it is around here anymore," the guard laughed. "Come on, stand aside, you're coming with me."

"I assure you, he is *not,*" Rane said through gritted teeth. Her hand moved forward, and Tarr could see the tip of a knife's blade held sharp against the woman's gut. The guard's eyes flicked fearfully down to her belly, then back up to the blank stare on Rane's face. She raised both of her hands in a sign of surrender and took a step back.

Suddenly, there was a loud crash from behind them, followed by shrill screaming. Tarr and Rane whipped around, expecting more guards to come charging their way, but found that nearly the opposite was true.

A band of about fifteen men and women tore through the streets toward the guards at the exit. They brandished sharpened sticks, knives, and a few swords. The guards shouted warnings to each other and readied themselves for an attack. The oncomers halted a few feet from them.

"Stand aside," said a young man at the head. He was tall and broad with blond hair and a fierce expression of determination on his face. He brandished a sword. The guards eyed him and the others behind him. "This gate is free," the young man announced.

The lead guard merely laughed. "Take them!" he shouted to the others. The guards leaped upon the small band and a brutal, violent skirmish broke out amongst them. The townspeople began to scream and clear the area; in a few moments a circle of onlookers had formed around the fighters.

Immediately, Rane dashed forward, intent on helping the newcomers. Tarr wished that he knew some way to fight, but reasoned that it would do no good getting himself killed, so he took a step back behind the cover of one of the houses and watched to see if any wounded needed to be taken away.

One of the resistors dropped to the ground, clutching his arm, red blood staining through the sleeve of his shirt, and Tarr saw his chance. He darted forward out of his cover and tucked his hands under the man's armpits, pulling him slowly over the cobbles. Tarr was sure that he was going to be struck down as soon as one of the guards caught sight of them, but they were all so involved in the frenzy of the fray that no one took any notice of him at all. He dragged the wounded man back behind the house where it was safe.

"Here," came a quiet voice behind him, and Tarr looked over his shoulder to see a middle-aged woman peeking around the door frame. "Bring all the wounded in here; we'll care for them."

Gratefully, Tarr heaved the man up and helped him through the door, where the woman and what looked like her daughter wrapped their hands around the man's shoulders and helped him inside.

Tarr turned back to the battle, expecting to see plenty more wounded and dead, but to his surprise, only a few of the members of the resistance had fallen. Tarr still felt rather queasy; he was as yet unused to scenes of violence and tried to avert his eyes from the prone figures lying on the ground. Though they were largely outnumbered by the guards, the resistance seemed to be possessed of a certain grit and fire against which the guards stood no chance. The guards were being beaten back and, with a blissful wave of relief, Tarr could see Rane still fighting among them. The sleeves of her white shirt were stained pink, her auburn hair shook loose from its hood.

Tarr again went out and retrieved one of the wounded, a young woman who looked to be about Athela's age. The two women inside the house accepted her soundlessly, staring fearfully over Tarr's shoulder, hoping not to be seen.

By the third time Tarr had delivered an unconscious fighter to the women, the fight was over, and, much to Tarr's amazement, the resistance seemed to have the upper hand. He knew, however, that the victory was probably only temporary, since word would undoubtedly get back to the barracks and a gigantic wave of Kagaian reinforcements would be arriving at any minute to quash the rebellion.

The big, blond young man who had led the initial charge stepped up to the north gate, recently erected by Kagai's soldiers and now standing unprotected. "Now!" he called.

A huddled group of twenty or so Ashans and half-Ashans suddenly broke out of the front doors of a dozen nearby houses and ran for the gate. The onlooking crowd that had gathered began to applaud as the Ashans ran across the one-time barricade to safety. Some of the Ashans held the hands of their children, and others carried large bundles of belongings. Tarr watched them and felt a huge lump rise in his chest as the Ashans sprinted towards the field beyond and safety in the forest.

The resistance leader watched the Ashans go, then turned. "We will hold this gate until they have reached safety!" he announced. "Two Falls will be free again!" He reached up and tore the green flag of Kagai down from where it had been snapping in the wind, carried it to the banks of the river, and unceremoniously dumped it in, spitting after it. Gradually, it took on water and sank slowly beneath the surface. The people in the crowd cheered again, and the young man raised his fist in triumph. The escaping Ashans were long gone.

To his right, Tarr heard the sound of horses fast approaching. He put both his fingers in his mouth and whistled loudly to attract their attention. Rane immediately turned around to see what it was, and when Tarr indicated the approaching riders, Rane reached up, grabbed the resistance leader's arm, and hurried him over to where Tarr stood. The crowd was fast dispersing; the stronger fighters picked up their dead and wounded and carried them away, the others blending immediately with the crowd. Kagaian riders littered the ground, and Tarr pointedly looked away from them until Rane and the young man were beside him.

"In here," Tarr said in a low voice, pushing open the door of the house, making sure they were all safely inside before bolting it.

There were three women in the small room, all tending to the wounded that Tarr had brought them; wrapping bandages around arms and slathering on scented ointments.

"Thank you for your help," the blond young man said in a deep voice. The oldest woman nodded at him curtly. Tarr could tell that she was still nervous about the possibility of riders coming to knock at her door.

"What's your name?" Tarr asked the young man. He was rather generically handsome and looked as though he could be distantly related to Laith. He had a large square frame and jaw, which he held perpetually clenched in an attitude of defiance.

"My name is Ari," he said.

Ari. The name jogged something in Tarr's mind. "You didn't happen to be in contact with Pieter, one of the former Two Falls council members, did you?"

"Yes," said Ari, looking bewildered. "My father and I went to speak with him a while ago, but then he disappeared, and we have heard nothing from him since."

"My name is Tarr, and this is Rane," Tarr said quickly. "We're..." he paused, groping to make the words sound natural coming out of his mouth, "two of Morthenstar's Strikers." He winced inwardly, waiting for Ari to burst into laughter at how ridiculous it sounded.

Instead, Ari stared at them for a moment, seemingly unmoved by this information. In contrast, Tarr noticed that the three women had momentarily stopped tending to the wounded fighters and were gaping at him. Tarr gave them a pleasant smile and a casual wave, and they quickly returned to their duties, pretending as though they hadn't heard anything. Ari folded his arms and frowned thoughtfully.

"You do exist, then?" he asked skeptically.

Tarr sighed heavily. "Believe it or not."

Ari looked from Rane to Tarr, a sense of respect growing on his face. "I heard about your exploits at Faridor. Pretty daring."

"We were lucky," Tarr admitted. "I know the others would like to talk to you."

Loud, clanking footsteps pounded outside the door. Tarr eyed the door nervously. They had to get out, had to relocate. The soldiers would begin breaking down doors before too long.

"You're leading some sort of resistance?" Rane inquired.

"Nothing too organized," Ari sighed. "It's hard to know who is loyal to whom these days. We were able to arrange this march on the bridge, however, and it should do at least something to get people talking. I'll send some of my friends over here to move these people out," Ari nodded towards the wounded on the floor. The women smiled gratefully back at him. He faced Tarr again. "I think we should work together. Tell me where you live, and I will try to meet you."

Ari arrived at Ma's house in the middle of the night, swathed in a dark cloak. Introductions were swiftly made, and the lights in the house were all put out so as not to attract attention. Only a single lamp burned on the kitchen table, and all the curtains were drawn. Rane kept a lookout by the window for any suspicious activity. Si was already fast asleep.

"What sort of an operation do you have going?" Laith asked eagerly.

Ari frowned. He wasn't the sort to think quickly or speak fast. "We have a small organization, mostly set up by my father and myself. A few of his associates and their families are willing to house refugee Ashans and want to help formulate a bigger resistance. However, they are sorely untrained and undersupplied. The only reason we really were able to get the upper hand today was out of sheer surprise. But next time, the guards will be ready."

"It's something," Athela agreed, though Tarr could tell that she was slightly disappointed. "We're still in touch with Pieter, though, and he could point us in the correct direction. We can start organizing. Start training."

"Where?" Marc broke in. "How? Cira's got this place in a stranglehold. She's building a wall around the city to keep everyone in and has troops patrolling the perimeter in the meantime. I mean, to even have *this* meeting, we have to do it in the middle of the night by a single candle. I can't see us ever finding enough space to covertly train resistance members."

It was indeed a problem. Tarr sat back quietly, his hands folded across his chest.

"Well, the first thing we can do is start some sort of network as you suggested, places where Ashans can hide until we can find some sort of way to smuggle them out," Athela suggested.

"It's dangerous," Laith shook his head. "We're going to have to thoroughly investigate everyone who offers to shelter Ashans and keep them under close surveillance."

And anyone can be turned, Tarr thought to himself. *Given the right incentive.*

"We can try threatening people with the prospect of having to kiss Cira," Archer said, grinning. "That should be effective leverage." A few of the others laughed, but Ari remained stony-faced, his arms crossed over his chest. Archer stared at him. Tarr, stifling a smile, realized that it was probably the first time one of Archer's jokes had garnered no reaction whatsoever. Archer peered at him closely, searching for a break in the façade, but Ari remained completely impassive.

"I had to kiss Athela's sister, you see. Cira. Kagai. Revolting, but all in the line of duty," he clarified, golden eyes still trained on Ari, who barely even blinked.

"Oh," he said.

"It was quite wet," he narrowed his gaze, watching Ari keenly. "And toothy."

"I see," said Ari, his face absolutely devoid of expression.

Frustrated, Archer slouched back in his chair and crossed his long legs under the table. He didn't speak throughout the rest of the conversation and kept sending Ari little glares across the table.

An hour later, Ari stood up to leave. "Please keep us updated," Athela said. "We're going to try our best to find the name of Morthenstar's heir. Once we've found out who the heir is, we'll have a figurehead, someone to rally around, and maybe someone with powers great enough to defeat Kagai."

"Or at least someone we can use as a human shield," Archer joked doggedly. Ari didn't bat an eyelash or even move a corner of his mouth. Instead, he stared disdainfully at Archer as if he were a small child begging for attention.

"Thank you for inviting me; I'm glad to have met you all. I will keep you updated with any new plans or developments," he said in a deep monotone, then threw on his cloak and was off.

"I don't like him," Archer said as soon as the door was closed.

"What, because he didn't like your 'hope the heir of Morthenstar gets shot at' joke?" Athela asked sarcastically.

"People without a sense of humor," Archer maintained stolidly, "are untrustworthy."

"Perhaps he actually needs to hear something *funny* in order to laugh," Athela flashed back.

"Good grief, you two, shut up," Laith rolled his eyes. "Everyone get some sleep. Between decoding the prophecy, organizing a smuggling ring, finding shelter for refugees, stockpiling supplies, and training an army, we've got quite enough on our plate without you pulling out each other's hair. Got it?"

Archer and Athela muttered their assent, still glaring at one another, and they all started to separate and go up the stairs to bed. Tarr was still smiling to himself as he walked up the stairs behind Archer, sliding his hand along the smooth banister. "Archer," he said suddenly as they reached the landing, "why were you exiled?"

Archer swiveled around and fixed Tarr in his golden eyes. "You want to know?" he said softly.

"I do," Tarr said.

Archer looked like he might be on the verge, but hesitated. "You know, I think it's getting to the point where you might actually understand," he said slowly. "So I'll tell you. But not yet." He turned to go to his room.

"I don't care, you know," Tarr said abruptly, realizing as soon as the words were out that they were absolutely true. "I don't care that you were exiled."

A peculiar smile flashed across Archer's mouth. It was soft and a little sad, completely uncharacteristic. "I know," he said quietly, "and I'm glad of it."

And with that, he walked into his room and closed the door.

CHAPTER TWENTY-ONE

"I've got a feeling," Si sang at the top of his voice, *"That we're going to stay together until the world ends!"*

"I sincerely hope it doesn't come to that," Archer said.

"And if I could ever think that you could love me..."

"Maybe if I was really, *really* intoxicated," Marc grumbled.

The Strikers were sitting around a table at one of the town pubs, safely anonymous in a sea of faces. The night had been sanctioned as a festival to honor Cira (which Tarr thought to be in extremely bad taste, considering that Ari's demonstration at the north gate had happened only two days before.) Green lanterns had been hung across the tops of the alleyways and streamers were flying through the air, but the green light was bathing everything in a sickly sort of unflattering glow, and the atmosphere was considerably dimmed compared to the celebrations Tarr had witnessed in Two Falls before. The townspeople had tentatively emerged into the streets and some were dancing, though not too exuberantly, as there were Kagaian guards stationed everywhere to keep things under control. While initially the Strikers had considered boycotting the festival, Archer had pointed out that they had already begun an ironic tradition of attending their archenemy's parties, so why stop now?

Athela seemed mostly interested in meeting people who could be incorporated into their sheltering and smuggling ring, and had been laying some preliminary groundwork with a few individuals that Ari had brought with him. Ari, much to Tarr's surprise and Archer's chagrin, had agreed to come and sit with them, and try though they might, neither Archer nor Marc could manage to get him to crack a smile. He sat at their table with his arms folded across his chest, his blond hair covered by a cloak, looking every inch like he could pass for Laith's boring cousin.

Some of Archer's underworld friends, having heard of the recent shake-up in Two Falls, had come in from Riddleton and other small surrounding villages to investigate the situation. A seemingly never-ending procession of them had been stopping by Archer's table, so that much of the night had been spent regaling each other with stories of jobs and adventures. Tarr could barely keep track of them as they kept rotating in and out of the pub and the table. At each new face, Archer rose up for a fresh round of hugging and back-pounding. Tarr was surprised by the level of respect with which Archer was treated by each of the newcomers, as he hadn't had much of a desire to know about Archer's chosen profession. He was surprised to realize that he felt a bit jealous seeing Archer with a different group of friends.

The hesitant dancing had leaked in from the streets to the insides of some of the buildings. Despite himself, Tarr still couldn't quite resist the sounds of the beats and melodies. Music was still something new and wonderful, and he allowed himself to be carried away by the sounds, temporarily forgetting his worries as the songs swelled and rose and cascaded around them. On five or six occasions, Laith was approached by a blushing young woman and asked to dance, and each time he gallantly accepted, though his attention appeared to be elsewhere. Tarr kept to his seat beside Rane, the both of them listening to the chatter of their friends. Tarr briefly considered asking Rane to dance, but then remembered he didn't know how. Beside them, Archer was laughing with one of his friends, a smuggler from Riddleton, but then the joke was over and the friend stood up to get another drink. Archer mused over his cup of wine for a few moments before honing in on Athela, who was studiously ignoring him.

"Athela," he said declaratively. His cheeks were flushed with wine, and Tarr could tell that he was feeling emboldened. Athela arched her eyebrow and regarded him imperiously.

"Yes?"

"Care to dance with me?"

"Thank you, no."

"Who's going to make fun of you?" Archer exclaimed, spreading his palms flat and motioning around the table. "Laith won't. Tarr won't. I don't think Ari can physically manifest a smile. Si's about to fall asleep." Archer glanced around to see if Ari had registered the taunt, but his face was just as stoic as ever.

"Am not asleep," Si maintained, his boisterous high spirits of a moment ago suddenly dimmed. His head was drooping so low his chin was almost resting on his chest. It was a curious childlike aspect of Si's personality that while he could maintain a high level of energy throughout the day and occasionally far into the night, there came a certain hour when his body seemed to shut off and he suddenly fell asleep in the middle of anything he was doing.

"How about it, Athela?" Archer wheedled, hand outstretched.

Athela stared at him for a few moments, then slowly turned her head around to Ari. "Care to dance?" she asked.

Tarr was fairly sure that he was about to die of shock, but that was nothing compared to what came next.

"All right," Ari replied unenthusiastically and unfolded his arms. Athela didn't even glance at Archer as the two headed out to the floor of dancing couples.

Archer leaned back, his face blooming from astonishment into absolute delight. "Well, I'll have the last laugh. *She's* the one who has to dance with Ari."

Tarr glanced over at the dance floor where Athela and Ari were mechanically performing the most joyless shuffle-step he had ever seen. Archer's smuggler friend returned, bearing a tray of tankards, which he distributed with some careless sloshing and spilling.

Laith looked to Archer's friend. "So, where is it that you're from?"

"Riddleton," the friend replied.

I'm sorry, Tarr thought privately.

Archer's friend was short, much of the build of Marc, with broad shoulders, dark black hair, and light blue eyes. It wasn't a face that called much attention to itself, which Tarr had come to realize was an asset in the criminal underworld. "Heard about the party and couldn't help but put in an appearance, especially after I heard that Archer's over here."

"You came all the way from Riddleton to see Archer?" Marc asked incredulously.

"Sure," Archer's friend shrugged. "Archer was one of the most successful criminals in Riddleton. When he packs up his bags and suddenly moves out, people are naturally going to wonder where he got to. As soon as he popped up here, word got back to us. A lot of us have been waiting for an opportunity to come and visit."

"How are things in Riddleton?" Laith inquired. "There's been a lot of new security measures being put up around Two Falls. Makes it hard to travel."

"Same thing," the friend nodded, frowning. "Maybe not quite as bad. It's doing hell for business, I'll tell you that."

"Did you have many problems getting into Two Falls?" Tarr asked. Laith caught his eye and frowned, clearly wondering what Tarr was on about. Tarr gave him a "be patient" glance and returned his attention to Archer's friend.

"No, there was hardly any trouble coming in, just a few guards at the entrance, pretty much letting everybody pass."

"What are you getting at, Tarr?" Marc inquired.

"I just thought it was somewhat odd that Cira was throwing this festival thing," Tarr mused. In his mind he could picture it, a hand slowly squeezing its grip around the perimeter of the city. "I wonder if what she's trying to do is get some of the underground people from Riddleton to come here for the party and to trap them here, closer to her realm of control."

"I doubt that," Archer's friend guffawed.

Tarr shrugged, feeling momentarily foolish. "I don't know. It does seem like the sort of thing Cira would do."

"You said yourself that many of the best assassins and members of the underworld have come here for the celebration," Marc chimed in. "Why wouldn't she try to keep you all here and take you out?"

"You're paranoid," Archer's friend laughed again and turned

around, rudely showing their back, ending the conversation. Marc opened his eyes wide at the smuggler's turned back for a second in an expression of frustration, and then sighed. Laith met Tarr's gaze once more and mouthed *I need to talk to you*. Tarr arched a quizzical eyebrow, but Laith shook his head slightly and then turned in his chair.

The night and the party continued weakly on, and eventually the Strikers were pushed out of their comfortable seats in the pub to make way for some of the more dehydrated and enthusiastic partygoers. The streets were still choked with people, many of them now completely inebriated, which gave the rather tense celebrations an added level of desperate hysteria. While Tarr managed to laugh at some of the antics he witnessed, he was sobered slightly by the sight of Kagaian guards at every corner, keeping a close watch on the goings-on.

Athela announced (more loudly than usual, Tarr noted) that it was probably best for them to start heading home. They bid a tepid farewell to Ari, who inclined his head and walked off with only a grunt or two.

"You know, I'm actually beginning to like him," Laith said fondly, watching Ari's retreating ramrod back.

"Hmph," grunted Archer.

The band set off amicably, threading their way through the crowd. Marc was, as usual, tugging along a drowsy Si, whose head kept lolling against Marc's shoulder. Rane drew up beside Tarr and subtly slipped her hand into his. Tarr's stomach did a small tap dance, and he tried to conceal his delight. He glanced around, hoping none of the others had noticed, and it appeared that they hadn't—except for Archer, who had a pinched expression on his lips as if he were trying to keep from smiling. He gave Tarr a tiny wink and a thumbs up, and Tarr felt himself grin widely in spite of himself.

They saw a group of guards approaching and automatically pulled their hoods up higher and ducked down a side street. All at once, Tarr suddenly remembered that Laith had wanted to speak to him about something. He sent Laith a meaningful look, quickly squeezed Rane's hand, and dropped back to walk behind the others. Laith fell into step beside him.

"What's up?" Tarr asked in a low voice.

"Look, I have something I need to go do tonight," Laith informed him. "I want you to come with me."

Tarr felt his curiosity rising. "Does it have to do with where you go when you disappear in the evening?"

"Yes," Laith replied. "I've been...it's hard to explain. I need your help tonight. This may be my last chance."

Tarr blinked in surprise. "Why me? Whatever it is, I'm no good at fighting, you know that. If you need someone else there, why don't you ask Archer or Marc to go with you? I know Marc's already put out that you haven't told him what you're up to. It'd probably make him feel better."

Rane turned around and, noting the serious expressions on Tarr and Laith's faces, gave him a quizzical look. Tarr shook his head briefly and Rane, getting the point, turned around to walk forward once again.

"I need you there," Laith muttered. "Fighting's not a problem; I don't think it will be that sort of situation. Even if it was, I'm pretty sure I could handle it..."

"Where do we need to go?" Tarr asked, his curiosity finally getting the better of him. He saw a smile of relief flit across Laith's handsome features before settling back into the depths of his dark eyes.

"When we head back to the house, let the others go into their rooms, then, quick as you can, come back downstairs, we'll get Wolver and Arfolasth and then we'll go. Bring a dark cloak."

"All right. Laith, where are we going?"

But he refused to say.

After the other Strikers had gone off to bed, hauling a reluctant Si in their wake, Tarr went to his closet, slipped on his black cloak, and went down the stairs. He thought he heard a door creak open behind him, but didn't bother to wait and see who it was.

Once he got out to the barn with Wolver, he found Laith was already there, saddling Arfolasth. Wolver seemed to sense that something was up and was pleased to be out of the house after so many days spent cooped up (after Kagai's takeover, it had been determined that he was too attention-grabbing to be taken out of the house on a regular basis.) The wolf's ears were pricked and ready, and he nudged Tarr's hand with the tip of his cool nose as they walked. Laith was swathed in his long midnight blue cloak, and nodded to Tarr as he led the way out of the barn into the moonlight. He pulled the broad hood up over his head and grasped the pommel of his saddle, pulling himself easily up into the seat. He hoisted Tarr up behind him, and then they were off, Arfolasth's hooves clattering loudly in the stillness of the night.

The main streets of the town were still fairly full of people, and the music, while faint, played on. Laith kept to the back alleys and dark roads, out of the way of most of the partygoers and out of sight of the Kagaian riders, who were mostly stationed at the major intersections and avenues. Tarr was beginning to wonder how they would be able to manage to get out of the town at all, as all of the entrances that he knew of were being watched, and the perimeter of the town was being patrolled. He didn't have to wait long for an answer, for after about five minutes they drew up a shadowy back corner, which, to Tarr's surprise, led straight down into a drainage ditch that ran parallel to the outer edge of the town. They marked the path that the patrols were making around the border of the city; once a window opened up, Laith kicked forward and they shot through the gap like a black arrow. Before the patrols could notice a thing, they were flying east under cover of darkness.

Once they were free of the Two Falls border, Laith eased Arfolasth up into a rolling canter. Wolver easily matched the gait from the ground beside him, and the black horse and white wolf ran together, the only sound their rhythmic breathing and the pounding of hooves and paws against the hard ground.

Laith had still made no mention of what exactly they were doing or where they were going, so Tarr resolved to ask him at the first breather they took. That, it turned out, was about forty-five minutes later when Laith slowed his horse down to a walk to let him cool out and catch his breath. Wolver's tongue was lolling out of his mouth.

"Laith?" Tarr asked in a low voice. The prince's head turned, his face illuminated in the light of the low-hanging moon. "Can you tell me now?" He had a vague inkling of what their destination might be; had been suspicious since the first night Laith had disappeared.

Laith swiveled around further in the saddle. "After we ended up back here in Two Falls, I decided that I would try to go back to Joymaril and find out what was going on, to see if I could find out anything about Kagai's heir from people there. And," he added quietly, "to try and find my wife. To help her get out, if I could. The first few times I tried, I wasn't very successful. The guards on duty thought I was a bandit and chased me off. Had quite a few close scares. Finally, I just decided to come back whenever I could and make my move when I recognized a guard I could trust. It took about a month before one of my lieutenants showed up. I came up to him and asked him what was going on. He didn't tell me much, just that bounties had been put on Athela's and my heads and that if Rane or Marc was sighted then they were to be killed as well."

Tarr's stomach clenched at the thought. Laith continued nonchalantly, "That was to be expected. But he said he'd try to help me and get word to my brother Cade. The next day when I came back, my lieutenant wasn't on duty anymore; it was some other fool who sighted me and sent an entire troop on my tail, took me half the night to outrun all of them."

Tarr seemed to remember a morning when Laith hadn't shown up to the breakfast table at all, and had caused the others such worry that they had dashed up to his room to make sure that he was actually there in one piece. Laith had been found sleeping soundly in his bed. The only strange thing about it was that his face seemed to have been cut in places by branches or vegetation. Tarr had found it decidedly odd, but none of them had wanted to ask Laith about it.

"I think I remember the night you're talking about," Tarr said finally. "Go on."

"After that, it was pretty much a no-go until last night when another one of the soldiers I used to command came on duty. I didn't think he'd help me at first; he was always a bit of a snot when he served under me, but he didn't run after me with his sword, so I stayed and talked to him."

"And?"

"He said that he'd be able to manage it. Help me get word to Ilaina. I've tried writing to her, but I'm pretty sure my letters got intercepted because she never wrote back. And then, with Cira's takeover and the wall she plans to build to enclose the city...I figured this was perhaps my last chance to get out. To get to her. So I arranged a meeting for tonight."

"Why on earth did you want me to come along?" Tarr asked, beginning to feel more nervous. He didn't like the sound of Laith's arrangement, didn't trust the word of the former soldier who'd agreed to facilitate the meeting. He realized suddenly that Laith's desperation to see his wife was clouding his ability to see clearly into a situation that was quite probably a trap.

"I want you to keep a lookout," Laith replied, and Tarr could hear the eagerness in his voice. "You can climb, right? I need you to take a look before we arrive and alert me to any danger you might be able to see from the trees."

"All right," Tarr said uneasily. "But why not bring Archer?"

Laith hesitated. "I don't know," he admitted. "I just thought... you'd met her. You'd know why it was important for me to come."

Tarr made no reply, and Laith seemed to take his silence as tacit agreement. He urged Arfolasth forward into a trot. Inside, Tarr was roiling. Laith's emotions had put them *both* in danger.

He knew better than to think that he could convince Laith not to go to the rendezvous he had arranged. The prospect of seeing his wife, of bringing her back to Two Falls with them, was too big a temptation. Tarr needed time to think.

"Tell me how you met," Tarr asked, and Laith smiled.

CHAPTER TWENTY-TWO

Three years before, in the palace of Joymaril, one of the future Strikers was running through the palace, late for a dinner engagement. Ebony hair shaking loose of its haphazard bun, Athela quickened her stride and dashed up a flight of stairs three at a time, responding to the bows of those who passed her with no more than the briefest of nods.

She careened down two hallways with arched white wooden ceilings; at the end of the last she nearly collided with a boy who was sitting by a window, reading a book. His head was crowned by a bright shock of white-blond hair; he glanced up at her with clear gray eyes (rimmed by surprisingly dark eyebrows and eyelashes), not moving his head as she approached.

"Cade," she breathed, using his presence as an excuse to catch her breath. "Is your brother in there?"

"I suppose so," Cade drawled. "What's up?"

"Having dinner with him and Marc," Athela replied.

"Sounds dull," Cade turned his gray eyes down to his book once more. Athela smiled. At thirteen, Cade was in the throes of being incredibly bored with anything that had to do with anyone besides himself.

Cade made no sign that he wished to continue his conversation with his cousin, which suited Athela just fine. She passed by him, murmuring in a low voice, "Nice book. Search for a girlfriend going well, is it?"

"Stuff it, Athela," Cade retorted pleasantly, turning a page. "They're all unworthy."

"Ah, adolescence," Athela sighed loftily, though she was still a teenager herself, and went through the handsome set of wooden doors into Prince Argolaith's apartments. When Athela entered the room, she saw that Laith, as usual, had set up a table on their favorite balcony right beside the waterfall so that they could enjoy the evening air together. Marc and Laith were already outside sipping wine and looking over the edge into the water below.

"You're late," Marc announced conversationally as she walked up to them.

"I know, I know," Athela rolled her eyes and poured herself a glass of wine. "I have an important announcement to make," she told them. Laith and Marc raised their eyes at one another and sat down.

"What is it?" Laith asked dubiously.

"I have..." here, she gave a dramatic pause, "a *friend*." Athela took a long sip of wine, eyeing Laith and Marc over her glass, anticipating their reaction.

"Oh? What color mane and tail?" Marc asked interestedly.

She glared at him. "It's not a *horse*," she said snippily. "It's an actual *person*."

Their mutual astonishment was not feigned.

"You what?" Laith gasped.

"Athela, that's wonderful!" Marc cried. "Tell us all about him... her...them...!"

Athela leaned forward conspiratorially, eager to impress them with her story. "Well, as you know, it was my day to do some instructing at the Academy, do swordsmanship and so forth."

"Don't I know it," Laith grumped. "I have to teach the little angels tomorrow."

"Well, you know how much I *adore* teaching at the Academy," Athela continued, with a note of sarcasm, "one of the little angels in the advanced class was a girl about our age, and she was doing pretty well with swordsmanship. I had her help me demonstrate a couple of things to the others. Well, when we got to the horseback riding section, she was a real natural. Because I was in a good mood, I decided to let them do some racing, just around the lake and that sort of thing, let them cool off. And this girl, she beat everyone! Except me, of course."

"Of course," Laith said drily. "Because she wouldn't be held in such high regard had she actually beaten you."

"Naturally."

"Athela, this is really a turning point for you," Marc breathed.

"I know!" Athela agreed. "She's very smart." She gave her cousin a rather shrewd look and said slowly, "Laith, I think you should meet her."

"Why should *Laith* meet her?" Marc guffawed. "He's already got every girl in this city after him."

"Correct, Marc," Athela pointed a finger at him. "But I actually *like* this one."

Laith looked dubious, but decided to humor her. "What's her name, then?"

Athela took a sip of wine and smiled. "Ilaina."

The Jelani Academy was made up of a number of small buildings in the north section of the palatial city, at the center of which was an open arena made of white sandstone and tile that was used for swordsmanship and combat training. Threaded through the cluster of Academy buildings were designated trails and areas of the forest used for equestrian instruction, spreading out to the open land to the east past the city walls.

The day after their chat in Laith's apartments, the two cousins rode up in front of their first class. It was a group of about ten students, all talking to one another and laughing. Each student was dressed in the loose white attire of trainees and had their wooden practice swords near them. Laith surveyed them curiously, wondering which one was the girl Athela had mentioned, and scanned the perimeter of the training area for any stragglers.

So keen was Athela to introduce Laith to Ilaina that she had actually volunteered to come and help Laith teach the "little angels" on her day off. They decided that Laith would teach the swordsmanship section of the class as he was more proficient in that area, and Athela, being more adept on horseback, would be in charge of that half.

Laith was slightly nervous as he rode into the ring, a feeling he hadn't remembered experiencing since the first time he had given a lesson years ago. Even more than usual, he was conscious of the way in which the students' chatter slowly died out as he approached, how their curious stares trained on his face. Athela had insisted that he dress up for the occasion, and so he rather reluctantly found himself attired in a royal purple combat jacket and clean boots, far more effort than he would have usually made. He had the impression that Athela was trying to show him off, and felt embarrassed about it.

"Which one is she?" he asked Athela in a low voice as they drew closer to the students, who had stood up in a gesture of respect for the approaching royalty.

"By the tree, the one with the hair," Athela muttered back, uncharacteristically gleeful.

"The *hair*?" Laith hissed. "Athela, perhaps if you could be a bit more specif—" His voice caught in his throat as he saw what she was talking about.

"Told you," Athela said serenely.

The first time Laith ever saw Ilaina, she had stood up directly into a shaft of filtered sunlight, and the effect was breathtaking. She had a full head of red-golden curls that spiraled down to her elbows and across her back, shining brightly like a beacon across the arena. Laith walked his horse a few steps closer and glimpsed her face, strong and extremely pretty, with wide-set eyes (what color were they? Blue? Hazel?) She seemed to regard the world with an innate intelligence and thoughtfulness.

Beside him, Athela was studying his expression with a smirk on her face. "Now, Laith, who's your favorite person in the entire world?"

"My horse, but you're running a close second, Athela," Laith replied, still taken aback.

"With anyone else I would take that as an insult, but I'll settle for what I can get," Athela unfolded her arms and dismounted, swinging one leg in front of her over her horse's neck. Aria, her gray, shifted excitedly to one side, bumping his nose into Arfolasth, who sighed patiently. Athela frowned at her mount, who paused momentarily and blinked virtuously, flicking his up-pricked ears forward and back with an expression of innocence.

"All right!" she called to the students. "You remember what you were working on yesterday. This time, you're really in for it because my cousin is here today, and he won't let you get away with anything. You five, with me; you five, go with Laith."

Laith gulped as he saw that Athela had assigned Ilaina to his group. He felt like an especially big twit now in his fancy jacket, and gave the collar a few disconcerted tugs before dismounting and throwing his cloak over Arfolasth's back. The five students assigned to him gathered around, and he tried not to stare. Laith hadn't thought that Ilaina could look any better than she had from across the arena, but up close her vibrancy came across even more potently. To his great surprise, he saw that she was inspecting him quite keenly and seemed to like what she saw. He quickly paired the other four students to work on forms together and took Ilaina as his own partner. Her face was slightly flushed.

"I'm Laith," he told her, extending a hand.

"Ilaina, my Lord," she replied, taking it and giving a small curtsy.

"Oh, don't bother with 'my Lord,' it's just Laith," he corrected gently, smiling. "Athela told us all about you yesterday."

"Lies, all of it," Ilaina scoffed, then let the edge of a smile creep into the corner of her mouth. "She thought I was all right?"

"You don't know what you've accomplished," Laith told her honestly. "It's a major coup."

He glanced around, heart doing graceful leaps and bounds within his chest, and considered briefly whether Ilaina would be put off if he performed a spontaneous pirouette. He decided against it and was immediately confronted with the fact that everyone else seemed to be practicing except them. "Oops," he cringed. "Okay, so Athela's taught you through fifth form, right?"

"Yeah. She's quite good, isn't she?" Ilaina observed, glancing over to where Athela was barking merrily at her students, occasionally sneaking a glance back to see how her cousin was getting on.

He cleared his throat. "Want to show me your form? Er—forms?" *You idiot*, he thought to himself. For a moment, he thought that Ilaina would balk at demonstrating her knowledge to him, but she gamely stepped back and began going through the graceful sweeps and intricate footwork of the second form of Jelani sword fighting. Laith sat back and admired her motion. Here and there her technique slipped a little, but she had innate talent.

Feeling that if he merely sat back and enjoyed the show the other students would take notice, he stopped her midway through the fifth form and stepped forward. The top of her head came up only to his shoulder, for even at nineteen he was already over six feet tall. He stood beside her, drawing his own sword and demonstrating the move, a spin and downward jab, crouching down onto one knee and doing a half-circle sweep near the ground. Ilaina mimicked his movements, but her sword was still at the wrong angle for her downward move. Seeing an opportunity, Laith sheathed his sword and walked to stand behind her, hunkering his height down so that he was closer to her level of motion.

"Okay, balance your hands on mine so that you feel where they're supposed to be," he instructed, and took her sword, holding it loosely between his fingers.

Obeying, she wrapped her right hand around his. Laith was in the middle of enjoying the sensation of their hands touching, his mind drifting away peacefully to their future wedding day, when he suddenly realized she was saying something.

"I like the third form better," she observed. "There's that fun jumping bit."

"That one is really great," Laith agreed enthusiastically, momentarily forgetting that he was flirting. "I've used it before in an actual combat scenario, and it's really hard to block. Back when it was first developed, it was said to have taken inspiration from the war horse drills that the Jelani cavalry were...uh..." he trailed off, embarrassed.

Ilaina had stopped and turned around to face him, her nose wrinkled, eyes sparkling mischievously. "Prince Argolaith," she exclaimed delightedly. "You're a *nerd!* A gorgeous *nerd!*"

Laith wasn't sure how to respond to this. No one had ever told him he was gorgeous to his face, but then again, no one had ever called him a nerd, either.

"...Thank you?" he replied hesitantly.

"Focus, everyone!" Athela bellowed merrily from across the room. She had clearly been keeping an eye on them.

"Oops," Laith muttered, and he and Ilaina hunkered down again, duly chastised.

Laith guided the free hand back in an arc, hers resting lightly on top of his, the two flowing together like a ship on the water. The hand holding the sword dipped around and down at precisely the correct angle, ingrained in Laith's subconscious by his early teachers. Not wanting to move from his close proximity to Ilaina, he continued the form, sliding easily down with her into the kneeling position and sweeping the sword around in front of them with the tiniest flick of his wrist. Their two bodies moved in perfect synchronization, sliding together like pieces to a puzzle as if they had practiced the movements for months beforehand. Laith stood and twirled the sword around in front of them, throwing it lightly behind his back and catching it in his free hand, unable to resist showing off a bit. Ilaina stood to the side with an expression of wry admiration, as if she was perfectly aware he was putting on a show for her, but couldn't help but enjoy it anyway. She was breathing harder than could be expected from such light exercise.

"I think I've got it now," she said with only a small tremor in her voice, and smiled at him. Laith wondered vaguely what she would think if he pirouetted, sang, proposed to her, and *then* fainted.

"Right!" Athela's distinctive bellow came from across the arena. "Take a few minutes' break, and we'll head down to the horses."

Ilaina, flustered, broke her gaze with Laith and walked over to the tree where the other students were convening. Immediately, a small group of girls descended on her and began whispering animatedly with not-so-surreptitious glances back in Laith's direction.

"Wait!" Laith called and jogged up to her. She turned eagerly, as if she had been hoping for him to stop her. The other girls around her stopped mid-whisper and stared at Laith with enormous eyes. He gulped and tried to ignore them. "Where do you live?"

"North section of the city," she replied.

"Which house?"

"Marisol."

"I'll find you," Laith said with a confident smile. Ilaina touched his arm and turned away. The whispering started up again, even louder than before. Laith watched her go, then turned to Athela as she approached, triumph barely concealed on her face.

"Why'd you stop the lesson?" Laith inquired irritatedly. "We barely gave them enough time to warm up!"

"I think the place was just about warm enough. Five more minutes and you'd be having your way with her on the arena floor, Laith," Athela said bluntly, smirking.

"You really think so?" Laith said, his voice faraway.

"Good grief," Athela shook her head, looking wholeheartedly pleased with herself.

"I can't stop thinking about her," Laith sighed a week later.

"Who?" Marc inquired sarcastically.

Laith was flung over a couch in his apartments, absentmindedly flipping a dagger up in the air and catching it. The setting sun poured in through the open windows, glinting off the metallic blade, making it wink and shine with every revolution. He hadn't seen Ilaina for a week, search for her though he did. The main problem was that she lived in the middle of the outlying city and therefore only came to the Academy for her lessons, which wouldn't resume for another three days. Three days was an absolute eternity. He wondered if she was thinking about him as well.

He flipped the blade down to Marc, who deftly caught it and tossed it a couple of times before he threw it back up to Laith. Marc furrowed his brow sympathetically. "I don't know what to tell you, mate," he sighed. "I mean, short of bringing her to court..." He caught the blade as it was thrown to him and slowly sat up. The two friends locked eyes.

"*This* is why I keep you around," Laith said, grinning. "These fleeting moments of brilliance."

"Fleeting is right. Keeping your expectations low is the only way I've managed to maintain my employment," Marc explained, standing up. "Come on."

"I'll see the Queen," Laith nodded, leaping up and heading for the door.

Across the city, Ilaina sat in her nightgown on her bed next to her older sister, Castille. A single candle flickered on her bedside table. The room was small but tidy, neatly and sparsely furnished. Ilaina's curly hair was tossed into a careless braid that hung down her back. She smiled secretively, and Castille regarded her closely. She was two years older than Ilaina, with steady hazel eyes, red hair, and a serious bearing. She had never quite seen anything like this.

"How tall is he?" she asked keenly.

"I don't know...tall." Ilaina's voice was dreamy, faraway.

"He really liked you?" Castille inquired curiously. Like everyone else in the city, she knew of Prince Argolaith and was intrigued that her sister was now in a position to give her firsthand details.

Ilaina simply smiled evasively, which was answer enough for her sister. Then her expression sobered.

"I did call him a nerd," she admitted slowly, frowning.

Castille stared at her. "Like...in a romantic way?"

"Yes?" Ilaina said hesitantly.

Castille groped for words that would sound encouraging. "I'm sure that he—" she stopped short as there was a knock on the front door downstairs. Ilaina looked at her sharply and grabbed her arm. The two sisters tumbled out of bed and rushed to grab their robes.

Ilaina's mother and father were seated at the table in the dining room on the first floor of the small apartment. They, too, started at the unanticipated noise, and Ilaina's father slowly rose from his seat and walked silently to the door, his wife a step or so behind. The door opened to reveal a tall, cloaked figure on their doorstep. He pulled the hood back, and Ilaina's parents fell to their knees, recognizing him at once.

"My Lord Argolaith!" Ilaina's mother exclaimed. "What...what are you doing here?"

"Please stand up," Laith said quickly, striding into the small, dimly lit room and shutting the door behind him. There was no hall or entranceway; the door led straight into the dining room. Laith took it in with one sweeping glance of the room and felt that he knew Ilaina's parents already. Hardworking, unpretentious, deeply devoted to their family. He turned around to them.

"To what do we owe this honor?" Ilaina's father asked, sliding beside his wife, looping a protective arm about her waist.

"It's—er...It's about your daughter," Laith said finally, grinning sheepishly.

From behind the door where they were listening, Castille and Ilaina gave a gasp and looked at each other excitedly. "It's him!" Ilaina whispered joyfully, her throat tightening at the sound of his voice.

"I met your daughter Ilaina while teaching at the Academy...and... er...well, I've secured her a place at court, if she wants it. She'll be a lady-in-waiting to Lady Athela. She can come back here anytime she wants, but she'll be given rooms at the palace, and can continue her lessons there. I...I wanted to ask your permission first, before I asked her."

Ilaina's father was a thoughtful, quiet man, and he waited for a while before he responded. Ilaina's mother, in her mid-fifties, was elegant and poised; her resemblance to her younger daughter was uncanny.

"Lord Argolaith," Ilaina's father said finally, "We have heard nothing but good things about you. My daughter has spoken very highly of you. But I also know that there are some at court...your cousin Cira, if you'll forgive me, who I feel Ilaina should be kept far away from."

"I don't disagree with you there," Laith said wryly. Ilaina's mother allowed the ghost of a smile to flicker across her face. "But," he continued. "Though I don't know her very well...I'll...take care of her. You don't have to worry. I...I just want to see her more. That's all."

There was something in the determination on Laith's face, something in his eyes that Ilaina's father recognized. It was the same look that had been on his daughter's face when she had first told them about meeting the prince. It was over, he realized, and there was nothing more he could do. He glanced at his wife, who nodded. She had seen it, too. "Ilaina," he called, knowing full well that she would be outside the door listening in.

Ilaina was gripping Castille's hand so hard that her knuckles were white, but at the sound of her name, she let go and smoothed out her long nightdress. Castille gave her a nod of encouragement. She came through the door, and Laith stood up, taking in the sight of her as if it was the first breath of fresh air he'd had in days. She was smiling nervously as she stepped forward.

"This young man says you have a place at court if you want it," Ilaina's father said, slightly heavily. "If you want to, your mother and I give our permission."

Ilaina paused only a second and nodded quickly. Her eyes never left Laith's. For the two of them, it was obvious that the room was empty of all others. There was a moment of silence before Ilaina's mother cleared her throat. "Well, then," she said briskly. "Would you like to come over for dinner next week sometime?"

"I'd love to," Laith smiled.

"And...er...your bodyguard...Lord Marcus?" she asked tentatively.

"I'd love to!" shouted a voice from right outside the door.

"Good heavens!" Ilaina's mother exclaimed after a spot of laughter. "Should we...let him in?"

"Nah," Laith waved his hand carelessly.

"I'm fine, thank you, ma'am!" Marc yelled.

"Well, I should get going," Laith said. "I'm not exactly supposed to be out and about the city after dark."

"It was good to finally meet you, Lord Argolaith," Ilaina's father said, shaking his hand.

"Laith, please," he smiled.

"Laith, then."

He was outside the door beside Marc and pulling on his hood when the door opened again, the sliver of orange candlelight escaping as she stole outside, shutting the door quietly behind her. Laith whipped around, surprised to see her. She stood in her nightgown and bare feet on the cobbled side of the street. Laith stepped towards her as if it were the most natural thing in the world, and took her by the arm. She looked up into his face and smiled, and without another word gave him a soft kiss on the cheek before spinning and vanishing back into her house. Laith watched her go longingly, then turned to his friend.

"Disgusting," Marc smiled broadly.

Shortly thereafter, Ilaina moved into a small apartment as a lady-in-waiting to Athela and became a fixture at court. She quickly learned the etiquette, when to curtsy, when to stand. When she made a misstep, she apologized with a lovely smile, and soon she was a favorite of everyone, from dukes and duchesses to the King himself (who even managed to learn and remember her name, which was more than he had done for most of his actual relatives.)

Laith was well aware that any romantic interest of his would be subject to more scrutiny than a single person could endure. To keep the gossip-hungry court at bay, Laith saw to it that his interactions with Ilaina were always above-board and usually in the company of Marc and Athela; there was nothing between them that even the servants could whisper about. While this worked well to keep Ilaina's name out of the mouths of any scandalmongers, it did mean that things between them progressed more slowly than Laith would have liked.

A year passed in this way, and soon it was autumn once again and time for Laith's birthday. As the prince was generally favored by his aunt and uncle, the Queen decided to hold a party for him to celebrate his turning twenty. The entire court was invited, and almost all of them turned up to pay their respects, which wound up making for a rather dull celebration for the guest of honor. Laith was forced to sit in the middle of the great hall in a chair, compelled to politely receive the well-wishings of every single dignitary. Marc and Athela were sitting beside him, keeping him company.

"This is a drag," Laith whispered to Athela, who was fiddling with the laces on her boot. "I have no idea who half these people are, and what's more, I'm not entirely sure they even know who *I* am."

"Offer free food, and you'll never know where you are or who your friends may be," Athela observed sagely.

"Not such a bad haul, though," Marc commented, raising his eyebrows appraisingly and looking back behind the chair at the pile of gifts that had been bestowed upon the prince. "I want one of those swords. You already got a Whitsun and you barely even use it. It's not fair."

"You can have it. I haven't even *seen* Ilaina yet," Laith grunted despondently. "She said she'd come."

"She told *me* she'd come, too," Athela agreed. "She'll be here, never fear." She paused for a good while, clearly wrestling with what she was about to say. "So. How are things...going...between you two?" she asked haltingly.

Laith turned around to look her straight in the eye. "Are you *really* asking me for details about my love life?"

"I've been sitting here on this step for three and a half hours, Laith," Athela snapped irritably. "There is literally *nothing* else to talk about."

"She's here," Marc elbowed Laith hard in the ribs and pointed. Laith craned his neck. There...he could see her. She was in white, the simplicity heightening the color of her hair and her cheeks. She looked over the heads in the room and caught Laith's eye. Laith stood up.

"I'm going to...er...take a breather," he announced, stretching rather unconvincingly. Athela barely managed to hide a snort. Laith winked at her. "Athela, you field the gifts. Marc, you field the women." This, they all knew, was a joke; Marc had had a steady boyfriend for about two years.

"I'll do my best," Marc said tragically and hauled himself into Laith's vacated chair, spreading his arms open wide. "Come unto me, all ye ladies of low self-esteem."

"What a king you'd make," Athela muttered, then arched one dark eyebrow. "Better dash off for that breather of yours, Laith, my parents might be heading over here soon to see why Marc is sitting in your chair."

Laith saw that she had a point and slipped to the back of the raised throne platform, disappearing behind a velvet curtain and down a small hallway out to a balcony. There, he waited until Ilaina slipped out beside him. The balcony was lit only by the moon and the light from a torch attached to the wall by an iron grate. Laith's breath caught as he looked at her, and when her eyes fastened on him, it seemed to him as though she blushed more in the low light. He hoped he looked all right. Marc and Athela had both told him that he looked all right.

In the year since they had met, things had barely progressed past the gentle flirting of their first encounter. It seemed that they were never alone long enough for anything except hushed whispers and a few brief touches. All too brief, in Laith's opinion. But tonight was different. There was something in the air, something about that night that made their longing almost unbearable. Laith couldn't wait any longer. He didn't want to spend any more of his time away from her.

She lowered her eyes for a brief moment, and then looked back up at him. "Happy birthday."

"Thanks."

The situation was getting to be a lot more tense than Laith would have liked, but he tried to ignore it. Ilaina looked from side to side. "I was going to make you a card that said 'Congratulations, you are old,' but I felt it was a bit on the nose."

Laith chuckled. After a moment or two of silence between them he said, "You know, I don't really want to go back inside."

She laughed. "Me neither. I don't see how you can stand this sort of thing."

"Who says I can stand it?" Laith asked gloomily.

They looked out over the surrounding hills and listened to the distant roar of the waterfall. Ilaina rested her arms on the balcony edge, hands clasped together. Laith was turned towards her sideways, his elbow on the railing, watching her.

"I heard a rumor the other day," Ilaina said suddenly, and Laith thought he heard her voice catch. "Your parents are trying to arrange your marriage."

"To a cousin, yes," Laith rolled his eyes. "I'm not too keen on letting that one get passed."

"You don't think..." Ilaina trailed off, then smiled, embarrassed and more than a little relieved. Laith cocked his head to one side, studying her. He reached out to her and touched her hair, stroking the curls all the way down her back, running his fingers along her spine. She stiffened a bit, shuddered, and glanced back at him for a moment, but made no motion to move him away. The look on her face told Laith all he had to know, and gave him all the courage he needed.

"You are what I love best about this world," Laith told her. He wasn't quite sure how the words were managing to come out of his mouth but was glad they were, for they were absolutely true.

She turned toward him now. Her eyes were glassy, looking straight through him. Laith hoped she could see that he was being completely honest. He continued, praying desperately that he wasn't being an ass. "If I asked you to spend your life with me, would you?" He rested his hand on the small of her back. She stared at him for a few seconds, then her face abruptly broke its serious demeanor, and her smile shone through. Laith felt as though he would explode with happiness. He pulled her to him and kissed her as he had been wanting to kiss her from the first moment he saw her.

A little over half a year later, Argolaith and Ilaina were married in state on a fine evening in early spring. Athela acted as Ilaina's second during the marriage, and since Laith's second had to be a direct member of the royal family, Laith's younger brother Cade ousted Marc from the honored position.

The marriage, as was customary, was divided into three days. On the first, the couple was separated and sent into seclusion. The bride was readied for the ceremony, with handmaidens sewing her gown and helping her to go through all the pre-marriage rituals of meditation and cleansing. Laith had a much easier time of it; he was mostly instructed to keep out of the way and avoid his bride-to-be, which meant that for three days he lounged around his extensive apartments with Marc and occasionally his younger brother, a situation which was altogether agreeable, even if it did make him impatient to see Ilaina again.

On the day of the wedding they met at the city square, at the marble archway built centuries ago for that very purpose. She was swathed in yards and yards of intricately embroidered burgundy cloth laced atop soft underskirts of creamy white, a streaming gossamer veil set atop her hair. Laith's wedding costume, though far less elaborate than Ilaina's, was nevertheless impressive, as he came arrayed in full Joymarillian battle dress, complete with a royal purple cloak and armor intricately engraved with images of the sun. The sigil had been bestowed on him by the Queen for the occasion of his marriage and the establishment of his own house.

The moment he saw Ilaina, something inside him relaxed and his nerves flew away, and he knelt beside her beneath the archway. As far as he was concerned, he didn't need any ceremony to cement his dedication to her. Seeing her face was enough; the rest was merely a show to impress his aunt and uncle. The tradition was that, after the King and Queen read the verses that bound them together as husband and wife, Laith's right hand would be wrapped with a red piece of cloth to Ilaina's left hand, and they would remain tied together until the sunset. Velvet pillows had been laid on the ground for them to kneel on so as not to become uncomfortable. The King and Queen recited the proper verses, and Laith and Ilaina murmured back the proper responses, and then Cade, Laith's second, and Athela, who was acting as Ilaina's, stepped forward with lengths of scarlet ribbon. They tied one end of each ribbon together, then wrapped the length around Laith and Ilaina's hands, joining them together, then stepped back. Laith avoided making eye contact with Athela, knowing that if he did he wouldn't be able to keep himself from giggling, so deathly serious was the atmosphere around them.

They waited in silence, side by side, for many hours, the witnesses to the wedding sitting in provided chairs. At the afternoon meal, food was passed around to the guests, and Cade and Athlela fed Laith and Ilaina the traditional tidbits of meats and nuts, followed by a series of sweets. Laith spent the time singing songs to himself in his head and thinking about various things. He studied the embroidery on the bottom of the King's and Queen's robes and ignored the malcontent expression of his cousin Cira, who was sitting in the place of honor at her parents' side. Apparently, she'd been quite put out at the announcement of his impending marriage; the look on her face was as though some spoiled food was being wafted about beneath her nose.

Laith chanced a glance over at Ilaina, wondering what she was thinking about and admiring the cascade of rose petals embroidered along her skirt. She felt his eyes on her and turned to him, giving him a small wink and a smile, then gave a minuscule grimace and flicked her eyes down to her knees. Laith winced in sympathy—hours of stiffness had set in, and he was quite sure his knees would buckle when he finally tried to stand on them, which wouldn't perhaps be the most romantic and debonair way to conclude his wedding.

Much later, sunset arrived and the ceremony was finally brought to a close. The Queen stood and walked forward, taking a swipe of red paint, and made three small dots at the bottom of Laith and Ilaina's throats, signifying that they were married. The scarlet ribbon was untied and Laith stood, beaming even as his knees creaked unpleasantly. A barrage of guests came forward to congratulate them and offer them gifts, and Laith was once more overwhelmed with the fact that he only seemed to know about twelve of the hundred people invited to the various royal gatherings his aunt and uncle organized.

Finally, Marc and Athela, who had been hanging at the back of the center until the throng had dispersed, walked forward. To Laith's great surprise, Marc's normally ice-blue eyes were red and rather bleary.

"Are you ill?" Laith asked in bewilderment as Marc seized him in a close hug, his stocky frame crushing Laith within his strong arms.

"I'm so happy for you!" Marc exclaimed, his voice choking. Athela rolled her eyes, eternally uncomfortable with any overt demonstration of affection. Laith patted Marc delicately on the top of the head.

"Marc, it's all right," Laith assured him, trying to break his vise-like grip. "I'm not *dead*." His bodyguard released him and stepped back. Laith took the opportunity to fill his lungs with air. "Nothing is actually going to change. We'll still all be together all the time."

Marc took a deep breath and shook back his silky yellow hair. "Sorry," he said finally. "I get a little emotional at weddings."

"As do I," Athela murmured flatly, her face expressionless.

They laughed, and then into the ringing air there fell an awkward silence. Athela glanced from Laith to Ilaina and cleared her throat.

"Well, time for us to be off," she announced. "Marc, let's see what Oren's up to."

The two of them strode off, leaving Laith and Ilaina alone together. The couple strolled to one side of the circle and sat, enjoying one another's company and the first few stolen minutes of peace and quiet together. They sat on the ground, Ilaina's dress pooling out around her. She laid her head on his shoulder. He kissed her forehead, more content at that moment than he ever had been before.

He wondered what the next day would be like with this change that had taken place. He wondered what the year would bring, what the year after that would hold. He wondered what their children would be like, what their names would be, if they would look like him or Ilaina. He hoped that if they had a girl, she would have her mother's hair and the way the corners of her mouth wrinkled when she smiled. He wondered whether they would come back to this place to remember this day when they were old, how he would hold her hand and still find her as beautiful as she was today. They would laugh at how nervous they had been the day they'd been married. How silly it would all seem, many years from now.

She stirred, sitting up and staring off in front of them. "I can't wait," she said finally.

Laith smiled, knowing exactly what she meant.

CHAPTER TWENTY-THREE

Tarr and Laith waited in the still forest, peering through the trees to the flickering surface of the lake below Joymaril. Through the screen of vegetation Tarr could see the many lights of the palace glinting over the top of the water. All at once, he could remember his first visit to the palace, how unsure he had been around Laith and Athela and the others. It seemed to him like it had been three lifetimes ago.

A few curved white archways were visible to Tarr from behind the trees, and here and there he could catch a glimpse of some distant motion. He was crouched on the ground, his head low, peering over a fallen tree trunk. Laith had left Arfolasth untied beside a tree well back from the path and was bent beside Tarr, his eyes trained on the lake, hunting for any sign of movement.

Laith flipped his hood up around his head, covering his light hair, and pulled on a mask that covered his nose and lower face. He slunk through the undergrowth beside the path, followed by Tarr, who was all too aware of the racket he seemed to be making as he brushed past low-hanging branches and snapped twigs underfoot. *Why didn't Laith ask Archer to go?* Tarr wondered again. *He'd be much better at this sort of creeping-around thing than I am.*

Laith led the way down a small hill to a dip in the land. The trees grew close around them, and Tarr saw that they were positioned close to the end of the mostly-obscured bridge beneath the water of the lake. Laith stopped and slipped to the ground. Tarr came up beside him.

"The night watch should be here soon," Laith informed him in a low voice, his dark eyes glinting keenly, mouth obscured by the covering over the lower half of his face.

"I'll keep a lookout," Tarr said. "How should I signal you?"

"I don't know, can you do any...bird sounds or something?"

"Not really," Tarr said, feeling rather stupid.

"Make one up," Laith suggested.

Tarr thought for a moment, then came up with a low trill at the back of his throat that he repeated a few times until Laith gave him a nod of approval. It didn't sound like any bird he was familiar with. He'd had to do a full unit on different bird calls when he was growing up back in the forest, and it hadn't been his favorite subject. Hopefully, the Jelani guards weren't familiar either, or at least wouldn't be listening very closely.

The code established, Tarr glanced upwards to the shadowy boughs stretching above their heads into the vast blue dome of the sky. The trees were all of fairly decent sizes, though not nearly as big as most of the trees in the forest where he had come from. There was a good-looking branch a short ways in front of him, about four or five feet above the ground. Tarr hopped so that his legs were coiled in front of him and leaped up onto the top of the branch, nimble as a cat, neither swaying nor losing any vestige of his balance. Glancing down, he saw Laith's surprised upturned face, and he gave a small wave before vaulting higher. A moment later, he looked down at the earth again and the prince had dissolved into the shadowy ground. He decided to get some more height and dove up through a few layers of branches before tiptoeing out to the bending end of a branch that dipped and rose buoyantly beneath his feet. Clinging to the swaying limbs, he let out a long breath and realized just how *right* it felt to be back there, high amongst the leaves. It had been so long.

He peered down to the water in front of him, where he could make out the silhouette of a band of riders heading across the bridge in the water toward the shore. Tarr slunk back along his branch until he was near the trunk, where the shadows of the foliage completely obscured him from view. He let out the slow trill in the back of his throat, signaling Laith that they had arrived.

He still didn't know quite what to do if it turned out to be a trap (which he highly suspected it was.) He wished that Laith had come to him before, that he had been there to help work out a plan, that he hadn't been dragged into a meetup where Laith's reckless desire to reunite with his wife outweighed the many potential dangers. He could have come up with something better than this.

In the meantime, he reasoned, he did have the element of surprise on his side. If Laith was ambushed, he could make a noise or try to spook the guards' horses, something to buy Laith a few seconds to escape. Deciding on this as a course of action, he slowly descended back down the tree, branch by branch, completely noiseless, casting about for any loose branches or other projectiles he could throw to distract attention.

The Joymarillian riders drew close and dismounted, leaving their horses at the edge of the water and walking up the shallow embankment onto the top of the ridge near where Laith (or so Tarr supposed) was located. As soon as they had drawn to a halt, almost directly under Tarr's tree, Laith stood up in front of them, appearing as if by magic out of the blue shadow. Two of the guards towards the rear started a little, clearly unaware that Laith had been there at all, though the other three seemed used to his sudden appearance. Laith kept the mask on the bottom of his face and his hood up around the top of his head. His eyes darted to either side, searching for any smaller figure that could be his wife. There was none.

"Lord Argolaith," the guard at the front intoned with a slight inclination of the head. Laith returned the gesture.

"Who are the others?" Laith asked, his rich voice distinctly lower than the higher register of the lead guard. "You told me that there would only be one other with you on your watch tonight."

"They're for my protection."

Laith snorted.

"You may laugh, my *Lord*," this was said with a definite sneer, "but you still are the most dangerous swordsman in the country, so I hope you will forgive me if I don't wish to risk my life."

Tarr could see Laith bristle in the way that his back straightened up. "It doesn't show very much trust, now, does it?"

The guard shrugged, spreading out his hands, helpless. "Do you wish to go on quibbling about this, or do you want to get down to business?"

"Please."

"You asked me if I could arrange a meeting with your wife."

"That's right."

"I have a message from her."

By this point, Laith's spine was like a ramrod. He took a breath, eyes darting from one guard's face to the other. He moved his broad shoulders around in small circles to calm himself. "A message? What's wrong? I thought I asked you to bring her here with you. Where is she?"

Tarr felt something sink in the pit of his stomach, low and hard like a rock. He tensed himself, ready to throw something down on the guards' heads, to startle them, to make a loud noise so that the horses would bolt. The guard drew something out of his pocket and threw it at Laith, who caught it in one hand. Tarr saw it glitter as it flew through the air, and he surmised that it was a piece of jewelry, though he couldn't see it well enough to identify it. Laith, however, inspected the item and looked up sharply.

"This is Ilaina's," he said dubiously. His fingers moved along its familiar length. It was her favorite hairpin, a blue cornflower made of sapphires, with a small cluster of freshwater pearls at the center, a few small diamonds dangling off the tips of the petals like falling dew. It winked at him in the darkness.

"That's correct," the guard confirmed.

"What are you playing at?" Laith's voice was razor-edged. Even from Tarr's high vantage point, he could see the main guard lose a bit of his bluster with Laith's icy tone. Laith took a step forward. The guard backed up instinctively. Laith yanked down the masking cloth from over his nose and mouth and stared deep into the guard's eyes.

"Where...is...my...*wife*?" Laith growled, his voice dropping down into a bass snarl.

"You asked to see her?" The guard smirked, though the others behind him shifted uneasily. The lead guard continued, with arrogant, cruel bravado, "There, in your hand. That's all that's left of her. Her body lies at the bottom of the lake."

Tarr knew before the last word was out of the guard's mouth that it was the wrong thing to say. Laith's dagger was at the guard's throat before his cronies could even move a muscle. Laith had the guard gripped by the cloak and was staring down into his face.

"What do you mean?" Laith asked, pressing his blade hard against the guard's exposed neck.

"She's dead," the guard said flatly, clearly both frightened and irritated at being humiliated this way in front of his troops. "She was killed the day that you and the others escaped from the palace."

A part of Laith seemed to collapse inside him, but he kept his dagger up and tried to keep his voice steady. "Who did it?" he asked in a whisper.

Cira, Tarr thought, as plainly as if the guard had said it aloud. *It must have been Cira.*

"There was no burial." The guard pointedly avoided Laith's question, relishing the last bit of pain that he was doling out. "Why don't you swim down now and say hello?"

In another instant, the guard gave a cry and dropped to the ground, a hand clutching his neck, and Laith lunged forward into the thick of black shadows. Seconds later, Tarr was on the ground and pulling Laith off of them, barely able to hold the prince back. Laith had made no outcry, no bellow of anger; he had darted forward like a striking serpent. The only sound coming from him was a frightening, animalistic, heavy breathing through his nose. As Tarr held Laith back, using every ounce of his body weight to force the prince's arm, he realized that his friend couldn't differentiate between him and the soldiers and that his own life was probably in mortal peril. Laith wrenched his arm away from Tarr's grasp. Once, twice, Laith missed him in his frenzy to get at the guards, but Tarr wasn't fast enough on the third, and a long tear was made in his left sleeve, a sharp slice of pain and something wet against his arm. The five guards scattered, frightened both of Tarr's sudden appearance and of Laith's blind rage, turning to run after their horses, which had bolted towards the palace after Tarr dropped from the trees.

Laith, blinded by pain and rage, left a wide opening as he swung back his arm (something he never would have done had he had full control of his faculties), and in that moment, Tarr somehow managed to knock him off his feet and onto his back. The prince, much stronger, was winded temporarily but then began struggling furiously, and Tarr knew he wouldn't be able to hold him for long. He looked up and whistled, knowing that Arfolasth and Wolver would soon be there. To his surprise, he heard the sound mimicked from a short ways away from him. A large rustling noise began to echo all around him, as if dozens of unseen creatures were creeping towards them. Tarr suddenly realized the full, dire extent of their situation.

"Laith, it was a trap; this place is swarming, that guard must have tipped your uncle and aunt off," Tarr said, holding up Laith's head with one hand and staring down at him. The dark eyes were still sightless, not recognizing him. It frightened Tarr to see his friend like this, as if he were just an empty space filled with nothing but a need to kill. "Do you understand me, Laith?" Tarr asked, forcing the prince to look at him straight-on. The rustling around them was growing louder; whoever was coming for them would be there soon. "We have to get out of here now!" Tarr shouted, not caring if anyone heard him or not. He shot a frightened glance over his shoulder, not sure whether he was imagining the dozens of figures moving through the brush towards them.

At that moment, Wolver and Arfolasth alternately bounded and galloped into the clearing. Tarr, still staring into Laith's dim eyes, gave him a little shake, and all at once the rage vanished. Laith seemed to crumple into a hollow, lifeless shell. Beside him, Wolver's legs were splayed out and his hackles were raised, ears pinned back against his head, not liking the sounds that were getting closer and closer; Tarr felt his heart beat faster up into his throat.

Struggling mightily, Tarr hauled the unresponsive prince to his feet and half-shoved, half-threw Laith up into the saddle, then clambered on behind him, ungainly and graceless. Tarr twisted around to look behind them just as a guard swung out into the moonlight, aiming a sword at Tarr's head. Wolver snapped his jaws at the exposed guard, who lunged forward with his sword. Wolver twitched his head to one side, avoiding the blade, and chomped down with his powerful jaws on the man's shoulder, tossing him to one side as though he were a rag doll. Tarr gritted his teeth and threw himself back so that he was lying flat on Arfolasth's spine as the sword whistled over his head, watched as it narrowly missed striking Laith. Wrapping one arm around Laith and taking up the reins in his hands, Tarr dug his heels into Arfolasth's sides, and the black charger sped forward into the blackness, Wolver close behind them.

Tarr could hear the guards crashing through the underbrush behind them, and kept glancing over his shoulder every few seconds to see if they were following. When nothing appeared out of the darkness, he had a moment to breathe and to collect his wits. He winced and felt the arm that Laith had cut, felt his torn shirt, soggy with blood. On the ground beside them, Wolver surged out in front, leading the way down the path.

After a long, exhausting stretch of running through the woods, Wolver suddenly banked a hard left and slowed his gallop to a trot, sniffing along the ground. He zig-zagged through a small grove of trees and paused, head straight up and ears pricked, testing the air. He turned his large white head around to Tarr and studied him with his light, reflective blue eyes. Tarr dismounted and patted his head. "Thanks, Wolver," Tarr said gratefully, and walked forward, leading Arfolasth behind him.

They found themselves in a small clearing, and Tarr left Arfolasth and Wolver there while he walked ahead. They were, he discovered, very near the edge of the trees that separated the land around Joymaril from the plains surrounding Two Falls. Dawn was just starting to show through the trees, yellow and pink and red. Tarr wondered if there was any way he could send word to his friends that they were all right, but felt that Laith shouldn't be left alone. If he sent Wolver by himself, Tarr worried that the others would think that something was seriously wrong with them and try to come and find them. He finally sighed to himself and hoped that the others would trust them to take care of themselves.

Heading back to the clearing he'd found, he saw that Arfolasth was silhouetted against the blue light amid the trees, and it appeared that Laith was sitting on the ground in front of him, legs bent up, head thrust forward, arms hanging listlessly on his knees. Arfolasth's reins were loose and draped on the ground, and foamy sweat caked the horse's chest and flanks. He raised his head and whickered softly as Tarr cautiously approached them through the trees. Tarr reached out and patted Arfolasth's muzzle once or twice and sat down a safe distance from Laith, who appeared to be staring at his hands. Tarr didn't feel that it was appropriate to say anything; he figured that Laith could speak when he wanted to.

Tarr and Laith sat near one another in the same manner for hours. The sun slowly crawled up through the clouds, which lightened from yellow to white. Laith made no movement at all, and Tarr, who was absolutely exhausted from the night's revelries and subsequent ride, allowed himself to doze off, while making sure that part of him was still attuned to Laith's actions so he could wake up at a moment's notice should the prince need him. In the haze of his mind, Tarr tried to make sense of what had transpired. Was Ilaina really dead? There was something so illogical about the thought. He had never known someone who'd died before, at least no one who was young and for whom it was unexpected. It felt as if the earth had tilted slightly around him and that everything was off-kilter now. Could it really be that Ilaina simply wasn't there anymore? That he had already said every word he'd ever say to her? Could it really be that she wouldn't ever spontaneously go for a walk, or make another joke, or have a child, or stub her toe? How could a person just vanish like that? The thought made him both exhausted and oddly wired; he tried to close his eyes while his mind kept churning. He couldn't even bring himself to look at Laith. If he was having trouble wrapping his head around it—he, who had had only a few short interactions with Ilaina—he couldn't imagine what could possibly be going through Laith's head at that moment.

Behind him, he heard Wolver's soft breathing and knew that the wolf had lay down and was sleeping lightly as well. Arfolasth had his left hind leg cocked up, his head slung low on his neck, and his eyes closed. Laith was the only one who seemed to be awake, his blank, expressionless stare focused on the hands hanging loosely in front of him. He blinked only a few times, and when he did, he did it slowly, almost as if he were closing them, resting, and then opening them again.

Midday passed, and Tarr began to rouse himself out of his light slumber. He knew beyond a shadow of a doubt that the others would be deeply concerned for them, but again could find no solution as to how to send word to them without leaving Laith. His stomach growled a few times, longing for the hearty breakfast they usually shared at the house, but he ignored it. Laith remained motionless, and Tarr wasn't too sure that he even registered that he was there, so he stood up, stretching from side to side, and walked around the clearing, unlocking his joints and putting some much-needed feeling back into his legs.

More hours passed. By this time, Tarr wished desperately that he had thought to bring some food along with him. Wolver was resting his huge head on his paws, eyeing Tarr with his level gaze. Arfolasth, sensing that something was deeply wrong with his master, stood where he was, not willing to move until Laith did. Tarr walked into the woods a short way, close enough so that he could still keep an eye on Laith, looking for any trees with berries or anything else that could potentially be edible, but found nothing. Frustrated, he returned to the clearing and sat down beside Laith, a little closer than he had done initially, hoping inwardly that Laith would come out of his trance.

About an hour later, Laith stirred. Tarr immediately snapped to attention, and Wolver raised his head from his paws. Arfolasth whickered slightly and took a step forward toward Laith, bumping his back with his nose. The touch seemed to bring Laith out of it. The prince slowly raised a hand and caressed Arfolasth's muzzle. He turned his head and laid it against Arfolasth's black forehead, patting the horse on the cheek. Arfolasth seemed to be relieved that whatever was wrong with Laith wasn't anything that *he* did and nickered louder. Laith turned back around and looked over at Tarr.

"How long have we been here?" he asked.

"All day."

Laith let out a breath and looked around. "I'm sorry you had to sit here for so long," he said.

Tarr shook his head. "Don't even think about that."

"I don't believe it," Laith said slowly.

"I know," Tarr felt completely inadequate. He had no idea what to say.

"No," Laith said sharply. "I *don't* believe it."

Tarr began to feel deeply uncomfortable and fidgeted slightly with his boot. His arm had stopped bleeding; it was crusted and brown along his bicep. Tarr absentmindedly picked at a few flecks of dried blood and gave Laith a sidelong glance.

"She can't just be *gone* like that," Laith said, his strong jaw in a stubborn set. "She can't just have gone. Without me knowing, without a chance to say goodbye. We..." he hunted for words. "We were so in love, I would know if she was gone. I would have felt something, I know it. I would have felt it if she died, and I didn't feel anything." Tarr was acutely aware of the desperation in Laith's voice, and wondered if the prince could hear it, too. Laith straightened up taller, as if facing off against some unseen foe. "No, that's it. She's alive; she has to be. Because she wouldn't just be *gone*. She can't."

His expression appealed, but Tarr couldn't bring himself to concur. *Laith's beliefs are strong*, he remembered with a sinking heart. *It takes a lot to shake them.* He managed a tiny nod and what he hoped was a comforting smile. *I won't let Laith walk into something like this again,* he told himself firmly. *I have to be more vigilant.*

After that, Laith rose to his feet and gave Arfolasth an affectionate pat on the neck. It was almost as if the previous night had never taken place. Laith mounted up with his usual ease and offered Tarr a smile and an arm to swing up behind him. The two of them slowly began riding back to Two Falls as dark, heavy rain clouds gathered in the sky, moving over the sun and casting a pall over the land and its people.

CHAPTER TWENTY-FOUR

After an hour's slow riding, they rounded the crest of a small hill and looked out over Two Falls. Though they had just made the same ride the night before, somehow everything felt different; it was as if a gray cast had settled over the world. Everything seemed quiet, but the stillness that hung over the city was not peaceful. Tarr wasn't sure whether this was because of the news about Ilaina or because the nagging, gnawing feeling of unease still hadn't left him. Laith drew Arfolasth up to a halt. His forehead creased, he scanned the land with his dark brown eyes, and Tarr followed his gaze to see what was wrong.

Just on the outskirts were freshly-made piles of gigantic stones, all in a row, and a few empty wagons. Tarr looked closer and saw that the piles of stones continued around the border of the city. A few workers were pulling sheets over the wagons to protect them from the oncoming weather.

Laith swallowed. "It's the wall."

Tarr looked over at him sharply.

"She's making good on her promise. Closing in the city," Laith murmured. "Making it impossible for anyone to get out. Like a spider's web."

Tarr shook his head disbelievingly, staring at the stones, the same sick feeling of dread circling around his stomach. Laith nudged Arfolasth with his heels, and Wolver followed them down the sloping hill.

It only took a little bit of sweet-talking to get back into the city. Tarr distinctly remembered what Archer's friend from Riddleton had told him the night before: that it was quite easy to get into the city, and quite another thing to get out. Tarr had actually come up with the ruse to get them past the gate. He had Laith bind his hands and pretend as though he were an Ashan captive being brought back into Two Falls for processing. The guards at the gate had been delighted by the prospect and had waved them in without question.

When they arrived in the center of town, a light drizzle had already started to fall, gathering on the rooftops and misting on Laith's and Tarr's eyelashes. The sky was a strange dark color, not quite gray, with tinges of yellow around the edges of the clouds. It was already near sunset; they had spent nearly the entire day sitting in the trees after their escape from Joymaril, and the oncoming rain was undoubtedly hastening along the onset of darkness. The people of Two Falls were clearly anticipating a great storm. Lamps were already lit in all the houses, and the citizens were hurrying to finish their evening chores and find shelter in their homes.

They walked toward the boarding house in a roundabout route, sticking to back alleys and avoiding main streets. They passed behind the library, once so majestic—now it seemed to loom ominously like a great hulking giant among the huddled houses surrounding it. Laith was choosing the route and seemed to Tarr to be dawdling a bit; he imagined that Laith was trying to put off having to tell Athela and the others where they had been all day and night. Tarr briefly considered offering to go and tell the others himself, letting Laith go off and find somewhere else to stay for the time being, but didn't relish facing Athela's wrath alone and unarmed.

Finally, they stopped in front of the house. Their street was strangely deserted, and the clouds seemed to have settled even lower over their heads. Tarr gazed up at them, mist settling on his upturned face. Laith sat back in his saddle and gave Tarr a wistful smile of thanks. Tarr nodded and dismounted, his thighs sore from the long day and night of riding. He gave Wolver a pat on the head, which the wolf returned with an affectionate nudge.

"Thank you for helping us last night," Tarr said. Wolver suddenly pricked his ears and whined faintly, taking a cautious step back. Immediately, Tarr's eyes went to the house. For a moment, he thought about trying to alert Laith with the bird call they'd practiced back by Joymaril, but Laith had already gone around the corner and out of earshot. Hesitantly, he followed Laith into the small stable around the back.

Laith was pulling off Arfolasth's saddle and bridle. He slung the headstall over one shoulder, grabbed the saddle by its pommel, and hoisted it up onto his hip. Laith nodded to his horse, who walked off, disappearing into the dark gloom of his stall.

"I'll give you a rinse off once we've checked in with everyone, boy," Laith said to Arfolasth's retreating back.

"Laith, I—Where are the other horses?" Tarr asked abruptly. Arfolasth was the only one there.

Laith's brow furrowed. "That's odd." His expression cleared. "They're probably out looking for us," he suggested, and heaved the saddle farther up on his hip.

Tarr didn't like it. He glanced around to where Wolver stood at the gate of the stable, his level gaze trained on them.

The two of them walked up the front stairs and entered the house. Tarr bid Wolver wait outside and keep guard. One lamp was lit on a table near the entrance; the rest of the place seemed completely deserted. Beside him, Laith set down the saddle by the front door, draping his bridle over it. He looked around the room, unbuckling the ornate gold-plated clasp on his sword belt, and leaned his weapon against the saddle.

"Athela?" Laith called. The house was silent. Tarr walked in from the other room, his brow furrowed. "Anything?" Laith asked.

"Nope, nothing." Tarr shook his head. "We need to get out," he said quickly, hoping that he didn't sound too alarmed.

Laith began to mount the stairs to see if any of the others were in their rooms. Tarr made to follow him, then his eyes traveled down to the table by the landing. A small note was tucked under the brass base of the lantern.

"Laith!" he said sharply, and the prince turned.

"What is it?" he asked, and Tarr handed him the note. In Athela's small, neat script, he read:

Laith,

We've just got word that Cira knows our whereabouts. We don't know how it happened, but we think that it had something to do with the party; someone must have recognized us and given her the location of our house. We've decided to find a place to hide and camp out until we're all back together and can figure out what else to do about this. We've all gathered in the alley behind The Cask; please come as soon as you get this. She might be having this house watched, so use extreme caution and be sure you're not followed.

Athela

Laith swiftly folded the note and tucked it into his coat. Before Tarr knew what was happening, they were sweeping back out of the room.

"They have our whereabouts," Tarr muttered. "How?"

"We come and go enough from this house that someone must finally have ratted us out." Laith grimaced. "We should have moved sooner."

"We're sure that that was Athela's handwriting?" Tarr asked suddenly.

Laith frowned and unfolded the note. The handwriting was unmistakable; even Tarr had to admit it.

Laith scooped up his sword and belt and re-buckled it around his waist, then the two of them walked out into the whistling wind. The door closed with a bang behind them.

"Are you armed?" Laith muttered in Tarr's direction.

"No," Tarr returned.

Laith reached around and withdrew a small sheathed knife that was strapped to the outside of his right boot, handing it to Tarr.

"I don't know how to use it," Tarr protested, taking the weapon in his awkward hands.

"I feel better that you have it," Laith told him. "Just stick it in the back of your pants or something." Tarr obeyed, pushing up his outer jacket and tucking the dagger into his pants. The hilt was curiously made, very flat and thin, so that it lay easily against Tarr's back. The rain had just begun to fall, and Laith pulled his hood up over his head. Tarr squinted against the drops and looked out over the street. There was no sign of Wolver. He whistled between his teeth. There was no reply.

"He probably went back to the barn where it's dry," Laith said. "We won't take them anyway; they'd attract too much attention. You know where the alleyway is that Athela's talking about, right?"

"Yes, I think so."

"Good."

They hugged the shadows of the buildings as they walked along. The streets were mostly deserted, and the rain was falling faster. Tarr could hear distant rumbling over the hillsides. In perhaps twenty minutes, the clouds would completely obscure the sky, and they wouldn't be able to see anything in the dusky gray light. Laith kept low to the ground as he walked along. From time to time, they intentionally went down a completely wrong street and then doubled back in order to lose anyone who might be following them. The trip to the alleyway that Athela had indicated would normally have taken about ten or fifteen minutes, but it was a full half-hour before they were a few streets away.

"Where is this place again?" Laith inquired.

"Two streets down," Tarr instructed. Laith straightened up, leaning his back flat against the wall, Tarr mimicking his movements. Laith glanced around them, then crossed one street, glancing either way as he went. He rounded the corner a few steps ahead of Tarr. The Ashan felt the dull pang of foreboding deep in his ribcage.

Seconds later there was a wild shout, and before Tarr could turn the corner after Laith, the prince came bolting back around the edge of the building, face white, mouth open. Tarr barely had time to register what was going on before there was a chorus of other yells, and something out of the shadows lunged out and struck Laith on the back of the head, the prince going down like a stone. Tarr whipped around, looking for a way to run, when something dull hit him on the back of the neck, and he felt his legs buckling beneath him. He fell face forward into the dirt of the street, the pain on the back of his head temporarily paralyzing him.

"An Ashan!" a voice crowed above him. "How about it, then? How's about I take a trophy back to Kagai?"

There was a hoot and a holler and blurry words of encouragement. Tarr tried to move his head, but the throbbing was too great.

All at once, he felt someone grab his left hand. Before he could register it, a searing pain nearly split him in half. He cried out and tried to snatch his hand back, his head swimming from the blow and from the anguish that bloomed out from his left hand like a rose. There was the sound of cackling, of hooting, of bellowing above and around him. Tarr felt himself going dizzy; the world swung round him in a nauseating arc; for a moment, he thought he glimpsed a figure leading Laith's horse, and then a flash of white fur, and a yelp. *Wolver*, he thought. *Wolver, what are you doing here? Run.*

His left hand was throbbing over and over as though his heart were beating through the ends of his fingertips. Dully, he reached over and felt his left hand with the numb fingers of his right.

One of his fingers, his sixth, was missing. They had cut it off.

Tarr closed his eyes slowly, the world spinning once again. He almost couldn't register it, and felt for it again. Where his finger had once been, it now just *ended,* covered in something warm and sticky. He retched, glad that he was only barely conscious.

Tarr tried to move and curl protectively into a ball around his mangled hand, but before he could, he was dealt another blow to his head and felt his body flatten out, limp against the cold, wet cobblestone. To his surprise, however, he didn't black out. Consciousness seeped into the corners of his eyes, and he decided, in a startling moment of clarity, that if he was going to survive, he was going to have to think.

He was tired, he realized. Tired of not being in control. Tired of being buffeted this way and that, like a boat in the middle of a hurricane.

Get control of the situation, he urged himself. *Get control now, or you're going to die.*

So he pretended to be unconscious, and with every passing second his mind scrambled to find a way out.

He felt hands on his arms, jerking them behind him, tying them with strong rope, and then the hands went up and down the sides of his legs, feeling for something.

"Clean," yelled a harsh voice, and Tarr realized that the hands had been searching for weapons. But, he thought in a rush, they had missed the knife tucked into the back of his pants. Whoever it was hadn't been able to see it in the darkness; hadn't thought to search there.

He heard a muffled yell to his left and wished that he could turn his head around to see what was happening, but any motion would give away his ruse of being unconscious.

"We need some help over here!" yelled another unfamiliar voice. The weight on Tarr's back raised, and Tarr quickly jerked his head around, squinting through the pouring rain to where the noise was coming from. Laith was on the ground with five black-cloaked figures on top of him, trying to hold him down and tie his hands behind his back. Arfolasth, his horse, was at the end of a lead held by one of the Kagaian guards, clearly having been retrieved from Ma's house. There was no sign of Wolver; Tarr felt a sinking fear in the pit of his stomach. Laith gave a terrific yell and shook his shoulders like a massive beast; more riders scurried in to try and pin him down.

Momentarily forgotten, Tarr saw his chance. Hands bound, blood from his finger co-mingling with the wetness from the rain, he wriggled his right hand under his jacket and withdrew Laith's knife from where he had tucked it into the top of his pants. He carefully, painstakingly pulled the blade from its sheath and turned the knife around so that it was facing upward and against the ropes binding his hands together. He sawed on the rope with the sharp knife, keeping a careful eye on the people fighting with Laith. The prince was putting up a magnificent effort to struggle loose from his captors, but the combined strength of the others was too much for him. Tarr winced as Laith was clubbed again in the head with what Tarr thought to be the hilt of a sword, and he went down hard. The fighters in black cloaks muttered curses at him, and one dealt him a kick. Tarr's heart quickened as he saw some of their assailants start to walk back toward him; all of a sudden, the ropes gave a snap, and he found himself free. Quick as a whip, he tucked the blade back in its sheath under his jacket and slumped back down in the mud. With his thumbs, he clasped the ends of the severed ropes on each hand, keeping his wrists together so it would look as though they were still tied. He gasped. The pain in his left hand was sickeningly sharp. He forced himself to stifle it, to fight back the pain like he was tamping down a flame. *Do not let yourself panic,* he told himself firmly, though he could feel the light of it flickering inside. *Keep your head. Keep your thoughts clear.*

Not a second later, a hand roughly grabbed his shoulder and hauled him up on his knees, then more hands found him, and he was moved onto his feet. Tarr lolled his head from side to side, keeping up the charade. Someone slapped him in the face and Tarr pretended to jerk awake, struggling with his arms, but was inwardly relieved not to have to act asleep anymore. His forearm was grabbed, and Tarr's heart gave a little lunge of fear. He looped his thumbs more tightly around the now-loosened ropes binding his wrists to secure them, hoping that the darkness would hide them from sight.

He found himself being half-pushed, half-pulled around the corner into the alleyway, which was cluttered with cast-away boxes and garbage. The alley had a dead end, the back wall of a stone building that must have been some sort of tavern or pub. There were only a few rear doors facing into the alley; all of them were bolted and the lights put out, casting the narrow street into total darkness. Tarr could only see the shadows of the soldiers in the green cloaks.

Suddenly, at the other end of the alley, someone lit a lantern and hung it on the wall, shining an eerie dim light through the rain. Tarr peered into the darkness and saw, to his horror, that the other Strikers were standing there, bound just as he and Laith had been. Athela had a cut beneath one eye, blood trickling down her cheek, her gray eyes masking what Tarr knew to be extreme rage comingled with fear. He realized that it must have been she who had shouted a warning as soon as she saw Laith, knowing that he wouldn't be able to escape. Si was beside her, eyes wide open, mouth closed in a thin line, and beside him was Marc, light hair plastered to his forehead with the rain. With a gulp, Tarr saw Rane, face caked with mud, eyes widening as she recognized Tarr. And, lastly, at the end of the line was Archer, looking like a ruffled hawk, his hair tousled and tossed, with cuts on his arms and one across his neck. He clearly had put up a fight upon his capture. He allowed himself the faintest rueful echo of his familiar grin upon seeing Tarr.

Laith, who had been dragged up behind Tarr with twice as many soldiers on his arms, was pushed into line beside Athela. The prince's head was reeling back and forth, and Tarr knew that, unlike him, he wasn't faking it. Athela stared at Laith, clearly wishing to help. Laith seemed to be regaining some of his senses as the guards dropped his arms, stepped back, and left him there in line. Laith barely managed to stay on his feet.

"Where were you?" Athela asked Tarr tersely.

Tarr opened his mouth to answer, but a shadowy figure yelled, "Shut up!" and Tarr closed it, sending Athela a helpless look. He watched as one of the cloaked guards walked up with Laith's sword and daggers and threw them into a pile on the other side of the alleyway. In the pile, Tarr recognized Athela's and Rane's curved blades, Morthenstar's ornate, ancient-looking sword, Marc's flat broadsword, as well as Archer's quiver, bow, and dagger. There were at least twenty cloaked Kagaian soldiers in front of them, and Tarr supposed that there were even more of them in the shadows at the entrance of the alleyway. *So this is it*, Tarr thought. *Cira captured us. There's no way out for us this time.*

Some Kagaian guards walked up to them and pushed the seven of them so that their backs were flat against the stone wall of the alley. They were lined up all in a row, similar to when Archer lined up targets for shooting practice. Tarr knew then, with wild fear throbbing louder and louder in his ears, that he and his friends were now in front of a Kagaian firing squad, and unless he figured out how to save them, they would be dead within a matter of minutes. *Think*, Tarr screamed to himself. *Take control and think!*

The first peal of thunder sounded overhead and one of the soldiers walked forward, casting back her hood and reading from a piece of parchment she unrolled in front of herself. "You seven are hereby accused of committing high treason against Her Majesty Cira Kagai. You are accused of conspiring to assassinate the Queen, of infiltrating her palace, of espionage, of murder, of theft, and of thoughts unbecoming servants of her Majesty."

Tarr's mind raced. It would be suicide for him to go and try to kill any of the guards. That would only speed up their executions. He wasn't a good enough fighter. He couldn't try to cut any of the others loose, either, even in the low light the guards would see him. He had to think of something. He had to...

"You are furthermore accused of attempting to form a band of rebels known as the Strikers and, under that banner, assemble those who wish to destroy this land and the noble ideals which her Lady-ship has established in the best interests of this country. It is for these reasons that you are now sentenced to immediate and painful death. Let it be known that your families will not be permitted to grieve for you and that your remains will be displayed in the center of Two Falls as warnings to those whom you thought to contaminate with your heinous and distasteful ways."

"*Contaminate?*" Archer scoffed. "A four-syllable word? No way did *Cira* manage to write this herself."

Without warning, one of the cloaked figures walked up and smacked Archer hard across the face. Without the use of his hands, Archer was powerless to stop it, and the force of the blow sent him reel-ing over onto Rane, who stumbled with his weight. He was pulled back up to standing height, and Rane was righted as well. Archer now bore a fresh cut beside his eye, which was trickling over his sharp cheekbone. He blinked a few times but made no noise, and had made no outcry when he had been hit. Athela grimly shook her head a few times. Tarr leaned forward ever so slightly. Archer raised his bound hands and wiped his eye momentarily and then lowered them back down. With relief, Tarr saw that all of Archer's fingers were still intact, and tried not to think about his own hand.

And then, all of a sudden, something clicked in his mind. *Archer's hands were tied in front of him.* He leaned forward and saw that Rane's were as well. Perhaps they had been tied by the same guard. Instantly, he knew what he was going to have to do. He prayed it would work.

The guard droned on, "Therefore, on this day, by the order of her Majesty, Queen Cira Kagai, you will be shot and subsequently stabbed through the hearts until each and every one of you is dead. This order is to be carried out by Captain Rike of the Queen's guard." She rolled up the parchment and tucked it into her shirt, motioning others forward. They began fitting arrows into their bows.

Tarr saw his chance. He fell forward onto his knees, bowing his head, and began speaking in rapid Ashan.

"Archer," he said, using the literal Ashan translation for the word, "I managed to cut myself loose, my hands are free, and I have a knife hidden at my back," he said quickly, not daring to look up. The guards had let out a shout, and some had started forward towards him to haul him back onto his feet, but once he started talking they had stopped. The head captain, the one who had read the proclamation, was laughing.

Tarr rushed on, not daring to stop, making sure that his voice had a desperate, pleading tone in it, hoping the captain would catch on. "Archer, when I stand back up, I will throw the knife to you."

"He's praying to his gods for deliverance," the captain was laughing. "What a coward! Look at him, on his knees in the mud! Right where he belongs. Her ladyship will laugh her head off when I tell her about this one. Ashan coward. Ashan filth. I'll give her the finger I cut off as a trophy for her to mount on her wall." The captain spat at Tarr, but Tarr didn't dare look up, merely continued speaking in a long rush of Ashan words.

"I cannot hit any of these soldiers on my own, Archer. I feel that our best chance lies with you. You must do this. Be ready. Wait for the moment after I am brought back to stand upon my feet."

The captain laughed again but flicked her hand forward, growing bored of Tarr's unintelligible speaking. Two soldiers rushed forward and pulled Tarr back up onto his feet, then backed away. Tarr chanced a glance down the row of Strikers. Athela was staring at him uncomfortably, plainly believing what the Kagaian captain had said about his cowardice. Laith was studiously avoiding his eyes, as was Marc. Si looked absolutely horrified. Rane was gazing at the ground in front of her. Tarr stared at Archer, but couldn't read anything on his face. Archer had told him many times that he didn't know how to speak Ashan anymore, but Tarr still possessed a dim sliver of hope that somehow it wasn't true. If he hadn't understood Tarr's message, then they would all be dead in a few seconds.

When we die, we become trees, Tarr remembered. *That's not such a bad thing.*

Tarr took in a gasp of a breath, unhooked his thumbs from the ropes around his wrists, and his hands were free. He moved his arm ever so slightly up his back, thunder pealing out above them, feeling for the knife hidden under his jacket, hoping that his motion was masked by the shadows. He drew out the blade, holding it now by its sharp point, resting his hands on his lower back. The archers were still readying themselves. Tarr had to act before they had raised their weapons to fire.

"Archer!" Tarr yelled, hurling the blade toward him, hoping as he had never hoped before that the other Ashan had understood him and was ready.

Archer didn't even glance over, but caught the knife in a fluid motion with one of his tied hands, shifted his weight, and hurled it at the lantern on the other side of the alley. The glass in the lantern shattered, and the knife blade clipped off the candle, plunging the street into complete darkness. There was a frenzied motion as each of the other Strikers galvanized into action on either side of him, using the night's dark cloak to dive to safety.

"Fire! Shoot them!" Tarr heard the captain scream, and he ducked, feeling Laith do the same on his left side. He heard dozens of arrows screech above them and heard them clatter on the stone wall and fall to the ground. A horrible cry sounded from beside them—Si. He whipped around from side to side, trying to find Si, but it was too dark, far too dark, and the frenzied rain was whipping furiously into his eyes.

"Pull me loose!" Laith yelled at Tarr, and though Tarr couldn't see, he felt Laith turn and bump his hands into Tarr's stomach. The Ashan frantically pulled at the knots with his painful, mangled fingers, and something must have been pulled the right way for the ropes around Laith's hands to come undone. The prince lunged forward toward the pile of weapons on the other side of the alley. Lighting flashed and the rain beat hard against their faces, and Tarr saw in the split second of illumination the freeze-frame outlines of dozens of Kagaian guards stumbling towards them blindly, swords drawn and flashing, raindrops streaming down the silvery blades in dozens of tiny rivulets. He backed toward the stone wall and felt along its length. His instinct told him that to stay in the alley meant certain death. He turned and shimmied up the side of the building, feet slipping here and there, severed finger throbbing, but after only a few seconds he heaved himself up onto the wooden roof of the building, rain streaming down between his fingers and around his boots, cascading off the edge of the roof like a waterfall.

From the other side of the alley he heard the first clash of steel on steel, which told him that Laith had at least managed to lay his hands on his sword. There were frantic shouts over the din of the thunder all around the street, the guards calling to one another, and the Strikers shouting one another's names, trying to get their bearings in the pitch black. Tarr crouched on his haunches, leaning back and forth, trying to see the others, but could only make out swiftly moving shadows like fish swimming at the bottom of a murky pool of water. The sound of swordplay escalated into not only one fight, but what sounded like two, perhaps three, and after that Tarr could no longer make out the individual percussion of battle, the sounds merging into one unholy din. Seeing a figure leap to his side, Tarr started and yelped, but it was only Archer, with Si's limp, senseless form slung over one shoulder. Archer jumped when he noticed Tarr, and it was clear that he hadn't seen him up on the rooftop, but had also followed his Ashan instincts to climb to safety. Archer was muddy, bloody, and completely drenched, but to Tarr's extreme relief, he saw that his friend had managed to lay hold of his bow and quiver. He lay Si down on the rooftop beside them, and Tarr steadied him with one hand, anxiously looking for any sign of life on the boy's face.

"Out cold. Got hit by an arrow, but I broke it off. Careful of his shoulder," Archer yelled over the roar of the wind, water pouring down the length of his nose in a steady rivulet. Tarr leaned over Si, and saw in the blue flash of lightning the stub of an arrow lodged in Si's shoulder. It had missed his heart.

"Can you see anything?" Archer cried.

"No!" Tarr shouted back. "What's happening?"

"Laith got his sword," Archer replied, slipping his quiver over his head, holding the leather in his teeth and nocking an arrow to his bow. "I think he took down a few guards. Rane managed to get herself loose, and she got my ropes off, and I think I got Marc. Athela followed behind Laith. He cut her free, and the two of them threw us all our weapons."

A crash of thunder sounded and Archer reared up, aiming down into the alley and loosing three arrows in the flash of light that followed. In that moment, Tarr made out Laith and Marc standing back to back in their combat stance, fighting three guards each, Rane with two and Athela cleaving her way through a crowd of dark cloaks. Two of Archer's arrows found their marks, and Tarr could see the soldiers drop. He reloaded and waited for the next crash of lightning. Tarr kept deadly silent, not wishing to distract Archer in any way.

The next thunder crackled above and the lightning flashed. Archer loosed another two arrows, this time in the direction of two guards who were coming up behind Marc. The lightning went out before Archer could see whether or not he hit them, but he didn't waste time trying to peer into the pitch black and fitted another arrow, rocking up on his heel, one long leg extended straight against the slope of the roof, stopping him from sliding down.

Tarr saw two shadows move right below them. "Down there!" he told Archer urgently. "I think one of ours is right down there, fighting someone."

Archer nodded and tipped himself forward so the shaft of his arrow was aimed where Tarr had indicated. The next peal of thunder, the next flash of lightning, and he loosed the arrow right into a guard who was leaning up, standing over what looked like Rane's prone body.

Tarr let out a cry and lunged forward, slipping on the wet surface of the roof, but Archer kicked out at him, stopping him at the edge of the wood. "Tarr, don't be an idiot; I need you up here, I need you to help me."

"I saw Rane!" Tarr bellowed furiously.

"And I saw Athela go down," Archer shouted back, half in frustration, half in order to be heard over the sound of the wind and the rain beating on the rooftops around them. "We don't know if they're dead, all right? I need you up here so I know at least one other person is all right and can help me with the others!"

Archer was right, and Tarr sat back on his heels. An earsplitting scream shot through the darkness at them, and Tarr craned his neck to try to see who it had come from. Thunder, lightning, the shriek of Archer's arrow as it sped from his bow, and Tarr saw that the number of guards had sharply thinned out. His eyes filled with rain, and he blinked angrily, brushing at the drops, but the illumination from the lightning had gone out and he couldn't see which of his friends were still standing. He gritted his teeth, gripping the slats of wood with anger. What if none of them survived? Would it have been kinder just to have given up?

Again, a crash shook the rooftop around them and Archer jerked his arm back. In the light that followed, Tarr saw only three guards left, two of whom were immediately taken down by Archer's arrows. To his horror, however, he didn't see any of his friends standing or fighting.

"Follow me!" Archer called, rolling Si onto his shoulder. He leaped onto both of his feet, sliding down the roof and slipping into the mud on the alley beneath them. Tarr followed, dreading what they might find. They stood together, feeling around with their feet. The ground was littered with prone bodies, but they couldn't tell which were the other Strikers and which were the Kagaian guards. A flash of lightning, and Tarr made out Laith's face, turned upward, perfectly still, caked with mud. He ran forward as the light went out, feeling around with his hands for the bare skin of Laith's face.

"I think there's still a guard left!" Tarr yelled. He had seen someone disappearing around the edge of the alley.

"She took off," Archer shook his head. "Probably to get reinforcements. We have to get the others out of here, Tarr. We have to find somewhere safe to go."

"You go get the horses; they're in a stable around the front of the alley," Tarr told him, still feeling around blindly in the direction of Laith. "I thought I saw Wolver, see if he's all right, I'll get the others. We'll figure out where to go then." Archer made no response. Tarr wasn't sure that he had heard him, but in the next peal of thunder and lightning, Tarr saw the Ashan disappearing around the corner.

At long last, Tarr's fingers brushed over a small area of smooth skin and determined that he had found Laith. He frantically pulled the prince's arms up and heaved him back a few feet. Laith did not move or make any response. Tarr felt around for his chest and put his ear above his heart, but in the din of the wind and rain could hear nothing. Frustrated, Tarr stood and looked around, seeing nothing. He would need a light if he had any hope of finding the others in time. He walked to a back door and banged on it loudly, hoping that the sound would echo inside. He hammered for a full three minutes before a small light shone behind the wood panel and it was tentatively opened. A man's fearful small face squinted out in the rain at Tarr and past him to the carnage in the alleyway.

"What on earth do you want?" the man asked.

"A light, nothing else," Tarr answered, breathing hard, fists throbbing from the effort of his pounding.

"Who are you?"

"Never mind, I need a light!" Tarr shrieked. He couldn't remember when he had ever been so frantic. The man must have sensed it in his voice and turned, disappearing into the gloom of the house, before reappearing with a glass lantern much like the one that Archer had broken. He lit it with his candle and handed it silently to Tarr before turning and slamming the door shut behind him.

Tarr turned back into the alley, holding up the lantern, sheltering it from the rain with his bleeding hand, a long scarlet rivulet running down his arm. The ground of the alley looked like a veritable carpet of bodies. He saw someone without a cloak and set the lamp down in the shelter of the doorway, rushing forward. It took him a minute or so of clearing arms and legs from atop the figure before he recognized the person to be Marc. He dragged Marc the rest of the way out from under three Kagaian riders and over to Laith, his head lolling sadly from side to side. Tarr closed off his mind to even the possibility that his friends were dead and continued to hunt around.

Athela he found propped up against a wall, sword loosely hanging from one hand. Tarr knew that she was in serious trouble as soon as he touched her shoulder, which moved irregularly as soon as his fingers had made contact. Her shirt was soaked, but it felt warm and Tarr had a sinking realization that it was blood. He pulled her forward as much as he dared and wrapped his arms around her waist, moving her up the rest of the way. He dropped her legs, then twisted around and picked her up in both arms, carrying her back over to Marc and Laith, laying her beside them.

Rane was beneath the section of roof where he and Archer had been perched, body twisted around, her sword lying a few feet away. Tarr frantically felt along her limbs for any major injuries or cuts and felt a few tears in her clothes, but nothing as bad as Athela's. He slid her arms around his neck and picked her up, her slight weight nothing to him, her head rolled back, rocking slightly as he walked. Tarr felt something warm on his cheek and realized he was crying but did nothing to try to stop himself. Rane was laid beside the others. Si was dragged over next, where Tarr could examine him by the light of the sputtering lantern. The arrow wound was dark and deep and caked in mud and blood. Tarr tried not to look and set him beside Laith. Si, at least, appeared to be breathing. Once all his friends were together, he set about collecting their swords and made a small pile next to them, then sat down to wait for Archer, the rain still pelting at his face, though he noticed that the thunder and lightning were subsiding into the distance.

At that moment Archer ran into the alley, leading Arfolasth, Kip, Aria, and the other horses. Wolver wasn't with them. His white face was streaked with blood and dirt, and his eyes were unblinking, intense. "We're going to have to leave immediately," he informed Tarr. "I can ride on Kip with Athela; maybe you can take Rane, and Si can be behind you. They're the smallest. I think we'll have to tie the others to their horses. We can use the rope they had for our arms."

"Where's Wolver?" Tarr asked, shouting above the din of the storm.

Archer gravely met his eyes and shook his head. "He's gone. Vanished. He wasn't there."

Tarr's head whipped around, eyes scanning the darkness for any sign of Wolver. Archer's hand caught him and stood him upright. "I need you to focus now," he said in Ashan, and something about hearing his native language snapped Tarr back to his senses like a hand shaking him awake. "Stay with me now, and help me save our friends. We do not have much time. We have to get out of here alive."

Mutely, Tarr nodded and forced himself to push his worry for Wolver to one side. The two of them ran over to a corner of the alley where they had seen the large length of rope used to bind their wrists. They cut long sections with Archer's dagger and returned to the horses.

"Arfolasth, come here," Tarr asked, and the black charger stepped forward obediently, ears pricked up, concerned. Archer walked up with Laith on his shoulder, and the horse whickered anxiously. Tarr patted his neck, and Archer walked around to his side, throwing Laith onto the horse's back.

"He's in great danger," Tarr informed the horse. "Take care of him, all right?" Arfolasth curved his long neck around and bumped Laith's knee with his silky nose, breathing in his master's scent, making a low whuffing sound, shaking his head against the drenching rain as it blew over and over them in unending sheets. Archer ducked under the horse's head and drew Laith's arms forward, tying them around Arfolasth's neck. Sensing what he had to do, the charger held his head high so that Laith wouldn't be knocked against him too much when they were moving. Archer then leaned down and tied Laith's legs to his stirrups. Once he checked that Laith was secure, Archer deftly repeated the operation on Marc with one of the other horses.

While he was busy tying ropes, Tarr fixed the large bundle of swords to the back of Aria's saddle. "Archer," he said anxiously, "where are we going to take them? No one in this town will take us in; they're all scared to death of Kagai. There's no place for us to go."

Archer straightened up from tying Marc's hands and thought for a moment. "Riddleton?"

Tarr's stomach convulsed. "*No.* They'd sell us out the moment we walk through the city border." Still, something about Riddleton jogged his memory. "You remember Silva? The girl who sold us the horses in Riddleton?

"Of course."

"She said her house was out of town, didn't she? Up on the cliffs north of here, by the sea?" He racked his brain, and her words rose up like a picture in his mind. "Something like the third farm down the road past Faridor."

"Tarr, that's a few hours' ride. We don't have a few hours! Athela is definitely losing blood fast; she's going to die if we don't get her help soon."

"Do you have a better idea?" Tarr demanded angrily. "We need shelter. We can't stay in this town. Once we leave the city, we're out in the middle of the wilderness with no medicine, not even a roof over our heads."

"You're right," Archer said after a second's pause. "You're right." He considered a moment longer. "I think I can get us there. I recovered a horse for her brother once, I think I know the way."

"Let's get out of town first, and then we can argue about directions. Help me get Si up."

Tarr moved Rane so that she hung over one of his shoulders, then with his spare hand pulled himself onto Marc's horse's back, and Archer hoisted Si behind him, tying him to Tarr so that the boy's head rested against his shoulderblade. Once Si was secure, Archer bent and easily scooped Athela up into his arms and mounted up on Kip, Si's horse. Aria, Athela's excitable gray, brought up the rear, snorting and huffing, his lead fastened to a silver loop on the back of Laith's saddle. They plunged out of the alleyway and into the night, hidden beneath the curtain of rain.

The night was pitch black, and everything in his head was so scattered and confused that Tarr had only a dim idea of where they were. It was lucky, he reflected, that he had Archer there to lead the way. Archer knew every possible secret alleyway, every back road they could take to sneak out of the city undetected. The sound of their horses was nearly inaudible over the din of the storm; Tarr kept shaking water from his eyes and peering through the darkness, trying to sense whether the oncoming shapes were approaching riders or whether they were merely buildings rising out of the gloom.

Archer finally turned and pointed them through a narrow opening between two buildings, barely wide enough for the horses to fit through. Tarr could feel his legs being squeezed uncomfortably against the walls as they passed. He was close enough to have knocked on the windows of the houses on either side of them. But the alleyway spilled them out onto a short ledge above a small canal overflowing its banks with rushing water. The horses, led by Arfolasth, waded out into the water and up the other side. At every passing moment, Tarr expected a rider to come swooping down at them out of the blackness, but none came. Perhaps he shouldn't have been surprised. It was nearly impossible to see further than five feet in any direction; none of the sentries Cira had posted around the city were likely to be able to spot them. Still, Tarr felt his breath catching in the back of his throat for at least half an hour after they left the city walls. It was only after they'd turned north and hit the merciful cover of the first grove of trees that he finally exhaled; the rain was quieter now, and he could at least hear himself think. He kicked Marc's horse up to fall into step alongside Archer.

"Which way?" he asked.

"We're going north. Once we're well clear of the city, there's a path that leads up past all the clifftop farms." The wind seemed to be dying down; either that, or the trees were providing enough shelter from the storm that the din was at least slightly muted.

"How did you all get captured?" Tarr asked, shifting Rane's weight in front of him. He glanced over his shoulder to make sure that Laith and Marc were still tied in place to their mounts.

"Well, I might ask you the same question," Archer retorted. "Where did you and Laith go?"

"Laith went to go try and bring his wife back from Joymaril, but that was an ambush," Tarr informed him, feeling the swell of anger rising in him. *Two ambushes in one day. Never again.* "We came back and had gotten a letter from Athela asking us to meet her in the alley."

"We all did, apparently," Archer shook his head, sending a spray of water out around himself. "We had split up earlier in the day to try and look for you two, and Athela, Si, and Marc had gone together. We were going to meet back at a tavern for dinner, but they didn't show. So we went back to Ma's, and there was a note from Athela telling us to meet her in that damned alley. We showed up, got clubbed in the back of the head, and then they tied us up and waited for you to get there."

Tarr swallowed. They had only made it out by the skin of their teeth; he felt almost giddy, considering how close they had all come to meeting their end. Tentatively, he reached out and touched the stump of the finger on his left hand, still throbbing. He snatched his hand away, felt the earth reel beneath him; he tightened his grip on Rane's waist to stay upright.

They rode on through the night, mile after mile. When they left the comparative shelter of the woods, the rain continued to billow down on them, punctuating its steady beat with crashes of thunder and lightning, the horses finding it difficult to slog through the ever-thickening mud. Tarr had never felt so tired. The adrenaline that had coursed through him during the fight was beginning to wear off, leaving in its place a hole of dull exhaustion. If they didn't reach Silva's house soon, then he would be in danger of collapsing and falling off of his horse, taking Si and Rane with him. The rain was unrelenting, pounding at him, making it difficult to take a breath. Every now and again during the brief flash of lightning, he glanced over to Archer. After a few hours of riding, Archer's head was lolling back, and Tarr could see him reeling in the saddle.

"Archer!" Tarr called, reaching out and shaking him, and he felt the other Ashan jerk upright. "Stay awake! How much longer?"

"I don't know," Archer replied groggily. "We're on the right road, going north. But I don't know exactly where we are."

Tarr felt dread growing beneath his exhaustion and fought to control it. Suppose they had missed Silva's house already? It was very late; perhaps they didn't have their lights lit. The rain was falling so thick and heavy that Tarr could barely see his horse's head in front of him. Time was running out for his friends. With each heartbeat, blood was pumping out of them, and their lifespans narrowed evermore. Tarr tightened his grip around Rane, burying his face in her sopping strands of hair, pulling his loose sleeves around her shoulders to shelter her from the rain.

The horses came to the crest of a small hill overlooking a plain, open below them like the palm of a hand. Tarr gamely set out first, Arfolasth following, delicately picking his way down the slippery slope so that Laith wouldn't be jostled out of the saddle. Tarr turned to make sure that the other horses made it down all right, as the path was close to being completely liquid. Then, just as he had turned back around, he heard a frightened animal scream. One of the horses—the one carrying Marc—had missed a step and was sliding down the hill on its side, four legs thrashing to find a foothold.

"No!" Tarr yelled, but he didn't dare try and jump free, or else Rane would have fallen on the ground. Archer, who was taking up the rear to make sure that they all made it safely, pulled his horse to a halt, leaning Athela forward as best he could and slipping off. Kip, Si's horse, knew that something was amiss and stood stock still in the spot where Archer had leaped off, occasionally raising a hoof to try and step over the oncoming pressure of the mud and shifting to keep Athela from falling. Tarr squinted through the pelting rain and saw Archer withdraw a knife and rush to the fallen horse at the bottom of the hill. He cut the ropes binding Marc to his saddle and heavily dragged him out from under the horse.

Free of its burden, Marc's mount hoisted itself heavily back up, standing awkwardly, holding its off-hind leg gingerly above the ground. Archer whistled at Aria, who perked his ears and came sliding down the hill, barely maintaining his stability. Quickly, Archer transferred Athela to her horse and mounted up behind Marc. Balancing the whole operation as best he could, he urged Aria and Kip forward. Tarr kept his eyes on their painstaking progress down the rest of the hill, desperately praying that the horses would keep their sure footing.

Once Archer and the others drew near to him, Tarr peered down to try to get a look at Marc. Tarr could barely recognize his face in the few flashes of lightning that crackled through the sky, so caked it was with mud and muck. When Aria was close enough, Tarr leaned over and grabbed the shank of the bit, leading him forward and steadying him.

"Is Marc all right?" Tarr asked.

"I don't know," Archer replied in a low voice so that Tarr could barely hear him over the din of the rain. "We've got him, though, and that's what matters."

Tarr wiped a sheet of rain from his face, feeling his throat close as if he were close to tears.

"There was a sign," Archer shouted.

"What?" Tarr asked.

"A sign. For a farm. We're on someone's land now."

"What did it say?" Tarr asked, feeling desperate.

Archer shook his head. "I don't know. But the sign was in the shape of a horse."

Tarr was almost afraid at how much he clung to that small glimmer of hope as they urged their horses forward into the torrent. Now, out of the shelter of the trees and in an open field, the ground was almost pure mud and the rain pelted straight against their faces, unfeeling and uncaring.

They had gone for another mile and were beginning to lose all hope and what little energy they had left when suddenly Archer sat bolt upright in the saddle.

"What is it?" Tarr asked quickly.

"Either I'm seeing things, or there are lights up ahead, I'd say in about a mile and a half," Archer replied. "Start bearing slightly more to the right."

Tarr obeyed, motioning for his horse to turn in the direction that Archer had indicated. He himself couldn't see anything at all, but if Archer had said that there were lights, then he had to hope that he was right.

They slogged on, and Tarr began to think that Archer was merely delirious. All at once, a faint twinkling caught his eye, high up on a bluff right by the coastal ridge. He blinked the water from his eyes, peering through the sleeting rain. Again, there it was, a light. He couldn't know whether or not it was Silva's house or not, and at this point it didn't matter to him whether it was Faridor fortress itself—it was a shelter of some kind. If nothing else, they could beg to be let in for the night and seek some medical aid.

"I see it!" Tarr exclaimed.

"Ride faster!" Archer called, though Tarr thought that this was asking a little much. The horses were lagging behind due to the effort of wading through a foot and a half of mud, and even Aria wasn't making his usual show of trying to run off in all directions at once. Tarr was relieved to see that Athela was still safely slung atop his back.

They drew closer to the lights, twinkling like beacons before them. Tarr could make out the outline of the house now. It wasn't so much of a house but a large mansion, with three stories stretching out for a good long way down the coast, right by the cliffs that divided the land from the sea. The lights they had seen were mounted in weatherproof boxes on the front walk leading up to the front door, cheerily unaware of the storm raging outside. The small band turned down the walk and half-walked, half-stumbled up to the front door.

Archer unbuckled himself from Marc and slid off of Kip. He untied Si from Tarr and hoisted the boy up in his arms. Tarr carried Rane up to the front door, a gigantic, ornate wood carving with a large knocker in the center. Archer walked straight to it, Si in his arms, grabbed the handle, and began pounding it against the door, so loudly that Tarr could hear the echoes inside the house. He himself balled up his fist and began beating the wood with it, feeling his energy sapping away with every blow.

They were standing right beneath the eaves of the house, so a good current of rain was continuously running down their faces. Tarr shook it off of him, continuing to desperately beat against the door, beginning to shiver uncontrollably, the cold gnawing into his skin. *What if they can't hear us? What if they're not home? I suppose we could break in...we have to get them out of the rain,* he thought, turning back to look anxiously at the horses. He stepped back from the door as Archer continued to pound against it, and saw that on the second story lights were beginning to turn on. He took an excited step back to stand next to Archer.

"I think they're coming!" he told him. Archer made no indication that he had heard him, but kept railing on the door. Tarr beat against the door again, once, twice, Rane's head rolling against his shoulder, her hair plastered over her face like dark strands of seaweed.

The door burst open, and Tarr found himself face to face with three extremely tall, dark men, one burly, the other two more slender, all with suspicious looks on their faces. Tarr thought that he could make out the silhouettes of more people behind them in the hallway, but he couldn't be sure.

"We're looking for Silva," Tarr managed to choke out. The tallest man had shoulder-length black hair and a beard. Tarr recognized him as the one who had sold them the horses.

He furrowed his eyebrows. "Archer?" he asked, eyeing Tarr's companion suspiciously. Silva's brother turned to the others standing behind him and made a curt jerking motion with his head. From between the two others, a small figure, no higher than the men's biceps, pushed its way to the front. It was Silva, red-eyed, with a little sleeping cap on the back of her head. Her eyes registered at first surprise, tentative recognition, then shock as she realized who it was at her door.

"Come in!" she said hurriedly, pushing the men back from the door and motioning them forward into the blissful stillness of the house.

"The others are on the horses; we have to go get them," Archer told her, handing Athela to one of the men, whom Tarr had ascertained were probably Silva's other brothers.

"These are some people from Riddleton. That's Archer," she said, pointing, "whom Cass has told you about, and this is..."

"Tarr," he panted.

The brothers all grunted, seemingly unimpressed, but one moved to take Rane from him, and the other two followed Archer back out to the horses, Tarr on their heels. Archer, Tarr, and two of the brothers untied the unconscious Strikers from the horses. Cass, the burliest, took Laith from Arfolasth, slinging him easily over a shoulder and striding back to the door. Tarr grabbed Athela, and Archer heavily heaved Marc over his back. The smallest brother, who'd been loitering just outside the door, nodded to Tarr, took Arfolasth's bridle, and led the string of horses around the side of the house, where Tarr surmised there must be a stable of some sort nearby. Tarr heaved Athela into a more comfortable position and entered, stamping the mud from his feet and shaking the rain from his face.

The hall was mercifully warm, with soft yellow lighting from lanterns hung here and there. Silva was flitting about like a silvery moth, lighting them up like a series of beacons up and down the stairs. The house was vast in its proportions, but it gave Tarr the distinct impression of being a *home* rather than a palace; there were multiple paintings of horses on the walls and a little horse figurine on one of the nearby tables. The rooms around the hall were dim; Tarr could not see into them, and for once, he didn't care. He was only interested in getting his friends to safety, his hand bandaged, and himself into a hot bath and then a bed. Cass led the way up the main staircase, Laith's hair hanging down limply in thin bloody strands, lifeless arms bumping gently against Cass's back with each step he took. Tarr gulped and looked instead at the heels of Archer's boots heading up the stairs in front of him.

On the landing, Silva materialized out of the gloom carrying a lantern, beckoning them to follow her. "We're going to put them in the north wing," she informed her brother, who grunted and headed off past her. Silva hung back for a moment in order to fall into step with Tarr and Archer. "You're bleeding," she said in a hushed voice, her eyes on Tarr's mangled hand.

Tarr quickly snatched it away. "It's mostly stopped," he said. He could feel Archer's eyes on him, but refused to look at him.

"I'll help you dress it," Silva said with a kindly touch to his elbow. "Don't worry, Tarr. I've known horsemen who have lost parts of their fingers, too. They healed without a problem."

Tarr nodded mutely. How could he explain to her what it meant?

It almost felt as though a part of his Ashan identity had been stolen from him and cast aside. He ducked his head, staring again at the backs of Archer's mud-caked boots.

"Who did this?" Silva asked, surveying the extent of the damage to the others as they passed by her on the landing.

"Kagai's guards. We're the Strikers," Archer told her. Tarr looked up at him.

Silva's green eyes widened. "*You*? How…"

"We were ambushed," Archer informed her gravely. "Tarr saved us. He saved us all."

Silence fell, and Silva and her brothers looked around. Tarr could almost see their minds re-assessing him, could almost hear them thinking, *that's surprising, he certainly doesn't look like he could save anyone.* He shifted uncomfortably, wishing he could dig a hole in the rug that would swallow him up.

"Tarr and I made it out all right," Archer continued. "We didn't even know if the others were alive; we just got out of there as fast as we could."

"You were right to come here," Silva told him firmly, shaking back a strand of her silver hair. Behind her, two of her brothers exchanged dubious looks, as if they didn't quite agree with Silva's assurance. "The rain is thick enough, any tracks are going to be washed away." She beckoned them down a dim hallway, lighting the way with her cheery lantern. "There are two rooms at the end over here with three beds in them. That's where we're going to put your friends. You and Archer can have the adjoining room."

"Do you think you'll be able to help them?" Archer asked.

"I haven't been able to look at them yet," Silva shook her head, businesslike. "So I can't answer that. I know a lot about medicine, though. So do my brothers. We care for the horses when they're injured; it's much the same principle. We'll do everything we can for them."

"Thank you," Tarr whispered, hoping that she knew how much it meant to him. She smiled and gave his arm a squeeze.

"In here," she told him, pointing.

Tarr and Archer walked into a large rectangular room with space and more to spare for the three beds it contained. Each bed was canopied and big enough for at least three people. Silva's brother was adjusting Laith on a mattress on top of a few towels he had spread out to soak up any blood. Archer carried Marc to another bed and laid him down gently, Tarr mimicking the motion with Athela. Silva rushed up to one of the beds, setting down her lantern and pulling out a few towels from the dresser on one end of the room. Archer and Tarr hung back, unsure of what to do as Silva began unbuttoning Si's shirt.

"His shirt has stuck to his wounds, Sil," the brother announced, squinting down at Laith. "The blood's beginning to clot."

"Cut the shirt out around the wounds—and get him out of those wet clothes, we don't want to have to deal with pneumonia in addition to everything else," Silva told him. "We'll get rid of the rest of the shirt in time."

"What can we do?" Archer asked. Silva turned, looking as though she was about to tell him something, but then stopped. She took in Archer's haggard, bloodstained face and Tarr's wet hair plastered against his scalp. She shook her head.

"There's hot water for a bath downstairs, I'll have my brother fetch you some. And there are fresh clothes in the dresser. You're exhausted, you can't do anything right now. I'll be there in a moment to tend to your hand, Tarr."

"Silva—" Archer began to protest.

"I mean it. Go," Silva ordered, then turned back around to her work, the straight set of her back lending an air of finality to the conversation. Tarr looked at Archer and shrugged helplessly. The two backed out of the room and into the hallway, nearly colliding with another one of Silva's seemingly interchangeable brothers, who was carrying a small towel and a pan of water into the next room. Tarr made a motion to follow him, but Archer laid a hand on his arm and shook his head. The two of them walked into the adjoining room, where a small candle was burning atop the dresser. Tarr felt sleep beginning to overcome him, despite the blood and the dirt. He stripped off his wet clothes and changed into the loose shirt and large drawstring pants that he found in the dresser and fell into one of the beds, his mangled hand held awkwardly away from his body. He heard the other bed creak slightly as Archer rolled onto it. As soon as his eyes closed, he was asleep.

CHAPTER TWENTY-FIVE

The next morning awoke misty and bleary-eyed after the previous night's torrents. A sweaty, hazy gray light slipped through the white curtains hung across the windows into Tarr and Archer's room. Tarr moaned a little, rubbing sleep from his eyes and stretching his long legs to the end of the bed. Then abruptly he sat bolt upright and remembered where he was. His left hand was clean and neatly bandaged with white dressing; with a lurch, he realized he hadn't dreamed his finger being cut off. A new wave of revulsion overtook him. He forced himself to look at his hand to try and accept it. It was easier to look at with the bandage covering his missing finger. It would be quite a different prospect when the bandage came off.

He glanced around the room and saw that Archer was already gone. He threw the bedcovers to one side, leaping across the room in two bounding steps, and went down the hallway toward the rooms where his friends lay.

He went in first to Athela and Rane's room. Two of Silva's brothers, the tall, slender duo, were there already. They were sitting on either side of Athela and muttering something in low voices. They had identical heads of dark wavy hair and the same dark tan, olive-colored skin, quite close to Tarr's own. They glanced up as Tarr entered and gave terse grunts of welcome. The entire male side of Silva's family seemed to lean towards the taciturn.

Rane and Athela were both neatly tucked under the covers of the beds, and from what Tarr could see of Rane, they had changed her into a simple, loose white sleeping shift. Tarr approached carefully, almost unwilling to ask what her condition was. Her skin was pale, with bruising along the sides of her face. He took her hand in his and felt no response from her. Alarmed, he stepped back, but then saw the undeniable movement of her breathing beneath the tightly pulled blanket. Sighing with relief, Tarr brushed back a bit of her drying auburn hair from her forehead and stepped back.

One of the attending brothers was watching him when Tarr turned around. "We gave her something to ease the pain," he informed him. His voice was low and had a slight rasp to it, a husky quality almost like Silva's. His smile was kind. "The medicine also induces sleep. She should be fine. She's in far better shape than your other friends."

Tarr swallowed, his throat dry. "We haven't...lost any of them, have we?"

"No," the brother to his side answered in a deep voice, comforting. This one had long sideburns; otherwise, it was almost impossible to tell him apart from the other. "It's a miracle, really. They were in a bad condition when you showed up."

"I know."

"That doesn't mean they're home free by any means," the first brother cautioned quickly.

"Thank you," Tarr said, edging closer to check up on Athela. The brother with sideburns was sewing up a gash at the base of her neck while the other held a knife to cut the string. Tarr winced, not liking the sight. In the forest he had never seen anyone sew another up; the Ashans usually just resorted to poultices of medicinal herbs. Usually, the worst injury any Ashan sustained was a broken leg or arm after a fall from a tree; blade wounds were virtually unheard of.

The pink was completely gone from Athela's cheeks, her dark skin flat and dull. The area around her eyes looked almost bruised, and sweat on her forehead was sticking to her curly black hair, which had been pulled back with a thin strap of leather to keep it out of the way. A thin slit of her eyes was open, and Tarr could see the tiny line of gray beneath her dark lashes. Her mouth was slightly ajar, and Tarr supposed that in addition to being unconscious, the two brothers had probably drugged her to keep her asleep while they operated.

"Her shoulder was dislocated," a brother told him. "But we put it back." He clearly meant this to be comforting.

Tarr nodded, feeling queasy, and backed out of the room, heading into the adjacent one. This room seemed to be far busier. Silva and her burly, raven-haired brother were walking from bed to bed with purposeful strides, occasionally calling out a medicinal need to one another. Archer, who was seated in a small chair by Laith's bed, looked up and gave Tarr a thin smile when he entered the room.

"Morning," Silva said, patting him on the arm as she passed by him. She held a pan of dark red water. "How's the hand?"

"How are we doing?" Tarr avoided her question about his hand and approached Laith's bedside.

"We could be doing worse," Archer replied, reaching over with one long arm and drawing up a nearby chair for Tarr. Laith, Tarr could see at once, was still breathing, but the clean towels that had been laid beneath him the night before were now stained a dark brown. Laith's chest was bare from the waist up, the blankets drawn around his hips. He had a long gash across his chest that had already been tended to and was shining with what looked like ointment. Laith also had a jagged raw cut running from halfway back on his head to just in front of his right ear, where his sand-colored hair had been cropped close to his scalp.

"They say that Rane, Marc, and Laith are going to make it for sure," Archer informed Tarr, crossing his arms. "They're not sure about Si and Athela."

Tarr closed his eyes for a moment, then re-opened them and looked to the other beds. Marc looked like he was merely sleeping, his head to one side, light yellow hair splayed out across his pillow, chest rising and falling evenly. Si, however, stood in stark contrast to Marc's peaceful demeanor, his skin an awful ashy-gray color. Silva's brother sat beside him, watchful.

"Let's go outside," Tarr said suddenly, not wanting to stay there any longer, needing air, needing a place to think. Archer shot him an inquiring look, shrugged, and stood, pausing briefly to touch Laith's arm before following Tarr out of the room. Silva was coming toward them with a fresh pan of water and stopped, smiling.

"We're going out to get some air," Tarr informed her. "And...thank you," he said awkwardly, holding up his bandaged hand.

"There's some bread and things in the kitchen if you're hungry. The kitchen is down the stairs, then you take a left and then two rights," she told him. "And you're welcome. It will heal nicely."

Tarr again didn't meet Archer's eyes as he lowered his hand. Together, they strode out into the light of day.

Silva's mansion was made of grayish-brown weathered stone with white trim around the roof and around the windows. It looked many centuries old, even to Tarr's untrained eyes. He imagined the house must have been in Silva's family for a very, very long time. It certainly seemed to have been built to house a great many more people than currently lived there. Tarr wondered where all the others had gone.

The two Ashans walked slowly off the step and away from the house, wandering out into a broad expanse that stretched out for miles up and down the coast. The house, except for a path leading up to the front door, was surrounded by broad fields of long waving grass, rippling back and forth with the wind. The day was overcast but surprisingly bright, moisture still hanging heavy in the air from the night before. The ground beneath them was sloshy and wet, but Tarr didn't mind the feeling on his bare feet. The rain had pulled the rich scent of earth up around them, where it co-mingled with the salt from the nearby sea. Tarr drank in deep, refreshing gulps of it, glad for the chill rising from the water below the cliff, glad for the bracing sensation of being alive.

The two Ashans meandered across the field, then slowly made their way to the edge of the cliff overlooking the sea. The house was set closer to the sea than Tarr had guessed the night before. Archer peered over, whistled in admiration at the sheer drop below, then strode back from the edge to an area in the grass. He plopped down, Tarr beside him, stretching his arms out and lacing them around his bent knees. The bruising and cuts he had sustained from the night before stood out starkly against his pale skin; it made Tarr's stomach turn to see them.

Neither of them spoke for a while. It was their usual companionable silence, comfortable in its quiet, not crying out to be filled with idle chatter. The wind whistled around them, ruffling Archer's hair, stinging Tarr's green and brown eyes; the push and pull of the sea was hypnotically soothing. It was getting chilly with the gusts of ocean air billowing up from below, and Tarr drew his long legs up and hugged them to keep warm. He glanced over at Archer, who was staring unblinkingly out at the sea with his golden eyes.

"How did they find us?" Archer wondered aloud. "Kagai's soldiers?"

Tarr shook his head. He had thought about that same question long and hard during the night's exhausting ride. "We were too careless from the start. There were too many people who knew who we were and where we were likely to stay. Any one of them could have turned us in to Kagai."

Archer peered at him searchingly. "But if you had to guess?"

"If I had to guess..." Tarr said slowly, "I would guess Pieter's nephew Nicolas. He knew exactly where we lived, as he sent us the carriage. He also had a sample of Athela's handwriting to fake the notes. We gave Pieter a copy of the first part of the prophecy she'd translated."

Archer shook his head, impressed. "So Pieter is in danger."

Tarr shrugged. "I can't be sure, but my guess is that he traded us in order to keep his uncle alive."

"Dear of him," Archer muttered.

"We'll write to Ari, the blacksmith fellow who was organizing the resistance in Two Falls. See that he gets Pieter out," Tarr said. "He and the others will have to be much more careful from here on out if they're going to stay alive."

"'They'?" Archer echoed, eyeing him shrewdly.

"Us," Tarr said quickly. "*We* have to be more careful."

Before them, a bird rose up into the air, carried aloft by a gust of sea wind. The bird eyed the two of them, its wings shifting infinitesimally back and forth as it caught the edges of the breeze. After a moment, it gave a lazy flap and soared off down the edge of the cliff.

"I don't suppose we'll be tracking down Morthenstar's heir very soon," Archer commented.

"No, I don't think so," Tarr agreed. "Our priorities have shifted somewhat." The prophecy and all its import seemed like a frivolous game compared to what they'd just been through. Tarr decided to change the subject. "So," he said conversationally in Ashan, "you still speak it after all."

"My grasp of it is probably terrible now," Archer returned obstinately in the Common tongue, not looking over at Tarr. "I haven't spoken it for years."

"Try," Tarr suggested, but Archer rocked his head side to side with indecision. "Why did you tell me that you did not speak it when I asked you?" Tarr inquired, still speaking Ashan.

There was a long stretch of silence before Archer spoke. He seemed to be wrestling inwardly. "It is a long story, Tarr," he haltingly returned in the same language. His accent was strange to Tarr's ears, as he had never spoken to any Northern Ashans before. It was more lilting, and the vowels were longer, more languorous. Tarr could see immediately the reflections of Archer's way of speaking the Common language. The humorous inflections he added to the ends of his sentences, Tarr realized, were a byproduct of the naturally melodic lilt of his Ashan accent.

"We have time," Tarr shrugged. "And what should I call you? I cannot call you Archer; it sounds very strange when said in Ashan."

"Do what you did before," Archer suggested. "Use the translation. I have no Ashan name."

Tarr wanted to press him further, but acquiesced. There would be time. "So, then, Archer," Tarr continued. "Why was it that you were exiled?"

Archer turned now and stared straight at Tarr with his intense golden eyes. He didn't respond for quite some time, and Tarr merely stared back at him, not intimidated by the hawklike gaze. Archer finally looked away, back to the gray sea rolling before them.

"I suppose that you would like to believe that I was exiled for some noble reason, something honorable," Archer flicked a small insect off his pant legs, then squinted up at the horizon.

"Was that what happened?" Tarr asked hopefully.

"No," Archer replied flatly in Common. "I killed another Ashan. A boy."

"Oh," Tarr could think of nothing else to say.

The Ashan boy's body reeled back a few steps. There was a startled look on his face as his hands groped numbly towards his chest, the blood spreading out like a scarlet flower opening its petals towards the sun. He wavered, a look of astonishment and pain clawing across his face before he finally wobbled and toppled into the snow. His arm sprawled across the ground, one hand still clawing at his chest before it gradually fell still. His reddish-orange eyes were still open, staring sightlessly into the void before him, gray hair gradually soaking up the melted water from the snow and clinging damply to his scalp. The spattered blood looked strangely beautiful against the white canvas.

Another Ashan boy was standing a little ways away from him, shirtless, up to his knees in the drift. His nostrils were flaring, steam coming off of his shoulders like rising mist. He was skinny, a green leaf tattooed on his narrow chest, blue-white skin, and black-tipped hair, his piercing golden eyes trained on the sight before him. He slowly looked from the still figure on the ground to his own hands. They were stained crimson, all over his palms and up his arms, over his twelve spiderlike fingers. He looked again. The fire, the burning *anger* that had absolutely consumed him moments before was still flaring and crackling within his chest. His mind skipped off in all directions. He wondered what it had been, what had been said to light the spark. He found that he couldn't remember. He couldn't even remember what the argument had been about. *How strange*, he thought vaguely.

His mind went in lurches, flashes of the struggle, the knife that he had pulled from his pocket—he still had it from harvesting bark in the morning, what now seemed like years ago. Peka's face, taunting, pulled back in rage, and then the fear, and then that grotesquely shocked expression. It was frozen now. The Ashan boy wished it would change. And when it didn't, he grew irritated and took a step forward, his baggy pants swishing softly through the knee-deep snow. His brow furrowed, his eyes focusing themselves, hawklike, on Peka's body. *Move*, he thought to himself. *Move.* "Move," he said out loud. "Move!" he shouted, but the other Ashan lay motionless, stiff, imprinted in the snow, outlined in a scarlet pool. And then the fire within his chest died out, and there was a horrible, sickening pull from his heart all the way down to his feet. "Move," he whispered. "Please move." But Peka didn't.

The Ashan let go of the dagger then, letting it fall with a whisper into the snowdrift. There were voices, people running towards him, shouts of anger, of fear. But the Ashan boy didn't hear them. He couldn't hear anything. Why wouldn't Peka move? The wind blew cold against his bare chest, but he didn't feel it. The coldness inside was much worse. He shook his head, uncomprehending. Then—hands were laid upon his arms, shouting, all of it just a dim echo. He was pulled backward, his feet unknowing and unwilling. He stumbled, off balance, but the hands at his arms just hauled him along, uncaring of any resistance he put up. There was chattering in his ear—*why do they sound like birds?* The boy wondered. They sounded just like a flock of birds calling hoarsely and roughly to one another from branch to branch.

Down they went through the clearing, dragging the young boy first, then the bloody body of Peka following, a cluster of others behind, all shouting and calling to one another, cursing the first boy, lamenting the second. One of them had the boy's sharp wooden harvesting knife in one hand, as if they needed any further proof. Further and further down the side of the mountain, until they reached the beginning of the birch wood in which their tribe had their homes. The trees were slender, but they were tall and strong, and the Ashan treehouses had stood for many, many years, longer than any of the surviving elders. Everything from the wood to the heavy seasonal windows was a pure, creamy white. It was winter there in the mountains, winter almost the entire year, save for a month or two of beautiful greenery and rejuvenation, where the trees could grow their leaves and soak up the sunlight. But for the rest of the time, it was a land of endless snow, harsh and cold and as wild as the mountains themselves.

The tribal houses were built in a series of concentric circles around the enormous meeting house, which lay at the very center of the birch forest. On a day like this, it looked—with the snow on the ground, the sky a forbidding shade of gray, and the Ashans themselves with their white skin and black, white, or gray hair—almost as if the entire world were monochrome. Everything except the eyes, the boy thought numbly as he was pulled along. The eyes were always brilliant, yellow, orange, red, ice blue, piercing green like emeralds. It was the eyes. And the blood still on his hands.

He was pulled up the largest tree in the center of the forest, upon which the foundation of the tribal meeting house was built. So many hands, on his back, on his arms, pulling, pushing, tugging so hard that he knew it would hurt if he could only manage to feel something, get the spark of life back into his limbs and skin. His golden eyes rolled around, taking in his surroundings uncomprehendingly. He hadn't even realized that they were going up, and then all of a sudden, they were through the door in the bottom of the meeting house, and he was pushed into the center of the cavernous circular room as the other members of his tribe filed through the opening around him like ants swarming out of a nest. Some eyed him with deep loathing and suspicion; others ignored him completely; some were crying, their shoulders racking with sobs. The inside of the room was a soft amber, but somehow the color seemed harsh and grating.

There was the billowing sound of the tribal horn, played on a hollowed-out tree trunk, the deep reverberations echoing through the forest, calling all the tribe together. It was used only in times of great emergency or on days of celebration. The boy stood at the center of the circle, unable to move as the other members of the tribe silently gathered around, sitting around him, staring at him from all sides with their glittering brilliant eyes. The boy didn't even care if they were looking. He saw his hands. The blood that had been so shiny, so red, had turned dull and brown, drying against his palm, his knuckles. If he looked closely, he could see the little cracks of the fabric of his skin peeking through.

The elders slowly came in, their heads of hair completely white, their glittering eyes like jewels. They watched the boy as they took their seats at the north side of the circle, the most holy point. And finally, a large Ashan man came through the trapdoor, the dead body of Peka in his arms. He laid the body down by the boy's feet and backed away, sitting in an open area near the southeast section of the circle. There was silence around the members of the tribe. The boy didn't bother to look at them.

There was always a ritualistic few minutes of silence before a tribal meeting. It was said that to sit back and say nothing would help clear the mind and help inform decisions. There was time enough for emotion to die down and for rational thought to take the upper hand. The Birch elders saw to it that nothing was ever done too hastily; no decision was ever made that was later regretted. It was their duty to the tribe, and they took it very seriously.

The chief elder was extremely thin and incredibly tall, her flesh stretched thinly out over the wireframe of her skeleton. She wore her hair cut close, unlike many of the other members of the tribe; some of the other women's hair even reached down to their shoulders. The chief, in her younger years, had had brilliant magenta eyes, but age had taken much of their color away so that they were now a dull red, the whites slightly yellow. Her voice shook slightly when she spoke. It was she who decided when the silence would be over.

"You have killed," she said finally, and the boy looked up. It was the first thing he had heard clearly over the rushing in his head and the throbbing in his ears since Peka had toppled over into the snow. "You have killed another member of your tribe. And it does not matter whether he insulted you, or whether he threatened you. It is the most grievous crime of all, to kill. You, as a member of this tribe, knew that before you let the blow fall. And you, as a member of this tribe, must now pay the price for what you have done. As long as you live, you will never cease to atone for what you have done."

The words fell upon the silent room. The boy could feel the eyes on his back, the condemning stares, the sympathetic gazes as they rested upon the dead body of Peka. Peka had not been exclusively liked amongst the tribe; he had a brash way of speaking that grated against their conservative ways. He hadn't been too bright, either—not like the boy at the center of the circle, who, even among the more dismissive older members of the tribe, was known to have a sharp and cunning mind, far more clever than most of the Ashans even three or four years older than his own nine years of age.

"You are hereby exiled from the Birch tribe," the chief elder said in a low voice. There was not so much as a whisper or a ripple from the silent faces staring back at him, merely a stiffening of shoulders, resilient set to their jaws that conveyed their unanimous approval at the decree of the elder. The boy heard the words but didn't feel them, just a sudden thud at the center of his chest. His legs buckled, but he controlled it. *Exile.* The word was foreign to him. He knew the meaning. Or at least he thought he did.

"You have no name," the elder continued. "You have never had a name. You have never been born. You never existed, nor were you ever a part of this tribe. We have not heard your voice, we do not recognize your laughter, we do not know the gait of your walk or the color of your eyes. While in form you are Ashan, in spirit you no longer are. You are a thing hated; you are a thing to be feared and despised. The Birch trees will never again support your weight, nor will their bark or leaves nourish your body. These mountains will forget that you ever stood upon them. You will never have a family, never have a history tattooed upon your spine. And when it is your body finally dies, you will walk, blind and unnamed, in search of a land that you will never find. You will never again plant roots in the earth."

The boy blinked, each word ringing in his ears like a bell.

"Go. And if you return to the land of the snow, your blood shall mark the spot." The elder finished this, the traditional Ashan curse of banishment, and closed her mouth, watching the boy closely with her eyes.

The boy took a step backward, his golden eyes wide. He swept along the rows of silent faces, searching for something, anything, but it might as well have been a wall barring him from his former tribesmen. There were his friends, those with whom he harvested bark and leaves, those with whom he laughed and told jokes. They looked foreign, alien to him now, their hooded expressions.

Behind him, a hand reached out and laid for him a pair of boots and a shirt. The boy's heel collided with them, and he stumbled, looking blindly towards the ground. He picked them up, sliding the boots up his long, gangly legs, lacing them slowly. The shirt he pulled over his head, and without another word, he opened the door in the floor and slid easily down the trunk landing in the snow below.

Go? He thought vacantly. *Where am I supposed to go?* He looked to one side, through the stark black-and-white trees to the sloping edge of the mountain. He looked to the other side. More trees, more bleached landscape, dotted here and there with the lavender shadows of footprints pressed into the snow. The wind whistled harder, picking up and ruffling his short black-tipped hair. The shirt he had been given was far too thin to keep him warm for very long; if he went north, there would just be more snow, more mountains to climb. He had been told vaguely of what was in the lands to the south; members of his tribe only traveled there if they weren't selected after the Choosing, and when they returned, few, if any, chose to speak of the lands they encountered.

But the boy didn't know where else to go, so he slowly turned south and began to walk, tucking his hands beneath his armpits and squinting into the oncoming wind. He did not look back as the tribal houses slowly dissolved into the gray sky. The snow blew around him in little flurries, catching on the tips of his hair and eyelashes, frosting over his dove gray eyebrows. The boy gritted his teeth and walked on. The feeling was furiously beginning to seep back into his limbs, painfully, horrifically. He was well-adapted to the cold, but this chill bit into every inch of his body like a series of stabbing knives.

Knives, he thought dully, and looked again at his rust-colored hands. The friction from the fabric of his shirt had rubbed some of it off, but it still looked as though he had some sort of disease, patches of his pale skin peeking through the reddish brown. He wondered if he could wash it off, but thought that if he stopped, the members of his tribe would find him and kill him. Would that be better? Would it be better to be dead as well? The fact that he wondered frightened him, and he pushed on harder, trudging through the snowdrifts. Even though he was tall for his age, the snow was now well above his knees, so he didn't so much walk as wade as he pressed forward through the blustering wind, tears streaming out of the corners of his eyes. Whether they were from the cold gale or from something else within him, the boy didn't know. He only knew that he had to keep on moving.

He walked for days through the frozen wood of the Birch tribe, sleeping when he could, eating bark peeled off of the sides of the trees, and holding snow in his mouth until it melted and he could drink it down. Not once did he see another Ashan, or anyone else for that matter. No one who could help him. His clothes were becoming tattered after the continuous wind and weather had whipped them around his thin body again and again. The boy wondered, *is the entire world made of snow?* He didn't know. He didn't think so. Where were the lands to the south, of which he had heard his fellow tribesmen speak?

And then, after seemingly endless days of walking, the ground tapered out. The snow slowly melted away, revealing dark earth and moss-covered boulders that divided the land between the Birch realm and the other tribes of Ashans. The boy stumbled forward, the last of the snow slipping off of the edges of his boots. He sat upon a nearby rock and looked around himself. He had never seen trees as large as these, so thick around that even if he had arms three times their normal length, he could not wrap them around the trunks. He looked up, squinting, and even with his razor-sharp eyesight could barely see where the canopy of the forest began; it seemed as if it were only a light green blur in the far distance. It was still slightly cold, being near the edge of the snow, but the sun shone in golden shafts through the branches onto the soft earth. The young Ashan breathed slowly, taking in the scent of rotting leaves and moist ground.

After having rested and regained some of his strength, he began to walk again. The trees were so different there that he had no idea what he could eat for food and what he couldn't. There was a bush only a short ways away from him that had small colored fruit nestled within its leaves—some of the fruit was red, some of it black, and it looked inviting to his hungry golden eyes. It looked a little bit like a type of berry he remembered collecting in the forest back home during the short harvesting months. He reached out and picked a few of the berries. He wasn't foolish enough, hungry as he was, to gulp all of them down. He hesitantly slid one berry into his mouth. It was dark and had a bumpy texture. He tested it gently with his tongue before he finally chewed it and swallowed, then waited, his heart pounding. The fruit was slightly sour but had a certain sweetness to it that appealed to him, and reminded him very much of the berries with which he was familiar. After a few minutes, when he found that he was still all right, he picked more, shedding the remains of his tattered shirt and putting as many berries as would fit into the cloth. He tied it and carried it along as he continued on his way.

Farther down the slope, his quick ears caught the sound of rushing water, and he turned, heading off towards it. He came upon a small but powerfully moving stream flowing south. He bent by the side of the clear water and ducked his hand in, scooping great mouthfuls and gulping them down, grateful that he didn't have to drink any more snow. He rubbed the water over his face and bare chest, scrubbing along his arms and over the green birch leaf tattoo he had been given in his fifth year. Pausing, he brushed his hand over the tattoo, then fastened his hand around a sharp-looking rock at the bottom of the stream. Perhaps it would be better if he were to scrape the tattoo off...but no, he thought quickly. It wouldn't do to lose that amount of blood while he was still hungry and fairly weak. He shook his head, droplets of water sprinkling out to either side, his short black-tipped hair spiking together. He sighed and glanced down the length of the stream. If he followed it, then he was sure to at least have a good water supply for the duration of his journey, and it was common sense that the stream would be heading somewhere. He stood, swinging the bag of berries beside him as he began walking again.

He followed the stream for days. Occasionally, he took to the trees when he was sure that there was absolutely no chance of any other Ashans seeing him or following him. Like all Ashans, he was far more comfortable in the trees—and what trees these were! It was sheer exhilaration as he ran easily up the side of one trunk and launched himself haphazardly into space, one long arm shooting out at the last moment to catch a branch and hurl himself back up into the boughs.

By night, he camped by the river, nestled in the crook of a branch and the trunk of a tree. If he heard something that startled or woke him, he would merely run farther up the tree and go to sleep once more. The first few nights had been horrible, with sounds of animals and birds he had never heard before hooting and cawing at all hours of the night. Initially, the boy had been sure that the wood was plagued with demons, but then he actually caught sight of a large owl with tufted ears making its mournful call, and he was no longer afraid. After a few days, he got to the point where he could sleep through almost anything.

During his travels, he encountered another tribe of Ashans three times, and each time he had kept his distance. He had seen the large round and square shadows of the treehouses, safely tucked away in the spreading boughs, black and foreboding from their perches. The boy would veer away from the river for a time until the treehouses were out of sight, then he would slowly make his way back and continue southward. On a couple of occasions, he even saw a few other Ashans, though they looked incredibly strange to him. Their skin wasn't white, as his was, but light or dark brown, and their hair was the same color as tree bark: honey, chestnut, ash brown, black. The first time he had seen one he hid for a time, wondering if there were, in fact, evil creatures lurking in the forest, but when he saw them take to the trees, and when he saw that except for their coloring they did resemble the members of the Birch tribe, he realized that they were nothing to fear. Still, he didn't want any of them to see him and to know he was an exile, to chase after him or try to kill him. Was his guilt written on his face? Would they know what it was that he had done? The blood had long ago been rubbed off of his hands, but the boy wasn't so sure.

After weeks of walking and living on nothing but berries, bark, and leaves, the boy's trail wove all the way down until he came upon a most intriguing sight. The shield of trees thinned out until there were no more left, and beyond them was a field and then a sheer rock wall, nearly as tall as some of the trees. And on that rock wall were two cascading sheets of water, truly beautiful to behold. Enraptured, the boy walked closer, his golden eyes wide and his mouth slightly open. He had never before seen anything so lovely in his entire life. The water fell to the ground, where it foamed in a huge pool of water at the base of the cliff. The stream that had led him there emptied into this pool, and from there the water flowed out of the pool in a western direction.

And, even more intriguing, there were people! He walked hesitantly forward, drawing nearer and nearer to the edge of the trees. The water roared out at him like one of the beasts he had heard during the night, but he was no longer afraid of such things. Yes, there were *people*, many of them, walking in a straight line like a group of ants the boy had once seen on a tree trunk during the short springtime in the mountains. They were all walking in the same direction on a narrow road that wound up the side of the rock wall. The boy thought that since the stream had ended, he might as well find another path to follow. If all of these people were headed in the same direction, there must be something at the end of it. He was determined to find out what it was.

He fell into line beside an old man and a young girl, who was perhaps a member of the old man's family. The man cast a single suspicious look at the odd-looking creature beside him. Embarrassed, the boy wished that his clothes weren't so ragged, that he had some way of hiding himself. The little girl, not knowing yet the rules of etiquette, stared unabashedly at the Ashan boy.

With a twinge of dismay, he saw that there were two people standing at the base of the path, blocking the way up the side of the cliff. The boy's eyes widened. They weren't Ashan! He could see that. They were short and certainly bigger around than any of the Ashans he had ever seen. And they were talking to each person as they walked past. The boy's heart fell even further as he got closer to the two men. They were talking in a strange way, not Ashan, not any dialect he had ever heard before in his life, quick and rough. It spun his head to even try and follow the words to pick out anything that he might find familiar. He had a horrible feeling that if he couldn't speak the correct words to the two men, they wouldn't let him go past. And he couldn't go back. He had to keep moving forward.

The old man and the little girl were ushered along. It was his turn. He stood in front of one of the men. Even though he was an Ashan of only nine, he stood as tall as this man. He couldn't help but stare. Not only was the man as large around as a tree trunk, but there was actually *hair* growing out of his *face!* The boy was at once nauseated and slightly fascinated. How could it be that the other people could stand to look at him and not want to run away in fear or exile him as well? The man said something in that odd language. The boy listened carefully, but not a single word made any sense to him. He slowly, regretfully shook his head, his cheeks burning red. Someone behind him in the line yelled out angrily. The boy didn't need to know the language to understand what had been said. The big man in front of him growled and called over his shoulder. In a few moments, a young woman approached them.

"Where you going?" she asked. The boy could have shouted in relief. She spoke in stilted Ashan, with an odd accent and far quicker than he was used to, but it was Ashan, and he could respond.

"I am going to the lands to the south," he replied, and the woman turned to the fat man and relayed this. The boy stared at her. She knew how to speak to him? Could it be possible that he, too, would learn how to speak the big man's language?

"Why is it that you have not been taught Common language?" the woman asked.

"I do not know what the Common language is," the boy replied honestly, tongue stumbling over the unfamiliar name.

"You are Ashan? What tribe?"

The boy opened his mouth, then closed it quickly. "I am not Ashan. I have no tribe."

A shadow passed through the eyes of the woman, but she obediently turned to the man and relayed his words. The man grunted and waved the boy along, clearly fed up with having anything to do with him. Blissful relief washed over him, and he stumbled forward a few steps, jogging to catch up with the old man and the little girl, the latter staring at him suspiciously underneath the old man's arm.

They went up and up until the young Ashan's legs began to ache with the effort of climbing. Finally, the ground leveled out and the clifftop flattened, and the boy strained his eyes to see what lay ahead. He let out a small gasp as he tried to take it all in.

The village was made up of more houses, more buildings than he had ever seen in his life; it seemed to stretch on forever, covering a large hill to the west and stretching out over the plain. Structurally, it looked like an Ashan village, but the houses were all inexplicably on the ground. Some were even built on what looked like tiny branches, perching themselves precariously over the rushing water of the river. The buildings were far larger than any of the treehouses the boy had ever seen, most of them even bigger than the tribal council house of the Birch tribe. He wanted to walk up to the nearest one and go inside, but as they drew closer, he saw that the line of people he'd been following up the cliff was spreading apart and going down separate paths in between the houses, none of them actually going in.

The boy tagged along behind one of the older women in front of him, but she started to weave away from the larger crowds and the boy became fearful that she was leading him into some sort of danger. He shied away and followed the next wave of passersby towards the center of the village. Sights and sounds assaulted him from all sides: people, more people than he had ever been close to, brushing past him and bumping him even though they were perfect strangers. Some of them looked at him strangely, and the boy couldn't help but be self-conscious again about his appearance. He ducked his head down, trying to avoid being seen, wishing that he had a shirt or jacket to cover his threadbare rags. He slipped along to the side of the street, out of the way of the bustling traffic, catching his breath, his eyes darting around like fluttering birds.

There were people everywhere, talking and jabbering to themselves in their odd, chattery language. Was he the only one who didn't know how to speak to them? The boy was startled as he realized that most of the people around him were as tall or shorter than he was. Were they not fully grown? He had certainly heard of humans before, but he had never been told what they looked like, what their customs were. It was all so strange. And then, all at once, he heard something peculiar, something like the sound of the tribal alert, the low, hollow, sonorous tone that called the tribe together. But it was lighter, and its tone changed. Frowning, he stepped back out into the street and followed the sound until he came to stand in front of a man with a small round wooden object in his lap, a long wooden plank coming out of one side. There were strings stretching across it, and the man pressed and plucked with his fingers. Miraculously, sounds came out, beautiful and sad at the same time. The boy stood as if in a trance. The sounds were so strange; they made him want to weep and smile, to move and to stand stock still. He stood there for a full fifteen minutes before the man with the object looked up at him curiously and with an edge of suspicion. The boy was startled by the sudden attention and backed up hurriedly, not wanting to attract any more notice than he had to.

He walked down the street, which emptied out into a wide plaza much as the stream he had followed through the forest emptied into the pool at the base of the waterfalls. Even more people were here, and the boy sank to one side, completely overwhelmed. There were strange smells wafting towards him, and his golden eyes caught sight of a series of stands across the square, bearing bright cartons of what looked like some sort of fruit like the berries he had found in the forest. His stomach gave an unkind lurch as he remembered exactly how hungry he was. He had lived on nothing but bark, leaves, berries, and water for the past weeks, and the diet was beginning to take a toll on him. He walked across the square, weaving in and out of people until he reached the stands. He realized that this area must be the place where the members of the village brought together their harvest for all the people to eat, and waves of relief washed over him as he understood.

An older woman was sitting on a stool behind one of the stands and eyed him narrowly as he approached her. He smiled to reassure her that he wasn't going to attack or harm her in any way. The fruit in the stand shone brightly with care, and the colors dazzled him as much as any of the other things he had seen in the strange town. He reached out and took a piece of fruit, smiling again at the woman. "Thank you," he said in Ashan, hoping that she would understand that he was grateful for the nourishment she had supplied him. He turned and began walking away when suddenly there was a terrific yell from behind him, and he whipped around, his eyes wide with alarm. The woman had leaped off her stool and dived towards him, her eyes like slits, shrieking noisily at him. The boy was so startled that he raised his arms to protect himself, and the woman walked towards him and began cuffing his head, still shrieking at him. The boy was abjectly confused; he looked from the woman to the piece of fruit in his hand. Hoping to placate her, he extended it, and she snatched it out of his hand and walked away, still huffing and muttering to herself. The boy backed away a hesitant step, hoping that he could escape without any further problem. When it seemed like she would let him go, he spun and began to stride as fast as he could away from her, trying to ignore the accusing stares of the people close to the woman's stand.

What kind of tribe was *this?* the boy wondered to himself. They set up displays of food, far more food than they could eat, no matter *how* big they were. But when a member of the tribe tried to share the food, it was snatched away. He looked back over his shoulder, saw people approaching the stands, trading the food, saw the woman still glaring at him from atop her stool. He looked quickly back around and kept on walking. Maybe it was because he was Ashan, not a member of their tribe. Maybe it was because he was an exile. Maybe the blood *was* still on his hands; maybe his guilt *was* written on his face. So what was he to do? Starve? He crept along the side of the walls until he found a space large enough for him to sit, in between the stairs of one house and the side wall of a building. There were no trees anywhere to be seen, nowhere where he could climb and be safe. He crept into the open area and curled his long legs in front of him, tucking his arms around them and hiding his head behind his knees. He watched the people go past the small enclosure, and when he felt their curious glances, he lowered his brilliant golden hawk's eyes. And then, after a time, exhausted and hungry, he drifted off to sleep.

He slept through the rest of that day, all the way through the night and well into the next morning. Eventually he awoke, disoriented. He lashed out with one arm, thinking himself captured, but then relaxed and remembered with dismay where he was. He thought wistfully about waking up in his treehouse back in the safety and comfort of the tribe, with a light snow falling outside. He shook his head. That life was long gone.

More pressing was the problem of food. He had no idea why it was that he had been denied the single piece of fruit, but with no trees or berry bushes in sight and little or no inclination to tromp all the way back to the forest to get sustenance, the boy decided that he would have to try something different. The equation was absolutely simple in his mind. The woman had food. He needed food. She had far more than she could ever hope to eat herself; he had none. She would not give; therefore, he must take. Thievery was an unknown concept to the Ashans of his tribe—what one owned, the entire tribe owned. If one did not have enough food, the rest of the tribe supplied one with food. The boy knew better than to think that every single town outside the forest would operate in the same way as his tribe back home, but it seemed so *logical* that he couldn't fathom it any other way.

The only question was how to do it. He knew that he shouldn't approach the woman with the stand that he had been to before; he would be too easily recognized. He had received enough curious stares to realize that he would be very easily remembered.

He scoped out his first target carefully. Another fruit vendor, which seemed like the easiest quarry. He didn't recognize any of the vendor's wares and longed for something familiar, but reminded himself that since this would be his home from now on, he would have to change everything from the way he spoke, to his clothes, to what he ate. He was no longer Ashan. That was something that he had to remember.

He crept closer to the vendor. It was another older woman, whose eyes passed carelessly over him as he walked casually by. The boy stopped and glanced over his shoulder. The woman turned in her seat and began talking to the woman in a stall farther down the row. The woman she was speaking to was busy arranging the food in the front of her stall. Now was his chance. His heart was pounding, though at a flat-out run there was no way the woman could catch him. The vendor had completely turned to the side. Smoothly and swiftly, the boy slipped by, his fingers shooting out and scooping up a piece of fruit. He gritted his teeth and held his breath, waiting for the outbreak of shouting and scolding, but none came.

Elated, he walked faster and sat down by a large enclosed pool of water in the center of the square. He began to eat the fruit, feeling the sugar coursing through his body. The light shone a bit brighter around him, and suddenly, the hunger that had been gnawing at his stomach came back with a huge, ravenous force. He sat straight up, looking around for other vendors he could take food from. One of them, on the east side of the square, was completely unattended. The boy stood and walked towards it with focused purpose. He wasn't sure exactly what food item was being offered; frankly, he didn't even care. He approached and walked by, slipping his hand over the front of the stall, snatching up a stick with a number of round, soft brown objects stuck along its length. He walked out of the square this time, turning the corner. He inspected what it was that he had taken. He sniffed it. It smelled strange but inviting. Steam billowed off of it. He took a small bite from one of the brown lumps and yelped slightly. Whatever it was was extremely hot, and he blew on it a few times until the steam died down. He took a larger bite. It was chewy, rather like the softened bark that used to be served at the tribal festivals. It tasted good. He gulped the rest down, feeling slightly more satiated. He knew, though, that he would have to wait a while before he returned. Perhaps there were more areas like this in the village; it was so large that surely there would be more than one gathering point.

He wound his way around the streets, feeling more and more

confident with every single step he took. More open plazas were to be found, and everywhere he went, the boy collected food, gobbling his prizes hungrily. When the sun went down, he found another small area to sleep, and though he was racked with severe stomach pains throughout the night, it was better than being hungry. In the morning, he was up again, searching for food. This time, he wasn't so lucky. He was caught at the second stand he visited, and he ran as fast as he could the other way, even going so far as to scamper up the side of a building and rest on the roof, watching as his pursuers went the opposite direction. It took a while to calm his pumping heart, but then he descended and headed to the other side of the village, waiting for a few hours before he got up the courage to try again. But this time, he was successful, and his confidence began to rise.

And, for a number of days, this was how the boy made his life. He slept outdoors even in the rain, shirtless, his boots and clothes wearing away. Some nights, when he rounded the corner of an alleyway, he was confronted with the sight of another man being beaten, his things taken from him. The first few times, he had shrunk back, unsure of what to do. He didn't know whether such behavior was permitted in this town or if it was as forbidden as in his tribe. But, as the occurrences continued, he began to assume that such things were to be expected. It was right, he concluded, that they sent him here. He was no better than any one of the knots of people he had seen, armed with fists and knives, converging on someone sorely outnumbered.

During the days, he gathered food where he could. Sometimes he was caught, sometimes he wasn't. One lady, a kind older woman with a round belly and gray hair, would give him food whenever she saw him and never scolded him. He liked her, but he couldn't help but feel that somehow he was cheating her, so he didn't visit her as often as he could have. Occasionally, he forgot where he had visited before and was chased away before he could even make his approach; the sellers were quickly starting to remember him. He had to get quieter, more stealthy, more careful. He was living. But it was less than what the boy had wanted. Something had to change.

One morning he was making his usual rounds, swiping fruit where he could find it. He was chomping through the remains of an apple, sitting at the fountain in the middle of the square, when a woman sat down beside him, closer than he was used to. The boy shot an insecure glance her way, then edged over so as to be farther away.

"You have stolen that," the woman beside him said in clear, idiomatic Ashan. The boy nearly dropped the fruit, his eyes swinging hopefully up, wishing to see a familiar, friendly face. But what faced him was obviously a human. Hooded eyes, striking in a reserved sort of way, a brush of light brown hair curving over her forehead. She seemed small, even for one of the women of this village. The boy stared at her curiously for a few moments, and the woman stared back, a pleasant smile on her face.

"Stolen?" the boy echoed the strange word incredulously, his mouth still full of fruit.

"You have taken it without paying," the woman returned.

"Paying?"

The woman laughed, though it was not mocking. It was gentle, patient, as if the boy were a small child who had just fallen from the lowest branch of a tree while trying to show off. "In this village, you must exchange something in order to be given food. You may not merely take food. You must pay for it."

"I have nothing to pay with," the boy pointed out reasonably.

"No, I imagine not," the woman chuckled.

"You are not Ashan," the boy observed, his mind still turning over the concept of payment. He gulped down the last bite of apple.

"No, I am not. You are Ashan?"

The boy blinked. "No."

"I see," the woman murmured. "What is your name?"

"I have none."

"You are an exile."

The boy did not reply to this. He was almost embarrassed to. But the woman didn't turn away or look at him with disgust. It was the same sort of kindness in those hooded eyes, welcoming, almost inviting. The boy wanted to trust her so desperately it frightened him. He drew back.

"Where have you been living?" the woman asked.

"In the city, near the sides of the tribal houses."

"Just houses," the woman smiled again. "They are just called houses here. There are no tribes in this village. Every person is their own tribe in some ways." She paused, regarding the boy with a cautious eye. "Would you like a place to stay? Food? Shelter? I can teach you how to speak the language of this place. I can teach you its ways. I can teach you how to survive."

"Why?" the boy asked. He was suspicious at how appealing the offer sounded. "Is it as you said? I must pay you in order for you to give me food?"

"No," the woman laughed. "I have seen you in the streets from time to time. You are quick. You could help me. That will be payment in time. Besides," she added, smiling again, with only a hint of it actually in her eyes. "My wife is Ashan, and she encourages me to help those I find in need in the city."

"She is Ashan?" the boy asked apprehensively. "Then she will surely be disgusted to have me in her house."

"You are not Ashan, I thought," the woman asked, eyes twinkling. "I see no reason why she should mind."

The boy gulped again. There was a certain amount of apprehension in his heart, though he didn't know why. He had never had reason to be distrustful of any creature before he came to this strange land, but things were different here. Still, the offer of food and shelter was too much for him to pass up. He nodded, slowly, finally. The woman smiled. "My name is Nikaila, but you may call me Niko."

Niko's house was on the eastern side of the city, and when the boy was led inside, he could scarcely believe his eyes. The Ashan treehouses had always been spare and strictly arrayed for practical purposes, but in this house the boy saw things on the walls and on the tables that could have nothing to do with survival. He reached out and touched something shiny and metallic hanging above a bench, then immediately pulled his hand back, abashed at having overstepped himself.

Noticing suddenly that Niko was watching him with not a small amount of amusement, the boy withdrew immediately, ducking his head. Inwardly, his head was spinning. This wasn't so much like an evil place, was it? There was magic here, he was sure of it. He followed Niko through the hallways in the house, and the boy was startled by the sheer size of the enclosure, far bigger than even the council meeting house had been. They walked out into a square open area in the middle of the house, and the boy was pleased to see that there were trees there, a long patch of grass with flowers and bubbling water in the center. He walked forward eagerly, sitting down on the grass. It was so rare to see things like leaves and flowers. For the few months when the ground had sopped up the snow and the trees shot forth their green leaves into the gentle sunlight, it was celebrated day in and day out within the tribe; the Birch collected their food for the year of following winter. But the marvel before him seemed almost commonplace to his companion. Niko didn't even bother to look at the flowers or grass as she approached.

"So," Niko said conversationally, watching as the young Ashan boy walked to the fountain and dipped his hand in it, feeling the cold water rushing off from either side of his palm. "This is my house, and you are welcome here. I have sent word to the servants that food should be brought out. But, in the meantime, we must start looking to your future. What skills do you have? What is it that you know how to do?"

The boy paused, frowning. He knew how to climb trees, but in a place such as this, where trees were only to be found in special sections of the town, he didn't think that that would be much use. He knew how to track, he knew how to harvest bark, but again, he didn't think that this would help him survive. But then he remembered the people he had seen in the alleyway. "I know how to fight. To...steal? And to kill," he said quietly.

Niko took this in with only a fraction of a batted eye. "Interesting," she murmured. "Your eyesight, is it good?"

"Yes."

"Wait here," she commanded, and walked off. The boy wondered for a few moments what Niko could have in mind, then was distracted again by the blooms surrounding the small garden. He heard Niko approach a few moments later and turned. The woman was now carrying something: a long wooden arc and a bag with odd items in it, which looked like short, straight branches with feathers in one end. The boy stood up, keen to learn about this new marvel.

"This is a 'bow,'" Niko told him, holding up the long wooden arc, saying its name clearly in the Common tongue. "And these are 'arrows,'" she gestured with the full bag. The boy's golden eyes were wide, taking it in as best as he could. "You use the bow to shoot the arrows, and it is called 'archery.' One who shoots such things is called an 'archer.'"

"Archer," the boy repeated in the strange language, the word sounding foreign to his mouth, but not unpleasant. "Arrows, bow."

"Very good," Niko said. "Now, watch carefully."

She set down the bag of arrows and withdrew one. The boy saw that at the other end, the unfeathered one, there was a nasty-looking piece of pointed stone. Niko picked up the bow and set the feathered end of the arrow against the string. Then she fluidly moved it up, arching her back and pulling the long string. Then, suddenly, she released her hand, and the arrow sped forward with a mighty hiss, lodging squarely in a wooden beam holding up the second-floor balcony a good distance from them. A gasp had escaped the boy's lips at the sudden action, and his eyes sped back and forth from Niko to the arrow lodged quietly and neatly in the wood.

"Now you try," Niko instructed, handing him the bow, withdrawing an arrow, and holding it ready for him. The boy reached out uncertainly, grasping the bow. It was slick and smooth with polish; he could tell that it had been well cared for. He took the arrow, saw a small notch at one end where he assumed the arrow should be fitted onto the string. He aligned the two; felt the resistance as he pulled back, the thrum of pain as the string dug into the skin of his fingers, unsure of his strength and whether he would break the bow if he pulled too hard. He raised it slowly and fired haphazardly; the arrow only flew a small way before falling to the ground. But there had been a moment there when it had all made sense; he knew exactly what he had done wrong even before Niko had begun to gently correct him. The arrow had been too far down the string; he had been too afraid to pull back completely. That was his fault. He had to let go of whatever fear he had. He grabbed at another arrow, eager to try again. His fingers were more assured, confident in their placement. The arrow slid comfortably into place, and he raised the bow again, this time pulling back as fully as he could, arching his body as he had seen Niko do.

"Sight down the shaft, you'll be able to aim better that way," Niko counseled. The boy responded, leaning his head slightly to the side as if the bow was an old friend of his. He kept both eyes open as he sighted towards his target, pulling back, enjoying the strain of the bow against him. It was as if he was in a tug of war with it, each trying to outlast the other's strength. He waited until the tension had built to the ultimate degree before he released his hold, and the arrow sped forward towards the wooden beam, striking it and glancing off to one side.

Niko watched the boy carefully as he lowered the bow, and saw the visible disappointment on his face at his seeming failure. Getting the arrow to fly anywhere near a target on only the second try was almost unheard of. She had seen the look of an archer in the boy's eyes the first time she saw him, calculating, able to be swift or take his time. The boy didn't even bother to ask Niko for pointers, but silently reached for another arrow, fitting it and aiming. Again, the arrow glanced to the side. But the boy showed no signs of impatience or frustration, merely dogged determination as he reached again and again into the bag for another arrow. And when, at last, an arrow struck home, remarkably close to the shot fired by Niko, the boy lowered the bow with a look of satisfaction that told Niko that no accolade she could give would improve the boy's spirits.

The boy walked forward to collect the arrows lying on the ground around the beam, leaving the one he had shot successfully lodged in the wood. He returned to the patch of grass and prepared to go again. This was something he couldn't explain. It was as if the bow and the arrow were both extensions of his own body that had been separate from him until that very moment; now that they were reunited, there was nothing to keep them from working as an efficient machine. The boy had little or no idea what Niko had in store for him—he still didn't quite know whether to trust her—but for introducing him to this new wonder, the boy could do little other than thank her. He didn't notice when Niko slowly backed away, leaving the boy to his own operations.

A few hours later, Niko was watching from a second-story window when her wife approached from behind her, looking out into the courtyard at the sight of the tall, slender Ashan boy firing the bow and arrow over and over again, his speed, skill, and accuracy improving with every new shaft that now thudded confidently into the wooden beam.

"Your new project?" she observed with amusement. "Doing some repairs to the house's foundation?"

Niko shook her head. "He's the most natural shot I've ever seen. I'll be damned if he's not the top assassin in this town by the time he's fourteen."

"Strong words," her wife said. "Found him on the streets?"

"Yes."

"What's he like?"

"Seems nice enough. Doesn't talk much. Probably completely shell-shocked from being thrown out of his tribe. He's very young for an exile."

Niko's wife chose her words delicately. "There's nothing *wrong* with him, you think?"

"No," Niko frowned as the boy walked forward to collect his arrows another time. "No. I think he'll be all right."

"How long will you train him?"

"With the speed he's going, not long," Niko commented wryly. "But there are other things. We have to teach him to speak the Common tongue, for one thing. Have to teach him how to function."

She looked at her affectionately. "You know, half the time I think you don't do this for the profit," she said with mock accusation. "One would almost believe that you have a soft heart under there."

"Me?" Niko deadpanned. "Certainly not."

"Have the girls met him yet?" her wife asked.

"Kai and Rowan?" Niko asked distractedly. "No, where are they?"

"Should be coming home from their lessons soon," she replied and scrunched her nose, trying to gauge the time of day.

"Come down and meet him," Niko urged. "I think he would like to speak with someone who can converse in Ashan more freely than I can."

"All right," she returned, and swept her sleek brown hair over one shoulder with her hand, following her wife down to the courtyard. The boy heard them from far off, turning around and lowering the bow. He greeted the new face with a hesitant smile that wasn't much more than a thin tightening of his lips. Niko's wife took in his appearance. He was a good-looking young boy; his long, angular features and striking coloring made him all the more intriguing. There was a desperate vulnerability in the appealing expression on his face. She liked him immediately, her concerns about his behavior fading instantly.

"My wife, Carina," Niko swept a hand back and forth between them.

"What is your name?" she asked, smiling, not expecting a reply.

The boy opened his mouth as if unsure what to reply. He looked down at the instrument in his hand and thought for a few moments before looking back up, an expression of conviction in his eye. "Archer," he said firmly, with a smile that showed his teeth. "My name is Archer."

Tarr was silent for a few minutes after Archer had finished talking, processing the story he had just heard.

Archer leaned forward on his long arms. "I was younger than Si," he said, his voice full of wonderment, as if he were looking back at the life of someone quite separate from himself. "I was young, impulsive, and stupid," he paused for a moment, a flash of the old grin. "As opposed to now, when I am less impulsive, slightly older, and stupid. But I killed that boy back in my tribe. Over *nothing*. Over something I can't even remember now."

"Did you mean to kill him?" Tarr asked.

"Yes and no," Archer tilted his head to one side. "When you fight someone, you mean to inflict the most damage possible, don't you? Well, *you* might not know what I mean. But I remember the feeling. I was seized with my rage against him. Was it truly my intention to kill him? No, it was not. Should anyone be surprised that it happened? No, they should not."

Tarr glanced over at his friend, who was staring quietly out at the ocean, though he didn't seem to be taking in the scenery anymore. "Do you regret it?"

"I don't know," Archer said. "I regret it for his sake. He should not have died. But for my sake? I don't know."

Tarr wasn't sure he quite understood what Archer meant, and was reluctant to press him any further. They sat in silence again for a little while, the tall grass beneath them crushed down into a sort of cushion, the free blades waving about, tickling their necks as they bent close. Tarr thought for a moment, tried to take stock of what he was feeling. He *had* hoped that Archer's crime had been one of martyrdom and sacrifice. But now that he knew the truth, he found that he felt no different towards the Ashan than he had before.

"What happened to Niko?" Tarr asked. "The woman who took you in?"

Archer shrugged. "I grew up in their family. Alongside their youngest daughters, Kai and Rowan. Rowan, you already know, of course, from the club back in Two Falls. But Niko and her wife split up eventually; her wife went back to her tribe in the forest. I was sixteen, old enough to get into trouble on my own by then. Niko left Two Falls a couple of years later. I haven't seen her since."

Archer's tone was casual, but there was a hollow ring of abandonment to it. Tarr glanced sidelong at him as Archer inspected the edge of his boot and toyed with one of the laces.

"As soon as I learned enough Common to get by, I never spoke Ashan again," Archer said, fiddling with the bottoms of his pants. "I thought that that part of my life was over."

"I understand," Tarr said. *But it's not the same for me*, he thought. There was much about Archer's story with which he could identify. But he had a home he could go back to. The time to return was drawing closer with every passing day.

Feeling suddenly out of sorts, he glanced around at the waving grass and the sea around them. He squinted, seeing to his right a distant speck in the middle of the sea, black, close to the land. "Look over there," he lapsed into Ashan, nudging Archer with his elbow. "Is that Faridor?"

Archer trained his eagle-sharp eyes to where Tarr was indicating. "Yes," he replied, a note of distaste in his voice. "That is Faridor."

"We are closer than I thought we were."

"I would not worry about Cira finding us here. She will be searching Two Falls, maybe Riddleton, where she knows we have contacts."

Tarr stared towards the speck. It looked like no more than a tiny rock, something he could flick with his finger and send careening out into the middle of the ocean and never see again.

CHAPTER TWENTY-SIX

The Strikers' recovery came in fits and starts: periods of thrilling advances followed by long stretches of no improvement at all. Athela, who was one of the hardest hit, was past the point of danger but spent most of her days in a medicated daze or sleep. Laith, however, was up and walking around after only a day or two. On the third day, Tarr even accompanied him outside, more than a little overwhelmed by the sight of the prince's weakness. He leaned heavily on Tarr's shoulder for support, and could only go a short distance before becoming exhausted. Tarr thought it best not to tire him out, but Laith told him staunchly that he had done quite enough healing during his service as a soldier and knew exactly what he was doing. Tarr thought it best not to argue.

After a short time, Marc and Rane awoke as well. Marc nearly broke his stitches clambering out of his bed to make sure that Laith and Si were all right, but once he had been assured that the prince's life wasn't in any danger, he returned to his bed without further protest. His wounds weren't as bad as the others, though Silva ordered him to stay bedridden for another couple of days, just in case. Rane slept a great deal, and Tarr spent long hours sitting beside her so that he would be there in the event that she woke up.

With his friends still on the mend, Tarr had many hours to while away in the huge house, and spent considerable time wandering around through one hallway and down the next. As he'd assumed when they first arrived, it was a place clearly designed to house many more people than the four that currently lived there; there were entire rooms where the furniture was covered with white sheets, ostensibly to protect against dust. It gave the rooms a ghostly, haunted air, like a forest blanketed with snow. Portraits of family members lined the walls, many of whom bore passing resemblance to Silva and her brothers.

In quiet moments his mind would drift off, and a distant, increasingly nagging voice piped up, telling him he no longer belonged with the others. At first he chalked the feeling up to despondency related to Wolver's sudden, unexpected disappearance during the fight in the alley. He hadn't fully realized how attached he was to the wolf, and kept staring out of his window, searching the horizon in vain for a speck of white. He imagined Wolver suddenly reappearing on Silva's front doorstep, greeting him with a thump of his tail and an expectant expression implying that dinnertime was close at hand. But days passed, and Wolver did not materialize. Eventually, Tarr resigned himself to the fact that, for whatever reason, Wolver was gone for good. But the nagging questions he left behind—where he'd come from, why he'd followed Tarr that first day in the forest, why he left without saying goodbye—still plagued Tarr's mind as he lay in bed awake at night.

Eventually, Tarr was finally able to speak to Silva about the history of the old house. She confirmed that long ago, generations before she and her brothers were born, nearly two entire branches of her family had resided in the house, along with servants and staff to run the stables. It sounded to Tarr like a slightly smaller version of the systems in place at the palace at Joymaril. When he'd tentatively asked about what had changed the family's fortunes, Silva hadn't been at all abashed to tell him: the family's money, she said, had gradually dwindled over the years. Some family members left to seek opportunities across the sea; others had succumbed to old age, and still others (Silva's parents included) to illness. It sounded like quite a lonely life, and after hearing her tale, it was no wonder to him that the halls seemed haunted by the spirits of the full, happy household that had once lived there. Tarr imagined that Silva especially was glad to have them there, thankful for their company and for the respite from her otherwise insular life. She went from room to room, silver hair tied back at the nape of her neck in a thick, shining knot, delivering medicine and fresh water and bandages with a light step and an easy smile—the latter came easiest for Laith.

There were many books in the large mansion, and Tarr gobbled them up: collections of poetry and local songs, legends and folk tales. He was especially fond of those relating to the history of Two Falls and Joymaril and Vireg, the country across the sea. Some of the books even had illustrations, which Tarr studied with astonishment. Vireg was apparently a desert, which he learned meant that there was very little water and almost no vegetation. Tarr could barely wrap his head around it, nor the few drawings there were of the city and palace and royal tombs, all of which seemed to have sprung fully formed out of the sea of sand beneath.

He was curious to read more about the history of the Jelani, too, since by that point, he'd spent a great deal of time with a handful of them (and even had the dubious honor of occupying a cell in Joymaril's dungeon for a short period of time.) He was curious as to whether they were really a separate race from humans, as they seemed to like to present themselves; from what he had seen, and from what Marc had once told him, they were virtually indistinguishable from each other. After a few hours of reading, all he could suss out was that early Jelani had emigrated from a distant land across the sea and had the business sense to capitalize on the abundant natural resources of their new country. In essence, they were nothing more than humans with a lot of money, a tendency towards blond hair, and a penchant for self-mythologizing. Tarr was mildly disappointed to have the Jelani legend dimmed in such a way, though he took some comfort in the humorous irony of it all.

There was even one book that contained some accounts of the Ashans. At first, Tarr's interest was piqued to read an outside perspective on his own people and culture, but he soon found that the book was inaccurate to the point where he couldn't be sure whether to laugh or to be deeply offended (eventually, he found himself hovering somewhere between the two.) All at once, he could perhaps understand why he had been met with skepticism by some of the people of Two Falls and Joymaril when he'd first arrived. There were accounts of forest Ashans not washing themselves properly and not cooking their food, as well as bold statements declaring that their homes were rudimentary and their tools primitive. Most infuriatingly, the book implied that once an Ashan had "assimilated" and adopted the customs and language of humans, some (but not all) of this inherent Ashan incivility would be forgiven.

All of it was so outrageous that Tarr had trouble understanding how it could have come to be published in the first place. He was struck with a deep sense of injustice that he couldn't march straight up to the misguided author and give them a piece of his mind. He thought, too, how many people must have read the book and based their assumptions about traditional Ashan culture on what they'd read. The thought made him slightly ill.

When the opportunity arose, he asked Silva about the book he'd found. She scrunched up her nose quite prettily and said that she'd never read it, that it had belonged to her grandfather. She seemed quite unconcerned about the whole situation, and her answer actually made Tarr feel even more gloomy, since it was apparent that these prejudices and inaccurate accounts had persisted in Two Falls and the surrounding human lands for some time. After that, he lost interest in perusing the library and, the rest of the house having been thoroughly explored, found himself sinking deeper and deeper into a well of his own thoughts. His ennui was only temporarily alleviated on the occasions of his evening walks with Archer along the edge of the sea cliffs. Though they often lapsed into long stretches of silence, he never felt alone. For the first few days during their walks together he scanned the surrounding land, hopeful that Wolver would suddenly reappear beside him, but there was no sign of him. A strange sinking in his chest told him that, for whatever reason, the wolf was gone for good.

Shortly after Tarr and Archer had set out on one of their outings, Laith went creakily into his room and walked over to sit beside Marc, who was upright but had reluctantly been ordered to rest for one more day before attempting to get up and move about.

"How's the outside world?" Marc asked with a resigned sigh.

"Cold," Laith grimaced. "And wet. It's not helping with my aches, I can tell you." He rubbed a hand on his knee and adopted an expression of self-deprecation. "I'm feeling my age these days."

The two young men laughed, and then, after a moment, Marc's face sobered. "I heard about what you were told. About Ilaina."

Laith looked at him sharply. "It's not true. They lied. If she were gone, I would know."

Marc opened his mouth to reply, perhaps to gently reason with the prince, but then thought better of it. "I'm sure you're right," he agreed. "She's clever. She'll have gotten herself out of it."

"I'm just surprised she hasn't sent word yet," Laith frowned.

Marc looked at him sadly. Tentatively, he said, "Cira may have seized control before she moved to Faridor. The whole city may be locked down."

Laith glanced at him sidelong. "Have you...have you had any word from Oren?"

Marc shook his head. "No."

Laith nodded. "I figured. I figured if you had heard from him while we were in Two Falls, you would have said something."

"I barely had time to see him before we had to get everyone out of the dungeons and make a run for it," Marc's eyes drifted, a faraway look taking them over. "It all happened so fast. And then we've been scrambling ever since."

"You..." Laith rooted around for the right words. "You think you would feel it? If he was gone? You would, wouldn't you? Because you love him."

"I do," Marc replied thoughtfully. "I do love him. I haven't felt anything, so I guess...I guess what we have to do is hope. Hope for the best. Hope that they made it out, and that we'll see them when all of this is over. Or if they manage to escape."

Laith nodded firmly, as if satisfied with this answer. "That's right. You're right. That's the best thing to do."

Marc couldn't bear to look at Laith's resolute face any longer and occupied himself for a few moments with the pretense of adjusting one of the bandages on his side. In a short while, Laith touched his shoulder and stood; Marc could hear the creak of his mattress across the room as he settled down into it. After a few minutes Marc pretended to be asleep, though in reality he was wide awake. He listened carefully to the sounds of Laith's breathing to see if he had fallen asleep as well, but the prince, to the best he could gather, was lying motionless, staring up at the ceiling above. Marc's heart lay heavy within his chest.

After a few sleepless hours, Laith stole back out of the room and went over to Athela and Rane's room to check on their progress. He was surprised to see that Archer, returned from his walk with Tarr, was seated beside the unconscious Athela, paging through the first few pages of a book.

"I—oh, hello, Laith," Archer said, leaping to his feet and casting the book down as soon as he realized that the prince was standing behind him. "I was about to start reading something aloud. I figure it's worth a shot. Athela would cross the eternal sands of time in order to get me to shut up," he grinned.

Laith managed a small laugh and sat down across from him. They were silent for a few moments, both watching Athela as she slept. "She's been through a lot," Laith said suddenly.

Archer nodded. "I'm glad she's going to make it through. She's a fighter."

"That's not exactly what I meant," Laith shook his head. "Her life... hasn't been easy. She was a princess, yes, but people have been building up her hopes and betraying her and trying to bump her off since she was old enough to walk. She didn't have a single friend in that palace until Marc and I came back from the Meadows." He paused. "She was fourteen. Fourteen years essentially alone."

Archer made no response. He looked back over to Athela. Her chest softly rose and fell; her hand draped loosely over her stomach. It looked almost as though her brow were furrowed with worry as she slept. He tugged the blanket up a little higher.

"I know," Laith continued awkwardly, "that it's all mostly a game for you. I don't know any details, and I don't want to, but I want to ask you, as a favor, both for myself and for her...if you don't mean it, don't lead her on. Because it won't be something she could take lightly."

Archer looked sharply up at him.

Laith winced and pushed himself higher in the chair, where his wounds weren't affected by the rough wood. "Be kind," he concluded finally. "Be kind to her."

THE STRIKERS

Archer managed a lopsided grimace. "Quite the warning."

"Not a warning," Laith countered. "A request. On behalf of someone I care deeply for."

Archer seemed on the verge of making some sort of witty quip, but thought the better of it and fixed Laith instead with a resolute nod. Laith stood from his chair and placed a hand on Archer's shoulder. "Come and get me if there's any change," he said, and shuffled painfully out of the room. Archer sat motionless for some time, watching Athela's steady breathing. Finally, he kicked his long legs up to rest on Laith's vacated chair, and tossed the book into one hand, flipping to page one.

"'Chapter one,'" he read aloud. " 'My long, arduous journey begins.'" He lowered the novel, looking disgruntled. "I tell you what," he said to Athela's sleeping form, "unless this book improves considerably from its first chapter, you had better wake up soon."

The next day was crisp and cool; fall was settling in, and winter was just around the corner. "Up you go," said Marc, hoisting Si against his shoulder. The boy's knees wobbled and nearly buckled, but Marc hung on tight to him, propping him up. Si winced in pain and hung on doggedly, his teeth gritted with determination.

"I've got it," he croaked through his clenched jaw. "I'm going to make it outside if it's the last thing I...blasted...well...do!"

"Watch your language," Marc chided, and the two of them made it down the last step. "There. You're outside."

Si inhaled deeply, looking around with his bright, freckled face. A deep chill from the nearby sea swelled up over the cliff and rolled across the plain. The rolling fields of grass rippled and swayed all around them like waves upon the ocean. Si watched for a moment in wonderment, his red hair fluttering in the wind. He took a better grip on Marc's shoulder. "It feels better," he said enthusiastically. "I feel better when I'm out here."

"That's where the phrase 'fresh air'll do you good' comes from," Marc informed him knowledgeably. "Easy does it, we don't have to run any races."

"I feel like running around," Si said eagerly. "I feel like I've been in that bedroom for weeks."

451

"You *have*," Marc corrected with a gentle grin.

Si was staring about himself as if he were just seeing the outdoors for the first time in his life. "So this is the house?" he said, twisting around. "I've never seen one look like that before. Even your house, Marc. But it was bigger."

"Yes, you could say that Joymaril palace was *slightly* bigger than this," Marc said wryly.

"It was probably the biggest house I ever saw. My houses were all very small. That night I came to the palace, it wasn't *really* to rob anything, like I said. It was because I had heard so much about the palace from different people in the city, about kings and princes and so on, that I didn't believe it could possibly be real, until someone told me how to find it."

"They did, did they?" asked Marc patiently. The sound of Si's chatter comforted him greatly.

"So I went where they told me, and there it was! Across that huge lake. I watched someone go across the water on that bridge thingy and into the cliff, and I just sort of snuck in, you know?"

"Very stealthy of you. Archer would be impressed."

"You think so?" Si said eagerly. "I brought the sword so I'd blend in."

Marc hid a smile at the illogical progression of Si's childlike thoughts.

"You know, when I get older, I want to be just like you," Si mused. "Go around saving people and fighting and having adventures."

"Getting shot at and escaping from a load of guards isn't enough adventure for you?" Marc asked mildly. "It's quite enough for me."

"You know what I mean," Si tilted his head and looked thoughtfully off into the distance. "I want to be...." He stopped, searching for the word.

"You're a good person; that's an achievement in itself," Marc maintained stoically. He glanced down and saw that Si was starting to pant with the exertion of walking. "Hey, there," he said, "why don't we sit and have a rest? I'm getting tired out."

"Perhaps a break would do us good," Si admitted breathlessly and plopped down gratefully into the soft grass. The tips of the blades tickled his cheek, and he smiled and swatted at them as if they were flies.

He lay on his back with his hands tucked behind his head and gazed at the clouds as they rolled by in the forbidding gray sky. "Marc," he said after a time, "we nearly died back there, didn't we?"

"Yes, we did," Marc agreed gravely. "We were very lucky."

"What do you think dying is like?" Si wondered.

Marc turned his head and studied Si for a few moments. "I don't know," he said honestly. "I don't think anyone does. Different groups of people come up with different stories to explain what happens."

"The lady who ran the boys' home that I lived in for a while said that when I died, I'd be in a place where I'd be forced to sweep up all the glasses and vases that I'd broken for all eternity," Si said dreamily. "What do they say where you're from?"

"Well, they mostly just say that you get to go somewhere where you can reunite with all your loved ones who have passed away," Marc told him. "I asked Tarr, and he said that Ashans believe that when you die you are reborn as a tree."

"But," Si asked, his face wrinkling, "don't they chop down trees to build their houses?"

Marc coughed. "I think as far as the Ashans see it, you're then providing shelter to your family and fuel to feed them and keep them warm."

"Oh," Si's face cleared. "That's a bit less weird, then."

Marc hid a smile.

"Someone said Laith's wife is dead," he commented after a while. Si had a way of phrasing his questions as outright statements, but by this point Marc was able to detect them.

"Someone told him that, yes," Marc said cautiously, with a sharp look at the boy.

"Do you believe it?"

"I don't know, Si," Marc said honestly. "I hope not."

"Laith would be able to see her, though, if she was," Si pressed. "Like how the Jelani believe, where you see the people you love after you die."

"If she was properly buried, yes," Marc agreed.

Si wrinkled his nose. "What's that mean?"

Marc sighed. "Oh, it's this whole extended thing, a Jelani tradition.

That you have to say these rituals and bury the body in this special place, and observe a period of mourning for a specific amount of time. I don't hold with it much."

"Yeah, that's stupid," Si said, mostly just to agree with Marc. "Who would believe that?"

Marc gave a sigh. "Laith," he said quietly. "Unfortunately."

"*Laith* does?" Si said disbelievingly. "*Really?*"

"Well, his parents died when he was very young, you see," said Marc. "So some of his earliest memories were these funerals that they had. They never found his father, you know, when he died in the Meadows. So getting told that you'll never see your own father, even in the afterlife, because he hasn't been buried properly is bound to make an impression."

"Yes, I see," Si nodded. "So...Laith's wife...?"

Marc considered whether he should be honest with Si, or whether he should gloss over the truth. He decided, after a brief debate, that if Si was old enough to ask the question, he was old enough for a direct answer. "If she died the way those people said she did, then she wasn't properly buried. And if that's the case, and if she really is dead, Laith believes he won't see her again," Marc told him in a soft voice. "Ever."

Si, who had sat up to hear the last of this, furrowed his brow. "But Laith believes she's still alive," he said slowly.

"That's right."

"Then he must know," Si stated. "He would know if she's dead."

Marc shrugged his shoulders, feeling a low, curious weight in his chest. "I don't know, Si. Sometimes, I think when people die, they're just...*gone*. And there's no easy way to understand it. It doesn't always get tied up the way we'd hope." Marc watched him in sympathy. *It's a lot for him to digest*, he thought. The boy was absentmindedly rubbing his shoulder, where the arrow had been removed. "You all right?" Marc asked quietly so as not to embarrass him. "In any pain?"

Si shook his head and squinched his face down to try and get a good look at his own shoulder. The injury was healing slowly and was truly horrible-looking, red and black and blue around the edges. Si had had a very narrow escape. Marc, who had seen his share of battle wounds, swallowed numbly.

"Quite the mess you've got there," he said lightly.

"Yeah, it's pretty gross," Si agreed happily and looked back up at him. "Think it'll go away?"

"You'll probably have a scar," Marc told him.

Si considered this for a moment, then looked back up at Marc, his face brightening into a glowing grin. "Like yours!" he exclaimed.

Marc was taken aback for a few seconds, and felt his throat tighten. "Yes, like mine." He reached out and affectionately ruffled the boy's red hair with one big hand. "Only *much* more impressive. Let's get you back to the house," he suggested, and stood.

The days melded quickly together, a long succession of gray, cloudy afternoons that brightened suddenly into a late fall sky of bright blue, where the sun caught the shine on the blades of sea grass, sending them shivering and shimmering back and forth in the wind. The clouds rolled and heaved their way heavily over the sky.

Since he had learned the story of Archer's exile and exhausted his explorations of Silva's house, Tarr had felt strangely withdrawn from the rest of the group. He was glad to see that they were all alive and on the mend, but as they grew stronger and began to talk once again of finding Morthenstar's heir, he found himself feeling increasingly separate from their conversations, as though they were discussing something he had no part of. Occasionally, he would even come up with some excuse and leave the room if one of them happened to bring it up. He was glad that they were as yet in no shape to continue on their quest; Si was still much too weak to ride, and the others seemed relatively content to stay in the safety of Silva's home for as long as they could.

Tarr fell into bouts of sleeplessness and, in the wee hours of one morning, found himself staring up at the roof above his bed, at the chipping white plaster in one corner, gossamer cracks spreading out like a spider's web. He sighed and tried to sort out the tangle of thoughts that were clamoring for room in his mind.

He found himself replaying the fight in the alley, where they'd all nearly been killed by Kagai's soldiers. It was easily the closest to death he'd ever been, and the memory of the darkness, of the screams, of the clash of weapons beneath him—not knowing if his friends were alive or dying—was truly terrible to remember. But there was something else, something that gnawed at him, that wouldn't let him go, that had been circling through his mind over and over for nearly an entire week. He remembered the moment when he'd thrown Archer the knife, how Archer had reached out and caught it, and the thrill that had gripped him. He remembered in that moment how it had felt to see his plan slide into place, to see the pieces fit together, to see that it had worked. He'd outsmarted Kagai's soldiers. Even the mere memory of it filled him with excitement, with a satisfaction that he'd never felt before in his life. Nothing had even come close.

He sat bolt upright in his bed, the swell of remembered gratification punctuated by the echo of a scream from the black depths of the alley. He shook his head, wondering if he was sick, wondering if there was something seriously wrong with him. *I have to get out*, he thought. *I have to get as far away from here as I can.*

In a flash, he had packed his bag and stood, surveying his surroundings. The other bed was empty; Archer had either slept somewhere else or was out for an early morning walk. Tarr felt a momentary pang at the thought of leaving without telling him goodbye, but told himself firmly that he owed Archer nothing. Perhaps Archer would understand better than the others. Tarr had to go home. It was time for him to go home.

It was odd. Once Tarr had made up his mind to leave, he couldn't bear to waste another second at Silva's house. He crept out the door and down the stairs. The house was blue with the shadows of morning; no one else was yet awake, and it was eerie how cold and lifeless the house was without the sounds of steps ringing along its halls, the voices echoing up from the kitchen. He reached the front door, gave an almighty heave, and let himself out.

The brisk morning air braced him as he stepped into it; it cleared his head as surely as if he had splashed cold water across his face. With each step, he felt increasing resolve. He would leave, go back to the forest. Perhaps the Aspen would allow him back, even though the year was not yet up. If they wouldn't, he would travel to another tribe, and if they welcomed him he would live amongst them for a time. Or he would live out in the forest until the year was up, eating what he could and making a solitary life for himself. Over time he would forget, forget the

Strikers and Morthenstar and Kagai. It would all seem a distant dream, something completely divorced from him, from the peaceful life he intended to lead. Later on, if news came of a distant war between Kagai and Morthenstar, fought on far-off battlefields and mythical fortresses, he would say something like, "Humans and Jelani have no idea how to conduct themselves," and go back to organizing the scrolls in the library.

Contenting himself with this imagined scenario, he felt his footsteps speeding up as he traveled along the path from Silva's house back towards the screen of the trees and the forest beyond. He wished there was some more cover, so that if someone at the house did happen to look out, they wouldn't see him leaving. He felt the imagined eyes on the back of his neck, tried to picture what the others would say when they found him gone. "Ashans are a strange sort of people," they'd say. "Perhaps he wasn't cut out for this sort of thing." Even Archer, he thought, wouldn't disagree with that.

You had the wrong person all along, he thought to himself. Now that Wolver had left him, there was nothing to prove that he was the Ashan foretold in Morthenstar's prophecy.

He rounded the top of the hill that they had slid down the night of their escape, the wet gash in the earth where Marc's horse had fallen. There were still thick grooves of mud torn up, and Tarr used them as soggy handholds as he clambered over the slippery turf and down the other side, glad to have the shelter of the hill behind him. They wouldn't be able to see him from the house, not now. He was safe. The way was clear, and he could return to the forest in peace and live out his days quietly as he'd always intended to do.

"Good morning," came an easygoing voice behind him. "Awfully early for a walk, isn't it?"

Tarr whirled around and saw Archer standing at the top of the hill, his black coat like ink against the gray sky, black-tipped hair rustling in the breeze. How he had crept up behind Tarr without him noticing was quite beyond Tarr's realm of comprehension.

"Erm—yes," Tarr said lamely. "I'm just—"

It was obvious what he was doing, and Tarr knew it. There was no way to bluff his way out of it. He straightened up and squared his jaw, and gripped his knapsack a bit tighter. His eyes held an unspoken challenge to Archer, as if daring him to try and stop him.

As if sensing this, Archer held up his hands in a gesture of peace and slowly picked his way down the hill. "I wish you would have said goodbye."

"I didn't want to draw it out," Tarr said shortly.

"I understand," Archer nodded.

Tarr tentatively took another step down the road, and was surprised when Archer simply fell into step alongside him. The two walked in silence for a moment.

"Do you think they'll take you back?" Archer asked, clearly referring to Tarr's tribe.

"I don't know," Tarr admitted, then remembered his resolve. "But I'm going anyway," he added forcefully, with a sideways glance at Archer, still half-expecting the Ashan to put up some form of protest.

But Archer shrugged equably and kicked a pebble off the side of the dirt path so that it skittered into the grass. "The night in the alley was difficult, I know," he said, as if he'd read Tarr's thoughts. "I've been in many close situations, but that was by far the worst."

"We were lucky," Tarr nodded.

"No, we weren't," Archer shook his head. Tarr looked at him curiously. Archer stopped and faced him full-on. "It wasn't luck. We had *you*."

The words still caught him by surprise, and he faltered for a moment. "I'm not a fighter," Tarr said quickly. "I don't know how to fight."

Archer shrugged. "So what?"

"So, I'm not even supposed to be with you all. There was a mix-up. It's not supposed to be me."

"And you're supposed to be...what? An Ashan librarian?"

"Maybe," Tarr shot back.

"All right," Archer said coolly. "Fine. You can absolutely have the rest of your life to be an Ashan librarian. Right now, we need you."

"You don't need me," Tarr shook his head. He shot a glance towards the open road before him, to the line of trees that led back to the forest, so much closer than they had been before. It was only a little farther. He wished Archer would stop talking.

"We need you, Tarr. You can see things."

Tarr's head whipped around and he stared at Archer, who regarded him, his golden eyes perfectly level.

"What things?" he demanded, irritated by how comparatively calm Archer seemed to be. "Puzzles and clues? Athela can sort them out without my help. People's names? Who put a paper in their boot? Which guard was on duty at the north gate a week ago? Anyone who pays the slightest bit of attention can do as much."

"That's not what I'm talking about," Archer shook his head. He took a step forward and took Tarr's thin shoulders in his hands. "That night in the alley, you saw a way to get us out. No one else. Only you."

Archer let the words fall and took a step back from him. Tarr looked again towards the line of trees, which somehow seemed to be pulling away, little by little. He tightened his hand on the leather cord of his knapsack.

"So, Tarr," he said in Ashan, before grinning self-consciously and lapsing back into Common. "I am formally asking you, on behalf of all of us, of all the people who may be drawn into this war, to stay. To keep us safe. To see the way out when no one else can."

The weight of it settled on Tarr's shoulders, and he felt himself sagging underneath it. He tried to look away from Archer, but he couldn't. "Archer," he whispered. "That night, in the alley—"

"I know. I know it's hard. To come so close—" Archer began, his expression sympathetic.

"That's not it," Tarr shook his head. "The moment I threw you the knife, and you caught it, and I knew you'd heard me and understood…" he groped for words, but it all sounded too awful. To say that he had enjoyed it, when they had all danced so close to death.

Archer's furrowed expression cleared, and he nodded slowly. Tarr saw that he didn't have to explain it any further. He searched Archer's face for some sign of judgment, of disgust, but there was none. *He understands it*, Tarr realized.

He thought suddenly of the members in his tribe, about the Elders. He wondered whether, if he ever spoke to any of them about the night in the alley, tried to describe what he'd done, the emotions he'd felt, whether any of *them* would understand. He knew unequivocally that they wouldn't. They would shame him for feeling the way he did. He would have to hide it, to never speak of it, to keep it buried down deep for the rest of his life. He looked down at his left hand, at the missing nub of his sixth finger. He swallowed, his throat dry and scratchy.

"Archer, I don't...I don't ever want to have to kill anyone," Tarr said quietly. "I know that when you were exiled and came to Two Falls, that was all they said you could do, and that is why you had to take the path you did. But I don't...I don't ever want to come to that. I don't want to reach that point." *I could*, he thought wildly. *If I go back to the house, if I follow them, that is where I may end up.* He could hear the sound of desperation in his own voice, almost pleading.

"You won't," Archer shook his head firmly.

"How do you know?" Tarr whispered.

"I won't let it," Archer said simply. "As long as I am there with you, you will never have to kill anyone. I promise it. I'll protect you from that. You protect the rest of us."

Tarr slowly looked from Archer, away to the thin line of trees slowly receding into the distance. He looked back at the Ashan standing next to him. For the first time, he saw real understanding, true recognition, looking out at him from the eyes of another person. Archer had seen him for who he truly was, and he had not looked away.

Slowly, Tarr reached a hand up and clasped it on the nape of Archer's neck, the traditional Ashan greeting exchanged between members of the same tribe. Slowly, he saw a smile of recognition spread across Archer's lips. His hand lifted, and Tarr could feel the cool touch against the back of his own neck. Their foreheads briefly touched, and then their hands released.

"Come on," Archer indicated the path back to the house with a jerk of his head. "I'll walk with you."

If any of the others had noticed Tarr's temporary departure that morning, they said nothing. The next day drew pleasantly into the next, and the next. Athela woke and spent long hours walking through the stables down near the cliff with one of Silva's brothers (Tarr still had trouble sorting out exactly how many Silva had and which name went with whom), and Laith even ventured out to sit for a time on the rocks overlooking the sea. Tarr watched him there from time to time, a small black dot wrapped in a cloak, swallowed up by the sea beyond.

One rainy morning, much to his surprise, there was a soft knock at his bedroom door. Tarr was perusing some of the prophecy papers (which Athela, true to her word, had kept on her person ever since their excursion to Faridor.) He and Athela had been trading them back and forth every few days in an attempt to translate and decode the rest of the prophecy. He threw them down and sat up quite straight as Rane entered his room.

"Hello," she said pleasantly in her low voice. She had her hood pushed back from her auburn hair, and came over to sit on the bed beside Tarr as if it were the most natural thing in the world. He felt his heart begin thudding. She indicated the papers strewn on the bedcover. "How are you getting along with this?"

"Not bad," Tarr replied, which was a slight exaggeration. The prophecy was written in a language called ancient Elyrian, which had been spoken in Morthenstar's time. It was a precursor to the Common tongue, so there were some points of reference, but the sentence structure was hard to puzzle out. Luckily, Athela had dug up a book on Elyrian translation in Silva's library (apparently, her family had once had business dealings with the Jelani), and she and Tarr had been using it as a way to splice the sentences together, bit by bit. It was slow going.

Rane nodded quietly, and didn't seem to feel the need to tell him why she had popped in for a visit. Tarr began to feel very nervous indeed. It had been lovely, the few bouts of hand-holding they'd had in Two Falls and in the carriage to Faridor, but he wasn't sure where it was supposed to progress from there. Was she expecting him to kiss her? Would she be appalled when she realized he didn't know how? Maybe she'd just be content with a few more months of holding hands so that he would have a chance to ask Archer about how to—

"I'm glad you decided to stay," she said abruptly, and Tarr's attention snapped back up.

"How did—how did you know?" he stammered. "Did you see me leave?"

She shook her head and shrugged. "I had a hunch. I could see it in your face." She smiled slowly. She raised one finger and tapped lightly on Tarr's forehead. "I'm like you, Tarr," she said, her voice in a conspiratorial whisper. "I can see things, too."

Tarr stared at her as she smiled and lowered her hand again to rest loosely in her lap. It was not at all like how he had felt with Archer—the feeling of opening a book, of being able to read the words on the pages and truly understand the contents within. Rane sat before him, smiling at him quietly, a complete and utter enigma. Reading people usually came so easy to him, but try as he might, he could not puzzle her out. He realized that he would never truly know what was going on inside of her head. It was slightly scary and rather exciting.

Trying to still his racing heart and grasping for something complimentary and clever to say, he said, "We're not *completely* alike. You can fight and use a sword. I can't."

Rane shrugged as if it mattered very little. "Together," she said slowly, "I think that you and I would make...a very effective team."

Tarr stared at her, trying not to look stupid or sound too hopeful. "Together?" he asked tentatively. "In what way...together?"

Her smile widened, and Tarr could see a gleam of flirtation in her eye. *She actually likes me,* he thought wildly to himself. *She wants to be with me.*

Suddenly, overwhelming the feelings of hesitation and terror he felt, he was gripped with the incredible urge to kiss her. He had only vague notions of what he was supposed to do, but he figured he would start with the lips, and they could progress from there. He leaned in tentatively, worried that she would suddenly back away, but she didn't. He pressed his lips to hers and was struck, through his racing, buzzing mind, how soft and warm they were. He felt one of his hands rise up and gently touch the side of her face.

He leaned back and swallowed, searching her face for a reaction: revulsion, discomfort, disappointment. But she merely smiled softly and stroked his cheek with her finger a few times. She looked happy.

"Was that all right?" he asked anxiously.

She nodded. "Lovely."

"I...ah...kissing isn't a big thing in Ashan culture," he explained. "Not unless you're married."

"How very forward of you," she murmured, and he could tell she was teasing him. "I guess you *really* can't go back now."

"The Elders may have some questions, yes," Tarr joked, surprised that the pang from her words was less than he expected, and the threat of the Elders' discipline seemed like something strangely disconnected from his new reality.

Abruptly, he leaned forward again to kiss her, but she wasn't expecting it, and his lips landed somewhere beside her left eye. At first, he drew back, feeling mortified, but after a moment she laughed and he felt himself joining in. Then she stood up beside him and regarded him softly, gently running her fingers along the edge of his jawline.

"You're leaving?" Tarr asked, surprised at how much he sounded like a petulant child.

"For now," she said. "We have time."

She turned away from him and went out the door. Tarr stared at the spot where she'd vanished for a few bewildering seconds, then flopped back down on the bed atop all the old prophecy papers and wondered how on earth anyone could expect him to focus on anything other than her ever again.

By that evening, rain was rattling outside the windows, pounding on the door like the fists of Kagai's guards. Tarr, for his part, felt quite content to be huddled up beside the others near a roaring fire in Silva's drawing room, with a book draped lazily in his lap. Silva's eldest brother Cass had gone to Two Falls to deliver Tarr's letter of warning to Ari about Pieter's nephew and to pick up supplies; he was due back at any moment. Tarr couldn't help but pity him for the soggy, freezing ride he had to endure. He could see that Silva was anxious for his return as well. She kept glancing up from her leatherwork to the clock on the mantelpiece and then towards the house's front door. When, finally, there was a creak and a slam at the entrance, she bolted upright and hurried to greet him, the others following, slowly unfolding themselves from the various chairs and couches in which they'd been comfortably ensconced.

As Tarr reached the front door, he saw that Cass's face was even graver than usual; he stomped the mud off of his boots and shook the rain from his shoulders with considerable force. Silva took his sodden coat off to dry it by the hearth in the kitchen and brought back a steaming mug, which she pressed into his grateful hands. Cass began to lumber toward the living room, and Tarr fell into step beside him, curious and slightly apprehensive to hear whether he had brought back some news from the city.

"I looked around your house," he told the others, who had gathered at the noise. "I brought back what things I could find from your rooms." He gestured towards the front door where a few knapsacks had been set down.

"Any sign of a white wolf?" Tarr asked hopefully.

Cass shook his head. "No. There doesn't seem to be anything strange going on around the house. I've asked a neighbor to take care of it for now. I'm going to head back to the city in a couple of days, and I'll be sure to check again, make sure that there isn't anything amiss."

"What's wrong, Cass?" Silva asked anxiously, as her brother inhaled deeply from the steaming mug and settled himself into the high-backed chair that Si had hurriedly vacated. He looked around at their faces, his beetle-black brows knit in consternation. Cass gave a sigh as if he had been hoping to put something off for a while longer. He drew a small parcel from his pocket and set it on the table. "They've been hanging these around town," he grimaced.

The others glanced at one another, none of them wanting to reach forward and uncover whatever it was. Finally, Athela made an impatient *tsk*ing sound in the back of her throat, leaned forward, and began to unwrap the small parcel. Layer after layer of fabric fell away, and a few of them gasped at the grisly object that lay before them. Out of the corner of his eye, Tarr saw Archer give a visible start. On the table lay the severed sixth finger of an Ashan.

Tarr's right hand at once flew to his left, the nub throbbing unpleasantly. Athela sharply recoiled, snatching her hand away from the finger. Marc caught her and guided her back up onto the couch. A wave of shock visibly rolled around the others, and Tarr had to swallow quickly to stifle the sick feeling that welled up in him.

"They're *hanging* these?" Athela demanded in a deathly low voice.

Cass nodded unhappily. "On the bridges. Street posts. Public places. They've set up a competition, you see," he continued tiredly.

"Among the Kagaian guards. See which guard can rack up the most fingers in a week."

"A few weeks, that's all," Marc said huskily. We're gone for that short a time, and something like this could start to happen?"

All of them were studiously avoiding looking at Tarr or Archer, and Tarr could sense their guilt that it was *his* people who were being mutilated instead of theirs. After the first wave of horror and revulsion after he saw the finger, all he felt was cold anger, and for the first time in his life, Tarr began to understand what it was to want violent revenge against another person. It was not an emotion with which he felt comfortable. He glanced around at the others, whose faces all registered shock or dismay or guilt. Si's, however, was a mixture of horror and a childish morbid curiosity. Tarr could tell that he was having to restrain himself very hard from reaching out and poking the finger as it lay there.

"From what I can tell, most of the Ashans and half-Ashans in the city are hiding out in their homes, have found shelter, have escaped or been arrested," Cass told them. "You'll hardly see one if you walk down the street anymore. It's the strangest damn thing I've ever seen. Like something's missing that you can't quite put your finger on." He grimaced at his unintentional slip of the tongue. "Sorry."

"Ashans have been living in Two Falls for a long time," Silva's middle brother chimed in. "Nearly as long as some of the human families. The city's so close to the forest."

"They can escape, though, can't they?" said Si hopefully. "They can sneak out. Like you said, the forest is close. It wouldn't be that hard."

"The security is getting tighter and tighter. It's nearly a stranglehold," Cass shrugged. "The wall is half-built, and it's going to be nearly impossible to get through once it's done. It took me ten minutes to give them my papers and get processed for an entrance. Hardly anyone wants to get into the city anymore. And no one is getting out."

They fell silent after that, each one of them deep in contemplation. The finger lay on the table in front of them, and Tarr stared at it until his eyes burned. None of them spoke for a long while. Eventually, the prince stirred from his seat and clasped his hands together in front of him.

"We've stayed here for far too long," Laith whispered, his voice scratchy.

"You've been healing," Silva chided him sharply, but Tarr could see the truth in the other faces around him. Like Tarr, they, too, had been content in staying at Silva's, far away from the troubles of prophecies and Two Falls and Cira. In each of their expressions were traces of unmistakable shame.

"We've got to leave as soon as we're all able to ride," Athela whispered. "For all we know, everyone in the city has given up hope. They probably all think we're dead."

"So much the better," Marc said grimly. "Give Cira a nasty surprise when we show up again, won't we?"

"What are you going to do?" Silva asked anxiously, looking from one of them to the other. She could see that there was no point in trying to argue with them and make them stay any longer. Her eyes slid desperately to Laith. "Please don't do anything foolish."

"We won't go as long as the rain holds out," Laith agreed. "We can take that time and plan our next move. Maybe we can stage a covert operation to sneak into Faridor, just the seven of us, and finish Cira once and for all. We could end this thing by next week."

"I think that counts as something foolish," Silva joked faintly.

"What about finding the heir?" Si pressed.

"From what Tarr and I have been able to decipher, it seems as though the next clue points towards the mountains," Athela sighed. "Some sort of hideout. But I'm not sure that's where we're most needed right now. Maybe the heir, whoever they are, will just come and find us."

"So we're giving up on finding them?" Si asked. Tarr could tell he was disappointed that the treasure hunt was coming to an unanticipated end.

"For the time being," Athela said firmly, her eyes glancing towards the grisly finger on the table.

"Look," Silva cut in again, "I'm not trying to force you all to stay here, I'm just thinking that another week, another two weeks can't hurt anything. You could make sure that you're all fully healed; there's no reason to go running off—"

"Silva," Cass said quietly, "let them go."

Silva's mouth stayed open as she struggled to find the words. "But what if...what if you all are taken? What if something happens? Who is going to save you?"

"I don't know," Laith said simply.

Silva looked down at her lap, biting her lip.

"It's very ungrateful of us," Marc said softly, soothingly, "to just breeze in here and abruptly leave. But it's due mostly to you and your brothers that we were able to survive at all. We won't ever forget it. None of us will."

"Well," Silva looked up, green eyes glistening. "For heaven's sake, you're not leaving yet; no need to make speeches, especially ones that exaggerate the truth. We just did what anyone would have done in our position."

Athela looked around at the rest of them. "It's settled then," she announced firmly. "Everyone, tell your bones and any other injuries to fix themselves immediately. Archer, you start thinking of some creative ways to smuggle Ashans safely out of the city. And when the rain clears, we ride for Two Falls."

CHAPTER TWENTY-SEVEN

Archer awoke Tarr at the crack of dawn, his cold hand sliding over Tarr's mouth, shaking him awake. Tarr jumped, then relaxed as the white Ashan slid into focus, the sleep falling unsteadily from his eyes.

"Silva was just here," Archer whispered. "There are Kagaian guards downstairs, starting to search the house."

They followed Cass from our house in Two Falls, Tarr thought immediately. *Careless again.*

"We've got to get out," Archer said urgently. "Quietly. Cass is trying to stall them at the door, and Silva was just able to slip upstairs to tell us."

Tarr's heart immediately began to race as the reality of the situation crystallized in his still half-conscious mind. His right hand flew unconsciously to his left, where the nub of his finger gave a sudden, painful throb.

He rubbed his eyes and threw back the bedsheets. Archer was already tossing his few meager possessions into his knapsack, which Cass had recovered in Two Falls the day before. "What about the others?" Tarr whispered.

"They've been alerted," Archer replied tersely.

"Silva," Tarr said, his stomach giving a lurch. "Archer, they're going to see that there were others living here; they'll never let Silva and her brothers live. They'll be arrested for sure."

Archer paused and considered. "Strip the bed. I'll tell the others. If we make it look as though we were never here..."

He paused at the door and listened for a moment. Tarr could hear the soldiers now, loud voices echoing through the hall. Archer slipped out into the hallway beyond.

Tarr snatched a sheaf of papers from the table beside his bed and shoved them in his bag. He threw on a coat Archer had lent him, which afforded him greater mobility than a cloak. He ran to the door and peeked out. In the dark corridor beyond, he could hear the voices coming from the floor below and saw lantern lights being thrown roughly against this wall and that, casting the dull morning light of the house into exaggerated, eerie shadows. Quickly, he shut the door. It looked as though the troops were already about to mount the stairs.

Out the window, he thought, and dashed over to throw open the shutters. The cold air hit him like a blast to the face. It was still just after dawn, the sun barely starting to peek over the edge of the cliffs, spilling across the broad plain surrounding the house. He looked down at the stone wall of the house to the ground many, many feet below. It would be simple enough, as an Ashan, for him to go out the window and to scale down. Archer, too, could accomplish the climb without much of an issue. But the others would have to descend using some form of rope, and that would take time.

He whirled around, his mind racing. He dashed again, quietly as he could, to the door. This time, he could hear footsteps on the stairs, Kagaian troops coming up to investigate. Archer would be helping the others out. He had to buy them some time.

He opened his door just a sliver, enough so that he could see outside. Sharp beams of light swung back and forth from a lantern held aloft by a Kagaian guard, green cloak dim in the dark hallway. Tarr watched as the guard mounted the stairs and came to the landing. Behind him, the stair was crowded with others, their swords out and ready. Tarr swallowed.

The lead Kagaian guard paused and pointed to the end of the hall opposite Tarr's, where the door was firmly closed. On the other side of that door, Archer and the others would be scrambling to find some way to get out of the window and to the stables where the horses were kept. "Start there," the guard ordered.

Saying an internal prayer, Tarr stepped back and gave his door a firm shut so that the sound could be carried unmistakably down the hall to the guards. Their voices now muffled, Tarr could nevertheless hear the lead guard call a halt, alerted by the noise.

Tarr turned and flew across the room, swinging his knapsack over one shoulder and springing onto the ledge of the windowsill. As easily as stepping off the curb of a street, he swung out onto the stone wall of the house and began to shimmy his way up the side towards the roof. He carefully picked his way up and over so that he was positioned just above the frame of his open window and looked down to see if his ruse had worked.

He was relieved when, a few moments later, three heads clad in green cloaks thrust out of the open window. The heads turned to the right and the left, but didn't bother to look up. Tarr nearly smiled in satisfaction.

"I don't see anyone down there," said a female voice tentatively. "They can't have run around the side of the house; we would have seen them."

"Maybe the wind from the open window pulled the door closed," another voice suggested. "That happens sometimes, you know."

"Have you searched the rest of the room?" a third voice, the Kaga-ian officer, barked. The reply, when it came, was muffled inside the house, but Tarr got the feeling that they hadn't found anything. He took another few steps up the side of the building so that he was nestled just beneath the eaves. It would actually be quite a nice morning, he thought, gazing out around himself at the open plain and the sea stretching beyond. The salt wind ruffled through his hair. *If we manage to live to see it.*

"Get back, then, search the other rooms," the officer barked, and the head withdrew.

Praying that he'd bought Archer enough time to get the others safely out, Tarr extended one arm, caught the edge of a beam, and swung up onto the slatted roof of the house. He skipped nimbly along the edge of the slanting rooftop until he came to the other side of the house and looked down.

To his relief, he could see that Athela and Laith were already across the field, vanishing into the stables beyond. On the ground by the side of the house was Marc, who was looking up expectantly. He gave a start when he saw Tarr, then a little wave. He pointed up at the window and mouthed something indecipherable.

Tarr looked down from his perch on the roof and saw three small heads poke out of the window below: Rane, Si, and Archer. They didn't have much time. Tarr felt like screaming at them to hurry up. They had fashioned a makeshift rope out of a sheet, and Tarr watched as Si clambered out the window, a little unsteadily with his bad shoulder.

As if he were watching a pantomime, Tarr saw Marc wave his hands at the three Strikers in the window and point up at the roof. The three heads paused for a second, then twisted up; the effect was almost comical as shock and recognition washed across all three. Si gave Tarr a jolly wave.

"Marc, go!" Tarr hissed, waving his hand urgently. "No time!"

Marc nodded his comprehension and took off running towards the stables. For someone so short and stocky, he was actually quite fast. Tarr leaned down. "Archer, they're coming! Throw me the rope! Take Si!"

Archer sprang into immediate action, and Tarr felt a momentary wash of relief that Archer never seemed to need Tarr to explain a plan twice. Archer threw the end of the sheet rope up to Tarr and handed the other end to Rane; he leaned down and Si fixed his arms around Archer's neck. Then Archer swung out onto the side of the house, just as Tarr had done, and began scaling upwards until he reached the eaves of the house. He hoisted himself and Si onto the roof and set Si down beside Tarr; the boy, less sure of himself around heights than either of the Ashans, sat down immediately, looking terrified at their precarious position.

Together, Archer and Tarr took hold of the rope, and Tarr watched as Rane swung out of the window into the air. They began hauling her upwards, and no sooner had she cleared the open window than a head thrust out of it, searching around to the left and the right.

Tarr and Archer held their breath. Rane remained as still as she could, swinging ever so slightly at the end of the makeshift rope, dangling just a foot or two over the guard's head. If she so much as sneezed, the game would be given away.

"Sir!" the guard exclaimed suddenly, and Tarr gritted his teeth, bracing for it. "There's someone at the stables!"

Archer and Tarr met each other's eyes, and Tarr heard his friend swear under his breath. They both looked over to the stable, where Marc was just disappearing inside. Tarr's arms were quivering with the strain from holding Rane aloft. Below them, the head disappeared from the window and the shutter was closed. There was a great deal of muffled ruckus within the house, and Tarr knew it was only a matter of time before the guards headed out to inspect the stables.

"Get them down," Archer told him. "And we'll get out."

Below, Rane glanced up at them, waiting for their next move. "We'll send you down," Tarr called as loudly as he dared. "Hang on."

Together the two of them lowered Rane, hand over hand, until she was swinging at the very end of the sheet about six feet above the ground. Tarr held his breath as she released and fell softly through the air, landing lightly in a roll that broke her fall. She stood, drawing her sword, ready to keep watch.

Si hooked his good arm around Archer's neck again, and the three of them swung over the side of the house. Si let out an unheralded yelp as they left the safety of the roof and met the open air beyond. Tarr's hands and feet automatically found their minuscule holds as they slipped smoothly down the side of the building, landing with a thump beside Rane.

Archer set Si down, and they glanced around themselves, listening for sounds of approaching guards. There was the distant clamor of raised voices; Tarr wondered if Silva and her brothers had taken advantage of the guards' distraction and begun to fight back, or had taken the opportunity to hide. He hoped fervently that they would be able to escape as well.

In the distance by the stables, Tarr saw Laith, Athela, and Marc, all mounted and leading the other horses in a pack. Archer watched them with his golden-eyed stare. "Here's hoping the guards don't have arrows," he muttered. "Run."

The four of them lit out as fast as they could across the open field to their friends and the waiting horses. Tarr had never run so fast in his life; his heart seemed to be beating up in his throat, and he didn't even chance a glance behind him to see if the Kagaian guards were in pursuit. He hoped they didn't have arrows. He tried to push the thought from his head.

Laith and the other two were riding towards them now, the distance between them slowly closing up. Tarr's chest was burning with the exertion of running for so long, but he forced his limbs to keep moving until they finally drew up alongside the others. Rane swung up onto her horse, followed by Archer; Si mounted up on Kip, and Tarr scrambled atop his. Athela's gray horse Aria was clearly thrilled with the entire production and was tossing his head and performing a series of half-rears, which Athela was sitting patiently.

Laith waited only as long as it took for them to touch the saddles before he tossed Archer his bow and quiver and wheeled Arfolasth around, pointing him northwest to the line of trees. The horses, clearly seized with the intensity felt by their riders, took off together like a flock of birds bursting into flight. Tarr, still not terribly comfortable with riding a horse at such high speeds, could only trust that his mount wouldn't purposefully sabotage him and focused all his energy on staying in the saddle, wrapping the reins and mane around his hands, steadying himself as best he could.

It seemed like an eternity before they hit the cover of the trees, and they plunged haphazardly through the brush for a minute or two before Laith held up a hand, and they slowed their mounts to a panting, steaming halt. Athela's horse's eyes were bright and thrilled; he was clearly unhappy with the prospect of stopping and gave a squeal before attempting to bite Kip, who was clearly not in the mood for his antics.

Tarr finally dared to look over his shoulder. Off in the distance was Silva's house, with black specks swarming around it like flies. As he watched, a few of the specks came together into a pack and began moving in their direction.

"What about Silva?" Tarr asked again.

"She may be able to get out," Laith said grimly. "They have horses. Maybe they'll get away."

Maybe, Tarr thought to himself, and felt like screaming. *Maybe is not good enough.*

"Change of plan, everyone," Athela announced. "How's about we head to the mountains and see about solving this stupid prophecy once and for all? We need to get the upper hand."

Agreed, Tarr thought privately, trying to push the image of severed Ashan fingers from his mind. *We need to stop, to gather ourselves, to make a plan.* He studiously avoided looking at his hand.

"I'm game," Marc agreed. "If this is any indication, Two Falls is not going to be a terribly welcoming place for the next few weeks."

Athela swiveled to Archer. "What's the best way to reach the mountains?"

Archer looked to the north. "There's a path along the edge of the forest and a few outlying villages. We may be able to lose them in the foothills."

Athela nodded. "We split up now and then meet back up on the main road going north. I'll make sure Kagai's guards follow me. I'm the fastest rider; I'll shake them."

"Athela..." Marc frowned.

"Look," Archer slid off Rane's horse. "Once you're back on the main path, follow it until you come to the foot of two mountains. There's a little town right between them. We'll meet you there at sundown."

"Be careful," Tarr said in Ashan. Archer winked, hiked his bow farther up on his shoulder, then slid a hand over the back of Athela's saddle and vaulted up behind her. Aria, Athela's horse, snorted and tossed his black mane to the other side, then began scratching impatiently at the ground with one delicate hoof.

"Ugh," Archer said with distaste. He wasn't a horse enthusiast.

"If you're going to ride with us, you don't get to say anything rude to Aria," Athela told him sternly.

"Fine," Archer muttered, settling himself and looping an arm casually around her waist.

Athela gave the others a nod. "Meet you there tonight. Let's go," she hissed. Laith nodded and urged Arfolasth forward, bending him off to the north along the main path, then veering into the cover of the trees, followed by the others. Athela watched as her friends went zig-zagging into the wood, doing their best to cover their trail until the colorful glimpses of their clothes had been swallowed between the trees. After a few seconds, everyone but Athela and Archer were safely hidden by the cover of the forest.

Aria was bouncing up and down, about to explode with frustration that the others had been able to run off but he hadn't. Athela had the reins choked in so close that the horse's nose was touching his chest, neck bent in a perfect arc. She looked over her shoulder, sliding Aria's flank around in a circle with her heel so she could get a better look. Archer scooted himself closer up to the saddle. Athela could feel his breath on her shoulder.

"Come on, come on, ride faster, you lot," Athela growled through gritted teeth, her gray eyes trained on the approaching mob of riders. Aria was pawing the ground, snorting, breath coming out in white puffs of steam from his nostrils, ears flicking wildly in every direction.

"Athela, I've never told you this, and I hope you don't take this the wrong way," Archer said carefully. "But your horse is nuts."

"I know," Athela said happily, giving the arched dappled neck an affectionate pat.

"Ugh," Archer muttered again. By this point, he could easily make out the features of the approaching riders. "Look, we *are* going to ride off sometime soon, aren't we?"

"Well, we want to give them a good run for it, don't we? We don't want to lose them in five seconds," Athela said impatiently.

"Athela," Archer pressed, a sense of urgency growing in his tone, "the rider five horses back has three moles on his face and a freckle right on the end of his nose."

"Fine. Hold on."

Archer barely had time to tighten his grip around Athela's waist before she loosed the rein and Aria exploded forward in a flurry of hooves and churning muscle. In that brief suspended instant, Archer reflected that it was probably like being shot like an arrow from his own bow. It took Aria a few midair leaps before he settled into a flat run, careening straight through the trees. For a wild second, Archer was afraid that they would crash into a trunk, but Athela was a better rider than that, and Aria was a much more well-trained horse, despite his exuberance. He dug down deep into his turns with his front hooves, swinging his neck down and around, whipping his riders around the trees where there was barely enough space between them for him to fit through. Athela had given him complete control of his head and had the reins wrapped around her hands, clutched in a thick handful of Aria's dark mane. The only guidance she was giving him was the gentlest of touches from her heel or calf muscle; Aria was so light that he bent at the slightest pressure.

"How many are behind us?" she asked. Archer swiveled around in the saddle, tightening his grip on Athela's waist to ensure that he would stay on the horse's back.

"Most of them," he replied. "I counted twenty-five riders; we've got about twenty behind us."

"Good. We'll get out of this thick wood so Aria can do some open running, and you can try your hand at a couple of them."

"Gladly."

Archer ducked his head down so that his chin was nearly resting on Athela's shoulder, squinting his eyes in anticipation of the branches that were flying into their faces. Athela used her free hand to ward them off as best she could. Archer sent a glance over his shoulder and saw that the riders were falling back.

"Better ease up; we're losing them already."

Athela swore under her breath and took in the rein. Aria snorted unhappily, trying to charge through her grip, but she sat back deep in the saddle and the horse resigned himself, deeply bending his neck but letting his stride extend far past his nose.

"I think we're nearly out of the woods," Athela yelled to him. "After that, once we're on the flats, it should be easier for them to keep up."

Archer let go of her for a moment to get his bow free from over his shoulder, right as Aria vaulted over a fallen tree trunk, nearly dislodging him from the saddle. Had he had anything but his Ashan sense of balance, he would have been deposited soundly on the forest floor, but he held on gamely, looping his arm snugly back around Athela to anchor himself, his free hand holding the bow ready down by his thigh. A little ways ahead of them was a clearing in the trees, and beyond that Archer could see fields that stretched on for at least a few miles. When they reached the edge of the wood, Athela choked Aria back for a few more strides, the horse nearly twisting upward in protest. Then, as their followers were nearly upon them, she cast the reins down at Aria's neck and grabbed onto a hunk of mane. Archer grinned in anticipation, letting go of Athela, trusting that she would steer.

He rocked his upper body around in time with Aria's pounding stride and fitted an arrow into his bow. He calculated the up and down beats of Aria's gallop and, as soon as he was able to balance his hand with the movement, sighted down the shaft and loosed it straight at the foremost rider, who gave a small gurgle and toppled from the saddle, right beneath the pounding hooves of his comrades' horses. The other riders eyed him with dismay, and a few of them took out bows themselves.

"Keep your head down, if you can, please," Archer requested politely, leaning in towards Athela so that she could hear him over the screaming wind. He squinted one eye and fired again, and was rewarded with a small cry from one of the riders as he fell. "Oh, hell—"

One of the riders reared up from his saddle and fired an arrow point-blank at them. Archer, faster than lightning, leaned to one side and fired back at a slight angle. His arrow went straight into his opponent's and knocked it harmlessly to one side, the small sliver of wood skipping off through the air and landing in the soft earth. Archer immediately whipped another arrow to his bow, and with a hiss the rider was propelled off his horse by the power of the blow.

"Oh hell what?" Athela asked keenly, chancing a look around over her shoulder.

"Nothing," Archer said coolly, straightening up, his nimble fingers fitting another arrow. "It's fine. Would you please steer the damn horse?"

Archer took down five more riders before they hit the trees, and again Athela was forced to rein in Aria, who was far quicker on his hooves than their pursuers' horses. Athela led them on a zig-zagging course through the wood, then banked a hard right and doubled back so that they completely reversed direction, and they went screaming back across the open field again. Archer was getting into his stride and took down half of the remaining riders before they once more flew into the dense trees. The remaining six riders were certainly no fools and were capable riders themselves; they had seen what had happened to their comrades and took to ducking around the trees as much as Aria was. Archer snarled as he tried to aim, but failed to get a clear shot.

"Athela!" he yelled over the wind. "Get some more distance between them!"

"Gladly," Athela nodded and chucked Aria the reins. Aria seized the bit in his teeth and powered forward, the distance between the riders gaping wider and wider with each churning stride of Aria's haunches. Finally, when Archer saw that there was enough of a chasm between them, he reached out one long arm and caught the branch of a tree right as he passed beneath. He swung forward off the saddle, the momentum propelling him upward. He let go of the branch just at the right moment and flipped up to land on a higher branch. He immediately knelt, perfectly balanced with his knee resting on the wood, and fired. One-two-three-four-five-six, the riders fell to the earth below him.

Archer blinked a few times and slid his bow back up on his shoulder. He skipped lightly down the branches until he reached the bottommost one; there he perched, with his long legs dangling down. He swung them idly back and forth, whistling to himself, waiting for Athela to notice that he had gone.

A few minutes later, there was the dull pounding of hooves on the moist leaves, and Athela atop her dapple gray came rollicking back into sight. Athela picked him out easily, his white skin standing out like snow against the dark bark of the trees. She pulled up alongside him, Aria halting reluctantly, bracing on his front legs, breath whoofing in and out of his nostrils, eyes wide and bright and clearly looking for more things to outrun. Athela silently eyed the riders groaning on the ground, then her gaze shifted to the riderless horses standing amongst the trees, watching with wary expressions on their faces. She looked back up to Archer, who was grinning down at her from the branch, back slightly slouched, black-tipped hair in disarray, hands resting easily on his knees.

"Hullo," he said pleasantly.

"Couldn't have done that earlier, could you?" Athela asked crossly, sidepassing Aria to stand beneath Archer's branch so that he could slide on.

"Aria seemed like he could do with a bit of exercise," Archer shrugged, dropping down to hang from the branch for a moment and stretch his firing arm before swinging onto the back of the horse behind Athela. He again looped an arm loosely around her waist, momentarily enjoying the feeling of her dark curls softly brushing his cheek. Athela twisted around in the saddle to face him fully, her mouth opening to retort with some sort of clever rebuttal. But instead their eyes locked together, and for once, Athela fumbled over her words.

"Archer..." she said slowly.

"Hang on a minute," he said, and raised one hand to brush a strand of curls from her eyes. Athela swallowed. "What were you going to ask me?" he said smoothly.

"Nothing," Athela muttered. Aria, clearly impatient with both of them, tossed his head and gave out a disgruntled snort. Athela had to look at him quickly and pick up the reins to steady him. "Let's catch up with the others," she said finally, and the two riders vanished in the space of a single breath.

CHAPTER TWENTY-EIGHT

The tiny mountain village was just as Archer had said: nestled snugly in the foothills at the very base of two towering blue peaks, with a river flowing right through the center. Exhausted from yet another escape followed by a long day of riding, Tarr nevertheless took in his new surroundings with interest, staring out over the country as they picked their way up the mountain path to the little town. It was remarkable what a bit of elevation did to heighten the grandeur of the sweeping country below. Everything shone out bright green and blue after the fall rains, and Tarr could see that vast swaths of the Ashan forest in the valley below them had already started to change color, red and gold leaves blooming like spreading flame in the unending current of trees.

The mountain town into which they walked had a character all its own. The buildings were short, wooden, and very old, clustered together for warmth with the mountains looming up behind them. At the head of their group, Laith urged Arfolasth farther up the street and took a left, then a right, and there saw the swinging outdoor sign that denoted a tavern. There were only two people in the street, old men, who stopped talking and stared at him as he rode up and dismounted.

Laith met Tarr's eyes. "We have to find somewhere to hide," he said in a low voice. "Odds are there will still be some riders on our trail.

They'll guess we're coming up here. This is probably the only town for miles."

Laith slipped his hood over his head, opened the tavern door, and walked inside. A few bar patrons were sitting at tables over mugs of ale, talking quietly. A man was tunelessly sawing on a musical instrument in one corner. The murmur and clink of glasses stopped immediately as soon as Laith entered, and a few pairs of round eyes focused on him. Laith didn't even notice them and walked straight to the bar. Behind the counter was a plump young woman of about ten or twelve, her cleaning rag and an empty mug frozen in her hands. Her eyes traveled up the arms, the broad shoulders, and came to rest on Laith's face, and her expression changed completely. With amusement, Tarr watched as her eyes softened and grew strangely glassy, as if she couldn't bring herself to look away.

"Marc," came a weak voice from behind them.

The others whipped around and saw that Si was swaying where he stood. Marc instinctively rushed forward and caught the boy before he swooned. "It was too much for him, all this riding," Marc said sharply.

"He'll need a poultice for his shoulder," Rane volunteered. "Something to help with the pain."

"Laith," Marc urged. "Do your thing."

Smoothly, Laith swung around and fixed the young barmaid with his dark brown eyes. "Hello," he said in his rich, deep voice. "My young friend over here is in need of some food, possibly some medicine. Is there any way you could help us?"

"Oh, yes," breathed the girl, though Tarr was quite sure she hadn't registered a word he'd said, as she made no move to get help.

This also seemed to occur to Laith, who took a beat and began again. "What's your name?"

"Winnie," she squeaked.

"Winnie," he repeated quietly. "Do you have a place we could take him? A back room?"

"Oh, yes," she nodded, as if waking from a dream. "A storeroom."

"And do you think," he leaned forward, and Tarr watched with amazement as Laith seemed to somehow conjure a smile from deep in his eyes without actually moving his lips, "that you could tell the other fellows in the bar that it's closing time?"

Mutely, the girl nodded and set down the tankard on the bar. Laith turned back to Tarr and gave his characteristic little frown and shrug. Tarr shook his head.

Winnie ushered them into a storeroom just behind the bar, then bustled off to begin dispersing the bar's patrons. The storeroom was cold and dank, not intended for any form of habitation, and was filled with casks of varying sizes stacked atop one another. A squat table stood in the center, and Winnie reappeared to light the lamp as Laith helped Si lie down atop it. The boy looked absolutely exhausted, and his shoulder was an unpleasant shade of purple. Tarr winced reflexively and looked away as Rane calmly peeled down his collar and asked Winnie for a bucket of hot water, soap, and a towel.

Tarr glanced to the door of the storeroom where a little boy, much younger than Winnie, was standing and watching them solemnly, a few of his fingers thrust in his mouth. Tarr gave the boy a tentative wave, which was not returned.

"Who's that?" Tarr asked as Winnie bustled back in, looking harried as she sloshed some steaming water onto the floor of the storeroom.

"My little brother, Nat. I think I should call my father in," she said, frowning. "There are some riders coming up the street knocking on doors, and I don't know what to do if they come here, or what to do..." she trailed off, but Tarr could clearly tell that she was about to say "about you." He couldn't blame her. He imagined her bartending duties didn't usually include a band of southerners showing up demanding medical aid.

At the mention of the riders, Laith's head had snapped around. "Were they in green cloaks?" Laith inquired.

"Yes," Winnie replied anxiously. "What's wrong?"

"Those are very bad people," Marc answered. "Go back out and stall them, all right? They can't know we're here."

Winnie began to look very frightened, but Marc gave her a nod and a friendly squeeze on her arm. "You can do it, don't worry." She gave him a tiny smile and went back outside.

"Put out that light," Laith ordered. "And lock the door."

"Try to keep him quiet," Rane added, nodding to Si. Marc gave the boy a pat on the arm and whispered something in his ear. Tarr turned the light down and bolted the lock, laying his ear against the wood to hear what was going on outside. In the darkness, he heard Marc slowly unsheath his blade and move to stand beside him, sword out and at the ready.

Winnie's hands were shaking as she took her place at the bar and began to slowly clean one of the cups. Nat, her little brother, came up beside her and tugged at her skirts. Startled, she glanced down, then picked him up and set him on the counter. He watched her quietly as she scrubbed one of the tankards, glancing nervously towards the door every few seconds.

All at once, it crashed open, and five tall soldiers in long green robes strode in with swords out and at the ready. Winnie nearly yelped out loud, but swallowed her cry in her throat. Nat looked at the riders with wide, curious eyes.

"Can I help you?" she asked in a small voice. The lead soldier paused in front of the bar.

"We're looking for a group of people who might have ridden through here," she growled in a deep voice. "Five of them. Have you seen them?"

"No," Winnie replied. "I haven't."

The rider nodded slowly and drew back, walking around the tavern. Her comrades hovered near the doorway. "Slow night, is it?"

"People usually start coming in after dinner time," Winnie stammered.

"Funny, I just ran into a few people outside who said they were already in here when you asked them to leave. Just after a troop of mysterious riders showed up." the guard said, walking back up to the bar. She looked down at Nat, who was watching her, sucking on his fingers. "And you, have you seen any of those men?" Nat made no reply. The rider leaned in closer. "I'll give you some candy and some nice treats if you tell me," she cooed.

Nat eyed her and slowly shook his head. Winnie let out an inward sigh of relief. The rider stepped back again, frustrated, then noted the small door behind the bar.

"What this?" she asked silkily.

"That leads to our storeroom," Winnie said quickly. "It stays locked all the time."

The rider put her hand on the doorknob and gave it a hard shake. The door remained still. "Really? Open it."

"My father has the key," Winnie stuttered. "I...I don't..."

"Break it down," the rider ordered, motioning for the other guards to come up, which they did.

"No!" Winnie yelped anxiously, trying to move in front of them. The guard roughly threw her to one side, and Nat let out a distressed wail. Winnie quickly gathered him into her arms and stepped back. The rider eyed her distastefully.

"If they're in there and you've been lying, I'll kill the child, and then I'll kill you," she hissed. Winnie clutched at Nat, who had his fingers locked about her neck, clinging to her for dear life. The guards braced themselves against the door and heaved against it. The wood shook and bucked on its hinges. They leaned back again and pushed with all their might, and the door whined in protest. It wouldn't withstand another blow. Winnie closed her eyes and buried her face against Nat, who was crying loudly.

Suddenly, the silhouettes of two people filled the open door of the tavern. They leaped inside, and Winnie caught her breath, stumbling backwards to shelter herself behind a wooden barrel in one corner of the room. The green guards jumped back at the noise of these new intruders, and Winnie could now make out the newcomers. The tall one was unlike any person she had ever seen before, with skin so pale it almost shone blue, piercing yellow eyes like a hawk, and strange, spiky, black-tipped hair. The shorter one was a woman with dark brown skin, ebony hair, and pale gray eyes that seemed to be rimmed in black kohl. The woman had a curved sword out and at the ready, and the tall man had a bow and arrow. The guards gave a yell and ran towards them, and Winnie was quite sure that it would be over in a matter of moments. What could two do against five? She covered Nat's eyes and then her own for good measure.

The white one raised his bow and sent an arrow speeding into the nearest rider with an angry sound like a diving wasp. The woman leaped atop one of the tables and jumped into the air to avoid a swipe from one of their swords. The flurry of fighting was so fast that Winnie could barely follow it with her eyes; in only a matter of seconds it was nearly over, and there was but one rider left. The two newcomers whipped around to face the final guard, but he had bolted through the door and onto his waiting horse outside.

"*Damn*," the woman swore, and careened out the door after him.

The tall thing—whatever he was—turned and saw Winnie and Nat huddled in the corner, frightened beyond belief.

"Hello, sorry about that mess on the floor," he said cheerily, peering down at her. "It's safe now for you to come out. We'll get this place mopped up, don't you worry. Where are my friends?"

Winnie extended a shaking finger and pointed at the back room.

"Thank you," said the strange creature. "Sorry about all that," he apologized, indicating the room. "My name's Archer, that was Athela."

"Are you a demon?" Winnie squeaked.

"Some of my ex-girlfriends would tell you as much," he smiled.

He didn't *seem* like a demon, Winnie thought, and gulped. "I'm Winnie."

"Hello, there. We'll have this place cleaned up in no time, don't worry." he smiled.

A moment later, Athela strode back into the tavern and saw Archer squatting next to an extremely traumatized-looking Winnie.

"All good?" Archer inquired.

"All good," she replied. "Where are they?"

"Storeroom," Archer indicated with a jerk of his head.

Athela strode to the door and pounded a few times against the solid wood. "Laith, it's me," she called. A moment later the door opened, and she vanished inside.

Winnie let out a long breath. "*What* is going on?" she asked aloud. She thought momentarily about fetching her father, but blanched at the thought of what he'd say if he saw the state of the bar. "I'd better go get those herbs." She scooted Nat up on her hip and walked out of the door towards the garden behind her house.

After the herbs had been applied in a wet poultice to Si's shoulder, the Strikers sat exhausted around the table in the storeroom, while

Winnie brought them food in from the main tavern. After a quick cleaning job by Archer, Marc, and Athela, it had reopened its doors to customers, and Winnie's sister had joined her to help her with her bartending duties, and to deflect all of the questions about her strange guests. News of the Strikers had spread like wildfire through the tiny village, and the small tavern room was crowded and noisy. Each townsperson kept peering at the door to the storeroom, as if willing it to open and reveal the contents within. Some said that they had seen a person with two heads and four arms waving swords around; some said that they had seen a forest demon with yellow eyes. Gossip hung like a swarm of flies.

Winnie slipped through the storeroom door and set down another bowl of stew and bread in front of Marc, who smiled thankfully and dug in. The barmaid paused by Laith, who was just finishing up his bowl.

"Anything else?" Winnie asked hopefully. Laith glanced up, a smile deep in his eyes.

"No, thank you, I'm full," he replied. Winnie gave a girlish, high-pitched giggle as though Laith had just proclaimed his everlasting love. She took his plate and gave a neat curtsy, then skipped towards the door. Marc rolled his eyes.

"All right," Athela sighed, leaning back in her chair. She seemed to be slightly frustrated and withdrew a dagger from her belt. She began toying with it, spinning it on its point in the middle of the table. "We have a head start, but we'll have to leave here at least by tomorrow morning, the way the people in this town are talking. The search party Cira's going to send out after us is going to be combing over this country inch by inch. They'll know we came this way. I'd be surprised if someone from this town wasn't already riding down the road on the way to alert Cira."

"Where does the prophecy say to go?" Si asked curiously.

Athela's cool gray eyes swiveled around to Tarr. Her expression was entreating. "Tarr," she said in a low voice. "*Please* tell me you brought the papers with you."

For a second, Tarr debated drawing out the moment just to see what would happen, but decided that Athela's nerves wouldn't be able to take it. "They're right here," he assured her, withdrawing them from his knapsack. "And I think I have the translations done. They should be mostly right. You can check them if you like."

Athela looked as though she were on the verge of throwing her arms around him and hugging him, but to everyone's relief, she was able to restrain herself.

They took turns on watch that night. It was only a matter of time before the next wave of Kagaian reinforcements showed up. Si badly needed to rest, however, and it seemed better to sleep at the tavern than out in the open elements. They hoped that the riders wouldn't manage to make it back up to the mountain town before morning.

Though it was well before his hour to keep watch, Tarr found himself oddly unable to sleep, and after a protracted period of tossing and turning, he rose and headed from the storeroom, where the others huddled in snuffling, snoring piles. Athela was seated by one of the windows, her forehead leaning against the cool pane of glass, her eyes trained out on the dark street beyond. There was a faraway look on her face; she stirred as Tarr approached.

"Couldn't sleep," Tarr told her and drew up a tall barstool, folding his thin arms across his chest. Strangely, in all the days they'd spent at Silva's house while recuperating from their injuries, he had never found himself alone with Athela, other than the few times they had traded notes over the prophecy papers.

"Good job on the translation," she complimented him. "Here's hoping it actually leads someplace." There was a strange look of melancholy in her eye. Tarr wondered what she'd been thinking about.

"I think Winnie left a pot of mulled wine for us on the hearth; it may still be warm. Do you want some?" he volunteered.

"Thanks," she said.

Tarr withdrew and came back a few moments later with two mugs. "Careful, some spilled," he cautioned her, and she took a grateful sip. She sat back and leaned her head against the window again, gazing into the black beyond. Tarr let her be still. The silences between them were no longer uncomfortable.

"Laith said you were with him," she said abruptly. "When those guards at Joymaril told him what happened to Ilaina."

So that's it, Tarr realized. "I was," he confirmed.

She turned and searched his face. "Did you believe it? Did you believe what they said?"

Tarr didn't answer for a moment. "I don't know," he said finally. "Laith doesn't."

"I asked if *you* did," she repeated. When Tarr didn't reply, she nodded. "You did. You did believe them." She sighed and leaned against the window. "Ilaina was smart, and she was capable. There's no way that she would have stayed at Joymaril and not even found a way to contact Laith, not find a way to get out and join us."

"Her family, perhaps," Tarr suggested, feeling as though he were grasping at straws. "She could have stayed for her family. Or she could have been captured and imprisoned. She would have had no way to get word out to us in Two Falls."

"She would have come," Athela shook her head. Suddenly, she winced, as if the pain she felt were something physical. "She would have found a way to get away. Nothing would have kept her apart from Laith. That I know for certain."

"I don't know," Tarr said again, feeling rather useless.

"She was my best friend," Athela said, mostly to herself. "From the first day, she didn't care who I was, or who my parents were, or whether everyone else in the entire city thought I was weird. She was just...my friend. And now," she twisted around and shot a look back towards the closed door of the storeroom, "now I can't even grieve for her. Not while..." Her voice trailed off, but Tarr could clearly sense her meaning. *Not while Laith believes she's alive. Or rather, while he wants to believe it.*

Tarr could think of nothing to say, so he simply extended his long, bandaged hand and placed it on her shoulder. Athela gave another shuddering sigh, then straightened up taller and flashed Tarr with a brave, grateful smile.

"You knew her, Tarr," she said. "You knew her. Even for a little while."

"I did," Tarr smiled faintly. "She taught me to ride."

"We *both* did," Athela corrected him, looking put out.

"You both did," Tarr agreed. "She was my first date. To my first party."

Athela shook her head. "It's funny; all I want to do is talk about her. All the small things I remember, all the tiny things she used to do that now seem so important. Like when she ate something with a spoon, after the last few bites she'd sometimes leave the spoon hanging out of her mouth for a few seconds while she was listening to whatever you were saying with her eyebrows up like this." She mimicked the exaggerated expression, and Tarr laughed. She shook her head and folded her arms more tightly over her chest. "All those stupid little things."

"They're not stupid," Tarr insisted. "That's what made her...*her*."

Athela fell silent again after that. Tarr sat with her, watching the street beyond. The figure of a man came up the street, stumbling slightly. He lurched against one of the buildings and then made his way unsteadily past them and into the night.

"I can take over," Tarr volunteered. "If you want to go get some rest."

"I'm all right," Athela shook her head, smiling tightly. Her guard was back up, Tarr could sense it. "I'll come and wake you when it's time."

So Tarr left her and returned to the storeroom, shutting the door quietly behind him. He went over to the table, leaned over, and checked to make sure that Si was still sleeping and comfortable. Then he made his way back to his makeshift cot (which was not much more than a sack of grain and a thin blanket) and lay down, conscious of Rane, curled up on her side and sleeping silently only a foot or two away. He wished that he could draw closer to her but didn't know whether that would be overstepping his bounds.

So he laid awake there for an hour or more, listening to Marc's gentle snuffling snores and Laith's heavy breathing. Though he expected Athela to fetch him before long, she never came.

CHAPTER TWENTY-NINE

Marc shook them all awake the next morning. Tarr blinked a few times, feeling stupid, but then remembered where he was. Around him, the others were groggily rousing themselves. Athela had fallen asleep behind the table, her head resting on the pit of Archer's stomach. He was also still asleep, one of his arms curled reflexively around her shoulders.

"Laith sighted guards on the outskirts of the forest," Marc told him. "We've got to leave now. Are you awake?"

"Not quite, give me five seconds," Tarr returned, standing and stretching the kinks out of his muscles, shaking his head and running his hands through his hair. It was still strange to only have eleven, and he shuddered involuntarily. "Someone needs to wake Athela and Archer up."

"Not me," Si said dubiously.

At the sound of his name, Archer's eyes opened a slit, and Tarr could see the situation dawn. He disentangled his limbs and gently shook Athela's shoulder a few times. She rubbed her eyes, looking tired, her black curls spilling over Archer's chest. A moment later, she got her bearings and shot straight up as soon as she realized that she had been using Archer as a pillow. "I'm awake," she announced aggressively, and indeed, she looked it. "What's going on?"

"Guards on the outskirts. They'll be here soon. We've got to leave, try not to leave tracks," Marc informed her quickly.

"It's snowing," Si observed. The night of rest and the medicine had left him much improved; he was no longer holding his arm at a painful angle, and some of the old spark was back in his youthful eye.

"We're high up on the mountain; it's cold enough to snow here," Marc told him.

"If we get out fast enough, the snow may cover some of our tracks," Athela stretched, studiously avoiding making eye contact with Archer as she leaned forward and gathered her papers and things from the table in front of them. "Might as well take the medicine too, we'll probably need it." Rane nodded and stepped forward, scooping the supplies into a sack.

Winnie and her sister were already in the tavern, cleaning and mopping the place down, when Tarr and Athela came out to try to coax them for any additional information that could help them in their search. Tarr had the impression that this was much earlier than they usually did their chores, and that perhaps they'd been keeping watch so as not to miss a glimpse of the Strikers as they awoke. The girls were only half-listening to Athela as she asked them for directions and completely lost interest once Laith appeared at the storeroom door. He gave them a friendly nod as he strode by, pulling on his cloak and flipping the hood over his sandy-colored hair. He went out the door and around the corner to where the horses were stabled, and Winnie's sister gave a faint whimper of complaint at his disappearance.

Athela cleared her voice and looked back to the parchment she was holding in front of Winnie. "Now, do you have a map of this area or anything that would be useful?" she asked.

"Maybe," Winnie replied, her eyes still following after Laith. "So, he's your brother or something?"

"He's gay," Athela said shortly. "A map, then?"

"Oh," Winnie said, disappointment sagging down her features. Athela noted the expression, and felt unwanted sympathy creeping up inside her. She met Tarr's gaze and threw up her hands in exasperation.

"Fine, he's not gay," she intoned through gritted teeth. "But *please.*"

Winnie's face brightened back up. "Well, we have this map here," she said, rooting beneath the bar and withdrawing a paper and handing it to Athela. Athela took it in. It was elementary, sketched out quickly, but pointed out some of the major mountains and surrounding regions.

"This will do," Athela nodded and folded it up. She looked Winnie straight in the eyes. "I want to thank you for all the help you've given us. We won't forget it. None of us." She stopped, briefly debating the ethics of commodifying her cousin, and finally shrugged. "I could ask Laith to give you a hug or something, if you'd like."

"*Really*?" Winnie asked breathlessly.

"Lucky," her sister muttered over her broom from down the bar.

Athela walked out and explained the situation to Laith, who gave her a withering look, but nevertheless gamely fixed on a winning smile and strode back in to give Winnie and her sister a hug. The expression on the girl's face looked as though it had been and would remain the crowning moment of her entire life.

Some of the townspeople had been alerted to their presence and had drifted out of their homes to catch a glimpse of the strangers as they left. Marc jogged his horse back and forth slowly down the street to make sure that everything was free and clear, but the majority of the onlookers seemed content with peering out of the shutters of their windows, rather than venturing out into the street.

The others were soon on their horses. The light was still dim; the sun was just beginning to ease up over the eastern hills, casting a golden-rosy glow through the gray village. Athela shaded her eyes, looking down the road to the southeast to scope out whether there were any approaching riders, but it was too hard for her to see.

She moved Aria up to stand beside Laith. "I got a map from Winnie, and it corresponds directly with the translation of the prophecy. We're heading up there," she announced, pointing. Tarr twisted around, staring in the indicated direction. He had never before been in the mountains, and the one to which Athela was pointing loomed up taller and more forbidding than any of the others. The tip was crested a snowy white, and he could see where the snowfall was beginning to cover the trees and rocks that knitted together the surface of the slope. It looked forbidding, insurmountable. He wished, with a twinge in his heart, that Wolver could be there to go with him.

Tarr turned back around to where Archer was watching the mountain with level golden eyes. "Is this close to where your tribe lived once?" Tarr asked in Ashan.

Archer looked surprised, then shook his head, replying in the same language, his northern lilt like a musical cadence. "No. I do not know for sure, but I think our mountains were even farther north. There," he pointed, indicating looming shapes farther on the horizon. "But I have not been in the mountains for a long time."

"You can help us," Tarr assured him. "You will remember."

"Perhaps," Archer shrugged, his eyes grave. Tarr could see that he wasn't eager at the thought of going back.

The Strikers moved out, loping slowly down the streets, heading towards the north. The snow fluttered down around them, twisting into little flurries by their horses' hooves. It would stick, at least while they were this high up.

Once they reached the edge of the town, they began to gallop faster and faster until the road sloped upwards and they reached the first hill, after which they slowed and began to climb, higher and higher and higher. As the vista swept below them, Tarr kept a hopeful eye out for anything that could be Wolver, but he could see nothing.

Marc took the lead in directing them to hide their tracks. He made them splash down a river for some time, and scurry across a slippery sheet of black volcanic rock. By the middle of the day, they had scaled the foothills and began their ascent into the very heart of the mountains. The craggy peaks towered above and around them and Tarr had to crane his neck back to take them in as they rose up over him, pulling the column of riders in. He was overwhelmed—looking at them was one thing; experiencing their cold majesty up close was something else entirely. Tarr could see the details of trees and the intricate crevices of rock and earth much better as they drew up and up. The trees began to thin out in places, and snow gathered on the tips of the rocks like soft shearling blankets. The air was cold and crisp and stung his throat; he found himself having to breathe harder and faster to keep up. His ears popped as they climbed over the first ridge of hills, and he twisted around from time to time, gazing down as the land beneath them gradually dropped away. It seemed so peaceful from the high vantage point, so quiet, just a slow *whooshing* sound like the sea, and the clopping of the horses' hooves. He could see even better now where the land dipped down into the valley of the forest, the thin silver ribbon of river splitting Two Falls, and even, far down along the coast to his left, the black rock of Faridor sitting low and heavy in the sea. It looked so tiny, so insignificant.

So enrapt was he in gazing at the landscape below that he barely noticed when Athela reined to a stop. Her eyes were fixed on a landmark just ahead of them. Tarr swiveled around to see what they were looking at and was so surprised he nearly fell out of his saddle.

A tree rose up before them, ancient and massive, seemingly out of place amongst the smaller, weedier growth around it. It had three massive boughs that spread up and out, almost in a perfect triangle.

"This is a tree in the prophecy; it has to be," Athela told them, then beckoned Tarr up to ride beside her. "Tarr, help me figure this out," she said, handing the parchment to him. "The first half of the inscription gives clues as to where we're generally supposed to go, so I was able to get us here all right, but the second half is what we're supposed to do when we get to this tree. We have a map, but I'm not sure what to do to get there. It's all so damned cryptic." As usual, Athela's conceptual love of puzzle-solving was at odds with her inherent impatience.

"Give it here," Tarr took the paper from her. It read:

> IT IS THE MOUNTAIN BENEATH THE STAR
> WHITE AMIDST THE DARK
> FIVE TO THE LEFT
> THEN TO THE NORTH.
> FOLLOW THE ASHES
> FOLLOW THE STONES
> PUSH AT THE MOUTH OF THE WOLF
> TOGETHER THEY ALL SHALL MOVE IT
> AND DESCEND BELOW

"Hmm," Tarr mused, scanning his eyes up and down the lines a few times. "Hand me the map, would you?"

Athela did as she was told. "What does it mean, the mountain beneath the star? There are a billion stars, there's no way we could find a mountain beneath *one* star... Does she *want* to make my head explode?"

"Probably," Tarr said distractedly, then something fell into place and he pointed at the map. "No, wait. It's this mountain here."

Athela looked over his shoulder. "How do you know?" she asked dubiously.

"Because the other mountains make a star-shaped pattern here," he traced the outline. "And this one is the one beneath the star."

"Fine," Athela said curtly, folding the paper back up. Though she didn't show it, Tarr could tell she was pleased.

"What does the rest of it mean?" Si asked, wrinkling his freckled nose.

"We'll find out when we get there, I suppose," Tarr shrugged.

They fell into a single-file line, picking their way delicately across the slippery rocks made even slicker by the falling snow. They were safely screened by the thick trees, and they wound their way across the seam of the hills up into the arms of the thick stone. Long rolls of earth and trees spread out around the ridges of the mountain like the roots of a tree. Eventually, they found themselves standing on a slab of rock that jutted out like a balcony, offering them a wide vantage point of the surrounding country. They were far up the side of the ridge now, and Tarr felt completely exhilarated by the height. Marc took one look over the side of the rock, muttered something dark and incomprehensible under his breath, and promptly walked his horse as far away from the edge as he could.

"This is where we're supposed to stop," Athela told them. "Now to find 'white amidst the dark.'"

Tarr took a deep breath and took another long look at the prophecy. "White amidst the dark," Tarr muttered and squinted against the wind and snow, quickly scanning the mountainside. "Up there!" he shouted suddenly, and pointed to the west. The trees all had black trunks, their branches mostly bare at the onset of winter, but tucked away into them were a few white birch trunks, gleaming in stark contrast against the dark earth.

"I could've told you that," Si groused, setting a hand on his hip and cocking his head up at the trees.

They rode up the twisting mountain trail towards the grove of birches, the path growing steeper and steeper until Laith dismounted and led Arfolasth up on foot. Rane's horse slipped a couple of times and she loosed her reins, giving him control of his head so that he could catch himself if he started to fall.

Finally, the Strikers reached another plateau on the side of the mountain, where they paused to let the animals have a bit of a breather. The small grove of birch trees was only a short ways away, and Tarr and Archer went over to get a closer look.

"Now what?" Tarr muttered in Ashan. "Was the clue the trees themselves?"

"Trees change," Archer shrugged, riding between them. To Tarr's shock, it suddenly seemed as if the other Ashan had vanished, his white skin and black hair perfectly camouflaged against the trunks and shadows of the birch trees. The only thing that allowed Tarr to pick him out was his black coat. If Archer had been standing there amid the birches in a snowstorm, he would have been almost invisible.

"I don't think that Morthenstar would leave clues that could change so much," Tarr frowned, looking around the trees. "She would have taken some sort of precaution."

"Tarr!" Archer exclaimed suddenly. "Look here!"

Tarr slithered his way between the thin trees until he came up beside Archer, who was pointing to the ground. On the ground, at the base of five of the trees, were five broad stones, all with a large engraved star pattern on the top.

"Did you find something?" Athela shouted.

"Yes!" Tarr replied. "Come up here!"

The others quickly found their way to where Archer and Tarr stood, their horses' legs braced against the sloping earth.

"Heck!" Si exclaimed. "Archer, you're camouflaged."

"Watch your language," corrected Marc automatically, though he, too, was staring at Archer with a look of wonderment.

Rane was leaning over the engraved rocks and ran her fingers over the carvings. "Read the clue again, Tarr," she said softly.

"'Five to the left,'" Tarr muttered, guiding his horse forward. "'To the north...'" he counted as he passed five trees. He looked down. Another stone was there, with a star pointing off to the left. "This way," he pointed. "Follow the stones."

They went along in silence, leading their horses, the excitement mounting between them as the object of their longtime quest seemed to loom ever closer.

"What about the ashes?" Athela inquired. "Are we looking for something burned?"

Tarr honestly didn't know, and shrugged. "We'll see what comes up."

Then, after a few minutes, they hit a new grove of trees. Archer glanced around himself at the spreading boughs, and caught Tarr's eye, giving out a hearty laugh.

"How clever," Archer said in Ashan.

"What is it?" Athela asked crossly. "And would you two keep your infernal code-talking down to a minimum?"

"The trees," Tarr informed her. "They're ash."

"Clever," Laith nodded.

"That's what I said," Archer grinned toothily. "We follow the grove up, I suppose."

They stayed within the winding grove of ash trees, following it like a path. They climbed upward, occasionally having to grab onto a nearby trunk to steady their mounts as the footing grew decidedly more precarious. Finally, they reached the northern border of the wood where the ash trees ended and came to a halt.

"Now what?" Athela inquired.

"I don't know," Tarr replied, dismounting. He climbed up a few feet until he came to the edge of a slight escarpment. Farther in towards the mountains was a cluster of gigantic rocks that continued upward as the trees thinned out and eventually disappeared. "Up here," he called, and the others obeyed.

Si gulped and looked over the side. "Ha ha, certainly is far up," he commented in an unusually high voice.

"Something about a wolf's mouth, right, Tarr?" Marc asked, hands on his hips, face upturned, pondering. His ice-blue eyes glanced around. "Maybe we need to find a wolf pack, grab the alpha male, and stick something in his mouth."

There was a protracted pause. "Yeah, something tells me that's not it," Archer murmured.

"Puzzle deciphering isn't for everyone, Marc," Athela told him with a comforting pat on his arm.

"I was just thinking out loud," Marc grumbled defensively.

"What about up there?" Athela inquired suddenly, pointing at the lip of a rock wall a little ways above them. Tarr craned his neck and walked forward, feeling around with his sensitive fingers. The pads of his hands moved along the grooves in the rock, calculating, and after a moment, he scaled up the sheer face and stood at the top. In front of him was a rock formation, worn down but unmistakably in the shape of a wolf's head: a snout protruding out, triangular rocks pointing down like incisors. A large boulder was wedged into the wolf's throat.

"You're right, Athela," Tarr called down. "Can you make it up here?"

"We'll try," came the reply.

A few minutes later, the train of horses picked their way carefully onto the top of the cliff. The surface was broader than the one before, and the horses stood more comfortably, Si edging closer to the flat side of the wall, not liking the edge.

"I guess we have to move that rock, huh?" Athela inquired, standing beside Tarr and pushing on the boulder with one hand. It didn't budge. She made a clicking sound in the back of her throat. "I don't know, Tarr; I think it's too big for all of us to be able to move it at all."

"Well, the clue said we should be able to. Come on over here, give me a hand," Tarr suggested. Tarr and Athela gripped the boulder with their hands and tried to pry it away from the opening, but it wouldn't budge; the stone was too slippery for them. Marc watched their effort, glaring at the rock.

"Well, that's frustrating," he commented, frowning.

"We need your shoulders, Marc, get over here," Tarr said.

"Oh, well, we gave it a good try. Back down the mountain, I suppose," Archer said sarcastically.

"Wait, wait, we're missing something," Tarr fluttered a hand at his friends. He looked around. "'*They shall all move it,*'" he said. "Come here, everyone," he ordered. "Put your hands here." The others stared at him incredulously but did as they were told, each laying a hand on the boulder.

"Right, everyone," Athela announced, rallying them together. Tarr expected nothing to happen, for the boulder to remain dormant, but at the slightest pressure of their hands, the boulder gave a groan and rolled backward into the mouth of the cave, revealing a cavernous opening.

"How did *that* one work?" Si asked.

"Dunno," Marc replied, eyeing the stone suspiciously.

Tarr glanced into the cave, then turned and stared back down the side of the mountain. If anyone was trying to find the entrance, they would have to have very specific directions. The arrangement of the rocks made it almost impossible to see unless one was standing just a few feet away. The cave yawned up before them. Tarr looked back at the others. "Anyone want to go first?"

Unsurprisingly, Athela volunteered, stepping forward into the pitch black, followed by Rane, whose hand was resting lightly on the hilt of her sword. After a few steps, Athela turned and looked back at them.

"There's a flight of stairs, and I think there's a torch on the side, someone hand me a match," she ordered. The matches were summarily retrieved from one of the saddlebags and handed to her. With a bit of coaxing, the ancient torch was lit, casting its glow along the craggy walls of the cave. There was, indeed, a staircase winding its way down into the pit of the mountain.

Athela went first, the others behind. They followed the staircase around and around, their footsteps echoing along the walls of the cave. Tarr wasn't afraid. In fact, it almost seemed familiar, as if he had been in the same place before, at a different time.

Finally, they reached the bottom of the staircase and entered a huge, circular room. Athela raised the torch up, but the light wasn't enough to illuminate the entire area. A single shaft of light shone in through a hole in the roof. Athela moved to one side, looking along the walls and finding more torches bolted to the walls. She went around and, with some effort, lit them one by one. The room slowly grew lighter and lighter until they could see the full extent of the cavern in which they found themselves. As the torches were lit, the light from the roof seemed to grow brighter. Dust filtered through the shaft of light, falling atop a large stone table. The Strikers spread out, mouths open, staring about themselves with astonishment.

"This was Alder Morthenstar's camp," Athela breathed.

CHAPTER THIRTY

"Do you really think this was it?" Laith inquired, gazing around.

"Must have been," Tarr replied, agape. It was easy to imagine the cave being full of people, swords lined up against the walls, plans and maps spread across the table before them as Alder Morthenstar and her generals inspected them. There was a sense of history about the place, the feeling that at any moment he might turn to find a ghostly figure from long ago standing just behind his shoulder.

"Up here!" Archer called from one side. The others looked over. There was a small flight of stairs on one side of the circular floor that led up to another alcove. They followed Archer's motion and looked inside. There was another circular room with little nooks branching off from it. In each nook there was a raised stone platform; the spaces were larger than they looked from the outside.

Archer grinned. "Rooms," he said. "Dozens of them."

Tarr didn't respond, and the others all glanced at one another. The cave seemed to be part of a vast network of spaces: meeting rooms, bedrooms, training areas.

"There's enough to shelter and house quite a significant force here," Athela murmured to him. Tarr agreed, growing more excited by the minute. They returned to the broad circular room into which they'd first descended, which seemed to be the main gathering area.

"Think of it, Athela," Laith muttered. "Dozens of people could live in here, we could store weapons, supplies. The light isn't all that bad. Not a far cry from Two Falls, all things considered. Impossible to find, unless you know where to look. This could be our new home." His voice was slightly hushed, excited. They had wandered for so long, at last it seemed as if there was a place where they *belonged*, somewhere that had been intended just for them. Athela heard her cousin's words and nodded silently, running her hand along the pink and yellow rock. There was an uncharacteristically soft look in her eyes that told Tarr that she was feeling the same excitement he was.

"That's what we'll do," Athela agreed eagerly. "We'll set up camp here. We need to contact Ari."

We need to place spies at Faridor, Tarr thought, running his hands along the edge of the smooth, sandy stone, looking around at the tunnels crisscrossing through the network of caves surrounding them. It was almost like an insect's nest. *We need spies at Two Falls. I'm going to crumble Cira's rule from the inside out, eat at her foundations like termites in the wood.* His heart began to race.

They made their way up the stairwell: broad steps and a groove cut into the rock wall for a railing. It took them around the corner and led them up into a circular room with no roof. Tarr glanced up at the sky above them, gray, the snow slowly filtering in through little gusts of breeze. He smiled and looked back down.

"What is this place?" Laith asked, running his hands up and down the stone pillars throughout the room. "There are engravings everywhere."

"And here," Si pointed out, kneeling down. In the very center of the floor was a gigantic star shape cut into the rock, the same six-pointed pattern that had been emblazoned on the stones that had led them to the cave.

"Oh, yes, well, there is that, too," Marc remarked offhandedly.

"This must be the room in the second part of the inscription," Athela breathed, hurriedly taking the papers out of her pocket and shuffling them into order. She looked eagerly around at the rest of them. "This is where we find out the identity of Morthenstar's heir.

You ready?"

Not really, Tarr thought to himself, and exchanged looks with a few of the others. He wasn't sure what was going to happen, whether a lightning bolt would suddenly strike—or, worse, if they went through the ritual and nothing happened at all. *Or,* perhaps even worse than that, if they went through the ritual and somehow Tarr was designated as Morthenstar's heir. He swallowed, feeling sick. Long gone were the days when he could blithely dismiss the entire business as something in Laith's imagination, a series of remarkable coincidences. There was more going on than Tarr could hope to understand.

It can't be me, he reassured himself. *I'm not even supposed to be here.*

"Read it, Athela," Laith said quietly.

The shuffling papers echoed about the chamber as the others fell silent. Tarr gulped.

Let it be Laith, or Athela, or even Marc, he thought to himself. *Or someone we don't even know. Let it be Ari.* Someone who knew how to fight, knew how to lead. That was what they needed. That would be best.

Athela's gray eyes skimmed down the papers. Tarr sidled up alongside her, to try and see if he could offer any assistance in deciphering the clue. The prophecy read:

AT THE POINTS OF THE STAR
FOUR FOR THE FOUR
TWO FOR THE TWO
AND THE HEART OF THE ONE

Tarr met Athela's eyes, and for a few comical moments the two of them silently mouthed the words back at one another. Tarr looked down at the floor to the six-pointed star emblazoned beneath their feet. He slowly began to feel the words clicking into place. As they did, he felt a rush of goosebumps sweep up his arms.

"What is it?" Athela asked as he gave an involuntary shudder.

He motioned the others to come closer and pointed down at the star pattern. The north and south points were the largest, with four smaller ones surrounding the center. "There," he said. "Two Ashans, four Jelani. And Si." He looked over at the boy. "We all need to stand on the points of the star."

"Where do I stand?" Si asked, looking anxious.

"In the center, I think," Tarr frowned.

"Great!" Si's face shifted into eagerness at the prospect of playing such a literally central role, and he dashed forward, looking carefully around at his feet to make sure they were positioned at the direct central convergence of the star's six points. The others were slower to get into place, looking sidelong at Tarr as though they couldn't quite believe him.

Finally, they were almost in position. Archer stood at the north point of the star, the four Jelani clustered closer to the center, Si in the center. Tarr looked down at his own feet, where he stood only a short way from the south point of the star. *I wonder if it will matter*, he thought, *that it's not me who's supposed to be here. Perhaps it will work with any Ashan.* Steeling himself, he slowly stepped forward and placed both of his feet so that they were standing on the point of the star. He felt his breath catch in his throat as he waited, the seconds ticking by interminably, to see if something would happen.

For a moment, nothing did. Tarr looked up and met Archer's eyes, then Athela's. His mind began to race, trying to think of something he'd missed, some other clue he'd overlooked. He had been so sure he was right. It had all fit together—two Ashans, four Jelani, one human—if only there was some other—

All at once, the room around them began to hum and to throb as if it had suddenly come to life. The light grew bright, so bright that Tarr shielded his eyes against it. The color flew from yellow to red, to green, to blue, back to red again. It was too much for him to take. He heard the others yelling around him, tried to tell them to stay in the same place. The rocks seemed to press inward, moving them all together. Tarr tried to shift one of his legs, but it was as if his foot had been physically attached to the stone beneath him. Tarr's arms reached out, grabbing for someone near to him, clutching for Archer, Rane, anyone. But they couldn't move. His eyes burned; he tried to close them but couldn't. And then it was as if the light was focusing in on him and was splitting him completely in half. It wasn't painful, but he had the distinct sensation of being pulled apart.

And then, his head snapped forward and the light began to focus itself. He was surrounded by the haze of a red glow, and he could see shapes shifting in and out in front of his eyes. Had the others been able to free themselves? He tried to pull his foot loose, but it was still lodged in place. The movements continued in front of his astonished eyes; there was heat emanating from them. The shapes—he could almost make them out, could almost see who and what they were. His shoulder blades were being pushed apart; his chest was thrown to the sky, his arms spread. If he was crying out, he couldn't hear it.

The movement, Tarr could see now, was focusing, getting clearer, ever clearer, as if he was just waking up and was rubbing his eyes. He was still in the cave, but in a different area than he was before, back in the area with the table and the bedrooms. The cave was decidedly different, with sacks and swords leaned here and there against the walls, and maps and papers spread on the tables, almost exactly as Tarr had imagined there would be someday. There was a fuzzy, hazy light about everything. And there were people...at first, Tarr thought they were two of his friends and he tried to reach out for them, but found he still couldn't move. He could only watch.

One of them turned, and with a jolt Tarr recognized the face of Alder Morthenstar.

"Alder!" Tarr tried to call out, but no sound issued from him. Alder looked past him as if she couldn't see him. She looked tired, a bit drawn, and her shoulders were held heavily. A few other people walked in and out of the bedrooms above, but as Tarr waited one by one they vanished until he and Alder were alone.

Alder sat down at the stone table and glanced through a few of the papers, slightly disinterested. Almost unconsciously, she reached into her shirt and withdrew a broad silver medallion that winked and flickered in the dancing orange torchlight. Tarr's eyes were dazzled.

Suddenly, a change seemed to come over Alder. Her head rocked forward as if she had lost control of herself, and her body sunk to one side. "Daemun!" she yelled as loud as she could, and fell onto the floor. A moment later, someone ran in right past Tarr's field of vision and knelt beside Alder. Tarr assumed that this was Daemun, Alder's general, who was quite a strapping individual and bore no small resemblance to Laith. He helped Alder back up into a sitting position where the young woman reeled heavily, weakly, as if all her balance had gone. "Get...a parchment," she whispered. The language was different, strange and ancient to Tarr's ears, but for some reason, he found that he could understand every word. He watched as Daemun's face grew dark.

"A vision?" Daemun demanded urgently.

"*Go!*" Alder urged, and Daemun immediately left her, returning a few seconds later with a parchment and quill. He waited expectantly for Alder to speak, the pen hovering over the paper.

"It'll all happen again," Alder murmured, her eyes glazed and vacant, staring ahead. "All of it."

For a moment, Daemun didn't write anything; he simply gaped at his friend. "What will?"

"The war." Her voice was a deathly whisper.

Daemun hesitated. "You're sure?" he asked, hushed.

Alder intoned, unseeing, "All of it again."

"The people won't let it!" Daemun exclaimed angrily. "They can't! Not after everything we've gone through, everything we've fought for. They won't just sit back and let this happen again!"

"*Write what I tell you,*" Alder hissed. "There will be...a woman..." she paused, her eyes whizzing back and forth, her voice still strangely muted. "The woman has gray eyes, black hair. And an Ashan...an Ashan at the center of the falls, with a wolf. And my sword...my sword will be reborn."

Daemun was furiously scribbling away, his pen scratching against the rough paper. He paused, looking back up at his friend, and Tarr could see his dubious expression.

"The others...I can't see their faces," Alder murmured, squinting her eyes as if to clear her vision. "I can't see their faces, but they're there."

"Your heir?" Daemun asked. "Who will lead them?"

"I will mark my heir as my own," Alder intoned slowly, then reeled heavily and fell onto the floor, senseless. Daemun threw down the pen and rushed over to help Alder sit back up. The young woman shook red hair from her eyes and scrambled wildly before she recalled her setting and recognized Daemun.

"What happened?" she demanded.

"You made another prophecy," Daemun told her matter-of-factly, pulling her up onto the chair. "There you go, upsy-daisy."

"*Another* prophecy?" Morthenstar said, leaning her head in her hand and squeezing her temples. "This is getting ridiculous."

"It *is* a tad bit stressful," Daemun admitted, his tone light. "Perhaps if you shut away the medall—"

"No," Morthenstar cut him off shortly, glaring. After a moment, she returned her head to her hands. "Well, what was it this time?"

Daemun cleared his throat uncomfortably and rustled the papers back and forth. "*What?*" Alder demanded, noting his odd behavior.

Daemun gave a sigh. "You said that Kagai's heir would rise and a new band of Strikers would come and oppose him. You predicted the appearances of two of these new Strikers, and something about your sword, then said you would mark your own heir. That was all."

Alder stared at him, disbelieving. "I...can't..." she stammered. "I...this...this can't all happen again."

"That's what *I* said," Daemun agreed. "And then you basically told me to shut up," he added rather peevishly.

Alder abruptly shoved herself away from the table and stood. Tarr could see that her nerves were very close to snapping. Daemun looked down at his hands. He didn't like to see his friend so upset.

"What are we fighting for, then?" Alder yelled loudly. "What...is all *this* for? Our friends, who have *died* believing it was worth something!"

"It could be," Daemun interjected. "Maybe we can do something, something to change what's going to happen." Tarr could hear the desperation in his voice.

Alder's shoulders sagged, and she looked a little deflated. She turned to meet Daemun's eyes, and something significant passed between them. It was almost as if Tarr could hear them thinking *we have to believe that it is going to change.* "You're right," Alder said softly. "My visions have altered before. This will, too. It has to."

"That's right," Daemun said firmly.

Alder returned to the table and sat again in her chair. Her red hair spilled over her eyes, and there was something about her posture that reminded Tarr of someone, but he couldn't pinpoint exactly who. "We've got to take precautions," she told Daemun. "I want this prophecy to be well-hidden. I don't want anyone to be able to find it. I need you to bring in the Serpens, see what magic they can cast, see if they can create a spell to lock the power in. We've also got to figure out how to hide the caves. If there are other Strikers, I want it to be here that they find my heir."

"It will be done," Daemun assented briskly, though Tarr detected a note of skepticism still playing at the backs of his eyes. After a moment, however, a slow smile snuck across his face. "Alder," he said tentatively, "this is just a thought, you understand, but say we do win the battle and take back Faridor. Wouldn't it be quite the trick to hide part of this prophecy *in* Faridor? Probably the last place Kagai's heir would be looking, that's for sure."

Alder let out a barking laugh. "It's a deal. If we make it through this, we plant clues in Faridor. We'll lead a trail for the next Strikers to find. If, of course, there are any other Strikers at all. I hope I'm wrong."

"There won't be," Daemun assured her confidently. "After us, it will all be over. But I will do as you ask. I'll put the Serpens," (again, a slight note of distaste as he said the word *Serpens*) "in charge of laying the trail."

"Good," Alder assented and rested her head on the back of her chair, staring up at the ceiling. Daemun scribbled for a few minutes on the sheet of paper before him. After a time, he paused and looked up at his friend.

"You didn't see the face, did you?" he asked tentatively. "Of your heir?"

Alder was motionless for a long time, then finally shook her head. "No," she murmured. "I did not see their face."

At that moment, it was as if the last tendril of a ragged string snapped, and the vision slipped into darkness. Tarr felt himself falling and landed with a dull thud on something very hard. He opened his eyes. There was nothing but blackness around him. He blinked a few times, confused, but his vision hadn't returned. He moved his hands, felt something rough beneath him, identified it as stone. He must still be in the cavern. But why couldn't he see? He felt the motion flow back through his body, moved his feet, wiggled his fingers, became aware of every small hair on the back of his arms, the dull pain on the back of his head as if he had been slammed down on the ground.

"Archer?" he asked, but his voice was only a croak. He swallowed, coughed a few times. Light was beginning to seep in around the dark edges of his vision. "Archer?" he asked again.

"Here," came a voice in the dark. It was weak, but it was Archer. Tarr breathed a sigh of relief. "Athela? Laith?"

"Here as well," Athela said, her voice shaking.

"And I," came Laith's deeper tones. "Is everyone all right?"

The others assented. "Can anyone see anything?" Marc asked from somewhere to Tarr's right.

"I can't," Athela said. "I can't see a thing."

"What happened to everyone?" Marc asked weakly. "We all just passed out...there was a really bright flash of light."

"Are you all right?" Laith asked.

"Wait, where's Si?" Marc yelped. "I can't sit up!"

"My vision's getting better," Tarr countered, and tried to will his limbs to allow him to sit up, but they wouldn't. "Can't move, though. Where's Si?"

"I'm here," Si's voice came, softer than usual, almost inhuman.

The light was growing clearer, so that Tarr's vision was starting to become just a fuzzy gray blur. He could dimly make out the outline of the top of the cave roof, and thought that he could even perhaps assume that some of the bright gray areas were the pearly sunlight shining down.

"I can almost see something," Archer announced. He coughed and began again. "Did you guys see what I saw? Alder talking to her general, giving him the prophecy? Talking about magic and serpents and stuff?"

"Serpens," Marc's voice corrected, "whatever a Serpen is."

"I saw them, too," Tarr said. There. One of his arms was moving. That was positive. He rolled his shoulder around a few times, feeling it loosening.

"I as well," Archer said.

"I think we all did," Laith agreed.

"It was *Daemun's* idea," Athela's voice griped bitterly, gaining strength by the second. "His *stupid* idea to hide the *stupid* prophecy in *stupid* Faridor. He is the cause of every headache I've had for the last three months."

Tarr blinked once, and everything slid into focus and vivid color. The shock of it made him sit bolt upright, and he looked around. The others were spread-eagled on the cavernous floor in the same star-shaped pattern in which they'd been standing. Archer jerked up a few seconds later, rubbing his head with one long hand. More slowly, Athela, Marc, Rane, and Laith all sat up. Si was still lying in the center of the room.

"Well, who is it?" Athela asked keenly, wrinkling her brow and looking around at the others. "One of us? Or do we have to go around hunting for someone new?"

Tarr stared around as well. The heir of Morthenstar would be marked, or so the prophecy said. Could something have gone wrong? He didn't see anything visible on any of his friends. His eyes ran up and down their faces, their arms, their legs, their own curious, searching expressions. And then he saw, and he stopped stock-still. Athela registered his lack of motion and followed his stare. One by one they all froze, shocked into absolute silence.

Rubbing the scarlet six-pointed tattoo imprinted on his skinny, freckled forearm, Si, the heir of Alder Morthenstar, opened his gray eyes to the afternoon sun.

ACKNOWLEDGEMENTS

I would first like to thank my sister Piper for reading literally every version of this book that has existed over the past twenty years, and for telling me each time that it was great (it wasn't.) And to Peter, who has also been reading iterations for over a decade and has supported, advised, edited, and cheered on everything from plot twists to dialogue, fonts and line spacing. I love you so much. You are the best thing.

Thank you to all the friends (Scott and Sarah especially) and family who read this and passed it around over the years. Your encouragement has meant so much to me.

Thank you to Kat and Rosie, whose talents helped me hone in on the book's look. Thank you to Luke for illuminating the deep, dark dungeon that is U.S. Copyright law. Thanks to Daphne for catching all the little mistakes and for asking the important questions.

Thank you to Elli, who was the first person to make me believe that someone (not obligated by marriage or blood relation) might actually enjoy this story. You are the reason this book exists in its current form. I am more grateful to you than you know.

A final thank you to Mom and Dad, who have always encouraged me to express my creativity in any way I wanted. I love you both enormously.

www.ingramcontent.com/pod-product-compliance
Lightning Source LLC
Chambersburg PA
CBHW072011020726
47501CB00006B/1767

* 9 7 9 8 9 9 0 0 0 6 9 9 7 *